Bry

FAMILIAR STRANGERS

QUICKSAND

ARROW

This edition published by Arrow in 2002
an imprint of The Random House Group
20 Vauxhall Bridge Road, London SW1V 2SA

Papers used by Random House UK Ltd are natural recyclable products made from wood grown
in sustainable forests. The manufacturing process
conform to the environment regulations of the
country of origin.

A catalogue record for this book is available from
the British Library

Printed and bound in Germany by Elsnerdruck,
Berlin

ISBN 0 09 187008 9

Familiar Strangers

'Many a man commits a reprehensible action, who is at bottom an honourable man, because man seldom acts upon natural impulse, but from some secret passion of the moment which lies hidden and concealed within the narrowest folds of his heart' – Napoleon 1, *Maxims*

For Bunter, Sheila, Brickman,
Eve, Roger and Louisa –
familiar friends in times of need.

1

I T WOULD HAVE appalled Theo even to have contemplated that his final resting place would be Slough. As a matter of fact it would appal me to die in Slough, since I can think of few English towns that depress me so instantly; Theo's body must have welcomed the consuming flames. Even the name 'Slough' – a constant source of confusion to foreigners – conjures up an Orwellian present. *Sluff* is how most strangers understandably pronounce it, and they get closer to the pictorial truth than the correct *Slau* as in *sow*, which in itself is hardly a celebration of our perverse language.

To be accurate and to calm his ghost, Theo did not die in Slough. He died in a rented bed-sitting room in a Victorian mansion with Gothic pretensions just off the neighbouring Englefield Green, a small and relatively unspoilt hamlet bordering Royal Windsor Great Park. He died alone, and from the coroner's report it is conceivable that his death took place on Christmas Day. The body wasn't found until the New Year. Nowadays, England being morally and financially bankrupt, we treat ourselves to longer and longer national holidays and nobody, not even the proverbial milkman, noticed poor Theo's absence from the festive scene during the six-day hangover that now dignifies the birth of Our Lord. Eventually his landlady stirred herself to enquire when one of Theo's three neutered cats expired on her doorstep. Using a house key she doubtless had no mandate to retain, she entered Theo's section of the building to find him long since dead.

He was lying across his spartan single bed clutching an ancient hot-water bottle to his chest, rather as a victim of religious persecution embraces the true Cross. Rigor mortis had set in, driving his fingers into the perished rubber of the bottle. Rusty water had stained his striped pyjamas, giving her the false impression of a dried chest wound sufficiently realistic at the time of discovery to send her into hysterics. An electric fire was burning at full strength and the atmosphere, I gather, was somewhere between a sauna and a charnel house. In all events, the body had started to decompose and it was with difficulty that the ambulance men prised him from the cheap mattress and took him to the mortuary.

It was hardly a fitting exit for one of England's most distinguished men of letters, somebody widely tipped for an eventual O.M. I don't suppose I would have had any prior notice of the tragedy before the obituaries appeared, for we were not close in the decade preceding his death, but by coincidence, or possibly a premonition, I had sent him a Christmas card that year. The local police found my seasonal greeting by the side of Theo's bed, and since I had appended my address and a vague invitation for a long-overdue reunion in the New Year, it was me they contacted to identify the body. We were related on my father's side of the family.

I drove to the mortuary at a speed that evoked rage and frustration from my fellow road users, but it was not a day to be hurried. When one is past fifty death seems all too close for comfort and the deaths of our contemporaries an almost weekly reminder that we are on the wrong side of the insurance statistics.

Much to my surprise the mortuary proved to be a pleasing example of modern architecture. I think I had been expecting some Burke and Hare establishment reeking of formaldehyde, but the entire building was air-conditioned and the only detectable scent that of freshly-polished floor tiles. There was also a refreshing lack of bureaucratic red tape and indeed, Mr. Pollard, the official who greeted me, behaved with more warmth than your average British hotel keeper.

My first impression was that Theo looked younger than his years, but as Mr. Pollard explained, death, unless it comes violently, often achieves this cosmetic effect. I was reminded of the famous death mask of Napoleon, a leader whom Theo greatly admired, I might add. The skin was truly wax-like, the face babyish, plumped, the lips slightly curled and suggesting a smile, though I noticed that he had lost more hair than me and that what remained looked as though it had been artificially coloured. Theo was a great one for patent medicines, believing anything he read in those health magazines he subscribed to, though I suspect he purchased them for the frolicking and, to my mind, always unattractive nude photographs of middle-class families engaged in improbable games.

"Satisfied, Mr. Stern?"

The tone was that of a tailor soliciting approval for a final fitting, and was hardly the right choice of word in the circumstances. I nodded, since I always believe in humouring minor officials. One can't be too careful as 1984 draws near.

"Perhaps you'd be good enough to say it then, sir."

I stared at him, then back to Theo. I had no idea what was expected of me – was I supposed to produce an instant wake, murmuring some suitable eulogy or prayer?

"We have to observe the statutory requirements required of us," Mr. Pollard continued, in the same faintly condescending voice, revealing in his thin smile a complete set of grotesque false teeth. These, more than the presence of poor Theo between us, gave me a jarring glimpse of life on the other side.

"I'm sorry?"

"We have to formally identify the deceased person, Mr. Stern. The law requires it."

"Ah, yes. Of course. How stupid of me."

"Take your time, sir."

"That is, or rather that was, my relative."

"I'm afraid we have to be more precise than that, sir. We need the full name of the departed. You say to me, 'That is Mr. So and So' – or, at the other extreme, 'That is Miss So and So, or Mrs.,' according to the marital status, adding if you wish, 'to the best of my knowledge and belief'. It saves any possible misunderstanding thereafter."

I repressed a desire to giggle. I felt Theo would have enjoyed this part of the proceedings – my discomfort and Mr. Pollard's delivery – for he had a sardonic sense of humour when it suited him.

"Right," I responded. "Well, we must do it by the book. That is my second cousin, Theo Gittings."

"And . . .?"

"And?"

"Did I detect the merest hesitation, Mr. Stern?"

"No, I don't think so. Did you?"

"Just a whisker, I fancy."

"Well, it wasn't intentional. I mean that *is* Theo."

"Can I suggest that – just to be on the safe side – we add the words 'to the best of our knowledge and belief'."

"Our knowledge? You mean my knowledge, don't you?"

"Yes, you've got me at it now, sir."

"Okay, I'll say the whole thing again, shall I? To the best of our – my – knowledge and belief, that is my late second cousin Theobald Gittings. How's that?"

"Perfect, sir. You said it very nicely."

I felt I had passed the audition and the role was mine.

"Now then, sir, unless you'd like to linger, I think we can tuck Mr. Gettings away."

"Gittings," I murmured.

"Quite so." His manner became brisker all of a sudden, as though he had been caught out in some shameful act.

"What happens now?" I asked. "Is there to be a post-mortem?"

"That is on the cards, I believe. What was his line of business, your cousin?"

"He was a writer," I said. "Quite a famous writer," as the sheet blotted out Theo's face and the drawer slid back into the wall.

"Wrote books, did he, sir?"

"Yes."

"I've always thought it was a nice hobby, writing. 'Course, I could write a few tales myself, if I had the time. You see it all here."

"I'm sure."

"Oh, yes. Death be not proud, what price glory, et cetera."

"Very apt."

Perhaps he detected in my voice that note of coldness professional writers employ when their craft is so lightly regarded. At any given gathering one can always count upon being button-holed by some would-be author and told that, were it not for the pressures of more important business, 'I could write a book.' It sometimes seems there is an Irving Wallace lurking inside half the population.

I signed the necessary papers in triplicate and drove away, thinking of the complexities of other people's lives. What sort of ambition or necessity leads the Mr. Pollards of this world to spend their years filing the dead? It's easy to say, somebody has to do it, but that is never the complete answer. I am aware that there was never any shortage of applicants anxious to break the Pierrepoint family's monopoly for the job of public hangman, and whilst Mr. Pollard was a long way down the line of spectators to human misery, there is no escaping the conclusion that suffering is addictive.

That last glimpse of Theo stayed with me as I drove through Datchet, past Windsor Castle walls, and headed for Runnymede and the London road, fully intending to return straight home to my chambers in Albany. I live alone, in what used to be called 'style' in less egalitarian times; a fairly routine existence, set in my ways, as the expression goes, since the death of my wife. I answer correspondence in the mornings, venture as far as the Garrick for lunch – the whole day a slow gathering of energies for the nightly stint at my Carlton House desk. I am always fascinated to read about the working habits of fellow writers, envying those who are most creative in the early hours. I find comfort in noting the eccentricities of others – their superstitions soothe me, for I share many of them. We are all programmed, we know what pressure points to touch, working like acupuncturists in reverse, seeking to reproduce the pain of past creative bouts. At various stages in my career I have made determined efforts to break away from my self-imposed drudgery, but like an old-time convict, I have found the ball and chain of routine has proved too strong. Even if I break the links I have no idea where the frontiers of freedom lie. I know my own limitations. I am not content with them, but I am enslaved by them.

Theo was totally different. Secretive by nature, he could seldom be drawn to discuss his own work in progress or his working habits, but over the years I gleaned enough to know that our distant blood relationship pulsed through separate

13

artistic veins. We had both lived through the pen (or in my lazy case, the electric typewriter) and to that extent we were alike, but in thinking of his death I realised we had little else in common. The memory of his calm, dead face troubled me. A vague, nagging doubt, such as parents experience when they drive away for a dinner engagement leaving children alone in the house. I had left something undone and it wasn't until I came to the intersection leading up the hill to Englefield Green that I realised I had one other task to perform.

I had no idea at that point which other members of our farflung family would eventually appear out of the woodwork (grief and avarice frequently leave the same visiting card), but I was aware that poor Theo still had the power to shock from the grave. I didn't really give a damn about the relatives, for they had never appreciated his true worth, but I did care about his reputation. From time to time he and I had discussed our literary estates, not too seriously, for Theo shied away from illness and could seldom be persuaded to attend a funeral or even a memorial service. We talked about some loose arrangements such as people do when they are in the best of health. I would look after his papers, he would look after mine, whoever went first – that sort of thing. It was never a formal undertaking and in my own case, since I have a horror of files and old letters, I had no real cause for concern. As to the rest, I am indifferent. I never had Theo's mania for the trivia of one's life. I would rather people speculate than be certain.

With Theo it was another story. I remembered something he had once said to me during the war when nobody was spared the inconvenience of sudden death.

"Have you ever given a thought to the skeletons?" he asked.

"Skeletons?"

"Yes. The proverbial kind, that rattle in cupboards."

"No, I can't say I have."

"I think about them all the time."

"Perhaps you've got more than me."

"Perhaps. It isn't the number, it's the quality of them."

"I'm sure yours are superior to mine."

"I doubt that."

It was one of those passing conversations we think little of at the time, but like certain social diseases they lie dormant just below the surface, erupting when we believe we are completely safe.

Although, as I have said, Theo and I had drifted apart in his final years, there had been a time when his friendship meant much to me. Perhaps I was not being totally altruistic, perhaps my predatory writer's instinct shared the honours with my concern – at this remove, and bearing in mind what later came to light, I can't be certain. In any event, I turned the wheel of my Mercedes and headed up the steep hill, changing gear to protect his memory.

2

I PARKED MY CAR on the grass verge outside the house where Theo died. It was set back from the road, the front garden protected by a crumbling brick wall daubed with the inevitable graffiti. Its daily dose of dog pee had caused the words to run, but I could still make out the message – ENOCH RULES OK. The garden itself was over-run and when I entered through the small iron gate I had to duck to avoid the branches of a weeping birch. The house had been converted into two separate dwellings, the original large front entrance split in two, so that now two front doors stood side by side, both glassed and both badly in need of a lick of paint. I hesitated, not knowing which bell to push and eventually pressed both of them. I had never visited Theo there when he was alive.

Why is it that houses where there has been a recent bereavement seem to have an aura surrounding them? Was it just my imagination, or merely the general gloominess of the façade that made me shiver as I stood waiting? Distant shouts reached me from a group of boys kicking a football about on the green. I heard the yap of a small and, even sight unseen, boring lap dog.

A few moments later one of the doors was opened a fraction. The dog pushed its repulsive face through the crack. A rodent-like head with eyes protruding like burnt sultanas, it exuded hatred – yapping and urinating simultaneously as it advanced towards me. I took a step backwards to avoid my trousers being fouled.

The woman in the doorway had certain marked similarities to her repellent pet, in that her head was out of proportion to the rest of her body. The effect was further distorted by a mass of Carmen rollers in her hair, fixed so tightly that they exposed areas of pink and scurfy scalp.

"Yes?"

"You don't know me," I began, speaking louder than normally in order to pitch my voice above the incessant yapping of the dog. "And please forgive me for disturbing you without warning, but I'm a relative of the late Mr. Gittings."

"Yes?"

"As a matter of fact I've just come from identifying his body."

"Oh. Shouldn't have thought that was necessary. I saw to all that."

"Well, the usual red tape, I suppose."

"I found him."

"So I was told. It must have been a great shock."

"New Year's Day."

"Not a very pleasant beginning."

Her dog had a bladder capacity out of all proportion to its size and by now was killing what remained of a cankered privet bush, all the while fixing me with its maniac eyes.

"That's enough, Elsie," the woman said. She slipped the chain from the lock and opened the door. "You've done your business like a good girl, now just be quiet."

The animal was suddenly, blissfully silent, but stood transfixed, one front paw raised as though petrifaction had set in.

"My name is Stern," I said. "I'm sorry, but I don't think we've ever met before."

"Davis. Mrs. Davis."

"Well, obviously, Mrs. Davis, you were very kind to my cousin. And on behalf of the family I'd like to thank you for that."

"I did what I had to do."

"Had he been here long?"

"Seven years."

The conversation was getting nowhere. She was not the kind of woman who volunteers information.

"Has anything been done about his things?"

"I haven't touched anything," she said, immediately on the defensive. "Not a thing. Apart from stripping his bed. I had to do that; it wasn't sanitary."

"I'm sure you did everything properly. But obviously, at

17

some given time, things will have to be sorted out. Forgive my ignorance, but did Theo . . . did my cousin own his part of the building, or was he renting it?"

"The house is in my name. The late Mr. Davis left me well cared for."

"So, presumably, you'll want to rent it out again as soon as possible?" I had an idea Mrs. Davis could best be approached through the cheque book.

"Well, naturally, although I'm comfortably off, I can't afford to let it stand empty for long."

"No, that's why I thought I ought to call. To try and be of some help."

"Tell me your name again."

"Stern. Anthony Stern. I'm a writer, like my late cousin." I paused. We authors always live in expectation that mention of our names will immediately elicit a smile of delighted recognition. Mrs. Davis was obviously not a patron of contemporary literature. "Not such a distinguished writer as he was," I added.

"Yes. I read a couple of his. He always gave me copies. Deep, I thought. Not exactly my cup of tea. All right for people who like that sort of thing."

"Did he ever mention me to you?"

"He might have, yes. Yes, the name is slightly familiar. Not that he was a great talker, and not that I ever pried. He respected my privacy and me likewise."

"I'm sure he appreciated that. Look, I don't want you to be bothered in any way, but somebody has got to tackle the business of clearing out his personal effects. D'you think I could take a look around? I think I must be his closest surviving relative. His parents died years ago and as you know, he was single."

"Yes, he was a very bachelor sort of man. You want to go inside, do you?"

"If that's possible."

"Into his rooms?"

"Yes."

"They're not very tidy. He was a regular payer, but not a great one for tidiness."

18

"All the more reason," I said, "for getting things sorted out."

She regarded me in silence for a few moments. "I hope I'm doing the right thing."

"Well, naturally, if you want to come with me I've no objections."

"Yes. Yes, all right. Well, I'll get the key. One can't be too careful these days."

"I quite agree."

"Come on in, Elsie. If you'll just wait here." The animal produced one last spatter before following her back into the house.

My first encounter with Mrs. Davis added to my bewilderment concerning Theo's last years. What could have possessed a man of his intelligence and distinction to bury himself in such a backwater with such a crone as his closest neighbour? I had no idea at that point what his financial situation had been. Although his novels never figured in the best seller lists, his sales had been respectable over the past decade, two of the novels being required reading for exams. I had never imagined him to be poor, yet the house seemed to be the last retreat of a man of declining means. The Theo I remembered had liked living well, had driven a hard bargain whenever his services were required for a Hollywood stint and was always a generous host with a nose for the best wines and cuisine. It seemed incomprehensible that he would choose to exist in such mundane surroundings, devoid of any stimulating conversation. Where Mrs. Davis was concerned, the effort of maintaining day-to-day politeness, however minimal, would have been too much for me.

It wasn't that the house was squalid, or that Mrs. Davis was slovenly. The house was merely depressing and his landlady the sort of neighbour I would take a sea trip to avoid. That is what really puzzled me as I waited for her return. I remembered Theo as a witty, gregarious companion, somebody who enjoyed the cut and thrust of debate, a man of pronounced opinions and unafraid, indeed anxious, to air them.

I was still pondering these contradictions when Mrs. Davis reappeared. She opened the adjacent front door and led the way. The conversion had obviously been done on the cheap, for Theo's door gave on to a narrow partitioned hallway, the staircase rising steeply to the upper storey he had occupied. The place smelt damp; I got an immediate impression of neglect, but nothing, not even my own fertile imagination – for which I have often been taken to task by my critics – had prepared me for the revelation of his bedroom, the room in which he had died.

Mrs. Davis stood to one side and made no attempt to cross the threshold.

"As I said, tidy he wasn't."

I shall need all my restraint to describe the state of his bedroom. Perhaps I should start by evoking the memory of Miss Haversham's fabled room in *Great Expectations*, for that was the comparison which leapt into my mind at first glance. The squalor was horrendous. Admittedly, there were no dead rats or decaying wedding cake, but the room – of average size – was crammed from top to bottom. Stacked all around the single iron bedstead were piles, three or four feet high, of old newspapers and magazines, the top layers faded with age. A desk was pushed tight into one corner and alongside this, without an inch to spare, was a cheap wardrobe, itself so full that the door had been forced from one hinge. Both the top of this and the desk were stacked high with an assortment of bric-à-brac: filing boxes, books with their spines broken, jam jars full of pencils and old coins, here a mass of what appeared to be old bus tickets, there a collection of cigarette tins, numerous ashtrays, bottles of patent medicines, batches of manuscript, a large biscuit tin overflowing with rubber bands, one shoe with a tea cup pressed into the heel, the saucer somewhere else serving as a receptacle for cigarette butts that had been smoked down to the filters. There was scarcely any room between the foot of the bed and the chest of drawers facing it. The top of this was also heaped with debris, and behind the bed Theo had massed more old newspapers, lining these up to form a crazy shelf on which he had arranged more books. The whole scene resembled a police photograph of a room that had been deliberately wrecked by intruders, and the curious thing is that I saw it all in black and white, just like such a photograph, all the colour bleached out. To tell the truth there was very little colour in that room, for everything had a dull sheen of dust over it. What clothes I could see were crammed in an open corner cupboard and looked like the garments one sees on second-hand stalls. It was one of the saddest rooms I have ever been in.

"See what I mean?" Mrs. Davis said. "'Course, I was never allowed to clean it up. Hated having anything disturbed."

"Didn't he have any help?"

"They never stayed."

"It's amazing," I said.

"There's two other rooms and the usual."

I followed her through into the tiny kitchen. In stark contrast to the chaos of the bedroom, this was bare except for the essentials, and betrayed the fact that this was where a bachelor had prepared his solitary meals. A few recipes cut from newspapers were pinned over the sink, and I noticed that the only objects that seemed to belong were three cat bowls with the names of their owners inked around the sides: Billy, Fluff and Mr. T. Lying beside one of the bowls was a toy mouse, the tail bitten away.

There was a sitting room adjoining, comfortless and furnished in appalling taste. Over the mantelpiece was a framed photograph of Theo taken during his undergraduate days at Cambridge. As I looked at it, the old expression, The Lost Generation, came to mind.

"Did he leave a Will?" Mrs. Davis asked.

"I don't know. I suppose that's one of the things I shall have to look for."

"He always talked about leaving me his grandfather clock. Not that I'm counting on it, mind, but that's what he used to say."

"Well, I'm sure if that was his wish it'll be honoured."

She brightened at this. "Would you like a cup of tea? I should have asked you before."

"Yes, that would be very welcome."

"I'll make it downstairs in my pot."

As she retreated I heard her call to the dog, "Go back, Elsie precious. You can't climb these stairs with your little legs, and this isn't the place for you."

I went back into the bedroom and eased my way to the desk. I had no idea where to begin, and in any event to examine another person's private papers is always distasteful. I would hate to be a policeman. Few of us make adequate preparations, for the myth of immortality is the hardest to discard. So much of what we leave behind for others to uncover betrays us. Happy the people whose annals are vacant.

I stared down at the cluttered desk. There was an open box of manuscript, the top page scribbled over with Theo's corrections. Work in progress, that would never now be finished. Then I saw a copy of my own last book, a review copy as it happened, presumably sent to Theo by some over-enthusiastic literary editor who thought that the family connection would maybe produce some controversial copy. It had the look of a book that had never been opened.

Not one of the drawers in the desk was locked, and I opened two or three at random and was appalled by the task ahead, for it was obvious at a glance that Theo had no system. I sifted through an assortment of unpaid bills, some months overdue, and my immediate thought was that he had died penniless and felt guilty that I had allowed us to drift apart. A moment later I came across a bundle of uncashed cheques and some quick mental arithmetic dispelled my first fears. Most of them were dividend cheques, and even to my untrained eye I could see that they represented sizeable investments more than sufficient to take care of his creditors. It was the first paradox of his secret life.

I turned my attention to the bedside table. Lying open on it amid a welter of odd scraps of paper was a school exercise book. I saw that the exposed page was dated at the top – December 22 – and I sat on the edge of the bare mattress and began to read the handwritten entry beneath.

10 a.m.   Got up. Felt very slightly sick. Made cup of choco-
               late. Laid and lit fire in lounge.

11.05	Ate porridge before the fire, felt very cold. I have been dreading this day, although I know it must be faced.
11.20	Practised deep breathing until feeling of dizziness wore off. Shaved and dressed.
1.20 p.m.	Caught train to Euston. What compelled me to make the journey? Was it merely the agony of expectation? I should know, but I don't. Didn't notice the train rocking so much as usual. On arrival at Euston I went to the snack bar and bought a cup of tea, cheese and biscuits and two mince pies. I quite enjoyed the rest and the bustle of the station. It's the season, of course. Everybody going home. Home for the holidays. Home.
3.45	Took various bus routes, then the Tube to Swiss Cottage. Was pushed several times. Noticed that most of the staff are black. Train filthy, seats ripped. Felt dizzy again and had my first cigarette of the day. Middle-aged woman shouted at me – I was in a non-smoking carriage. Extinguished cigarette but did not apologise. The episode unnerved me.
4.20	Had difficulty finding A's address. House next door has been pulled down since my last visit and this confused me. He kept me waiting on the doorstep for at least five minutes before answering my ring. Gave me a Dubonnet and said I could not stay. He had another appointment and it was too dangerous. Said the whole thing was impossible and had to end. Made a fool of myself by pleading. All to no avail. I was stupid to go in the first place. He explained he no longer received at home, that it was madness, the place was being watched. This may have been just to scare me, but I am past scaring. Anyway it ended. I left before he did since he refused to be seen with me. Walked part of the way back to the station then felt dizzy again and hailed a taxi.
7.15	Arrived home. Fire out, of course, and too tired to re-light it. Felt terribly lonely. Dog barking incessantly. I've made such a mess of it all, doing all the wrong things for the right reasons, or do I mean the other

way round? Too tired to think it out. To bed with a
hot water bottle.

I covered the notebook with some magazines at the sound of
Mrs. Davis returning. She brought the tea on a tray, together
with a plate of digestive biscuits. I needed the hot comfort the
tea provided, for the unheated room had chilled me. I had to
concentrate to hear what Mrs. Davis was saying.

"He was a good payer, I couldn't fault him there. And a
real gentleman, of course. One of the old sort. I suppose, in a
way, it's quite something to have a famous person die in your
house. He was famous, wasn't he?"

"Yes. Not famous like a footballer or a pop singer – times
have changed – but very distinguished."

"'Course, some people get a morbid pleasure out of that,
don't they, like living in a house where there's been a murder.
I mean, some people will pay more for that."

"So I've heard."

"Funny, isn't it?"

"People can be very odd," I said.

"I did think of ringing the local paper. I expect they'll want
to interview me, seeing as how I was the one who found him."

"D'you think we could put on the fire?" I said. "I find it
very cold in here."

She pulled an ancient electric fire into the open space by the
door.

"It was on when I found him. Like a furnace in here. Been
on for days, you see, and of course the you-know-what – well,
to be crude, the smell, you know."

"Very unpleasant."

"Yes. Gave Elsie a nasty turn; she wasn't herself for days.
They sense things, don't they, animals? And of course she's
highly strung. On account of her breeding. She's pedigree."

"I could see that."

"Yes, lovely little thing. Would you like another cup?
Plenty in the pot."

"I can see why he stayed with you all those years," I said.
"You obviously spoilt him."

"I did what I could. I did my best."

"Was his rent paid up to date? Because, if not, I'd be only too happy to take care of that. Until things are sorted out."

"He owed a month," she said quickly, and I knew I had found the way to her heart.

In the short time I had been left alone in the room I had made certain decisions. I knew I had a task ahead of me. There was the funeral to arrange, of course, but beyond that – beyond the dismal formalities – I had the feeling that my instincts had been sound. It's difficult for me to speculate on my true motives at that moment, for in the rush of the day's events I had experienced a variety of emotions. Perhaps uppermost in my mind were horror and pity, for the state of the room, the way in which Theo had obviously spent his declining years, was something my imagination had not previously embraced. They say that an author's inventions always outstrip reality, but I have found most human acts too dreadfully obscure for us to pronounce judgment with any finality.

Yet there was something else, no more than a vague uneasiness. The last entries in Theo's journal hinted at a muted nightmare. The fact that he had used words like 'dangerous', 'madness'; that he had written 'I am past scaring'. Most journals and diaries are banal, pre-edited versions of our daily lives that we write from habit rather than conviction, but in Theo's case, from the little I had read, there were undertones of quiet horror. The careful tabulating of exact times suggested he had a need to record everything, as though he was aware that time was running out in more ways than one. A writer never knows when the pool of his imagination will allow the submerged evidence to surface. I had come to that house to protect that portion of Theo's memory I knew better than anybody else, but now I needed more time alone to think things through, and the presence of Mrs. Davis was too distracting. I gestured towards the desk.

"Look, there's going to be a post-mortem, but once that's over and the necessary authorities have been granted, I'll sort through this lot. In the meantime, perhaps you'll allow me to pay you two months' rent."

I wrote her out a cheque there and then, and she willingly

agreed to my suggestion that the room be left completely undisturbed. While she removed the tea things I pocketed Theo's journal, then we locked his portion of the house and exchanged warm farewells under the weeping birch, the small dog still performing urinary wonders as I drove away.

Let me quickly deal with the mechanics that set this account in motion. The post-mortem revealed nothing untoward. There were the usual signs of deterioration in some of the vital organs commensurate with his age, but the final verdict was that all-embracing comfort, 'death by natural causes'.

The funeral was a simple one. I placed In Memoriam notices in *The Times*, the *Daily Telegraph* and the *New Statesman*, in addition circulating the Cambridge newspapers since I thought it possible that some members of his old college might care to pay their last respects. In the event the mourners numbered eleven. Apart from Mrs. Davis and myself, there was a representative from the Arts Council whom I vaguely knew, but the rest were all strangers, and although I carefully noted their names when the short cremation service was concluded, they meant nothing to me. There was no family and I was therefore spared the embarrassment of even a token wake. The young clergyman who conducted the service introduced a brief element of farce into the empty proceedings by referring to Theo as 'our sister who has just departed' before recovering the thread.

There was talk of a memorial service in the Abbey, but nothing came of it. Theo's publisher, acting with an enthusiasm seldom visible when Theo was alive, announced that he was 'privileged' to rush reprints of four of the best-known novels into the bookshops, but within months I noticed they had been remaindered on the station bookstalls. I dare say Theo will have to wait another decade until the next generation evaluates his true worth.

His bank contacted me revealing that he had not only left a Will but, surprisingly, had named me as his Executor. It was a simple document. He asked me to make suitable provision for his three cats, a request I could not honour, for one had already expired and the other two had vanished, as animals sometimes do when their routine is broken. I went through the motions of placing advertisements in the local newsagent's, but Fluffy and Mr. T failed to reappear. There were a few other minor bequests to charities he had supported and a donation to the Festival of Light (a typical piece of cynicism on Theo's part), and I was instructed to apply the residue of his estate for the preservation of his manuscripts and private papers. In particular, he left detailed procedures for the future handling of his journals, charging me to ensure that they were not to be published for twenty years after his death. I was given full authority to dispose of the remainder of his effects in any manner I thought suitable and to deduct such reasonable expenses for my pains as the situation demanded. He had not made any provision for the anxious Mrs. Davis, a fact I successfully concealed from her, and I used my discretion where the grandfather clock was concerned.

I took the precaution of telephoning her in advance before paying my next visit to the house. She greeted me with somewhat flirtatious warmth and a tray of tea already prepared. I had the suspicion that his bedroom had been altered slightly, but the chaos was still such as to defy the perceptions of a Maigret. Having finished her tea and biscuits I managed, by a series of increasingly obvious hints, to penetrate her thick skin and she eventually grasped that I would prefer to work alone and undisturbed.

"You just treat it like your own home," she said, as though Theo's squalor was the natural habitat of writers.

In the interval since my previous visit I had had ample opportunity to consider the scattered evidence in that last volume of Theo's journals. It did not make happy reading. I now knew what I was looking for, but since there was no system to Theo's various collections it seemed a waste of time to impose one of my own, and for the first few hours I delved in haphazard fashion, throwing away whatever was patently of no lasting interest.

I was again dismayed by his dismal wardrobe, for I remembered he had once been what we used to call a 'snappy dresser', immaculate when the occasion demanded. But the clothes I found jumbled together that afternoon revealed no trace of past elegance. One drawer contained a quantity of sports clothes — rugby jerseys, socks and shorts, all soiled. I found this curious because like many of us who toil by the pen he was not one of nature's hearties. Yet another drawer in the same battered chest was crammed with lederhosen, decorated leather and the like, and these seemed to my inexpert eye to be in a variety of sizes.

I have said that I knew what I was looking for. But let me correct that. I *thought* I knew what I was looking for.

I knew only too well that by the time he was in his twenties Theo had settled for being homosexual. The popular description now is 'coming out of the closet', but in the period between the wars nobody 'came out' publicly except debutantes, and for good reason, since queers were still the blackmailer's favourite quarries and I stood sad witness to several of my contemporaries' suicides.

Theo was reasonably discreet, as far as I could tell. On those occasions when we openly discussed the subject he revealed little of his affairs. He would merely say, "I came across a new friend the other day who I think might amuse you," and on two or three occasions he invited me to make a threesome for dinner. I never found his companions even faintly amusing. They all seemed cast from the same mould: rather bovine youths, who drank his wine like draught beer and scarcely uttered, though, presumably in an effort to justify his choice, Theo would laugh immoderately at their unsophisticated jokes, granting them a wit that was scarcely discernible to an outsider. I found such evenings trying. Not that Theo was 'camp' in the theatrical sense, or at least he never parodied his tastes when I was around. He dressed, as I have related, with stylish conservatism, and never gave any clues in his published novels.

So in my preliminary search through the contents of Theo's room I was prepared for revelations of a certain kind, but I confess that I was surprised by what I actually found. There was no clever attempt at concealment — the first box of photographs I came across was stored inside an ancient fibre suitcase, still festooned with old Cunard labels. It wasn't even locked, though the hard-core stuff was under a layer of family snapshots which might have diverted a casual searcher.

I suppose, if I am honest, what surprised me most was not the easy discovery but the nature of the discovery. There was a selection of more or less standard poses showing fellatio and anal penetration between youths dressed partially in scouting uniform, presumably stock items that can be purchased in most dirty bookshops. It wasn't until I came across a batch featuring Theo himself that I was forced to acknowledge that perhaps I had never known him at all. They were amateur efforts, some of them taken in that very bedroom by flashlight that had bounced back from the shiny surfaces of the walls, giving them a milky appearance. In almost every case they showed Theo clad in football gear, complete with studded boots, bent across the laps of various middle-aged men wearing a form of Nazi uniform. They had obviously been taken over a long period, for Theo's appearance was noticeably different in many cases: I noted changes in the colour and style of his hair and the fact that he had acquired a paunch between sessions. Equally, his 'military' companions were seldom duplicated. None of them could be said to be oil paintings; they looked like their real-life wartime counterparts, dreary little men who had had all pleasures blotted from their faces.

Immediately I had brought them to light I felt compelled to check whether Mrs. Davis was anywhere in the vicinity. I went into the kitchen and made myself a cup of black instant coffee from a half-empty jar I found in a cupboard. Looking at the cat bowls, I found myself wondering whether Mr. T and his companions had ever been silent, unimpressed witnesses to the events depicted in the photographs. My novelist's brain began to map out the stage directions that must have accompanied such tableaux. The conjectures proved accurate, since I was later to establish that Theo recruited his contacts by a variety of pen names and box numbers, and it was therefore safe to assume that in the majority of cases his midnight Nazis were total strangers. They must have come to the house and mounted that steep staircase to the upper floor. I imagined Theo offering them a glass of sherry or, more bizarre, a cup of hot chocolate that he seemed to drink in preference to tea or coffee. Then, presumably, they got down to the serious business. Did Theo greet them already wearing his football gear? Did they ever exchange their real names? Was there a scale of charges to be haggled over before trousers were dropped? My imagination was not broad enough to supply all the answers. What I could believe, looking again at the photographs, was the bleakness of it all. I hope I am not being unduly sentimental about this, applying my own conventional standards out of ignorance. I may have got it all wrong. Perhaps it wasn't as joyless as the photographs suggested. Perhaps human loneliness is so complex that the unthinkable can, for a few brief moments, be transformed into an act of compassion.

And Theo? What post coitus emotions did he endure? Did he go straight to his desk, feed a clean sheet of paper into that ancient portable and commence another of his polished, elegant paragraphs – the creative impulse regenerated by sexual fulfilment? I have heard it is quite commonplace with footballers and boxers, and Edmund Kean is reputed to have sampled up to three whores immediately prior to one of his major performances. A highly successful playwright once confided that whenever he fell victim to our recurring complaint, writer's block, he resorted to masturbation. "Nothing like it for clearing the brain. It's the guilt, you see, old man. You feel so bloody guilty afterwards, especially at my age, you have to get back to work. And of course one doesn't have to be polite afterwards. That's what I always hate about conventional sex. To have to waste so much time romancing the creatures. You can say goodbye to yourself so easily."

I don't know how many hours I spent in Theo's room that first day of discovery. I became grimed with newsprint and dust, forgetful of time passing, unaware of hunger, and it wasn't until Mrs. Davis suddenly reappeared, spruced and drenched in a sickening, cheap scent to invite me down for supper that I returned to the world of the living.

I accepted as graciously as I could and endured her small talk over a meal of curry that in itself was justification for the Race Relations Act. Her own brand of loneliness was of the aggressive kind, as though some of Theo's sexuality had seeped downstairs and impregnated the flock wallpaper of her garish apartment. Her conversation, when she was not probing for details of the value of Theo's estate, was saturated with innuendo that I found as bitter as the coffee she served.

As soon as was polite, I excused myself and returned to Theo's room. I packed two suitcases, filling one with the pornography I intended to burn, and the other with selected bundles of letters and documents together with some forty of the identical exercise books he had used for his journals. I had tidied up the worst of the debris and parcelled most of the tattered magazines for eventual collection as salvage. I dare say that would have been the end of it had I not, at the last moment, been drawn to flick through the pages of an old copy of *Country Life*. My initial interest was to compare the price of houses in the Sixties with current values. A photograph fluttered to the floor, falling face downwards. I picked it up and found myself staring at a man who had once featured on the front pages of every Western newspaper. It was the face of a once handsome youth gone to flab; a weak face, the lips moistened in a smile devoid of any warmth. Written across the photograph were the words *To Theo with too much love*. One corner was torn, obliterating most of the signature, but I had no difficulty in identifying the face. It was a photograph of Guy Burgess.

3

THEO REALLY BELONGED to the turn of the century. Connolly once described him (in an otherwise uncomplimentary lead review) as an 'Edwardian monument to the English novel', a remark which prompted a particularly arid correspondence in the *Times Literary Supplement*. He was often spoken of in the same reverent tones as Forster and Beerbohm, though his output was considerably more than their combined efforts and he had no time for either of them. He dismissed Beerbohm as a dilettante and felt it was an outrage that he had been knighted. "He should have had the decency to refuse it," Theo said, "and been satisfied with a widow's pension. That was more his mark." He was no less scathing about Forster, dubbing him a 'back passage to India' and was never so angry as when a critic bracketed him and Forster together.

I can understand how difficult it was for his critics to net him, for it was almost impossible for a complete outsider to get his true personality down on paper. He seldom gave interviews, and although he could have written his own ticket for any of the television talk shows he was seldom seen on the box. Unlike Willie Maugham, Theo never had a constant male companion and thus the gossip columnists were denied the field of innuendo and, in those far-off days before the dawn of the permissive society, were forced to scatter their clues with circumspection. "Hell," he used to remark, "hath no fury like a homosexual critic who senses that his more exalted victims are getting away with it," adding that, "Although it has always been an unwritten law that everybody closes ranks when the yahoos advance on the camp, there is little mercy shown to those within the city walls."

Theo gave no personal clues in his published works. He wrote elegant prose, being closer to Henry James than most of his contemporaries and his narratives centred on a way of life that has long since disappeared. He shared, with Hartley, a belief that the past is a foreign country where people do things differently. He had an affinity with the past, a hankering for time lost, searching back for an age of innocence that probably never existed but which seemed preferable to the world he was compelled to inhabit. The major novels, fourteen in all, were spaced out at regular intervals, and those readers who care about such things will doubtless have noted that the majority of his plots deal with unrequited love. The novels constitute the bulk of his output, but he did publish two collections of essays, both of which were taken apart and degutted by Leavis, thus ensuring that the other critics over-praised them.

Within the family he and I were both regarded as misfits, I perhaps less so than Theo because I was more recognisably successful. My novels, though never accorded the respect that Theo commanded, sold in far greater numbers, especially in paperback editions which many of my relatives favoured since, as one of them put it, 'you don't feel it's such a waste of money'. My mother, who regarded Theo as a second son, remained steadfastly sorrowful about his lifelong bachelor status. "Such a pity," she would say, "Theo never found a nice girl. They were all too flighty for him" – betraying her own sex *en masse*. In her later years she found it convenient to embroider her basic fantasy and spoke knowledgeably of Theo having been jilted. "It broke his heart," she would confide. "That's why he took up writing." Somewhere tucked away in her memory, like the small lawn handkerchief she always kept up her sleeve, was a folded misinterpretation, easy to mock. It satisfied her moral sense of the order of things and I dare say that in her true innocence, typical of her class and generation, her inventions were no more reprehensible than the realities of Theo's secret life. I was sometimes tempted to explode the myth in her presence, but lacked the killer instinct that divides families more easily than the axe. There is always a point when the attitudes of the previous generation make paper Lizzie Bordens of us all.

She was, I am sorry to say, a snob without a glimmer of

justification, for we were not even *nouveau riche*, we were just plodding middle-class ordinary – though, as my mother remarked, bending many a bored ear, she came of 'good stock'. There was always the unspoken implication that she had improved the bloodline without any assistance from my father. Even as a small child I detected the heady aroma of my mother's pretensions, sometimes as strong as the Chanel No. 5 with which she drenched her ample bosom when she and my father had 'an evening out' – a Masonic dinner or one of those annual obligations, so revered in close communities, known as The Mayor's Open Day. We once entertained a canon to tea, and this sent my mother into a frenzy of pre- and post-exaltation.

My father suffered in silence, never challenging, giving no sign that every fresh obsession of my mother's was a criticism of his personality. They were bound together by the conventions of the time, for divorce in our family was akin to leprosy: those who strayed, no matter how distant the relationship, were for ever struck off The Christmas Card List – my mother's equivalent of the Almanach de Gotha.

For reasons that time has partially obscured, I spent most of my school holidays with Theo and his parents in their large house outside Norwich. It was called Westfield, a dark Victorian horror with 'later additions', as the estate agents say. Whatever else may have displeased my mother regarding the character of Harry Gittings, Theo's father, the size of his home and the life style he affected weighed heavily in his favour. By our own standards the Gittings were rich. They took holidays abroad, they kept two horses, had a housekeeper, a maid, and ran a car. Harry Gittings was a senior partner in a long-established firm of country solicitors, a profession where the pickings have always been substantial. Naturally, the fact that he was a member of the legal profession impressed my mother. Out of his hearing and careful of her company she would often inflate his standing, referring to him as 'our barrister relative'. I suspect that Harry Gittings retained scant knowledge of the day-to-day workings of the courts. Early on in his career he had taken stock of his own abilities and concentrated on the intricacies of the laws pertaining to Death and Estate Duties. He enjoyed a reasonable reputation in his field and was certainly never short of elderly widows for clients, all of whom had seen their husbands laid to rest and lived on to enjoy what Harry salvaged for them. My father, giving one of his rare verdicts, once pronounced that Harry sailed close to the wind. In my then innocence I took this to mean he had nautical leanings. He was a man of many parts, taking a keen interest in the local community, a church warden who rode with the local hunt and was on the Board of Governors of the County Reform School for wayward girls – of which more later.

Theo was an only child, born prematurely by Caesarean section in France, Harry Gittings having insisted that his wife accompany him on an exhaustive tour, 'doing' the châteaux of the Loire. More than anything else, the Gittings' travels set them apart from my own family, for we seldom ventured further than Bournemouth and then always putting up in what the British term 'private' hotels. I cannot recall that they were ever private or merited being named hotels, but they came halfway between my mother's pretensions and my father's income. For many British families most of the year is a storing of the energy necessary to survive a British holiday. We journeyed by train, second class, and took a taxi from Bournemouth station. Every morning, rain or shine, we would troop down to the beach and hire deck chairs to stake our claim to a section of the over-crowded sands. My brothers and I would immediately start to acquire third-degree burns, assuming the sun shone, or else streaming colds, when the sun did not shine. Occasionally, accompanied by father, we would thread our way through the crowds to sample the icy qualities of that holy stretch of grey matter known as the English Channel. My mother would sit, protected from the sun by a large flowered hat, a fugitive from death in Little Venice. All around people would be struggling to change into swimming attire, hopping on one foot, swathed in towels, knickers and trousers entwined around their ankles, bras and vests quickly crumpled and concealed – a series of prudish conjuring tricks not yet mastered, so that at times when one looked up through the heat haze the whole beach seemed to be populated with a tribe of voodoo dancers.

Such were our dismal summer holidays, and it was with mingled fear and relief that I escaped most years to Westfield: fear because of justifiable suspicions of Theo's father, and relief because for a few weeks I could be relieved of my mother's suffocating concern for the proprieties. The moment I arrived at Westfield Theo entered into an unspoken conspiracy, giving me a relationship I never enjoyed with my twin brothers. There was an element of hero worship, of course, and a feeling of superiority since my brothers were never invited. Perhaps I was quieter than they or, improbable though it now seems, perhaps I gave the impression of being better mannered.

Theo was my senior by some three years and yet the age difference was never apparent to me, and I cannot recall that he ever used it to his own advantage, or condescended to me. I suspect that Theo was somewhat undeveloped, for he had been kept apart from children of his own age. He reputedly suffered from chronic ill health as a child, and as a consequence never attended school until he was in his late teens, but instead had a series of tutors, few of whom lasted longer than six months. Illness fascinated me, and I envied Theo what I imagined was a halcyon life free from the drudgery of the classroom. He never seemed particularly sickly during the holidays we spent together, and it wasn't until long after those early years that I pieced together the many clues and came to realise that his reported weaknesses were mostly his mother's inventions – a form of self-protection she had devised to keep him with her.

I don't suppose I am alone in my habit of finding literary comparisons with real life; a chance sentence from a favourite book can transport me back through the years in an instant. I have long cherished what I believe to be one of the finest novels written this century: Ford Madox Ford's *The Good Soldier*, that ironic tale of passion and deceit, so evocative, so erotic that it puts most of today's fiction to shame. It begins with the words 'This is the saddest story . . .' and whenever I re-read it my thoughts surge back to Westfield, and I can see as clearly as I now behold the bowl of freshly-cut roses on my desk the image of Theo's mother, pastel-shaded, her face too heavily powdered, her eyes blurred as though she cried too often, lifting thin hands to her throat in a constant, nervous gesture, and always speaking in a hushed voice. I never saw her laugh when Harry was present, unless it was in anxious response to one of his coarse jokes. At the dining table her eyes never left him; she was like some inexperienced umpire at Wimbledon, terrified of making the wrong call. Away from Harry she would relax and take an interest in our childhood games, but she always seemed to have one ear cocked for his return; the sound of his latch-key in the front door was sufficient to transform her. If this now sounds melodramatic, I cannot help it. She lived in a state of perpetual tension, torn between an unhealthy concern for Theo and terror of her husband. There was an atmosphere of fear about that house, a sense of things happening off-stage, as it were – things which, to a child, remained unexplained but which nevertheless made themselves felt in everyday life.

Looking back, I can fill some of the blank squares in the then unsolved crossword of our immature lives. I remember one occasion when Theo and I had the house to ourselves for a whole afternoon. His parents had both gone to some garden party and the housekeeper had the afternoon off. We were put on our honour – a promise given loosely and immediately disregarded. It was inevitable that with the insatiable curiosity of the young we should jointly settle on the idea of invading the holy of holies: Harry Gittings's study, or 'library' as it was generously termed.

I think I turned the door handle. There was a stillness about the room – forbidding, as though the personality of its regular occupant had permeated the very fabric of the walls. Facing us was a tall, mahogany, glass-fronted bookcase, its shelves housing the standard collection for solicitors, a uniformly bound set of the Law Reports. The partner's desk in the same dark wood stood in front of a leaded bay window, and beside the desk was a brass ashtray with a half-smoked Havana poised on it, the tip black-sodden and flattened. I have always found this a curiously repellent sight.

Committed now to total folly, I advanced into the room

and unprompted by Theo performed what to his eyes must have seemed an act of unparalleled heroism. I went and sat in his father's chair behind the desk. The leather seat was dimpled from his weight and emitted a soft fart as it was depressed. This reduced both of us to helpless laughter.

"Don't touch anything," Theo said, when he had recovered. "Don't leave any fingerprints." He was an avid disciple of Sexton Blake.

I took a grubby handkerchief from my pocket in the best traditions of that super sleuth and gently tried the centre drawer of the desk.

"For God's sake!" Theo said. He had not moved further than the doorway.

"They won't be back for ages."

"Well, I'd still better keep look out."

He advanced a few more paces into the room, standing to one side so that he could keep the street under observation.

The centre drawer contained some blotting paper and pens. The heavy scent of stale cigar smoke was making me feel queasy, but Theo's continued timidity spurred me to other acts of bravado. I took a fresh cigar from the drawer and placed it gently between my lips. Theo covered his eyes.

"I'm not at all satisfied with your behaviour," I growled in an unconvincing parody of his father's voice.

"Put it back, put it back," Theo moaned.

I complied because my nausea was stronger than my boastful intentions. I tried another drawer. This was deeper and had dividing sections in it. I saw what I at first thought were some rags in the nearest section. I poked at them.

"What're you doing now?"

"Nothing. Hey, look at these."

"What?"

"Come and look."

Theo edged closer to the desk and peered into the drawer. "What are they?"

"Knickers," I said. "Girl's knickers."

We stared at them.

"They must be your mother's. Why does he keep them in his desk?"

"I don't know," Theo said.

"Let's see what else there is."

I pulled the drawer further open, revealing the back section. This had a lid to it. I lifted this. The first thing we saw was a small, square packet with the emotive word *Durex* printed on a violet background. We were not so innocent that we did not immediately realise the implications of such an astounding discovery. On Saturday mornings when my brothers and I paid our fortnightly visit to the barber shop, we were always drawn to the same word engraved across a small mirror to the rear of the salon. Waiting our turn for the chair, we had observed the furtive transactions whereby the self-same packets changed hands without a word being spoken between barber and customer. Further evidence came our way when we picked up discarded packets on the Common, that sparsely-grassed arena of sexual initiation for many of my contemporaries. Total knowledge had come when a sixth former inflated a sample of the forbidden wares and floated it across the Assembly Hall during morning prayers, a crime of such enormity that he was caned in front of the entire school before being expelled. Although I had never carried out such advanced experiments myself, the grapevine of smut had ensured that I had a rudimentary knowledge of the true function of the damning objects. Even to say 'French letters' aloud was considered daring, suggesting a world of such blazing depravity as to pass all comprehension. To think that such seemingly innocent articles, so close to the Christmas balloons that exploded on the holly tips when batted between us, could hold the key to the ultimate sexual mystery inspired feelings of the keenest intensity. We were triggered into instant tumescence whenever the subject was discussed.

"God!" Theo said.

"Your father," I said. "He uses *them*!"

"God," Theo repeated.

I lifted a corner of the packet with a finger nail, exposing the flaccid white skin of rubber. It was like lifting a heavy stone and finding something loathsome beneath. We both stared at it. I think that, simultaneously, we arrived at the same inescapable conclusion: Theo's father, although patently past his prime by any standards we normally applied, still indulged in the sins of the flesh. And of course the idea was repugnant to us, as well as fascinating – more repugnant to Theo than to me, because it naturally followed that his mother was on the receiving end.

The packet lay on top of a large white envelope. "D'you think there's anything else?" I whispered. It seemed right to whisper in the presence of such mysteries.

"What else could there be?"

I took the question to be rhetorical and, once again using my handkerchief for protection, slid the envelope out of the drawer. Then I lifted the flap with a pencil. Inside were half a dozen postcard-size photographs. Using the pencil as a lever, I pushed the top photograph into view. It depicted what I took to be a French legionnaire sitting on a garden swing, the ropes of which were entwined with flowers. He was wearing a legionnaire's peaked cap and black socks, but apart from these two items he was naked. He was not a particularly healthy-looking specimen and had a reedy body, but he was endowed with a truly enormous penis standing out from his groin at a forty-five degree angle. Kneeling between his legs was a nun. At first I thought she was praying to be spared rape, and then I realised that her mouth was resting on the tip of his penis, the lips parted as though she was poised to take a bite.

We stared at the picture in silence.

Although neither of us were strangers to reproductions of the nude female body and had often discussed the more prominent attributes of the opposite sex, the revelation of such blatant male sexuality – the visual evidence of adult life in the raw, albeit not fully understood (since we were unprepared for and had no comprehension of fellatio) produced in us feelings of excited revulsion. Whereas lust in the abstract, lust directed towards those demure female nudes we searched for so diligently in forbidden magazines, with their sweet pointed breasts and hairless genitals discreetly shadowed, was without conscious depravity, the evidence now before us pointed towards a world of satanic proportions. Had we chanced upon the photographs in some natural setting the immediate effect would have been the same, but we would have been spared the true horror of connecting the sexuality with anybody we knew. But there, in that cold room, Harry's holy of holies, there was no such escape route. The tunnel towards maturity had not yet been dug. The evidence was conclusive. It was Harry's desk; nobody touched it, therefore the photographs could not have been planted.

Fear smothered our further curiosity. We had seen enough. The envelope was hastily replaced, the packet of contraceptives carefully positioned as we had found it, the drawer shut and then wiped of all incriminating evidence by my less than pristine handkerchief. We crept out of the room, went through the house and into the garden. Neither of us could find the right words.

"I think," Theo said finally, "I think he must have bought them in France, don't you?"

"Probably."

"On holiday."

"Yes."

"As souvenirs."

I nodded.

"Without mother knowing."

That thought hadn't occurred to me, but as Theo searched my face for confirmation I hadn't the heart to disagree.

"I'm sure Mother doesn't do that."

"She was a nun," I said, as though that was the perfect explanation.

"A real nun, d'you think?"

"They have temptations, too." For the first time in our relationship his advantage in years was not so apparent.

"Wasn't it extraordinary?"

"Yes."

We walked up and down the garden path.

"What d'you imagine it does to you?"

I couldn't answer that. "Maybe it's only in France," I said, trying to be helpful.

4

I SEE NOW, HAVING read and re-read the journals, that
betrayal was Theo's life's work. In the end I honestly
believe that what killed him was the incurable drug of
deceit itself. Even his published work, the external evidence of
his view of life, so carefully sifted and 'cleared' by his peers,
was an industrious fabrication. He deliberately chose to lead
everybody away from the real trail by concentrating on
themes bleached of all political content. All those books, all
that application over so many years, and not a single clue that
could be isolated and used against him. One has to have a
grudging admiration, and if logic revolts against the evidence,
releasing the inevitable questions as to why he was never
exposed, one has only to turn to the post-mortems held for his
erstwhile companions in arms – Philby, Burgess and Maclean
– to see how openly most of the people who shouldn't be
fooled can be fooled most of the time.

My knowledge of Cambridge in the late Twenties and early
Thirties was acquired second hand. I missed any personal
exposure to the 'loss of innocence' Theo's generation
experienced and which he recounted to me. He was eighteen
when he went up to Trinity in 1929, the very year that Philby
became an undergraduate at the same college. Burgess didn't
arrive until the following year.

I suppose, looking back, I was the most deceived, for in
those formative years I doubt if anybody was closer to Theo:
nobody, to my knowledge, shared his confidence as I did.
Both our families survived the sullen aftermath of the
1914–1918 war. Harry Gittings, having escaped the trenches
with a staff appointment, picked up where he left off – there
was, after all, no shortage of widows to comfort and advise.
His practice flourished as never before. My own father was
not so fortunate. He was gassed, and although he made a

recovery was never the same man again. More by good luck than compassion his old job – that of a quantity surveyor – was kept open for him. He was able to tread water, but that was all. Any plans he might have had for sending me or my brothers to university were never spoken of again. My mother lapsed into another of her periodic declines and their relationship became a bitter truce easily broken. Whenever she saw a crack in my father's thin armour she would lunge to draw blood and somehow she was always at her most dangerous when comparing Theo's advantages in life with my own. Her maternal instincts had always been spread thin; she was never so happy as when she was describing the difficult circumstances of our births. "'Course I never wanted children," she would say. "I wasn't built for them. The doctors said it was a miracle I ever came through" – this with a sidelong glance at father – "not that some people gave any thought to my feelings in the matter. Too intent on their own pleasures."

My brothers found some compensating comfort from the fact that they were twins, being alike in temperament if not in looks. I was never close to either of them, for they lacked any urge to escape from the environment I found so stifling. I thought of Theo as my brother and longed to emulate his attitudes towards life. I gradually came to understand part of my mother's sad snobbery, her sense of outrage that she had missed out on things, and for self-protection I became the Switzerland in the family Europe, surrounded on all sides by hostile forces that I willed myself to ignore.

I began writing at an early age, first as a form of escape, and before the age of seventeen I had completed two turgid and, happily for my future reputation, unpublishable novels. They drew heavily on my limited experience of life, but since I had neither the wit nor the sophistication to be objective, the results were predictably puerile. At the time, I laboured in the belief that I would shortly be challenging Arnold Bennett. Every publisher in London was bombarded with my soiled manuscripts; only one replied with any compassion and a few sparse words of encouragement, and these sustained me for many a fresh attempt. I finally accepted defeat where the novels were concerned and started to write short stories. Here I had a modicum of success and was able to place two of them, since in those halcyon days there was a surfeit of small magazines only too anxious to fill their pages with cheap submissions. I seem to remember I received ten and sixpence for one and a cheque for a guinea for the second, and that the cheque bounced. However, I had proved my point: I was capable of being published. The sight of one's own work actually in print is perhaps the most potent drug for a writer, and my resolve never faltered from that moment. Because of our reduced circumstances I was forced to leave school at sixteen and find a job to help supplement the family income. Armed with my published works I attacked the local newspaper, and must have been sufficiently brash to overcome the editor's reluctance to hire anybody in those depressed times, for I was taken on as a glorified tea-boy. I was deliberately, grotesquely sycophantic to everybody in that grimy establishment, and the ploy paid off, for I was finally allowed to handle those assignments that the rest of our small and jaded staff scorned. I covered weddings, funerals and the local Petty Sessions, turning in copy that was seldom less than purple and was inevitably subbed unmercifully.

It was a boring and in many ways soul-destroying period, but marginally better than the nine to five occupations that my twin brothers willingly embraced. At least I was not chained to the routine of a shop assistant; I had a reasonable amount of freedom and although I loathed journalism at the level I was exposed to it, I was not completely separated from my chosen vocation.

This was the same year Theo went to Trinity. He was the only person who gave me any real encouragement with my writing. Without his understanding I doubt whether I would have stayed the course, since my further short stories slid down the same slope as the novels. Rejection slips corrode ambition after a time. It was Theo who urged me to look outside my own immediate circle.

"The trouble is," he said, "your novels and stories aren't about real people. Or, put it this way, they're not about people anybody wants to read about. Your characters don't

44

have any sexuality. They're neuter." I listened to his criticism with a respect I accorded to nobody else. "What you've got to write about is what's happening up here at Cambridge. Kiss your suburban background goodbye, forget writing abut life in a Bournemouth lodging house and young love triumphant. That's gone, all that's old hat."

"It's all right for you. You're at Cambridge."

"Well, live vicariously through me. I'll give you some copy. The next time we meet I'll give you a plot that'll make your hair stand on end."

"What sort of plot?"

"Life in the raw."

"Meaning sex?"

"Sex comes into it. I mean, sex comes into everything."

"Have you done it yet?"

"It?"

"You know."

"There are some things one doesn't boast about."

"Don't be rotten. We always said we'd tell each other. We had a pact, remember?"

"Well, I will tell you, but I'm in the middle of it. I'll tell you the unhappy ending."

"Why will it be an unhappy ending?"

"Because those are the only affairs worth having."

Ever since our fateful exploration of his father's study, the topic of sex had obsessed us. I had lost my initial advantage where Theo was concerned, partly because of my semi-detached environment and partly because of the age difference between us. I was just turned sixteen when Theo went to Cambridge and there were little or no opportunities for experiment in Little Venice. There were two secretaries at my place of work, but one was married and the other, although only her late twenties, seemed almost as old as my mother. I met girls of my own age, but none of them was emancipated and any fumbling approaches I made from time to time were hastily and conclusively repulsed. I lived in a fever of expectation, starting every fresh assignment for the paper with my imagination recharged, able to convince myself that in the best tradition of a foreign correspondent I

45

would be exposed to voluptuous temptation. The effort of sustaining the image of a foreign correspondent while covering a church jumble sale or a Rotarian lunch daily proved too much and I remained resolutely virginal.

It never occurred to me to envy Theo in the way that my mother sought to envy the Gittings's entire way of life. As the years went by my admiration for Theo became a lifeline. We still spent holidays together and I was no longer tongue-tied at his family meal tables, and could even, on occasion, raise a smile from Harry Gittings with my descriptions of life in London. But I was in no doubt that there was something faintly sinister about him. His speech had a curious delivery, precise, somewhat sibulant and pitched low, maybe a professional affectation he had developed to impress his clients. Having begun by ignoring me completely, I think he grew to tolerate me. I spent Christmas with them the year of Theo's first term at Trinity and was amazed by the amount and variety of food on the festive table. The first time I ever tasted venison, Harry Gittings carved it and after lunch on Christmas Day he offered me a small cigar.

"I don't smoke," I said. It was a white lie because I had several times attempted to puff my way through a Gold Flake stolen from my father.

"No vices, eh?"

He cut the end of his own cigar with a patented penknife which, he demonstrated, could only be opened if held at a certain angle.

"Given to me by a grateful client."

He licked the end of the cigar in a way I found curiously unpleasant. Our conversation took place in his study and it took all my concentration to refrain from staring at his desk; memories of that extraordinary afternoon came crowding back.

"One should always have one vice," he said after the first inhale. "I mean, where would I be if everybody was perfect? Vice of one kind or another paid for your Christmas lunch." He regarded me as somebody in a witness box. "I understand you're not going to university like Theo."

"No, sir."

"Why is that? Don't you want to go?"

"I don't think my parents can afford it."

"No, I don't suppose they can. D'you want a glass of port? You do drink port, I take it?"

"Oh, yes," I said. I didn't, but there was something about his attitude towards me that provoked a spurious courage. He poured two glasses from a decanter and pushed one towards me.

"Put down before you were born."

"Very nice," I said.

"Port is never nice. It's either superb or undrinkable. Remember that. This particular port is superb. Otherwise I wouldn't serve it. Tell me more about yourself."

"I'm a reporter."

"Enjoy that, do you?"

"Well, I don't intend to make it my career."

"What do you intend?"

"I want to be writer. I've been published already. Several magazines have taken my stories."

He regarded me with narrowed eyes for several seconds. "What sort of stories do you write?"

"Oh, all sorts."

"Such as?"

I struggled to think of words to describe my unsophisticated efforts.

"Are they all about the sweet mystery of life?"

"Yes," I said, "more or less."

He poured himself a second glass of port. "D'you like animals?" he asked.

The question took me by surprise. "Animals? Yes. Very much."

"Cats?"

"Yes, we've got a cat."

"Cats are my favourites," he said. "Very proud creatures. Independent. In fact there's only one thing I dislike about them. D'you know what that is?"

I shook my head.

"They always show their bottoms. Have you noticed that?"

"Yes, I suppose you're right. I'd never thought of that."

"I've thought about it a great deal. They always show their

47

bottoms," he repeated with slow relish. "Apart from that they're fastidious creatures, much cleaner than dogs. They bury their excreta."

His words came to me through a haze brought about by the unaccustomed port, but I was sufficiently aware of the situation to think he was insane.

"As a matter of fact they're much cleaner than human beings. We wash our faces and our hands, do we not? but most of us never wash our arses. Most of us in this country, that is. The French, who leave a lot to be desired in other directions, do at least employ the bidet. Ask the average plumber in this country to install a bidet and he doesn't know what you're talking about. Most of them can't even pronounce it. Now that would be a good subject for you to write about. Why don't people wash their arses when they've been to the toilet?"

He stared at me.

"The paper I write for doesn't really go in for that . . . that sort of article."

"But it is an interesting comment on our society don't you think?"

Mad, I thought, stark staring mad.

"I have a bidet installed in my own bathroom. Imported from the Continent, at no little expense. I use it every day. Every day. Because I know how to live."

He seemed to leave me at that point and we sat in silence until, mercifully, Theo came in search of me and I was able to make my escape.

"You'll never guess what he told me," I said, the moment we were safely out of earshot.

"What? Something about me?"

"No. He talked about cats and their arses, and then he talked about his own. How he washes it every day."

The revelation did not have the anticipated effect on Theo.

"Oh, yes," he said. "Conversation normal. I've had that for years. It's his favourite topic. Anything scatological. I think he's off his chop. You know he's on the Board of the local naughty girls school. Well . . . he doesn't give up his spare time to improve their wayward minds. He just likes to see them punished. Have their little bottoms whacked. All legal. It has to be carried out in front of witnesses, you see. So, he witnesses."

"What d'you think he gets out of it?"

"The mind boggles," Theo said. "You know those knickers we found in his desk? Well, we were both so bloody naïve in those days. I mean, we both thought they belonged to Mother, didn't we? Not a bit of it. Know where they came from? The girls' reform school. He brings their dirty knickers home."

"Christ!" I said.

"I'll tell you what my dear father is. He's a filthy old sod."

I suppose what impressed me as much as the secret itself was Theo's calmness in the telling of it. Occasionally my paper ran heavily censored accounts of some sex deviant who had been caught committing an act of public indecency in the local swimming baths, but I had no idea that such aberrations could apply to a man of Harry Gittings's standing.

"How did you find out?" I asked.

"I put two and two together. And of course like most perverts he can't resist dropping hints. That's their kick, of course. Shocking other people. He's always coming out with some new piece of sexual wisdom."

"Like what?"

"Oh, what was his latest? Yes, when I went up to Cambridge he warned about the dangers of promiscuity. 'Always remember,' he said, 'an upright phallus has no conscience.'"

"My father's never ever mentioned anything like that to me."

"No, well, your old man's normal. Dull, but normal."

"He can't help being dull," I said. "He was gassed."

"Gassed on the Somme and gassed at home by your mother's boring conversation – a lethal combination."

"Yes, well, it's sad rather than dull."

"But you mustn't get like them. If you want to be a writer, then you've got to broaden the old horizons, say goodbyeeee, turn your back on all that."

I noticed that even in the short time he had been at Trinity his way of speaking had changed. He was much more self-assertive, perhaps even a little pompous.

"It's easy for you," I said. "You've done it, you've got away."

"Listen, Tony, dear boy. Never envy people. This is never going to be a land fit for heroes to live in, so face up to it early on. Envy is corrosive. It'll destroy your writing and it'll destroy you. By all means try and change this piddling society, but don't base your whole philosophy on envy. It's a dead end. You should hear Kim's views on the subject."

"Who's Kim?"

"Oh, somebody I know."

I felt a sense of apartness. There was Theo, the epitomy of the 'Rupert Brooke' undergraduate, in his expensive flannel bags and tweed jacket, his Hawes and Curtis shirt mono-grammed on the pocket, that casual elegance that sits easily on the privileged few — in strict contrast to my own appear-ance, usually classified as neat but undistinguished. Try as I might I could not stifle those shameful feelings of envy, for I wanted what he was able to take for granted. I wanted Cambridge's beauty and freedom — that cushioned, intoxi-cating life, a mixture of quiet scholarship and hilarious social conventions. It was a period in British history that will never come again, for the old order had changed — the Great War had seen to that — and on both sides of the Atlantic those who had survived were determined to enjoy themselves whatever the cost. But the flamboyant pleasures, the pleasures that were reported, belonged to those who, buttressed by private incomes and by admiration of the masses, tried to perpetuate the security and opulence of the pre-war society by grafting on the sexual emancipation of the Twenties. It was not a Jazz Age for the majority, but a time for survival, a time of dreary cynicism as the brave experiment of the League of Nations rotted at the roots, a time of drift — the tide bearing us all towards the next holocaust.

I used to visit Theo in Cambridge and on one occasion managed to persuade my editor to let me cover the university scene in depth over a series of three articles which, for the first time, carried my by-line. I remember thinking it was strange for a man in his position to be so impressed with my contacts in the outside world and was amazed that I had sold him the idea so easily. Perhaps he was persuaded by the fact that it wasn't going to cost him anything extra, for I roomed with Theo in Trinity during my stay. Theo having bribed his bedder to turn a blind eye. The ease with which the rules could be bent impressed me in turn.

It would be satisfying to be able to relate that I had an immediate perception of what was happening behind the scenes in the Cambridge of 1931, but I saw only the surface; and whether by design or accident, Theo, while acting the perfect host, never took me backstage. In many ways it was the turning point in my own life, for I felt that I had been given a glimpse of paradise. If that seems an over-statement it can be excused by my adolescent lack of sophistication: I was so anxious to be welcomed even on the fringe that all critical faculties were cheerfully abandoned.

I imagine I behaved like the tourist I was, punting on the Cam for the obligatory pilgrimage to Granchester, enjoying strawberry teas, joining in the earnest but shallow conversations which Theo and his set continued far into the night. I turned in three articles of acute banality, which revealed nothing new about Cambridge or its undergraduate population, but presumably I wrote what the public wanted to read and even got a modest rise in salary.

I recall that the main topic for debate was a copy of the privately printed *Seven Pillars of Wisdom* which Theo had acquired. He was greatly attracted to the enigmatic personality of Lawrence – the double and indeed treble life he led.

"It's amazing what he got away with, right under everybody's noses. 'Course, he enjoyed all that other stuff in the desert, I'm convinced of that. It was like the Greeks, you know. He went to battle with his boy mistresses. So he had to be brave in order to impress them."

The detailed and exhaustive discussions concerning Lawrence's sexual proclivities bored me. I was far more interested in discovering whether any of the Cambridge girls, dismissively referred to as 'blue-stockings' or 'bottled snakes'

(I am not quite sure whether I fully understand Julian Bell's much quoted remark), shared the freedom enjoyed by their male counterparts. My attempts to draw Theo on the subject met with little success.

"Boring. The whole lot of them are boring. Without exception. One doesn't even acknowledge their presence."

It was not a view I could share. If the sight of Theo and his set induced a feeling of envy, then the girls of Girton and Newnham inspired positive worship. I indulged in intellectual and sexual fantasies about them, convinced that somewhere in their midst was my ideal companion – a mixture of passion and purity of thought. More than once I walked the three miles down the Huntington Road to where Girton had been sited beyond the male citadel walls. In an effort to belong I borrowed a silk shirt of Theo's for these trips, convinced that this would give me the necessary poetic look so vital in the early stages of a seduction. Alas, the girls of Girton were not on the look out for poets that season, and I drew a series of blanks. Hope, like tumescence, sprang up afresh every morning, but I never even got to first base.

5

M Y FIRST SUCCESS when it came was of a totally different order, for I struck up an acquaintance with a chocolate-box-pretty young waitress in a café close to Trinity. I often went there to spin out a coffee and sticky bun for a couple of hours while waiting for Theo to join me after one of the few lectures he attended. I used the time to make notes for my articles and for future stories, since it was inevitable that the next novel I attempted would be set in Cambridge.

Her name was Judy. She was a year or so older than me, refreshingly aware of her sexual attractions and, more astonishing, quite happy to discuss them. She had one of those pert, slightly exaggerated figures, prominent, conical breasts and a delicious bum. I had never met anybody quite like her, for the confines of Little Venice had not harboured such teenage sirens. I was immediately enamoured, my appetite sharpened by my Girton failures. It is surprising how easily, at that age, one can renounce intellectual ambitions.

Poor Judy had little or no stimulating conversation, a fact that Theo criticised the first time I made my intentions known to him.

"But she can't utter, dear boy. It's all she can do to repeat the orders. Now, we know that in the dark all cats are grey, albeit some greyer than others, but even allowing for the poverty of your tastes, I really think you should aim a little higher."

"But don't you think she's pretty?"

He stared at her across the café.

"Very. Slightly bovine, but I'll allow you, pretty. Over-developed, of course."

"Nothing wrong with that, is there?"

"Too pneumatic. I hate sleeping on feather beds."

53

"You're just jealous."

"My dear Tony, that's the last thing I am. I mean, don't let me put you off. If your thrill of the chase lies in that direction, go to it."

"Well, easier said than done."

"Have you asked her?"

"Asked her what?"

"What? he says! Is she prepared to surrender what Frank Harris terms her box of delights?"

"It's too early for that," I said.

"How can it be too early? Tony, dear, you mustn't ask me for advice. She doesn't happen to be my type, which is of no consequence; after all, that's what makes the world go round. I think she's a very pretty little piece and knowing her class I'm sure she fucks."

"That's a bloody snobbish remark."

It was the closest we had ever been to falling out.

"Well, I'm sorry," Theo said. "I didn't mean it to be. Just stating what I take to be the facts. But don't get upset. It isn't as if you're intending to marry her."

"I might," I said, since sexual convictions are the easiest to defend.

"Well, fine. Congratulations."

"I suppose like your beloved Lawrence you're looking for an Arab boy?"

"Not Arab. They're too unwashed. But you're warm."

He got up from the table as Judy approached. "Look, I've got to cut. Don't take offence. It really doesn't matter one way or the other. You do what you want."

"You're always in here together," Judy said, looking after Theo. "Are you at the same college?"

"I'm not at college," I said. "I'm just here working, on a visit. He's my cousin."

"Very good looking."

"He said the same about you."

"Did he? What did he say?"

"He said I ought to ask you for a date."

"Cheeky!"

"So I'm asking you."

She stared at me, wrinkling her full mouth. "Don't know about that. How old are you?"

"Old enough."

"Oh, we know all the answers, don't we?"

The manageress was staring in our direction. From long training Judy seemed to have eyes in the back of her head. "Another cup of coffee, right, sir," she said loudly, then added for my benefit alone: "I'll see if the other's on my menu," and winked.

Having taken this first step I found her more desirable than ever. Watching her swing away from me through the crowded tables I felt those first pangs of a hunger that is never satisfied when one is young and the sap is rising. I envied Theo for other reasons, envied him his self-assurance and his money. I could not help comparing my appearance with those all around: how could she possibly prefer me when she had such superior choices?

By the time she returned I had prepared myself for the expected rebuff. She poured the coffee with maddening slowness, glancing at me as she added sugar and milk. Then she made out another bill, licking a stub of pencil in a particularly provocative manner.

"I don't get off 'til eight," she said. "I'll meet you by the bus stop round the corner."

"You mean tonight?"

"Yes."

She had a trayful of other orders to serve and I had no opportunity of prolonging the conversation. I could not believe my good fortune. It was as if I had just been awarded a First after an examination I was certain I had failed.

Something warned me not to rush and tell Theo the good news. I went to the public baths and spruced myself, then had a haircut. There my courage left me, for I must admit that my visit to the barber's was not without ulterior motives. When I was asked if I wanted anything 'extra', I could only stammer a request for a little pomade. It was lavender scented and slightly nauseated me.

I took up my position by the bus stop half an hour ahead of time. She arrived promptly. Doubtless she was always ready to escape from her twelve-hour shift.

"Where are we going?" she asked.

I hadn't thought of that.

"You smell nice," she said, waiting for my answer.

"It's something I use on my hair," I said. I was desperately seeking not to make any mistakes. "I didn't know whether you'd want to eat," I went on. "Having been in that place all day."

"Oh, I like my grub. Especially when I'm being taken out."

Instinctively my hand went to my trousei pocket. I tried to count the coins without jingling them.

"Fine," I said. "Anywhere you prefer? I don't know the best places, being a stranger."

"All right, I'll take you somewhere. But let's get out of here, shall we?"

She put her arm through mine as we walked off. I could feel her warmth as our bodies touched.

"Did you say you're from London?"

"Yes."

"Is it like they say?"

"Haven't you ever been?"

"I've never been outside Cambridge. Oh, that's a lie. We did go to Hunstanton once. That's the seaside. We went there when me dad was alive."

"Your father's dead, is he?"

"Yes," she said. "He come back from the war with half his face shot away. There wasn't much to live for. He had a lovely face when it was all there." She tightened her grip on my arm. "Tell me more about London. Did you ever see the King and Queen?"

"Yes, several times."

"Really?"

"Yes. At the Trooping of the Colour and on Armistice Day."

"Is it true what they say about the King?"

"What do they say?"

"That he wears make-up when he goes out."

"Who says that?"

"I don't know. Some friend at work told me. She reckons they all do. Prince of Wales and all."

"Well, not that I've noticed," I said airily.

She stopped outside a small restaurant. It had a menu stuck in the window and to my dismay I saw that the set dinner was priced at one and sixpence.

"This is nice," Judy said. "I ate here once before on me last birthday. And don't ask how old I am, because I shan't tell you."

I wasn't able to concentrate at that moment, being too busy working out complicated sums in my head. Without actually counting my money in front of her, I could only guess at the exact state of my finances.

"We'll go dutch, of course. I made quite a bit in tips today. It was one of the good days."

"But I'm taking you out," I said bravely.

"Yes, so what? You always go dutch the first time, otherwise it isn't fair. I mean, I know you haven't got any money."

"How?"

"Look, I wasn't born yesterday, you know. Anybody who makes a sticky bun and a cup of coffee last two hours isn't exactly flush. Come on."

She more or less pushed me inside. I couldn't get over her. The fact that she had accepted my invitation had been wonder enough, but she continued to amaze me. Her conversation as she prattled on through the simple meal was mostly gossip based on famous people she had read about. I learnt that she lived alone with an invalid mother on the outskirts of Cambridge. Several times during the course of the meal she made reference to the fact that her one recurring dream was to escape from her present environment and go to London. I confess it did cross my mind that perhaps I was being used, but I misjudged her. More than any other woman I have ever known she was devoid of guile; she just said what she meant, and there were no strings attached. She enjoyed her food and I was content to watch her eat, for the anticipation of what might lie beyond the meal had destroyed my own appetite.

"Hey, aren't you going to eat that?" she said. When I shook

my head she speared my lamb chop and took it to her own plate. "Can't waste it. I love lamb. Don't like to think about all them little sheep jumping about, but you've got to live, haven't you? D'you think they know?"

"Maybe."

"I don't think they do. Same with everything really, isn't it? If you thought about it, you'd never do anything. You've got to enjoy it while you can. That was what my dad always used to say. I'll show you his photo when we get back."

"Back?" I said. "Back where?"

"Well, you're taking me home, aren't you?"

"Yes. Yes, if you want me to."

"Aren't you funny? You've gone all white. Little white patches on both cheeks." She smiled at me across the table.

"Won't your mother mind?" I asked.

"She's an invalid, I told you. She's been in bed for six years. Rheumatoid arthritis. We haven't had much luck, our family."

"Who looks after her when you're at work?"

"Oh, neighbours come in. She's great, my mum. Never complains. She always says, you have a good time while you're young, because it ain't going to last."

"Six years. That's awful."

"Yes. Doctors say she could go on for another six, or it could all be over next week. They don't really know, do they? They're all about the same." She laughed. "Bloody useless."

We caught the last bus and the journey to her home took twenty minutes. We sat close together and she felt for my hand and squeezed it. "Hope you brought your pyjamas," she said.

I looked around quickly to see if any of the other passengers had overheard, and this made her laugh again.

"Perhaps you don't wear pyjamas."

"Depends," I said, in what I hoped was a calm voice.

"Only teasing you."

It was a short walk from the last bus stop to the house where she lived. It was in the middle of a terraced row, red bricked, with a small bay window in front. I hesitated at the gate.

58

"I wasn't really teasing on the bus. You can come in if you want."

"But your mother . . ."

"Listen, I'll tell you something about my mum. She ain't religious, 'cos she's got bloody little to be religious about, and she ain't narrow-minded. So she don't worry about me going in fear of mortal sin. When you lie on your back for years like she has, you don't think too much about the bleeding life hereafter. You say sod it!"

I was beginning to have second thoughts. Marriage, I thought ignobly. That's what she's looking for; she wants to trap me into marriage. She and her sick mother have probably worked it all out.

Judy had her key in the front door. "Come on, nobody's going to eat you."

I cast a glance down the deserted street. She opened the door and went inside to light a gas bracket in the small hall-way.

"I tell you what, I'll borrow a couple of pennies if you've got them. For the meter."

I stepped into the hallway and closed the door behind me. She came to me and kissed me on the lips, her mouth opening as we touched. I felt her breasts against me.

"I'll just see me mum," she said when the kiss was over. "Go in the back room and make yourself comfortable. The meter's under the sink." She started upstairs.

I walked with some difficulty into the kitchen-cum-parlour at the back of the house. Striking a match, I found the gas jet and lit it. Then I put two pennies in the meter. The room was spotlessly clean. There were two armchairs on either side of the iron range, a scrubbed pine table and a dresser. On the tall mantelpiece above the range was a photograph of a Tommy, stiffly posed in an ill-fitting uniform. I took this to be her dead father, for there was a distinct resemblance about the eyes and mouth. A cat appeared, uncurling from behind the coal scuttle, back arched, suddenly purring loudly as though somebody had switched it on. I bent to stroke it and it threaded in and out of my legs, frenzied with affection.

"That's Kitchener," Judy said.

I looked up to see her standing in the doorway.

"He's one of the old contemptibles usually. You're very favoured." She had taken her coat off upstairs.

"Like a cup of tea?"

"If you're having one."

"I always make one for Mum when I come in." She moved to the sink and filled a heavy kettle, blackened from standing on the open grate. "You can help me. Cups and saucers on the dresser there."

"How is your mother?"

"How is she ever? She's a bloody miracle, she is. Lies up there all day, sometimes she can't even brush a fly from her nose. Sometimes it's worse than others, you see. But we've got good neighbours either side. They come in and out all day. She can't do anything for herself."

"Does she know I'm here?"

"Yes, I told you. We don't have secrets, Mum and me."

She brewed the tea, having warmed the pot in traditional fashion, moving about the kitchen in bare feet, the cat following her everywhere, its purr like a motor.

"Give him a saucer of milk while I take this up, otherwise he'll give us no peace."

She left me again and in the quietness I could hear her talking to the sick woman upstairs, chattering on as she had with me in the restaurant. I tried to imagine what it would be like to be bedridden, then I poured some milk into a saucer and the cat jumped up on to the table and tried to lap it there.

"Don't be so ruddy anxious," I said, as much to myself as to the cat.

"Didn't you pour yourself a cup?" Judy said when she returned. "You're a daft one. Be stewed by now. My dad used to like strong tea. You could skate mice across his cup."

She poured two cups, adding at least four spoons of sugar to her own, then sat opposite me in the other armchair, lifting her legs and placing them in my lap.

"Oh, that's a relief. Best part of the day, this." She blew the steam off her cup and smiled at me over it.

"Are all London boys like you?"

"How d'you mean?"

"Quiet."

"I'm not always quiet. I was just enjoying this, being with you."

She stared at me. "Do you want to stay the night, sleep with me?"

I didn't answer at once. Her frankness utterly amazed me. "If you want me to," I said, not looking at her.

"Wouldn't ask you if I didn't, would I? I'm not a tart, you know. Is that what you're thinking?"

"No, 'course not."

"I haven't slept with anybody in, oh, over six months. I'm very choosy. I have to . . . like somebody, I don't mean love them, 'cos that, well, that's something else, but I have to like them. I like you. You're so serious."

"I like you too," I said.

"So you'll stay, will you?"

"If you want me to."

"There! You've said it again. It's not just what I want. I know what I want, it's you we're talking about. Look at me. I know what's worrying you. You've never done it before, have you?"

"It's not that," I said.

"What is it, then? You got a girl in London? Because if you have just say, I won't get mardy. But look at me and tell me straight."

I raised my eyes to hers. There was no malice in her face: it was as devoid of malice as it was of make-up. There was a bloom about her, a kind of innocence, the look of somebody who would never betray you.

"No, I haven't got anybody like that."

"I was right first time then. You haven't been to bed before?"

"Not all the way."

"Well, you either have or you haven't. Nothing to be scared of, you know. It's lovely, better than you've ever imagined." She put her cup down and came and sat in my lap. "You are a silly. Sitting here all buttoned up. You look like our vicar Give me a kiss, and open your lips this time."

61

We kissed, then she said, "Give me your hand. Put it there."

She took my hand and placed it on her right breast. I could feel the nipple beneath the cheap fabric of her waitress's blouse.

"Is that what you ordered, sir?"

She kissed my eyes, the corners of my mouth, the side of my neck, my ear. "I wasn't lying," she said. "What I told you. I'm not a tart, don't think that. Oh, I've done it before, but that's a good thing, because it's morbid if neither of you have a clue. I've only done it three times, all with boys I liked, and never for money. I've just got the taste for it, you see, and I'll make it all lovely for you, you just wait. Look, I'll show you, I'm proud of these and I know you've been looking at them in the shop. I always know when boys are looking."

She unbuttoned her blouse. She was wearing only a vest underneath. "Slip it over my head," she whispered. "Two buttons at the back."

I did as I was told. "My hands are cold," I said.

"They won't be for long."

I lifted the vest over her head. Nothing I had ever seen could compare with the beauty of her young breasts. The gaslight seemed to bathe them in a golden haze. They were bigger than I had imagined and I was scared to touch them.

"Kiss them," she said. "I like having them kissed."

I bent my head and put my mouth to one nipple. It seemed to jump at my first touch and she pressed herself into my face as I tasted her.

"Oh, that's it, that's it, I love that."

Her head was thrown back and I lifted my face from her breasts to kiss her neck, seeking to trace the patterns she had recently taught me.

"No, kiss them again, kiss the other one, I love to feel your mouth on them."

It was no hardship to satisfy her. I felt as though I was suspended in time. I put my hands under her breasts and lifted them as I kissed them. I dare say I would have been content to please her in that fashion the whole night through, but the mood was suddenly shattered by the cat jumping on to our laps.

"Jealous, you see," Judy said. "Like all men. Will you be jealous?"

"Don't know, do I?" I said. "Will I have anything to be jealous about?"

She didn't answer that, but took my face in her two hands and stared into my eyes for several seconds. "Don't think badly about me, will you? I can't help myself."

Then, a moment later, "I fancied you, you see. I know girls aren't supposed to say that, but if they waited for the right man to ask them, they'd die old maids most of the time. I like fucking. Does that shock you?"

It did, but I pretended otherwise. I had never heard a woman say the word before; in some stupid chauvinistic fashion I doubted whether women even knew of it. It didn't come out as a swearword when she said it, that was the biggest surprise. It sounded gentle from her lips and after all, I thought, it is only a *word* – why do we attach so much importance to it?

"Come on," she said, rising from my lap, her breasts brushing my face. "We mustn't shock Kitchener. Let's go to my room."

"What about . . . ?"

"Don't worry. You worry so much."

She turned out the gas and led the way upstairs. Even then I still couldn't believe it was happening to me. I had imagined the scene a hundred times, conjuring up version after version, but I had never cast myself in the role of the seduced.

Some women have an aptitude for love, and to this day, nearly fifty years after the event, I can still recall the excitement Judy's body gave me.

"Just don't think about it," she said, "because there's nothing to go wrong. You see? There, you see! See how easy it is? Doesn't that feel nice? It's the best feeling in the world, isn't it?"

She was so feminine – clever enough, thank God, not to make me feel I was being used. Because she made everything seem so natural, my nervousness left me, I believed I was the teacher not the taught. We are so conditioned to expect the worst, to think of failure and humiliation. Judy enjoyed me because she enjoyed the very act of sex. Her pleasure was more intense than mine, but then, perhaps she had more need of love than me that night. I was consumed with simple lust, not the frenzy that destroys us in later years when our bodies need to be goaded to triumph, but the trembling urgency of ignorance. I had no idea that pleasures and sorrows were so inexorably mixed, and her tears dismayed me, for when I eased out of her body that first time she cried uncontrollably. It was as if the act of loving had released all her hidden fears. She lay in my arms, her nudeness touching every part of me, her tears running between us. I can put explanations to it now, since the whole business of living seems an endless preparation for sorrow, but that night I had no such perceptions. I was too dazed with the wonder of it all.

Afterwards, it was like watching somebody come round after an anaesthetic. "Oh, I needed that," she said. She pushed wet strands of hair from her forehead and lifted herself above me. Her breasts quivered a few inches from my mouth and I could not resist suckling them again. Many future choices were made in that small back bedroom, for I judged the women who came after by Judy's nubile body.

"When shall I see you again?" I said.

"You're seeing me now. All of me."

She raised herself higher before sitting down on my legs. "Was it like what you imagined?"

"Better."

"Well, I take that as a compliment."

"But shall I?"

"Yes, if you want to. But don't get soft on me, will you? I don't mean this sort of soft either."

"Why not?"

"Because I won't make old bones."

"That's a dreadful thing to say."

"Is it? Not really."

"I want to be with you for ever."

"Now you do, and that's nice, that's how it should be, but you don't have to make any promises. I'm not looking to catch you. I bet you thought that, didn't you? Be honest now."

"No," I said.

"I wouldn't blame you. I mean, I'm very brazen when I want to be. I knew I'd have you from the first moment you walked in. You couldn't take your eyes off my titties, could you? I like that. They are pretty, aren't they?" She cupped and held them, stroking them as she would smooth a piece of velvet. "Pretty for now, anyway. Won't last, of course. They're too big, they'll be down past me waist by the time I'm thirty, so you'd better enjoy them while you can. Why're you laughing?"

"You say such funny things."

"I face up to the truth. My dad taught me that. He used to make me look at his face. See, I never could, not when he first came home. I used to run away and hide. You won't *really* want me, not for life. You think so now, because I've just made you happy. And we can go on doing that, but don't make promises you won't be able to keep, because then you'll feel guilty and it'll all be spoilt."

She lay across me, her head on my stomach.

"Talk to me about London."

"It's just bigger than Cambridge, that's about all. I live in a place called Little Venice. There are canals, but they're not as pretty as the Cam. I'll take you on the Cam."

"Have to be a Sunday, then. I work the rest of the week."

"Yes, well I have to work too, you know. But I'll save my money and come and see you at weekends."

We talked far into that night. She was curious about Theo and asked me what our relationship was. "I thought you were his fancy boy until you looked at me," she said. "We get them all in there, you know. You can always tell. Or I can. Makes you laugh, don't it? I mean, I'd rather have me than some boy, wouldn't you?"

"Well, I've shown I would. Theo's not like that."

"Want to bet? If he's not, he ought to be. And he's stuck up."

"Really?" The thought had never occurred to me.

"Oh, yes, I'm always made to know my place when I serve him."

I told her about Harry Gittings and his peculiarities,

relating the story of how Theo and I uncovered the secrets of his desk that afternoon.

"Dirty pictures are for dirty old men," Judy said. "I've seen some — one of the girls at work had a boy friend who was always showing them to her. I mean they don't shock me. You can't be worried by pictures, can you? Just boring, I think, especially when you can have the real thing. Your friend's father sounds like he just needs a good fuck."

"But some of the pictures were very odd. I mean, really odd."

"What way?"

I told her of the nun and the legionnaire.

"You mean like this?" She slid her head down to my groin. "Nothing odd if you love somebody. 'Course, you don't have to dress up like a bleeding nun to do it. You just do it, like this." And to my further amazement, she did it.

"You said 'if you love somebody'," I whispered when the sweet agony was finished. "Did you mean that?"

"This is love, isn't it? What we've been doing."

"But I want you to love me, not anybody else."

"I can't promise that," she said. "You have to take me as I am. Don't be so serious. Look, that's serious, in that room next door. And there's plenty of that around. Too much. Half the people don't know they're alive, and the other half wish they were dead. We're both lucky, you and me, for the time being anyway, and that's all you've got to think about. You start thinking about for ever, and you're in trouble."

We slept in each other's arms and the following day I had to return home. I saw her every other week for the best part of that year, using Theo as my excuse to the family — an easy enough lie to carry off, for anything to do with Theo met with my mother's immediate approval. Judy never changed. She didn't seem to have moods, and could always laugh me out of my sombreness. I began another novel, leaning heavily on the affair for my plot with somewhat transparent attempts to disguise the personal experience as fiction. For the first time in my life I didn't consult Theo, or show him work in progress. He knew the real reason for my frequent visits and adopted a lofty tolerance towards me. But some instinct for self-preservation held me from telling him the whole truth, and of course the whole truth was that I loved with an intensity that amounted to a sickness. I could think of nothing else but Judy between visits, my existence at home and at work a necessary interval of pain that could only be relieved when I was once again in her arms.

I was so proud of her. She seemed without fault. I kept trying to convince her that nothing she could ever say or do would weaken my resolve. We seldom quarrelled, nor did she ever give me cause for jealousy; our only differences sprang from my insistence that I would one day marry her. I made elaborate plans, saved what little money I could and when apart from her wrote endless letters protesting my intentions. The only sorrow she ever brought me stemmed from her reluctance to put pen to paper in return.

"You wouldn't want my letters," she said. "I don't know how. I'm not educated like you; my letters would be proper tripe."

"No, they wouldn't, and in any case I don't care. I just want you to write that you love me."

"You're like the government, you are. You want a Means Test before you'll believe anything. I do love you, you great stupid."

"Well, just write that. You could write that."

I gave her pen and paper and sat over her while she wrote to my direction in large, curling letters. Then I put the sheet into an envelope and addressed it to myself.

"Now post it," I said.

"You're daft. Waste of money, that is. Take it with you."

"That wouldn't be the same."

In the end I posted it myself. Obsessive love leads us all into traps of our own making. From pride we become careless. I made the mistake of forcing Theo to invite Judy to join one of his boating parties.

"But it'll embarrass her," he said. "It always embarrasses those sort of people to move outside their own circle."

"What a toffee-nosed bloody attitude. I go to bed with her, for Christ's sake!"

67

"Well, we know that. What's that got to do with it? Unless of course you discuss Proust in bed."

"You'll like her. She's funny and amusing. And I want her to come."

"Then be it on your head, Tony dear. I assure you I'm not thinking of myself, I'm only warning you for your own sake."

Judy bought a new hat for the outing, spending what to her was a sizeable amount of money in order, as she put it, 'not to let you down'. If Theo had raised doubts in my mind, I was forced to keep them to myself. For the first time in our relationship I had the feeling that she was vulnerable, something which had never occurred to me before.

I travelled up on a night train, arriving at Cambridge with the milk churns on the morning of the trip, and called for her before she was up. She greeted me in her shift, her eyes and face blurred with sleep. I had never found her so attractive, and we made love in one of the armchairs with Kitchener looking on with bland indifference.

"Let's have breakfast in the nude," I said. "I want this to be a day to remember."

"What's got into you?"

"I just feel very good. And you look marvellous – you always do immediately after we've done it."

"Just as well, isn't it? You didn't give me much option. What d'you want for breakfast?"

"A lot. I need to replenish my strength."

"I'm not eating a lot. I want to save room for all the posh food you say we're going to have."

We set off in high spirits, arriving at the riverside rendezvous before the others. "Are there going to be many of them?" Judy asked. "You know I'm not very good with names. I can only remember faces and orders. Like, I think to myself, the poached eggs were for the red face in the corner, and the cheese sandwiches were for the one with spots by the window."

"Oh, tell them that, they'll love that."

"I shall do no such thing. I want to put it on today."

"You don't have to put it on," I said. "Just be yourself and they'll love you as much as I do."

Theo and several companions arrived with the picnic hampers. I was slightly disconcerted that there was only one other girl in the party, the sister of a rather reedy undergraduate called Flesch. Her name was Rachel. She had the arrogant, spoilt manner of a Jewish princess. Theo introduced everybody by their first names, but hesitated when he got to Judy.

"And this is Miss . . ."

"This is Judy," I said.

"Judy," Theo repeated. "A friend of Tony's."

"Are you up here?" Rachel asked. She was wearing expensive clothes and rather too much perfume.

"No, I live here," Judy said.

"Oh, a local girl. How interesting."

I looked around at the rest of the party. In varying degrees all the young men had that easy manner, bordering on insolence, that comes with total acceptance of their social lot. Theo caught my eye and gave me a knowing smile, as if to say, Well, I did warn you. I took Judy's hand and helped her into the boat.

"Are you going to row?" Judy asked me.

"No, I think we'll leave that to the experts," Theo said. "It's too early for falling in."

"It won't sink, will it?" she said.

"No, dear. The only thing that will sink today are my principles."

This came from a young man who had been introduced as Guy. He had epicene good looks and I immediately singled him out as a potential rival. He took one of the oars and sat facing Judy and me. I had to admit he rowed extremely well and I was still so unsure of myself that I imagined this would impress Judy. Another young man called Stephen took the other oar and we set out in great style. It was one of those perfect days in early spring, just hot enough for comfort. Judy trailed one hand in the limpid water as we glided past the bright greenery of trees that had just burst their buds.

Rachel and her brother sat in the prow smoking Balkan Sobranie Russian cigarettes in long holders, while Theo announced he would read selected passages from *The Ancient*

Mariner to encourage, as he put it, 'the galley slaves'. This suggestion was immediately shouted down, and Guy began to sing an obscene version of the Eton Boating Song which began, 'Jolly old homo sailors' and went on in similar vein.

"Did you know," Theo said, when the song was finished, "that Dennis has gone to see Freud in Vienna to seek a cure?"

"Ah, a clear example of don't be afreud," Guy said.

The rest of them found this funnier than the retelling of it suggests.

"Who's Freud?" Judy whispered, and Theo immediately pounced.

"Now, can somebody explain to our charming guest? Guy, how would you describe Freud?"

"B.B.B."

"Let me translate," Theo said. "Professor Burgess, world-renowned authority on the sexual habits of policemen and engine drivers . . ."

"And postmen," Guy shouted. "Don't leave out the postmen."

". . . Professor Burgess is of the opinion that the Viennese saga can best be described under the heading Bums Before Butter. Am I right, Professor?"

"Absolutely."

"Personally, I would challenge the Professor's finding. As we all know he is somewhat blatant in his view of human nature, having been frightened by his nanny who had a moustache bigger than Lloyd George. In fact some people firmly believe that his nanny *was* Lloyd George, which perhaps explains all."

If Judy was disconcerted by this exchange at her expense, she gave no sign other than to squeeze my hand. She kept a smile on her face and pretended to enjoy the joke as much as the others.

"How long before we sight land and break open the champers?" Stephen said.

"We shall shortly be entering the erogenous zone, Stephen dear, so just continue doing your impersonation of a hearty Blue. Take the stroke."

They decided to moor at a suitably deserted spot another

two miles up river, and as the boat slid under the alders lining the bank one of the overhanging branches swept Judy's new hat from her head. It started to float out towards the opposite bank.

"Oh, no!" she screamed.

"Hat overboard!"

"Well, come on, Tony, do the decent thing and swim for it."

I started to take off my jacket.

"No, don't," Judy said. "It's not worth it."

"'Course, it's worth it," Theo said. "And we all want to see Tony do his stuff."

"No, the sight of naked flesh this early would be too much for me," Guy said. "Come on, Stephen, pull her round. We'll get it."

We went chasing after the elusive hat, bobbing like some red buoy on the current, and Flesch eventually fished it out. It was completely ruined.

"What a shame," I said.

"Doesn't matter."

"You must buy her a new one," Rachel said. "There are so many pretty new colours this season."

"It'll probably dry out," I said, trying to be helpful.

"Talking of which, let us wet ourselves with a little bubbly. Break out the hampers, men! Guy, dear, apply your well-known muscular strength and remove the first cork."

We scrambled on to the bank and with the boat tied off prepared the picnic. I took fresh heart, stifling my fears that the whole trip had been a mistake as far as Judy and I were concerned. The first bottle of champagne was quickly disposed of and a second opened. Theo took the empty bottle and strode down to the water's edge.

"Attention, please! Quiet, please! I call upon Dame Nellie Burgess to launch this ship."

The others applauded as Guy got to his feet and joined Theo by the boat. Taking the bottle and assuming a high-pitched voice he proclaimed: "I name this ship, *Repulsive*. God Bless All Who Sail in Her." Then he smashed the empty bottle against the hull.

"Not a good year," he said in his normal voice, while the rest of us applauded loudly.

"Aren't they funny?" Judy said. She was slightly flushed from the unaccustomed champagne, which I noticed she had drunk rather too quickly.

"Those who go down to seamen shall not perish from the face of the earth. There is some corner of a foreign whatsit, as we all know, where England's sons dropped their trousers while gentlemen now abed thought themselves accurst they were not there." Guy put on another voice for this recital, a sort of Church of England gothic. "I now call upon Father Gittings to give the Blessing."

"Thank you," Theo said. He put his hands together. "Let us pray. Oh, Lord, who has seen fit to let us buy this food on tick, grant us now the courage to eat it without a conscience. Look down, O Lord, upon this humble sod – green sod, I mean – and give us the strength to stay sober. In the name of our fathers, our mothers, or anybody else misguided enough to let us dissipate our lives in this holy place, for ever and ever, Amen."

"Amen," we all intoned.

There was caviar, and smoked salmon, and strawberries out of season which Rachel had brought with her. Judy eyed the caviar suspiciously to begin with, but was easily persuaded to try it.

"It's the start of a lifetime's romance," Stephen said. "If only people ate more caviar there'd be less unrest in the world. Don't you agree, Theo?"

"I not only agree, I intend to take positive steps to spread the good word. I'm going to start a new political movement – The Workers for Caviar Party. We shall march on Downing Street and hurl whole sturgeons through the windows."

I suppose I was somewhat of a prude in those days, a secret prude to boot, because although I found their dialogue too arch and not really funny, I lacked the courage to say so. In an effort to convince Judy that it was all terrific fun, I joined in the general merriment, occasionally making my own vapid comments. I couldn't make up my mind whether Judy was enjoying it or not. She seemed to be, but of course she had no idea what they were talking about most of the time, and they for their part made no real effort to include her. She had to take them or leave them.

The lunch over, Theo suggested one of those elaborate word games, so beloved by my generation. His choice had very complicated rules, almost impossible to follow, which he refused to repeat when Judy asked for guidance. The game consisted of one member of the party choosing a famous historical figure while the others had to seek the identity by a series of oblique questions, such as 'If I was a piece of music, what would I be?' or 'If I was a flower what sort of flower would I be?' I have suffered such after-dinner games all my life and they never fail to irritate me.

The whole thing was over Judy's head, of course. When I tried, tactfully, to guide her, they shouted me down.

"No helping! Unfair! Disqualified. You've lost your turn. Next."

They played at least six rounds before the effect of the champagne wore off. Then, with the spring air turning chill, we re-embarked for the journey home. Judy was very quiet and sat fingering the ribbon on her ruined hat. It had dried, but was patently beyond saving.

"I'll buy you a new one," I whispered.

"Don't bother," she said.

Flesch and Theo rowed home, while Guy sat with his arm around Stephen. I thought I saw Guy's hand fondle Stephen's groin, but in the fading light I couldn't be sure. When we said our goodbyes Theo was the only one who troubled to be politely effusive to Judy – the others, intent on their own further pleasures, could hardly be bothered to acknowledge her presence. It was made quite obvious to both of us that we were not welcome to continue the day's festivities over dinner.

Judy made light of the snub on the way home. "Do you really enjoy that sort of company?" she said.

"I don't know. I haven't been exposed to them that much. What did you think of Theo?"

"He was the nicest. I didn't know what they were talking about most of the time."

"What did you think of Rachel?"

"I'll ask you that question."

"Well, I didn't fancy her, if that's what you mean. I fancy you. I'm so sorry about your hat."

"Teach me, won't it? Shouldn't waste me money. That Guy, he was a card, wasn't he? Full of himself. Wouldn't trust him with anything."

"I gather he prefers the boys."

"What about your cousin?"

"I don't know about Theo," I said. "He's changed a lot since he came to Cambridge. He didn't used to be like that. He's sort of brittle now. As though he's putting on an act to impress people."

"I think he likes a bit of the other."

"I don't really think he's made up his mind," I said.

"You're so nice about everybody, that's your trouble. You don't see through people. If you want to know the truth, I thought they were a snotty lot. Taking the piss out of us all the time."

I defended them, not for my own sake, but for hers. I knew she was right, but I tried to steer her away from the obvious hurt. We walked hand in hand in the sharp evening air, and I could scent the dangers ahead. I had a premonition of losing her, for even in love we are none of us so constant as totally to ignore the opinion of others. My defence was half-hearted and I doubted if she was taken in by it.

When we reached her home she turned at the door and kissed me on the lips.

"Don't come in tonight," she said. "I don't feel like it, and I must spend some time with me mum."

"Nothing wrong, is there?"

"No."

"I mean, nothing I've done?"

"'Course not. Just that I'm tired."

"I'm sorry it wasn't a nicer day."

"That's all right. Wasn't your fault."

"Shall I see you next weekend?"

"If you want to."

"You know I want to. We'll spend it on our own."

"We were on our own today," she said.

6

THAT SUNDAY ON the river marked the beginning of the end between us, though I was too blinded by my own romanticism to see it at the time; at nineteen it is difficult to perceive we are equipped to love more than once. I was doing well on the newspaper, being now entrusted with the occasional book review, a minor leg-up which eventually led to my appointment as 'Literary Editor' the following year. This was a grandiose title for a humble occupation, but which carried with it certain perks, since it has always been an unwritten tradition that book critics can supplement their meagre wages by selling their review copies at half the published price. I was required to plough my way through innumerable historical novels, since our readership was pointedly 'down-market' and non-fiction seldom came my way, unless by mistake. I tried my best when judging these worthy efforts, and laboured in the belief that I was meant to take them seriously. I was swiftly corrected by my editor.

"You're not here to bury them," he shouted. "You're supposed to praise the bloody things. Look, let me show you. Take out all this rubbish" – the blue pencil went to work on my polished prose – "and concentrate on three things. Tell them the plot without comment, add the odd description like 'masterly' or 'seldom have I read a more compelling account', that sort of thing, and then, most important, put the name of the publisher and the price. You don't have to be bloody Bernard Shaw. You're just giving information, that's all. See, let me give you a tip. The more you praise, the more they'll send us, and you'll make a few more bob. Plus the fact we might be able to twist the bloody publishers' arms to take a few ads. It's a cynical business, lad."

I did as instructed, but was able to slip in the odd serious review when the page needed making up. I can claim to have been one of the first to recognise the worth of H. E. Bates who arrived on my desk like a breath of fresh air, dispelling the heady pollution of my average fare. Unless one is drawn to the role of critic, sitting in judgment of one's fellows is a dispiriting business, making executioners of us all, since it is easy to fell a tree in a matter of seconds without giving thought to how long it has taken to grow. I was glad of the extra money while hating how I had to earn it.

Armed with what was then a decent living wage, I tried to convince Judy that my repeated offers of marriage could be taken seriously.

"No," she said. "It wouldn't last."

"But, why? Why do you keep saying that?"

"Because it wouldn't. I'm not the marrying sort. It isn't all having your oats in bed, you know."

I used every argument I could think of to make her change her mind. I thought the main reason for her reluctance to contemplate marriage was her mother. "If we got married," I said, "we could do more for her. You never know, they keep finding new cures for these things, and at least she'd feel happier knowing there was somebody to take care of you."

I used to sit and read to her mother, who was like a print made from an under-exposed negative. The only thing about her that the disease had not touched was her hair: it was still thick and glossy, not unlike Judy's – a young girl's halo surrounding the wasted face of a prematurely aged woman. I used to help Judy turn her in the bed and one weekend I made a window box which we planted with flowers, moving the bed so that she could see them without effort. Her body was grotesquely thin; years later when the first photographs of Belsen were released I was reminded of Nature's imitation, seeing again that pitiful frame in the iron bedstead, the skeleton hands lying motionless on the white counterpane, the outline of the body like a twisted log. I think she knew what I was trying to accomplish with Judy and approved, but she hadn't the energy to influence her daughter. What little religious belief I still retained was obliterated in her presence: I could not contemplate the sort of God who condoned such a living death. Yet it was to the same God I pleaded, away from Judy, asking Him to help me change her mind.

I continued to take Theo partly into my confidence, but although he listened politely he found it more and more difficult to conceal his irritation.

"Why do you cling to your middle-class origins? That's what baffles me. Here you are with apparently every young man's dream – a nubile mistress who fucks like a stoat, who doesn't want marriage. So accept it! The boot's usually on the other foot. You don't know how lucky you are."

"I do, really I do, it's just that I can't bear the thought of ever losing her."

"Well, you're going the right way about it. From what you tell me her mind's quite made up. If you force her into marriage just to satisfy your morbid taste for respectability you'll end up the loser. Her very obvious charms will swiftly be ruined by the arrival of a puking son and heir – since I'm sure you'll want to go the whole hog once the ring's on her finger – and you'll be sitting by the conjugal hearth wondering how the hell your Juliet became the Duchess of Malfi."

"It doesn't have to end up like that."

"Tony, dear, if you want to be a writer then read the writing on the wall. It's staring you in the face. In words of fire. Marry young and your creative balls shrivel."

"If I don't marry her I shall lose her."

"Yes, probably. Not lose her exactly. She'll always be a shining memory. You'll just move on, that's all. There's a great deal to be said for the thrill of the chase, you know."

"You speak from experience, of course?"

"I speak from a certain kind of experience."

"I don't think you've ever had a woman."

"Now don't get personal."

"Oh, I see, it's all right for you to dish out the advice, but no one's allowed to give you some."

"But I'm not asking for advice."

"Okay. But you still haven't given an answer. You haven't, have you?"

"Yes, as a matter of fact."

"Who with?"

"You really shouldn't ask me. Gentlemen don't kiss and tell."

"I don't believe you."

"As you choose. I can assure you that I'm telling the truth."

"Well, all right. How was it?"

"Different, shall we say?"

"Was she a tart?"

"You're such a stickler for detail, Tony. If by that you mean, did I have to pay for the experience? no, not in the accepted sense. No money changed hands."

"Well, why didn't you tell me before?"

"In the first place you never asked me, and secondly, whenever we meet it's difficult to get beyond your endless saga of love amongst the ruins."

He refused to be pressed further, and since he could usually get the better of me in any argument I was forced to let the matter drop. I sometimes found his pose of bored superiority very hard to take, yet I still yearned for our relationship to continue on the old, intimate footing. The fact that I had to earn my living and he didn't drove a thickening wedge between us, but I clung to the sacred and profane fragments of our childhood friendship. I suppose I always wanted to impress him in those days.

Judy was right when she said that I was still an innocent about so many things. I had no idea that the pattern of Theo's life was forming there, in Cambridge, on the loom of youth. If I gave any real thought to his hedonistic way of life, it was just ordinary curiosity, the fascination we have when a close friend shocks, or dares to stand aside from the mainstream. While not flaunting his homosexuality like Guy Burgess (transparently bogus when talking of his 'two nephews'), Theo was at no great pains to conceal it. I suppose I was square enough at that time to believe that, in Theo's case, it was just a passing phase, something he would discard the moment he left Cambridge. He was not a peacock queer or a member of the green carnation set, nor did he ever make the slightest attempt to convert me to the cause. Burgess did make one pass at me, a blatant one, easy to block, but then I gather he groped at anything that moved. It's even possible that Theo put him up to it, as a sort of double get-even ploy, the kind of joke he greatly enjoyed. Knowing what I do now, anything seems possible.

There were so many deceits, all interwoven, dovetailing together like the components of a Chinese puzzle box. Now I can immediately find the pressure points: the box opens at a touch and has no power to surprise. We were saving money in 1931, not souls. Being the outsider, I saw only the surface currents of that Cambridge generation, the obvious whirl-pools of discontent. Politically, I had no awareness. I dare say my all-consuming passion for Judy left little room for any-thing else: people in love make poor revolutionaries. I was conscious of the changes taking place all over Europe, but they seemed so remote, so tedious when set against the day-to-day realities of my own struggles for identity. If I listened at all to political voices, I preferred Ramsay Mac-Donald's soothing lullabies to the siren songs of the doomsday crowd. In that respect Theo and I appeared to be as one. He, too, professed a total disinterest for the political arena. He was sardonically amusing, at his vitriolic best when discuss-ing the middle-class Marxism that attracted so many of his contemporaries. "They say they want to use the same bath water as the hunger marchers, yet the poor dears protest they can't get though life without two dressing gowns." On another occasion he described the Cambridge political scene as 'the flight to the herd', quoting, without due credit, what I later learnt was one of the better remarks of Professor Joad.

Obviously it wasn't difficult to fool me, but as subsequent events have shown, he managed to hoodwink the authorities as well. He was a Pitt Club man and was also elected to the Apostles, a fraternity so exalted that it was known as The Society. Modesty became nobody in those days. But having arrived he was content to remain anonymous. I saw him standing on the fringe, quizzical, faintly condescending, the face nobody can remember when looking at old wedding photographs.

He always knew how to slip the blade into my back when I was least expecting it, drawing blood but never touching any

79

vital organs. He pricked away where Judy was concerned, always careful to give the impression that he was doing it for my own good.

What disconcerted me most was his casual admission one day that he had written a novel.

"It's my dusty answer to *Chrome Yellow*," he said. "I decided that all the smart young men want putting in their places, so I've written a novel that is so old-fashioned it practically screams to be remaindered on publication day."

"What's it about?" I said.

"It's a stroll through the past, a tender look at the age of illusion."

"Has anybody seen it?"

"Yes," Theo said, with that casualness that always conceals triumph. "Yes, I've really had the most amazing luck. The first publisher I sent it to must want his head examined, because he accepted it."

"Just like that?"

"Just like that. A contract, advance, the lot."

"How much?"

"Seventy-five pounds, would you believe?"

"Well, that's fantastic," I said, trying hard to keep the pack-ice out of my voice. "Congratulations. I never knew you wanted to be a writer."

"Nor did I. It just sort of happened."

"When are they going to publish it?"

"They're rushing it through for their autumn list."

"What have you called it?"

"*Burnt Umber*. A bit self-conscious, don't you think?"

"No, I think it's good. I shall have to try and review it," I said, in a pathetic attempt to get on to the score board: "Can I have the first copy?"

"It's dedicated to you," Theo said, and the salt really burnt into my wounds. "I won't sign it, though."

"Why not?"

"I have the feeling the unsigned copies will be the rare ones."

Nothing upset me more. I thought about my own abortive efforts, the long hours I had struggled to arrive at that point

80

which Theo had achieved first time out. Friendship demanded that I conceal my bitter sense of the injustice of it all, but alone in my room that night, staring at the thick pile of manuscript representing all my hopes, I gave way to a bout of self-pity. I had been so open with Theo about my own work in progress, discussing the chronic lack of interest shown by publishers, asking his advice, soliciting his help, reading selected passages in expectation of his blessing – and all the time he had been working in secret. Maliciously I hoped his debut would be ignored by the literary world. I even entertained the idea of giving him a bad review myself, but in the event he confounded us all. When eventually I read *Burnt Umber*, I was forced to admit that he came fully equipped to the novel form. His narrative had a disarming elegance, as though no effort had been required in the writing, technique concealing the technique as it were, so that the reader was carried forward with lulling ease.

I had to admire his cleverness. There was I trying to ape the current literary darlings, borrowing from all and sundry – the starkness of Hemingway, the tightrope daring of Huxley, the cynicism of Aldington – with the inevitable result that what finally found its way on to paper was a hopeless jumble. Theo, on the other hand, had spurned all previous map references and struck out on his own. His timing was impeccable: most young writers of the period were desperate to parade their disenchantment, and yet here was a new novelist with the courage to say goodbye to all that, cock a snook at current trends and write about the old values without irony. He had somehow chosen a theme that his contemporaries had ignored, rightly judging that the older generation provided a wider readership, one that felt out of touch with the innovators – out of touch and perhaps threatened by them. The present, he told his readers, is always chaos, its morals always false. Only the past has any meaning for us if we are to survive.

I had no trouble persuading my editor to let me give *Burnt Umber* due prominence on my weekly page, since my more exalted colleagues had already prepared the way. Mr. Howard Spring found it 'impossible to lay down', Mr.

Swinnerton pronounced it a 'minor masterpiece', Mr. Godfrey Wynn found it an experience 'to make your heart sing' and Mr. Ralph Strauss capped it all by stating 'a work of genius'. My own review, my first exercise in back-scratching, followed the example set by my peers. It was an act of considerable generosity in the circumstances.

Thus was laid the first deceit, bearing no resemblance to the rest of his life, but the foundation stone, solid, respectable, on which he built the entire edifice. To operate as Theo did for so many years without detection requires relentless dedication. I followed as closely as anybody the flight and exposure of Burgess and Maclean, closing ranks with the rest of that motley band of armchair critics who never fail to appear in the wake of such a scandal. How could those in authority have failed so miserably in their duty? we asked. I even went into print with my own meagre contribution and asked Theo to check my copy for any obvious mistakes of memory. Theo was approached by the *Sunday Times* to give his version of the origins of such species, but declined on the grounds that it would interfere with his more serious work in progress. I remember admiring him for that.

Later, when the Third Man theory was finally exploded with Philby's appearance and canonisation in Moscow, we met over dinner and shook heads in common bewilderment.

"It's the most extraordinary thing one could possibly imagine," Theo said. "First Guy, then Donald and now Kim. It's like suddenly discovering that Oscar Wilde, Bosie and Frank Harris were all founders of the T.U.C."

"Did you have any inkling at Cambridge?"

"I can't have had. I mean, I always thought Guy would end up on the front page of the *News of The World*, but for normal reasons, like buggering a whole boys' choir at evensong on a Sunday. I suppose I vaguely knew they were taken up with all that communist hysteria in the Thirties. They were always urging me to support some lost cause. But Kim, you see, he supported Franco. What was it he said in his statement? 'Many of us who made the choice in those days changed sides . . . I stayed the course.' Well, that doesn't add up, does it?"

"Nothing adds up as far as I can see, except that we've been made to look ridiculous. I feel sorry for poor old Macmillan."

"One must never feel sorry for politicians. In opposition they are just tolerable, in office insufferable."

Theo never joined any political party. He was much too careful for that. He layered his many deceits like a master pastry chef. To achieve their maximum purpose spies must either live totally in the shadows or else openly appear to be what they are not. It still seems incredible to me that Theo could have mapped out the rest of his life while writing *Burnt Umber*, for although the-writer-as-secret-agent is a familiar figure, embracing such distinguished names as Maugham, Buchan, Greene and Fleming, from their own accounts their recruitment appears to have been by accident rather than design. I was vaguely caught up in intelligence myself during the last war and there again my own involvement stemmed from a typical War Office bog-up rather than an inspired piece of planning. What came first in Theo's case – the literary chicken or the deceptive egg? Now that he is dead I doubt if we shall ever trace the truth to its source, but from a careful study of his journals all the evidence would seem to point to a conscious, meticulously plotted synopsis from which he never deviated. The only thing that could have gone wrong from the beginning was his own writing talent. Had he failed to convince the world at large that he was a literary force to be reckoned with, becoming almost overnight a respected Establishment figure, then it is possible that the rest of the story would have been different. He might have joined Guy and Donald, forming an unholy trio, lost pensioners of that 'élite force' Philby was so proud to serve. It is doubtful whether his Russian masters would have done him the further honour of keeping his books in print, for he wrote glowingly of a way of life that Lenin so ruthlessly destroyed. The chances are, given his sexual tastes, he might have been granted Burgess's last, sad prize: the accommodating factory hand playing the accordion to the drunk with the Eton tie.

As a writer of fiction I am at a disadvantage in setting down this story. Long service at the typewriter has trained me to give my public what it wants: characters with sharply defined motives, heroes with heroic qualities, villains who pay the price. Real life is not so tidy. Today the murderers are literally in our midst, just as the foxes now scavenge in urban dustbins. The village policeman can be armed, Miss Marple is hardly a match for the Baader–Meinhof gang. It is only in films that the Bonnies and Clydes look more glamorous than the boy and girl next door and set next season's fashions in the pages of *Vogue*. The realities are more terrifying than our fictions, for we can live with what we invent. It's the truth that scares.

7

THEO GITTINGS'S JOURNAL: entry dated Sunday, May 15, 1930.

Guy began the day with an argument. He had brought one of his latest 'nephews' with him. This one was called Stephen and he apparently met him on a train and boasts that he masturbated the youth twice in the W.C. "You do that with gun dogs, too, you know," he told me in that boring tone he always adopts when he sets out to shock people. "Always take a new gun dog into the woods and play with it. It's yours for life after that." I asked him whether, in that case, he wanted Stephen for life. He really annoys me when he's so brazen in public.

Despite my prior warnings Tony insisted on bringing his little Nippy along. I have to admit that she is attractive in a bovine sort of way. If she didn't have such large tits I could actually fancy her myself. She was wearing a ridiculous hat, as though dressed for a wedding rather than a trip on the river. Tony should have told her the form, but he probably doesn't know any better himself. He hasn't developed at all and his attempts to appear sophisticated are embarrassing. He's actually convinced himself he wants to marry his Judy, which of course would be a disaster and put a full stop to any hope he has of breaking out of the rut. The moment her looks have gone, as go they will, he'll start to loathe her for ruining his life. The inevitable result of marrying beneath one's class. Writers need to be utterly free.

I suppose the trip itself was quite a success, and the weather stayed good. Leon ('The Flesch is weak,' as Guy describes him) and his sister make such a point of being Jewish. She has obviously been spoilt from the cradle and is determined to be spoilt all the way to the grave. Still, like most Jews, they feel compelled to flaunt their wealth amongst the Gentiles, which worked to our advantage today, because she brought strawberries out of season. I don't think Tony's Judy had ever tasted caviar before – she ate it like fish paste.

We got back reasonably early but I couldn't face another meal with Leon and Rachel, so excused myself on the grounds of tiredness. Came back here and changed into my shop assistant's outfit to go cruising. Got lucky almost immediately. Went to one of my favourite haunts, the lavatory on the green behind the church. Sunday evenings are usually fruitful, probably because there is such a direct relationship between religious fervour and sin. There was a man standing there as I walked in. Late thirties, I would imagine, quite well built and a little shy at first. We stood side by side in silence for a few minutes to make sure the coast was clear, then he put his hand across and felt me. "I only suck," he said. I noticed he had very bad teeth when he smiled, but by then I was too excited to call it off. He was quite good at it and extremely grateful, as they say. I would have returned the favour, but we heard people outside and only just got ourselves together before they walked in. I really must avoid that place for a few weeks. Familiarity breeds danger.

One curious thing. All the way back to college I kept thinking about Tony's Judy and whether I could get her to perform. The idea intrigues.

There were several other entries for the same month (he didn't always make daily notes) and most of them were graphic descriptions of his sexual anarchy. There is of course a pathetic sameness to all pornography, endless repetition being required to sustain the reader's interest, and Theo was no exception. He collected and tabulated his nightly conquests with the industry of a dedicated lepidopterist, pinning them to his pages before they had stopped fluttering in his memory. Never less than explicit, he used the journals to rid his imagination of those carnal descriptions he so religiously excluded from his published novels. There was a kind of exaltation in the written confessions, a spitting in the face of cosy, conventional British life.

I had been prepared for the pornography; it was the rational passages that curiously had the power to confound and wound. So much so I could not continue reading, but had to pour myself a much stiffer brandy than my heart specialist permits these days. It took me a good half an hour to collect myself and be sufficiently calm to read on.

July 20, 1930
I don't know what got into me today. Perhaps my father's letter started the ball rolling. He gave me his usual boring lecture about

86

over-spending, followed by his even more boring lecture about the importance of personal hygiene. I really think that stupid old fart is going off his head. I can't bear to think what Mother goes through day after day, because she must know what he's up to. Curiously enough he doesn't frighten me any more. Getting away from home at long last has changed all that. He frightens Mother, though. I noticed the last time I saw them that she has totally withdrawn into her shell. All that pious stuff he spouts about the sacrifices he has to make to fulfil his social obligations. I think he suspects I see through him and is worried about this; that's why he tries to probe me. What I'd really like to do would be to shock him, and maybe that'll come. He's such a hypocritical snob, churching himself twice every Sunday and then going straight to the Reform School for his mental wank.

His letter put me in a bad mood and I skipped old Dawlish's lecture and instead went out and bought myself an expensive pair of shoes. I wore them out of the shop and then walked to Bright's where the bosomy Judy works. I sat at one of her tables and chatted to her until the Gorgon at the cash desk glared at us. She's exactly the sort of girl who would drive my father over the brink. That's what gave me the idea. It'll take time and effort to work out, of course, and I shall have to tread carefully where Tony is concerned. But I think it could be done. We shall see.

July 23, 1930

The more I think about the idea the more it appeals to my doubtless perverted sense of humour. The first thing is to gain her confidence. She mustn't feel rushed – that would be a big mistake. I'm convinced that the best approach with girls like her is to make them believe they are performing an act of charity. The first moves are very critical. I must say the plan intrigues more and more, and at the same time excites. I felt so keyed up last night that I had to find what is laughingly known as relief. It was willingly granted by a very engaging postman that Guy obligingly passed on. Too old for him, but very acceptable to yours truly. Had a sense of humour too, because I was quicker than usual. "Oh, special delivery," he said. Which I thought was reasonably witty, given the circumstances.

July 30, 1930

Tony was here at the weekend, so it was impossible to progress matters. But I laid some more groundwork. We went out into the country for tea on Sunday at my suggestion and I deliberately went out of my way to charm Judy. At the same time I presented a picture of quiet melancholy. She noticed this and asked if there was anything worrying me. I said no in such a way as to imply yes, but it doesn't matter. Women are always intrigued by sorrow and always jump to the conclusion that they are the cause. (It's a theme I could usefully employ in the novel. I want to create an English Bovary if I can, but set at the end of the last century in a large country house. Grander than Flaubert and turning his plot inside out.)

But Madame Judy. I feel more and more confident that I can pull this off. One can't really feel sorry for Tony. He's so slavishly devoted to her that even I can see he gets on her nerves at times. I'm sure women really prefer a touch of the cad. That is what is wrong with his writing. All the women he writes about are impossibly perfect and consequently incredibly boring. His trouble is that he thinks Hemingway has discovered the secret of the universe. I'd like to write a parody called *A Farewell to Nurses*, a sort of literary enema. Taking the longer view, if I can carry through my plan I might be doing Tony a favour, not that I would expect him to appreciate the fact at the moment, but it might shake him out of his suffocating complacency and be the making of him as a writer.

When we said goodbye I kissed Judy on the cheek. The first kiss between us. Tony looked approving and in a whispered aside thanked me for being so nice to her.

August 3, 1930

Changed my tactics today, and went to Bright's with Kim. Made a point of not sitting at one of her tables, but smiled and waved to her. Always the perfect gentleman. Kim was breaking in a new pipe. I thought it made him look faintly ridiculous, too much the prototype earnest student. We were joined by David Haden Guest wearing his hammer and sickle badge – defiantly, I surmise – and only too anxious to bore us with another repeat performance about his recent experiences in a German clink. Politics bore me, especially foreign politics. Our own lot are tedious enough, with Ramsay Mac and his cloth cap choir singing hymns of praise for The British Working Man. Have to be careful what I say since Guest's father is of that breed, and gets very touchy. From what he tells us about the workings of the Nazis they sound the ideal party for my aged father. Very much up his street. Guest is all for recruiting people for the cause. Kim infected to a lesser degree, and with his pipe gives the impression he would rather be a spectator than a participator. I tried to stifle my yawns and kept a watching eye for Judy. Whenever she looked my way I tried to convey I was sorry not to be served by her.

Started to apply a gentle pressure today. Went to Bright's alone and was lucky enough to find one of her tables empty. Told her how disappointed I had been yesterday. While she was making out my bill I asked her whether she'd ever consider coming out to dinner. I said I wanted to ask her advice about something. "That is, if you don't think Tony would object," I said.

"Why should he?" she replied. "You're his best friend."

"It's just that he's very possessive where you're concerned."

"No harm in going out to dinner, is there?" she said.

It was all too easy. We made a date for Friday night when she gets off work an hour earlier. So far so good. But I mustn't rush things. Before people betray they have to have total trust.

Could hardly wait to get back here and write it all down. Without undue modesty I must record that I was absolutely brilliant tonight. Left nothing to chance in the preparations. Booked a table for two at the Cloche Hat, a discreet restaurant about six miles out of town which serves passable food. Hired a car and picked her up at her home on the dot. Gave her full marks for being ready. Didn't say much on the way there and made sure that we sat apart in the back seat of the car. Merely said how grateful I was she had accepted my invitation.

She seemed amazed by the menu. Funny how, like most pretentious establishments around here, they feel compelled to disguise average British cooking by describing it in French. After translating I ordered for us both, and chose a bottle of claret to have with the main course. Talked glowingly of Tony for a great deal of the time which had the desired effect, for by the time we reached the dessert (she had the sickliest concoction on the trolley) she could hardly contain her curiosity. What was the advice I wanted?

"Oh, I've thought better of it," I said. "You'll think it stupid."

"No, I won't. Tell me."

We were sitting opposite each other and I put out my hand and let it rest on hers briefly. "I don't really know how to put it," I said. "But if you promise you won't laugh, I know I try and give the impression of being somebody who knows his way around, but I had a somewhat strict upbringing. I suffered from ill health as a child and never really mixed with other children. Tony was my closest, my only friend really. So when I came to Cambridge, I really wanted to make up for lost time and find other friends. Well, I've done that to a point. I mean I've got lots of male companions, some of them very nice, and some of them . . . well, you've met a few, and how shall I put it? They're . . . they've got a different attitude to me. I'm not sure what I am really, that's what worries me. I'm not really very good with girls." I paused there for effect. I had her complete attention. "You see, I envy Tony having somebody like you. You don't have any sisters, do you?"

She shook her head.

"Well, there it is," I said. "I've managed to tell somebody at last. Got it off my chest."

"It shouldn't be difficult for you to get a girl."

"Easier said than done. You can't have girls in your room, and anyway most of the girls I meet are so stand-offish. Not like you. I don't mean that rudely, please don't think that. I just mean that you're easy to talk to."

"Have you talked to Tony about it?"

"No," I said. "I don't really think he'd understand, to tell the truth. Or else he'd turn it into a joke. Which it isn't."

"It's awful for you," she said.

"Well, thank you for listening. It's just such a relief to find somebody who will listen sympathetically."

I didn't press it after that, and I must say that she surprised me. I hadn't expected her to have that sort of sophistication. I knew I'd planted the seed. I changed the subject then, and over coffee I asked about her mother and told her what a good daughter she must be. We didn't linger and I drove her home, only reaching for her hand as the car pulled up. "I can't thank you enough, Judy," I said.

"Nothing to thank me for," she said. "I've had a lovely evening."

I saw her to the door, but made no attempt to kiss her.

"I'm spoilt," she said. "Coming home in a posh car."

I said I would try and look in for morning coffee later in the week and thanked her once again. I could hardly have wished for the evening to have gone better. I was so pleased with myself I nearly made a pass at the chauffeur, but rightly thought better of it.

There was a three-week gap in the narrative at this point and I can only assume (having no diaries of my own for the same period) that I was too much in evidence for Theo to progress his scheme. I wish I could look back and state that I had premonitions, but I had none. That much I do remember. My relationship with Judy continued smoothly. We made love as frequently as possible and I proposed at least once a week. Suspecting nothing, I had nothing to fear. I seem to remember that all three of us spent more time together than before, and that Theo no longer tried to score points where Judy was concerned. I attributed this to her personality rather than his sudden change of heart, because alone with me he was as caustic as ever.

It was a time of national turmoil, of course. The country was boiling up for the inevitable collapse of the Labour Government, though few envisaged their total annihilation and MacDonald's inglorious defection. Without much enthusiasm or political awareness I was forced to play my part on the fringe, for there were political meetings going on all over London and I was required to cover my quota. We were in the third year of the Depression and there was a general feeling of disillusion, heightened by the Japanese invasion of Manchuria and the shattering strike in the Royal Navy at Invergordon, an event thought by many to herald the approach of civil war.

Harry Gittings paid a visit to Cambridge during the autumn, inviting me to have lunch with him and Theo at The George. He spoke darkly of revolutionary forces on the march and warned us both of the dire consequences should Europe's madness cross the Channel. I think merely to goad and display his new-found courage to me, Theo deliberately opposed his father's argument. Harry Gittings was not accustomed to being crossed, especially by his son, and the meal was a disaster. It astonished me to see Theo stand his ground, for his father was formidable when aroused, his voice growing ever lower and more intense as his fury increased.

"Father, don't take it all so seriously," Theo said. "You'll have a stroke. We're merely having a friendly argument."

"It is not an argument. There is nothing to argue about. I am telling you the plain facts of the situation and you are contradicting me. You're supposed to be here to educate yourself, not live in some ivory tower. When the war comes you'll have to fight."

"Not necessarily."

"What're you talking about?"

"I could be a conscientious objector."

"I'll tell you something," Harry Gittings said. He leant across the table, knocking over a cup of coffee. "If you ever refused to fight for king and country, I'd take a gun to you myself."

"Well, I dare say you'll be spared such a display of paternal love, Father, because there isn't going to be a war."

I was amazed at Theo's self-control. "I'm sure Tony here is as disgusted as I am," his father said. He summoned a waiter to bring him a fresh cup and a napkin to cover the coffee stain. "Unlike some people he has to work for his living, not live off the fat of the land at other people's expense. You don't know how bloody privileged you are."

"If I don't I'm sure you'll remind me. You're very good at that, aren't you, Father? Reminding people how grateful they should be. If you don't want to pay for my education, just say so. I'd be quite happy to leave."

"Then what would you do? You'd be lost."

"I should earn my own living."

"What as?"

"I might surprise you."

"The only time you ever surprised me was when you were born. You weren't expected to live, you know."

They seemed to have forgotten that I was present. I welcomed the return of the waiter, hoping this would calm matters, but Harry Gittings was not the sort of man to worry about staff. He really was one of the grossest men I have ever come across.

"I take the trouble to come up here," he said, "and I'm treated like this. I shall have no hesitation in telling your mother *exactly* the sort of son she brought into the world."

"Of course she did have help. Unless you're trying to tell me I was an immaculate conception."

Blood rushed into Gittings's face, rather like the cat in some of the early *Tom and Jerry* cartoons.

"You bloody little blasphemer," he hissed. "If we weren't in a public place I'd smash you down."

Still Theo held his ground, though I noticed that he did ease his chair a little further from the table.

"Then I'm glad we're in a public place," he said. "Because you might not have it all your own way. The time has passed, Father, when you can threaten me. I hate to ruin your day totally, but the only person you frighten is yourself. You're awfully red in the neck, which is never a good sign in a man of your age."

Gittings jumped up from the table. There was a second or two when time seemed to be suspended. I was conscious that the rest of the diners were looking in our direction and that the head waiter was approaching. Gittings fumbled for his wallet, extracted a few notes and flung them down in front of me. "Pay the bill," he said.

"Is anything wrong, sir?" the head waiter asked with a total lack of spirit. Gittings ignored him and left the dining room.

"Nothing wrong," Theo said. "The meal was excellent. But we'd like some brandy, I think."

"Well," I said, when heads had turned away. "That was quite something."

"Now you know. I don't suppose you ever believed me before. He's mad, of course. Let's hope it doesn't run in the family."

He poured two very stiff brandies. "Did I ever tell you he once held me out of my nursery window? When I was about two."

"What did he do that for?"

"I'd been crying. I had tummy ache or something. Kept him awake, so he held me by the legs, face downwards until my mother fainted. He's the genuine article, my dear father. He makes Mr. Barratt look like Pickwick."

"Christ!" I said. "I'd no idea it was as bad as that."

"Oh, I could tell you more, but it's too boring. The twist is, I think he wanted a girl. Somebody he could dominate or worse when Mother's gone."

"Do you think he will cut you off?"

Theo shrugged. "Yes, probably. Except he's such a pious snob, he wouldn't want to lose face with his fellow Masons. He's the absolutely perfect one-man reason for a revolution."

I came away from that lunch with increased respect for Theo. Having never been exposed to such family traumas I found it hard to imagine how people survived them. Added to which, the fact that the whole episode had taken place in the stately surroundings of The George's main dining room on a Sunday gave it a surrealist flavour. The row had flared up so quickly. One moment we had all been eating our roast beef, the next moment the table had been struck by lightning. I didn't want to think about what was in store for Theo's poor mother.

I saw Judy later the same day and gave her a fairly graphic reconstruction. She was amazed, of course, but perhaps not as shocked as I had anticipated. I remember being surprised by her reaction.

I didn't see Judy or Theo for three weeks after that. The General Election meant I was kept busy in London. I won't pretend that the paper I worked for made any vital contribution towards a greater understanding of the political morass, or that my reporting of the local scene heralded the debut of another Stephen King Hall, but I did get exposed to the seamier side of democracy in action. It was a dirty election, and I had a ringside seat for some of the minor bouts. It was illuminating stuff to somebody of my tender years, conditioned to the belief that by some mysterious process unknown to ordinary mortals the electorate is blessed with choosing from the cream. All I saw was a succession of dreary little men making dreary little speeches, generating less passion than a sackful of dead mice.

There was a spurious excitement, to be sure, mostly generated by hot air, but Ramsay MacDonald's eventual betrayal of his previous convictions in the name of patriotism introduced me to a cynicism about the political scene I have never had cause to renounce. Over the succeeding decades success has brought me into social contact with many of our leading politicians and I am inclined to Turgot's dictum that 'scrupulous people are not suited to great affairs'. Most of those who have come within my passing orbit have easily persuaded me of their mediocrity.

In the hiatus caused by the General Election I was touched to receive a note from Theo saying he missed seeing me and that in my enforced absence he would try and give Judy a night out. I thought it very noble of him and wrote back and said so. Of such is the Kingdom of Heaven.

October 19, 1931

I think I shall go mad if I attend another political meeting. I would rather look at Comic Cuts than read a single line of any of the manifestos. The King is dead so let's re-elect the King Land of Hope and Glory. I have resisted all calls to join in the campaigning. The only discernible advantage of this election from my own point of view is that the public lavatories seem to be frequented by a better class of queer. Have cast my vote three times in two days with three separate parties. One was a labour of love, one was extremely liberal and the third a shade too conservative. But I was the good time had by all.

Such activities left me with little opportunity to pursue The Great Plan. Wrote to Tony. A subtle touch, this. Received his enthusiastic blessing by return of post. This morning took my place at the coffee table and was gratified by her obvious pleasure at seeing me again. She asked if I was feeling any better and I told her that she had been a great help. We talked about Tony and I let slip that he was delighted she and I were now such good friends. Asked her to accompany me to the cinema on Saturday. Invitation accepted.

October 23, 1931

On reflection the choice of *The Blue Angel* was a lucky one. Heavy Germanic romanticism, but just what the shopgirls ordered. She loved it. Clutched at my hand during the sad parts and I lent her my handkerchief when the lights went up. Said she had never seen a film like it, which I suppose is true enough, because none of us has. We managed to get a drink before closing time and then I walked with her for what seemed like ten miles to her depressing little house. She linked arms part of the way and talked mainly about Hollywood stars and were they really as wicked as they were made out. It was obvious that she wanted to believe they were, and I did my best to hint at erotic delights. "Don't they kiss beautifully?" she said. This as we reached the street where she lived. "I suppose they do," I said. "I haven't got much personal experience to go by." She asked me in for a late night cup of tea and after a show of reluctance I accepted.

Inside, the house lived up to its depressing exterior. Large and friendly cat which immediately proved dotty Father's favourite theory. She made the tea and took a cup upstairs to crippled mother. Everything seemed familiar, as though I had been there before, a criminal revisiting the scene of the crime, as it were. Decided that this was because Tony has described it all in such detail many times over. We sat on either side of the fire with Kitchener the inscrutable Sphinx between us. Conversation soon returned to earlier discussion about the sex life of the stars. I invented lurid stories of orgies which she swallowed without question. Dialogue bordered on the explicit and I detected that it was exciting her. Funny how dirty talk levels us all. Gradually worked around to my alleged dilemma.

"But you must have had girl friends," she said. "Good looking chap like you. Didn't you ever smooch?"

"Well, I know it sounds ridiculous, but I honestly didn't. My father wouldn't let me bring a girl near the house. Tony's very lucky, having somebody like you. I expect you'll get married one day."

"What makes you think that?"

"Well, I assume you will. You're both in love."

I must say she surprised me with her next remark. Tony has always given me the impression that she is as keen as he is.

"He wants to," she said, "but I shan't let him." I didn't have to fake my reaction. "I like him too much to wish that on him. It wouldn't last, you see. I can't make him see it now, because his head's full of nothing else, and in any case I don't want to hurt him. There's probably something wrong with me. Well, I know there is. I keep telling him not to get too fond of me, but it goes in one ear and out the other."

"Perhaps he'll find a way to make you change your mind?"

She shook her head.

"Why're you so sure?" I pressed.

"Because I am. Because I know me too well. I know what I'm

like. I couldn't promise to be faithful, you see. I like variety. I know girls aren't supposed to say that, but I can't help it."

I often read that one of the solaces of growing old is that we can look back without anger. The sorrows and mistakes of our youth, whether misspent or not, are supposed to fade with the passing of time, but I have discovered that I must be one of the exceptions to the rule. I find that whereas I am often hard put to remember who I dined with a week ago and frequently forget my own telephone number, my recollections of distant events remain unbearably vivid. In particular I seem to have retained every detail of my time with Judy: none of those who came after her has ever effaced her memory. The fever and the fret of those days and nights in Cambridge still have the power to disturb. Reading these sections of Theo's journals became too painful at times. I can understand Judy — she was at least consistent — but Theo's role is harder to take. It is not necessary to trust to stay in love, but friendship is more fragile than love.

I have edited some of Theo's eroticism from the remainder of this episode, not for reasons of prudery — it's too late for that — but because it is not a pain I wish to share.

I judged the moment ripe to advance more boldly. As Guy always says, 'One can always apologise, the important thing is to have something to apologise for.' I knew that she and I were talking in a kind of shorthand. We stared at each other and she smiled.

"What're you thinking? How awful I am?"

"No," I said. "If you must know, I was wondering what it's like to kiss somebody like you."

"Only one way to find out, isn't there?"

She came and sat in my lap. Her lips were more pliant than I had imagined. I missed the accustomed roughness of my usual partners and the fact that her breath was untainted by tobacco. Altogether very curious. I was careful not to appear too anxious.

"Just relax," she said. We tried again.

"I don't think I'm very good at it," I said.

"Never mind about that. You're all tense, that's why. Did you enjoy it? Was it nice?"

97

"Yes," I said. "But I don't think we ought to take the lesson any further, do you?"

"Why not? You mean because of Tony?"

"Yes, I suppose so."

"What about my feelings?" she said. "Don't I have a say in it?" She wriggled about on my lap. "You know what they say, you can't get off the train while it's moving. You men are all alike, all such babies, crying for the bottle and then when it's given to you pretending you don't want it. You're not really worried about Tony, are you? You wouldn't be here if you were."

I must say I gave her ten out of ten for that.

"If you're not going to buy," she said, "you shouldn't have fingered the goods."

"But aren't you worried about Tony?"

"Yes and no. I would be if he found out, because I wouldn't like to hurt him. But he won't find out from me."

I decided that my bogus show of resistance had gone far enough, because rather to my surprise I was by now more excited than I had thought possible. Visibly so, which she was not slow to notice. We undressed with what is known as unseemly haste and the last of life's great mysteries was revealed to me. Definitely a sight to gladden the aged father's heart, in fact probably a sight to put paid to it. I did have certain preconceptions, but photographs don't really prepare one for the living flesh. Tony had described her breasts, of course, but even so at first glance quite alarming. The nipples intrigued me, and remembering her remark about the baby's bottle I closed my eyes and thought of Nanny. I think what struck me most was the overall softness.

At the time I dare say Judy felt she had struck a blow for the cause, since women can make a virtue out of adultery more easily than men. Whether they ever repeated the experiment is nowhere recorded. There are a few further references to her in the journals, but nothing that elaborates on the joint deception. It is even possible that for once Theo felt some guilt, though it is more likely he became bored once he had achieved his original objective.

I've thought about it a great deal. I even went back to Theo's first novel the other day, since few writers can resist the temptation to make use of their own secrets. And I was right. There as aspects of Judy in his character of Masie

Price, the first love of the hero of *Burnt Umber*, but Theo turned her inside out, like one of those reversible jackets. He was nothing if not a consummate technician. None of us creates entirely from the imagination: there is always a starting point. Alone at our desks we dredge forgotten pools, searching like a murder squad for bodies that disappeared long ago. When eventually they rise to the surface, time may have bloated them and distorted the features, but we can still make use of the corpses.

8

I HAVE NOTICED THAT when people begin to suspect, rightly or wrongly, that the framework of their society is disintegrating they are seldom over-particular in the conduct of their own lives. We were all careless, it seems, during the late summer of 1931 and the months following the election. There was a feeling of hopelessness in the air that contaminated everybody. It reminded me of those pyramid letters one sometimes receives, unsolicited, through the post. You know the sort of thing: you must either send six copies immediately or else the chain will be broken and misfortune will be heaped upon you. As a child I was terrified of them and followed the dire instructions explicitly, though I never received the postbags full of bounty that were supposed to flow in return.

Certainly there seemed to be such a chain of ill luck. My mother died in the spring of 1932, surprising everybody. Mercifully there was no lingering illness, as had been the case with Judy's mother. The diagnosis was made and within three weeks she was buried. The word 'cancer' was only slightly more socially permissible than 'syphillis' in those days, and my father asked me and the twins to keep the cause of her death a secret. "Just say she passed away," he told us. "We don't want people talking about it." He showed little emotion at the graveside and in truth I had to force myself to shed tears, for we had never been close, a fact borne out by her Will, since she left her small personal estate, amounting to a few hundred pounds, to be divided equally between my two brothers.

Harry Gittings and his wife made the journey down to London for the funeral, but he spoilt the sympathetic gesture by telling us that it had proved quite convenient since he had to consult Counsel in chambers. He invited me to have lunch with him at the Strand Palace, a hotel he favoured because of its proximity to the Law Courts. On arrival, I found we were dining alone. He ordered for me, briskly, choosing from the set, and therefore cheapest, menu of the day.

"You don't drink at lunch, I hope."

I did, given the chance, but his question demanded a refusal.

"We'll have Malvern water. Good for the bowels, flushes out all the toxins. Regular bowel movements are the secret of good health. Your mother would have been alive today if she'd only followed my advice. But women don't, you know. The only time you can get a woman to take advice is when she's concerned about money. Then they're all ears. People think it's only doctors who see human nature in the raw. Quite wrong. It's we lawyers who see people with their trousers down. How's your father taken it?"

The non-sequitur took me off balance.

"Not too badly."

"Will he marry again?"

"I don't know."

"They weren't happy, you know. Never got on. Did you know that?"

"They seemed to get on all right," I said.

"Children never notice these things. Unless there's actual violence in the house. Your father ought to get out more, broaden his horizons, meet people. Find himself somebody young and marry again."

I wasn't shocked by his reference to my parents' relationship, but I found his talk of remarriage so soon after the funeral in poor taste.

"You got a girl, have you?"

"Yes. Sort of."

"I'd like to meet her."

The idea filled me with horror, and I bent low over my grilled mackerel.

"Has Theo got a girl?"

"I'm not sure," I said.

"Really? I'm sure he confides in you."

"I think he's got a lot of friends in college."

"My son is a great disappointment to me, did you know

that?" He leant across the table to emphasise the point. "Great disappointment. You saw the way he behaved to me that Sunday. Didn't that disgust you? Let me tell you something, something for your further education . . . Theo is well on his way to becoming a bloody nancy boy. D'you know what I mean by that?"

"I think so," I said.

"Somebody who goes to bed with men instead of girls. They perform unnatural acts, do disgusting things to each other. I'm not going to spell it out for you over a meal, but I'm sure you get my drift. And if I'm right, if what I suspect is true, then God help him. You tell him that next time you see him. Will you tell him?"

"I'm not sure it's my place to tell him," I said with a sudden surge of courage. The conversation was turning into a nightmare.

"Well, you try. If you're his real friend, you try. Because I'll tell you something, Tony. This country we live in is morally bankrupt . . . *morally* bankrupt as well as down the drain financially. All the decent chaps, the men of my generation, were killed in the trenches. You wouldn't be here, any of you, if we hadn't fought and died for you. And what is happening now, what's happened since? We've got a lot of namby-pamby politicians running round in circles wetting themselves when they should be cracking the whip. And we've got a generation, your generation, who think life is a joke that parents pay for. They don't know the meaning of the word patriotism. They're all nancies, nancy boys. I *know*. I don't read about it like most people. I see it, every day, in the courts, face to face. People behaving like animals. Animals. Having sex like animals. Gratifying their perverted desires like dogs in the street. D'you understand what I'm saying?"

"But not everybody's like that," I said.

"We're not talking about everybody. I'm telling you about people who should know better, who've been given all the advantages in life. We know the lower classes can't help being what they are, but the real people, the people born to govern who should be setting an example, they're the ones who are letting the side down. You mark my words, you're going to see blood run in the streets before very long. Anarchy. Yids and communists and nancy boys, inflaming the British working man, giving him ideas. It'll be the end of England as we know it."

The sheer volume of gloom bordered on the ridiculous. Harry Gittings was such a bogus character, reminding me of something out of a third-rate touring melodrama. He affected smart clothes, always wore a buttonhole and a silk pocket handkerchief. When he talked he nodded his head downwards, like a chicken taking water. As he warmed to a favourite subject he closed his lips tightly at the end of each sentence in a curiously prissy manner. I found him repulsive – all my childhood fears had been replaced by loathing. I don't think I have ever disliked any man so much before or since.

Over coffee he continued the monologue, telling me of his dedication to public service, how things would be different if everybody followed his shining example. "Duty! That's a word this generation's never heard of. D'you think I want to spend my spare time making sure that a lot of sluttish little girls are set on the right path? Of course I don't. But I consider it my duty. We've got girls in that reform school who were pregnant by the time they were fourteen." He put his head on one side to emphasise his disgust. "Fourteen!" They'd had carnal knowledge of their fathers, some of them. The sin of incest. You can't deal in ordinary terms with those sort of people. They're degenerate. But you have to *try*, that's the point I'm making. People like me *have to try*, we consider it our duty. And for no personal benefit, you understand? We get no thanks in return."

He had made himself red in the face. By now I was desperate to escape. I realised I had been used. He had no interest in me, but his estrangement from Theo meant that I was his only contact and he had elected me the go-between, a role that carried no rewards whatsoever. I think even then I saw through him. Even though I lacked any clinical comparisons, my instincts alone made me aware that the origins of Theo's revolt were to be found in his monstrous father's intolerance. Now, of course, I can be persuaded to draw some parallels with Philby's father, an eccentric of other dimensions from Harry Gittings, but both dominant personalities with a burning sense of their own importance.

I left the hotel feeling vaguely sick. He had extracted a final promise from me that I would convey his displeasure and threat to Theo. I gave it with fingers crossed beneath the table. The after-taste of his dialogue added to my queasiness, and I nipped into the nearest pub for a quick beer before closing time. I found myself looking with new curiosity at the people around me, seeing them through Gittings's suspicious eyes, wondering what hidden vices their sullen faces concealed. The trouble with the Harry Gittings of this world is not that they have the power to disturb us, but that they are capable of infecting us with their prejudices.

It would have been unthinkable, of course, to have relayed his message to Theo verbatim. The young seldom betray each other in such bald terms. I would sooner have shattered the smug virginity of my twin brothers than voice any criticism of Theo to his face. Our arguments, and we had many, were never on that personal level. There were many aspects of Theo's way of life that I did not understand, but I did not try to analyse them. Even after Gittings had forced me to recognise the true nature of Theo's sexuality, I still did not actively relate the physical details to Theo. If I thought about it at all, it was still in the abstract. Since I was totally ignorant of his seduction of Judy at that time, I felt no personal threat. If Theo preferred the company of men to women, then if anything it gave me a feeling of superiority, a certain pity for him at the thought of what he was missing. Had Gittings directed all his venom towards Burgess, then I might have reacted differently. In his blundering, offensive way Gittings had stumbled on the truth – his definition of duty was light years away from Theo's and I dare say he was disturbed enough to have committed violence had he ever discovered the real facts of Theo's life.

None of these thoughts was uppermost in my mind at the time. I had dared to challenge my own luck and the tide had turned against me. Now that my mother was dead I could no longer keep up the pretence of enjoying the family hearth. The smugness of my brothers was all-embracing. They even treated mourning like a form of holy orders, silently reproachful of me like two prematurely-old spinsters. I made up my mind to leave home as soon as possible.

I was still convinced that Judy could be persuaded to marry. My first plans embraced the fantasy of moving to Cambridge, claiming Judy for my own, finding a job there and living a life of pastoral bliss while I laboured to become a published writer. The fact that Theo had done it was the added spur I needed, for nothing provokes like the success of a close friend.

It all seemed cut and dried for twenty-four hours. Then I was sacked from my job on the paper. Following the election, I suppose the demand for local newspapers slackened as people tightened their belts, and all such minor luxuries were dispensed with. The editor was apologetic and gave me a generous testimonial letter, but the good old maxim of 'last in, first out' applied and I added one more statistic to the growing ranks of the unemployed. I had no money saved; all I had was my final week's wages and a new sense of injustice.

I was too proud to reveal the news to my father or the twins. My job had always demanded erratic hours and for two weeks, until my money gave out, I tramped the streets following up every lead I could. Having no special qualifications I usually got passed over, and at the end of the fortnight all I had to show for my efforts was an evening's casual labour washing dishes à la Orwell in a Soho restaurant. In my ineptness I dropped a whole pile of plates, the cost of which wiped out my meagre earnings. I returned home defeated and confessed the true situation to my father.

"I really think it would be best if I left home and tried for work elsewhere. It would be one less mouth for you to feed and less of a wrangle."

"Where would you go?"

"I haven't really decided," I lied. "Maybe Cambridge. Lodgings are cheaper there and I've made some contacts through Theo."

"Well, you'll need something to tide you over." Although we had never discussed it my father was well aware of my hurt at having been completely excluded from my mother's bequests.

"I can't give you much, as you know." His own salary had been cut along with many others, but he drew fifty pounds out of his Post Office Savings – an enormous sum of money to my eyes. I protested it was too much.

"No," he said. "I'll give you a tip. When you lend people money, always make sure you lend them enough to sustain their dignity. If you give them too little they resent you for it and have no compunction about forgetting it."

"I won't forget."

"I'm sure you won't. That's why I'm giving it to you. Just take care of it and don't waste it. I've got no worries; I know you're going to make it. We're just all going through a bad patch. I was thinking of selling this place anyway, getting somewhere smaller. We don't need all the space now that your mother's gone."

"She wasn't a very happy person, was she?" I said.

"No, I don't think she was. Life didn't give her what she wanted. I didn't have enough ambition for her, you see. I often wondered why she married me."

It was the first intimate conversation we had ever had, and it came too late for me to be able to be of any comfort to him.

"Perhaps," I said, "perhaps she changed."

"No, I don't think so. I think she was always the same person. A lot of people marry just to escape, you know. They don't quite know what they're escaping from, or to. It's just the idea that appeals to them."

"At least she didn't suffer when she died."

"No, that's true. She did most of her suffering before."

I felt a stab of remorse for my selfish lack of perception, and when I said goodbye, kissing my father awkwardly – the first time in many years we had allowed ourselves any outward show of affection – I found I was crying.

I took a coach to Cambridge, beginning my economies, and went straight to Judy's place of work on arrival. Much to my surprise she wasn't there. I made enquiries of the woman at the cash desk.

"She's left," the woman said.

"Left? You mean left for good?"

"I don't know. You'll have to ask the manageress."

I went in search, but that lady was busy and couldn't see me. I asked one of the other waitresses.

"They fired three last week," the girl whispered. "They said food was missing from the kitchens, and since nobody owned up, they fired three girls to make an example."

I lugged my suitcases all the way to Judy's home. She greeted me warmly enough, but I immediately sensed a subtle change in her. I put this down to her recent misfortune.

"Well, that makes two of us," I said. I told her of my parallel experience, trying to conjure up the courage to talk of it lightly, but the suddenness of our change of fortune had chilled us. I said nothing of my wilder plans for our joint future.

"I suppose you want to move in?" Judy said.

"Is that all right? I haven't had a chance to look for anywhere else."

"Neighbours are funny," she said. "They turn a blind eye as long as it isn't stuck under their noses. It's easier while you're able to pay the rent regular, but the agent doesn't miss a trick."

"I've got some money my father lent me, and two can live as cheaply as one."

"Three can't," she said.

"You'd rather I didn't, then?"

"I'm not going to kick you out tonight. All I'm saying is, things are different. Moving in is different from just sleeping with me. You don't know how narrow-minded people are around here. And I've got me mum to think of."

"Yes, I see."

"We're a pair, aren't we, you and me? I haven't got over what that mean old sod said to me at work. Wish I had nicked stuff from the kitchens now, but I never even brought scraps home. None of us did. It was the bloody chef; he's been at it for ages. We all knew."

"I've got an idea. They probably need help at the college. We can ask Theo to make enquiries. He'd vouch for you."

"No, I wouldn't want to put on him."

"Have you seen him recently?"

"Not for a bit. What're you going to do?"

"Oh, I'll try the obvious, have a go at getting on the local paper. And if that doesn't work, I'll take anything. Just 'til I get my head above water. And whatever I've got, or get, is yours. That goes without saying."

"You're sweet," she said. "Too good for me."

"Balls," I said. "Double balls, in fact. It's the other way round from where I'm sitting."

"Oh, sure. I'm a great catch. All tits and no prospects," she said with a flash of her old humour. "Go and talk to Mum while I get us a meal. But don't let on that I've got the boot. I haven't told her."

I kissed her. Her lips were colder than usual. "It'll all work out, darling," I said. "You'll see."

I sat and chatted with her mother until Judy had prepared the meal. As I looked at her frail, motionless figure in that condemned cell of a bed, the remainder of my courage drained away. I realised I had no idea where to begin.

After a sparse meal of soup Judy left me alone while she prepared her mother for the night. I took out the pages of the new novel I had been working on, rereading them by the dead fire with Kitchener on my lap. I had made a better start, but I forced myself to recognise my work still lacked any form of passion; it was all half-digested experience bought second hand. I put the pages in the grate and set a match to them.

"What're you burning?" Judy said as she returned.

"My past," I said dramatically.

"Your writing, wasn't that your writing? Why're you doing that?"

"Because it's no good."

"But last time you told me you were pleased with it."

"Well, I was wrong," I said.

She made love with a kind of quiet desperation that night, as though trying to make up for her lukewarm welcome earlier. There is something about lying in the dark with the girl you love, the warmth of her soft belly pressed against you, legs entwined, the damp hair against your cheek – the rest of the world shut out completely. There is something primitive about it, a throwback to childhood nights when a storm is raging outside and only the warmth of the blankets pulled high gives any hope for survival.

"I must try and see Theo tomorrow," I said.

"You set great store by him, don't you?"

"He's my best friend."

"It's funny that, really. You're both so different," she said.

9

"Is THAT WHAT the old merde actually said? Did he actually use those words?"

Theo seemed far more interested in his father's threats of future action than in my own present dilemma. He was nothing if not consistent.

"Yes," I said. I had prefaced the tale of my own misfortunes with a colourful account of my lunch at the Strand Palace.

"God, he's so pathetically bourgeois! One really should choose one's parents more carefully. They're such an embarrassment in later life. I suppose you had some of the usual, did you? A clean bowel is a clean mind *et cetera*. Well, we mustn't disappoint him. I shall have to think of something quite conclusive. I don't want him to spend the rest of his life being constipated by doubt."

Theo's evocative phrase is an accurate description of my present state of mind. Even now, with all the evidence so neatly set out in those schoolroom exercise books he used to record his treasons, I still have doubts. They are mostly doubts about my own intelligence. My own horizons were so narrow in those days that I was totally unaware of the outside forces which were even then shaping the lives of Theo, Guy Burgess, Maclean and Philby. I suppose I can be excused where the other three are concerned, for they were never intimates, but I am amazed at my own cupidity with Theo. Did I overlook all the clues, or did he share with Philby and the others such a consummate and natural talent for the double-life that there was none to overlook? This must have been the period when they were all recruited and it would be a savage exaggeration to imagine that any of them were master spies overnight. They were undergraduates, with no influence, no access to State secrets; they were not familiar with the corridors of power . . . And yet they were part of a long-term strategy, quick frozen in a manner of speaking for future consumption.

In order to illustrate how innocent our lives seemed on the surface, mine genuinely so, and Theo's judged not by the knowledge I now possess but by the events I witnessed, it is necessary to set down the various stages of our emotional development. If I anticipate later knowledge for the sake of convenience I shall be cheating on myself, pretending intuitions I never had. If that presents me in an unflattering light, well, I must take that risk. In writing of betrayals one should always guard against becoming too apt a pupil.

Theo did change around this time, but like many others I misread the plausible explanations for such changes. The publication of *Burnt Umber* had not only given him the means to withstand his father's financial blackmail (his first novel earned him £1,000, a not inconsiderable sum in 1932, plus the Findlater Memorial Prize for Fiction) but also immeasurably strengthened his public self-confidence. With that brand of modesty which makes sure that one's friends are aware they are rubbing shoulders with success, he had subtly informed me that he was now the centre of attraction, lionised by the literary set, his mantelpiece festooned with invitations from those members of society who cannot resist claiming every new hero as their own special property. "Such a bore," he said, "but I suppose one has to suffer them; it's good for sales. I doubt if a third of them have actually *read* the book, but at least they've bought it. The really amusing thing is quite a few think I've written about them, their family and way of life."

"Still, it must be terrific," I said, "to see yourself in print."

"I must admit it is a bit of a giggle. And getting a prize as well. My publisher's tickled pink."

He seemed to have gathered a whole new set of friends, names unfamiliar to me, and while he had not abandoned his previous cronies he was disinclined to talk about them. "Guy?" he said when I enquired. "Fine as far as I know.

He's become so rabidly political, that's his trouble. Proper little revolutionary. One should never take politics *that* seriously."

Listening between the lines I had the impression that part of Theo's disenchantment stemmed from the fact that Burgess and his set disapproved of Theo's choice of subject matter in *Burnt Umber*. It was not fashionable to write a nostalgic view of the upper classes, and smacked of betrayal. "The heart of England," Kim Philby had said in an election speech for a Trinity contemporary, "does not beat in stately homes and castles. It beats in the factories and on the farms." Despite such fighting words, I did not notice that many of them wore cloth caps. Whatever their personal habits, sexual or otherwise, it was the adultery of the soul that claimed most of their spare time.

It had taken me a week to get Theo on his own and explain my predicament. He listened sympathetically enough, but volunteered no immediate solution.

"I can quite see Judy's point of view," he said, when I explained her reluctance to let me move in with her on a semi-permanent basis. "An outward display of morals is the hallmark of the poor." It was not the answer I wanted to hear.

Having spent the first night with Judy I had done the honourable thing and sought lodgings elsewhere, eventually landing up with a Mrs. Pike, a widow in her late fifties who had lost both her husband and only son in the war, the son being killed a few hours before the Armistice. Their pictures were everywhere in the small house. I had the dead son's bedroom at the back of the house, overlooking a distant view of the colleges like a constant reminder of Xanadu. Of necessity her conversation was coloured by the joint tragedy, but she was a kindly soul and within a strictly limited scope cooked me ample meals for the two pounds and five shillings a week I paid her for full board. She fussed over my laundry and I didn't have the heart to tell her to use less starch on my shirts: she seemed to dip them in concrete and I had a permanent rash on my neck where the razor-like collars chafed. There was no electric light, only gas in the downstairs rooms, and I went to bed with a candle, a comforting source of illumination before sleep, but a strain to work by. I wrote every night until the candle gutted, and when inspiration faltered, as it frequently did, I made copious financial calculations in an effort to stretch my dwindling capital for as long as possible. All luxuries were out. I attempted to grow a beard, not only to save the cost of shaving but in the hope that it would make me look older, since I convinced myself that what few jobs there were going would first be offered to more mature men. The effect, alas, hovered between the ludicrous and the unsightly: my beard grew in patches, giving me the appearance of a demented gypsy. I allowed myself five Woodbines a day in the beginning, and bought a cheap holder to prolong their thin delights to the last centimetre. Alcohol was forbidden, save for the occasional half pint of bitter if I treated Judy at the weekends.

As soon as I had finished Mrs. Pike's breakfast of fried bread and fatty bacon washed down with strong cups of tea – her panacea for all ills – I started the day's search for work. My early efforts to get back into local journalism were quickly smothered. The editor's letter didn't even produce a personal interview; dog didn't help dog in those days. I applied at the local library, who directed me to the labour exchange, who in turn directed me to the back of the queue. My only success in the first month was a chance encounter in a workmen's café, where an elderly sage let slip that there was a chance of employment in what he described as 'a high quality butchers'. I ran all the way to the address he gave me, only to find it was an establishment specialising in horse meat, ostensibly for consumption by cats and dogs. The sight of slabs of horse, with their curious yellow fat being attacked by swarms of large flies, was enough to quench my thirst for security at any cost. Beggars, I decided there and then, sometimes had to be choosers.

In an effort to cheer us up, I took Judy to the cinema one night. Cinemas gave better value for money in those days: there were always two full-length feature films, a newsreel, or two cartoons and a trailer for forthcoming attractions. For the princely sum of sixpence (in the old coinage) one could escape reality for three hours or more. We chose a comedy bill – Will Hay and gang, and Ernie Lotinga in another of his Josser roles. I noticed that the somewhat hangdog manager was jack of all trades, taking the money at the box office, then rushing up to the projection booth when, as often happened, the film broke down. Feeling lighter of heart when the programme finished, and emboldened by previous humiliations, I stopped by his tatty little office and asked if he was looking for any assistance. He proved to be practically stone deaf and I had to repeat my enquiry before it penetrated.

"Haven't got an assistant," he said. "I'm the manager, so if you've got any complaints you tell me. I can't do anything about the toilets until next week."

"No, I was enquiring whether you wanted any extra staff."

"Staff? I am the staff."

Judy had to walk away at that point. "Yes," I persevered, "I just thought that possibly you might be looking for some help. I-am-seeking-employment."

"Seeking what?"

"Employment. I-am-looking-for-a-job."

"Oh, I see. Thought it was a complaint. What sort of job?"

"Any. I'll tackle anything."

"Do what?"

"I don't mind what I do. I'm very keen. I'll work very hard."

"Yes, well, I can't help that. It's the war. Burst my eardrum. Exploded right next to me. Say it slowly."

I gave every word the same deliberate emphasis. "I-would-be-very-grateful-if-you-would-consider-giving-me-a-job."

He stared at me for a long time. "Here?"

I nodded.

He seemed surprised that anybody would wish to join his tottering organisation. He shifted some papers from under a stained tea mug. "I'll show you something. Just so you don't think I'm making it up. It's my own business, you see. I'm not in with any of the big boys. What am I looking for? Oh, yes, here it is. Look at that. That's last week's take. Makes you bloody cry. See what they left me after charging rental? I'm being ground into dust, I am."

He thrust a piece of paper under my nose. I looked at the figures on it. "Look at the last figure. That's what I was left with." I forget the exact amount but it was less than twenty pounds. "That's why the toilet's not mended, you see. And I've got to buy a new lamp. Nearly had a fire tonight."

"I'll work for very little."

"You can say that again. What d'you call little? People have different ideas."

"Anything you say."

"Well, I could say three quid."

"I'll take it," I said.

"You what?"

"I accept."

"Haven't offered it yet, have I? I was just talking aloud. How do I know you're any good? Do you know anything about running a cinema?"

"No, but I could soon learn."

"I see. I've got to teach you, have I? Might as well carry on as I am."

"All right," I said. "I'll make a bargain with you. You don't have to pay me at all for the first week. If you think I'm useless at the end of the week you owe me nothing. But if you keep me on, it's three pounds a week."

He looked at me and then at Judy. "That your wife?"

"No, I'm not married."

He stared at his pieces of paper again, then back to me. "Are you any good at mending toilets? Because that's likely to be your first job. You have to wear a tie, you know. When the public comes in. I like to see people neat."

He was wearing a crumpled dress suit and black tie, giving him the appearance of somebody playing a waiter in an early Hal Roach comedy.

"Don't have one of these monkey suits, I suppose?"

"No, I'm afraid not."

"Well, can't have everything, can I? All right, it's a deal then. Eight o'clock tomorrow. I'll be here. What's your name?"

"Tony. Anthony Stern."

"Stirr?"

"No, Stern."

"Tony, is it? Mine's Clifford Pinkwater."

That sent Judy off again, but fortunately he didn't hear. I kept a straight face.

"Very nice of you, Mr. Pinkwater."

"I'm the manager and the owner. The whole works."

"Yes, well, I'm very grateful. I'll be here at eight o'clock sharp."

I shook his hand, which surprised him. "Thank you very much indeed. You won't regret it."

I backed out of his office, grabbed Judy's arm and rushed her outside, just in case he had second thoughts.

"There, you see! I did it. Isn't that fantastic? I mean, that's a real bit of luck."

"Pinkwater," Judy said, and was off again.

"Clifford," I said.

We both fell against each other in an excess of hysteria.

"Do you know anything about toilets?" Judy said.

"They flush with success. Like me."

Arms entwined, exchanging snatches of Mr. Pinkwater's dialogue, we walked home discussing my new fortune, stopping en route for a fish and chip supper, an extravagance I felt I could now afford.

I presented myself for work the following morning, taking care to arrive a quarter of an hour before the allotted time. Clifford arrived on an ancient bicycle, still wearing the trousers of his evening suit well hoisted with cycling clips.

"Tony, isn't it?"

"Yes," I said anxiously. For one awful moment I thought he had forgotten our arrangement.

"I'm not good on names."

He removed his clips and hung them on a nail behind his desk. Then he took a small mirror from one drawer and, propping it against some cans of film, carefully arranged his sparse hair. I was to discover that he was very vain about his appearance.

I waited for his instructions.

"Can you boil a kettle?"

"Yes."

"Over there. Gas ring. Needs something in the meter. Here." He gave me a couple of pennies. "When you get paid, we'll share that. But I don't mind treating you this week. Take your coat off."

He brewed us both a cup of tea.

"Listen . . . what's your name?"

"Tony, sir."

"I'll get it in time. Listen, Tony, what you've got to learn about the general public, is they've got no respect for other people's property. Take that broom, and go in the auditorium and sweep up. I've given you a cup of tea, because you'll need a strong stomach. You'll find a bucket of sawdust over in that corner. Put some of that down first, it helps mop up the mess. They spit, you know. All over the floor. It's not a pretty sight. If there's anything worse, use the disinfectant. Any lost property, bring to me. When you've done that we'll get cracking on the toilet."

It took me the best part of two hours to sweep between the rows of seats. I noticed that most of the consumptives seemed to sit in the first five rows. Mr. Pinkwater looked in several times to see how I was progressing. He spent his morning rewinding the films for the first performance. The cinema opened at noon, the programme commencing fifteen minutes later.

"Never many here for first house," he said. "Usually out of works and old age pensioners. They get in half price, you see, until two thirty. Sit anywhere they like. Oh, and any ex-soldiers wearing a badge. Just take the money, you don't give them tickets. Give them tickets and half of them'll try it on the following day. Swear blind they've paid already. And watch out for kids sneaking in through the fire exit once the lights are down. Just sling 'em out, don't argue."

Our efforts to repair the men's toilet were unsuccessful, since it was obvious even to my untrained eye that his clients had totally wrecked it. "Put a notice on the door," he said. "Don't put 'Out of Order', because they'll ignore that. Write 'Keep Out, Danger of Infection'. That might do the trick for those of them that can read. And wipe some of that filth off the walls."

I removed as many of the obscenities as I could. They had a depressing sameness about them, being mostly crude drawings of the male and female sexual organs and accompanied by pencilled samples of the artists' poetic wit, such as *Stand on your arse, not on your feet, shit down the hole, not on the seat* – a piece of advice that appeared to have been ignored by many. I could not help comparing my lot with the life led by Hollywood stars. Norma Shearer seemed a far cry from the lives led by her Cambridge admirers.

I spent the rest of the day supervising the patrons to their seats and acting as policeman for the small boys attempting to effect free entry. Mr. Pinkwater seemed reasonably pleased with my progress and there were odd moments when I could slip into the auditorium and enjoy snatches of *Will Hay*. I made up my mind to survive, come what may. There was only one other person on the staff, George the projectionist, a borderline maniac whom I was rightly warned to avoid at all costs. He spent most of his time reading Bible tracts and as a result frequently missed the changeovers. When this happened the audiences went wild, hurling debris towards the screen and whistling loudly until normal service was resumed. I noticed that this behaviour was not confined to any one section or age group, nor were the frequent interruptions resented by our audiences. On the contrary, they seemed to welcome an opportunity to let off steam. In the case of a major breakdown, Mr. Pinkwater would advance to the front of the auditorium and crave their indulgence. He was greeted with even wilder applause. These episodes had a ritual all of their own and were considered part of the entertainment.

On Saturdays Mrs. Pinkwater put in an appearance to help cope with the most popular matinée of the week. The programme times were altered and customers were given an extra short film to prolong the value for money. Half the house was given over to children and was known as The Tuppenny Rush – with good cause. The entire programme was changed twice a week, with special films on a Sunday. This meant that cans of film were constantly arriving and being collected, and the paperwork drove Clifford into short sharp furies — from time to time he would sweep all from his desk.

Mrs. Pinkwater confided to me that she had been on the boards, a claim which later boiled down to one appearance in the chorus during the war, her career being curtailed the moment Clifford spotted her. "I think it can be said, I swept Clifford off his feet. Not all the nice girls love a sailor, you know, and the moment I clapped eyes on him, I said, Ruby, it's going to be a khaki wedding. He's a very passionate man, Clifford. Hidden depths."

Certainly he was a pleasant man to work for, and not ungenerous. Despite our arrangement he insisted on paying me for the first week and never asked me to contribute to the cost of my twice daily cup of tea. Together we managed to spruce up the entrance and I impressed him by finding a brand-new toilet at cut price in a bankrupt builder's yard. We made some simple frames to display the still photographs that the film companies provided, and I persuaded him that there was extra profit to be made by selling bags of peanuts and sherbert dabs. I can't pretend that The Splendide, as it was proudly named, was anything but a flea-pit, but we did try and the business gradually improved. I was able to take over a lot of the paperwork for him, and since the flirtatious Ruby had also given me her seal of approval, my future seemed reasonably secure.

Judy's situation was not as happy. She was still without a regular job, and had been forced to accept a few mornings charring in the larger houses on the fashionable side of town. She was paid a few pence an hour and her efforts hardly kept her and her mother in the bare essentials. I tried to get her to accept part of my wages, but all she would allow was to let me buy the occasional cheap joint of meat which she cooked and which she and her mother shared with me.

Although I had little spare time to spend with Theo, to his credit he was most solicitous whenever we did meet and generous with his hospitality. His favourite topic of conversation was ways and means of getting even with his father.

"I think I've finally got it," he announced one day. "The

master plan, and it requires your presence."

"Mine?"

"Yes, I don't want to waste it. I have to have a committed audience. Can you get a Sunday off?"

"Doubtful."

"Well, try. You must try because this is going to be too good to miss."

"What're you going to do?"

"Well, for several weeks now I've been writing home to Mother and dropping certain calculated hints. Very subtly, and since he reads all her mail as a matter of course he's bound to be intrigued. I've told Mother that I've met a very nice girl. In the last letter I put my tongue firmly in my cheek and said that I'm getting rather serious with this girl and that I hope Father will approve."

"But what girl? Have I ever met her?"

"There isn't a girl. That's the whole point. She doesn't exist, as such. But what I'm angling for is an invitation to take her home to meet the aged parents." He paused for effect. "And when that happens, you've got to be there."

"If she doesn't exist, how can you take her home?"

"*She* doesn't exist, but *he* does. Have you ever met a character called Raymond Blake? No, you didn't come to the last revue, did you? Well, the amazing Raymond happens to be extremely presentable, and when done up looks more like a girl than most girls. He does a fantastic impersonation of Jessie Mathews, high kicks and all. So, we've been rehearsing. Raymond is going to become Miss Angela Pritchett, only daughter of Sir Charles and Lady Prichett, who live abroad of course. Sir Charles retired to Bermuda for his health. I mean, we've really worked it out in great detail. We rehearse all the time."

"You'll never get away with it."

"Yes, we will. I promise you, made up and dressed, Raymond is the real McCoy. We've had a couple of trial runs. I've taken her out to restaurants and you'd be amazed how many heads turn. He's got marvellous legs and an absolutely flawless complexion. Don't think it's going to be your average female impersonator. Raymond is an artist."

"And you are actually going to try and pass him off as this Angela to your parents?"

"Yes. Don't you think it's a marvellous idea? I can't wait. Now listen, you can help. I've thought about it a lot. I want you to write to Mummy, just a chatty letter telling her all your news, and somewhere in the middle slip in the odd sentence about meeting Theo's Angela and what a charming girl she is, you know. That's all. Nothing too pointed."

"Gosh," I said. "Well, okay, but I hope you know what you're doing. Your old man will have a heart attack if he ever finds out."

"He won't. I know him too well. He won't be able to resist taking a look at the lady of my choice. That's quite beyond his powers of resistance. All I hope is Raymond isn't too much of a hit and Daddy tries to slip a hand up her skirt."

"Oh, God, that would really be a corker."

"And when the great day comes, you've got to be there. I'll make sure it's a Sunday, and we'll all arrive together. So speak to your improbable Mr. Pinkwater and write that letter."

Despite considerable misgivings I managed to compose a casual reference to Angela in writing to Mrs. Gittings, and I broached the subject of a day off with Clifford. Adding my own fantasy to Theo's, I explained that my closest friend was getting engaged and had invited me to the engagement party. I chose a time when Ruby Pinkwater was present, knowing that anything vaguely sentimental always made her eye-black glisten. I was entitled to half a day off a week and said that I would work two whole days to make up for the Sunday. Ruby did all the work for me.

"Of course he must go, mustn't he, Cliffy?"

"Yes, I suppose so."

"'Course he must. You go, my duck. We never had an engagement party. Wasn't time, you see, what with the war on and that. 'Bout time you got yourself a girl, too. Give you ideas, this will. Nothing like a wedding to get things rolling."

"Well, they're not getting married just yet."

"Nice girl, is she?"

"Very," I said. "Her parents are titled."

"Titled! Fancy that. My, you do move in posh circles, don't you? Did you hear that, Cliffy? She's titled."

"What title?"

"No, the girl, love. The girl's titled."

"What girl?"

"His friend's, Tony's friend, the one we've just been talking about. He's so deaf, poor love. Never mind, I'll tell you later."

I reported back to Theo, who related that he thought my letter had done the trick.

"Let me read you this," he said. He produced the latest letter from his mother. "Blah . . .blah . . .blah . . . where is it? Here it is, yes. 'Your father and I are very pleased with your news, although it did come as something of a surprise. Tony wrote to say what a nice girl Angela is, and as you know, I go a lot by Tony's opinion. I've discussed the matter with your father who thinks we ought to be allowed to meet her before things become too serious. So why don't you bring her over for lunch one day?' You see! Hooked! I shall write back immediately of course, very excited and thanking them for being so understanding. I might even humour the silly old sod by saying how relieved I am to have Father's approval at long last. It's all working out quite beautifully."

"Listen," I said. "I'd better meet Raymond before the actual day, otherwise I could quite easily put my foot in it right off and ruin everything."

"Yes, you're right. That's a good point. Well, we'll arrange that. You're in for a very big surprise, you know."

"I'm not the only one. I still don't know how you've got the nerve."

"It isn't nerve. I just have a malicious urge to get even."

It was arranged that Theo and Raymond would organise a dress rehearsal for me in Raymond's rooms. I went there after work the following week and the door was opened by a very good-looking girl in her early twenties. She was very trim, with a slightly angular face, hair cut fashionably short, and wearing the regulation blouse and skirt. I was completely taken in.

"You must be Tony," she said. "Do come in, we were expecting you." She put out a well-manicured hand and then suddenly jerked me across the threshold with more than feminine strength.

I half fell into the room and looked around as Theo gave a shriek of triumph from his hiding place behind the door.

"You see! I told you! Now admit it, he fooled you. This, dear Tony, allow me to introduce, is Miss Angela Pritchett."

"Hello, Tony," Raymond said, reverting to his normal voice.

I had to admit that the deception had been perfect. It was all the more impressive for the fact that I had gone forewarned. Over a bottle of very good sherry, we spent the rest of the evening planning strategy for the promised luncheon. Theo and Raymond instructed me in various aspects of Angela's character, where she had been brought up, what her interests were, and so forth. I became as involved as they were, and we had to restrict our inventions which were always in danger of becoming too farcical.

The date of the luncheon had been fixed for the Sunday following, and it was agreed that we would travel to Norwich by hired limousine.

"In for a penny, in for a Rolls," Theo said.

It was arranged that Raymond would change and make up in my lodgings since we didn't want to risk exposure before we had left the college precincts. Our explanation to the good Mrs. Pike was that the impersonation was in aid of a charity Rag, something she accepted without question having long been familiar with university pranks of this nature. We used her as a final guinea-pig before setting off in the chauffeur-driven Rolls.

"Don't cross your legs," was Theo's last instruction. We all three noticed that the chauffeur gave 'Angela' the eye as he opened the rear door for her, and we took this to be a good omen.

As Theo had predicted his parents had made a real effort for the occasion. Genuine last-minute alarm doused our inner hysteria and the formal introductions were accomplished without mishap. Harry Gittings produced his special sherry.

"Angela doesn't drink," Theo said quickly. Raymond picked up his first cue.

"No, I don't thank you. Daddy doesn't approve of women drinking."

"Very sensible," Gittings said. "I gather your parents live abroad now."

"Yes. Poor Daddy's got a gammy leg."

"The war, I take it?"

"Yes. The doctors said that he had to live in a warm climate. Of course, he misses the old country."

The rest of us had our drinks by now. I saw Raymond lick his lips. There were beads of perspiration pushing through his make-up.

"D'you think I could be very rude and ask for a glass of lemonade?" he said.

"Yes, how remiss of us," Theo's mother said. "I'll get it. We don't have lemonade, but I've got some barley water."

"Lovely. I get a little car sick on a long journey."

"Just like me," Mrs. Gittings said.

"Well, I must say, this is a very pleasant surprise, Angela. We're delighted to welcome you to our humble home. I often wondered what sort of girl Theo would eventually land up with."

"Now don't embarrass Angela, Father."

"I have no intention of embarrassing Angela. I was going to say, if you'd allowed me to finish, that you don't know how lucky you are."

"Oh, I do, Father."

"Are you at college, too, Angela? This Girton place?"

"No. I'm taking languages privately."

"Languages, eh?"

"Yes. Daddy's a great linguist. He speaks eleven Indian dialects. Of course, I shall never be as good as him. But I think French is useful, don't you?"

"Yes, I suppose it is. Can't say that I'm overfond of the French. Very unreliable as a nation."

"But I love French things, don't you? French knickers especially."

There was a long pause before Harry Gittings spoke again. I buried my face in my glass of sherry, Theo looked out of the window, and Raymond kept an absolutely straight face.

"That barley water to your liking, is it?"

"Very refreshing."

"I was telling Angela, Father, of your keen interest in young people. The work you do at the Reform School."

"Yes, I do my bit."

"It's a girls' school, I believe?" Raymond said.

"Yes."

"What do they get sent there for, exactly?"

"Oh, well, all manner of things. Stealing and stuff like that. 'Course, there's a lot of talk about social causes these days, but personally I think that's all claptrap. We give them discipline and a sense of moral values."

"Very important, I'm sure."

"What're you up to, Tony?" Mrs. Gittings asked me.

"I'm still working in the cinema."

"I don't approve of the films they show these days," Gittings said.

"You don't go to the cinema, Father."

"I sit on the local Watch Committee, that's enough."

"What do you watch, Mr. Gittings?" Raymond asked sweetly.

"Well, we have to decide what's good for people to see, young people that is. There's so much licentious stuff around. Semi-nudity and the rest of it. That's what fills the reform schools."

"But they don't see the films, Father."

"I don't want to go into it, Theo. It's not a suitable conversation for a Sunday, or in the presence of ladies."

"We'll have lunch in a minute," Mrs. Gittings said. "Perhaps you'd like to wash your hands, Angela. I'll show you." She led Raymond away. We watched him leave the room. He gave the slightest wriggle of his bottom as he left.

"Well, Father," Theo said when we were alone, "do you approve?"

"Seems a charming gel. I hope you respect her."

"I'm so relieved you think I've made a wise choice. I know we haven't always seen eye to eye lately."

"How serious is it?"

"Between Angela and me? I think she's very fond of me."

"Well, I'll tell you something for your own good. For your good too, Tony. I don't mind admitting that I've had grave suspicions about you, Theo. I don't want to spell it out, but it seemed to me you were mixing with quite the wrong set."

"I don't quite follow."

"I think you do. Tony knows what I'm talking about. I think Angela's arrived on the scene just in time. We'll leave it at that, shall we?"

Theo and I nudged ourselves as we went into lunch. The first part of the meal passed off without incident. Raymond kept up amusing small talk and laughed at Harry Gittings's more banal jokes, which obviously charmed him. Mrs. Gittings, I could see, was not quite so charmed. From time to time she stared at Raymond as though something was puzzling her.

"Must be so interesting to be a lawyer," Raymond said.

"Yes, I suppose it is."

"You must see human nature in the raw."

"In a manner of speaking, yes."

"Daddy always says human nature is basically animal. Would you agree with that, Mr. Gittings?"

"Well, I think most criminals, er, people with criminal instincts, are, yes, closer to animals than, er, human beings."

"Daddy used to tell awful tales about what went on in India?"

"Really? Did he, yes."

"What sort of things?" Theo asked.

"Well, I hesitate to say. I mean they weren't very nice things."

"They have different customs out there."

"Oh, it wasn't the Indians' customs. He was talking about ours, the British. Some of the young officers didn't always behave as they should."

Once again I intercepted a look from Mrs. Gittings at the other end of the table. I folded and refolded my napkin, unable to contain my mounting tension.

"Yes, well, I suppose some of them did cut loose, being in a foreign country," Harry Gittings said. "What about coffee, Lucy?"

126

Mrs. Gittings rang a small china bell.

"Perhaps I shouldn't tell tales out of school," Raymond continued.

The scene had started to take on the appearance of something out of *Pygmalion*. A fuse had been lit, as pre-arranged, and it was slowly burning towards the charge.

"Oh, do," Theo urged. "I love hearing you tell about the old Khyber Pass and life in the hills."

"Well, of course, I was too young to appreciate what was going on. But sometimes when Daddy got, well, shall we say, the teeniest weeniest bit pissed, he did let his hair down." Raymond pulled himself up and looked at Mrs. Gittings in wide-eyed innocence. "Oh, dear, perhaps I shouldn't have said that. I don't know what came over me. I've given myself quite a hot flush."

Coffee was served at that point and we had a merciful interval of silence until the housekeeper had left the room. It was difficult to decide what Harry Gittings was feeling. His neck had coloured when Raymond uttered the word 'pissed' and I noticed his hand tighten on the stem of his wine glass. Surprisingly enough I didn't think Mrs. Gittings had reacted at all.

"I think perhaps I should apologise," Raymond continued.

"That's all right, Angela."

"If I hadn't been drinking barley water I would have said I was pissed myself. Oh, there I go again."

"Is this some sort of joke?" Gittings said.

"No, of course not, Mr. Gittings."

"We're not used to that sort of talk at our table, young lady."

He could sense that something was wrong, but still hadn't put his finger on it.

"I think it's just the excitement of meeting you all."

Theo exploded at that point. He tried to turn his hysteria into a fit of coughing, but without much success.

"It's not funny, Theo," his father said.

"Oh, I just feel so awful," Raymond continued. "I mean I so wanted to make a good impression, and I've absolutely fucked it, haven't I?"

Theo fell backwards off his chair, unable to restrain himself any longer. Gittings's face, which I was studying behind my napkin, seemed to break into pieces. I had never seen a man so astounded. It was obvious that the final climax was at hand and I prepared myself for escape. Raymond rose to his feet, fluttering a hand around his pearls in a show of nervousness.

"Always a bridesmaid, never a bride, that's me. I never learn. Daddy always said he wanted a nice, well mannered girl and instead he got me."

"Oh, God!" Theo choked. "No more, Raymond. Don't go on!"

The penny finally dropped for Gittings. He pushed his own chair back and, shoving Raymond aside, strode out of the room.

Using his normal voice Raymond called after him. "No offence, Mr. Gittings, sir. Just harmless undergraduate fun."

I suddenly became conscious that Theo's mother was laughing. I turned to her and the tears were rolling down her cheeks. I had never seen her laugh like that before.

"I'm sorry, Mother, really. But we just couldn't resist it. Did you see his face?"

Mrs. Gittings had her handkerchief to her mouth.

"Oh, it was worth it," she said. "It's the best joke I've ever heard. Serves him right."

"I hope I didn't really go too far?" Raymond said. He started to wipe off his lipstick.

"Yes, you did, you did go too far," Theo said. "I thought you'd gone mad. That wasn't what we rehearsed."

"No, well, I mean I just got carried away."

"You'd better all get out of the way," Mrs. Gittings said. "Oh, it's been such a lovely day. I've waited for a day like this. Just to see the look on his face." She started to laugh again. "Go on, off you go."

"Will you be all right with him?" Theo asked.

"Yes, of course I shall. Goodbye Tony."

I kissed her.

"Goodbye . . . it's Raymond, isn't it? You didn't really fool me, you know, but you make a very good girl."

"A rather rude one," Raymond said.

"Well, that was the joke, wasn't it?"

She kissed Theo and bundled us outside to the waiting car. "You're sure you'll be able to handle him?" Theo asked anxiously.

"Quite sure. After all, he can't blame me. But I don't suppose he'll be too keen to talk about it, anyway. Write to me, dear. I do so look forward to your letters. And take care."

She waved us out of sight. We collapsed into the back of the Rolls and went over the entire scene line for line all the way back to Cambridge.

10

THE FAMILY BOAT burnt at last. The success of Sunday's inspired adventure exceeded wildest expectations. Raymond was incredible, even though he deviated from the set plan, carried away, no doubt, by his own cleverness. I never knew revenge could be so sweet. *Vindicta docili quia patet sollertiae* or perhaps it was better expressed by dear old Seneca – *Ultio doloris confessio.* Certainly my long-awaited revenge was a confession of many past pains. I feel absolutely no remorse. On the contrary, for the first time in my life I have a sense of complete freedom. He had it coming, as they say in the gangster movies, the dirty rat.

I think Tony was as amazed as anybody. Still unable to break loose from his suburban chains. I probably shocked him as much as the aged father, although he would never admit it. But shocking people is a rewarding pastime, I've found. Not in the sense that Guy shocks; that's too crude and obvious. One has to conceal motives if one is to survive. That is where I part company with them all. K, for instance, is becoming too openly vehement. I warned him against this the other day. Apparently he has received approaches from the same source. I haven't made up my mind yet, but as and when I do, I certainly intend to be more circumspect. Otherwise, I think the groundwork has been carefully prepared. Have removed all incriminating fingerprints. The biggest mistake is to admit to any beliefs. One must appear to be an atheist in all things bright and beautiful. Give us this day our daily dose of subterfuge and lead us not into public temptations.

Reverting back to Sunday's joyous episode, I was interested to note my own reactions to Raymond. As himself he attracts me greatly, although we have never laid hands on each other. But his impersonation which, according to popular belief, should have made him that much more attractive in my eyes, totally failed to excite me. I could admire the sheer beauty of it, but 'Angela' left me cold. I have tried to analyse why this is so. Why am I only attracted to the other end of the scale? Is it that I can never take what is there for the asking? I have to put myself in a position of danger; the real excitement comes when I am at risk. Another reason, I suppose, why I am drawn to K's philosophy. That seems to me to hold promise of a lifetime's romance. But I must approach it in quite a different way.

June 27, 1933

Guy's behaviour gives increasing cause for concern. He has just announced that as soon as he has finished here he intends to go to Russia and help further the Revolution. A typically crass idea, since it is doubtful whether he would be welcomed with open arms, given his basic personality. It's also second hand, borrowing from Donald, whom he is infatuated with, though professing otherwise. Methinks Miss Burgess protesteth too much. I refuse to be drawn into their mesh. If I proceed at all, and it is by no means certain that I shall, I shall proceed at my own pace and in my own way. There is no one to betray us but ourselves. That is my constant reminder. Write nothing, join nothing, make no speeches. Time is always on our side. Let the Klugmans* and the like take all the outward glory, since this serves another purpose, necessary to sustain the public image. But that isn't our purpose. Our aim must be long-term, a slow accumulation which, if properly carried out, will never be recognised. That is the attraction for me, since it is entirely in character.

June 29, 1933

Burnt Umber now in its third edition and still collecting bravos, which is satisfying on two levels. Tony, who I saw yesterday, is guarded in his praise. This was predictable, since his own efforts to scrabble into print have so far been abortive. He came round last night and read me work in progress from his current opus. Could hardly conceal my irritation because he arrived unannounced and wrecked what I had hoped would be a night on the town. Recent events have left me with little time for pleasures.

I encouraged him with false words, and then he proceeded to bore the arse off me with more talk of Judy. He still clings to his pathetic idea of everlasting happiness, and it was all I could do to stop myself blurting out a few home truths about the young lady. He also kept dropping hints that I should write to Chatto and Windus on his behalf and put in a good word, but I don't want to

---

* James Klugman, eminent historian and member of the British Communist executive. A.S.

131

spoil my own market. We can't have too many geniuses in the family.

July 2, 1933

Celebrated my birthday with three assignations in three different locations within three hours – blowing out several candles, so to speak. Have had no contact with aged father since the great day, so wasn't expecting any birthday greetings from that quarter. Did have a card from Mother, but assume he now censors her outgoing mail as well because there was no letter with it. I miss seeing her, but one has to be resolute.

I chose today to commit myself irrevocably. Apparently I passed the initial tests with honours, and have convinced my masters that their trust will not be misplaced. Can't say that I am greatly attracted to them as people; squalid, ordinary, dull creatures devoid of humour, but perhaps this is normal in their vocation. They have set me another problem to solve – far more complicated than before and one that will need a great deal of thought. It is the problems within the problem that fascinate me. And of course everyday life has to go on since it is vital to give the appearance of total respectability. They don't mind my extra-curricular activities since they are devious enough to see that these can lead to useful contacts in the future, but they have urged discretion. I hardly followed the advice tonight, but I had promised myself a birthday fling and don't think I took any undue chances. I went to London for my birthday dinner, since Lilly Law has been having a purge locally. My trouble is that permanence bores me. I can't bear the thought of a lasting relationship. Those loyalties are promised elsewhere.

July 15, 1933

Have made good progress on the second novel, despite having to finish my thesis. I find that one stimulates the other. Have now worked out the plot in some detail and committed five chapters to paper. Have taken fragments of the aged father and grafted them on to the character of Lord Brandel, and this works a treat. I shall leave in just enough clues to satisfy my own sense of humour, and if the final result comes out as anticipated I have the thought of dedicating it to him, which I know will infuriate. So much hard work has made Theo a dull boy sexually and I doubt whether I shall be able to sustain good intentions much longer. Nocturnal dreams hardly compensate.

Still on the subject of the new novel, I find that I am also making use of Tony's character. Brandel's eldest son who brings disgrace on the family by running off with the local whore was subconsciously based on Tony. I recognised this last night and can see ways and means of improving it now that the truth has surfaced.

He did use me as the model for his character, giving me the only title I am ever likely to have. With the benefit of hindsight, having read his journals, I can discern traces of my early self in young Lord Brandel scattered through the pages of *The Gilded Aviary*. It is not a flattering portrait. I can now also detect the moral change in the area closest to him at that time, for his second novel is a story of deception. Perhaps failure is always closer to the human condition than triumph.

I remained besotted with Judy. Our relationship seemed on the surface as secure and content as I imagined marriage to be. My romantic pride dictated that I continue to pursue that goal, and I was confident that my insistence would one day wear her down. I was totally unprepared for the blow she dealt me.

She met me outside the cinema one night. I had not been expecting her, but was overjoyed to see her.

"Nothing wrong, is there?"

"No, not wrong. I've just got something to tell you."

"Your mother's all right?"

"Yes, it's nothing like that."

I linked my arm through hers as we started to walk. "I know what it is," I said. "You've finally changed your mind and you couldn't wait to tell me."

"Well, I've changed my mind, that's for sure. I am going to get married."

"Say that again."

"I never wanted to hurt you, you know that."

I stopped her under a street lamp and for the first time I could see her face clearly. There was no good news in her expression.

"I'm going to marry Mr. Fraser."

"What're you talking about? Who's Mr. Fraser?"

"He's one of the people I work for. A widower, and he's

asked me to marry him and I've decided to say yes. But I wanted to tell you before I told him."

"That was big of you."

"Don't be like that."

"Well, what am I supposed to be? How can you just say it like that? You always told me you never wanted to get married. God, I asked you often enough."

"I didn't say that. I said I wouldn't marry you. Because you're different."

I felt sick and angry. I couldn't believe what she was telling me.

"I suppose he's got money, this Mr. Fraser."

"Yes."

"Yes, he would have. But you don't love him; you *can't* love him."

"No, you're right, I don't love him. I could never marry anybody I loved."

"What sort of answer is that?"

"It's the truth. Why d'you think I always said no to you? I'd only hurt you more."

"But he's different?"

"Yes. He's just lonely."

"How old is he?"

"Oh, I don't know. Fifty maybe."

"It's disgusting. How could you think of marrying an old man like that?"

I paced up and down the street, anguished and totally at a loss to know how to deal with the situation. Coming back to her I returned to the attack.

"It can only be his money," I shouted. "Why don't you come out and admit it?"

"But I do admit it," she said calmly. "Of course that's the main reason. I thought you'd understand that."

"Why should I understand? I don't have to understand anything."

"You think we should just go on as we are?"

"Yes."

"You know how it'd end, don't you? You'd hate me."

"How d'you know I don't hate you now?"

"I just hope you don't. Listen, Tony, you have to try and understand. What else have I got? There's me mum, I've got to think of her. He promised to take care of her, get her proper treatment. He's not a dirty old man, and he's not getting a great bargain in me. He's just lonely and want's company."

"You won't ever sleep with him, I suppose?"

I had a sudden vision of her body pressed against the unknown Mr. Fraser and it blinded me to everything else. "You'll just take his money, is that what I'm supposed to believe?"

"Well, I've told you," she said. "If you can't understand, there's nothing more to say." And with that she started to walk away.

I ran after her and caught her by the arm, pulling her round, searching for her lips. I had the arrogance to think that I could kiss her into changing her mind.

"But you love me? How can you do it with anybody else?"

She made no attempt to move out of my embrace, but she was passive, all passion spent. It was like kissing a stranger.

"You'll only make it worse for yourself," she said. "I never pretended, did I? You can't say that I ever pretended with you. I always told you the truth, and I didn't look for this to happen. It just did. People like me don't have much choice."

"But I could take care of you, if you'd let me. All right, look, we won't get married, I won't ask you again, I promise. But let's just go on as we are. I'll earn more money soon. I can ask for a rise in a month or so, and maybe my book'll be published. But don't go with this old man; I couldn't bear that. I'll do anything else you ask me, but just don't marry him."

My sudden jealousy of the unknown Mr. Fraser rose in my throat like bile, distorting my voice. Some lovers are only jealous of the past, of the years they didn't share, yet I have always felt the worst pain stems from the unknown. We can sometimes come to terms with the rivals we know, but future lovers have an advantage we can never smother. It is difficult to believe that love can ever take any other form than one's own, that those bodies we have worshipped can mould themselves against a stranger, that those cries of loving pain that

135

we produced can be conjured up by others. I had no weapons to fight her with.

"I have to marry him," she said. "It's my only chance."

I dropped my arms. We stood like statues. I couldn't find the right words to repay her for the hurt she had done me. It was like the nightmare within a nightmare, when one part of the subconscious fights to convince us that we shall shortly wake and find everything normal – then the horrors take command again and the headlong fall into the pit continues. I tried to believe that we had never met that night, that before long my eyes would open and I could reach out to touch the gutted candle in my familiar bedroom and face a day suffused with the old happiness.

"I know you hate me now," she was saying, "but later you'll see I was right."

"You and your right," I blurted. Pain had made me stupid. I had no idea what I was saying, what I wanted to say. "Well, go to him then! Go and crawl into bed with that fucking old man, take his money, be safe, be what you want to be, you little whore, do anything you bloody well like. Go on – what're you waiting for?"

She stared at me for a few moments and then walked away. The pubs were closed; it was too late to get drunk, too late for everything. I walked the streets aimlessly, first going to Theo's college, and then circling back, past the cinema again, coming back to the very spot where we parted, like some mad traveller lost in the desert. Then of course, I wanted to apologise and I ran all the way to her house. There were no lights showing and I hammered on the door and called her name. A neighbour opened a window and told me to shut up. I went to the back of the house, but everywhere was dark. The window of the room where she slept had the curtains drawn. I threw gravel up to it and pleaded with her, but nothing happened. I imagined her lying in the bed we had shared so many times, as motionless as her mother, listening to me, hearing me without pity. I stayed there in the weed-wet garden, staring up at the blank window, telling myself I would always remember, wondering how much more there was to discover about hate.

For a period I went slightly mad. I became unable to converse normally, taking refuge in fantasy and lies, saying the first thing that came into my mind whether it made sense or not.

I wrote Judy long, passionate letters, sometimes taking them round by hand at night and slipping them under her door, fearful they might go astray if trusted to the post. She never answered them. I even wrote to Fraser, finding his whereabouts from the Electoral Register. My letter was returned unopened, readdressed in Judy's childish handwriting. I scanned the local newspapers for any announcement of the marriage, intending to make a dramatic appearance at the ceremony. Whenever I was not at work I hung about at the corner of the street where Fraser lived, hoping to catch sight of her, but he seemed to have spirited her away. A 'For Sale' notice went up at her old address and I could see straight through the empty house. Alone in my bedroom at night I found I was talking to myself, carrying on two-way conversations with her.

I debated whether to give notice and leave Cambridge, disappear from everybody who had ever seen us together. I longed for some violence in my life. The mushy, romantic films I was compelled to watch day after day intensified my sense of loss, for I was reminded that whereas the love scenes on screen would be repeated at the next performance without change, my own were gone for ever.

11

WHILE MY LOVE affair came to an end, Theo's was just beginning. Being so obsessed with my own loss I failed to discern any change in him, but it was then, during his last year at Cambridge, at a time when he was least able to hide what was happening to him, that the commitment was made. It was all going on under my very nose, and I saw nothing.

During that crucial year he made a conscious decision and never-again allowed self-doubt to put a foot in the door. He must have believed, like Auden,

> To be young means
> To be all on edge, to be held waiting in
> A packed lounge for a Personal Call
> From Long Distance, for the low voice that
> Defines one's future.

At some point during those Cambridge years the fatal connection was made, the low voice from a distance gave him the definition he had been seeking and he accepted the call. Perhaps, given the slightest leaning towards religious belief he might have turned towards Roman Catholicism, for he was ripe for some form of paternalistic dogmatism, and the concept of sin was important to him. Yet that would probably have been too simplistic for Theo; he needed something beyond mere faith – he needed danger.

I repeat, I saw nothing, I suspected nothing, I challenged nothing, I lacked all perceptions. Now I can savour the various ironies, salt them away for future use, but that does not make my present task any easier. I can only set down this story as an act of contrition, my own rather than Theo's, for apparently the God he worshipped never failed him. While others wavered, Theo, like Philby, held the faith. Such steadfastness provokes a grudging admiration, especially when set against his other career. Even the comparison with Philby has holes in it, because Philby could take refuge in other things when the going was rough – his marriages, his socialising, drink, the companionship of the bed and the bottle. Even an unsuccessful marriage is better than none when other deceits make the mind a celibate. Theo denied himself such mundane comforts, for there he was at the end of his days hidden away uncomforted, comfortless, only able to communicate with total strangers.

It is all in such contrast to those steamy Cambridge years. He soared then, a daring young man on a literary trapeze, sufficiently outrageous to attract the attention of the authorities without incurring their outright condemnation. He was early marked as a coming force, and because his novels deliberately went against the tide they partially excused his public excesses.

If it was all plotted, as I am now forced to believe it was, then it was a campaign of diabolical cleverness. Theo was the only variant in the group, an isolated figure from the rest, but again this was entirely in character: he loathed officialdom and would have scorned to take the Establishment route mapped out for the others. Once trapped into service he must have convinced his Russian masters that his own individual form of cover was the only one with which he could survive. He enjoyed being recognised as a literary figure, and as his reputation increased so his cover became more and more secure. It enabled him to travel widely without arousing comment, it gave him an income in half a dozen countries, and the opportunity to mix with and study all classes of society. His writing was so far removed from current political thought as to totally disarm suspicion, and he never allowed himself to be grouped with the literary set of fellow travellers. Nobody ever suspected that a writer regularly recommended by The Book Society could ever be a threat to its members. It would have been as unthinkable as the previous generation accusing Galsworthy of being a child molester. None of his fellow defectors enjoyed such a safety valve, and although it failed him in the end he outlasted them all. Just as his novels were plotted with impeccable care, so he applied the same technique to the pattern of his secret life. Ultimately, like any spy, he became the prisoner of his own convictions, but until those last lonely years he made sure that the cell he willingly inhabited was comfortably furnished and to his own taste. The world of the one-night stand, the casual pick-up, the quick impersonal gratification, was sufficient for his sexual needs – or at least one hopes that it was – and I am sure he reasoned that the additional risk of betrayal that any permanent relationship brings might have proved his undoing.

I know little of the inner workings of the Communist Party, though I suspect that its officers are as rigidly conventional in their own way as any Empire Loyalist. Theo's individuality must sometimes have alarmed them as well as impressed. They could only have tolerated his eccentricities in the belief that he could deliver the goods. Every political creed acts from expediency and Theo was a risk they judged worth taking. All the same, he must have given them their share of anxious moments. He ignored the baneful repressions forced upon most people, just as his sense of the ridiculous rejected the jaunty Marxism openly practised by those who jumped on the passing revolutionary bandwagon. The use of the word 'comrade' appalled him: it was only in the sexual act that he felt any urge to identify with the so-called masses. He could take 'the people' into his bed, but not into his heart – though, again, I don't know why I am so emphatic. Perhaps that philosophy was just another sleight of hand he fooled me with; perhaps in his shadowy relationships I find so difficult to comprehend, he deceived neither himself nor others; perhaps they were his only acts of unselfish honesty.

Theo and the Cambridge cell traded on that enduring trait, British 'reserve' – used it, perfected it. They played the game, spoke the official language, knew the umpires on first-name terms. Spies are supposed to be figures who live in a twilight world, semi-fictional creatures existing in that hinterland that lies between le Carré and Fleming. They are not supposed to wear Savile Row suits in real life, talk to Ministers as equals, write novels that can be obtained from Boots' lending libraries.

I recall the furore that swept England when Guy Burgess and Maclean defected, the sense of personal violation that so many people felt. Squalid little figures like Blake are considered ideally cast for their roles, but not symbols like Guy and Donald. As a nation we are seldom so ridiculous as when we surrender to one of our periodic bouts of outraged moral indignation; and when questions of so-called national security are coupled with a measure of sexual innuendo outsiders might be forgiven for thinking that the Martians have finally landed. In trying to determine why this should be so, I am reminded of something Orwell once wrote – 'the *privateness* of English life'. Appearances may not be everything, but by God they count for a lot.

Certainly the outward appearance that Theo presented to me in those far-off days aroused no suspicions. I merely thought of him as lucky – lucky not to be in love, lucky not to have loved and lost. Following Judy's departure out of my life, I had avoided him for several weeks and finally he sent a note round to the cinema asking if I was ill. I forced myself to make the effort and went to his rooms on my day off.

I found him with Guy and the man he called Kim, to whom I had never been formally introduced. Kim regarded me critically as we shook hands, a pipe clenched awkwardly between his teeth, like a stage prop that an actor hasn't fully rehearsed with.

"Sorry. Kim Philby," Theo said. "Cambridge's answer to Stanley Baldwin. So: where have you been hiding? I was worried about you. Tony works at the splendid La Splendide, did you know?"

"No," Philby said. There was a pause. "But then, I'm not . . . not a great film fan." He had a pronounced stammer which I will not attempt to reproduce here; it gave the immediate impression that he considered every word before committing himself. "Films don't reflect ordinary life. I like newsreels, though. 'Course, they're all slanted, just like the capitalist press."

He seemed to use quantities of matches to keep his pipe alight.

"Christ, why don't you have a gasper like everybody else and give up that hearty stuff?" Guy said.

Philby just stared at him.

"I'm sorry if I interrupted something," I said, as the conversation sagged.

"No, we were just having a drink," Theo said. I was suddenly conscious of my own shabbiness in their midst, for since Judy's departure I had neglected my appearance.

Extinguishing yet another match, Philby turned to me and with that same agonising slowness, giving each word equal value, he asked if I was a genuine member of the working class. The question took me off guard.

"Working middle-class," Theo volunteered for me. "Don't let his Jarrow outfit fool you. He only hires that."

"What do they pay you at your cinema?" Philby asked.

"I get three quid at the moment."

"Bloody . . . exploitation."

"Oh, I don't know. I suppose I'm lucky to have a job at all."

"Nobody's lucky. It's your right," Philby said. He seemed touchy and aggressive about something. His pipe had gone out again and he searched for a fresh box of matches.

"What the masses want," Guy said, "is free beer, free fucks and freedom. That's rather good, isn't it? Should have used that in the last election. Our candidate would have romped home. Voting for free fucks, dear? Yes, well, put your cross just there. Kim, why don't you throw that pipe away? You really do look like Baldwin."

I could see no way of entering their world. In their company Theo took an unaccustomed back seat. He sat with his legs across the arm of a battered easy chair, sipping his sherry, slightly quizzical, raising the occasional eyebrow to me behind their backs.

"I must say," Guy continued, "changing the subject, or rather not changing the subject, I heard a marvellous story about Mrs. Baldwin the other day. Apparently she was opening some girls' school for Tory virgins and somebody asked her about married life. She said, 'Whenever sex rears its ugly head in Stanley, I close my eyes and think of England.' Don't you think that's good?"

"You made it up," Theo said

"No, I didn't."

"What do you think about when it raises its ugly head in you?"

"Yes, that's a good one. Let's invent a new game. We all have to say what we think about at the moment of truth. You can first."

"I don't want to go first," Theo said. "In fact I don't want to play the game."

"All right, well, I'll start. What do I think about? Certainly not England. I mean, it's absolutely true, though, isn't it? Half the time one has to think of something else, otherwise the whole process is too boring."

"Speak for yourself," Philby said.

"I am speaking for myself, dear. Never the one to relinquish my favourite topic. Lenin. I think of Lenin. D'you think he did it often? Be a marvellous conversation piece, wouldn't it? A real stopper. You know, you're with some boring little thing and doing all the work, and you suddenly stop and say, 'You're not half as good as Lenin. He was just amazing on that train.'"

I looked quickly at Philby to see if he found it as amusing as Theo. He was pressing the ash in his pipe with a dampened finger and appeared not to have heard any of it.

"Now you, Kim."

"I don't do it that often," he said. "And when I do I happen to enjoy it."

"Do the girls talk as much as the chaps? I was at it the other night with quite a pretty little thing, just over the age of consent, and it never drew breath. I said to it, 'Don't talk with your mouth full, dear.'"

Then he turned to me. "Tony, you must be an expert on the ladies. I remember that bosomy little whatsit you brought on the boat. D'you still see her?"

"Not very often," I said.

"We were all very taken with her, weren't we, Theo?"

143

"Very."

"Was she very good at it? I'm told they don't move about much. You have to do it all for them; is that so?"

"Not that I've found."

"Oh, I'm relieved to hear it. It's a closed book to me, you see. Never having done it with the fair sex. God, is that the time? I said I'd meet Lady Maclean an hour ago. Nice to meet you again, Tony."

He kissed Theo goodbye, but happily was more formal with me.

"I wish he wasn't so bloody one-track," Philby said as the door closed. "You can't have any conversation with Guy without him turning it around to his favourite topic."

"Oh, I don't know," Theo said. "At least it's more amusing than his political drivel. The spectre of our Guy as champion of the downtrodden masses is hardly one of the most convincing performances."

"You must have found it very boring, Tony."

"Well, I haven't met many like him," I said.

"No, Tony leads such a sheltered life by comparison. And strictly moral, too. Tony believes in the institution of marriage."

"Marriage is a lunatic institution," Philby said.

"Actually, I agree," I said.

"Oh, we've changed our minds, have we?" Theo eased himself out of the armchair to pour liberal replenishments of sherry. "What happened?"

"Nothing. I just decided to concentrate on my writing."

"Well, I'll drink to that. I must say, being published does lead to the most extraordinary encounters. The mail one gets – mail as in Royal, that is. Some of the letters I receive are quite bizarre. I had one yesterday from a vicar in Cornwall. He'd read *Burnt Umber*. Hadn't bought it, of course, borrowed it from the library, but one has to be grateful for small mercies. Went on and on, pages of it, saying I was the new Trollope, which I hope was not a veiled nudge in the wrong direction. But he ended up asking if he could have a lock of my hair. What d'you make of that?"

"Hair today and gone tomorrow," Philby said. He smiled at his own atrocious pun.

"Oh God!" Theo moaned. "I shan't quote you."

"What're you writing, Tony?"

"A novel."

"Everybody I meet seems to be writing novels. It's an epidemic. Life isn't a fiction. All the smart young men trying to be Firbank or Huxley, completely out of touch with what is really happening in the world. What's happening is that the world is changing. People endlessly writing about unimportant issues, delving back into our boring past, as if any of it mattered." He turned away suddenly, as though he had not meant to be caught out in such vehemence.

I wanted to answer him, to justify my own efforts, but somehow the words did not come. I was the interloper in their society. Part of me admired them, part of me found their attitudes tiresome. I realise now that they were a new breed of revolutionaries, not the traditional student anarchist, shabby and bearded, but drawn from well-to-do families, in Philby's case the son of a distinguished Civil Servant, who shouldered the white man's burden as his birthright. This is what made them so hard to detect. They were like the murderer in Chesterton's story, who turned out to be the postman: everybody saw him, nobody saw him. Because of their backgrounds, because of the ease with which they moved through society and exploited their connections and inner knowledge, they appeared to pose no lasting threat. Early flirtations with the Communist Party were excused – undergraduates had always had a radical destiny to perform. While our politicians were mooning about Europe gathering the flowers of appeasement, bringing home the wilted blooms like wedding bouquets, all serious-thinking young people were up in arms.

In this climate the Philbys and the Burgesses and the Macleans could operate without attracting undue attention, their own future designs easily concealed. The real threat was thought to come from Germany, not Russia. Heroes and villains were scrambled together, distant figures in a foreign landscape, our island mentality ensuring that we did not heed the warning signs in our own midst. The poets were ignored, preaching only to the already converted – *Evolution the dance, revolution the steps*, in Day Lewis's clarion slogan. The general hope among my generation was that revolution and pacifism could go hand in hand, the religion of non-intervention, Gandhi the Father, the Son and the Holy Ghost. Any sort of protest was acceptable, the important thing was to join the universal club. Even Theo's homosexuality was, I believe, more a part of this movement than the more Freudian explanation – a tradition inherited from the 'Apostles' – because to be queer was to be on the inside, a privileged, if sometimes fearful, member of an élite group, knowing what the public at large seldom suspected, having free access to a sexual speakeasy. It is a natural progression for the sexual fugitive to gravitate to undercover political activities, and those who were looking to recruit found no shortage of willing disciples.

Of course it has all been so faithfully documented since and seems so obvious in retrospect, but at the time the real clues were well hidden. We were the young seeking to be old, youth having its fling belonged to the Twenties. Previous literary giants were dying, and only Wells from the old guard remained to give us his great dream of the future. Perhaps betrayals have become too commonplace, they no longer have the power to shock. Yet it was with a feeling of shock that, a few days ago, I came across Theo's membership card to the Communist Party. It fluttered from, of all things, a copy of Virginia Woolf's *The Waves*, when I was deciding how best to dispose of his effects. It was dated October 1932, something of a vintage year, it would appear for the Cambridge cell. I don't know why I was quite so shocked – perhaps it was the final confirmation of my own naivety. Seeing his name written on the faded card took me straight back to his room in Trinity all those years ago, and the true significance of his mocking smile when Burgess and Philby were sounding off. I compared the casual elegance of his life then to the way in which he spent his last years and for the first time I could trace the connection. Only death released him from deceit, and he passed it on to me – the last joker, as it were, in his pack. In many ways he took greater risks than his more notorious contemporaries, for the journals might have exposed him at any time, yet he carried his secrets to the grave.

When my affair with Judy came to such an abrupt end, I made serious attempts to transform my personal anguish into fiction. The results were banal and fortunately I retained enough common sense to recognise the fact. Even though I knew I had lost her for ever, I was still driven by the need to justify myself in her eyes. I wanted to show her evidence of material success. So I abandoned my Scott Fitzgerald efforts, turning instead to more immediately saleable plots. I embarked on a spy novel, heavily influenced by Buchan and to my surprise (since the writing of fiction is always a surprise) I found that the writing came easily. Naturally Theo was the first person to be taken into my confidence.

"But what an extraordinary choice," he said. "Spy stories are dreadfully old hat, aren't they?"

"Why should they be?"

"I don't know. Perhaps I'm wrong. It just seems a strange decision on your part. Why don't you write about something you know?"

"I tried that. It didn't work."

"Detective stories, yes. But not spies, I would have thought. I mean, does that sort of think really go on now?"

His replies disappointed, but did not flatten me as had often been the case in the past. I was slowly finding my own feet again, and the creative adrenalin was flowing back – even Theo's critical tourniquet could not stem it. Every night after I had finished at the cinema I could not wait to get back to my room and pick up where I had left off. I became a virtual hermit for months on end, my energies unfettered by sexual demands. I spent little money and was happily able to repay my father the fifty pounds he had loaned me. He had sold our old home by now and was living in a flat overlooking the zoo in Regent's Park. My twin brothers had gone their separate ways at the time of the removal and he confessed to me that it was a great relief to live on his own. We were drawn closer to each other by virtue of this common isolation. He hinted that he had formed a liaison with another woman, 'nothing permanent, but quite good for the old ego, I've found,' and seemed anxious to earn my approval for such an arrangement.

When I had finished the new novel something made me cautious where Theo was concerned. I still wanted his praise, but I was not prepared to risk his condemnation. I had saved enough money to have the manuscript professionally typed, but when I received the pristine pages, stapled, the title and my name pasted on the front cover, I might have been looking at a work written in a foreign language. I stared at the neatly typed pages, reading words that seemed to have come from a stranger. After living with a book for months on end a writer often feels such a sense of alienation.

I parcelled it up and sent it by registered post to the first publisher of my choice, having spent some time in the local public library deciding which list was most likely to accommodate my new style of writing. Then followed a six-week agony of waiting that will be familiar to anyone who has ever attempted to earn their living by the pen. Outsiders never realise the extent of an author's misgivings.

I went through the whole gamut, sometimes racing back to my lodgings during my brief lunch break to see if the second post had brought the long-awaited reply. It was the longest six weeks of my life. Then, suddenly, one morning, the letter was there on the doormat. I carried it up to my room and propped it against my dressing table mirror while I shaved. I could not bring myself to open it at once for fear that it contained yet another rejection. Symbolically, I shaved my throat first, preparing for the tumbril. I dried my face, put on my one good suit, polished my shoes and flattened my hair with water and Brylcream. Only then did I feel calm enough to open the typewritten envelope. I sat on the edge of the bed and extracted the crisp, single sheet of headed paper.

Dear Mr. Stern,
My partner and I have now had an opportunity to consider your unsolicited manuscript entitled *The Death of Innocence*. We think it shows sufficient promise to ask you to be good

enough to come and see us. Perhaps you will be so kind as to telephone this office for a convenient appointment.

Yours sincerely,

Nicholas Brogan

I must have read it ten times before I became aware that Mrs. Pike was shouting for me to come and have my breakfast while it was still hot. I studied every word. 'Sufficient promise' had to mean something. Guarded, yes. But then that was to be expected from a business man. Still, he would hardly ask to see me if he was going to reject it. That would be a waste of his valuable time. Or perhaps it was his way of letting people down gently. 'Yes, I meant what I said, Mr. Stern. It does show sufficient promise for the future if not this time. Go away and stick at it, and show us your next.'

I had difficulty in swallowing my tepid boiled egg, causing the motherly Mrs. Pike to enquire whether I was under the weather. I had decided to withhold all information from my circle of friends until success was confirmed.

I went to a public call box during my coffee break and telephoned Mr. Brogan's office. My stammered introduction was translated by a friendly female voice and an appointment made for the following week. Without giving too much away I asked Clifford for time off, a request readily granted since our relationship was now secure.

During the days that followed I rehearsed several speeches designed to accommodate anything Mr. Brogan might put to me. In the event, of course, all such careful preparations went by the board.

Brogan's offices were in Bedford Square, that still elegant oasis of Georgian splendour, surrounded as it now is by the concrete building bricks and tourist flotsam of Oxford Street and Tottenham Court Road. I had been away from London a long time and the contrast between the quiet of Cambridge and the packed pavements of the capital unnerved me still further. I was treated as an expected guest by the receptionist and shown up to the first floor without further ado. Brogan rose from behind his book-cluttered desk to greet me.

"This can't be Mr. Stern?" he said.

"Yes."

"The Mr. Stern, author of *The Death of Innocence*?"

"Yes."

"Amazing."

He went to a side door and called into the next office. "Arthur, come and meet our new author."

He was joined by another man who was later introduced to me as Arthur Skilton, Brogan's partner. They both regarded me with amusement.

"How old are you?" Skilton said. His manner, though brusque, was not unfriendly. I told him.

"Well, now, I'd never have guessed. We were expecting a much older man. You know, university don, dabbles in writing spy stories; tricky customers most of them – hate changing a line and very good on contracts. I think this calls for celebration."

"What d'you think?" Brogan asked. "Wait a minute, before you tell me, let's see what we've got."

He went to a cupboard and fished out two or three bottles from behind a mass of books.

"I don't know why we live in such chaos," he said. "Who was it said 'a cluttered desk is a sign of genius'? Well, whoever it was I wouldn't have published him. We'll get organised and down to business in a minute. To you, Mr. Stern."

The neat whisky went straight to my head. I had eaten nothing since breakfast and this, combined with my nerves and the unexpected manner in which I had been greeted by the two men, rendered me immediately tipsy.

"Do you mind if I sit down?"

"'Course not, how rude of us. Shift those manuscripts off that chair."

Brogan searched amongst the debris of his desk and pulled out what I recognised as my own manuscript. It looked well-thumbed.

"Now, then. Let's talk about this. First effort?"

"No."

"No, couldn't be. How long have you been at it?"

"Oh, I wrote three, no four novels before that."

"No good?"

"Rubbish."

"This isn't rubbish, you know. Well, you know that, don't you? Authors always know. They may pretend they don't. We like this, don't we, Arthur?"

"Yes, we're very taken with it."

"We're even thinking of publishing it."

I tried to clear my head.

"Got a few rough edges, the odd split infinitive, but I don't mind those. Critics do, though. The lazy ones. They always pick them out, makes it look as though they've read it from cover to cover. You want another whisky?"

"No, thank you."

"Yes, we've discussed it, Arthur and me. Never publish anything we don't both like. House rule. If we go down, we go down together. No women and children first. Now, who else has seen it?"

"Nobody," I said.

"Got an agent?"

"No."

"Oh, it gets better and better, doesn't it, Arthur? And it's all your own unaided work?"

"Yes, of course."

"Have to ask it, because we've been caught out once or twice. I mean, nothing personal. Well now, think I've exhausted all the usual excuses. That's just my warped sense of humour." He consulted the title page of my manuscript. "Anthony – can I call you Anthony? Why did you choose us?"

"I don't know. Yours seemed the best bet. I studied some of your other publications."

"Well, I can see why you don't need an agent. But let's be serious for a moment. If you want to go away and get yourself an agent, I'll recommend one. I'd send you to Peters. He's as tough as they come and he'll look after you. I don't want you to think we're taking advantage of you, you see. Don't want that, do we, Arthur?"

"We certainly don't."

"We like to keep our authors. Start off as we mean to go on.

I mean, Peters won't better your terms on this one, but he might in the future. If you sell, that is."

He picked up some papers and waved them at me. "Now this frightening document – have you seen one before? – is what is known as a publisher's contract. Drawn up by the best legal brains to ensure that authors are kept in a state of abject slavery. This one's got your name on it. I suggest you read it very carefully, and when you've recovered from the shock, let us know if you want to sign it."

"Oh, I want to sign it," I said.

"You haven't read it yet."

"I'll sign it anyway."

"Arthur, are you and I men of integrity?"

"Average integrity."

"Well, I'll tell you what we'll do, Anthony." He took out a fountain pen, crossed out something on the contract and wrote something else. "Because we happen to like your book, and because we happen to have got you a bit on the ropes, I've crossed out the first advance I thought of, and put this."

He pushed the open contract under my nose. I dimly made out the figure of seventy-five pounds which had been substituted for the original fifty pounds. "Now, that's slightly above average. Plus the usual scale of royalties. Now I'm not saying you couldn't get a bit more elsewhere. Not saying that, are we, Arthur?"

"No. 'Course, he could get a bit less."

"True. No names, no pack drill. But what you'll get from us is dedication. See, we're not too big that we can't give your book our individual attention. I'm the brains and Arthur here's the salesman. Or is it the other way round?"

"I'll go and look it up," Arthur said.

I watched them like a spectator at a tennis match. They seemed to me two of the wittiest and most perceptive men I had ever met, or was ever likely to meet. The whisky had penetrated to my feet by now.

"We think a lot of your book," Brogan continued. "Looking at you I don't know how you came to write it, but then I've never understood authors. I can't predict what'll happen to this, you know. We shall publish it, I hope, and do our best, but don't expect the moon, will you? It might go out there and sink like the proverbial stone. There's no justice."

He drained his own glass. "I'll tell you what we're going to do. We're going to go out and have a bite of lunch, and if you still want to sign after a couple more hours of Arthur and me, I won't stop you. How's that?"

"Sounds great," I said.

"We'll walk down to the Garrick and you can tell us all about yourself."

"I have to be back in Cambridge by six o'clock."

"Six o'clock? Oh, I think we'll be through with lunch before then, don't you, Arthur?"

"Yes, we'll make it a quick lunch."

Over lunch they introduced me to several well-known actors and authors as their new find. My head, already swimming from the previous experience in their office, now seemed likely to burst. When I got to know them better in the years ahead I realised that their double-act was not entirely spontaneous. They knew how to flatter, which is half the game, I suppose, since writers desperately need the assurance that they are not alone. They could also be tough when the occasion demanded, as it often did in their cut-throat business, for despite publishing being an occupation for gentlemen, survival went to the fittest.

I shook hands on their contract over coffee in the Garrick, had a double brandy on the strength of it, and was bundled into a taxi just in time to catch my train back to Cambridge. I slept the entire way and was lucky not to go past my station.

It was the beginning of a long association. They remained my publishers until Brogan died. After his death the firm was taken over by a conglomerate and the relationship was never the same. By then I could name my price, but that first seventy-five pounds always remained the most important sum I ever earned.

12

FOR SOME ODD reason Theo seemed irritated by the modest
success that *The Death of Innocence* achieved. I had dedicated it to him and the thought did occur that perhaps he
suspected some personal innuendo in my pretentious title. He
had no real cause to feel jealous, for the sales of the book were
hardly stupendous. It was ignored by most of the 'heavies',
the only reviews of any note appearing in the provincial
papers. My royalties just exceeded the advance and although
I was downcast at the time, Brogan and his partner seemed
pleased enough, and gave me a hundred pounds for my
second.

I sensibly resisted the temptation to chuck in my job at The
Splendide, some inner voice urging caution instead of
euphoria. In many ways the life was ideal: I met a variety of
people, the actual work was not onerous and Clifford seldom
bothered me. I was well cared for by Mrs. Pike and had
adopted a routine well suited to a writer's needs. The only
thing lacking in my life during this period was romance.
Unlike Theo I was not claimed by the smart set, and indeed,
apart from a few isolated fan letters, mostly from readers who
felt they could write just as well as me given my luck, the
publication of my first novel caused not a ripple.

"You should count yourself lucky," Theo said with the air of
a man who has the generosity to pay a beggar fourpence for a
penny box of matches. "I'd love to live like an ostrich, but I
seem to spend most of my time answering mail from dotty old
spinsters of both sexes who imagine they can recognise themselves in my books. It's too boring."

I excused some of his behaviour at the time, first because I
was in awe of his greater experience, and also because his
mother was dying. Unlike my own mother, Lucy Gittings's
terminal illness was protracted and ghastly. She endured

three major operations, becoming in the process little more than a shell. I went once to the hospital with Theo, but found the experience too distressing to repeat. Theo was remarkable, for although he found his regular visits just as horrifying, he never allowed his mother to see his anguish. It was only when he came away from the hospital that the mask slipped. He sometimes cried bitterly when we were alone together, reviling his father for past and present wrongs.

"Why did it have to be her?" he said. "Why couldn't it have been that evil sod instead?"

When eventually she died he went on a monumental binge. I like to think that I was closer to him at that period than I had ever been, but who knows? Perhaps I was just the nearest shoulder to cry on — or should the word be 'safest'? In tracing back over the memories of those years I seem to have become infected with the virus of doubt, as though the pages of his journals are still the carriers of his particular disease, making me wary of pronouncing any certainties.

He came round to my lodgings late one night to break the news of his mother's death, bringing with him two bottles of brandy which he solemnly consumed until he passed out. I undressed him and put him to bed in my room and he slept for the best part of a day. I had never witnessed grief on such a scale and I contrasted his behaviour with mine when my own mother had died. Perhaps I envied him — real grief only comes with love.

I sobered him up for the funeral and supported him at the graveside. It was a large funeral — Harry Gittings had seen to that, though the majority of the mourners were his friends. It was touch and go whether Theo's smouldering hatred of his father blazed into a public confrontation, but he managed to keep himself under control. The principal mourners went back to Westfield after the burial and it did not escape my notice that Gittings had already installed a much younger housekeeper. He mingled amongst the guests making pious statements about his late wife. Knowing what I did, it was sickening to watch. As soon as was socially acceptable Theo made his mumbled excuses and left. Gittings followed us to the waiting car.

"Well, a very sad day," he said. "But I think your dear mother would have been gratified by the turn-out."

"Yes, people always look forward to their funerals," Theo said.

"What does that mean? You can't resist it, can you? You have to be bloody snide and clever, even on a day like this."

I tightened my grip on Theo's arm.

"I don't suppose I shall see much of you now, shall I?" Gittings went on. "Well, I can't say I shall be too sorry about that. I'm not too keen to have a pervert in my house, even though he is my own son."

"No, one under one roof is enough, isn't it, Father? You can really go to town now."

"What're you talking about?"

"What am I talking about? You, Father. All those lovely treasures you keep in your desk. You can bring those out now, can't you? Have cosy evenings showing them to your new housekeeper. What will you do, dress her up in a gymslip and give her a smacked bottom when she breaks your best cups?"

"I'm warning you, Theo!"

"Oh, you can do better than that – that's very cliché, almost East Lynne. I tumbled you years ago. You're the one who needs warning. One or two hints from me in the right quarters and you'd be right in the shit. Don't you ever threaten me, Father, not ever, because I wouldn't hesitate to drop you in it."

We left him there, his mouth wide open, outrage staining his features brick red.

"I've waited a long time to do that," Theo said as we drove away. "My only regret is I never did it while mother was still alive . . . though I suppose the truth is, incredibly enough, she must have loved him once."

"Takes all sorts," I said lamely. "But don't make yourself ill. She's out of it now, he can't hurt her any more. Nobody can." I heard myself saying all the things others had once said to me.

"You're my best friend," Theo said. "You know that, don't you? I couldn't have gone through it alone."

His guard seemed to drop for those moments, but in

writing of that incident I find it puzzling that he makes no reference to his mother's death in his journals. It's almost as if he had to blot it out completely. He wanted love as much as the rest of us, but with Theo love was something he had to buy under the counter; he didn't trust the genuine article.

Whoever recruited him must have traded on this, have known him as well as he knew himself. They picked carefully and they picked well, since the four we know of could hardly be considered failures. I feel it was no accident that their four most successful recruits were all taken from the ranks of those who considered themselves unloved. Yet it would be a mistake to think of Theo as some wistful victim of his own lonely abnormality. That would be too pat. I think the mentality of a traitor must be more complex than that. When caught, the majority of them plead a love of humanity as a whole, that convenient blanket that has smothered so many freedoms. The secrets they steal are always for the benefit of all, it seems, and fellow travellers are much taken with this outwardly persuasive argument, finding it easy to stomach the basic flaw – namely that the love of humanity is curiously selective, since few spies seem disposed to share their thefts with anybody but the Soviet Union.

Time was on their side, time is always on their side. The democracies seldom galvanise themselves except in times of crisis; for the most part they remain sleeping clergymen while their enemies shunt backwards and forwards, exploring every branch line of human fallibility, deliberately taking the longest route, but always in motion, in the sure knowledge that the vital element is not the journey but the ultimate destination.

They found Theo and they salted him away, adding him to the collection. One has to admire their foresight. It must take a particular kind of patience, alien to the Western character, to recruit a number of undergraduates (and there could well be more than the four we know of) at a time when most eyes were lowered over the Bingo cards of appeasement, and prepare them for a war that nobody had thought of. And why Cambridge? That is the other enigma.

There are some of us who are drawn to violence and at this

distance I can't be sure whether Theo was a total innocent who was trapped, or somebody who deliberately placed himself in a position of danger. Sometimes the motives of murderer and victim coincide, which perhaps explains why so many crimes of violence go undetected. From the incomplete account he gives in his journals, Theo had premonitions of disaster, yet he still felt compelled to keep his appointment in Samarra. The year was 1934. A vintage year, it would appear.

I don't know what to make of last night's episode. I had misgivings about going in the first place, but he was so persuasive that I finally couldn't help myself. Part of me suspected that he wasn't quite what he seemed, but I fancied him. (No, let's be honest, I didn't fancy him, he excited me beyond belief.) Thirty-ish, and a fascinating mixture. He dressed like a labourer, but was obviously intelligent. Wouldn't let me touch him the first time we met, said he never gave himself to total strangers. I showed myself to him but got nothing in return, which of course only increased my excitement. He let me meet him again, and we had a few drinks together, but he refused to let me buy him a meal. He said he had to very sure before he allowed intimacy. He actually used the word 'intimacy', which I found odd because it seemed out of character. Told me he had been hurt on several occasions and this had made him wary. I told him that he had a terrible effect on me, but was careful not to reveal too much of myself. We talked about love and pain and compared tastes, finding many common interests. He says his name is John, and I allowed him to know me as Ken.

Saw J. again last night. Met him by chance in that pub by the Catholic church. Had the feeling, I don't quite know why, that he knew I would be there. He insisted on buying me a drink and said that he had been thinking a lot about my proposition. "If we're going to have intimacy," he said, using that word again, "it has to be right, in the right surroundings. I can't bear a quick gobble in some sordid cottage. That isn't my cup of tea at all."

There were one or two rugby hearties in the pub who started to make snide remarks in our hearing, so we drank up and went for a walk. I found out that he drifts around a lot, seldom staying long in any one place, but takes labouring work where he can find it.

At the moment he is working on the Appleby Estate, digging drains, and has been given the use of one of the bungalows on the estate while the job lasts. He suggested that I come there Saturday night. "I'll give myself to you then," he said. "I can be very loving with the right person."

He let me kiss him when we said goodbye. I can't remember feeling like this about anybody, but the way he put it and the expectation of Saturday made me quite light-headed. I slept soundly all night and woke this morning still feeling elated.

Sunday

Followed J.'s directions and found the bungalow without too much difficulty. It is about a mile from the main house and fairly isolated, being away from the road and surrounded by a spinney. He is only occupying two of the rooms since the rest of the place is unfurnished. Not much in the way of creature comforts, but he had done what he could and was touchingly houseproud. I took drink with me and some food. "You shouldn't have done that," he said. "This is my treat." I helped him gather some firewood and we lit the fire and drew the curtains. I had made up my mind not to hurry things and we ate the meal he had prepared. I can't say that his cooking impressed me, but I made all the polite noises and pretended that it was to my liking. I suddenly had a glimpse of the the sort of domesticity that Tony longs for and for the first time could see what he means.

We chatted about a number of things and he surprised me with his awareness of world affairs. We decided the bedroom was too cold, so after we had cleared away the remains of the meal we brought the mattress and laid it in front of the fire. It was like one of those Warner Brothers movies where the boy and the girl are trapped in the mountain lodge in a snow storm, the world outside completely cut off. I told him this and it made him laugh. "What a romantic you are," he said. "I like that." He liked a lot of things. I have never known anybody quite so passionate. I usually find that people of his class have a sort of brute aggressiveness.

At one point, when we had finished the first bout and we were having a drink, I asked him, "Is that what you call intimacy? Don't you ever call it something else?" I wanted to draw him out. Dirty talk always excites me. We were totally naked in front of the fire and instead of answering me he started to play with mine again. I noticed his hands were surprisingly soft for a labourer

159

and I was driven by unreasoning desires. We did things to each other I have only previously dreamed about. I stayed all night, and over breakfast he told me that he had fallen in love with me. I am besotted about him.

Wednesday

We have now fallen into an old married couple's routine, though J. quite properly cautioned me about falling into any pattern that might arouse suspicion. We have already had one narrow escape when one of the gamekeepers knocked at the door the other night we were bathing each other in an old hip bath in front of the fire. I hid in one of the empty rooms and the man apparently went away unsuspecting. I agree with J. we have to be careful, because if he was chucked out of his job all this would have to end. For the first time in my life I don't feel the need for anybody else. We satisfy each other in a way I didn't think possible. My work is going well because I have no frustrations.

When I saw Tony at college today he remarked on the change in me.

"What sort of change?" I asked.

"You just seem very relaxed."

I gave him my Gioconda smile and went out of my way to praise his latest novel when he read me a chapter. I felt very generous, though what he read seemed terribly mundane. He is what he writes – well meaning and dull.

Friday

Don't know how to describe my feelings at the moment. J. has been very moody of late and last night after we had slaked each other he said he had a confession to make. "An old friend has turned up out of the blue," he said. "Somebody out of my past. It's all over, it was over years ago, but he won't take no for an answer. I told him about you and me, but he thinks I'm just making it up to get rid of him. Would you be willing to meet him? It's the only way he'll be convinced."

I was torn. This is something I have always been at pains to avoid, some ghastly triangle situation, especially if this friend is the possessive type. They get so hysterical. J. says he's already threatened suicide in the past. I had a sudden vision of this bliss ending. J. went on protesting that the other was a burnt-out case, but was obviously still under some sort of compulsion, because otherwise why would he be so insistent? I suggested we bought this character off, but he was adamant that this wouldn't work.

"I know him too well," he said. "He's a very determined one is Harry. I mean, don't misunderstand me, I've nothing really against him, it's just that I'm so happy with you and I don't want anything to spoil it."

I couldn't put up much of an argument after that and we finally agreed a plan of campaign. We'd invite Harry to have supper with us, treat him kindly, but make him see that his cause is lost. I can't say that I'm altogether happy about it, but there seems no alternative.

Tuesday

Harry, cry God for Harry. Totally, but totally different from anything I had imagined. First impressions not favourable. Skin rather yellow and unhealthy looking. Older than expected, and indeed looks older than J. described him. Would guess in his late thirties, well mannered and with just a trace of an accent. Not a foreign accent exactly, but something grafted on as sometimes happens when people have lived abroad. Was perfectly polite to me, though somewhat removed for the first hour or so. I had made up my mind to charm him, feeling that charm in this case the better part of valour.

We had quite a pleasant dinner, roast chicken which I provided and J. cooked rather well. Plenty to drink. Conversation skirted round the problem but couldn't be avoided for ever so I broached it when I judged the atmosphere sufficiently thawed. He listened in silence to my statement of the defence and didn't seem too disturbed when I explained that although I knew J. still had great affection for him, our present situation could not be attacked.

Then he said a rather sad thing, I thought. He told me his whole life had been made miserable by passion. "I can't remember a time," he said, "when I was free of it."

He didn't only mean J., it was something deeper than that. I was relieved to see that he would accept defeat so gracefully, because although he several times repeated that J. was the one decent episode in his life, he was very unemotional. I suspect he might have been somewhat in his cups by then, for we had all drunk a great deal. I drank to calm my nerves in the first place and could hear myself slurring my words. I didn't see any traces of the hysteria that J. had spoken of. On the contrary he seemed flat and ordinary, and I warmed to him.

Looking back, I don't quite know how the rest of the evening developed, but I suppose that confession time breeds a certain relaxation. Perhaps J. and I were anxious to show there was no hard feelings, or perhaps the underlying eroticism of the occasion, heightened by the drink, took over at a certain point. All I know is that we were suddenly all three naked – an absurd, bizarre scene in that stifling little room, the firelight playing on our entwined bodies. Harry and I were both rivals for J.'s attentions. I have never minded sharing in any case, and it was a time for extra generosity. In other circumstances I might have found it farcically sordid, but we were all swept up into a collective madness, a frenzied saturnalia. Then Harry produced a camera, saying that he wanted something to remember us by. He took a series of photographs of J. and me in the act – again a new experience. Variations on scenes from a nunnery. I played nun to J.'s Legionnaire, a conscious echo of the discovery Tony and I made all those years ago. There is something very special about making one's own pornography. It's the ultimate in narcissism. All in all a unique evening.

Tuesday

I spoke too soon. J. has disappeared. We had arranged to meet as usual at the bungalow, but when I arrived the place was dark. No sign of him anywhere. I tried to break in, fearing something might have happened to him, and although I broke a pane of glass in one of the back windows I still couldn't open it. I waited around for over an hour, then spotted the gamekeeper in the distance and thought it wise to keep out of sight. I have a feeling of panic.

Thursday

Still no sign of him. Have been back to the bungalow twice more, and today I was so distraught I went in daylight. Was able to look in the windows and could see none of his things. Have no idea what to do next. Can't go to the police for obvious reasons. The only clue I have is that he once told me his parents lived in Liverpool. The whole thing is inexplicable. I can't believe that there is any connection between his disappearance and the evening we spent with Harry. That would be unthinkable. Unthinkable, but something I have thought about.

Friday

Took my courage in my hands today and called at the Appleby Estate Office. Had rehearsed what I was going to say, inventing some distant relationship with J. I was going to tell them that I had to break some bad news to him. Just in time I remembered I had no idea whether John was his real name. It was too late to turn back, because I was inside the office by then, so I quickly changed my story. I said that I had heard that some of the bungalows on the estate were for rent and could they tell me which ones were available. They were rather shirty and said that it was not their policy to rent any property, that the bungalows were reserved for staff. I was forced to admit defeat. Came back here and was violently sick.

Monday

Stayed in bed over the weekend, unable to think straight. The whole thing is a nightmare. I feel unreal. I am one long nerve-end.

Tuesday

Forced myself to get up and went back to the bungalow. I don't know whether it was horror or relief that I found it was occupied. Smoke was coming from the chimney and I rushed to knock on the door. The door was opened by a gypsy-like woman with a baby at the breast. Had to pretend I had lost my way and asked for directions to the main house. It is obvious that J. has gone for ever. I keep hoping that I shall have some word from him, some explanation. Anything would be better than this vacuum.

Thursday

Another week and still nothing. Can't concentrate on anything. When Tony came round last night I was abrupt to the point of rudeness and had to apologise, saying I had neglected my thesis and needed to placate my tutor. No idea whether he believed me or not, nor do I care. My writing has gone to bits. After Tony left I dressed in old clothes and went looking for some sex, I didn't mind what. Picked up a stockbroker in The George and we did it in the back of his Morris Oxford. It was like cold mutton, as Oscar said to Yeats. Felt worse afterwards and got away as soon as it was finished.

Monday

News at last! Received a letter from Harry this morning, postmarked London. Brief and to the point. In it he said he was sure I was worried about J. He apparently knows his present whereabouts and hinted that J. has had some sort of breakdown. Asked me if I could meet him in London this Friday when he will explain all. There was no address on the letter, but he gave me a time and a place. I shall go.

Saturday

How polite he was. He might have been inviting me to join the Salvation Army. Polite but straight to the point. I thought it was just blackmail at first, alarming enough in itself, but something I could have come to terms with. Nothing was an accident, I realise that now. Meeting J. was not the happy chance I once imagined. Everything had been planned; they had had me in their sights for a long time. Guy was the pimp, a willing convert who had suggested I might like to join the club.

I asked him why they felt they had to go to such lengths, that perhaps the direct approach would have been simpler.

"We like to be sure," he said. He told me that J. was too enthusiastic in my case. "One can't afford to be emotional in this job, as I hope you appreciate. Just as there's nothing personal in my proposition to you. It's just a matter of business, a commercial transaction if you like." All said like a salesman trying to hawk his samples. Nothing overt.

He greatly regretted the necessity of reminding me of the existence of the photographs. The negatives had been lodged with his superiors who would not hesitate to make use of them should my answer be other than the one they were looking for. "Think of them as an insurance policy for loyalty," he said.

His superiors had the greatest respect for my talents. This was merely a preliminary talk, a clearing of the ground as it were. I would be contacted at a later date and given more detailed briefings. They just wanted an answer in principle. I could take my time, because time was on their side. They just felt from what Guy had told them that I was sympathetic material. "Would you disagree with that?" he asked. "Could I say that much?"

I suppose I was too amazed by the whole scene to put up much of a counter-argument. His politeness was somehow more threatening than anything else. He even apologised on J.'s behalf. "He wanted to write you a goodbye letter," he said, "but we don't encourage a lot of written evidence." When I asked him if I would be allowed to see J. again, assuming I agreed to their terms, he said he thought this might be arranged. "But give it a while," he said. "He's not in the country at the moment. We felt he needed a holiday. He takes his work so seriously. Such a conscientious young man."

I asked how long I had got to make up my mind.

"Shall we say two weeks?" he said. "We don't want to leave it too long, things go off the boil. I'm sure we haven't made the wrong choice. You'll find that once you've taken the decision everything falls into place. We look after our own."

I found a little of my old self-confidence and complimented him on his tact and the choice of venue (Lyons Corner House in Coventry Street). We shook hands when we parted.

I stayed in town overnight. Was propositioned twice in Leicester Square, but declined.

Tuesday

Having thought of nothing else, I finally took the plunge and talked to Guy today. He couldn't resist smirking of course, when I told him some of the history of my case.

"Crude, I suppose, but effective," he said. "I had no idea I was letting you in for all that. I thought it would be straightforward, like it was with me. I dare say they thought it wasn't worth wasting film on me. Mind you, I wouldn't have said no to a little liaison, a little icing on the cake. I'm all for that."

He must have known what I wanted to talk about because he insisted we took a punt out. It was bloody cold on the river, but poetically the right setting for what we were about. And so it begins.

Sunday

They have contacted me again. I shall go and I shall agree. What Guy says makes sense. It's comforting to feel part of a family. Funny how quickly one learns and adapts. I have already taken certain precautions with these journals. After all, it's a game that two can play.

13

THE THIRTIES WERE years when we all did our fair share of crystal-gazing, predicting, arguing, violently disagreeing as to which way the world was going. I used to envy those who had no doubts, some to whom *The Times* leader was gospel, others to whom anything printed in the *Worker* was immediately Holy Writ. Lacking the courage of anybody's convictions, I fluctuated daily. I once consulted a fortune teller at a local fair, since we all need that necessary flirtation with the unknown from time to time. It turned out to be a farcical encounter, for the advertised medium had slipped out for a cup of tea when my turn came, her place being taken by her daughter.

"But are you qualified?" I asked.

"Oh, yes. It runs in the family. Do you want the large ball or the small one?"

"What's the difference?"

"Five bob."

"I'll take the small one."

We sat opposite each other across a rickety card-table covered with a tablecloth patterned with the signs of the zodiac. She produced the economy-sized crystal ball from under the table and placed it between us with nicotine-stained hands. It immediately rolled off, which I took to be a discouraging sign.

"That's never happened before."

She examined it for damage, then wiped it with a piece of velvet before going into the statutory 'trance', passing her grubby hands over the ball in series of ludicrous gestures. I became more interested in her behaviour than in my own future. Once the preliminaries were over she bent forward and stared into the crystal.

"Concentrate," she said.

I stared fixedly at her cleavage.

She suddenly staggered back from the table. "Oh, my gawd!" she exclaimed. "Oh, my gawd, I've seen something. I've never seen anything before."

The experience unnerved her so much she was unable to continue and after a wrangle she gave me my money back and left the tent in search of her mother, desperate to share the revelation. I never did find out what she saw.

The episode seemed to sum up my own life at the time. I was conscious that I had embarked on a journey without maps, in a state of mind that could best be described as muddled. I had some sympathy with the unknown author – the only non-pornographer amongst the clientele of the male lavatories in The Splendide – who scrawled the despairing question, IS THERE A LIFE AFTER BREAKFAST? on our walls. Breakfast in my case had been the publication of my first novel; what had followed had been anticlimax. I suppose the truth of the matter was I was still living in the emotional vacuum that the end of the affair with Judy had bequeathed. A state of grace without religious beliefs is difficult to sustain, and in cutting myself off from all normal social intercourse during the period when the novel was being written I seemed to have lost the knack of making new friends. The solitary life can lead us into areas of quiet madness, and for a brief period I embarked on a strange quest. I chanced upon a photograph of an unknown girl in a magazine which inflamed my imagination. I convinced myself that here was somebody to whom I could entrust my affections and wrote to the editor of the magazine stating that I was convinced the girl was my dead sister's child I had lost touch with for ten years, and could he kindly supply an address for her. My enquiry was treated with the contempt it deserved, though I was to make use of the idea a decade later in one of my novels.

My own loneliness prevented me from perceiving Theo's dilemma. I had no inkling of his affair with the *agent provocateur* called J. – that secret lay buried for forty years until the squalid bedroom in Englefield Green gave up its treasures.

Time and time again over the past few months I have puzzled over the contradiction of the journals. It seems such an extraordinary risk for him to have taken – after Burgess, Maclean and Kim Philby were exposed he could not have been that confident of his own safety: there must have been many moments when he listened for the tread on the stairs in the early hours. And yet he never destroyed them, he ignored even the elementary precaution of depositing them elsewhere. We all like to be amateur psychologists, and never more so than when we are judging our friends. I am as guilty as anyone, applying a little knowledge in dangerous doses. Where Theo is concerned I am driven to believe that the only explanation worth entertaining is that he tempted his own fate, but lacked the conceit which finally makes criminals boast of their secret life. He needed to leave some record of his guilt, and a lifetime's devotion to the written word dictated the form it would take.

Theo's day-to-day existence was so different to mine. He worked amongst noble buildings, conjuring his plots in Wren's great library while I slaved away in Mrs. Pike's mundane back bedroom. He was surrounded by contemporaries intent on like hedonistic pleasures; I met only those concerned with buying a few hours respite from the drab repetitions of their everyday lives. I noticed that whenever parties of under-graduates came 'slumming' to The Splendide they frequently mocked what the rest of our audiences found romantic. But they saved their real malice for the bourgeois traditions of the middle-class; they channelled their anger into pacifism. For the first time in their lives most of them came face to face with actual poverty, not some classical exercise in historical neglect but the poverty that marched with brave songs through the streets of Cambridge. The bleak reality of the Depression suddenly had a human face, and for many of Theo's con-temporaries this was the moment of political awakening. Coupled with the growing awareness of what was happening on the Continent, this was the culminating disillusion with the old order. It was as if, as was the case with the substitute medium I encountered in the fairground, they had suddenly seen the future for the first time, and the collective shock frag-mented, driving many of Theo's generation to the four points of the political compass.

I wish I could record that I was part of that awareness, but my life continued to be made up of fictions: the realities passed by. I know now that people like Burgess and Philby went to see for themselves – Burgess to Russia and Philby to Austria. Whether their journeys were part of a master plan or merely prompted by wanderlust I shall never know. Theo stayed at home, never openly associated with any cause, the detached observer, the rising young novelist who took the longer view, giving the appearance of being a liberal democrat too involved in his vocation to descend into the sawdust of the arena.

After he had taken his Tripos in 1934 (a few months after the affair with J. came to an abrupt end) he announced that he had made a decision for both of us.

"It's absurd to waste your life cleaning out cinema toilets," he said. "I've got enough for us both to live on. We should move to London. I've found a little place behind Flask Walk in Hampstead. It's just big enough for us to live together and apart, if you know what I mean. We can both write and lead separate lives under the same roof. You can pay me what you can afford, but there are no conditions. What d'you say?"

His gesture took me completely by surprise. Until that moment I had formed the impression that Theo had outgrown our childhood friendship – that he still tolerated me out of family loyalty, but that the old intimacy of our relationship had gone for ever. Whether by chance or design, he had timed his offer well. I was increasingly dissatisfied with my lot. I found Clifford and Ruby stultifying; they were kindly and well meaning people, but totally content with what life had offered them. I would always remember them with gratitude, but I had all but smothered myself under their blanketing complacency.

Yet I hesitated. "You've really thought it through, have you? I mean, I don't want to seem ungracious or ungrateful, but the arrangement could present problems."

"What problems?"

"Well, can't you guess? We do have different tastes, after all."

"Oh, that! Tony, dear, as far as I'm concerned you can bring anything home. And I shall extend the same courtesy to myself. We'll sign a non-aggression pact, strict neutrality. The only favour I shall demand as landlord is first claim on the bathroom."

I travelled to London with him on my first free day to inspect our new home. It was a charming, three-storied house tucked away in a mews and had obviously once formed part of a stable-block. It was unfurnished, and although Theo suggested that he be responsible for the entire decor, I insisted that I made my own contribution and furnish my own two rooms. I had saved the odd fifty pounds, and by scouring the second-hand shops I managed to purchase the essentials for just over twenty pounds, acquiring a solid mahogany bed, a simple pine desk, an armchair and a collection of odd pieces of china together with a roll of carpet salvaged from a warehouse fire.

Clifford and Ruby received my news with genuine dismay. I kept in touch with them for a few years but the best of intentions are whittled away and it wasn't until near the end of the war that I learnt that the old Splendide had been gutted by a freak accident involving a Home Guard exercise. Apparently the cinema had been used for a lecture to demonstrate the best way of dealing with incendiary bombs during the Blitz; the demonstration had gone disastrously wrong.

It was with the same mixed feelings that I departed from Mrs. Pike. Clearing my things from that bedroom I remembered the pain of my time with Judy, the long hours spent writing my novel by candlelight – it was like a monk leaving his cell to venture into the real world. There are some places one never forgets and others where memories are erased immediately.

To compensate, of course, there was the excitement of moving into Hampstead – the feeling of accomplishment, never to be repeated exactly, at having achieved a place of one's own for the first time. The fact that I could now close the door and look around at my own possessions was a pleasure that stoked my creative energies. Out of necessity I had to get to work quickly, for I was determined not to sponge on Theo, but pay my own way through my writing. I began as

I meant to continue, keeping to a strict, spartan regime, cutting out all luxuries except my daily quota of Player's Navy Cut, since this was the age when lung cancer was scarcely spoken of and young and old were assailed from every hoarding to accept the pleasures of nicotine as part of life's rich harvest.

Our arrangement seemed to work perfectly. We kept ourselves to ourselves for the most part, and I was at some pains to let Theo see that I respected his privacy. It was usually Theo who disturbed the peace, for he could never resist relating the latest gossip. I was aware that he entertained a variety of 'midnight callers' but they were seldom in evidence during our working hours. "The captains and the queens have all departed," was one of Theo's most repeated remarks if ever we met at breakfast. Perhaps because writing is such a lonely pursuit, one that only a fellow writer can respect and understand for long periods, we need to have a sympathetic companion on tap without the complications of an emotional relationship. Theo and I were able to discuss our works in progress, and the fact that our two styles were so different rendered the criticism we offered each other that much more valuable: we were not in competition except to have the last word on occasions. Being the more successful at that time, Theo was already showing signs of a magnificent disdain for the critics, an attitude I was not confident enough to imitate.

I could not help admiring his self-confidence, for he blossomed as never before the moment we came to London.

"So much to choose from, my dear. There are sections of this fair city positively swarming with talent. As you know, I prefer rough trade to the more obvious queens."

"Aren't you ever scared at the risks you take?"

"Yes."

"Why do you do it then?"

"Because I like being scared, dear. Your trouble is you don't get about enough. You don't meet anybody. This whole literary thing is a game, dear. If you want to get on you've got to join in, dip your toes in the muddy waters and splash a few people. I shall take you around."

He was as good as his word and the following week I went with him to a cocktail party given by the wife of an elderly and extremely rich art dealer, a Mrs. Steel. "We call her Madame de Steel, dear," Theo said, "if you'll excuse the pun. All the money in the world. Her aged husband made a mint selling quite frightful pictures to war profiteers. The point is, she knows everybody, and it'll be very good for you."

I was taken to an elegant house in Eaton Square where we were received by a butler in livery.

"T.B.H., dear," Theo whispered as we waited to be announced.

"What's that mean?"

"To be had," he said, with a nod in the direction of the butler.

Mrs. Steel wasn't at all what I had been led to expect. I guessed her to be in her middle thirties, possibly half the age of her husband. From Theo's description I had imagined her to be vulgarly obvious, but she was soft spoken and gave the impression of being somewhat shy. She had that pampered look of the very rich, and I felt like Gatsby seeing Daisy for the first time.

It was a crowded party with a strong literary emphasis and I knew nobody, though I was able to recognise several famous faces. Sensing my discomfort Diana Steel took me in hand and introduced me to a group. Nerves blurred my perceptions at the time and I confess I have no accurate recall, though I seem to remember that during the course of the evening I exchanged a few pleasantries with the young H. E. Bates, a fellow lost soul. For the most part I stood on the fringe of conversations, never quick enough to catch up with the constantly changing threads, so that by the time I had thought of a witty contribution the dialogue had moved on to another subject. Eveybody gave the impression of being very successful and at the same time indifferent to that success. But the food was good and the drinks plentiful.

After the meal I wandered off to look at Steel's personal art collection which, contrary to Theo's earlier verdict, I found exciting. Perhaps Steel only sold the rubbish to his *nouveau riche* clients and kept the best for himself. He had several exquisite Marie Laurencins, a Picasso of the Blue Period, one huge van Dongen, a Marquet, a whole collection of Bakst (whom I later found he had known intimately before settling in England before the First World War), a little-known contemporary of Renoir, Marval, and two or three superb Braques. But what caught and held my attention was a large female nude hanging above the fireplace in Steel's study. It was done in the style of Boldini, the model depicted as just stepping from her bath, the head turned away, one arm outstretched to pick up a towel so that the breasts were taut and prominent.

"You like that, do you?"

I turned to see my host standing behind me.

"It's very disturbing," I said.

"Do you know anything about painting?"

"Not a great deal."

"I was lucky. I knew most of them at a time when they were either unknown or unwanted. I was lucky. Very lucky. Of course, now they say I had an eye. Well, they were looking at the same things, but they didn't buy them. I did. But I'm glad you like this one. It happens to be one of my favourites, that's why it hangs in my study." He smiled at me. "It's very comforting to be reminded of youth and beauty, don't you think? No, of course you don't, because you are still young. But it will be comforting, take my word for it. I'm sorry, forgive me, I don't think we were ever introduced?"

"Tony Stern."

"Ah, yes. You're the friend of . . . Oh, I'm hopeless on names."

"Theo."

"Of course, the amazing Theo, our rising star. And what do you do, Mr. Stern?"

"I write too."

"Novels?"

"Spy stories. Well, I've only had one published."

"I'm not very up on the literary world. That's Diana's province. I only steal from the rich. And I never dissuade them from their own mistakes. I learnt that lesson a long time ago. If money wants to speak with a common voice, then why try and change it? All artists have to live, even the bad ones. Of course if people really want my opinion, I give it, but I don't volunteer it any more. I'm not a Duveen, that seems like too much hard work."

At that time I had never heard of Duveen, but I nodded politely. He seemed as though he wanted to talk. He was fascinatingly ugly, reminding me of photographs of Frank Harris, and I could detect traces of a mid-European accent when he became animated about his favourite subject. His descriptions of life in Paris at the turn of the century which he decorated with highly personal anecdotes held me spellbound.

"I was a painter myself for a time. At least I called myself a painter, but I laboured under one great disadvantage. I had no talent. A facility, yes, but the spark was missing. One should always be aware of one's limitations, don't you agree? There is nothing sadder than a competent artist. I remember the real moment of truth. It was many years ago, when I still entertained some hope for my own career. I was taken to Matisse's studio and when I looked for the first time at what he was doing, I felt that my whole life was a sham. It seemed impossible for me ever to pick up a brush again. So I never did. I became the next best thing. I started to sell the works of people I admired. It wasn't easy. Nobody accepts original art in the beginning. Nobody. I don't care what it is, people are frightened of what they can't immediately comprehend. Sometimes it's a book, a poem, sometimes a piece of sculpture, or a painting, or a symphony . . . on occasions it's a woman. A woman like that perhaps." He stared up at the nude. "I'm glad you find it disturbing. Beauty should be. She's still beautiful, don't you agree?"

"I'm sorry?"

"My wife. I thought you recognised her. That's a painting of my wife."

I have the feeling that I blushed.

"It's a curious thing. The artist who painted that had a great future, in my opinion. But he never lived to fulfil the promise. He was killed at Verdun. I've tried for a long time to discover more of his work, but with no success. I bought it for very little money and then I set about discovering the model."

"What a romantic story," I said.

"Yes, I suppose it is."

We were interrupted by Theo and his wife at that point. "There you are," she said. "We thought Tony had taken fright and disappeared. What's Anton been telling you?"

"I've been admiring your portrait."

"Hardly a portrait."

Again I felt the blood rush to my face.

She turned to Theo. "You wouldn't call it a portrait, would you, Theo?"

"No. I like my portraits to be realistic, and you're much more beautiful than that, Diana."

"Oh, such flattery."

"Don't misunderstand me, Anton, I'm not speaking from memory."

The sophistication of the exchange only added to my embarrassment. I found it odd to be discussing a woman's nudity in front of her husband. To be standing next to Diana Steel in the flesh, both literally and figuratively, was unnerving.

"Why don't we all have dinner?" she said. "Are you two doing anything?"

"Free as the wind," Theo said, answering for both of us.

"Well, then that's settled."

"I can't," her husband said. "I have to have dinner with those Americans."

"Oh, that's right. Well, don't suggest we join you. Right, well give me time to powder my nose. Theo, ring up the Savoy and get us a table. The Grill, I think." She kissed her husband. "Poor darling, you're going to have such a dull evening."

Mr. Steel excused himself a few moments later and Theo and I were left alone.

"What d'you make of them?" Theo asked when we were on our own.

"They're both very nice. He's a fascinating character."

"In small doses. Don't you like her?"

175

"Yes."

"I saw you colour up when we were discussing that." He pointed to the nude painting. "She's T.B.H., too, you know."

"How d'you know? You just say that about everybody."

"Theo knows, dear. Take his word for it. Poor Anton isn't up to it any more. She's very discreet, though. I mean, she's not about to say goodbye to all this for the sake of a little bunk up. You should cultivate her."

"How could I do that?"

"Do you mean, how could I do that from a moral point of view, or *how* could I do that? If it's the latter, quite simple. Don't rush it, just let things take their course. I know she's got the eye for you."

"You're absurd," I said.

"Okay, have it your way, but I'm never wrong about these things. Why d'you think she invited us to dinner?"

"Well, it's not going to happen, so the whole conversation is academic."

"Did you meet anybody else interesting?"

"Not really. They all seemed very full of themselves."

"Writers always are, dear. And always a disappointment to meet, present company excepted. Were you introduced to Arnold Bennett?"

"Arnold Bennett? He's dead."

"Did I say Bennett? I meant Walpole. Hugh Walpole."

"No, I hardly met anybody."

"Oh, you ought to have met him. He's very kind to up and comings. It's no good me trying to widen your horizons if you behave like some shrinking wallflower."

Diana Steel rejoined us before Theo could expand on his favourite topic of the moment. The Steels' Rolls was waiting outside to whisk us through the evening traffic to the Strand. I sat next to Diana while Theo occupied the jump seat and kept up an endless stream of chatter, for which I was grateful, since it absolved me from making a fool of myself. Diana seemed to have drenched herself in a particularly heavy perfume and from time to time the soft suspension of the Rolls nudged us together.

Dinner was an equally heady experience. Diana insisted

that I order oysters once I had stupidly revealed that I was a stranger to their oily charms. She seemed to know all the waiters on first-name terms and I was suitably impressed by the impeccable service and atmosphere of The Grill. Noel Coward came in with a party after the theatre and stopped by our table.

"Isn't it awful about poor Lottie," Diana said when Theo and I had been introduced.

"What's happend to her now?" Coward said.

"She was playing tennis, fell down and broke her leg in two places."

"Are there two places?" Coward said in his most clipped of mandarin voices.

"Do you think he rehearses those sort of lines?" Theo said maliciously when Coward had gone.

"No, I'm sure he doesn't."

The conversation then turned to the current theatre, another topic about which I was abysmally ignorant. I became more and more conscious that I had done nothing with my life, seen nothing, met nobody of consequence. There I was sitting next to a beautiful and witty woman, drinking champagne in close proximity to the famous, and without a word to say for myself. I thought, how dull she must think me, what a clumsy bore. She and Theo monopolised the conversation, for they talked the same language while I could only interpret the occasional word. What had begun as an evening of enchantment rapidly became an agony. I drank too much and allowed myself to be guided towards a series of over-rich courses, so that by the time coffee was served I was feeling distinctly queasy.

To my horror I heard Diana say, "Shall we go on somewhere?"

"Oh, what a lovely idea," Theo said. "Unfortunately, I can't. I have a certain assignation which I daren't break. But why don't you and Tony go somewhere? He's dying to live it up, aren't you, Tony?"

I had no opportunity to head him off.

"Then Tony and I will enjoy ourselves. Where would you like to go, Tony?"

I had no idea other than to find my way to the nearest men's room.

"You choose," I said. "But don't think you have to just for my sake."

"Oh, Diana never goes to bed," Theo said. He ignored the look I gave him.

"Will you excuse me for a moment," I said. I picked my way through the tables very carefully, only making a bolt for it when I was out of their range. The Savoy's cuisine was wasted on me that night, for I gave back what I had received. After splashing my face with cold water I felt just able to face the world again.

By the time I returned to our table Theo had disappeared. I wondered whether I should make a token effort to offer to pay for the meal, but no bill was presented.

We drove to a night club in the vicinity of Berkeley Square, subsequently closed down during the war for its black market activities. I was grateful for the semi-darkness. Diana ordered more champagne. "Can I ask you a very rude question?" she said. "Are you and Theo a twosome?"

"How d'you mean?"

"Well, you live together, don't you?"

"Yes, we share a house."

"Do you share anything else?"

"Oh, I see what you mean. No. No, we don't. Theo's my best, my oldest friend; we're related, second cousins."

"Then it was rude of me. But perhaps forgivable in view of Theo's reputation."

"Does he have a reputation?"

"Amongst those in the know."

"I think I should tell you, if it isn't already obvious, that I'm not in the know."

"Do you want to be?"

"I'm not sure. Theo says that it's important if you want to make your name quickly."

"I haven't read your book, but I shall get it tomorrow. That's two things you have to forgive me for. Do you?"

"Of course," I said.

"Would you like to dance?"

"Look," I said, "I may as well be honest. I'm not in the know and I can't dance. I'd probably cripple you."

"Oh, I doubt that. Take your shoes off. Nobody'll notice here. And there isn't room to dance on this floor, you can only shuffle together."

I was relieved to find that my socks had no holes in them; since leaving Mrs. Pike my limited wardrobe had suffered from neglect. I lead Diana Steel on to the crowded dance floor where most of the couples seemed to be joined together with glue. Diana took my right arm and placed it firmly in the middle of her bare back. "Just relax," she said. It seemed to me that every woman I met gave me the same advice. I had only taken a few tentative steps before she nestled her cheek against mine.

"It's such a relief to find somebody who isn't queer these days," she said.

The band was playing Vivian Ellis's 'Faster, Faster!' from Cochran's new revue and the words seemed particularly appropriate for the occasion – 'step on the gas, boys, and let's save some time' – for the pace of the evening had suddenly accelerated: I was not so naive as to mistake the pressure of her body against mine as we swayed together.

"What're you thinking about?" she said. "You're very quiet."

"I was concentrating, otherwise I should fall over. I'm not very good, am I?"

"You don't have to be good, you're young," she said. "Did Theo tell you much about me?"

"No."

"Unusually discreet of him, and totally out of character. I can't believe he said nothing."

She spoke close to my ear and to my amazement she suddenly closed her teeth on the lobe.

"But you admired the painting, didn't you? You're in the know to that extent."

"Can we go and sit down?" I said. "I've an idea I'm going to pass out."

"Oh, well, we can't have that."

We went back to our seat in the corner. She poured herself another drink.

"What is it – the wine, the food, or me?"

"A combination."

"How sweet. I'm being very wicked, aren't I? Teasing you. I don't usually cradle snatch, but I might make an exception where you're concerned."

"What about your husband?"

"Is that what's bothering you? We have an arrangement. Does that shock you?"

"But he's so nice."

"Yes," she said, drawing out the word. "Yes, he is. He's also thirty years older than me."

She emptied her glass of champagne and picked up her handbag.

"It's past your bedtime," she said.

"I'm sorry. I didn't mean to offend you."

"I'm not in the least offended."

She took took two five pound notes from her bag and placed them under her glass. "Let's go, shall we?"

Once outside she shook my hand. "You don't mind getting a taxi, do you? It's been such a pleasant evening."

She got into the waiting Rolls, the chauffeur nodded to me with just the hint of a smile, and then she was gone. I walked to Trafalgar Square, then down Whitehall and on to the Embankment. Derelicts were dossing down for the night, like characters from a Chaplin movie. I stood looking down into the sluggish waters of the Thames until my head cleared, angry with myself for lacking the courage to take what had so obviously been mine for the asking. I thought about her nude body in the painting, then I thought about her husband and felt sorry for both of us.

Perrins Walk, NW3
Wednesday

I must guard against becoming 'camp'. I hate it in others, yet find myself sliding down the same slope. Last night, having dinner with Diana and Tony at the Savoy I heard myself being falsetto. In enjoying the wider freedoms of London I must be careful not to overdo it. I led myself into the trap, too anxious to impress Tony with my social contacts. Work suffers, everything suffers.

Excused myself after dinner and left Tony to Diana's tender mercies. She will eat him given half an opportunity. Met with Harry who again refused to disclose J.'s whereabouts or pass on any message. He also mentioned that I was drawing too much attention to myself, which suggests that I am being watched. I will play their game, but not necessarily strictly according to their rules. When I asked him exactly what is required of me, he was vague to the point of irritation. It is my belief they are just collecting people in a haphazard fashion with no concise plan in mind. Most of the literature he has given me (which I read and destroyed) is banal, written by idiots parrot style and patently handed to them from afar. They believe they can step straight into the vacuum created by the collapse of the Labour Party as a political force, but again they completely misread the character of this country. Strangely enough both opposing extremes are flirting with the intellectuals at the moment, while the Continental pot is coming slowly to the boil. But any attempt to have a rational argument with Harry is a waste of time – he goes by the book rather in the manner of a sergeant major who has displaced his brains by too much foot stamping. Not a pleasant little man. eaten up with class hatred and determined to impose his will on anybody he senses has any intellectual advantage. He cannot understand that whereas I am attracted to the concept in its purest form, I have no illusions about the basic squalid nature of the human race. People *en masse* are repellent. He is concerned with abstracts. I am fascinated by realities.

Perrins Walk
Friday

When pressed, Tony revealed that his evening with Diana ended abruptly and unconsummated. He was non-committal about his feelings towards her. I have turned over a new leaf, no longer seeking endless social diversions and have cancelled all future engagements. I have been putting in six or seven hours a day at the new novel and now feel that I have it by the throat. It will be my most ambitious book to date, a hideously complicated plot which I am struggling to simplify. Like James I am drawn to 'the wasting of life', with passions that might have been. Two people groping for each other in the darkness. The idea of love that is formed too late. It's all there in my head, but needs digging for.

Perrins Walk
Friday

The idea that my every movement is being watched is both fascinating and alarming. I may have misjudged their application, which since it is basically small-time civil service in essence, hideously concerned with ephemera – the kind of details that the average person forgets in a day – is that much more dangerous. I was contacted yesterday and ordered to make certain social excursions, thus negating all my good resolutions. Knowing of my friendship with Diana, they want me to cultivate some of her political friends. In particular Mosley. He is going to dinner with her next week and my brief is to get myself invited. This is bound to irritate Diana since, being a single man, I always present a seating problem. She has a fetish about odd numbers.

Saturday

Finally got Diana to come to the telephone and flattered her into an invitation. She says that I will have to escort old Lady Howarth to make up the numbers. Better than I could have hoped for, since she is stone deaf, dotty but pleasant with it. Always has some scandal to impart, which will come in useful for the new novel since I am short on incident. I can't imagine that such an occasion will yield much for the cause, but they are convinced that we must infiltrate at all levels.

Perrins Walk
Thursday

There was no danger, not the slightest chance of being suspected, and yet I found the experience of sitting at Diana's dinner table last night very frightening. At one point old Lady Howarth asked me whether I was feeling all right. Since she is deaf she tends to shout her questions and the whole table stopped talking. I hastily explained that I found the room somewhat hot and her conversation too stimulating, turning the whole thing into a vague joke. Fortunately Diana agreed with me, blaming the temperature on Anton's compulsion to have the heat at tropical level.

Mosley I found fascinating, a brilliant speaker, with all his facts at his fingertips and very persuasive. He is much better looking in the flesh, a somewhat dashing figure, reminding me of Douglas Fairbanks. He was at his best when describing his vision of the next few years. His convictions seemed to carry weight and were listened to with respect around the table. I sat across from Harold Nicolson who was most complimentary about my last novel.

I enjoyed myself on an intellectual plane because it is the first time I have ever been exposed to political talk on this level, face to face with people who actually have the power to change our lives. But at the same time the inner feeling, the knowledge that, however circumspect, I am actively committed at last, gave me butterflies. If this sort of social occasion can bring such a reaction, I wonder how I will react when put to stronger tests? Forget nothing, I was told. We will decide what is important, not you. Deception gives a curious feeling of superiority – I hadn't realised that before.

Perrins Walk
Sunday

I went to church today for the first time in years. Why? I wonder. The mumbo-jumbo still nauseates me, and I totally reject the idea of Christ as a divine. I can embrace the conception of a unique man totally possessed, but then belief comes to a full stop. Perhaps the petulance and spite of the Old Testament arrested my faith during Sunday School days. I was terrified of those stories, with their endless wrath and wailing and gnashing of teeth, the smiting and the ritual murders – they gave me nightmares, I remember. I would try and creep into Mother's and Father's bed, only he would never have it. I suspend judgment on anybody who set themselves up as God. So why today's return to the fold? Am I testing myself? Religion always wears my father's face. I saw him today in the pulpit.

Wednesday

They appear satisfied with my report. I used the opportunity to make another enquiry about J., but drew the usual blank. They are playing cat and mouse with me. The time is not yet ripe to take a stand. I must choose that moment carefully, and at a higher level than Harry. I am convinced that he is very much the office boy. He takes a sadistic pleasure in reminding me how much damage the photographs could do. Retold last week's Old Bailey trial of the stockbroker and the guardsmen with great relish, insisting that they had a hand in the exposure and that this is only the tip of the iceberg. I suspect he is lying and that the boast has no real substance, but one can't be sure.

I have picked up the threads of the novel once again, but feel that I have made a mistake in cutting myself off from all socialising. I have been very good lately, yet like Proust I need to seek contacts – the vanity that comes from being admired fires my creative energies in the same way that sex provokes a surge. A curious paradox this, that a roll in the gutter and the stimulation of intellectual conversation produce the same results.

The arrangement with Tony still holding together. I find it amusing to think that he sits downstairs manipulating his fictional spies, blissfully ignorant that the real-life counterpart uses the same bath. I sometimes have to make a concentrated effort not to spill the beans, the urge to shock him is so strong.

14

LOOKING BACK ON the novels I wrote during the years 1935-1939, I am astounded at the contradictions that leap from my pages. There I was churning out thrillers which dealt with the assassination of mid-European dictators, civil wars and international spy rings, consolidating my reputation as an author who anticipated history, and yet the full implication of what was happening in the world never seemed to penetrate. I am not only think of Theo – he was a separate issue – I am referring to my share of the collective myopia. I saw the newsreels, had all the right feelings about Abyssinia, applauded Eden, was shocked by Guernica, admired Hemingway, laughed at Mussolini, read Geoffrey Dawson's pontifications on disarmament, rearmament, pacificsm, public morality and the rest, listened to Baldwin's 'appallingly frank' speeches, was disturbed by Mosley's excursions into the East End, joined the Left Book Club for a period, allowed Churchill my qualified admiration, welcomed Einstein in our midst, found Hitler grotesquely fascinating, Goering merely grotesque, was fanatical about Len Hutton, attempted to read *Mathematics for the Million*, felt comforted by the proliferation of Odeon cinemas, adored Our Gracie and *Quiet Weekend*, fell in love with Jane Baxter in *George and Margaret*, sent flowers to Kay Hammond in *French Without Tears* – in fact behaved like any other young man about town who should have known better, analysed more deeply, cared more passionately, wasted less time.

My books began to sell, the third novel going into several editions. I bought some hideously uncomfortable modern furniture for my part of the house, had a small Augustus John on my wall, acquired the beginnings of a library, ordered my suits from Sackville Street and had my hair cut at Trumpers. I joined the Garrick and the Savile, smoked Balkan Sobranie cigarettes, paid income tax for the first time in my life and spent the rest.

The house in Perrins Walk seemed to bring both of us luck. Theo was equally prolific and wrote with apparently effortless grace, reaching a different audience than mine; smaller, more selective, less middle-brow. Critics now spoke of his 'matchless virtuosity', he was applauded for his 'strange, haunting fermentations from the past'. ("They'll put me down like port," he said.) And we were told that 'Of all the writers of the younger generation, it is Gittings who arouses our boldest hopes.' It would be wrong to suggest that all this acclaim went to his head. He enjoyed his success, but was not unduly impressed by it. Whereas I was interviewed by the Beaverbrook Press, his views of the literary scene were solicited by rather more august publications.

It was about this time that he became noticeably pro-German and we had several non-conclusive arguments about the purity of German youth. This appeared to be his main attraction to the emerging Nazi ideal. He inclined, like so many of us, to dismiss as mere propaganda the increasing number of disturbing reports of German militancy, since it was generally agreed that the Treaty of Versailles had been self-defeating in its punitive clauses. The French, with their constant changes of government, seemed the more suspect, unreliable, a nation without backbone and arrogant to boot. There was a curious undercurrent of sympathy for the Germans, perhaps because they had cast themselves in the role of the underdog, always an irresistible challenge to political punters.

"I thought of joining the Anglo–German Fellowship," Theo said one morning.

"Why?"

"Why? Well, for one thing I like to repay a debt, and my German publishers are quite the nicest people I have to deal with. So generous with their advances. And secondly I think we ought to do something to counteract all this anti-German hysteria."

"Well, which is it, money or conscience?"

"You know me too well. Mostly money. But I do think that

186

everybody is going lulu at the moment. A lot of scrubby little Reds rushing about stoking up the hate. Anyway, I'm told the Fellowship holds very good dinners."

A few weeks later he asked me if I would like to be his guest at one such dinner.

"You joined, then?"

"Yes. I think it's worth while."

It was a formal, black tie affair at the Savoy and the guest list was formidable. I confess I was impressed, especially as the first person I was introduced to proved to be a fan: there is nothing like flattery to appease a conscience.

"Well, look who's here!" Theo said.

He raised an arm to somebody in the distance. I turned and saw Kim Philby sauntering towards us.

"You remember Tony?"

He stared at me while struggling to make his lips form the right words, finally managing to say that he remembered me very well, his stammer seeming, if anything, more pronounced than I remembered.

"What are you up to these days?"

"I've been doing a little journalism, so called, nothing very spectacular and now I've been asked to edit the Fellowship magazine. I constantly read about your success." He turned to include me. "And yours, of course. Seems a long time since Sundays on the river."

"Who's the guest of honour tonight? I did know, but I've forgotten."

"It's on the invitation," Philby said. "The Kaiser's daughter, the Duchess of Brunswick."

"Just as well we didn't hang him, then. Might have cast a gloom on the evening. It's quite a turn-out."

"Have you seen Guy recently?"

"Not recently, no. He rang me some time ago and said he was off to Berlin for the Olympics. He's probably still there. After all, it must be his idea of wish-fulfilment."

We were separated after that and took our places for dinner. I found myself seated opposite Diana Steel. After our previous encounter I fully expected her to ignore me, but she seemed to have forgotten, or perhaps forgiven, my refusal to get to know her better. There was no sign of her husband.

The food was excellent, the speeches predictably boring, though I remarked that most of the guests received them as tablets handed down from the mountain. I got a spurious pleasure from being amongst the famous and near-famous, since I was still of an age when titles impressed.

When the dinner broke up we found an angry demonstration had formed outside the riverside exit, and the guests were jostled by a mixed bag of Jews and communists as they made their way to the waiting cars. Although the police were in evidence, and some arrests made, there were a few ugly moments. Theo and I got separated in the crush and I found myself pushed against Diana Steel.

"Have you got transport?" she said.

"No, we were going to get a taxi."

"Well, you won't get one now. Come and share with me."

I hesitated, but she took my arm firmly and we elbowed our way to the outskirts of the crowd and spotted Diana's chauffeur who had sensibly parked on the Embankment. As we drove away more police reinforcements were arriving.

"Such excitement," Diana said. "I must say it makes some of the speeches very apt. Bloody Reds. I hope the police wade in. I'm all for that."

"I didn't see Theo, did you?"

"No, I didn't. Are you worried about him? I wouldn't be, he can take care of himself. I must say I never expected to see you here tonight."

"I'm not a member," I said. "I came as Theo's guest."

"Do I detect a note of disapproval?"

"No, not really. I'm neutral."

"You can't afford to be neutral these days. Surely you were impressed with the speeches?"

"The faces change, but the actual words seem remarkably similar."

"I disagree."

"Are we going to have another row?"

"Another one?"

"Well, I got the impression that out last meeting wasn't exactly cause for celebration."

"Really? I can't honestly remember."

"Oh, dear. And there was I thinking I had made a memorable impression with my Fred Astaire impersonation. I can actually get through a fox-trot now without crippling my partner."

"I thought you were very young, that's all. I've read your novels, by the way."

"I'm flattered. Did you enjoy them?"

"Oh, I enjoy most things. I read everything that comes out. Mostly in bed. It's my only bedtime activity these days."

"How is your husband?"

"You're right on cue, aren't you? He's well. Boring, but well."

I glanced to see if the glass division of the Rolls was closed.

"Why do you stay married to him, then?"

"Because it suits me."

The chauffeur slid the glass partition open. "Where to, madam?"

Diana turned to me. "Where would I like to go?"

"I've no idea."

"Didn't you want to show me where you and Theo hibernate?"

"Yes, if you like."

"Could we have a little more enthusiasm?"

"It's not up to your standard," I said. "But you're very welcome to take pot luck."

I gave the chauffeur the instructions and we headed for Swiss Cottage.

"What I like about the Germans," Diana said, "is they're positive. We're such a nation of drifters. I'm also mad about the uniforms. They're so theatrical. I mean, what have we got? Boring old Lloyd George."

"I thought he approved of Hitler?"

"Doesn't make him any less of a bore."

"You seem to find most men boring."

"Well, you are. You have very few uses."

"You charm them into your bed, I take it?"

"Am I going to charm you?"

"Well, not into your bed," I said. "On the other hand,

189

providing I'm not too boring, I might let you charm me into mine. It's rather narrow, like my mind."

"You haven't forgiven me, have you?"

"Yes, I think so. You were very aggressive."

"That put you off?"

"I like my women to be pliable."

"What a ghastly word."

"Soft, then. Look," I said, "I may as well ask you once more, because I'm not an experienced adulterer. What is the position between you and your husband?"

"Darling, you do harp on it, don't you? Does he know, is that what you're asking? Yes, I think so He doesn't know names, nor do I give them. I mean, you won't suddenly be hauled through the courts, if that's what you mean. You aren't rich enough for me."

"Fine," I said. "At least I know where I stand."

The Rolls was too large to manoeuvre into the narrow entrance to Perrins Walk.

"Kenton, why don't you drop us here and come back later."

"Any specific time, madam?"

He avoided looking at me, and there was a certain intimate insolence in his manner. One day, I thought, you're going to have trouble with Kenton.

"Oh, three hours," Diana said carelessly.

There were no lights on, indicating that Theo had not yet returned.

"Do you think he's all right?"

"Yes, I'm sure. He met an old friend at the dinner, from his Cambridge days. Well, this is it," I said, turning on the lights in my study. "Not what you're used to, I'm afraid, but as the saying goes, it's home."

"How d'you know what I'm used to?"

She flung her coat down with that lack of concern that often distinguishes the haves from the have-nots. "I take it there is a bedroom?"

"Oh, yes, all mod. cons."

"I was never a great one for sofas."

I poured us both a drink.

"Did you really enjoy this evening?" I said.

"I met you again, didn't I?"

"Well, that may not prove a blessing. Seriously did you?"

"Yes, those sort of functions amuse me. You obviously didn't."

"I don't know enough about them. It seemed a strange sort of evening, really. Gave me an uneasy feeling."

"But we're closer to the Germans than any of the others. After all the royal family is related. You have to prefer them to the French."

"I don't know the French. Or the Germans for that matter. I've never travelled, you see."

"Well, we must remedy that. I'll take you with me next time I go."

"My only impression of Paris is Orwell's."

"Oh, I couldn't read it. Who wants to know what goes on in kitchens? I've never set foot in my kitchen, and I certainly don't want to set foot in anybody else's."

"If you like Germany and the Germans so much, why don't you go there?"

"I've been, several times. One goes to Paris for the clothes and the food. One goes to Germany for something else."

"What's that?"

"Sex. Decadence."

"Sex is very important to you, obviously."

"Why obviously?"

"You talk about it all the time."

"It's the first time I've mentioned it."

"By name, yes."

"Oh, darling, I love that little boy look. I bet I can guess about you. You think a lot about it, but you don't do it often. Had maybe a couple of affairs, not very happy and think that it should all be romantic. Yes? Am I close?"

"You're a bitch, aren't you?" I said.

"Yes, darling. I don't want romancing. You don't have to make any effort in that direction. No ties either side. I can't bear being anybody's private possession."

"That's not so unique. I've been through all that."

"Oh, was that your little Nippy? Theo told me about her."

"Did he? That was loyal of him. Then he probably told you she was much younger than you, or perhaps he left that bit out."

"We're wasting an awful lot of time, you know. Why don't you show me the rest of this mansion. Take me into the west wing."

"I might have changed my mind."

"I don't think so."

She stood up and kissed me full on the lips. We went into the bedroom.

"Oh, it's like a *wagon-lit*," Diana said. "I love having it in sleeping cars. We'll take the night train to Paris when we go. Undress me. You can tear the dress if you like. Tear it, go on, be impatient, pretend you can't wait, pretend we've just met."

I tried to follow her instructions, but she had judged me correctly, I was too romantic to enjoy her playacting and in the end, impatient with me, she ripped her own clothes. I found her behaviour slightly ludicrous and became icy cold, detached, looking at her naked body writhing about on my single bed with the eyes of a voyeur rather than a lover. She fascinated me because I had never come across a woman like her. I was excited by her, since she knew how to excite. Part of me was repelled by her, and that too is a form of excitement that we may not always wish to acknowledge. Diana had needs that were alien to me, and the fact that I was able to satisfy them did not signify that I shared them. During our spasmodic affair I came to use her in the same way as, in the beginning, she so obviously used me. I have no illusions that I was ever her only lover. After that first night we spent together (the unfortunate Kenton had a longer wait than three hours) we met whenever the mood took her. It is not so difficult to accommodate lust when one is young.

I can see now how nearly I was drawn into the net. Had it not been for my sexual romanticism I might have followed a parallel route to Theo, for the seduction of the gullible is more easily accomplished in bed than in the classroom, and Diana was a persuasive teacher. It was such a patient process where Theo, Philby and the rest were concerned. They were told it didn't matter how long it took to penetrate British

Intelligence, and in a way outside events smoothed their paths. The inexorable progress towards a second world war provided the necessary self-justifications as well as the necessary cover. There were complimentary tickets to be had for the dress-rehearsal in Spain, a chance to see if all the war toys worked when wound up. It was a time when heroism could wear many disguises. The real nature of the struggle was obscured by the propagandists of both sides, for the age of compromise was upon us.

When Theo announced that he was going as a freelance journalist accredited to Reuters to cover the Spanish civil war, I greeted the surprise statement with awe rather than suspicion. Again he had been provided with an external alibi which I accepted without question. Some time earlier he had shown me an item in the Personal columns of *The Times* with a fine display of disgust.

"God, how sickening!"

"What's that?" I said.

"The aged bloody father. He's marrying that teenage, so-called 'housekeeper'. Fucking old hypocrite."

"Well, what does it matter? You don't see him any more."

But even I had to share his disgust when Gittings actually had the lack of taste to send us both a wedding invitation.

As the date for the wedding approached he suddenly mentioned his plans for going to Spain.

"Get out of the country altogether," he said. "That's what I want to do. Do you think it's a good idea?"

"Well, yes, but not for that reason alone, surely?"

"No, it was just coincidence, but it's come at the right time. I want to go anyway. And I can make him squirm a little, because I shall write and tell him that I intend to put some distance between us."

"How long will you go for?"

"I don't know. It's a fairly loose arrangement, and everybody thinks it'll be over very quickly. I happened to be having lunch with my publisher and he mentioned he'd been asked to suggest an impartial observer, and could he put my name forward. Apparently they jumped at the idea."

"Well, it's certainly a new departure for you."

"Yes. I thought that. I'm a bit bogged down with the new novel and this thing has unsettled me so much, I thought I'd give it a whirl."

"How do those things work?"

"What d'you mean?"

"Do you rove around? I mean are you accredited to one side, or both, or what?"

"I shall be with Franco's lot," he said. Perhaps he felt it necessary to explain the choice in more mundane terms. "You know me, I'm not one of Nature's heroes. According to Diana that's going to be the winning side." He smiled. "Lacking any strong convictions of my own, I thought I'd take the safest bet."

Despite his self-denigration, there was an element of heroism in his decision which I applauded. The role of foreign correspondent had long been one of my fantasies, and I certainly did not suspect him of any sinister ulterior motive in selecting to report on the Franco campaign. The whole Spanish civil war seemed to me a strange mixture of good and evil on both sides, the issues being far too complex to be judged in black and white terms.

Theo departed without fanfare. He showed me the letter he had finally written to his father and I was relieved that he had omitted most of the actionable abuse. He promised to write to me, but it was a promise he did not keep. I certainly had no idea of his experiences in Spain until the journals came to light, and reading them I can see why.

Salamanca
March 15, 1937

The most surprising thing about this war is the politeness. Everybody I have met so far is full of old-world courtesy – doubtless a characteristic of the Spanish race which strikes a new-comer more forcibly than the old hands, but I had a preconceived notion of conflict which has been knocked sideways. Not that I have seen any fighting so far; only the distant rumble of guns and ambulances bringing back wounded from the front lines. I must

194

learn a whole new vocabulary. War creates new words, new ways of describing old horrors, and most of my fellow correspondents speak the language with irritating superiority. They also seem to treat the whole thing as a gigantic binge interrupted by bouts at the typewriter when they file their stories. I haven't got the hang of it yet.

I am living in a semi-derelict hotel with half a dozen others. The service is primitive and the food strangely unappetising to my taste, though I am beginning to live with it. Spent most of the first week on the toilet, which gave me plenty of time to think about what lies ahead.

Although official sources give us daily bulletins, I gather the form is to ignore these unless one is desperate. Most of the hardened journalists rely on rumours – either rumours they exchange in the bars, or else those they invent and circulate. The actual war itself is so totally confused at the moment, and it is surprising how many of the rumours eventually become true in the end. I suppose a war of this kind, where – excepting the foreigners who have joined in – Spaniard is killing Spaniard is the purest form of conflict. Like a family who systematically set about destroying each other. It would be unacceptable to write this for public consumption, but in a way civil war is more excusable than one where you fight total strangers.

The natives are not only polite, but extremely friendly. I don't know who first pronounced Latins are lousy lovers (are Spaniards Latins?) but they couldn't have done any extensive homework on the subject. No field trials, as it were. I have already experienced a variation of death in the afternoon, though far from the bullring.

Because most of the big names are reporting the other side, we are treated very well indeed. It is a far cry from Perrins Walk, and I have been mildly surprised at my ability to adapt to the changed circumstances. I am still not entirely clear exactly what is required of me, but have been told to be patient. Contact will be made when they are ready, and more explicit instructions issued. They are thorough, very cautious indeed. I live in expectation.

Salamanca
April 28, 1937

I feel like a criminal. Today I looted a single book from a ruined house. I must be curiously unfitted for such everyday tasks, since nobody else pays any attention, but I found myself shaking as I walked away. Having stolen it, I felt compelled to read it. It was a book of French aphorisms; odd to find it here – bygone culture stained with brick dust, fond memories of a world that will never come again. Much taken with a saying of Bjion's that I had never come across before: "Although small boys kill frogs in sport, yet the frogs do not die in sport, but in earnest" I will now add to that with a pompous on-the-spot observation – I can state with the utmost authority that there is very little difference between a dead communist and a dead fascist. They both died not in sport, but in earnest.

Of course Guernica is the only thing being talked about at the present time. Opinions sharply divided. The official line is that the town was blown up by Basque communists as a propaganda exercise, though it seems fairly obvious that this is not a version that will be swallowed by many. Unofficially there is great satisfaction that the Germans have at last flexed their muscles in no uncertain fashion. I have filed a factual dispatch, including both stories and leaving the reader to form his own opinion as to the truth. I doubt whether it will be printed intact, but there it is.

Contact was made last week. The sheer cynicism of the operation takes one's breath away, but I listened and was finally convinced of the long-term strategy. I appreciate that initial sacrifices have to be made here in order to prepare for the inevitable. I am given to understand that this is already regarded as a lost cause, to be kept alive for the sake of appearances only. The lethal rain in Spain is to be endured only to test the umbrellas. My present job is to establish a subtle leaning towards the Right which, I am assured, will stand me in good stead in times to come. I was warned about being too brash and complimented on progress made. My informant also gave me news of Kim who is out here too. We haven't bumped into each other and I was advised not to attempt to make contact. This proved difficult, because the moment my German departed I walked into the bar here to find Kim with his mistress propping up the counter. He gave himself airs, as befits a correspondent for the London *Times*. Perhaps the surprise of seeing me accentuated his stutter, but at times he was almost incoherent, waving his hands in the air as though trying to clutch the words and cram them into his mouth. The lady I found somewhat tiresome. When he got his words together K. was vehement on the subject of world communism as the real threat to civilisation. He convinced me, though I dare say he was putting on a show for the benefit of the others in the crowded bar. Some of his stuff didn't go down too well, but he appeared not to notice. He is much more adept than I shall ever be.

I don't know how to put my present thoughts down on paper, yet I must make the effort, otherwise I shall go mad. I think perhaps I am slightly mad already. In the past two hours I have drunk a whole bottle of Scotch, for which I paid through the nose, and it hasn't had the slightest effect. I wish to God it had, for then I might be spared these nightmare images. I went to the hospital today intending to file a story on the wounded, since London has asked for more personal stories. I was shown around the wards and, using an interpreter, got some useful human interest stuff. The suffering of the wounded takes a stronger stomach than mine – I had no idea how obscene gaping wounds can be, and I am amazed that the human body can be blown half to pieces and yet deny the soul release.

Just as I was preparing to leave, a new batch was brought in from the front. The journey had been a long one and many of them were dead on arrival. I stood as the stretchers were passing close enought to touch and blood dripped over my shoes on more than one occasion. I have never seen anything like it and never want to again. Most of the wards are full and as more and more ambulances arrived they were forced to put the bodies down in the corridors. I had to step over them in order to get out and as I reached the last stretcher, which was half in and half out of the building, I had a sudden premonition of my own death. I looked down at this last stretcher – the shattered head of the young man lying on it was turned away from me and pressed close to the wall. The body was partially covered with a piece of blanket and from the twisted outline it was obvious that there wasn't much left below the trunk. I don't know why, but I felt compelled to bend and look at the face. I think I knew what I was going to see, but I could not stop myself. It was J. Half of the jaw had been shot away, that beautiful mouth I kissed was like something seen on a butcher's slab, the flesh whitened, the gums exposed, only his top teeth showing. The shock was so terrifying I actually fell across the body and his blood stained my clothes. My interpreter helped my up and I was led outside to vomit.

I hardly know what I am writing, I can't get that last image out of my mind, or what remains of my mind. I wish I could die myself, drink and drink until a black curtain of nothingness descends, but I am stone cold sober and nothing comes between that poor lovely face. I wish to God I could pray, or smash this room, or had the courage to end it all, anything but this agony, anything.

15

M Y OWN LIFE was not coloured by such momentous
events. While Theo went to Spain, I went to Denham.
Out of the blue I was suddenly summoned to meet
Sir Alexander Korda, that flamboyant messiah of the
emerging British film industry who brought his Hungarian
panache, two brothers and considerable charm to bear upon
the confused scene. One of his acolytes telephoned me to say
that Alex had read my novels and would like to discuss the
possibility of me writing a film script for him. I knew nothing
whatsoever of the intricacies of film-making, but could not
resist the flattery. I duly presented myself outside his office in
Denham Studios.

In those days Denham was an oasis of concrete in the unspoilt countryside of Buckinghamshire, situated close to a
picture-postcard village where many of the stars took up
temporary residence. I was greeted by an attractive secretary,
given coffee and asked if I wouldn't mind waiting, as Alex had
been forced to take a meeting with a group of City financiers.
The explanation was hardly necessary as I could, without
straining, overhear the shouting match coming from the inner
sanctum. It sounded as though the participants would shortly
come to blows, and I was impressed that the secretary and
others bustling in and out of the office paid no attention. It
was quite obviously a commonplace happening. I drank my
coffee and leafed through some film trade papers. I thought,
what have I let myself in for? The row in Korda's office
continued unabated, rising now to a new crescendo. Then a
lull and the buzzer sounded on the secretary's desk. She
picked up the intercom phone and listened briefly. Then she
took in an unopened box of Havana cigars. As the door to
Korda's office was opened I glimpsed the great man pacing,
and in front of him a group of City gents, nattily attired in the

standard bankers' uniform. The door closed again.

Left to myself I studied the photographs on the walls. Here were many of the screen greats smiling down, the women heavily re-touched, their mouths outlined like the slots in pillar-boxes, the men looking like the famous Brylcream advertisements. All were signed with messages of undying affection for Korda.

"Is it still going on?" a voice said.

I looked round to find a somewhat wild young man in baggy trousers and moth-eaten sweater.

"You mean in there? Yes, I think so."

"Oh, Christ! Well, look, as soon as you can, try and get word to Alex that Carol wants him on Stage Four. Betty's refusing to shoot that additional scene. She says the dialogue is fucking awful. Tell him, will you?"

"Er, yes, if I can."

"Well, it's absolutely vital. I mean, we can't shoot."

"Betty?" I said.

"Yes. The stupid cow, she should be grateful she's even in work. But she's already phoned her poncey little agent, so the shit is flying."

"Right. Well, I'll do my best."

"Thanks," he said and left.

The row had died down in Korda's office and much to my surprise I heard the pop of a champagne cork and afterwards laughter. I waited for another twenty minutes, during which time the frantic young man returned.

"Any luck?"

"Not yet."

"Oh, well. There's been a new development. She's taken all her clothes off and gone to her dressing room. Alex is the only person who can do any good now."

He seemed much more cheerful than before.

"You're not the bloke from the insurance company, are you?"

"No."

"Oh, thank Christ for that. Just occurred to me, you might have been. I'm not supposed to talk to him, you see."

He disappeared again, having helped himself to some

cigarettes from a packet on the secretary's desk. Finally the meeting came to an end, and the deputation was ushered out by Korda. They all seemed in a remarkably good mood, several of them were smoking the cigars and there were handshakes and smiles all round. When they had been shown to the door, Korda turned to me.

"My dear Mr. Stern, please forgive me for keeping you waiting, but I had to deal with a certain urgent situation. Such a bore, but there it is, these things are sent to try us. Please come in. Would you like some champagne? Darling, open another bottle."

His secretary did the honours.

"They were bankers, as you could see. Lovely people, but no comprehension of what we creative people have to live with. I mean, they should feel privileged to lend me their money, don't you think?"

"Yes," I said.

"Of course. But one always has to start from the very beginning every time. See, they don't understand how we have to spend the money. They don't appreciate that one isn't making pots and pans. They think everything is a balance sheet. Films aren't balance sheets."

"I suppose they only think in one way."

"Well, it happens to be the wrong way, dear Mr. Stern. Is that cold enough? Warm champagne is hideous."

"I have a message for you," I said, as soon as I could get a word in. "About Betty. On Stage Four."

"Such a talented artist. You know her?"

"Er, no. It was just that this young man came by while you were engaged and asked me to relate an urgent message about her. She's apparently refusing to say the lines, shoot the scene or something, and has taken all her clothes off."

"She does that every day. Such an exhibitionist. And she really should keep her clothes on, because what is revealed is not, shall we say, God's gift to the British film industry. Her face is her fortune. How long ago was this?"

"About twenty minutes, at least."

"My dear, excuse me again." He turned to his secretary. "Get me Carol on Stage Four."

I had time to admire the paintings on his walls while the secretary dialled. They were very impressive even to my inexpert eye. The whole office reeked of affluent good taste.

"Carol, dear, I understand we have another little problem? . . . Yes, so tiresome. Is she still there? . . . And there's nothing else you can shoot round her? No, good, you did the right thing. I'll come over."

He turned to me. "Mr. Stern, how can you ever forgive me for such bad manners? Unfortunately the situation requires my presence. Listen, my dear, it's quite simple. You are a great writer. I'd like you to write for me. Have you an agent?"

"No."

"Oh, that's good. They always make problems between creative people. Don't worry, we'll send you a contract, and you write for me. It's all very pleasant; you join the family and we make lovely films together. So kind of you to come. Next time we have a real talk."

He shook my hand and wandered out. I swallowed some more of his vintage champagne.

"What did all that mean?" I asked the secretary.

"It means you're hired. We'll send you a contract."

"Just like that?"

"Yes, Alex never wastes words. He liked you."

"But what am I supposed to do when I get the contract?"

"Well, if you've got any sense you'll sign it."

"I meant, after that."

"Then you'll write us a script."

"Any script?"

"It depends. Alex gets an idea and he just follows his nose. You'll love working for him."

"Is it always like this?"

"Always."

"Well," I said. "It's been a pleasure, as they say. I hope I see you again."

"I'm sure you will, Mr. Stern. Alex never breaks his word where artistic people are concerned. Do you smoke cigars?"

"Not those," I said, "but I'm willing to learn."

I took one. I never smoked it. It remained on my desk for the best part of two years until it dried and flaked away to dust, like so much of the film industry.

In due course a fat contract arrived through the post. I read it carefully, but was unable to understand more than a few paragraphs. It appeared that London Films Ltd, would own all my vital organs for a period of twelve months, during which time I might be required to write an original film script of not less than eighty pages, three copies of which had to be delivered in bound form, and for which I would receive the amazing sum of two thousand pounds, payable in fifty-two equal instalments. There were options to retain me in this elegant slavery for a further two years at the discretion of the said London Films Ltd. I didn't hesitate. I signed it before anybody had second thoughts. Then I heard nothing. Three weeks went by and, amazingly, the cheques started to arrive. Still I heard nothing. Having deposited the first two cheques, I rang Korda's office. He was abroad, I was told.

"What d'you think I should do, then?"

"About what, Mr. Stern?"

"Shouldn't I start writing something?"

"Oh, you've got an idea, have you? Alex will be pleased."

"No. I'm not quite sure what he would like. I mean, is there any particular sort of story he's looking for?"

"Not really."

I got the distinct impression that she found my questions amusing.

"Well, I hate to take money under false pretences."

"Oh, nobody would think that of you, Mr. Stern. We don't work like that."

"When will he be back, d'you think?"

"His plans are a little vague at the moment, but as soon as I have any news I'll let you know. Don't worry, Mr. Stern."

I put the phone down and stared at the latest cheque. It was the beginning of a lifelong romance with the idiocies of the film industry.

In the midst of all this I finally heard from Theo. A postcard arrived, stamped in Berlin. It gave only the briefest of details. He had left Spain and was researching a new book. I was to expect him when he arrived. He was well and hoped I was, too. It was the sort of duty postcard one writes on holiday and then forgets to mail, so that it arrives after one has returned home.

Korda was back in England and I had a further audience with him, only slightly less baffling than the first. He hoped I could come up with an original idea that might serve as a star vehicle for Robert Donat. Arrangements were made for me to have dinner with Donat, but I was denied that pleasure, since Donat was an asthma sufferer and had to cancel at the last moment. I set to work with enormous enthusiasm and the vaguest of guidelines, because in those days I was embarrassed to take money under false pretences.

I continued to see Diana at odd intervals and although the relationship left much to be desired, she did pump the sexual adrenalin along my veins – a necessary relief from my daily stints at the typewriter. She was as good as her word, though, and took me to Paris, a trip I justified as being useful for my work. I found that I behaved like any other tourist set loose in that enchanted city for the first time and was immediately enslaved, reviling myself for what I had missed.

I suppose it was a time when we wanted to cling to some form of permanence, for the clock was moving towards Munich. Looking back, I can see a bitter irony in our activities: there was I bent over a typewriter inventing a spy plot for Korda's celluloid dream factory and there was Theo in Berlin already leading the double-life he sustained to the end of his days. Word filtered through that he was being fêted by the Nazi hierarchy since he was one of the few literary figures of any consequence who seemed sympathetic towards the German problem. He was careful not to burn his boats in every direction, and unlike the Duchess of Roxburghe did not go so far as to suggest that the peace of Europe could be stabilised if only Goering were invited to England for the grouse season, but he allowed his name to be associated with a plea for closer understanding between the two countries. He had asked me to deal with his mail during his absence and I opened several abusive letters from friends as well as strangers who were appalled by his behaviour. I confess that as time went by I became more and more perplexed by his apparent disregard for the changing climate of opinion.

At home we were just beginning to come to terms with the gilded amateurism of Chamberlain as he pushed everybody's darling from the centre of the stage and assumed the star role for himself. The soon-to-be-familiar initials of A.R.P. entered our lives and the spectre of war, far from being a foreigner's distant game, became almost overnight a familiar in our midst.

Autumn in Paris notwithstanding, there was something basically squalid about Diana, and our relationship came to an end the night she took me to hear Mosley speak.

"He's divine," she said. "The only man who makes any sense at all."

What I witnessed that evening depressed me unutterably. We left her Rolls a few streets away from the location of the meeting, and despite my increasing misgivings joined the throng milling around on the Whitechapel pavements. There was a good turn-out on both sides: hand-picked bully boys sporting black shirts, and an equal number of the Jewish Brigade, while in the side streets the mounted police waited with staves drawn. It was quite obvious that the evening had to end in a near riot and I tried to dissuade her from going any further.

"There's going to be a fight. You know that, don't you?"

"But that's half the fun."

"How can you call it fun?"

"Oh, don't be so dreary. Go home if you're scared. I can take care of myself."

I should have accepted the offer – there was never any need to act the gentleman with Diana, and I was scared. Perhaps I was more scared of showing I was scared, and I stayed. Predictably, the moment Mosley started to speak the bottles started flying and there was soon a pitched battle taking place in front of the platform. The police moved in on cue, the crowd breaking into chunks as the horses appeared and we were lucky not to be crushed against the boarded shop windows.

"Satisfied?" I shouted. "Now come on, for God's sake,

while we're still in one piece." I dragged her to safety in a side street and we made a circular detour back to the parked Rolls.

"You bloody wet," she said, as soon as we were inside the car. "What are you, a Jew lover?"

I didn't answer her.

"I wonder you're not circumcised, go the whole hog, you boring little fart."

"One thing I shall always remember about you, Diana, is your amazing command of language. Now, do you mind if I get out?" I rapped on the glass partition. "Let me out here." The chauffeur pulled over to the kerb and stopped the car.

"Yes, get out and piss off. You'll feel at home here, this is Yid country."

I have always wished I could carry off such scenes with dignity, have some brilliantly witty and cutting remark to hand, but somehow it never happens. I just walked away quickly as the Rolls continued towards the City. I never saw Diana again.

That evening made me more conscious of the growing crisis and the fact that we were patently all living on borrowed time. I attended some Civil Defence lectures given in Hampstead, a futile gesture since it was fairly obvious that when the war came I was the perfect age for cannon fodder and hardly likely to be classified in a reserved occupation. But it was better than doing nothing.

There was an element of farce about those early days of Civil Defence. The class barriers hadn't yet fallen, and the strangers who gathered together in drill halls all over the country were linked by a potent mixture of patriotism and fear. I think we were all convinced that within hours of any declaration of war the whole of England would be blanketed by a cloud of mustard gas – for some reason death by gas topped the horror poll; it was as if everybody chose to forget that death from a bullet or high explosive bomb is equally final. The farcical aspect was supplied by our well-meaning and dedicated instructors, for many of them treated the subject as something akin to religious knowledge. Lacking any practical experience themselves, reading from government pamphlets which in retrospect often resembled Dead

Sea Scrolls, they were often the blind leading the blind. I remember with particular pleasure the lecture on fire drill. Our instructor found it almost impossible to get past the procedure of how to couple the hose to the pump without his own face becoming a conflagration of embarrassment. "One takes the, er, how shall I put it, male element and, er, in accordance with standard practice, er, inserts it into the, er, well the, er, female counterpart." This invariably earned him a round of applause and was eagerly awaited by the old hands.

There was no general exuberance such as my father had described to me when recounting the outbreak of the 1914 war, but in contrast the general mood seemed to me to be one of grim resignation.

On my third visit to the course of lectures I noticed a particularly attractive girl of my own age sitting by herself against the lukewarm radiators that barely took the chill off that draughty Hampstead schoolroom. With that casual air that most men assume when they are on the make, I took the vacant chair next to her.

"First time?" I asked.

She nodded.

"All sounds fairly horrific, doesn't it?"

"Horrible. Do you think it'll happen?"

"Well, the way things are going."

I offered her a cigarette which she accepted. I noticed she was not wearing any rings on her wedding finger. During the tea interval (the war never interrupted that, and we started as we meant to continue) I found out more about her. I had already decided that the national emergency would have to take second place to personal need.

"What d'you think you'll do if it comes to the crunch?"

"I don't know. I suppose women will be called up as well this time. That's what all the papers say."

"What accent is that?" I said. "Not London, is it?"

"No, I come from Lancashire. I thought I'd lost it."

"You work in London, do you?"

"When I'm working. I'm an actress."

"Really? What a coincidence! I work in films myself," I said.

She was gratifyingly impressed. I introduced myself and discovered that her name was Jill Perry. I think what first attracted me to her were her eyes; they were extraordinarily pale, and violet rather than blue. Actresses in those days made no attempt to look like the girl next door, for glamour rather than an assumed dowdiness was considered a necessary adjunct to talent, and Miss Perry had obviously taken some pains to make the most of her physical attractions. I thought she was one of the most stunning girls I had ever seen and could hardly believe my good fortune that we had been brought together by a shared curiosity about the male and female functions of a fire hose.

"Why do you think there has to be a war?" she said.

"I don't know."

"Everybody's telling everybody they don't want it, but here we all are getting used to the idea."

"There's still a chance, I suppose. Are you in a play now?"

"No. I've just done a tour, but they ran out of money. I had quite a good part, too. Still, that's the way it is with this profession."

"I can't think somebody like you will be out of work for long."

"Oh, there's no shortage of me. You should come to some of the auditions."

As fast as I tried to turn the conversation, she just as skilfully reversed back into the topic that obsessed her. "It's the gas attacks that frighten me. I can't even sleep in a room where there's a gas fire. Do you think the Germans will use gas?"

"I suppose they might," I said, thinking of my own father. I could recall his hawking cough that had disturbed so many of my childhood nights.

"I mean, they're going to issue gas masks. They wouldn't do that, go to all that trouble and expense, if they didn't believe it's going to happen."

"Well, they have to take precautions."

"I think I'm a terrible coward." she said. "Even coming here and listening to this frightens me."

"I don't suppose any of us feel very brave. I don't. But is not knowing better than knowing?"

"I think so. I wish I hadn't come."

"I can't agree there," I said, plunging. "If you hadn't come, I wouldn't have met you. So at least Hitler's done something good."

She gave no indication that my awkward flattery had registered.

"D'you think Germans feel the same as we do?"

"Well, I expect they believe what they're told, just as we do."

"It all seems so futile," she said. "We're helpless, aren't we?"

We went back to our seats for the remainder of the lecture. This consisted of illustrating ways and means of making a room gas proof, and in listening to the instructor's voice tabulating the coming horrors in officialese, I caught something of Jill's fear. Panic spurred me to take risks, so that when the lecture ended I was prepared to shed my previous personality and become just a man on the make.

"I don't live far from here," I said. "Perhaps you'd like to come back for a drink or a coffee?"

She looked understandably dubious.

"I couldn't stay long. I share a flat with another girl and it's my turn to cook. She's a dancer, and luckily she's working. What do you do in films?" she said, and doubtless the non sequitur sprang from previous encounters with predatory casting directors.

"I'm a screenwriter. I'm working for Korda at the moment."

My reply seemed to allay her worst fears and after another token hesitation she accepted the invitation. I can't say that I blamed her – she was, after all, absolutely correct in her assumption. My intentions were never honourable.

The sight of Theo's luggage in the hallway pulled me up short. I had deliberately omitted to tell the delectable Miss Perry that I, too, shared a residence, and my surprise at his sudden reappearance confused not only my plans but also my powers of speech.

"How extraordinary. He must be back."

"Who?"

"The friend, my cousin, who . . . we share this house, but he's been away. In Berlin."

"Berlin?"

"Yes. He didn't let me know he was coming back."

Hearing our voices, Theo came out of his study. Perhaps because I was so unreasonably shattered by his return, I found the physical change in him more pronounced. He was much thinner, his clothes seemed to hang on him, and his hair, usually so carefully groomed, seemed to have been cut inexpertly, giving him the look of a shaggy, overgrown schoolboy.

"Well, thanks for letting me know," I said. "This is Miss Perry. We just met at the school, and . . . well, how are you, for Christ's sake?"

"Fine. What d'you mean, school?"

We were talking across her and he suddenly remembered his manners and put out his hand.

"Tony didn't introduce me. I'm Theo Gittings."

"Sorry. Yes, Jill this is Theo."

His name obviously meant nothing to her. Not a great reader, I thought.

"What school did you meet at?"

"School?" I said. "Oh, yes. Civil Defence lecture. They hold the meetings in the local infants school, and we just met there."

"Did Tony say you've just come back from Berlin?"

"I have been in Berlin, yes. Today I came across from France."

"Is it the same over there?" Jill asked.

"Is what the same?"

"The war scare."

"Yes, I suppose so. I don't know what it's like here."

I noticed Theo seemed very uneasy. He seemed reluctant to answer her questions in any detail.

"I don't understand politics," Jill said. "But what do ordinary people think in Germany?"

"They're very pro-British," Theo said. He took a cigarette

from his case and tapped it at both ends before putting it in his mouth. Again I noticed something different about him. His hands, formerly so well manicured, were stained with nicotine.

"Do you think that's a good sign?"

"Look, don't let's have a discussion in the hall," I said. "I invited you back for a cup of coffee."

"Now that your cousin's back you probably want to talk. I'll get off," she said.

The thought appalled me. "Well, stay and have a cup of coffee."

"No, I think I'll get back. It's quite late."

"Can I walk you home, then?"

"No, don't bother. You stay and talk to your cousin. I'm sure you've got lots to talk about."

"There's another lecture on Friday," I said. "Will I see you there?"

"Probably. Depends."

"Let me see you home," I was behaving like an overgrown schoolboy myself, and very conscious that I had lost control of the situation. I felt an unreasonable irritation towards Theo.

"No, really, I'm fine."

She said goodbye to Theo and I walked with her to the end of the road. It's now or never, I thought. I was well aware that I was pressing my luck in the circumstances, but I needed to have one vital piece of information.

"I'd like to see you again," I said, "and if you don't come on Friday, how will I ever find you again? Are you on the telephone?"

"Not really. There is a telephone, but the landlady doesn't like us having calls. Unless it's an emergency."

"This is an emergency." I smiled as I said this, because I had the sudden thought that she must be staring into the face of a sex maniac.

"I'd better not give it you, but I live in Mount Vernon. Number four. You have to go past the graveyard to get to it."

"Doesn't that bother you at night?"

"Not really. Not when you've been in as many flops as I have," she said with a flash of humour. She returned my smile. "I would like to see you again, but I think you should go and talk to your cousin tonight. He doesn't look very well."

I watched her walk off, thinking what pretty legs she had. She moved like an actress.

I thought about her last remark when I got back to the house. Theo was sitting at his desk looking through the pile of mail I had collected for him.

"You're not ill, are you?" I said.

There was a pause before he answered. "No. Just tired from travelling. Why, do I look ill?"

"Not to me, but then I'm not very perceptive. That girl thought you didn't look very well."

"I'm sorry if I ruined your plans for the evening."

"Oh, just wishful thinking. I doubt whether I would have bedded her tonight. I don't think she's the type for immediate seduction."

"Is there anything to eat?"

"Not much, I'm afraid. I wasn't expecting you."

"No, well, I decided on the spur of the moment. I should have let you know."

"We could probably go out to eat. There might be somewhere open."

"It doesn't matter. A boiled egg or something will do."

We went into the kitchen to scrounge around.

"You know me," I said, holding up some very curled bacon. "The perfect housekeeper. I never seem to bother about food when I'm on my own."

"Have you been doing a lot of work?"

I told him about my screenwriting debut and he seemed suitably impressed, especially when I told him what they were paying me.

"How about you? Did you get some useful material in Berlin?"

"What d'you mean?" he said sharply.

"The new book. I thought you were out there researching a new book. That's what you said on the only postcard I got from you."

"Oh, that. Yes. Yes, I did get a few ideas."

"What's it like in Berlin?"

"You can't tell, really. Nobody wants to talk. They're very polite to us, very anxious to convince us we're their natural ally."

"But . . .?"

"Well, it's like meeting a lot of people at a wedding party. You get very friendly while it's all going on, and exchange addresses, and yet you know that the invitations will never come to anything."

"You seem very on edge."

"Do I?"

"How many minutes?"

He stared at me blankly.

"The eggs, how d'you like them?"

"Oh, four minutes, four and a half."

"I suppose it will happen sooner or later, and that means us. If we have any choice, what would you go in? Army or what?"

"You have to pass a medical, don't you? I might not pass."

"Assuming you did."

I served his eggs on toast and he sat at the kitchen table to eat them while I made some coffee.

"I've tried not to think that far," he said.

"I think it's all fairly gloomy, though. I mean, pathetic old Chamberlain is bleating around. He always looks like something out of Madame Tussaud's to me. Of course Eden's gone, you knew that?"

"Yes. The Germans were pleased about that."

"You keep saying Germans, but you mean the Nazis?"

"There's not that much difference," Theo said. "I'd say that most of them think the sun shines out of Hitler's arse."

"But all these stories we hear; is it as fearful as they make out?"

He stared down at his half-eaten egg. "I met him, you know. Hitler. I was introduced at some official reception."

I stopped what I was doing. "Well, go on! What was he like?"

213

"Impressive," Theo said. "I could see why they follow him."

"Did you meet any of the others?"

"Only Goebbels – repellent, face like one of those awful lap dogs, which I suppose he is – and a man called Bormann. They all think the real enemy is Russia, you know. It's not the Jews they're after, it's the Reds."

"But they're kicking the Jews out."

"Put it this way, they're not encouraging them to stay. There's a lot of talk about the purity of the race. Most of the young men are very handsome, hand-picked, I'd say, for the benefit of tourists like me."

"But you weren't tempted?"

"I didn't say that."

"And Spain," I said. "I want to know all about Spain too. I read some of your pieces, of course."

We drank coffee and talked for the next two hours. I kept noticing how nervous he had become. He wasn't very forthcoming about the Spanish experience and at one point I almost thought he had tears in his eyes, but I could have been mistaken. He seemed to be waiting for something, and when the doorbell went he was on his feet before me.

"That's probably somebody for me."

"For you? But nobody knows you're home."

"Yes. It's somebody I met on the boat."

"Oh, I see. I thought you were a bit on edge. Why didn't you say?"

"I'm not on edge."

"Fine. I can take a hint. You can do the same thing for me when eventually I get Miss Perry to nibble at the bait. See you in the morning."

I went to my own room to plan future strategy where Jill was concerned. I heard Theo admit his visitor, but curiously the conversation between them was held at the front door. It seemed to me that they were both talking in a foreign language, and I heard my own name mentioned once. Then the door slammed and all was quiet. I listened and it became obvious that Theo had gone out with his visitor. I went to the bathroom to brush my teeth, amazed he had the energy even to contemplate whatever he was contemplating, and slightly miffed that everything always seemed so cut and dried between Theo and his lovers. If only Miss Perry could be so easily persuaded, I thought.

16

DURING ALL THAT unreal summer of 1938 we made a conscious effort to push outside events to the back of our minds. Theo seemed to become more his old self in the weeks following his return from Berlin, though he still couldn't be drawn into any serious discussion of his foreign experiences. He started work on a new novel, the one eventually published under the title of *The Burnt Heart*, and in all probability when the time comes for a definitive biography whoever undertakes the task will discern traces of his Spanish episode and the death of the boy he loved. We writers often think we cover our tracks completely, but some words force themselves on to the page.

My affair with Jill progressed slowly. She was not another Judy or Diana, prepared to tumble into bed just like that. I enjoyed her company because she cared about so many things. She wanted to be something more than just a decorative piece of scenery and I respected her for that. God knows she could have taken a far easier route to further her career in the pre-war theatre. Girls as pretty as she was could usually find a couch with a contract under the cushions, and she often came back from an interview to relate some narrow escape from the fate that was commonly thought to be worse than death. Of course, she might have been exaggerating to keep me in line, since it is always more difficult to play the cad when you are listening to an account of somebody else's seduction attempt. Not that I felt caddish towards her. I was anxious to get her into bed, but at the same time I felt protective. She had none of the conceits usually associated with young actresses who have repeatedly been told they are beautiful. I went to see her act on a couple of occasions – Sunday try-outs, I think they were called – and although I was predisposed in her favour, I had to admit that she was hardly likely to challenge Peggy Ashcroft. What she had was a presence. She knew how to place her body under the lights: it's a sort of instinct that some actresses have which has nothing to do with acting talent, and careers have been made with less. But in Jill's case the timing was all wrong. Wrong for her, wrong for all of us. It was difficult to think of permanence in 1938.

When Munich happened I shared that general, shaming relief – like getting away with cheating in an exam – that gripped us all. I didn't go to Downing Street, or stand outside Buckingham Palace to cheer, but inwardly my heart sang. I have little memory for dates, but September 30th, 1938 is likely to be the Calais on my heart – not for the right reasons, but because that night in celebration of the snatched peace, I finally persuaded Jill to share my bed.

The landscape of our lives changed drastically after Munich. There were trial 'blackouts' and preparations for war were increasingly in evidence. The garden at Perrins Walk wasn't large enough to accommodate an Anderson Shelter, so we fortified an area under the stairwell, really nothing more than a glorified cupboard, which we reinforced with corrugated iron and sandbags. We also laid in a store of emergency supplies, going about such inherently terrifying preparations with that typical British mixture of mock seriousness and black humour that has so often confounded our enemies.

Theo and I discussed the inevitability of war on many occasions. It was the only time he ever referred to his Spanish experience, describing the effects of aerial bombing in graphic detail. Like everybody else we fully expected London to be devastated within the first few days of the commencement of hostilities. It was entirely characteristic of us that we both, independently, packed our most valuable books and manuscripts before thinking of anything else. We also gave consideration to the desirability of volunteering ahead of time rather than wait to be directed since it was obvious that conscription would come.

With this in mind I took myself off for an interview with the Board of an outfit called The Officers' Emergency Reserve.

There my sparse qualifications were noted with an embarrassed lack of enthusiasm by an elderly gentleman who looked as though he had spent the greater part of his life passing the port.

"Can't hold out much hope of a decent regiment," he muttered. "Present occupation writer, is it?"

"Yes."

"Yes." He stared at me, fingering his buttonhole. "Not likely to change, I suppose?"

"I don't think so."

"Difficult to see where you'd fit in. You are British, I take it?"

"Yes."

"That helps, of course. Well, Mr. Stern, we must just wait and see. 'Course, it may not happen. The Hun is no man's fool, and there's always a chance the old balloon won't go up."

I came away with a keener appreciation of the encounters Jill had to suffer and even more convinced that our days were numbered. It was in this depressed state of mind that Jill and I made plans to take what we rightly surmised would be our last holiday for many years to come. We decided to rent a houseboat and explore the Norfolk Broads. ("My aged and disgusting father has been exploring them all his adult life," Theo told Jill.) It's funny how one can plot pleasures in an atmosphere of fear, but it seemed the only route to sanity at the time.

Towards the middle of August and just before Jill and I took off, Theo confided that he was going to accept a government job.

"What sort of job?" I asked him.

"Oh, well, it's all a bit vague, but I gather they're going to set up some sort of propaganda department in anticipation of Armageddon, and they've asked me to be part of it."

"You crafty sod! Didn't row me in, I suppose? When was this decided?"

"They've been pestering me for some time," he said.

"And it'll be classified as a reserved occupation, of course?"

"Probably, yes. Yes, I imagine so."

"You double-dealer," I said. "So while I'm fighting for you, you'll be here in some cushy office with a willing secretary on your knee."

"As long as it's a male secretary. Anyway, who's to say London won't be the most dangerous place?"

"Don't you believe it. Propaganda departments will be buried under ten feet of concrete reinforced with steely lies. When do you start?"

"I suppose I've sort of started already."

"Well," I said, "you've ruined my holiday. You crafty sod, I repeat. I shall never trust a single government communique."

In retrospect, that last August of peace seems the best holiday I ever had. Jill and I cut ourselves off from everything and everybody. We didn't take a radio with us and we didn't buy a single newspaper. Most days we ambled along in our rented houseboat, reminding ourselves of Kenneth Grahameland, the calming feeling of drifting on water in glorious contrast to what was happening in the outside world. I have never slept so well or made love so often. To be in love and cut off from the rest of suffering humanity is to sample the age of illusion. Those hot summer days seemed to consist of nothing but gentle bouts of love-making in the curtained cabin, watching the green, ever-moving light play across Jill's nude body – an Ondine borrowed for a few brief weeks. I remember her tumbled hair and the breakfasts we took on deck when everything was still, the sun just starting to burn through the drifting patches of river mist, while birds flew low over the water to snatch at our thrown crumbs.

We were still there, innocent, uncaring, on September 3rd when a small boy suddenly appeared on the far bank, running for dear life. We waved to him and he waved back, his face pink with excitement. "We're at war," he shouted. "We've declared war, on the wireless!"

Then he was gone, desperate to spread the good news. Instinctively we looked up into the wide skies, hearing the drone of a single-engined aircraft appearing on cue. We watched it out of sight and then we went down into the cabin and made love for the last time. All the holidays were over.

*

The implacable darkness of the blackout was the hardest thing to get used to – the rest was anticlimax. We had been expecting immediate horror and wholesale carnage, clouds of lethal gas blanketing the rubble of our ruined cities: what we got was minor officialdom shouting at us to seal the cracks of light. If we had been hoping for a new sense of urgency and purpose after the long years of drift, we were disappointed. Chamberlain was still there, his features set in a hurt expression as though Hitler had cheated him at the bridge table. After that first morning the sirens remained silent; it was business as usual, the only outward indication that anything untoward had happened, the appearance of Polish soldiers in our streets – sad reminders of our good intentions – with their slightly musical comedy hats and heel-clicking good manners, giving rise to the first generation of Polish jokes. We spent our time listening for the clarion call to duty and all we heard was the leaden voices of our masters who gave the impression that it was their collective intention to bore Germany into submission. The only acts of attrition were a series of R.A.F. leaflet raids, a war strategy of such benevolence it might have been devised by the Salvation Army.

I tackled Theo on this subject, accusing him of writing the actual leaflets. He denied all knowledge.

"Well, what exactly is your exalted department doing, then?"

"My lips are sealed."

"The whole thing is pathetic. Does anybody seriously believe that the Germans read what we drop? Apart from providing them with free toilet paper, what bloody good is it doing?"

"Greater minds than ours are at work," Theo said.

"Name one."

"Goebbels."

"At least Lord Haw Haw makes the occasional joke."

"Yes, but we're not supposed to listen to him," Jill said. "Personally, I love Alvar Lidell. Do you think he still puts on a black tie to read the nine o'clock news?"

"When that goes," Theo said, "we shall really be at war."

Apart from such frivolous exchanges, he was seldom forthcoming about his new occupation. He kept odd hours and often disappeared for days on end without explanation. I found it difficult to settle to anything. I had finished the Korda commission and sent the script to Denham and that was the last I heard of it. I tried to start a new novel but my fictions seemed to belong to a bygone age and I abandoned it after a few chapters. Jill moved in with us when her flat-mate went to join the Women's Land Army – a piece of war effort that provided a good proportion of the jokes that B.B.C. comedians beamed at us. There was little work going in the theatre, despite the fact that most of them had reopened after the early panic closures. She was as restless as I was and told me that she was seriously thinking of joining E.N.S.A. – that much-maligned entertainment organisation which did little to enhance its launching with posters that proclaimed: COME THE FOUR CORNERS OF THE EARTH IN ARMS, AND WE SHALL SHOCK THEM.

My own future was resolved for me. I received notification to present myself at a barracks on the outskirts of Chelmsford in Essex. Obviously the interview with The Officers' Emergency Reserve had been the dismal failure I had imagined. After a farewell dinner at Perrins Walk, during which we killed the last three bottles of decent Burgundy we were to see for the next six years, I took my Beau Geste exit and journeyed to Chelmsford.

There any remaining illusions about the Army were swiftly dispelled. I learnt to survive, to endure the brutalised camaraderie of my fellow sufferers, to shave in three minutes flat in cold water and run all the way to the open latrines and back in order not to be last in line for the congealed breakfast. I was given a rifle manufactured in 1915 that kicked like a mule, and a uniform that brought me up in a rash wherever it touched bare skin. I looked as dashing as an Old Bill cartoon and believed I was on the verge of a major heart attack whenever we went on a forced route march. As far as I could gather, the British infantry was still being trained to fend off Napoleon's Old Guard, the philosophy of most of our officers being that, although Hitler had broken the rules in Poland, once he came face to face with seven inches of blunt bayonet he would settle for a more civilised form of warfare. We were allowed five rounds of live ammunition on the firing ranges, since bullets were in short supply: those of us who actually hit any part of the targets were regarded as potential sniper material.

After eight weeks of such enlightened instruction I was posted to the Somerset Light Infantry which the barrack-room wit suggested was due to the fact I had once got drunk on draught cider. Much to my surprise I felt physically stronger, walked with a pronounced swagger and behaved as though a member of an élite force.

Granted a brief forty-eight hour leave, I went back to Perrins Walk with a lean and hungry look and fell upon the admiring Jill with the ardour of a man who has served a long term in the Foreign Legion. I also commandeered the bath-room for hours on end, much to Theo's annoyance.

"It's your privilege to take second place to we brave boys in khaki," I said. "How are things in the rumour factory?"

"Dull by comparison to your own exciting life."

"Written any good leaflets lately?"

"We also serve," he said, "who only sit and ponder."

I had no sooner joined the Somersets when my Company was posted overseas. We embarked for France as part of the ill-fated British Expeditionary Force – fully prepared, in the words of the then popular song, to do laundry service on the Siegfried Line.

In thinking of those extraordinary, far-off days, and trying to piece together Theo's parallel story, I wish I could provide myself with a rational explanation for everything. But every-where I look there are loose ends. The spoor marks have been mostly obliterated, some by time, some by deliberate acts by persons as yet unknown.

This much seems obvious: at some point during the period he spent in Spain and Berlin, Theo received the instructions that were to shape the rest of his life. It must have been then that his relationship with the Comintern moved from the shallows of an undergraduate playpool to the deeper waters where one either sank or swam. There is a definite gap in the journals after Spain. When the entries resumed they had a different, almost Kafka-like quality. Perhaps he was under orders, or perhaps he merely adapted his technique to suit the changed circumstances, but I can find no evidence of a code being employed. Instead, I believe he hit upon the idea of setting down fact as fiction, changing names and localities and employing the third person instead of the more dangerous, betraying 'I' of the earlier years. If so it was entirely in character, for he always maintained that British officialdom could never come to terms with literature. Doubtless pride in his craft as a serious novelist played an important role as he painfully doctored the entries in those identical exercise books. Even when he was deceiving others he could not resist trying to write well, and perhaps he knew that this final conceit was the one that would save him. The passages I am about to quote are Theo's version of hell – his Gilbert Pinfold's ordeal, if you like, the actions of a man who was a writer first and last. This was his war, the one he fought with himself.

If for 'Alec' you read 'Theo' then the whole thing starts to make sense.

17

. . . WHAT WOULD BE most painful to him, Alec thought? For the world to discover his worthlessness, or to remain dependent on those he no longer loved?

He woke covered in sweat, his mind immediately alert to the danger he carried within him like malaria. For a few moments he had no idea where he was.

"Wakey, wakey, sir," a voice said very close to his ear. He turned in panic and pitched on to the floor. In the act of falling he was conscious of a hot liquid stinging the hand he thrust out to save himself.

"Sorry, sir, very sorry. Didn't mean to startle you like that."

He was helped to his feet and found himself staring at a stranger in uniform. Memories of the country he had recently left came crowding back, and once again his instinct was to try and escape, but the room was moving and he lost balance again.

"Woke you up with a start, didn't I? That's a black mark, can't have that. Here, just sit down on the edge of the bed, sir, and get your bearings. You were in a real deep sleep."

Alec sat on the hard edge of the bunk, his eyes gradually becoming accustomed to the dim overhead light as he remembered where he was. The stranger in uniform had a Cockney accent and was smiling.

"Be in Victoria in under the half hour, sir. So I usually call my gentlemen in good time, in case they want to have a sluice and a shave. All right now, are you? My mistake but we'll put it to rights. I'll get you fresh cup of Rosy; we seem to have spilt this one."

He backed out of the sleeping compartment and Alec had an impression of a pitted landscape flashing by.

"Thank you," he said, as the door closed. "Thank you, stupid of me," talking to himself. He pulled himself upright and stared at his reflection in the mirror over the handbasin. Home, he thought, I'm nearly home and then he started to shake involuntarily, like a man suddenly struck with a virulent fever. He reached for a cigarette and had to strike three matches before he could get it alight Why am I fully dressed? he thought, looking down at the rumpled bed. Why not pyjamas? The cigarette calmed him, but he still had to struggle to find the answers. He pressed the cigarette into the serrated edge of the fixed ashtray and returned to the washbasin, splashing his face with cold water that tasted of iron on his lips. As he straightened he found himself reading a notice which said, *In Case of Emergency Pull The Chain Downwards. Penalty for Wrongful Use £5.* The words helped him focus on reality. He drew deeply on the cigarette again, his mouth full of the bitter taste of betrayal. I shall have to get used to that, he thought. It was like an alcoholic telling himself to become accustomed to an endless hangover. I'll give up smoking, he thought. To compensate, one addiction in exchange for another. But it was a further promise to keep and he had made too many in recent weeks.

There was a knock on the door, barely audible over the noise of the boat train travelling at speed over the suburban points. Alec opened the door with a hand that had stopped trembling.

"Here we are, sir. I made a fresh pot. Least I could do after that little episode. No offence taken, I hope?"

"No, it was my fault," Alec said, taking the fresh cup of tea. "I'm a very heavy sleeper."

"Now then, sir, have we got all we want? Razor, shaving soap? I always carry some just in case any of my gentlemen come unprepared."

"I think I have everything, thank you."

The man leaned across and turned on the hot water tap. "Watch this, sir. Scald you this would. Still, better hot than cold."

The strong tea completed the process of revival and when he had sipped half of it, he scraped a razor over his stubble, performing the routine actions like man under hypnosis. Why am I doing this? he thought. Just because that man suggested it, and it suddenly struck him that he had obeyed without question. They did a good job, he thought. I'm already conditioned. It seemed to him then that his whole life had been a preparation for betrayal, that he was going home to an old familiarity.

(This must refer to the night he arrived back unexpectedly and surprised me with Jill. Although writing with aplomb in a style hitherto foreign to him, I can detect a certain unease. A writer can never completely hide an element of self-destruction.)

They didn't waste any time. Alec wanted space to breathe, a chance to gather up old threads, make quite certain that none of the patches on his previous personality gave him away, but he was not allowed such luxuries. He realised that this would be the pattern of his life from now on, that his every act would be watched and judged. What had they told him? Things will happen that you won't understand, but accept our word that the right decisions are being taken in the right order. You are important to us and that carries heavy responsibilities.

The whole structure of his life had become a hideous novelty overnight. Until this point he had only half-believed in the existence of a malignant force operating from afar, but his recent journey abroad had robbed him of this last comfort. So much of his life had been a walk with fantasy and now the fantasy had been crowded out. Even so, the speed with which they worked took him by surprise. It was like being hauled back to school a few hours after the last term had finished, to begin again the education of himself. Forget everything you have learnt, begin again, discard the old values, trample on the honour code, it's all right to split, you have our permission. The new curriculum begins now.

Part of him was offended by the company he was now forced to keep. Although he had never thought of himself as a snob, he was appalled by his new set of friends. He had the feeling that the distaste was returned and this added to his sense of uneasiness, that no matter how hard he tried to please, his papers would never be marked ten out of ten. His previous circle were not slow to remark the change in him; it was as if he had come home scarred, a Dorian Gray denied a mirror that gave any true reflection.

(Sections of the narrative are heavily crossed out at this point, as though Theo had grown tired with the effort of disguising his plot with such a heavy layer of literary grease paint. To ghost one's own work is heavy labour. When he resumed, his prose became much more direct.)

"You must be patient with me," Alec said. "I don't come fully equipped to this sort of thing."

The man sitting across the table in the all-night Corner shop picked his nose with grave concentration. There were four cups of half-drunk tea between them and the remnants of a cheese sandwich sharing a plateful of cigarette ends.

"We have been patient," the man said. He took the result of his diligent search and rolled it into a ball between his fingers before carefully depositing it on the underside of the table. "You can't say we've hurried you, but now events are overtaking us. I think Berlin explained how quickly things are going. We don't want to be the ones who let the side down."

The voice was right but the appearance, the mannerisms suggested failure – a doctor who had been struck off the register and was determined to get his own back.

"Therefore we have to play our part in good time. Certain arrangements have been made to receive you." – again the suggestion of a medical opinion, as though I'm being admitted to an isolation ward, Alec thought. "You will be contacted quite legitimately. That's already been set in motion. It's a question of patriotism, you see. Don't be too anxious, too keen, that's always taken as a bad sign. You have to learn to understand the Establishment mentality; it's just another branch of the civil service moving in more mysterious ways."

It all sounded so plausible put that way, yet the thrill of staring into the abyss was only exciting until it became contemptible. How have I reached this point? Alec thought. A few months ago I was set in my rut, a respected Oxford don steeped in the classics, dull, ordinary, conditioned by an academic routine I thought would last me out my days. I could number my vices on three fingers, endowed with limited imagination and feeling, a passable analytical intelligence, a reliable memory. Now I am here, my world exploded: 'Here' was the outskirts of treason, the unknown bourn, face to face with a stranger who picked his nose while peace receded.

"How will they contact me?" he asked.

"Normal channels. It's another form of income tax, in a way. They want you to pay your dues, that's all."

"And then?"

"Just take things as they come. It's all very methodical, not at all like the thriller writers. That's just a smokescreen to fool the majority. The real thing is all routine, paperwork, something you're used to."

"I'm not used to any of it," Alec said.

"You should have thought about that earlier," his companion said. He opened a fresh packet of cigarettes, extracted one and replaced it with what looked like an identical paper cylinder he took from his jacket pocket.

"These are your brand, I believe?"

"There's a number you can call written on the inside. Memorise it, then destroy it. Call me when you've been accepted, but only when you've been accepted. You should hear within the next two weeks."

He slid the packet across the table.

"We've every confidence in you," he said. "Every confidence. You're going to be a feather in our cap."

Then he got up, leaning across the table to shake hands formally, saying in a somewhat louder voice: "Very pleasant to see you again. Good luck with the project" – though there was nobody to hear but a drunk sitting a few tables away, and a tired waitress clearing the debris of forgotten meals. Then he walked swiftly away.

He's left me to pay the bill, Alec thought. It was the only gesture he fully understood. From that moment onwards he would always be paying.

If he was honest with himself, the actual initiation had been easy. And quite different from anything he had imagined. He had moved from one extreme to the other. From the squalid absurdity of secret telephone numbers hidden in cigarette packets, to the cloistered calm of his club. Some ten days later he was enjoying an after-lunch cigar and leafing through the pages of *Country Life* (he had long nurtured a hankering for a thatched cottage in which to spend his retirement) when he was approached by a fellow member who settled down in the armchair next to him. Alec was aware that he was something to do with the War Office, though the main attraction of his club was that few of the members intruded upon others; it was considered bad form to talk too much personal shop.

"Chilly today. Should have thought they'd have lit the fire," his companion said.

"Yes."

"'Course the news is chilly enough without the weather adding to it."

"Yes."

"You take *Country Life*, do you? Some damn good articles in there, I always think. Better than the *Tatler*. Can't stand all that social chit-chat."

Having made the effort to appear unsociable, Alec resigned himself to the fact that he would have to enter into a conversation.

"I was looking at the prices of cottages," he said. "Thinking of my old age."

"Dorset. That's the county. Though I don't know that most of us will see old age, the way things are going."

"You don't think so?"

"I'm damn sure of it. We've bought a few months credit with that Munich job, but it's not going to last. He's not going to be satisfied with just that, not if I read it correctly. It's going to come and we won't be able to wriggle out of it next time. Nor should we."

"No, I suppose not. It seems a terrible prospect."

"Run out of options, you see. Should have called his bluff when he walked into the Rhineland."

"Yes. I'm not very well up in these matters, I'm afraid."

"Why should you be? You dons live in your ivory towers and very necessary, too. Always regret I never walked amongst the dreaming spires. Been Army all my life. You're not on the Reserve, are you?"

"No."

"I think we'll all be in it, of course, one way or the other. Going to be a different kind of war from the last one."

It suddenly struck Alec that the conversation was a probe. He felt a sense of enormous relief, like a man who has been consulting several specialists and is finally given a diagnosis – even bad news is sometimes preferable to the unknown.

"They're going to be looking for chaps like you. Chaps with brains. Not going to be six inches of cold steel when you get over the top boys. There's still a lot of that sort of thinking around, of course. Mistaken, in my opinion. It's going to be a war of nerves."

"Are we as unprepared as they say?"

"We're thin on the ground. Very thin. Need everybody we can muster."

I mustn't seem curious or anxious, Alec thought. If this is the approach I was told to expect, the important thing is to be totally ignorant. He stared down at the cover of *Country Life*, at a picture of an England that was destined to disappear for ever, an England he was just about to betray.

"I hear you travel quite a bit?"

"Yes. I try to. It broadens the mind, I find. Teaching the classics year in and year out is apt to solidify the old intellectual arteries."

There was a pause. How curious, Alec thought, I really believe that he's embarrassed, he can't quite bring himself to discuss what he's really here for. Not for the first time he was amazed by the comparison between the two organisations. His contempt for

229

the class his companion represented was tempered by a sort of awe – they have a purpose, he thought, and we muddle through, inhibited, half-articulate, desperate to observe the social conventions whatever the circumstances. The whole country was governed in the same way, strictly adhering to a set of Queensberry Rules that everybody else disregarded. Chamberlain waving that piece of paper, a bookie's slip for a horse that was never going to run.

"I'm sure that somebody like yourself has a role to play," his companion continued. He had the studied manner of a West End actor. "Not necessarily in uniform. If you were interested I could put somebody in touch."

"You mean some sort of propaganda work?"

"Yes, that kind of thing."

"I doubt if I'd be any good."

"Well, these people seem to think you might."

It was the first reference to third parties. I don't suppose he meant to say that, Alec thought. Still playing the innocent, he gave no sign he had detected anything untoward.

"Yes," he said, "by all means, then, if you think I could be of some value."

"Good. I've got one or two contacts and I'll pass your name along." He brightened a little, as though he had just discharged an awkward chore. "Be a relief in many ways when the old balloon goes up. Can't bear all this hanging around. Hope you find your cottage. Useful to have a funk hole, comes in handy."

(Theo is not straying far from reality in his fictional account. Reading various authenticated memoirs, one gathers that recruitment was often conducted in this gentlemanly, oblique fashion. Approaches were made in all directions, to academics, scientists, mathematicians, actors, lawyers, writers and even the criminal classes. There was doubtless an element of desperation in the beginning, with a few enlightened men casting the net wide in order to make up for lost time.

Inevitably one comes back to the apparent recklessness of Theo's journals-cum-notebooks, this overriding compulsion he had to document his own treasons. They give me the feeling that he might have welcomed being exposed, that the layers of deceit were his way of testing himself. He was not alone, of course: many of his fellow travellers could not resist the conceit, for there must be many moments in a double-agent's life when the burden becomes intolerable. There is always the early precedent of Casement's *Black Diaries*.)

Alec had never anticipated that his next contact would be a woman – an elderly woman at that, one of those brusque, capable ladies that the British seem to have invented as a third race. One couldn't imagine the French or German counterparts operating in the same way or at the same level. The British seem to accept such things, he thought. After all, the most popular woman writer of detective stories had actually got her readers to accept a female detective, a preposterous idea on the face of it, but swallowed wholesale and with every sign of relish. The lady who interviewed him might well have been the model for Miss Marple. Sensibly dressed, smart without being showy, the sort of woman you would expect to be in charge of a village jumble sale. Perhaps the faintest suggestion of a moustache on the upper lip, but powdered out. A hint of 4711 Cologne whenever she took her handkerchief from the sleeve of her jacket, and a no-nonsense manner of smoking her Kensitas.

She had greeted him as she might have welcomed a nephew she had not seen for several years. The telephoned appointment had been for four o'clock sharp at Brown's Hotel and she was waiting at a reserved table when Alec walked in at five to four.

"How very nice of you to spare the time, Mr. Morris. I'm Miss Malcolm. What sort of tea do you prefer? I ordered Earl Grey, but if you'd rather have Indian or China, we can soon change it. I believe your usual tipple is Earl Grey."

"Yes. How clever of you to know."

"I wouldn't say clever. Just efficient."

They all sat down and tea was served almost immediately, together with a selection of sandwiches that seemed to have been carved by a miniaturist.

Miss Malcolm got straight to the point. "I think I'm right in saying that you could be looking for some interesting, different employment in the future?"

"That was the idea, yes."

"And the fact that you've taken the trouble to keep this appointment means you're still interested?"

"I'm interested in exploring it further."

231

"Good. How many lumps?"

"None. I don't take it."

"Oh, you put me to shame. I like mud at the bottom of my cup. It keeps up the energy, or so I tell myself."

She poured with a steady hand, then lit another cigarette.

"Do you mind if I do?" Alec said.

"I can hardly object, can I? Tea, cigarettes and cats, my life revolves around all three."

"You're fond of cats?"

"Fond isn't the word. I am somewhat enslaved by them. Do you like cats, Mr. Morris?"

"Yes, I do. I prefer them to dogs."

"Oh, then we're going to get along. I always feel there's something odd about people who don't like cats. You've travelled quite a lot, I believe? How well do you know Germany?"

"Reasonably well. I studied there for a time and frequently go back for holidays."

"Yes. Well, holidays may be curtailed in the near future."

"I suppose so."

"The sort of employment we had in mind would be political in nature. Does that worry you?"

"I don't think so."

She asked her questions in a chatty, conversational manner and to the rest of the residents in the lounge they must have presented a conventional tableau.

"Very political in fact, involving, shall we say, a certain element of discretion. Do you follow me?"

"Yes."

"Of course it would be work of the highest importance; that is why we are approaching people of your standing."

"Very flattering."

"No, not flattering. Just a sensible precaution. We can't afford to make mistakes."

"Can you give me any more detailed idea of what might be involved?"

"Well, I know it sounds rude, but do you know, I can't. That really isn't my forte. They just think I'm rather useful getting to know people and making recommendations. How's your tea, need topping up?"

"Thank you. So, where do we go from here?"

"I go back to the office, where do you go?"

The sudden dart of humour took him by surprise. For the first time during the interview he became aware of her femininity. Be careful, he thought. She may look like your maiden aunt, but there the resemblance ends.

"The one thing we all have to learn in this line of business," she said, "is that things are never quite what they appear. It's a little confusing at first, but I'm sure you'll soon get the hang of it."

"Have I passed the first test?"

"I've certainly enjoyed our little talk. But could I ask you one last question? It's rather personal, I'm afraid, so please forgive me. Do you have any . . . emotional attachments that might preclude you from taking such employment, assuming it was offered?"

"No," Alec said, looking straight at her as he answered. "No, nothing to speak of. I lead a somewhat solitary life, as I'm sure you know."

"Don't we all?" she said. She gathered up her gloves and handbag. "Forgive me if I have to rush. Do stay and finish some more of those delicious sandwiches. It's all paid for."

Alec got to his feet to say goodbye. "I never thought I'd be a kept man," he said.

"Oh, you're not. I claim it all back on expenses. So nice to have met you. I'm sure we'll meet again."

He watched her walk briskly out of the lounge. Much to his surprise he saw that she had rather shapely legs.

He was asked to make a second meeting less than a week later. He made apologies and declined, pleading a prior engagement that was impossible to break. One mustn't appear too keen, he thought, and already he was training his mind to think one step ahead. An alternative date was agreed and on this occasion he went to an address off Grosvenor Square. This time Miss Malcolm was joined by his original contact from the club, and again he was put through his paces in more detail. He might have been applying for the job of headmaster at some minor public school, the only marked difference being he was offered Scotch instead of Earl Grey. He was told that, subject to his own final decision, an approach had already been made to his college. There would be no objection to his having leave of absence, though for the time being nothing was cut and dried. In the event, the story for general consumption would be that he was having a rest on medical advice. 'A slight patch on the lung, we thought, in view of the fact that you're a heavy smoker.' Alec had further cause to admire their thoroughness. It would be dangerous, he thought, to be fooled by the seemingly amateur approach. Once again the meeting ended with nothing actually resolved, though he came away convinced that he had passed their tests.

This was confirmed a fortnight later when a fellow don enquired about his health. "Heard a rumour and hope it's nothing too serious."

"Well, I have been told to take it easy. But reports of my death are premature."

"Have they told you to give up the weed?"

"Oh, yes. I'm cutting it down."

"Well, sorry to hear it, Alec. Take care of yourself."

Miss Malcolm phoned that evening. His medical report had now been carefully studied and they would like him to come in and discuss the treatment involved. "It would be tidier if we could start from August 1st."

He had a stiff drink before making his own telephone call. The number rang half a dozen times before it was answered. "I've been accepted," he said. "They're taking me in on August 1st."

"Congratulations," the voice said. "We'll be in touch. Don't use this number again." The line went dead.

The following day he attempted to trace it through Directory Enquiries. He was told that it was now a defunct line. It had been used by a firm of toy importers operating from a warehouse in Shoreditch.

18

THERE WAS LITTLE that was heroic about my war. Shortly after our arrival in France I was put in charge of unit intelligence. This mostly consisted of sticking flags in maps to mark the locations of local brothels, and resulted in my being promoted to unpaid sergeant. I was later transferred into the Field Security arm of the Intelligence Corps proper and had my own Section, most of them misfits who, like me, were considered liabilities as infantrymen.

Until the German invasion of the Low Countries, mail reached us without too much delay. Faithful to me in her fashion, Jill wrote regularly. She had managed to get herself into an E.N.S.A. troupe and was touring Army camps in Southern Command, appearing once nightly in a production of Edgar Wallace's vintage thriller, *The Case of The Frightened Lady*. "An apt title for this particular lady," she wrote, "since our coach driver is a monumental drunk and I am nightly amazed that we ever survive in the blackout."

I heard nothing from Theo, although several times I wrote to Perrins Walk and enquired after him through Jill. "I phoned him after I got your last letter," she wrote, "but there was no reply. If and when we get nearer to London I'll try and find time to go home." Her use of the word 'home' struck a comforting note. Then her letters stopped: by then the Allied armies were in full retreat and Dunkirk was upon us.

I was amongst the lucky ones who got out of France before the surrender. I landed at Newhaven in a dangerously overloaded fishing boat that had already made three trips to the beaches. I lay below decks with a dying man across my legs and another holding my hand as tightly as a scared child. Once we had disembarked it was every man for himself. Willing ladies handed out tea and buns and we were told to make our own ways back to our base units. I had no idea where I was expected to report, and instead took advantage of the general confusion to return to London. Nobody was likely to miss me and my consuming thought was to find Jill. Perrins Walk seemed as good a base as any.

I found the house deserted, looking as though it had been abandoned in a hurry: Theo's bed unmade, the sink full of unwashed crockery, my own room chill and dusty. I had no idea of Theo's whereabouts, but I rang E.N.S.A. headquarters to start my search for Jill. The phone was answered by a weary female voice.

"*The Case of The Frightened Lady* company," I said. "Do you know where they are?"

"The who?"

I repeated the question. "I'm trying to locate a Miss Jill Perry."

"Oh, well, I wouldn't know anything like that. I'm just temporary, just manning the switchboard."

"Is there anybody else? This is an emergency."

"Everything's an emergency," the voice said. "Are you a relative?"

"Yes," I lied. "I'm her husband and I've just got back from Dunkirk."

"Oh. Well, all I can do is take your number."

Without thinking, I started to give my Army number, then corrected myself. I knew that nothing would happen; the woman at the other end had that sort of voice. I took a bath and shaved. My skin was ingrained with grease from the deck of the fishing boat and there was blood from the dying man under my finger nails. I felt like a murder suspect. Even though I scrubbed myself the stink of smoke and death lingered, so I purloined Theo's only bottle of cologne. Then I cooked the only egg in the house. I was sitting at the kitchen table wondering what to do next when the phone went. I rushed to it.

"It's all set," a male voice said. "Exactly as planned."

"Who d'you want?" I said. "Are you calling Mr. Gittings?"

The line went dead immediately. I waited for the caller to ring again, but nothing happened. There was a calendar pinned to the wall above the phone and as I replaced the receiver I noticed that there was a circle drawn round one date. I'd lost all track of time but when I checked, I found it was that day's date that had been scored.

The quiet of Hampstead was unreal. I went upstairs to my room and sifted through my books and possessions, staring at them as though they belonged to somebody else. It was the same with Theo's room — I felt like an invader scavenging for loot. There was a copy of *Tit Bits* on Theo's bedside table and I remember thinking that was hardly his normal reading matter. There was something missing in the house and for a long time I couldn't think what it might be. Then it came to me: any trace of Jill was missing. She was not the tidiest of people and in the old days my chest of drawers had always been littered with the debris of her several handbags, the surface white with her spilled face powder, my ashtrays holding a collection of hairpins. Eventually I fell asleep on top of my bed, going out as though knocked unconscious and immediately plunged into nightmarish dreams, faces floating past me, drowned men spinning down into a vortex. The bang of the front door wakened me and with newly-acquired instincts for survival I rolled over, falling on to the floor.

"Who's that?" It was Theo's voice.

I appeared, still in shock, at the top of the stairs.

"Christ!" he said. "You made my heart stop."

I went to put on a light and he screamed a warning.

"Don't! I haven't fixed the blackout."

I did nothing to help as he struggled with the home-made shutters. Without any justification I felt the serving soldier's resentment of civilians: Theo's neat appearance contrasted sharply with how I felt and looked.

"Where's Jill?" I asked.

"Give me a chance. Haven't said hello yet. Listen, I'm glad you're back safely. I never expected to see you again. The news has been terrible."

"Well, the news is right. I want to know where Jill is."

"I'll tell you, just let me catch my breath. D'you want something to drink?"

He rummaged around and produced a third of a bottle of

237

gin. "Nothing to go with it, I'm afraid." He rinsed two glasses and poured generous tots.

"Welcome back."

"Tell me."

"God, you're one track. She's at home. She's gone home to her parents. I put her on the train myself."

"When?"

"Today."

"Today? Oh, Christ! you mean I've only just missed her?"

He nodded, and poured the rest of the gin in my glass. I was aware that I had drunk the first tot too quickly.

"She's all right, though?"

"Yes . . . Yes."

"What does that mean?"

"Just that. She's fine."

"But?"

"My God, you've come back in an aggressive mood."

"I'm sorry. I was asleep, and I don't know, I don't mean to be aggressive. I'm just anxious, that's all."

"She's been staying here for the last couple of weeks," Theo said. He seemed to be searching for his words. "She hasn't been too well, you see. But she's all right now. Don't look so worried, I promise you she's all right."

"There is a 'but', though. I can tell."

"Yes . . . Look, now don't get upset, but the fact of the matter is, and I may as well come straight out with it, she had an abortion."

I stared at him. His words meant nothing to me. They were just part of the general nightmare, sounds heard dimly through the increasing gin haze, part of the swaying journey in darkness with a dying man bleeding over my legs, just another aspect of the bloody war. Theo fumbled for a packet of cigarettes and lit one for me. My fingers still had traces of dried blood under the nails.

"Tony, dear, obviously I would have contacted you if I'd been able, but there was no way."

I nodded.

"Just no way."

"When? When did she have it?"

238

"About a fortnight ago, I believe. She didn't tell me all that much. Difficult things to arrange, so I'm told. I mean, they're not my line of country, and of course they're illegal. Anyway, she got it done somehow, and then it went wrong or something. A friend of hers, a girlfriend, another actress in the same company, rang me one night asking where you were and I couldn't tell her anything, so then she appealed to me, could I help? So I helped. Did the best I could."

I got up and walked around the room.

"The problem was my best was pretty useless, but I did manage to get hold of a reliable doctor — somebody in my outfit gave me his name and he agreed to come and see her. She was here by then, and not very well at all. I gave her my room. Not every doctor will touch these things, even after the event, but this bloke turned up trumps. Apparently, it hadn't been done too expertly; these back-street jobs never are, I gather. But he patched her up, came in twice a day for the first three days. I slept in the room with her, slept in a chair by the bed because she was delirious for a while and it wasn't safe to leave her. I'm telling you all this because it does have a happy ending. She's all right. I made sure of that. She's fine now. And she's gone home where she'll be properly looked after."

I finally managed to put the only other question that mattered to me.

"Whose child was it, did she say?"

Theo studied my face before answering. "Well, yours I presumed."

"How could it be?" I said. "I haven't seen her in over five months."

He looked away. "Oh. Well, I'm not very up on these things. She didn't tell me, and I didn't ask her."

I had the feeling the room was closing in on all four sides, like the remembered childhood terror of the Edgar Allen Poe story. I sat down again and found I couldn't stop myself crying. "I'm sorry," I said. "It's just reaction. That and the tiredness and the gin."

"Doesn't matter," Theo said.

"I'll be okay in a minute." The many ironies slowly began

239

to penetrate. Theo gave me his handerchief and I had a sudden vision of him playing nurse to Jill: well-meaning, half-embarrassed by the intimacy of it all, probably a little revolted by being confronted with such unfamiliarities, but doing his best.

"I'm really sorry," he said.

"Don't be silly. Thank God you were here. Why the hell didn't she tell me? I wouldn't have cared that it wasn't mine."

"Perhaps she did try. Perhaps the letter never reached you. On the other hand, she might have been too scared to tell you, seeing as . . ."

"Yes," I said, thinking back to those afternoons on the houseboat just before the war started. "I've ruined your handkerchief. Still got grime all over me."

"What's a handkerchief between friends?"

"Oh, God . . . I don't know. D'you have her home address?"

He went to the dresser and took a piece of paper from a jug. "They're not on the phone," he said, "if that's what you're thinking."

I was halfway towards the hall. "Well, I'll go there. Can you lend me some money?"

He gave me nine pounds, all he had on him.

"What's your own situation? I haven't asked you that. Are you supposed to rejoin your unit?"

"Yes, but sod that."

"Well, don't get into trouble. Everybody's very trigger-happy, looking for parachutists disguised as nuns."

"I'll risk it. Just go and change. If anybody stops me I'll say I lost my uniform on the way back."

I started up the stairs, then remembered the telephone call.

"By the way, somebody rang just after I got here."

"For me?"

"Could have been, I don't know. He didn't give a name. Just said something about everything's arranged exactly as planned. Then he got cut off."

"Strange. Did he ask for me?"

"No."

"Probably a wrong number."

"Unless you've got a secret lover. How is your love life, by the way?"

"Dull."

"I see you're now reading *Tit Bits*; thought perhaps you're on the turn."

"That must have been Jill's," Theo said. "She must have left it there."

I suddenly became conscious of what he had done for me. I went back to him and put my arms round him. "I'll never forget what you did," I said.

He seemed embarrassed. "I've always liked Jill," he said.

While I was changing he shouted up the stairs to me. "I have to go out again, see I wasn't expecting you. Take care of yourself. When will I see you?"

"I'll ring when I get there."

"I'll leave my office number by the phone."

"What're you up to now? I didn't even ask about you."

"Same old thing. They've given me the rank of major, so next time we meet, salute."

I walked all the way to Euston Station, keeping to the back streets. The station was crowded – a mass of servicemen and civilians milling around in the hope of finding room on those trains still running. There were long queues at all the booking offices and I waited twenty minutes before I got my ticket to Manchester. Then my luck ran out. I was at the barrier before I realised that the platforms were stiff with Military Police. All servicemen were being closely scrutinised, but I still believed I could brazen it out if challenged, forgetting that my army haircut and generally haggard appearance betrayed me. I got on to the platform but was headed off by a Provost Sergeant as I made for the Manchester train.

"Excuse me, soldier," he said.

I kept walking.

"Excuse me, sir." I couldn't ignore that. "D'you have any means of identifying yourself, sir?"

"Not on me. Why are you stopping me? I'm not in the Army."

"Just doing my job, sir. Be easier if you could provide some identification." He was staring at my hair. I was such an amateur at it.

"Okay," I said, bereft of any further inspiration. "You're right. I am in the Army. I'm a sergeant, Intelligence Corps, just back from Dunkirk. I'm trying to get to my girlfriend. She's just lost a baby. It was stupid of me, I know, but I'm desperate, so give me a break."

"Can I have your name and number, Sergeant?"

I gave them.

"No travel warrant?"

"No. I promise you I'm not on the run, and I'll report to my unit as soon as I've seen her. You've got tabs on me now, so turn the other way, will you?"

"Can't," he said.

"Why not? What's it to you?"

"My stripes, that's what it is to me, Serg. Nothing personal, but you should know the rules."

"Fuck the rules," I said. "What difference will it make?"

I might have persuaded him, but he was joined by his officer.

"What's the trouble, Sergeant?"

The sergeant came to attention with shattering, text-book perfection. "This sergeant travelling without a warrant, sah! Lost his uniform at Dunkirk, sah!"

I was grateful to him for that piece of embroidery. The officer looked me up and down.

"What's your unit?"

"Intelligence Corps, sir."

"Oh." We were nobody's favourite. "Well, you'd better rejoin them, hadn't you? Get him over to Chelsea under escort, Sergeant."

He walked away. He had a boil right in the centre of his shaven neck. I heard the guard's whistle herald the departure of my train. The lucky ones scuttled past me to grab at closing doors and swing aboard. The scene suddenly resembled the last reel of a Warner Brothers melodrama.

"Sorry," the Military Police sergeant said. "Did me best, but he's a right pisser."

"That's okay. I know you tried."

242

I followed him to the waiting room being used as a clearing house. It was crowded with a motley collection of dispirited men. I took my place amongst them and after a two-hour wait we were herded into Bedford trucks and taken across London to Chelsea Barracks where I was again interrogated. Resigned to the inevitable by then, I still kept torturing myself with images of Jill, imagining her loneliness and terror going to some squalid, anonymous house in the suburbs to end a life. There were other kinds of war, different betrayals.

After being rekitted I was sent to a holding unit just outside Aldershot. The camp there was under canvas and was crammed with remnants of the B.E.F. who had arrived from all points of the compass. At the first opportunity I persuaded one of the clerks in the adjutant's office to send a telegram to Jill asking her to get in touch. She phoned the following evening and I had to take the call in the Guard House, overheard by a leery group of squaddees. The best we could manage was an exchange of pleasantries, all the while skirting the main topic.

"I never thought I'd hear from you again," she said.

"You know me. Indestructible."

"I didn't mean that."

"I know what you meant, and you're wrong. Look, I'm having to share this conversation . . . We're confined to camp, but is there any chance of you coming down here? When you feel up to it, that is."

There was no answer.

"Hello? You still there?"

"Yes," she said, and I realised she was crying.

"Don't," I said. Then the time pips started to go and I hadn't got any more change. "Write," I shouted before the line went dead.

War plays so many tricks. She did write, but the letter never reached me, because by the time it arrived I had been moved elsewhere, having been singled out for an O.T.C. crash course. I found myself billeted in an elegant Lutyens house a few miles inland from Worthing on the Sussex coast. Things had hotted up after Dunkirk. There was a shortage of junior officers with any sort of field experience and my intake included several other N.C.O.s salvaged from the ill-fated French episode. Once again I tried to let Jill know of my changed whereabouts, but since I was now posted inside a restricted area any chance of her visiting me was ruled out.

The German invasion was expected any day and our training was pushed through at speed. It was a remote existence. The house was set amongst rolling farmland and had it not been for the dogfights tracing black and white doodles in the summer sky, I could have believed I was living in a part of England only seen in travel guides. Most of the civilians in the area had been evacuated; those few able-bodied men who remained were members of the Local Defence Volunteers, and marched up and down the lanes armed with a variety of antique and mostly useless weapons. Despite all the brave rhetoric that Churchill broadcast we were aware that, when the Germans came, we wouldn't be doing too much fighting on the beaches.

One can never exaggerate the absurdities brought about by wars. After I was commissioned I was seconded to MI 5 where I was not required to wear my splendid new uniform. The blow was not softened by the fact that a demented old woman pushed a white feather at me during the train journey to Farnham, my next temporary home. This time I found myself in another large country house that had previously been used as a private clinic specialising in colonic irrigation for rich dipsomaniacs. Naturally, we were immediately known as 'The Colonics' and an anonymous wit chalked 'The higher you go, the more you bring down' above the entrance as a unit motto.

I shared a room with an affable major named Miller (and for some inexplicable reason all Millers were called Dusty) who carried out valiant experiments with some of the abandoned medical equipment and managed to construct an efficient still. The moonshine he produced was commendably lethal once one had got beyond the taste.

Dusty was the only regular soldier amongst us and cast himself as the unit philosopher. Like many of the older hands he had seen service with the Indian Police. "Only outfit that would have me," he said. "Never a great one for exams." He was cynical about everything to do with the Army. "Officially, of course, we don't exist," he told us. "There are no secret services. Why? That's the way the Establishment mind works. Can't admit to anything underhand; destroy the whole bloody system that would. Very dodgy. Might lead to questions in the House. So, if we follow it through logically, if we don't exist we aren't here."

"You've been reading Forster," I said.

"What outfit's he in?"

"He's a novelist."

"Never read novels," Dusty said, and that shut me up. "No, I mean, if we're not here, we can do no wrong. Our job is quite simple . . ." and he slipped, quite unconsciously I'm sure, into a parody of Churchill's voice. "We are in a non-existent organisation, engaged in non-existent acts of deception against non-existent enemies. We should have quite a cushy war."

His cynicism was not too far removed from the truth at that stage of the war. The head of MI 5 at that time was a distinguished servant of the Crown who had received his baptism of fire in the Boxer Rebellion of 1900 and still administered his department with an Edwardian regard for the proprieties. He was renowned for his views on female staff recruitment, requiring his typists to be *Tatler* material and to have a good pair of legs. This admirable philosophy worked wonders for our morale but produced havoc in the filing system. Since the files were the backbone of the entire operation, his prejudices (which to be fair were social rather than sexual) constituted a major threat to the smooth running of his department. Dusty gave his own verdict on the girls of the typing pool, stating that their education had not concentrated on the traditional three 'Rs' but on the three 'Ds' instead. "They rely on being Debby, Dumb and Daddy's," he said with gloomy relish. Most of them were very young and were run by a ferocious dyke who hovered between acute excitement and an angry state of grace, though Dusty maintained that her lick was worse than her bite.

Shortly after I added my inexperience to the collective chaos our headquarters suffered a major disaster. A decision had been taken at the outset of the war to house most of the files in Wormwood Scrubs Prison, the actual prisoners being moved elsewhere. The transfer was not accomplished without mishap. An aged prison chaplain was somehow never informed of the changed circumstances and continued to conduct his weekly services to a congregation of MI 5 cynics in the devout belief that he was still addressing his criminal flock. He confided that, for the first time in his life, he really felt he was 'getting through' and when eventually the top brass discovered he was still operating *in situ*, a decision was taken to preserve his illusions. "Preached a bloody good sermon," Dusty told us. "He'd have made a criminal out of me."

It was generally understood that we could put our fingers on any undesirable political figure in a matter of minutes. Alas, this was a figment of many disordered imaginations, and the reality was quite the reverse. Dusty once made a routine check through the cards and discovered that a maiden aunt of his was listed as an undesirable on the grounds that she paid a yearly pre-war visit to Baden Baden. He added to the incriminating evidence, stating that his aunt kept a dachshund, only went to the Proms when Beethoven was on the programme and used a German bayonet as a fire poker.

A Luftwaffe incendiary bomb put paid to most of these astonishing documents and the gentle hero of the Boxer Rebellion was tactfully retired. Naturally, we of the lower orders based at Colonic Hall only heard faint echoes of such distant thunder. Our life continued to have something of the flavour of a long country weekend. Jill and I finally made contact and I set in motion my own piece of subterfuge, persuading her to come south and join me. I installed her in a small flat over a butcher's shop on the outskirts of Farnham, a move of considerable cunning since a tame butcher in wartime was a friend indeed. There seemed to be a bomber's moon every other night that autumn, and when the Blitz started in earnest Jill and I would often watch the distant battle from a high point on the Common. We were reasonably safe except for the occasional stick of jettisoned bombs, though I daily expected to receive a call telling me that Perrins Walk had been razed.

It was Dusty who discovered what Theo was up to. He had acquired some samples of the work being carried out by the 'Buxton' group, a quasi-propaganda outfit which was tenuously linked to the S.I.S., but more or less operated alone. The Buxton boys' activities supposedly came under Section D, and they had a reputation for dirty tricks which were frowned upon by the older hands.

"What d'you think of these?" Dusty handed me a batch of postcards. They were photographs done with a professional gloss. The first one I turned over depicted Stalin buggering Hitler, their respective heads having been skilfully superimposed on some original pornographic pose.

"It's going to be Buxton's Christmas card this year, I'm told," Dusty said.

I leafed through the rest. There was a set of Goering in the nude, his head superimposed on a gross female body, a gigantic medal hanging between pendulous breasts. The captions were in German, the humour basic. Another set featured Goebbels and Hess. Yet another Bormann, shown naked on all fours, pulling a sleigh with Hitler on board. Later in the war we discovered that a German counterpart to Buxton was producing material in the same vein, depicting Churchill and members of the Royal Family.

"Not really my taste," Dusty said. "Bit too sentimental for me. I prefer the hard stuff. Still, good for morale – Hitler's morale, that is. He's never looked so good."

I didn't think much more about them until a few days later I was handed a memo from the Buxton outfit soliciting our help in accurately identifying the names of certain German divisions believed to be poised for the invasion. The memo was initialled T.G. and the coincidence seemed too strong. According to the fictions we were living amongst, Buxton (which was a cover name) didn't exist anywhere, but Dusty had the number and I called Theo. When he answered the phone I could hear music being played in the background.

"You're obviously having a hard war," I said

"We're putting rude words to the German national anthem. Dangerous work."

"How are you?"

"I'm not quite sure."

"What about Perrins Walk? Has it been hit yet?"

"Still standing at the last count. We've lost some windows, though and some tiles off the roof. Over your bedroom."

"Oh, great! Look, any chance of us meeting for a meal? Jill's down here now and I think I could slip away for a few hours at the weekend."

"Yes. That would be fine."

I thought he sounded slightly guarded, but imagined that he couldn't talk freely.

"Where shall we meet, then? D'you know anywhere good? It's so long since I've been in London."

"There's a place in Berwick Street I've been to. They sometimes have steaks. Can't vouch for them, but they're eatable."

"Okay. What's the name?"

"The Golden Hind."

We arranged to meet there the following Friday evening. He seemed disinclined to prolong the conversation.

"Your memo," I said. "I'm dealing with that. That's how I tracked you down. You'd better be more careful."

It all seemed an absurd game in those days. We blundered about aimlessly, since no cohesive master plan existed. One classic example I remember resulted in our arresting a number of Section D operators in the mistaken belief they were German agents who had been parachuted in. In fact they were trying to set up secret ammunition dumps as a precaution against the expected invasion. Nobody had bothered to tell us they would be working in our area. Those genuine German agents who did manage to land seemed to have been trained in the art of immediate exposure, and most of them were apprehended within hours of coming ashore, not because we were ultra efficient but because they had neglected to memorise the intricacies of British licensing laws: even to this day there are few things more guaranteed to arouse suspicion in these islands than a stranger who attempts to get a drink after hours. I knew of four who were caught in this way. All four were tried and three were executed. It was the only time I believed the game was being played for real.

19

THERE WERE TWO distinct groups in the Blitz: those who lived like moles and those who ignored it. The clientele of The Golden Hind belonged to the latter category. They were mostly rich by the standards of the day, and getting richer, for people who could afford to eat regularly at black-market restaurants were having a good war. There might be a sprinkling of young officers out to impress their girlfriends, but generally the tables were well booked in advance by those who had steered themselves away from the Forces. The food was pretentiously ordinary, the menu un-priced, and the drinks exorbitant.

Theo had booked a table for three in his name. Jill and I arrived first. It was a big night for her and although I took an instant dislike to the place I wasn't going to spoil it for her. Our relationship had changed since the abortion, for few women go through that experience without scars of some sort. She was over-grateful for everything I did, and it had the effect of passing her guilt to me. Not that I blamed her. I didn't blame anybody, but all the same things had changed. One can never go back.

Perhaps it was the atmosphere of the place, or the over-satisfied faces that turned to stare at us as we took our seats, but I had the feeling that the evening wasn't going to live up to expectations. We had a couple of drinks, but when Theo still didn't appear, I made a phone call to Perrins Walk. There was no answer, and by now the Cypriot head waiter was getting edgy so we ordered our meal and started without Theo. The steak when it came could have been horse, but it was so smothered in a nameless sauce that only a pathologist could have given a final verdict.

"What could have happened to him, d'you think?"

"No idea," I said.

The air raid warning had gone at the usual hour, but apart from the odd rumble in the distance it seemed to be a quiet night. I later learnt that the docks at Dagenham had got the brunt of it.

"What sort of work does he do?" Jill asked.

"I don't really know. I think it's something to do with the Ministry of Information."

"He's really a very kind character, isn't he?"

"Yes."

"I never really knew him . . . before. Of course, you've known him all your life."

We sampled that curious British dish known as trifle, eating without enthusiasm. I felt like I sometimes do when I go to the theatre full of expectation only to find that an understudy has been substituted for the star. Jill and I were behaving like an old married couple who had long since exhausted any interesting topic of conversation. Without Theo the whole evening seemed pointless and I found myself staring at the other diners with growing resentment: I didn't want to feel part of them. I had worn my uniform that night to please Jill, and in a way that made me more of a collaborator.

I ordered a last round of drinks and paid the bill, which was a greater outrage that I had prepared myself for. The head waiter returned to the table and for a moment I thought he was going to complain at the paucity of the tip.

"I think there's a phone call for you," he said.

"Oh, right. Must be Theo at last," I said to Jill. "Is it Major Gittings?"

"No," he said. "It's the police." He watched me anxiously as I made my way to the pay-phone which was in the corridor between the restaurant and the kitchens.

"Lieutenant Stern?" a flat voice asked.

"Yes."

"Duty officer Cannon Row here, sir. Sorry to trouble you, but a friend of yours has got himself in a spot of bother, I'm afraid."

"Who?"

"A Major Gittings, sir. He told us you could be contacted

at this number and I wondered if you'd mind coming to the station."

"What sort of trouble?" I said.

"I think it'd be best if we told you that when you get here, sir."

"I'll come right away."

I didn't bother to explain anything to Jill until we were outside. A taxi was out of the question so we trotted through the all-but deserted streets. The air raid was still in progress and the sky behind us was glowing red, the first wave of bombers having come and gone.

"D'you think it's anything serious?" Jill kept saying.

"I don't know, do I? They never tell you anything over the phone."

The front of Cannon Row police station was heavily sand-bagged like all public buildings, and we pushed our way through the gas curtain into the dimly-lit entrance hall. There was a young girl sitting on a bench clutching a bright purple teddy bear, her make-up streaked. I tapped on the glass window of the reception office and after a pause it was opened by an elderly sergeant.

"You contacted me," I said.

"What name would that be, sir?"

"Lieutenant Stern."

"Oh, yes. Yes, well, if you just hang on a minute I'll have somebody take you down."

The window closed again.

"I hate these places," Jill said. "They remind me of hospitals."

The young girl stared at us. "He fucking did nothing," she said blankly. She had teeth missing at both sides of her mouth. Jill reached for my hand.

A plain clothes detective appeared from a doorway and approached us. "If you'd like to come this way, sir."

Jill and I moved forward.

"I think it'd be best if you came on your own, sir. If the young lady would like to wait."

I followed him through a series of doors and we went down one flight. He showed me into what I suppose was an interrogation room. Theo was sitting at a table, his head resting on his arms. He didn't look up when we came in.

"Your friend's arrived," the detective said. He turned to me. "You can identify him, can you, sir?"

"Yes, of course," I said.

I don't know what I had been expecting, but I was shocked by Theo's appearance as he raised his head. One eye was nearly closed and he had blood at the corner of his mouth. He was in civilian clothes and the front of his jacket was stained with dried vomit. He didn't say anything to me. He just looked.

"What's all this about?" I said. "What happened?"

"Well, we'll get to that, sir. I just wanted a formal identification to begin with. Only the gentleman hasn't got any papers on him."

"Yes," I said briskly. "It's my cousin and his name is Theo Gittings and he's a serving officer with the rank of major."

"Fine. Now I'd like a word in private, sir."

"Well, just a minute. Are you holding Major Gittings? I mean, has he been charged with anything?"

"Not at the moment, sir. We're in the process of deciding that and thought you might be able to give us some additional information. Won't take us long, sir."

I addressed Theo directly for the first time. "Are you all right?"

He nodded and mouthed the words 'help me'.

The detective ushered me into an adjoining room and closed the door.

"Now what the hell's going on?"

"Tell me something more about your cousin, sir."

"Well, first of all tell me something. Why have you got him here?"

The detective took out a battered packet of tobacco and a roll of rice papers and began to fashion a ragged cigarette. I suppose it's part of the standard technique for them deliberately to take their time.

"Your cousin could be charged – I'm not saying he will be – on a number of counts. Drunk and disorderly, liable to cause a breach of the peace . . ." He licked the gummed edge of the cigarette paper like a man preparing to play the flute. ". . . and gross indecency, sir. That's the one that concerns me most."

"Must be some mistake," I said.

He lit the cigarette, watching my face all the time. Bits of burning tobacco fell from the end and he ground them out with his heel.

"See, what makes it tricky, sir," he continued, ignoring my remark, "is him being an officer in the Army. We picked him up in civvies, but by rights we have to turn him over. Now I don't want to do that unless it's absolutely necessary, if you get my meaning."

"I still don't understand what you mean about gross indecency."

"He was picked up in a public urinal."

"But how did he get the black eye?"

"I imagine somebody clocked him. That's what usually causes black eyes. Somebody who didn't care for his sort. And I'll tell you something else, off the record. If he wasn't in the Army, I'd black the other bloody eye for him. I'm not too keen on queers."

I decided not to answer that.

"Now you say it's a mistake, and I might, just might, take your word for it."

"He's been under a lot of pressure," I said.

"Is that so?"

"Yes, he's got a very top secret job, a lot of responsibility. It must have got too much for him, and he got drunk and behaved in this totally uncharacteristic way."

"That's how you'd describe it, would you?"

"Absolutely. Believe me."

"Is he married?"

It was then that I took the plunge. "No," I said, "but that's his fiancée upstairs. Now, can I say something off the record?"

"Go ahead."

"She lost a baby recently. Only it wasn't his."

His homemade cigarette was curling upwards, burning unevenly, and he crushed it between his thumb and first

253

finger and put the stub in a tin lid. He made the action look as though he was gathering further evidence.

"Ask her," I said, pushing my luck now, but conscious that I had to convince him.

He looked at me for a long time. "Well, it's late," he said. "And I want to get home. I haven't been home for four nights. Most of that time I've been helping to pick up bits and pieces of people. Not something I enjoy, but I'll tell you something, it doesn't upset me half as much as queers. So you take your cousin off and tell him to stay home with his fiancée. He won't be so lucky if there's a next time."

"Thank you," I said. "That's very decent of you."

"Yes, isn't it? Especially since the whole thing is a mistake."

We went back into the interrogation room. Theo looked worse than before and needed my support as we made our way upstairs, the detective following. It was lucky that, without any signal from me, Jill instinctively put her arms around Theo the moment she saw him. I have no idea whether the detective really believed my explanation and the girl with the purple teddy bear distracted him as we made our exit. "You ought to be in the bleedin' war," she was saying as we made our way out into the street.

"D'you think you can walk?" I asked Theo.

"I'll try. Anything to get away from that place. I'm sorry."

"Well, we'll keep our eyes open for a taxi. We might get lucky, though I doubt it."

"What happened?" Jill asked.

"Theo got in a fight," I said. "You take his other arm."

Together we helped him find his feet as we headed in the direction of Hampstead. He had to rest frequently and was obviously in bad shape, although the cold air gradually sobered him. We didn't talk much on the journey and happily we only had to walk as far as Tottenham Court Road. There we found an empty taxi who was persuaded to take us to Perrins Walk.

We got him upstairs and I undressed him and put him to bed while Jill made us all some strong coffee.

"How did you manage to talk him out of it?" Theo said.

"Oh. Told him a few half-truths. What does it matter?"

"It matters a lot. I'll never be able to thank you."

"You don't have to be grateful. The only thing that concerns me is why the hell you ever got yourself in such a situation. I mean, I'm not going to preach at you, but you must have known there's always the risk you're going to pick up the wrong person."

"You don't have to tell me."

"Well, why tonight of all nights? We were looking forward to seeing you and having a reunion dinner."

"I know," he said. "But something happened."

"I can see that, I just don't understand why."

Jill brought the coffee in and a cold compress for his swollen eye. "Did the police get the man who hit you?" she said. It was typical of her that she didn't question the story I had concocted.

"Apparently not," I said. "He got away in the blackout."

"I think it's terrible. Did he steal any money?"

"It was my own fault," Theo said. "Tony's just trying to be tactful. There's no reason why you shouldn't know the truth since I ruined the evening. I got up to town early and instead of coming here, I went to a bar where I've usually been lucky. Tonight my luck was out. I had too much to drink and picked up the wrong man. Just a normal hazard for queens like me."

"Don't talk like that," Jill said. "You're not a queen."

"Well, I certainly behaved like one tonight," Theo said with a faint attempt at humour. He winced as she applied the compress. "Your turn to look after me. We're a pair, aren't we?"

It was the first time the topic had ever been openly broached between us all and I couldn't help thinking what a strange trio we made. I think, like a lot of women, Jill had the idea that she could somehow change him. There was a certain bond between them that I could never share.

We made him as comfortable as we could and gave him a couple of aspirins, then Jill and I went downstairs to share that curious aftermath of excitement that always attends the misfortunes of a friend. I can't remember that Jill and I had ever discussed Theo's homosexuality in explicit terms, but now that it had been forced into the open she couldn't resist questioning me.

"Is that how they go about it?" she said. "Just picking up strangers in pubs?"

"A lot of them do, I guess."

"But Theo always seemed different. Not obvious. I always imagined that he had a regular boy friend somewhere, if I thought about it at all. When you first brought me back here, I even thought you and he might be a twosome."

"Is that why you held out on me for so long?"

"No, I didn't really think it, but it just occurred to me the first time."

"Understandable I suppose."

"Have you always known?"

"More of less. Not when we were kids, but later when he was up at Cambridge."

"Were you shocked?"

"No. I don't suppose I understood it, perhaps I don't even understand it now, but I wouldn't say I was ever shocked. Does it shock you?"

"Not with Theo. It just seems he's looking for something he'll never find."

"That's true of most of us."

"It must take a very sad person to always love in secret," she said, with more truth than either of us knew at the time.

There was no question of us going back to Farnham that night. I rang the duty officer and sold him some tale of the trains having been cancelled, an excuse which was never questioned in wartime. Theo was sleeping it off by the time we went to bed, but I woke in the middle of the night and heard him groaning. Jill hadn't stirred, so I got up and went into his room to find him coming out of a nightmare. He looked like a broken boxer at the end of a lost fight.

"I was in Spain," he said. "They kept showing me dead bodies."

I made us some tea this time and sat on the end of the bed to keep him company.

"D'you want to talk about tonight?" I said. "Would it help?"

256

"There's not much to tell . . . I just had a shock and I guess I took the easy route. Or what I thought was the easy route."

"It's just the bloody war," I said. "It gets everybody down."

"Yes, I think you're right."

"Is it anything I can help about?"

"You've helped enough already. I thought I was for the high jump there. He was a real queer-basher."

"Did he give you a hard time?"

"Oh, he didn't use rubber hoses or anything like that. That job had been done for him. D'you think he knew who I was?"

"He knew your name, obviously."

"No I meant, do you think he connected the name?"

"He didn't strike me as a literary man," I said. "I think his education stopped with Oscar Wilde."

"I'm sorry Jilly had to see it."

"She's on your side. I think if you ever wanted to change, she'd make an honest woman of you."

He smiled at that, but the effort made him wince. His eye was completely closed now.

"Would you mind if that happened?"

"We could have a ménage à trois . . . Jill and I won't last for ever, if that's what you're asking. What happened sort of changed things. Nobody's fault. Blame the war again."

"I hate what I'm doing," Theo said. "But none of the alternatives are much better, are they?"

"It all seems madness."

I shall never know whether he was on the brink of a confession that night; perhaps if I had pressed him, albeit in innocence of the true causes, he might have shared the guilt, though what I would have done with the information I have no idea. We all betray each other sooner or later; even the most faithful husband commits adultery in his heart.

He told me all in the end, of course. The missing clues in the crossword are all there in his unpublished novel. He was too good a writer not to be selective, but try as he might he couldn't bury all traces of the personal crime, the guilt he took with him to that underground room in Cannon Row where, without my well-meaning intervention he might have found an escape from the continuing loneliness of the rest of his life. It's ironic, but in prison, he would have been safe.

The sense of unreality grew stronger every day. Alec felt he had entered a world that divided loyalty like portions of a wedding cake: everything neatly boxed, an equal amount of marzipan to each section, just a taste of the cake itself – and stale before you ate it. In the first few months it sometimes seemed to him that he was the victim of some elaborate practical joke, the pay-off for which was never going to be revealed. "Be patient," they had said, "all will be revealed." But nothing was. He was never contacted no instructions reached him. He was doubly anonymous. The war hadn't touched him; he read about it and there were minor inconveniences, but for the most part he had merely exchanged one backwater for another. The only thing he missed was young faces. He seemed to be surrounded by middle-aged strangers talking a foreign language, people who were adept at changing the subject if he ever attempted to have an intellectual conversation. They seemed strangely indifferent to the wider issues he had expected them to be concerned with, and spent most of their time plotting how to enlarge their own empires at the expense of others supposedly on the same side. One of them actually used Alec's simile of the wedding cake. "There's only so much to go round, old boy, and it's my job to see that we get more than our fair share."

He felt like a foreigner in London, just another displaced person in the basement flat they had found for him off Hyde Park Gardens – an area where the tarts patrolled in pairs. He moved some of his possessions down from the college – mostly his books and a few nineteenth-century watercolours to brighten up the sweating walls of the flat. The illusion of being a prisoner was strengthened by the bars let into the brick surrounds on all the windows: he could only glimpse a portion of the world outside – a series of headless bodies parading past, and the occasional dog lifting its leg against the railings. He had to keep the lights burning all day, even when the sun was out. Fear seeped in easier than daylight. He had little contact with the other occupants of the house, though he suspected from the comings and goings that one of the upper floors was being used as a brothel. He found himself remembering a fragment of Plautus – *Mulieri nimio male facere melius est onus, quam bene* 'A woman finds it much easier to do ill than well.' But there was nothing classical about the world he now inhabited and he felt oddly emasculated.

When, finally, contact was made again he had almost forgotten their existence. He was walking home across Hyde Park one evening during the autumn of 1940, hoping to be safely inside before the sirens went. The dying sun glinted on the rippling bellies of the barrage balloon, giving the impression that they would suddenly burst into flames. As he approached the Bayswater Road he noticed that some of the tarts were taking up their positions earlier than usual. Probably as anxious as I am, he thought, and not for the first time he pondered about their lives. He knew quite a few of them by sight and sometimes nodded in passing, confident that he would not be solicited – they didn't waste time on neighbours, the pickings were to be had elsewhere. Some of them operated in the park itself, giving what a randy colleague at work described as 'a quick knee-trembler' – lust against the trees, with one eye open for the police, and he tried to imagine a time when he would find himself that desperate for human contact.

Just before he crossed the road he noticed a potential customer negotiating with a young whore in front of a recently bombed house. As often happened the blast had been selective: half of a first-floor bedroom was still miraculously intact, the bed itself protruding over the edge of the jagged rafters, the bedclothes turned down ready for an occupant who would never sleep in it again. It gave a macabre symbolism to the scene and Alec hurried past with head down, turning the corner into Albion Street. He had only gone a few more yards when he became conscious of footsteps gaining on him from behind, and the same man who had been propositioning the teenage whore passed close to him. He felt something being thrust into his hand and checked the impulse to shout out. He had been given a scrap of paper. He kept it clenched in his palm while the man continued on without looking back. Alec waited until he was safely inside his basement living room with the blackout blinds drawn before examining the message. It was brief and to the point. "St. Giles High Street Tearooms. Tonight. 8.30. Look for a copy of *Tit Bits*."

(St. Giles High Street used to run from the unfashionable end of Shaftesbury Avenue to the junction of Tottenham Court Road and Oxford Street. Now most of it lies buried

259

beneath that monument to the property boom known as Centre Point. During the war it had a fairly disreputable appearance, the area alongside St. Giles' Church being somewhere to avoid after dark.)

Alec spotted his contact the moment he stepped through the blackout curtains into the steamy atmosphere of the tearoom. He was sitting at the furthest table from the door, nursing a cup of tea, with the remains of what look like a plate of corned beef and chips. There were perhaps a dozen tables, six to either side of the oblong room, mostly occupied by foreign servicemen. The stench of fried food was almost overpowering.

Alec took a seat opposite the man, having asked if it was free. The copy of *Tit Bits* lay open between them and he found himself staring at an inverted pin-up – an over-developed girl wearing a black negligee. The contact glanced at his wrist-watch and nodded approvingly.

"Have you eaten?"

"No."

A sauce-stained menu was pushed across. "Steer clear of the meat, it's liable to be horse."

"I've never eaten horse," Alec said. "Is it very different? After all, the horse is a clean animal."

"Sweet," the man said. "Hard to chew and sweet."

"I don't know why we're so sentimental about horses," Alec said, studying the depressing alternative choices. "I dare say we'll all have to make concessions if the war continues much longer."

He ordered egg and chips, thinking, they can hardly ruin those, but he was wrong. They seem to have been fried in rifle grease, and the cup of tea included in the price came in a chipped cup.

"I had an eccentric uncle who used to smash cracked cups," he said. The other man's continued silence made him nervous and he took refuge in small-talk. "He claimed they spread diseases, like lavatory seats." The crudeness of the anecdote offended him, but he couldn't help himself. From the kitchen came the sound of Tommy Handley and company. I'm insane, he thought. To be sitting here eating swill with a total stranger.

As if reading this thoughts the man folded the copy of *Tit Bits* and smiled at him.

"Don't look so worried. This is quite safe. When you leave take this with you." He tapped the folded magazine. "I've already done the crossword, but you could check it for me. I think you'll get the answers right."

"Are you ever going to give me anything to do?" Alec said.

"Yes, we want you to discredit somebody. We've got a serious family problem. One of our top agents has crossed the line. He knows enough about out set-up over here to do a lot of damage. Fortunately he doesn't know the names, but he'll talk enough to start a witch-hunt. So we want you to plant material to throw them off the scent. It'll be a good test for you." He smiled again.

"What will I have to do?"

"Nothing violent. Just destroy a man's credibility."

"Who?"

"Chalmers."

"But I know Chalmers."

"Yes. That's why we've picked you."

"But what happens to him afterwards?"

"Do you care?" The voice hardened perceptibly.

"No, of course not," Alec said. "I was just asking."

"It's all been worked out. You're merely the instrument; you needn't feel there's anything personal in it."

"Will he know it's me?"

"You mean will the plant be traced to you? Not if you go about it the right way." He stirred cigarette ash into a black paste in his saucer. "Just follow instructions and you can't go wrong."

"Does it get any easier?" Alec asked. "After the first time, do you get used to it?"

"You have to be a pragmatist."

"Yes," Alec said. "I'm not sure that I've ever quite understood what that means in human terms. It's always seemed to me a politician's excuse for something unforgivable."

"We don't concern ourselves overmuch with forgiveness. If we did everything would grind to a halt, the great revolutionary march forward, etcetera."

Alec thought he detected a note of sarcasm, but he wasn't sure of his ground. Anything might be a trap.

"We have to act quickly in this case," the man said. "So I suggest you start the ball rolling." It was a dismissal.

Alec pushed his sordid plate away and stood up. He took the copy of *Tit Bits*.

"I think you'll enjoy that issue," his companion said in a slightly louder voice. "Some interesting articles and some very saucy pictures."

From the kitchen a parody of a female voice screeched, "Can I do you now, sir?" and the studio audience laughter followed him out into the street.

(It is possible that Theo based this next sequence on the defection to the West in 1940 of a senior Soviet intelligence officer, Walter Krivitsky. Krivitsky told the British authorities that the Foreign Office had been infiltrated by 'somebody of good family and breeding' and from the description he gave, he could well have been referring to Maclean. For reasons that have never been adequately explained this information was never followed through. Maclean continued to operate without undue suspicion for many more years.)

In the end Chalmers's very blandness counted against him. There was nothing in his past, which in itself was a suspicious factor. Happily married with two perfect children and a devoted fluffy wife, dedicated to his work, educated at Winchester and Oxford, a member of Whites, the Carlton and the M.C.C., he epitomised the perfect servant of the State. He held his drink well, seldom gossiped and was well thought of by all his staff – who afterwards derived much pleasure from saying, "Isn't it funny how wrong one can be? He's the very last person one would have thought of."

When Alec returned home that evening he studied the copy of *Tit Bits* and deciphered the code contained in the completed crossword. It occurred to him that the instructions could just as easily have been passed verbally, but he was conditioned to expect the unexpected. Secrecy was a chain reaction, deceit piled upon deceit like layers of garden compost, and underneath truth lay rotting.

During his lunch hour the following day he went to a small stamp dealer's shop off the Strand and asked to see some Edward VII definitives. He was shown into a back room and left alone with a large stock album. From this he extracted a plain manila envelope, made a small purchase of some stamps and asked for a receipt for them. He put the stamps and the manila envelope into his briefcase and after having a hurried sandwich lunch went back to his office.

Later in the afternoon he visited Chalmers on a perfectly legitimate errand, asking for a particular file that only Chalmers had access to. When Chalmers left the room to fetch the file, Alec planted the manila envelope inside Chalmers's briefcase. They chatted about the lack of soap and clean towels in the men's washroom, then Alec checked one of the papers in the file in Chalmers's presence and signed the registry book. They parted on the best of terms with Chalmers insisting that Alec really must come and take pot luck for lunch one Sunday.

"Rosemary was only saying the other day, it's very remiss of us. We've been promising it for ages."

"I'd love to," Alec said. "I must admit Sunday in London on your own is a long day."

He found that he was sweating when he returned to his own office. "I think I'm coming down with a bout of flu," he told his secretary when she expressed concern. She brought him a cup of tea and two aspirins, urging him to go home early. It was almost as if the illness was self-induced, for by the time he got back to his flat he had a slight temperature. The sirens went early that night, but apart from some sporadic explosions in the distance, which he judged to be coming from the East End dock area, it did not seem to be a heavy raid.

After he had made his supper he dressed warmly and went out and walked to Notting Hill Gate Tube station. There he took a roundabout route to the Elephant and Castle and walked to the nearest public call box. He placed a call to a member of the Special Branch who worked closely with his own Section. The number was engaged. Taking no chances he boarded a bus and travelled back across the river, getting off as soon as he had spotted another call box. He rang the same number again and this time he got an answer. After verifying he was speaking to the right man he plunged straight into his rehearsed speech.

"If you want some useful information on the Stupolsky affair, search Chalmers's home."

"Who is that?"

"A very reliable source. Chalmers is your man," he said, and broke the connection. He ran from the call box, almost knocking over an air-raid warden.

"Don't bloody apologise, will you?" the warden shouted after him, but Alec ran on until his lungs started to burn. An ack-ack gun battery opened up quite close to, and he heard the familiar sound of Dornier engines. He leaned up against a wall, pressing his forehead against the cold brickwork until he could breathe normally again.

Shrapnel started to fall on nearby roofs and a voice shouted out of the darkness, "Get off the street, there's one right overhead." He turned and took refuge in a street shelter as the noise of the descending bomb obliterated all previous fears. The shelter was crammed with regulars, most of them well equipped with blankets and Thermos flasks. The atmosphere was fetid – a mixture of human sweat, tobacco smoke and the smell of fish and chips and vinegar. A dozen faces turned towards him as he slumped into the nearest space. It was almost as if he was contaminating them with some new menace.

An old woman wearing a man's flat cap and an overcoat tied round the middle with string cackled at him, exposing a mouth devoid of teeth. "The bleeders are at it tonight," she said. "Dropping them all over the fucking place. That one nearly had your bleedin' number on it." She laughed again and he could hear the phlegm rising in her throat. "Ain't got any fags, 'ave yer? I've done mine in."

Alec fumbled for his cigarettes and offered her one.

"These are fancy," the old woman said. "Ain't come across these before. What are they? Bit la-di-da, aren't they?"

Alec did not trust himself to answer her. He struck a match for her and found that his hands were still shaking.

"Gives you a turn, don't it? Fucking old 'Itler."

"Mind your language, you dozy old cow," another voice said from the opposite benches. "Got children here."

"Piss off!" the old woman said. She coughed herself puce. "Gor!" she said when she had recovered sufficiently. "What's in these, then?" She leaned in towards Alec and he was conscious of the smell of lavender moth balls.

Then there was a lull outside and on an impulse he got to his feet and blundered through the gas curtains to the fresh air. Behind him he heard the old woman say, "Now look what you've done!"

The bomb had landed two streets away and the fire engines and heavy rescue teams were just arriving. There were confused shouts all round him and the roadway was suddenly illuminated as a gas main went up, sending a sheet of flame above the roof-tops. Fear and shock had robbed him of a sense of direction, but he hurried away from the incident, hoping that luck would lead him to the river. He covered a mile before he came to another Tube station and was able to feel safe.

He had no need to feign sickness the following morning, but he felt compelled to go into work. If things had gone according to plan his own absence might look suspicious. He allowed his secretary the luxury of feeling concerned for him and tried to concentrate on routine correspondence, deliberately avoiding any mention of Chalmers. It wasn't until he went into the canteen at lunchtime that he was able to confirm that Chalmers had not reported in that morning.

"There's a lot of illness going around," Alec said. "Has anybody telephoned to see how he is?"

By the third day, with Chalmers still absent, the first rumours started. Morris, the number two under Chalmers, sent for Alec in the afternoon of the third day. He was with the Special Branch man Alec had telephoned.

"You know Commander Latimer, Alec?"

"Yes, we have met."

"We've got a situation on our hands, Alec, and the commander would like to pick your brains."

"I hate that expression," Latimer said. "Makes us sound like carrion. It's all informal, Alec . . . Can I call you Alec?"

"Of course."

"Just one or two loose ends I'd like to clear up."

He had the easy manner of the trained interrogator. "How well do you know Chalmers?" he said, with a smile that came like an afterthought.

"Reasonably. I mean, we see each other most days."

"In the course of work?"

"Yes."

"Ever meet him socially?"

"We've had the occasional lunch together."

"Never been to his home?"

"No. He's often talked of inviting me. As a matter of fact only the other day he said he wanted to have me back for a meal one Sunday."

"You know about the Stupolsky affair, of course."

"I know he defected, yes. It doesn't actually concern my Section. I have a limited knowledge."

"Did Chalmers ever talk about him?"

"He might have done. We all did when it became known. There was a certain natural curiosity."

"And?"

"I'm sorry?" Alec said. "I'm not quite sure what you're asking."

"The commander's trying to trace certain things to their source," Morris said.

"How exactly did Chalmers talk about Stupolsky?"

265

"He seemed excited."

"In what way?"

"Well, he felt it was a windfall. He seemed to think Stupolsky might have valuable information."

"That was all?"

"Yes."

"He didn't seem odd in any way?"

"Look," Alec said, "could I ask what all this is about?"

"It could be," the commander said, "that there's a connection between Chalmers and the Russians."

"Chalmers?"

"Certain things have come to light, Alec," Morris said smugly. He's already banking on promotion, Alec thought. "We can't take you completely into the picture, but it would appear that the evidence against Chalmers is fairly conclusive."

"Curiously enough you were one of the last people to see him on Monday afternoon," the commander said. "Did you notice anything different about him?"

"Monday afternoon?"

"You requested a file. It's in the registry book."

"That's right, yes, I did. No, he was the same as usual."

"What did you talk about?"

"Towels," Alec said.

"Towels?"

"Yes, we were both complaining that they're never changed regularly in the washroom."

Morris and the commander exchanged looks.

"Nothing very illuminating, I'm afraid," Alec continued. "To tell you the truth I wasn't feeling too hot. I thought I was coming down with flu, so I went home early. In case I gave it to anybody else. When Chalmers didn't come in the next day, I felt slightly guilty." He looked at the two men. "I say, he's all right, isn't he?"

"He took the top of his head off this morning," Latimer said. "In the garden shed. Not a very pleasant way of doing it. Shotguns never are, especially for those who have to find the remains."

"One of his children found him," Morris said. "Found bits of him, would be more accurate."

Alec groped for a chair and sat down. "Good God!" he said. "Excuse me, but I can't believe it." He had no need to act. The shock of what he had just been told relieved him of all sham emotions.

"Exactly my reaction," Morris said. "Quite incredible."

"Officially he died of a heart attack," Latimer said. "It's important that none of this gets out."

"But why?" Alec said. "Why would he do a thing like that?"

"We had a tip-off and when we searched his house we came up with this." He went to Morris's desk and picked up the manila envelope. He opened it and shook a key into his palm. "In itself nothing much. Just a key to a locker on Victoria Station. Chalmers couldn't explain it. He was co-operating at that point, and in fact I believed him. What was inside the locker told a different story, however."

He slid the key back into the envelope. "But even that wasn't conclusive in itself. Evidence can always be planted. But when we went back to Stupolsky we used a little more persuasion, and he named Chalmers. Gave us chapter and verse. It seems we all made a mistake about Chalmers. He was in it up to his neck, from Spain onwards."

Alec composed his face before he looked up. "He seemed so . . . well, it's beyond me. I'm somewhat of a newcomer to these things," he said, and the truth of how he had been used was just beginning to seep through. "But killing himself like that."

"No, I think that was in character," Latimer said. "And at least it saved us the trouble."

That night he did something that previously would have been unthinkable. After giving himself some liquid Dutch courage in the local pub, he walked across Bayswater Road and into the park to pick up one of the young whores. There was no attempt at selection; he struck a deal with the first one who approached him. She couldn't have been much more than seventeen and had a strong provincial accent. He was just sober enought to register that she was more concerned about the well-being of her poodle than the business in hand. She tied the dog to a tree and it fretted and whined all the time Alec took his quick, fumbled pleasure. It was the dog that gave them away and he just had time to adjust his clothing and run into the darkened park as the police approached. He could hear the girl shouting abuse at the police as he plunged further into the darkness and when eventually he felt himself to be safe he sat on the ground and cried. He remembered the girl's pinched, adolescent face and self-disgust made him retch. Chalmers's daughter was roughly the same age.

It was two weeks after Chalmers's funeral – an uneasy ceremony at a suburban crematorium attended by representatives from all departments – before Alec was contacted again. He received a single theatre ticket in his mail one morning. It was for a stall seat to the new Herbert Farjeon revue at Wyndham's Theatre. That was it. No message, no instructions. Staring at it, Alec had a transient moment of relief: they don't know everything about me, he thought: I wouldn't have chosen this particular show. An orchestral concert was more his mark – Brahms or Sibelius.

He went to the theatre on the appointed night. The aisle seat next to his remained empty until just after the curtain had risen, and then his contact, whom he now knew as Peter, eased into it. They did not acknowledge each other. Rather to his surprise Alec found himself enjoying the show and it wasn't until the interval that he remembered the true purpose of his visit. Peter made no attempt to join the crush making for the bar.

"Could I borrow your programme, please?" Peter said. "I came in late and didn't get one."

The request was made in a loud voice, presumably for the benefit of anybody who might have been listening. How absurd, Alec thought, to go to such ridiculous lengths, and then he had a sudden vision of poor, dead Chalmers – death in the potting shed, the child at the moment of discovery, seeing what remained of his face amongst the stored daffodil bulbs, the cobwebs flecked with blood.

Peter went through the motions of studying the programme for a few moments, and then Alec saw him insert a small piece of paper between the centre pages before handing it back.

"Very enjoyable first half, didn't you think?"

"Yes," Alec said. He desperately wanted a drink, but by now the audience was coming back.

Peter stood to let some people pass along the row, and when they had cleared Alec found he had disappeared. As the house lights were being lowered he glanced inside the programme. The slip of paper had an address on it: Flat 3, 98, Limerston Street, Chelsea. After memorising it, Alec tore the paper into minute pieces, sprinkling half under his seat and keeping the rest to dispose of in the street. He watched the remainder of the show with scant concentration and left while the cast were taking their first bows.

He was lucky enough to find a taxi, directing the driver to World's End rather than the exact address (it's becoming second nature, he thought) and then walking by a roundabout route to Limerston Street. He flared a match in cupped hands to read the nameplates on a front door that had been boarded up following previous blast damage. He rang the bell alongside the handwritten card for Flat 3 and after a short pause the door was opened by Peter. He followed him upstairs to the second floor of a three storey house, Peter shining a torch to show him the way.

The flat was surprisingly well-furnished and comfortable and this further disconcerted him, for he had prepared himself to accept something squalid, something in keeping with the company he was now forced to keep

"Scotch?" Peter said.

"Thank you."

"Gin or what-have-you, if you prefer. I've got everything."

"No, Scotch would be fine."

Peter handed him a generous measure and offered soda.

"No, I'll take it neat."

"Well, I think congratulations are in order. You did admirably. Admirably. Everybody's very pleased with you."

"Including Chalmers's widow?"

"You mustn't think of it like that." he said with fake concern.

"How should I think of it?"

"Just as something that had to be done."

"You lied to me," Alec said. He still hadn't touched his drink, since drinking while Peter had his glass raised would have seemed like a toast he did not want to respond to.

"I don't think so. Did I? In what way?"

"You said you only wanted to destroy his credibility."

"But my dear comrade, we didn't kill Chalmers. He put his own gun to his head."

"Yes. Very convenient all round. That's more or less what Latimer said. I didn't come into this to kill people."

"There's a war on, you know. People do get killed in war. It could happen to us, tonight," Peter said as distant sirens began to wail, soon to be echoed by those closer to hand. "The point is our deaths would serve little purpose. Chalmer's suicide was quite a different matter. I wouldn't waste too much sympathy on him. He wasn't what you thought. I'd save your concern for more positive matters. Look upon Chalmers's timely exit as a warning."

"For whom?"

"You. Me. All of us, comrade."

"Do you mind," Alec said, "not calling me comrade? It's not a word that has much meaning for me. You're not a comrade. You're just somebody I'm forced to know." The whisky had given him a spurious courage.

"Next time," he said, "If there is a next time, I want to know what the end of the game is before I start." The anti-aircraft batteries opened up across the river at that moment, but he felt curiously detached from the dangers of the outside world: all his faculties were concentrated on the man sitting opposite him. He was reminded of leaner days, facing a bank manager to whom he had just applied for a loan without collateral. He would have welcomed sudden obliteration at that moment – the direct hit, fear and shame wiped out in one last shrieking rush of descending German steel and explosive.

"All right, Alec, whichever you prefer. We'll dispense with the congratulations since they seem to disturb you. There'll be other things in the future, of course You can depend on that. It doesn't end with Chalmers's death. He was just a small cog. Don't waste too much sympathy on him; his widow and children will be taken care of by two grateful governments. They've got a bonus."

"You mean Chalmers wasn't innocent?"

"Now don't grasp at straws too quickly. I didn't say that, did I? Didn't give you that impression? Chalmers had something to hide like everybody else, though maybe it wasn't worth blowing your head off for. That's why we had to add a little more colour. That's where you came in. If you really want a guilty conscience, Chalmers had to go to save you."

Alec stared at him. The words refused to penetrate.

"He'd served his purpose a long time ago. He was burnt out. We never intended lighting him again. It was you. We think you're a coming man. You were one we had to protect. They were getting too close, you see. That bastard Stupolsky had led them very near; he knew most of it, but he didn't have your name. We had to give them a name. Now they're happy. They've buried Chalmers and they can close the file. You know what tidy little minds they've got."

"I killed him," Alec said.

"You're too sensitive, Alec. Doesn't do to take things so personally. I mean, it's admirable in one way, means you care, but at the same time it complicates matters. For you, that is. Once you learn to take the longer view, everything falls into place. Adapt to changing circumstances, Alec, and you stay alive."

He held his smile for longer than the occasion merited. Somewhere in the direction of Hammersmith a flare descended, brightening the room. They stood like figures in a stage tableau. Then they heard a noise impossible to identify, as though somebody had thrown a heavy curtain from a great height and a wind had caught it from below, flapping it like sail on a capsized ship. They looked at each other, and Peter shouted "Get down!" but before he could throw himself to the ground the entire window frame disintegrated, and blast lifted him into the air like a macabre version of Peter Pan. He was flung into a bookcase on the far side of the room and as that collapsed, part of the ceiling fell down on him and he lay there like some crumpled ghost until blood started to spurt, smearing the white plaster and the torn books. Alec crouched, unharmed except for a single cut from broken glass on the hand he had managed to shield his eyes with. Somehow the blast had missed him, adding another story to the various legends of the Blitz.

For a minute or more he lost all power in his limbs and remained there as though posing for a statue. His eardrums suddenly popped and then he heard the cries of confusion from other parts of the house. Somewhere a whistle was blowing, a nearby wall tumbled, shaking the room and he forced himself to a standing position. He picked his way across the debris to where Peter lay motionless. Blood was pumping out of a jagged hole in Peter's neck and a lump of glass from the window stuck out of his forehead giving him the appearance of a human unicorn.

He had never known such fear before, but part of his brain signalled that he had other dangers to face. He not only had to get out alive, but he had to avoid being identified. The door to the landing swung on shattered hinges. He groped his way out, a step at at time, into darkness that was thick with choking dust. Somebody below shone a torch and a voice called out: "Is there anybody up there?"

"Yes," he shouted.

"How many?"

"Only one," he answered.

The beam of the torch provided some slight illumination in the dusty gloom, and he picked his way towards it. Some parts of the stair rail were missing, and he hugged the wall as he descended.

"Hurry it up," the voice said, "the whole bloody lot's going to go any minute."

Suddenly he was close to the light source and hands reached out and grasped him under the armpits, lifting him down the last few feet, and guiding him towards the street. He had no sooner reached the pavement when he heard the upper floors collapse. Other hands helped him away from the scene.

"Sure there was nobody else up there?"

"I don't think so," he said, his brain working quicker now that he was safe.

271

"You injured?"

"Just a cut on the hand. Nothing. I was lucky."

"Get his name," another voice shouted. "We're making a check."

"Look, sit down here, sir, until we get an ambulance."

"I'm fine," he said. "You take care of people who need it."

"Can we just have your name?"

"Maybone," Alec said "Charles Maybone," giving the name of a form master he had once had at Prep school, and wondered why that name had suddenly leapt into his mind.

They left him alone, sitting on the kerbstone as a Heavy Rescue Lorry and an Auxiliary Fire Pump roared on to the scene. Fires were starting at the far end of the street, and helmeted figures ran in haphazard patterns. He heard one of them cry, "There's a kid trapped in number 43," and all the figures converged on one particular spot. I must get away, he thought. Now, before they come back and ask other questions. He seemed to have been forgotten for the moment. Shock, delayed until now, shook his limbs as he got to his feet. He found he had to lift his legs unnaturally high before putting them to the ground – they seemed to belong to somebody else, moving independently. He grasped at some railings for support and the wound on his hand began to bleed again.

"Maybone," he said aloud, "dear old Maybone. Why him? He always caned me," talking to himself as he forced his legs to transport him further and further from the scene. He started to laugh, binding a handkerchief round his wounded hand, a feeling of exaltation taking over from fear.

Another pedestrian arriving to give help loomed in front of him. "You all right, mate?"

"Happy," Alec said. "Very lucky, very happy," as though it was the best joke he had heard in ages.

The stranger stared at him uncertainly for a few seconds. "Good," he said, "good, you're happy, are you?"

"Going home now," Alec said. "Going home. To bed."

He walked on while behind him more rubble fell, burying old treacheries.

20

THEO WAS BETRAYED into betraying by an act of love, becoming in the process more dangerous, perhaps, than those who commit treason from a deep sense of political morality. There must have been a 'Chalmers' episode in his life. We all sent men to their deaths – that was par for the course; most of us were lucky; we did not have to put faces to our crimes. I also believe that it is more than possible they left him alone for a while following the fortuitous death of his control, the man he called Peter. They were ultra cautious and they had infinite patience. It's worth recalling that at this point in the war the convenient logicality of the Nazi–Soviet alliance was in the process of being set aside, an added reason for proceeding with care. Plans for the German invasion of Russia were well advanced as early as July 1940 when most informed sources were only looking towards the English Channel. Well documented warnings went out from our intelligence services and were ignored. The Soviets even dismissed their own double-agents' exact and accurate dates for the launching of Barbarossa, paranoically determined to believe that any information originating from the West had to be a plant. Deceit, like religion, has to begin with faith, and once any of us have taken the first step we are committed to the belief that the dogma we live by is shared by others of the same faith. But the double-agent has no priest to confide in, no ritual to comfort: hot chocolate was Theo's last communion wine. And what did his arms enfold as he died? Not a faith, not another body, not even a stranger's warmth, merely a leaking hot water bottle as he returned, full circle, to the nursery.

There is a conceit in deep friendships which allows us to cling to the hope that, given the opportunity, we can change another person's life. Had Theo and I been closer during that last decade, had I made that extra effort to break into his silence, would the end have been any different, I wonder?

Following the episode at the police station we saw each other more frequently. We never discussed our respective roles in any detail, it being an unwritten law that one maintained a front of ignorance. We usually met for a meal at an old established restaurant off the Strand which to this day is still frequented by government officials seeking a discreet venue. I remember one such occasion around that time, just before I was shunted off at short notice to investigate leakages and corruption in Cairo. We drifted into one of those conversations that follow no particular direction – the sort of dialogue that old friends resume when they have been apart for a period and which picks up the threads of their respective lives in a verbal shorthand strangers find unfathomable.

"I see somebody mentioned Auden and Isherwood again," Theo began.

"Some M.P. I suppose? Has to be."

"Yes. Usual stuff. Why are they seeking refuge abroad, being British citizens of military age?"

"Where are they now?"

"Still in America. Isherwood's in Hollywood, I think, working for the movies. Good luck to him. I hope he's eating better than we are today. What is this?"

"It said rabbit on the menu."

"Tastes like Beatrix Potter," Theo said. "Have you done any serious writing lately?"

"Not really. No time. Well, that's a feeble excuse; one can always make time to write something. I keep a sort of diary. Highly illegal, of course."

"Is it?"

"Yes," I said. "Definitely frowned upon in our trade."

"I don't sleep very well these days."

The non-sequitur seemed perfectly natural to me.

"The moment I put my head on the pillow I start to have the strangest sexual fantasies. They keep me awake for hours."

"Can you share them?"

"No, I don't think so. Hardly likely to be your cup of tea."

"Well, my cup of tea doesn't exactly runneth over at the moment."

"How's Jill?"

"That's over. Sad, but perhaps inevitable. She ended it, and I didn't stop her ending it, if I can put it that way. You should read Proust, like I do, if you can't sleep. Very soothing."

"Yes, he's always been the French cure for insomnia I'm told. I can't say I like him, you sometimes need a map to get to the end of some of his sentences, but I envy him. Envy the life style he led. The idea of a writer sacrificing his mortal body to an immortal work. That's a noble thought . . . He consecrated all his strength, you know, lying there in that comfortless cell he called a bedroom, working all night – that race with death – then taking veronal at dawn and sleeping until the afternoon."

"He believed a writer's first duty is to live for his work."

"I ought to like him more, really."

"Why do you say that?"

"Well, I'm likewise obsessed with the past. I think one of the truest things he ever wrote, and let me get it right, I'm always very shaky on quotations . . . He said, 'Love is less dangerous than friendship because . . . because being subjective, it does not turn us from ourselves.'"

"I'll have to work that one out," I said.

As parts of that conversation surface again, I can't help making the comparison with his own death. He found a cell, the isolation, but he had no Celeste at his end (one could hardly cast the predatory Mrs. Davis in that role) and he betrayed his true calling. He also proved his favourite quotation false.

From Proust we turned, incongruously, to his father. I remember suggesting that perhaps Harry Gittings was Theo's equivalent of Baron Charlus.

"No," Theo said. "The aged father doesn't have the imagination to be anything but disgustingly normal. I'll tell you something though, since we're on the subject."

"What subject?"

"Homosexuality. I was talking to a character the other day

275

who advanced an interesting theory. Did you know that before the purges Russian legislation decreed that an individual's sex life was private and therefore outside the law? Which perhaps explains why so many homosexuals turned to communisim."

He elaborated on this for a while, speaking in a detached, unselfconscious way about his own sexual attitudes, eventually bringing the conversation round to certain studies his department had made regarding the connection between sado-masochism and the appeal of Nazism. We exchanged views about the possibility of Hitler turning towards the Eastern front, both of us maintaining the pretence that we had no special knowledge.

"D'you think it has any effect, what we're doing?" I said.

"We'll know if we win. No, let me rephrase that. We'll know if we lose. The victors never give away their secrets; they may want to use them again. It'll be interesting, though, if he does attack Russia. They'll become our allies. Quite a few people will have to do an abrupt about-face."

"Including our mobs."

"Yes, there is that, of course. I don't trust the Russians, do you?"

"It's been drummed into me that we shouldn't trust anybody."

A few days later he rang me to say that Diana had been killed in an air raid. She was amongst the eighty-four dead when the bomb fell on the old Café de Paris. I was told that girls tore their evening dresses to make bandages for the badly wounded, and those waiters still alive poured champagne over wounds to disinfect them. "I imagine she died as she lived," Theo said, "with her tongue in somebody's else's cheek."

That was the last time I spoke to him for two years.

I travelled to Cairo in a converted Stirling bomber the next day and from the moment I landed I hated every moment of that assignment. The appalling comparisons between the luxury of the few and the squalor of the many, the corruption it was my duty to uncover and the corruption that went unheeded, plus the heat and the filth made it one of the most depressing periods in my life. I was engaged on a squalid mission and the man I was hunting tried to kill me, a botched attempt as clumsy as the rest of his life, but it resulted in my spending a month in a military hospital. During that time I fell in love with and proposed to a Scottish nursing sister. We were married on the first afternoon I was allowed out and spent a three-day honeymoon at the rest camp by the shores of Lake Timsah. Her name was Alison and I would like to think that I made her briefly happy. As soon as I was passed fit I was ordered back to London. By the time my troopship docked at Liverpool she was dead – killed during the disastrous campaign in Crete. I don't even know where she is buried, if she was buried.

The official notification didn't reach me until two months later and by the same post the authorities returned all my letters to her unopened. The few weeks we had together are like uncut pages in a book, and now I can't even recall her sweet face; the only memory I have is her voice coming to me sometimes during a dream as it once did in the blue darkness of that hospital ward: the words of comfort she used as she slipped the pain-obliterating needle into the vein. There was no such instant relief in the months following the news of her death. I took refuge in drink for a while, but nothing wiped out that particular pain and I sought my own destruction with an enthusiasm my superiors mistook for commendable bravery. Heroism is so often akin to a gambler's philosophy: if you go to the tables indifferent to your fate the odds of winning seem to increase. I finally persuaded my commanding officer that I was expendable and they parachuted me into Jugoslavia to join up with Tito's partisans. I can remember that dark descent when I would have welcomed the killing tracers from below, but my luck held and for the next eighteen months I lived a life of charmed recklessness; the more I tested Fate, the more I appeared to have been granted immunity and in the end my self-disregard was rewarded with a medal, the final irony, I suppose, of my personal war.

Smuggled back into England by a tortuous route, my first concern was to try and contact Theo. I found London greatly changed. The streets were poxed with bomb craters and people looked shabbier than I had remembered, but there was an atmosphere of hope now. The Yanks had arrived, of course, and were much in evidence, dispensing silk stockings to over-impressionable girls and depositing liberal dollops of chewing gum on the pavements. Nothing else seemed unduly disturbed. Ascot had been reinstated, elderly peers were still being cited in torrid divorce cases, the Russian Ambassador's portrait was hung in the Tate Gallery and Sir Oswald and Lady Mosley released from prison. Much to my surprise Perrins Walk had survived. Despite a few cracks in the brickwork and some missing roof tiles, it had withstood the worst of the Blitz, and my possessions, damp when they were not dusty, were intact. I had a whole month's leave due to me and what then amounted to a small fortune in back pay which I resolved to squander as soon as possible.

Of Theo there was no sign. His part of the house seemed as unlived in as my own. I made some enquiries at the last known address but the man who answered the phone was war-time cagey and, it seemed to me, deliberately vague.

"I'll make enquiries," he said, "and if we can help you I'll have somebody call you back. Can I have your name again?"

"Stern. Major Stern," I said, pulling rank to see if that would stand him to attention at the other end. But he seemed even less impressed than before.

"We'll check through, Major."

I sat down in that empty, dank house totally at a loss. Expectations of home had been so strong while I was living in the Jugoslavian mountains that the feeling of let-down was inevitable. I suddenly realised I had completely lost touch with my old life style. There was no Alison and no immediate substitute for Alison. On an impulse I rang one of my brothers. The phone was answered by his wife – a harassed, slightly common voice snapped at me, and in the background I could hear a child crying.

"Who?" she said. Then, "will you shut up and be quiet! Otherwise you'll get a good smack. Sorry. I didn't get that. Who is it?"

"Tony."

"Tony who?"

"Your brother-in-law."

There was a pause. "Oh, Tony! That Tony. Where are you?"

"In London. I just got back from overseas."

"No letters or anything, we thought you were dead."

My mood was such that I imagined I could detect a note of disappointment. "No," I said. I started to say, "How's . . . er . . ." and then my mind went a complete blank. I couldn't remember which of my brothers I was ringing, nor could I remember her name.

"Oh, so, so. He's doing war-work, of course. Reserved occupation. Had the usual flu he always gets, and of course we've got three now. That's little Martin you can hear."

I had sudden recall – a vivid picture of life at the other end of the phone: the well-meaning but claustrophobic homeliness, its set patterns of conversation, meals, sex. I listened while my sister-in-law gave me chapter and verse of what they had eaten for lunch the previous Sunday (food, I found, was a chronic obsession for many), how well my brother was doing in his job, what she intended to spend the clothing coupons on. She made it sound as though most of the burden of the war had fallen on her shoulders alone, and it wasn't until near the end of the conversation that she casually mentioned my father.

"Of course, we're just getting over that."

"What's that?"

"Oh, God!" she said. "Now what have I said? You don't know, do you?"

But even as she said it, I did know, for many times in the Jugoslavian mountains I had woken wet and cold from a nightmare premonition.

"Is he dead? Is that what you mean?"

"Yes," she said. "I'm sorry. Poor Father passed over two months ago. We had no means of letting you know, you see."

"No. That's all right. Did he have a bad time?"

"Oh, no. Quite peaceful, the doctor said. He was well looked after."

I tried to picture my father's resigned face the last time I had seen him and what troubled me most was the pointlessness of his whole life. It seemed I had been singled out to hear everything second hand, buying my sorrow in the antique market. At the other end of the line there was the sound of something crashing down, and the baby started to howl again.

"Oh, God, now look what he's done! I'll have to ring off, I'm afraid. Shall we see you?"

"Yes," I said, without enthusiasm, "I'll give you another ring." But as the line went dead I knew I had no intention of making good the promise. With the death of my father the last family link had been severed. It seemed hypocritical to pretend to a loyalty I had never enjoyed.

Before I could move away from the phone it rang again. This time it was Theo.

"You're just in time for a whole orange for Christmas," was Theo's greeting. "How are you, dear? All in one piece?"

"Just about."

"And a major to boot. Very impressive. I've always wanted to meet a war hero. Look, stay where you are and I'll come home. Take me about two or three hours, depending on whether I can scrounge a lift."

"Where are you?"

"That's classified."

"You don't seem to have been living here very much."

"Don't I? No, I suppose I haven't."

While I waited for him I spent the time sorting through a motley pile of mail, most of it referring to a life I had all but forgotten. There were polite reminders from my tailor rendering his account for the last suit I had ordered and which I now discovered had been colandered by moths, and a hardly decipherable note from my father, obviously written from his hospital bed, expressing the forlorn hope that he would see me once again before he died. I burnt this and my letters to Alison in the sooted grate, and the fire was still smouldering when Theo walked in. My immediate thought was that he looked older than his years. We were both in our early thirties, but I dare say the war had aged us prematurely.

"Getting rid of the evidence?" he said.

We embraced.

"Burning my past. Did you know about Father?"

"Yes. I happened to come back and there was a telegram. I didn't go to the funeral, I'm afraid."

"Why should you? Funerals are something to avoid."

"I managed to get this," Theo said. "Traded my butter ration for a month." He held up a bottle of champagne. "The widow before butter or guns, is my motto. I thought we ought to celebrate with something vintage."

The cork flew across the room with satisfying force. It wasn't cold enough, but it was still delicious, the best thing I had tasted in years.

"I know you can't give me map references, but are you a town or country mouse?"

"We've just been moved back to the town," Theo said. "The Yanks have moved in with us, which may have something to do with it. Plus something of a palace revolution. I often get the feeling that our boss sees his mission in life as the suppression of intelligence. Not good for morale."

"How are the Yanks?"

"Well, they go about it in a different way from us, of course. There's a slight whiff of Jimmy Cagney about some of them . . . In fact – well, I suppose I can tell you – I met Purvis the other day."

I must have looked blank.

"Melvin Purvis, the F.B.I. agent who killed Dillinger. Quite a glamour boy. The typing pool got very flushed."

"Are you glad to be back in town?"

"It might make my sexual life a little more varied. Bovine village youths pall after a while."

"I'm amazed you get away with it."

"Yes, doesn't say much for our staff security, does it? I'm very discreet, I never do it on my own doorstep. And I sprinkle my dialogue with hearty references to Rita Hayworth and Phyllis Dixey – whoever she is. The only person who might blow the gaff is Kim, but he's loyal to his old college chums."

"Kim?"

"Philby."

"Oh, yes. How is he?"

"Very much the coming man. Highly respected. Puts us all to shame, in fact. Works night and day. A somewhat transparent case of ambition, perhaps."

"Do you ever see any of the others?"

"Oh, they're all about, I believe. Doing their bit. Did you enjoy whatever you were doing?"

"It was different, shall we say?"

"I'm a bit late, but congratulations." He pointed to my medal ribbon.

"Oh, well," I said. "They pick names out of a hat, I think."

"Do we talk about our literary careers?"

"I don't know. Do we? I haven't written much. Collected a few plots, maybe, to store away. How about you?"

"Well, I haven't penned myself into the twentieth century, if that's what you mean. I mean, the characters I meet, they're all frightfully brainy, do *The Times* crossword in seventeen minutes flat and all that, but incredibly dull and uninspiring. The real thing that puts me off finishing a new novel is that ghastly toilet paper everything's printed on nowadays. I mean, I don't want to be published 'in accordance with wartime standards'. It sounds as though one has been instantly remaindered."

I noticed that he had developed several small nervous gestures, most noticeable when he was smoking a cigarette. He seldom used an ashtray, collecting the ash in the palm of his hand, or else standing the butt upright on the nearest flat surface and letting it burn down. I showed him a trick I had learnt in the field – that of placing a penny over the burning tip: it not only extinguished the cigarette immediately but allowed one to resmoke it at a later date.

"I must remember that," Theo said.

"I'll tell you something else I learnt. It's World War One stuff, but still useful in the survival kit. Never light three cigarettes from one match."

"Oh, yes, that's something to do with snipers, isn't it?"

"Yes, they see it the first time, take aim on the second, and kill on the third."

"You sound as though somebody tried it."

"Yes."

"I don't know what I'd be like, actually under fire. We seem to kill people by remote control. I suppose that's easier on the conscience, wouldn't you say?"

"I don't know. Is it?"

"No," Theo said. He stared at the ash in his palm. "And the thing is, who are the friends and who are the foes? Do you know?"

"You mean Russia?"

"Yes, they're so bloody suspicious, don't you find?"

"In a way. Where I've been nobody trusted anybody."

"It's all so frightful," Theo said. "I can't see anybody winning this one."

We talked about the horrifying reports that were then starting to come out of Germany. Like Theo I had been shown smuggled photographs of the concentration camps. They were almost beyond comprehension. What I found as sickening as the monstrous crime itself was the fact that the Germans had actually documented it in detail.

"Can you imagine the mentality of people taking those photographs?"

"Aren't murderers always supposed to return to the scene?"

"But they don't provide their own incriminating evidence, do they?"

Theo didn't answer that. If I had expected to feel elated from the unaccustomed champagne, I was mistaken. It seemed to have no effect on either of us; it was almost as if there was a third man in the room, a stranger, preventing us from enjoying our reunion or talking with our old intimacy. I realised that the war had changed both of us, but that didn't explain the feeling that stood between us at the time – only hindsight provides those answers. Theo didn't have the same resilience as Philby. He couldn't blur his misgivings with alcohol, he just didn't have the iron constitution for it. Philby came perfectly equipped for his mission in life, and of course he believed in what he was doing, which Theo never did. There we all were, literally shifting the dirt, like ants, carting it from one place to another, a human chain of deception. The host feasting on the host. And that year, 1943, was the turning point. By then the defeat of Germany was only a matter of time and future policy – the methods of penetrating Russia – was already being discussed in the stratified regions of our tawdry profession. The infiltrators were well established in our ant hill by then, blocking channels as fast as they were dug, while on the other side of the Atlantic the awesome secrets of Los Alamos were being mined by another set of idealists.

I was so dim, so stupidly innocent, playing my part like some overgrown boy scout, tracking down conventional spies, my villains cast in old moulds, post-William le Queux perhaps, but definitely pre-Bond. I was not alone, my school of old thought was not that rare. I wonder what I would have done had Theo suddenly lowered his mask – would I have given him an escape route? Friends did betray friends. There were so many ways and means, one didn't actually have to plunge the knife in the back. The game had to go on, and we turned people several times, sending them to certain death primed with false information, dispatching them with all the trimmings of honour. If it suited our purpose we could perform the ultimate act of cynicism and recommend them for some posthumous decoration – there were no rules that couldn't be broken, no graves that couldn't be desecrated, no bottoms to the pits we were prepared to dig.

I never suspected Theo. The only doubts that crossed my mind were concerned with his personal safety. In that respect I came close to the truth of the matter, but I approached it from the wrong direction. I always had a fear that his homo-sexuality would one day produce a scandal – the British will sometimes excuse a man's treason, but seldom forgive his sexual aberrations. I was fearful for his reputation as a man of letters, believing that if his true nature was ever revealed his readership would desert him. But as in the childhood game, I pinned the donkey's tail on the wrong part of the body.

. The game is still being played, of course. There is Philby telling all and telling nothing in his much-praised autobio-graphy, yet unable to stem the instincts of a lifetime – betraying his wife, betraying Maclean, switching partners just as he switched sides, without conscience. Who knows how deeply the worms have eaten? We all think we sleep safely in our beds, the mortgage payments up to date, the house insured, the burglar alarm operative: but we haven't read the fine print on the policy – our own treasons are excluded, and outside, the Philbys of this world are still at large, observing us from afar, listening to us through brick walls, photographing us with lens that pierce the night, recruiting the next crop of fellow travellers even as they discredit the old, detonating their minds with new lies. Thank God I haven't any children.

I understand now that the sad pattern of Theo's last years was established long before. In a way he is to be pitied. Unlike his Trinity companions he was never granted the catharsis of defection. His Moscow flat was situated in Englefield Green, but who is to say that his forced confinement wasn't just as absolute? The essence of what they all believed in and worked for is beyond the limits of comprehension for most people. We act as though we are not capable of making the effort to understand the *Communist Manifesto*, or penetrate its many disguises. Theo exiled himself in his own country.

He seems to have abandoned the 'Alec' manuscript after the 'Chalmers' episode. I have found some random notes for a continuation of the narrative, but they don't make much sense, being jottings such as writers make to themselves at the end of a day in order to trigger the creative processes the following morning. Knowing Theo as I did, I would imagine that the act of having sent a man to his death would have destroyed the last vestige of self-justification. He had been trapped and blackmailed into making his own commitment, the point of no return had been passed and for the rest of his life he was on his own.

21

I T PROVED TO be Theo's turn to be sent overseas, and he spent the remainder of the war out of the country, mostly in America, though for a period he was stationed in the Caribbean and it was there, when the fake peace came so suddenly, that he made his next home. He bought an enchanting house built of powdered coral on the leeward coast of Barbados. This was long before the tourist trade exploded, and the island was undefiled. I envied him the wherewithal to afford such a move and although I stayed on alone in Perrins Walk for a few years, it never felt the same and I sampled half a dozen addresses before being fortunate enough to secure a set of chambers in Albany where, if the Inland Revenue permits, I hope to end my days.

He was always inviting me to join him in Barbados, extolling the virtues of its near-perfect climate, the purity of the water-supply, the absence of mosquitoes and (probably the deciding factor in his case) the calming influence of the local youths. Our wartime exploits quickly receded in the astonishment of the first years of peace, and we were both very prolific – I had to be, I was very short of money. That was another piece of sales talk Theo gave me in his letters. He wrote that he had never found anywhere as conducive to work and detailed his daily routine. It certainly seemed to suit him and during those immediate post-war years he produced three of his best novels: he picked up where he had left off, but with greater authority, still writing of times past but in a way that caught the mood of the period. One forgets that rationing persisted long after VJ Day, the bomb sites remained, there was an overall feeling of anticlimax and people hankered for the return of the old values and felt cheated that victory hadn't brought instant affluence. The Forces vote had swept

Attlee to power but the great social changes that his government promised to bring about overnight didn't happen – the pinched, Bob Cratchit face of Cripps epitomised Christmases past rather than the much-heralded furture.

Although he had removed himself five thousand miles away, Theo seemed to realise the underlying dissatisfactions and, more than with many contemporary, trendy novels, his work caught this mood perfectly and the reading public responded. I must include myself in the rival camp, for the novels I published in the decade following the end of the war, although successful at the time, had no staying power. Perhaps I should have accepted Theo's frequent invitations; a change of scenery might have meant a change of perspective.

In the event, I stayed put, justifying the self-denial with the thought that my brain would addle in such a hot climate. My wartime wanderings had left me with little appetite for travelling; I functioned better in temperate zones, working amongst the cluttered familiarity of my desk, reference books to hand and a good supply of my favourite cigarettes which at long last had reappeared in the shops.

When at last we did meet it was in Hollywood, during the height of the McCarthy era – the early Fifties, in fact. Theo had written to tell me of his seduction.

They finally discovered this particular whore's price, so I have taken the plunge and am willing to lie back with my literary legs wide open. I have no illusions, but certain friends tell me that the place is not without charms, and really what they are offering is too ridiculous. A gentleman rejoicing in the name of Sol. B. Zeidman, though doubtless of sound mind, is suffering from the temporary delusion that 'Harriet's Day' is the perfect vehicle (his word, not mine) for a lady called Maria Montez, who he assures me is perfect casting for my Harriet. I dare say Miss Montez will bring an added dimension to the role of a late Victorian schoolmistress. They want me to go out there and write what you, with your superior experience of these matters, will be familiar with – namely something known as a 'Draft Screenplay'. They have sent me a first class ticket and I am also to be given free accommodation. The whole thing seems highly improbable, but a change of venue won't do me any harm (and in fact will relieve me of a somewhat tiresome emotional involvement that has run its course), so I am taking the boat to New York and then go by train to Los Angeles, on the Super Chief, I believe. Stand by for further news from the front line in due course.

It was a time when the major Hollywood studios were talent spotting all over Europe. They appeared to have money to burn, and I suppose I was somewhat miffed that Theo had been discovered ahead of me. By coincidence, I didn't have long to wait, for the very same day that Theo's letter arrived from Barbados my agent rang to say he had had an enquiry as to my availability from Twentieth Century Fox.

"I played it very cagey," he said with that irritating casualness agents sometimes adopt when changing the course of one's life.

"Not too cagey, I hope."

"Listen, Tony, you must never be keen where the Americans are concerned. Take it from me. The more you play hard to get the more they're desperate to have you. I told them you were considering an offer from M.G.M."

"But I'm not."

"You and I know you're not. You and I know your last novel didn't sell too well," he continued, displaying an honesty he reserved for his clients. "Now is the moment to play it close to the chest."

"But can't they check whether M.G.M. have made me an offer?"

"Tony, if – and it's a remote if – they check with M.G.M., you'll get the offer from M.G.M. That's the way it works. Nobody at M.G.M. is going to admit they're *not* after you, because an enquiry from somebody else will immediately make them wonder what they're missing." Then he spoilt it all. "They're signing anybody these days."

"You make it sound very exclusive."

"Just stay by the phone and trust me."

My pre-war experiences with Korda had conditioned me to accept that film people moved in mysterious ways, but even I was unprepared for the eventual outcome. Theo had written from Hollywood where he was now comfortably housed in the

Beverly Hills Hotel apparently coming to terms with un-accustomed luxury.

The most impressive thing is the laundry service. I resolutely stick to collar and tie, which clearly impresses the natives, and I am fascinated by the speed at which my shirts are returned. They have a special delivery service which gets them back, perfectly ironed, in three hours. It must be what makes America great.

I have completed the mysterious process known as The First Draft, which turned out be a précis of the novel that Frau Zeidman (birds of a feather stick together, dear) insisted need not exceed twenty-five pages. So I did my prep and they are now reading it, which would appear to indicate that they never read the actual novel, although they paid good money for it. I keep asking if I can meet Miss Montez, but I am told that this is not the form and might cause her agent to push her price up. I am invited out for every meal, but I have resolutely steered clear of *Les Anglais* – the few expatriots I have met inspire dread; they appear to have been put to sleep in 1939, and I am not going to be the one to kiss them awake. The natives, on the other hand, *very* approachable and friendly, mad for physical exercise of any description. Drink plentiful and very potent. The sun shines ever day and so do I.

I was forced to eat humble pie where my agent was concerned because in due course his predictions came true. I was offered a contract by M.G.M. at roughly twice as much as the opening bid from Twentieth Century Fox. I cabled Theo my impending arrival and sailed on the *Mary*, taking the same overland route from New York as Theo. I think the train journey was more of a revelation than the near-Edwardian atmosphere of the Cunard Line. Nowadays even America shrinks beneath the Jumbo jets, but to go from the East to West coasts in those early post-war days was a heady experience. I was totally unprepared for the vastness of America and the infinite variety of its terrain. I was also disarmed by the friendliness of my fellow passengers, since England had swiftly reverted to old and surly habits. Most of the travellers on the train appeared to be celebrating the end of prohibition, and I viewed the passing countryside through a 90% proof haze for most of the four days and was more or less poured off the train and into the waiting M.G.M. limousine when we arrived in Los Angeles. American hospitality may not always be sincere, but it is certainly generous.

I was driven to the Beverly Wilshire Hotel, my chauffeur proudly informing me that it had been the 'official air raid shelter' during the war, a piece of information I am sure he felt would be of great comfort to a Limey. My suite was festooned with unreal flowers and various gifts of liquor and fruit from my hosts at M.G.M. There was even a letter of welcome from Louis B. Mayer himself, though when I examined it closely I discovered that the signature was printed. A card in the bathroom proudly proclaimed: *The Beverly Wilshire stands, and will ever stand, as a monument to the loyalty and love that Walter Mcarty, the builder, bears for his home city.*

I had fully intended to telephone Theo as soon as I had unpacked, but I wasn't given the opportunity. All four telephones in my suite rang simultaneously. I picked up the nearest one and in the classic tradition of the movies a cute female voice immediately said: "Hi! Mr. Stern. This is Betsy. Welcome to Beverly Hills and the Beverly Wilshire. Mr. Wadsworth is on his way up. Have a good day."

Before I could enquire why Mr. Wadsworth was paying me a visit, there was a knock on the door. I was still somewhat unsteady on my feet when I greeted the unexpected Mr. Wadsworth, who turned out to be one of those rarities, a native without a suntan; young, formally dressed with a matching waistcoat to his dark suit and sporting a thin moustache in the style of Douglas Fairbanks. He carried two bottles of champagne, each gift-wrapped with festive bows.

"Mr. Stern, sir? May I welcome you on behalf of Alfred Somburn, sir."

"You may indeed," I said. "Who is Alfred Somburn?"

He deflated visibly. "Oh, didn't you know? You're working for Mr. Somburn. He's a very important producer on the lot, sir. I work for him, too. These are a gift from Mr. Somburn."

He proffered the two bottles of champagne.

"How very kind of Mr. Somburn."

"He's a very fine gentleman, sir."

"You're Mr. Wadsworth, I take it?"

"Yes, sir. Would you like my card?"

It was out of his waistcoat pocket in a flash.

"I have the limousine downstairs, sir. It's Mr. Somburn's personal limousine, which he's placed at your disposal."

"Well, I don't think I'll drive it just now."

"Oh, no, sir. I have to take you to him."

"Why don't you come inside?" I said, totally confused by now. "Would you like a drink? As you can see, I could open a bar. Perhaps you'd like some champagne?"

"Thank you, no. The fact is, Mr. Somburn is expecting us."

"Now?"

"Yes, Mr. Stern."

"What is he expecting us for? Dinner?"

"Gee, I don't rightly know, sir. All he said was to bring you to the studio. I'm sure he'd give you dinner if you're hungry."

"No, I was just asking. Well, we'd better go then. I'll just put on a clean shirt."

"May I use your phone, sir? I'd better advise Mr. Somburn of the delay."

"Take your pick."

I splashed some cold water on my face and changed my shirt. "Does your Mr. Somburn always operate at this pace?" I called into the next room.

"Oh, yes, sir. He's noted for it. He has no fewer than seven motion pictures under consideration at this present time."

One of the longest cars I had ever seen was drawn up outside the Wilshire Boulevard entrance. A black chauffeur opened the door for me (they still called them 'Negro' in 1952) and I sank into the custom-made interior. It was like climbing into a feather bed. Wadsworth occupied one of the jump seats. Throughout the twenty-minute journey to Culver City he gave me a sobering run-down on the many qualities of Mr. Somburn, leaving me with the firm impression that I was shortly to be ushered into the presence of a man of genius.

I was deposited in front of the Thalberg building, having

been closely scrutinised by the studio police at the gate. It was quite obvious from young Mr. Wadsworth's behaviour that he felt he was leading me into a holy place. I noticed he straightened his tie and pulled the points of his waistcoat before entering the building. I was given a printed security pass by another policeman sitting at the desk in the lobby. It bore my name and the description 'Contract Writer – valid for one month' which was not exactly reassuring.

Somburn's office was on the second floor, which I later learnt denoted that he existed somewhere between heaven and the ghetto. He had three secretaries, all of whom looked like Varga girls to my innocent eyes, and all three greeted me as though I was the sole survivor of Pearl Harbor. It was flattering but unnerving. The senior of the three, distinguished by her slightly larger desk devoid of a typewriter, buzzed Mr. Somburn in the inner sanctum. The office itself was of dazzling whiteness.

"Why don't you go right in, Mr. Stern?"

"Congratulations," Wadsworth said, as he opened the door for me. There wasn't time to ask what for.

In alarming contrast to the outer office, Somburn's room appeared to be in total darkness. The shutters were drawn, the only illumination coming from a picture light over a framed photograph of Louis B. Mayer, and I found it difficult to move through the wall-to-wall carpet, the pile of which came up to my ankles.

"Mr. Stern from England, sir," Wadsworth said.

I peered in the same direction as Wadsworth and finally made out a figure lying on a couch at the far end of the room.

"Did you get the champagne?" a voice said.

"I personally handed it to Mr. Stern," Wadsworth said.

"Of course you did, you prick!"

The body on the couch heaved itself up to a sitting position. By now my eyes had more or less adjusted to the gloom and I was able to make out Somburn's features. He had the face of a prize fighter gone to fat – the beard sparse and reddish in colour where he had neglected to shave, reminding me of the scalded skin of pigs in a slaughterhouse. I had no idea of his real age and he was careful not to volunteer it. When I looked him up in a trade reference book his entry merely said, 'Born Pittsburg, the only son of Stanley and Miriam Somburn.' He was a snappy dresser, had his finger nails manicured every day and affected two-tone brogue shoes.

His first rejoinder to the immediately craven Wadsworth took me off guard. At that time I was totally unfamiliar with his species.

"Tony, I'm sorry I didn't meet you myself, but I had a mess of dailies to look at. They take care of you at the hotel? You got everything you want?"

"Well, I've just arrived, but everything seems fine, thank you."

"You want anything, just tell Helena outside. You met Helena?"

"I imagine I have."

"She's terrific. The best. You want a drink?"

"No, I don't think so, not just for the moment."

"Pour me a Jack Daniels then fuck off, will you?" he said to Wadsworth, then added, "But hang around, I may need you later."

He opened a drawer and took a paper cocktail mat from it on which he placed his whisky glass. I noticed that the paper mat had a motif on it of two naked bodies closely entwined. This was repeated on his personal stationery with the words *Things to Do Today* printed underneath.

"Tony," he said. "I hired you for your reputation. You've got a great reputation. In this town that counts for something. Most of the writers around here couldn't write their way out of a fucking paper sack. But I've read your books, that's why I didn't turn a hair at your price. It's cheaper to live at the Ritz, that's my philosophy. Don't you agree?"

"Absolutely," I said.

"I treat my people well, you know. You work for me, the best ain't good enough. And you know something else? That man . . ." He poked a thick, pink finger at the photograph of Louis B. Mayer. ". . . That man is like Jesus Christ to me. Fucking saviour of this industry. What he doesn't know ain't worth knowing. I worship him. When you meet him you're

293

going to worship him. He put me here because he trusts me, because he know's my heart's in the right place, because I'm not a fucking pinko like some of the pricks who really sold him down the river. They sold that beautiful human being down the river. Took his money and sold him. But he's going to have the last laugh. We're going to run every one of those commie motherfuckers out of town. Let me show you something, see if it's still on."

He pressed a button and pointed at an oversized television set. After a few seconds a picture appeared. It was a commercial for a local beer called Brew 102. When this came to an end I found myself looking at Senator McCarthy's blue-chinned face. He was smiling.

"That's the man who's going to save America!" Somburn said.

At that point I had only the vaguest idea of the day-to-day workings of the House Un-American Activities Committee, but I remember being immediately appalled by the spectacle of witnesses being interrogated like participants in some spectator sport. It was so alien to my very British conception of justice and the fact that it was being presented on television like some grotesque soap-opera was more shocking than anything I could have imagined.

The close-up of McCarthy was replaced with live transmission from the actual sub-committee rooms. Not wishing to rely on the hazy memories of that afternoon, I have since verified the actual date of the first hearing I witnessed. It was May 21, 1952 and the witness on the stand that day was Lillian Hellman. The staff member who conducted the interrogation was a Frank S. Tavenner. There in Somburn's shuttered office I heard for the first time the constant reiteration of the basic question, and the monotonous denials by the witness.

"Were you at any time a member at large of the Communist Party?"

"I refuse to answer, Mr. Tavenner, on the ground that it might incriminate me."

"You might refuse to answer it. The question is asked, do you refuse?"

"I'm sorry, I refuse to answer on the ground that it might incriminate me."

"Are you now a member of the Communist Party?"

"No, sir."

"Were you ever a member of the Communist Party?"

"I refuse to answer, Mr. Tavenner, on the same grounds."

And so on. Somburn might have been watching a football game.

"Listen to the communist bitch!" he said. "She's fucking lying. They're gonna nail her like they nailed the rest of those red cocksuckers. You got any like her in England?"

"I don't think there's anybody like Miss Hellman," I said, but the nuance passed over his balding head.

"You know, sooner or later you're gonna hafta get after your own commies, because you take my word for it, your woodwork's infested just the same."

His mood suddenly changed and he switched off the sound and turned to face me again. The rest of the conversation was conducted with the mute face of Miss Hellman confronting her accusers always in my vision.

"Now, you're sure you're being taken care of? You want to change your room at the hotel?"

"No, the room's splendid. I haven't even unpacked yet."

"That's good, that's good. Long as you're being taken care of by my people. Now I expect you're wondering why I got you over here?"

"Yes, I did wonder about that."

"When you get to know me better, you'll get to know how I work. You got to keep moving in this town. Stand still and they'll take you to the cleaners. You're sure you don't want a drink?"

"Quite sure, thank you."

"Coffee? Hey, what about a cup of your English tea?"

"Well, maybe a cup of coffee. When in Rome."

"You been to Rome?"

"No, it's just an expression."

One of the girls appeared in the 'oorway in response to his buzz on the intercom.

"Get Mr. Stern a cup of coffee. How do you take it? You want cream and sugar?"

"Just as it comes."

"Well it comes black."

"A little milk then."

"We don't use milk, how about half and half?"

"Yes, fine," I said, not knowing what he was talking about. I could lip read Miss Hellman as she again stood on her constitutional rights.

"So, where were we?" Somburn said. "Yeah, let me tell you about my operation. I've got a wide open deal here, very kosher. I don't make waves for them, they don't make waves for me. Anything I want to do, L.B. listens to. You know what he's a sucker for? Pictures with heart." He thumped his initialled shirt pocket as he said this. "He likes to be hit right here. Because he's got a big heart, that man, and he likes to share it. I hired you because I like what you write. I loved that one, the last one, *Last Call For Dinner*."

"*First Call For Dinner*."

"Yeah, something like that. I was going to option it, but train movies are dying this year. And one thing I always stick by. Don't knock the public. They don't want to buy it, don't give it to them."

The girl returned with a welcome and excellent cup of coffee and the liquid called 'half and half' which turned out to be thinned cream. Before the door had closed behind her, Somburn again switched his train of thought.

"Listen, any time you want a little action, just drop the word. What are you, a leg man, or do you like to eat off the candy counter?"

"Tits," I said descending to his level, since subtlety seemed a lost cause. "I go for tits."

"You've come to the right town." Much to my horror he made a note on his pad, tore off the top sheet and handed it to me. "Have that on me," he said. "That little baby has a pair of jugs that'll put your eyes out."

"Very kind of you," I said.

"My pleasure. So listen, the point is, what L.B. likes, what I like, is class. I only make pictures with class. That's why you're here. You're a class writer and I'm a class producer. That's a great combination."

"Do you have any particular subject in mind or do you want me to think of something?"

"No, I've got something for you. Only we've got to keep it under wraps for the time being. Know what I mean?"

I didn't, but I forced my face to register renewed interest.

"You ever heard of a book called *Harriet's Day*?"

"By Theo Gittings?"

"That his name? Another English guy, right?"

"Yes." Something warned me not to blurt out my relationship with Theo.

"What d'you think of it?"

"It's a very good novel. Very good."

"You bet your ass it's good. The point is, and you're going to be part of the family from here on in, so I'm going to take you into my confidence . . . what's happening is that some guy who calls himself a producer over at Warners has got this Gittings character knocking out a script for him. But what he doesn't know is that we bought it from under him. And I'm going to put you on it."

I stared at him. On the television screen the committee room seemed to be in uproar. Photographers were clustering around Miss Hellman as she and her attorney prepared to leave.

"How does that grab you?"

"You mean, you now own the novel, but this other producer doesn't realise you own it?"

"You got it."

"Won't he object when he finds out?"

"He can object 'til he's blue in the fucking face, who cares? I wanted it, L.B. said you go buy it, I bought it. He's going to wake up to find his balls have been cut off."

"Does this sort of thing happen very often?"

"Sure. Like I said, you've got to keep weaving. It's just business. Warners weren't going to make it anyway. They grabbed at it when I made the offer. Grabbed at it."

"Amazing," I said.

"Listen, you stick close to me and I'll teach you the ropes.

When I like somebody, I share everything. That number I gave you, I don't give that out to everybody."

He opened another drawer in his desk and took out a copy of Theo's novel which he pushed across to me.

"Tony, we're going to get rich with this one. You start tomorrow. Helena'll show you where your office is. Now, I'm going to take a little steam and a rub. You want to join me?"

"No, I think I'll get back to the hotel. I've been on that train for four days."

"You take it easy tonight and in the morning you can start nice and fresh. But if you feel a little tense, use that number. She'll take very good care of you. You're going to love it here, believe me. You're never going to want to leave."

Safely back in my hotel room I found it difficult to believe that the entire scene had taken place. Somburn's personality and dialogue were a grotesque background to the tragic happenings on the television screen. I had strong premonitions of disaster and they sobered me more quickly than the coffee. I looked around the unaccustomed opulence of the hotel suite, taking in the gifts of fruit and flowers, thinking of the telephone number on the piece of paper in my pocket, and wondered how on earth I had been trapped. Survival was my immediate concern, and I reached for the telephone and asked to be connected to the Beverly Hills Hotel. When that operator answered I gave Theo's name. I was in luck because a moment later I heard his familiar English voice.

"Where are you?" he said. "Are you here?"

"Here and frantic. I must see you."

"Look, I know what you're going to say. And I take back everything I wrote about this place. It's a nightmare. You've no idea what's been happening to me."

"I think I do."

"You remember I told you they wanted to cast a lady called Maria Montez? Well, last week I found out she's dead."

"Shall we meet for dinner?"

"Can you believe that?"

"After what I've gone through this afternoon I could believe anything. Where shall we meet?"

"Why don't you come here? Have you got a car?"

"No. I've got a room full of flowers, some champagne and the telephone number of a tart, plus a copy of your novel."

"My novel?"

"Yes – *Harriet's Day*. I'll tell you about that when we meet."

"I'll pick you up. Half an hour?"

"Fine," I said. "Hurry."

At Theo's suggestion we avoided the more popular eating places and ended up at a small restaurant on Wilshire which was Belgian owned, had Mexican waiters and served pseudo-Italian food. We wasted no time in comparing horror stories and I gave Theo a blow by blow account of my encounter with Somburn.

"They're quite shameless," Theo said. "In a way I admire them. I mean they have this unbelievable capacity for self-deception."

"So what are we going to do? I simply can't rewrite your script."

"Why not? I don't mind. The whole thing is a farce anyway."

We ordered a second bottle of imported wine, being European snobs.

"I tell you what," Theo said. "I've got a brilliant idea. We must put our heads together – after all, we weren't in Intelligence for nothing. Play them at their own game. Is there anything in your contract which says you can't collaborate?"

"I don't think so, why?"

"Let's both write identical scripts and turn them in on the same day. I mean, do you care if you ever work here again?"

"Right now I don't."

"Me neither. I mean, I'm slightly ahead of you. My reading of the situation is that although they've bought my book from under Zeidman's nose, they won't tell him. They'll keep him in ignorance and let me go on writing as though nothing had happened. They like getting their pound of flesh."

"It's a great idea," I said.

"I'll let you see what I've done so far. Working to Mr. Zeidman's inspired instructions I've already turned Harriet into a demur girl from West Virginia – the whole thing's set in America now, by the way."

"You're kidding?"

"Alas, no. Look, like you I was seduced by their hospitality in the first few weeks, but then gradually I woke up to what was really happening. They've perfected the techniques, of course. They're all so scared, they grasp at any straw. Actually, I like them. They mean well, they're generous with the studio money, they're so sincere they make you puke, and the whole set-up is a fantasy."

"What happens when we've finished?"

"Well, now," Theo said. "Let's think it through." He finished his glass of wine. "The really clever thing would be for us both to plant a few rumours. You go around saying that you're amazed they rejected my script – because it's so brilliant – and I'll let it be known to Warners that they were insane to let the property go because you're turning in a work of dazzling originality."

"Will they take the bait?"

"They'll get the hook right down their throats. Yes, I know! I've got it. I know exactly how to do it. You get your story to Louella Parsons – you know who she is, don't you?"

"I've heard the name. Doesn't she write a column?"

"She's practically gaga. She doesn't write much of it herself. She has leg-men, or leg-women who collect most of the garbage they print. Then her great rival is she of the amazing hats, Miss Hedda Hopper. Between them they practically run this town. And they hate each other."

"And you think that's the way to do it?"

"I'm sure. I might even hire a press agent for a few weeks. In fact, that would be the smart way to do it."

We spent another half an hour embroidering the scheme before going to our separate hotels, highly pleased with ourselves.

Theo sent over a copy of his work-in-progress before I left for the studio the following morning. I had been allocated what to my eyes was a palatial office complete with a bright-eyed secretary called Carol who seemed to be dressed in a negligee, plus a generous supply of paper, sharpened pencils and two more bottles of champagne. Wadsworth was in attendance for my arrival and over-anxious to ensure that everything was to my satisfaction.

"I think I'll spend the morning reading the novel," I said.

"If you don't like your desk, we can change it," Wadsworth said. "Likewise . . ." he rolled his eyes in the direction of Carol in the outer office. "No sweat."

"Everything seems perfect."

"I'll call for you at lunch, then and take you to the commissary."

I had no sooner closed the door when my telephone rang. It was Somburn.

"How's it going? How many pages?"

I was not sufficiently tuned in to his subtle sense of humour in those early days and simply remained silent.

"Just putting you on, Tony. Did you get the champagne?"

"Sitting in front of me. Unopened, of course. I never drink when I'm working."

"That's my boy! How did you make out last night?"

"Last night?"

"Did you meet the little lady?"

"Oh, that. Er, no, I didn't feel I could do her justice last night."

"Well, she's on ice for you. Listen, I just want to leave you with one thought. The book. It's not the Bible. Understand?"

"The book? Oh, yes."

"You want to change anything, you go ahead and change it. Have you had any thoughts?"

"Well, the only thing that occurred to me, is that possibly the heroine, Harriet, is too English. I suppose you wouldn't want me to make her an American girl?"

"Tony. Let me say something. You're one of my people. You're thinking like I am. That is one *hell* of an idea. I can't wait to read the pages."

Begin as we mean to continue, I thought as I put the phone down and started to read Theo's unfinished script. This took me most of the morning and I made notes as I went along. I resisted ringing Theo to exchange progress reports: if our scheme was to succeed we had to maintain radio silence.

My first lunch in the studio commissary proved to be another emotional experience. I had a place reserved for me at Somburn's table in the executive dining room – the caste system was still rigidly enforced in Hollywood 1952. Like any other first-time tourist I confess I was impressed to come face to face with a dozen household names, but I found the locker-room conversation strangely disconcerting. The humour of the film industry is savage – 'as funny as a baby's open grave' explained one local sage when I questioned him on the subject. An onlooker at the perpetual feast, I had the feeling that most of the regular guests would self-destruct given time, for they all seemed to be living on their nerves, their keenest pleasures originating from the failures, artistic, commercial or marital, of their colleagues. Most of them appeared to be living on borrowed time, borrowed money and borrowed ideas and they kept one eye trained on the permanent officials – those who controlled the books. Everything seemed to be expressed in numbers: you scored with a tally of wives, girlfriends; inflated budgets, busts and box-office returns rated high; six-figure salaries, the profits that *Variety* were encouraged to exaggerate, even the gin-rummy stakes were discussed with a reverence never before encountered. Their total dedication to the pursuit of affluence was stunning when it wasn't frightening.

Surprisingly – for the place was inhabited by over-anxious gossips – our deception was not uncovered. Pleading devotion to duty, we resolutely declined the many social invitations; having sampled two or three we felt we could exist outside the Beverly Hills Circuit – that perpetual round of the same tight group going to the same parties, making the same conversation night after night. Equally, we felt it prudent to avoid being seen together in public. Our meetings and exchanges of progress reports took place in unfashionable restaurants.

The schoolboy prank we were playing visibly excited Theo and he could hardly wait for the dénouement. It was the sort of joke that appealed to him, just as years before his friend Raymond's impersonation of Miss Angela Pritchett had given him such lasting pleasure. If I had any misgivings about the eventual outcome Theo swept them aside.

"They deserve everything they get," he kept insisting. There was a touch of the old Cambridge élitism in his all-embracing dislike of the American scene. He was often unnecessarily supercilious with waiters when discussing the menu and wine list. He embarrassed me sometimes – unpleasant echoes of his father. I suppose I should have been more perceptive and realised that his frequently absurd anti-Americanism was a symptom of some deeper resentment.

Our stay in Hollywood came a year after Burgess and Maclean's flight. Given past associations, it was inevitable that we several times discussed their defection. Even at the time Theo's reaction struck me as odd, though I attached no particular significance to it: he was frequently perverse in argument.

I think I was morally shocked by the Burgess and Maclean affair, coming as it did in the wake of the Nunn May and Fuchs trials. I found myself curiously torn. Part of me abhorred the current American obsession with communist treachery, but at the same time I could not embrace the liberal theory that Russia's atomic programme would miraculously enhance world peace. Theo, on the other hand, appeared to have no such divided loyalites.

"I was questioned, of course."

"Were you?"

"Yes, I expect they'll get around to you in due course. Anybody who ever knew them."

"Well, I didn't really *know* them."

"No, but their knickers are in a right old twist. They've got to find a few victims to excuse their own total incompetence. I mean, I told them it was always right there under their bloody noses. Imagine putting Guy in Washington, or anywhere else for that matter! You only had to take one look at him to know he was a degenerate liability. He'd have sold anybody on a first come, first served basis."

"Now they're saying it's only the tip of the iceberg."

"Yes, well, it's equally obvious they weren't operating alone. Guy could just about find his way to the nearest toilet, but you'd hardly cast him as a master spy. There must be others."

"This Third Man theory they're pushing?"

"Oh, that's just journalese."

"The trouble is that when anything like this happens a great number of innocent people have their lives wrecked. Look what's happening over here — all these kangaroo courts. Have you watched any of it?"

"Yes."

"Well, don't you find it horrifying?"

"Not really. They all look as though they've got something to hide."

"You serious?"

"Yes, absolutely. I don't think it's all that horrifying. I mean, this great show of standing on their famous Fifth Amendment. They should try that in Russia, see how far it would get them."

"But most of them are just writers and actors "

"So?"

"Well, what threat could they pose, even assuming they are converts or party members or what-have-you?"

"Now you're being naive. We're writers and we did it. We were up to our necks in it during the war."

"But that was during the war."

"Well, the war's still on. Russia's the enemy now, Russia was always the enemy. Hitler's war was just the dress rehearsal."

"You are a cynical sod."

"I'm being bloody serious. And I'm certainly not going to get morally indignant because a few boring film stars and Hollywood hacks are asked some perfectly legitimate questions. I've got no particular love of all things American, as you well know, but I think in this instance they're perfectly within their rights. If these would-be martyrs are innocent they don't need to stand on anything; if they're not then they deserve anything they get."

I still thought he was merely goading me for the sake of effect. But there was another incident that made me wonder whether his new convictions were perhaps genuine, even though unfamiliar.

I don't quite recall how it came about, but on one of the

rare occasions when Theo and I did not have dinner together (he was cruising the bars on Santa Monica Boulevard after an enforced period of sexual abstinence) I accepted an invitation from a fellow writer on the lot. He had a pleasant house out in the Valley and had promised me that he and his wife had not 'gone Hollywood' and that I would meet some interesting people. "Not the usual crap merchants," he said.

When I arrived I found there were about twenty fellow guests, a small gathering by local standards, none of whom I had ever met before. The hospitality was generous but informal –barbecued steaks *al fresco* around the modest-sized pool – and it was my first glimpse of anything approaching normal standards of human behaviour. The conversation was still mostly film-industry shop, but it lacked that vicious cutting edge which characterised the higher echelons of Hollywood society, and I relaxed and accepted it. I gradually became aware that, unofficially, the guest of honour was a male star who had 'sung' before the Un-American Activities Committee, and had paid dearly for it. A few years previously his career had been one of the most publicised even by Hollywood's standards. Now it was non-existent. I have no idea what motives drove him to make his confession – fear assumes many disguises – or what he expected from it, but he could hardly have envisaged the eventual outcome. Reviled by his fellow travellers, he had also been shunned by those very reactionaries who should, logically, have applauded him. He was in limbo, a star name that nobody would put above the title, an embarrassment to friends and foes alike.

My host (described by another guest as a 'closet-liberal') was at some pains to tell me that he was acting purely out of charity.

"I don't sympathise, I don't condemn. He's just a considerable human being and right now he needs a little compassion."

I have frequently observed that the cardinal American sin is getting found out. It doesn't matter too much what you do, but don't get caught doing it. The fallen star had managed to violate all the codes at once, and they were making him pay for it. He seemed to me falsely, irrationally cheerful about his predicament, over-anxious to confide that this was just a temporary pause in his career, that good things were just around the corner. He still had that carefully groomed, slightly unreal look of the old-fashioned Hollywood leading man. "I go to class every day, just to keep in trim," he told me. Even his agent had abandoned him, and his wife was just about to, but he hung on for another eighteen months, keeping in trim, holding himself in readiness for the call that never came, unemployed, unemployable, until his savings ran out and then he opened his veins in his king-sized bath under a framed photograph of himself in his first major success.

The grapevine was visited by many little foxes that year and the following morning I had no sooner sat down at my desk when Somburn asked me to come and see him. He got straight to the point.

"Tony, you're my guest over here and a very important guest. I respect you, so don't take what I'm going to say the wrong way. I understand you had dinner out in the Valley last night."

"Yes, very pleasant."

"Look, me, I don't take sides. I'm strictly neutral, Switzerland on Coldwater Canyon, that's me. But I think you ought to stay clear of those people."

"What people?"

"You know what people. I don't have to spell it out for you. Some of your fellow guests last night are bad news in this town. One in particular. And who needs it?"

He took a Kleenex, blew into it and then carefully scrutinised the results before screwing the tissue into a ball.

"Assuming we're talking about the same man, I thought he'd washed himself in public," I said.

"You could be right. But I repeat, who needs it? You could have a ball here, Tony, write your own ticket, but you have to play it by the house rules. That guy is a no, no. Off limits. *Verboten*, you understand?"

I didn't answer him.

"See, I know you're innocent, but it doesn't look good. A lotta people are running scared. They jump to conclusions, and it's easier to jump to the wrong conclusions, you take my meaning? So why run the risk, for what? What d'you care whether this guy is kosher or not? I'll tell you something, he ain't that kosher. Personally, and I'll deny it if you ever quote me, I think he's paid his dues. I mean, I'm a great believer in justice and I think he had a lotta guts. But I'm not calling the shots. You either get off the pot or piss in it. Am I right?"

"I don't know," I said.

"Tony, I'm right. Believe me. I know the way this town works. Play your cards right and you've got it made here. So, let's talk about the script. How are the pages coming?"

"It seems to be coming along okay."

"You having a good time? Everybody treating you right?"

"I've no complaints," I said.

"So take a little advice. You're my boy, remember?"

I reported this nauseating conversation to Theo that evening. He gave me the second surprise of the day.

"Well, allowing for the fact that your Mr. Sunburn is as ghastly as my Frau Zeidman, he does have a point. Why get mixed up in local politics?"

"Nobody's going to tell me who I should or should not see."

"Oh, don't get all high hat and indignant. You betray your origins."

"I insist, nobody has that right. Certainly not a super prick like Somburn."

"Yes, but the way to get even with those characters is not to take up moral attitudes. Hit them where it really hurts, in the wallet. We're well on our way to doing that."

We argued backwards and forwards for most of the meal, but Theo refused to shift his position. I retired none too gracefully to my own corner, irritated, as one always is when somebody we know very well reveals that we know them scarcely at all.

Perhaps jokes of that nature never succeed after adolescence, or perhaps we underestimated the enemy, but in the event, despite the fact that our collaboration on the screenplay was a masterpiece of inspired mediocrity, the last laugh was on us. I hadn't realised that the Somburns of this world always take out insurance policies, and whilst Theo and I were happily engaged on our involved deception, Somburn hired a third writer – a tame, local boy noted for his ability to serve any number of masters at once. It was quite common practice (and probably still is) owing much to the industry maxim that 'you can't bullshit an old bullshitter'. We turned in identical scripts on the same day, then sat back to await the explosion. There wasn't even a whimper. After forty-eight hours of silence, I phoned Somburn to enquire what he thought of my effort. Theo did the same with his Mr. Zeidman.

"You did a great job," Somburn said. "Maybe just needs a little polish, which we won't bother you with."

I compared reactions with Theo. His Mr. Zeidman had said: "Theo, it's a classic example of the art form. Too good for these bums, they can only recognise crap."

On balance, we felt that Zeidman won by an expletive.

We suffered a feeling of let-down. I still have a tattered copy of the script somewhere and the last time I glanced at it I formed the opinion that manufactured dross seems to age in the wood. The awful thing is it was rather a good, bad script, despite our efforts. When the film eventually appeared it had been retitled *Heaven, Hell and Harriett*, our names had been removed from the screenplay credit, and the only reference to Theo's original was a line of small type which read: *Based on a novel by Theo Gittings*. I never saw Mr. Somburn again, though I still get Christmas cards from him. Full of the spirit of the Nativity they are always specially posed colour photographs of our hero himself and give details of his latest epic. They are collectors' items.

22

I T WAS SOME years after our foolish escapade in Hollywood that I finally accepted his invitation to take a working holiday in Barbados. Things have changed now, I believe: with the coming of independence the new government saw fit to rescind most of the labour permits for Europeans so that the islanders would have a better chance of advancement. Friends tell me that the exodus included most of the trained chefs and that subsequently the over-ambitious hotel menus lacked a certain piquancy, to put it mildly. But at the time of my first visit there was a happy lassitude about the whole island; the package tourists had not yet started to descend in their jumbo-loads and imports of plastic commercialism were still of modest proportions.

I took an ancient taxi from Seawell Airport and drove across the island through lanes shadowed by the tall and impenetrable fields of sugar cane. My local driver appeared to work on the same principle as those shire horses one used to see at harvest time in Norfolk: finding his way by habit. At one point I looked up and saw his reflection in the rear-view mirror: both his eyes were closed. Since the road we were travelling on was only wide enough to accommodate one vehicle at a time, I felt the need for urgent action if we were to survive the journey. I hastily engaged him in a conversation about cricket and at the mention of the national hero, Garry Sobers, his eyes flickered open and some resemblance of energy crossed his face. He stayed awake for the rest of the trip and in time we descended from the high ridge where the cool winds blow and drove along the coast road, reaching Theo's house at last light.

Theo greeted me with drink in hand, and appeared to have gone semi-native. He was dressed in tattered shorts with a loose fitting cotton shirt flapped over them. He was tanned and relaxed and seemed genuinely pleased to see me. I had brought a bundle of English newspapers with me, always the most welcome gift, I have found, for those who profess to have turned their back for ever on the mother country.

There was a young male house-boy called Thomas to attend to my luggage and it did not escape my notice that his relationship with Theo was hardly formal. We sat and chatted on the verandah, strangely contrasted in appearance, for like most arriving travellers I felt vaguely ashamed of my pallor and crumpled city clothes.

"Get out of them," Theo said. "Nobody wears anything here. I can lend you a beachcomber outfit. Take a swim."

"Now?"

"The best time. The sea is always warm, and bathing at night is sybaritic. But let me show you where. One has to avoid the coral and the sea urchins. Very painful if you tread on one of those and the cure somewhat bizarre. The natives piss on the soles of your feet and then apply hot wax."

"I think I'll give that a miss on my first night here."

"Yes. Personally I cheat and use lemon juice."

After my swim, which I found as relaxing as Theo had promised – the sea warmer than anything I had imagined and of a strange consistency – we had a meal of flying fish and sweet potatoes, expertly cooked and served by Thomas. He had threaded freshly picked hibiscus blossoms on thin wires and these fanned out from the centre of the round table and hung down over the sides.

"He's so artistic," Theo said with noticeable pride in his acquisition. "A positive little Lady Chatterley with flowers."

The house itself was cool and surrounded by greenery, so that one hardly noticed where the walls ended and the garden began. It was in the pre-air-conditioning days, but the room had a large circular fan on the ceiling and when I lay down to sleep that first night I found myself thinking of Kipling and the early travel books of Somerset Maugham. The sea broke on the coral shingle only a dozen yards from my bedroom window, and the small night frogs called non-stop. I felt the tiredness slake from me like a useless skin, and slept as I hadn't slept since childhood.

Theo had gone to immense pains to make me comfortable. He had set aside a small, bare room close to the beach for me to write in, and explained his own working method.

"One can't write after lunch," he said. "It's too hot and one must surrender to the customs of the island. My routine is to rise early, have a swim, then breakfast and work until about eleven. Then another swim and laze around all afternoon. Other good intentions prove ultimately useless. One can see why the natives burn the sugar-cane fields rather than go to the trouble of harvesting them. Why should anybody work hard in a climate like this?"

There was a cane factory set back from the beach about half a mile from the house, and on two days a week the heavy, sickly scent thrown off by the refining process would penetrate every corner of the house. More frequently the air would be full of floating black ashes as a distant field was fired, arson being the local pastime, and an ancient fire engine would race past with a crowd of naked children in its wake. These were the only excitements, and for the rest it was day after day of blissful sameness – perhaps gentle rain in the early mornings, which freshened all the foliage and steamed the verandah. There was a tulip tree outside my bedroom window and humming birds hovered round it, their wings beating so fast that they appeared to be china models suspended on invisible wires.

Some mornings Theo and I would walk the half a mile to the local market and choose fresh fish and vegetables. There was none of the clamour and dirt of the Middle East, no beggars or professional cripples, just brightly coloured women and school-children sedately walking in crocodile file, the girls wearing smart blazers and straw hats and white stockings. On Sunday mornings I could hear their voices raised in song from the church across the way, and in the afternoon they would rush to the beach, naked, gleaming, screaming with pleasure, turning cartwheels as they dived and leap-frogged into the foaming surf. I would watch the young men play beach cricket, utilising driftwood, roughly-shaped, for bats, making miraculous catches with headlong lunges that often ended with the fielder in the sea. It was a world apart, innocent and joyful and within a few days of my arrival I had totally surrendered to it and could scarcely recall the life I had left behind.

For the first time I could understand how some people come to such islands and never leave, the lotus existence seducing them away from old realities. In such a climate the past seems like a pawn ticket one cannot be bothered to redeem, for it is easier to cut one's losses. Time no longer retains its city meaning; clothes have no importance, personal appearance matters for little. After two weeks my skin was tanned and taut, cleansed and salted by the hour-long swims we took each day. I began to lose my writer's paunch and smoked less, though I had yet to learn the trick of Theo's discipline. I tried to write in that perfect setting, but the very nothingness of it defeated me. It was a time to contemplate my navel in traditional beachcomber fashion, to take stock. I had ideas for a new novel, but they swam beneath the surface – multi-coloured plots darting about in the coral of my mind.

I think Theo was amused by the transformation in me and kept reminding me I could have sampled this life style many years earlier.

"You see," he would say, "I told you what it was like, but you never believed me."

One night under the influence of too many rum punches prepared by the ever-solicitous Thomas, he talked with uncharacteristic sadness of his life.

"I've always envied you," he said.

"Me?"

"Yes. For as long as I can remember."

"Well, that's odd, because really I could say the same thing. I remember, if we're going to let our hair down . . ."

"Not so much to let down these days . . ."

". . . I remember feeling, well something stronger than envy, hate almost, the day you told me your first novel had been accepted. There I was struggling with my pathetic first attempts, and you just sailed home on the maiden voyage."

"Really, I never knew that. I dedicated it to you."

"Not very perceptive of you."

"I'm sorry," Theo said. "But I didn't really mean that, I

wasn't talking about your writing. That sounds very rude. What I said was – God knows what Thomas put in these tonight. Lethal! – when I said I envied you, I was thinking more of your love life."

"Which could be written on the head of a pin."

"Not always. You're just going through a temporary lull. At least . . at least you've had one *grand amour.*"

"Have I?"

"Yes. Judy."

"Ah," I said. "Dear Judy. That seems a long time ago."

"But while it lasted it was all or nothing."

"Catastrophic," I said.

"I never had that . . . Some queers don't, you know."

It seemed odd to hear him use the word 'queer' but I sensed he wanted for once to unburden himself.

"Even when we're settled and happy," he said, "we never stop looking. That's the main difference. It's a compulsion, a kind of love-death-wish, if you like. I sometimes think it's not really me. I'm standing outside a lighted window, looking in and seeing myself behave in a totally alien manner. It's the horror of a long dream. You know you're doing it, that you'll do it again and again, yet you can't stop yourself. That and the risks you take. The endless . . . stupid, hideously exciting risks. And I'm not talking about what you might call 'camp', not that. I don't mean those sad creatures who swish about the West End, defiantly female under their blue chins. Not them, that isn't me. They revolt me as much as I'm sure they . . . well, you must find them grotesque. No, the types I'm attracted to whenever I'm back in my own familiar hunting grounds . . . And that's what they are, you know: hunting grounds;" – he lingered over the phrase, bringing his eyes to meet mine and smiling – "well, you'd never suspect, not in a million years. Bank managers, postmen, long-distance lorry drivers, quite a few of them married with dull, mousy wives if one is to believe what they tell me . . . And of course, their risks are greater than mine. It isn't like the proverbial dirty weekend at Brighton with your secretary – two single rooms and clean sheets. It's usually somewhere exposed, dangerous and with a complete stranger. You often don't even exchange first names. Everything's anonymous and you get it over quickly, in a car parked on a bomb site, or else in a railway station toilet between trains . . . the risk, you see, that's so important, the need to feel that even the quick pleasure might be interrupted, that you'll be caught in the act. Fear is a very powerful aphrodisiac . . . Am I disgusting you with all this?"

"No," I said.

"I expect I am. Here, it's different, of course. There's a kind of pagan innocence about it. Perhaps it is something to do with the sea, the cleansing sea. I'm very happy here . . . fulfilled, as they say . . . and yet, I miss the danger, it's not quite the same without the danger. Did you ever feel like that?"

"I can't say I have. But then my sex life has always been very ordinary."

"What's ordinary? . . . If we knew that we could all live peacefully. No, I have the feeling that one day it'll destroy me. But I have to go on, I'm driven, I can't help myself."

"You've never brought any of this into your novels, have you?"

"No."

"Why not?"

He hesitated. "If you give people a murder weapon," he said, "sooner or later they're tempted to use it."

"But you could disguise it."

"Not well enough. Not and be honest. And there doesn't seem to be any point in the half-truth. Like all those boring novels which skirt around it, getting heavily praised in the *New Statesman*, written by lapsed Catholics."

"Can I ask you something? I presume Thomas has talents that extend beyond the kitchen and the bar?"

"Oh, yes. There have been quite a few Thomases over the years. As you probably suspected. I find them very good for the morale, though a little short on stimulating conversation. That's why it's so good to have you here. Quite like old times. It's funny our friendship, isn't it?"

"In what way?"

"Oh, I don't know. We've nothing in common, really and yet .. at the risk of embarrassing you . . . you're one of the very

314

few people I actually care about. I must have been a bit of a pain at times. Especially at Cambridge. I used to lord it over you, didn't I?"

"I don't think so. I was very dreary, always mooning over the delectable Judy. I wonder what became of her?"

"Yes, I wonder," Theo said, and looked away.

We replenished our glasses yet again and swopped anecdotes of those years, lapsing into mild hysteria at our own jokes. Our mood was half-induced by alcohol, half brought about by a nostalgia for things lost – a searching back for innocence.

The next morning Theo studiously avoided any mention of our previous discussion, and I did not press him. We spent the day like any other, and that evening enjoyed a sunset that was vividly unreal. The sea was without ripples, though far out to the right we could discern the glinting surf breaking on the reef. Small fishing boats were silhouetted against the fast-changing sky. One was closer to the shore than the rest and we could see two young, naked fishermen standing in it.

"Look at them," Theo said. "They're so beautiful when they throw the nets."

"What do they fish for?"

"I don't really know. 'I'm not very up on such things." He was silent for a while. "I don't think they catch much."

He turned away and walked back into the house. "Perhaps they only catch my eye," he said.

23

THE FIRST BAD omen that day was the discovery of a dead suckling pig at the water's edge. It was white against the sand and seemed weightless in the slight swell. It was perfect, like an exquisitely moulded bone china replica. The umbilical cord was still attached to the body, floating from the belly like a strand of purple coral. I carefully moved it with a piece of driftwood so that it remained in the sea, but when I returned an hour later it had again been shifted higher up the beach. After lunch I went back to the same spot a third time but could find no trace at first. Then I saw the membrane with the cord still fixed to it had come away from the carcass and was floating on its own like some giant contraceptive. The rest of the tiny body was trapped on the coral and was being pounded to pieces. I was somehow glad that it hadn't been devoured by the sand crabs, for at least the sea was cleansing and its very ruthlessness mitigated against the horror. I stood and stared at it for a while but the afternoon sun in a cloudless sky seared my shoulders, and I retreated to another section of the beach and plunged into the clear water, swimming alone for half an hour in an attempt to wash away my strange feeling of guilt – the guilt I felt for being human and alive in a world of meaningless cruelty.

Later, walking to post a letter in the village, I came across death in another form. There was a dead toad lying in the centre of the debris-strewn roadway. It had been flattened like a cartoon character so that it resembled nothing more than a brown suit of clothes for a toad: one expected to see buttons on the jacket, and it reminded me of a theatrical costume for *The Wind in The Willows*.

The whole day seemed filled with sinister portents. Leaving the post office I was approached by a total stranger, a European, quite well spoken and dressed with an insane disregard for the intense heat. His suit was dark with perspiration; the sweat must have been running down his body as rain from a roof, for I noticed that even his shoes were discoloured around the lace-holes. He asked me who I was, without any polite preamble, but when I told him betrayed no further interest. Then he told me he had been fishing on the North Coast earlier in the day and had caught some barracuda.

"D'you know what?" he said. "I'll tell you something fascinating. This man, this man I hired the boat from, very interesting character. D'you know how he killed the fish once we'd landed them? You'll never guess. He poked a finger through their eyes, straight into the brain. Never seen that done before."

Having distributed this information he trotted off. There was a small patch of wet where he had stood. The encounter left me feeling nauseated, for I could not rid myself of the image he had conjured up. I began to feel that I had somehow been selected as the receptacle of everything that was repulsive on the island: horror is always more pronounced, I find, for being introduced into idyllic surroundings – one expects it in graveyards and empty houses, but never in strong sunlight.

I took a stiff drink the moment I returned to the house, but even so I was witness to yet another incident. Two men suddenly appeared on the beach, one minus an arm, the other minus a leg. They undressed awkwardly, then helped each other in and out of the sea, all the time shouting at each other in German, which is not a language which lends itself to immediate humour. Theo joined me while they were still cavorting.

"There's going to be a storm," he said. "I can always tell. I saw the rain bird this morning when I got up, and now these. That's probably a rain dance."

"Oh, don't be ridiculous," I said. "They're just two cripples having a good time."

"You'd be surprised. Everything gets shaken up before a storm, people go slightly mad. I've seen it many times."

"You're not going to run amok, are you? Warn me if you are, because I've had quite an afternoon." I told him about the various incidents.

"Yes. Well, there you are, you see. Proves my point. By the way, changing the subject, or perhaps staying with it, we've been invited to a party this evening. But you don't have to go if you don't feel like it. I must, I'm afraid. I'm so antisocial most of the time that I have to make the occasional effort."

"No, I'll come. I assume I'm invited because I'm here with you and not because of my so-called literary reputation?"

"Oh, they'd invite anybody new," Theo said, ungraciously. "They're always desperate for new faces."

"Who are they?"

"A couple called Neisser. There's a standing local joke. The nicer they are, the more you should watch out. She's passable providing she doesn't get at the gin too early. He's a monster. Very rich, of course, which he needs to be, since she goes through it at a rate of knots. I don't know where he made his money, there's a kind of mystery about that. Some have it that he made a killing during the war, cornered the South American copper market or something. One thing I will say, they don't stint on food and drink. The guest list is pot luck, but I've found I usually come away with some good copy."

"Sounds intriguing," I said.

"It's formal, of course. At the beginning of the evening, that is. Most parties on the island tend to fall to pieces very quickly. They're so bored, you see, they drink to forget how lucky they are."

The Neisser's house was situated inland, near the golf course and standing in some thirty acres of land: a long modern structure, with two guest wings forming a pair of protective arms around an enormous swimming pool. The driveway was hung with lanterns and a steel band was playing at a discreet distance from the illuminated patio around the pool. We arrived slightly late because Theo's water pump had shown some temperament and delayed our showers. There seemed to be fifty or sixty guests with almost as many servants, coming and going with endless trays of food and drink. Introductions were haphazard, and it was some time before I met either of my hosts. We had no sooner been offered an enormous drink when we were approached by a tall, gangling man wearing a white dinner jacket at least two sizes too small for him.

"Theo!" he said. "Why you're just the man I want to see. You've saved the day."

He had a pronounced American accent, and pushed his very large hands towards your face as he talked to you. Instinctively one wanted to duck.

"Hi!" he said, turning to me. "I'm Bill."

"Bill is a society photographer," Theo explained.

"*The* society photographer, thank you. Not here, of course. I'm from Palm Beach."

"From whence you should never have strayed," Theo said.

"Listen, Theo, old dear, I need you desperately. I'm here on assignment and there's simply nobody on the island worth exposing."

"Say it louder," Theo said. "I don't think everybody heard you."

"Oh, shit to them," Bill said. His hands punched out within an inch of my nose. I stepped back and trod on somebody's foot.

"Excuse me," I said. I had nearly crippled an enormously fat man. He took my apology graciously and passed on.

"What I need," Bill was explaining, "is a really challenging lay-out. Something out of the ordinary. How I see it, is if I could get you against one of those really broken-down shacks with lots of naked little local kids – you looking very suave and terribly, terribly British, contrasted, you know what I mean, you get the picture? I mean, I think it would make a terrific set which I know I could place, and believe me I need the bread. I'll make you look like Edith Sitwell."

"What is the point of the pictures?" Theo asked.

"The point? The point is to pay my rent, dummy. Now listen, you loved the last lot I took of you. Your publisher used one on the jacket, though I can't say he paid my going rate. Listen, can we fix this? Can I ring you? Do I still have your number? Give it to me."

I heard Theo give him a false number, changing the last digit, though I had the conviction that Bill would not be put off so simply. I eased myself away before he knocked me flying with one of his expansive gestures, and went in search of the fat man, feeling that I owed him a more detailed apology.

He was sitting in a corner, taking up at least half of a large sofa. He was even larger at a second viewing, though like many fat men, his face seemed out of proportion to the rest of his body. He was gripping an unlighted full corona between his lips, turning it round and round to saturate the tip with saliva.

"I do so hope I didn't do you a permanent injury,' I said.

"Not at all. It was nice to feel my feet. I haven't seen them in years," he said with unexpected humour. "Do you have a light, by any chance? My name's Mannix, by the way."

"Tony Stern."

"Pleased to meet you, Mr. Stern."

I offered him a light and he went through a ritual with the cigar.

"Do you live on the island, Mr. Stern?"

"No, I'm just visiting."

"Likewise. I just came to case the joint. Thinking of buying a house here if I like it."

"And d'you think you'll like it?"

"What's your opinion?"

"Depends what you want," I said.

"I want somewhere peaceful to die," he said. "See, I've got a little problem." He tapped his chest with a pudgy hand. "Here. I've got a pacemaker. Quite a dandy, as a matter of fact. Made of plutonium. Ticks away at a steady seventy-five a minute if I behave myself. Got enough power to keep going for thirty years. Even if the rest of me falls to pieces, this little baby will still be pumping away."

"That's quite a thought."

"Sort of Edgar Allen Poe brought up to date." He regarded me quizzically. "What's your line of country?"

"I'm a writer."

"Do me a favour, will you? Reach me that ashtray. Do you accept commissions?"

"For books? Yes."

"How'd you like to write a book about me?"

The question took me by surprise. Although at several

stages in my career I have been approached to write what are known as 'house biographies' – the history of some brewery or chocolate manufacturer – I have always resisted. I'm sure it's an honourable way of earning a living, but I have not yet felt the need to succumb to it.

"Does the idea appeal? I'd be willing to pay generously."

"Why don't you write it yourself?" I said.

"Me? I can't write two words. Well, maybe two words. My name on a cheque." He smiled. He had a rather slack jaw which the most extensive dental surgery had been unable to correct.

"I take it you've had an interesting life?"

"I think so."

"What d'you do?"

"I make money," he said. "You know, that stuff that buys people who do the work that makes more money."

"I've heard about it," I said

I began to feel slightly uneasy again, as though some of the earlier happenings of the day had been warnings of worse to come. Far out to sea the sky was illuminated by violent electrical discharges and I felt the wind freshen on my face and saw it disturb the surface of the swimming pool. Behind me the crass photographer suddenly screamed: "The faggots won the war in the desert, not your Monty!" The party was beginning to fragment as the lethal drinks loosened tongues. The general level of conversation seemed shriller, rising above the insistent music of the steel band. I caught a scent of burning, something acrid, transporting me back to the Blitz, and saw that on the lawn a troupe of limbo dancers were preparing to stage an exhibition.

"Take my card," Mannix said.

He fumbled in a pocket and extracted it with some difficulty. Before putting it away I glanced at the address. There were three: Miami, Zurich and Hong Kong. "Any one will get me," Mannix said. "I'm computer-linked. I'll keep the offer open."

"You're taking me on trust. How d'you know I can write?"

"You can write." He rattled off the titles of my last three books. Then smiled again and tapped his cigar against the side of the ashtray. "I never make guesses in the dark. Glad to meet you, Mr. Stern."

It was with a feeling of some relief that I turned towards the limbo dancers. The performance started with an exhibition of fire-eating. I thought it particularly impressive set against the backcloth of an angry sky, though I noticed that many of the guests behaved with noisy indifference towards the artists. I have always had a sneaking sympathy for any form of cabaret act, forced as they are to display their talents to audiences intent on other pleasures, but to have to ignite methylated spirits for a living and still not gain attention seems particularly cruel. The steel band increased the monotonous rhythm and the spectacle on the lawn took on savage splendour. The leading man in the troupe imposed silence on the watching spectators, breathing out tongues of flame I swear must have been three to four feet long. It was then that tragedy struck.

A drunken girl, teetering on the edge of the swimming pool, suddenly veered towards the performers. The leading fire-eater, head thrust back as he brought the flaming taper close to the vapour he was expelling, did not see her and when he breathed the next jet of flame it shot across her face. Screaming, her hair on fire, she fell backwards into the pool. Two male guests immediately dived in fully clothed to rescue her. She was brought to the side and I could see that part of her face was blackened and that most of her hair was charred back to the scalp. The limbo dancer responsible for the accident came forward to help, his lips still wet with methylated spirit, but he was pushed away in the panic and confusion. Mrs. Neisser collapsed, moaning, as the half-drowned girl came to and began to scream. As the girl was carried into the house I could see that the skin on the burnt side of her face had bubbled and peeled away. Too many people were giving advice, but eventually a car was manoeuvred as close as possible and the girl carried into it. As it drove away the first heavy drops of rain began to fall, beating into the pool, the surface of which was blackened in places.

I heard the American photographer complaining, "Jesus!

why the hell didn't I have a camera? I knew I should have brought one."

I went in search of Theo and again stumbled into Mannix.

"What happened? I was inside."

"A girl got burnt."

He nodded. I might have been telling him that the Dow Jones Index had shifted half a point.

"That was nasty," I said, when I found Theo.

"And the rain," Theo said. "I told you. There'll be other things before the night's out."

"Don't be too cheerful, will you? I need a drink."

Outside, in the rain, the troupe of limbo dancers were packing their props and the members of the steel band were grouped together in a forlorn huddle as though they shared a collective responsibility for what had happened. Mrs. Neisser had been taken to her bedroom, and her husband moved amongst the guests attempting to save his party from total collapse.

"Silly little cow," I heard somebody say, "she was drinking like there was going to be no tomorrow."

"What d'you think?" I asked Theo. "Shall we ease our way out?"

"I don't think so," he said. "It's all part of life's rich pageant."

"Does that mean you've found something?"

"Could be."

"Well, let me know, won't you, because I'll need to get transport."

"Oh, I won't abandon you."

There is something primeval about a tropical storm. For a few moments the rain was so solid that it stifled all conversation and we stood gaping at it. Small rivers formed on the previously immaculate lawn and, as though seized by madness, some of the younger guests who must have come prepared for such an eventuality, changed into swimming costumes and plunged into the pool. Coming so soon after the girl's tragedy their antics filled me with revulsion, but most of the guests applauded them from the safety of the covered patio. I drifted around, wishing to God I had never come, and caught a glimpse of Theo in the distance. He was standing in the doorway of one of the bedrooms, earnestly in conversation with a young man with floppy, thin hair. Theo had one hand on his shoulder, and their faces were close together.

"Talk to me," a voice said. "I'm worth talking to."

I turned to find a woman of about my own age, flamboyantly dressed in a Pucci print dress.

"Where did you come from?" she said. "I haven't seen you before. You haven't got a drink. Don't tell me you're on the wagon, I couldn't bear it. Everybody's going on the wagon these days. It's so boring."

"I've just put one down."

"Oh, you've just put one *down*, have you? Well, why don't you pick one *up* and be sociable? This bloody party's gone to pot! First decent party for weeks and it's all ruined because of that dreary little Hamilton girl."

I looked around for an escape route.

"Don't look away when I'm talking to you. Most people like talking to me. I don't suppose you even know who I am, do you?"

"No," I said.

"Well, guess."

"I'm no good at those sort of games."

"My husband – he's that fucking bore over there – that dehydrated Prince of Wales – talking to, I don't know who he's talking to, nor do I care – well, anyway, he's one of the most important people on this shitty little island, and I'm his wife, thank you very much, though you wouldn't know it because he doesn't do it very often. Not with me at any rate. Are you from jolly old England? You look as though you're from jolly old England. Well, let me give you a tip. Don't, repeat don't, come and live here because it's fucking death. Death! Believe me, and I know. Sun, sand and the dear little blackamoors who don't do a fucking thing. They can't even pour water, most of them. Do you think I'm attractive?"

"Very," I said.

"Fucking liar. Let me tell you something. I don't know who you are – did you tell me who you are? – but I thought you had a pleasant face and that's why I talked to you. I've given up talking to everybody else, because they're all fucking bores. And the biggest bore of all is my husband. I am attractive, whether you think so or not. Very attractive. I'll show you, if you like."

She pulled her dress open, exposing one breast. "Does that do anything to you, or are you like the rest of the men on this boring island? You can see the rest if you like."

"Oh, put it away, Doris," somebody said. "You're always flashing those tired old tits."

She flung the remains of her drink in the man's face, and I was able to escape.

The whole party was like that, and as the evening wore on I glimpsed those hatreds that always lurk just below the surface in any closed community. As the interloper, I was therefore a new audience for old resentments, the recipient of many un-asked-for confidences and slanders. Perhaps only strangers could be trusted; those who remained on the island were too close for trust.

I finally went and sat next to Mannix again. He seemed reasonably aloof from the mob and shared my detachment.

"Have they come back from the hospital yet?"

"No idea," he said. "Tell me about your friend."

"My cousin, you mean?"

"Oh, he's your cousin, is he? Then you must know him very well."

"Reasonably well."

"He interests me. I seem to have seen him somewhere before. The face looks familiar. I was trying to place him."

Something in his voice put me on my guard.

"Mention my name to him. It might jog his memory. I'm staying at the Sandy Lane for a few more days. He might care to have lunch with me."

"I'll ask him," I said.

He heaved himself up out of the sofa and I noticed his neck turned a different colour with the effort.

"It was good to meet you, anyway. Think about my offer. It's worth thinking about."

I waited until Theo joined me with the fair-haired young man. By then I had drunk rather too much.

"Ready?" Theo said. "I think we've had the best of this. Quite an amusing party, as local parties go. This is Adrian, by the way."

I nodded. Adrian was swaying on his feet and needed Theo's arm to guide him through the crowd. Just as we were halfway to our car I heard the American photographer give one last shout. "Theo, you old queen, don't forget you're going to pose for me!"

It was fairly obvious that Theo had acquired another house guest in Adrian, who sat with lolling head in the front seat while Theo drove with a caution I was thankful for. Reaching the house was a triumph of concentration.

"I think bed, don't you?" Theo said. "Poor Adrian lives on the other side of Bridgetown, so I suggested he stayed the night."

"Where's the bathroom?" Adrian muttered.

"Let me show you," Theo said, grimacing at me behind his back. "We've got everything you need here."

They disappeared in the direction of Theo's bedroom. I was too tired and too irritable to care what they did, and for once slept very badly, waking at frequent intervals to hear the rain beating down on the flat roof. The sound of the phone ringing woke me another time. I listened to see if Theo would answer it, letting it ring a dozen times before groping my way into the living room. It was a long distance call, I could tell that from the echo on the line, and a slurred man's voice said: "Theo?"

"No," I said. "This isn't Theo."

The man did not speak again but the connection wasn't broken immediately and I thought I could hear an operator's voice in the background. It seemed to be Arabic. Then nothing. I waited, but it never rang again. On my way back to my room I heard somebody running past on the beach and registered that it had at last stopped raining.

I was awake again just after dawn. My lungs felt as though they had no air in them and I walked out on to the deserted beach. Evidence of the storm was everywhere – driftwood and bottles, broken but washed smooth by many tides, ugly, greasy piles of seaweed, and a palm tree, half-buried in the sand and sticking up at an angle. It looked like part of a dead elephant. The sea was calm now, just lapping the beach, and the sand was rippled in symmetrical patterns, reminding me of a yellow lawn that had recently been mown. Far out to sea was a single fishing boat, the sound of its outboard motor bringing back memories of Sunday mornings in suburban gardens. Fallen green coconuts lay like the heads of massacred brigands, and ravening hordes of sand crabs scrambled to unseen holes as I walked along the water's edge enjoying the feel of cool damp sand.

That particular stretch of beach ended after a couple of hundred yards and fingers of rock encrusted with limpets poked out into deeper water. The body was jammed into a crevice, pushed there by the last of the storm waves. I didn't register it at first. I was walking into the sun and the rays came back at me off the water. When I reached the rocks I sat down on them to enjoy the peace, elated as always by the sheer, deserted tranquillity of the beach. Putting out a hand to steady myself I touched something soft and looking down I saw it was a black arm, bent at an obscene angle. I pushed myself off the rock, losing balance so that I ended up on my knees, and there, with my face only inches from the water, I found the rest of Thomas.

His black head was under the water and even as I looked, shoals of small silver fish darted from the scene, and the ripples seemed to move his features, waving them in the same way that old movie close-ups used to dissolve into each other to denote the passing of time. I don't know how long I remained in that supplicant's position, for the shock had crippled me. He was naked except for a pair of striped shorts, but apart from the fact that the body was grotesquely twisted I could see no marks of violence.

I suddenly became conscious that the noise of the fishing boat was much closer and looked up to see it passing. I struggled to my feet and shouted to its single occupant, but he mistook my panic for a greeting, waved and kept on going. I ran all the way back to the house, heedless of the broken glass, straight through and into Theo's bedroom.

He and the young man called Adrian were both sprawled asleep in the bed, and Adrian had one arm thrown across

Theo's chest as though warding off a blow. Theo's eyes opened at my first words, but he couldn't take in the news immediately and I had to repeat my story before the full impact penetrated. I don't think Adrian had any comprehension at that moment, but he was forgotten as Theo and I raced back to the beach. Together we managed to drag the body out of the crevice and on to the dry sand.

"Twice," Theo said.

"What?"

"Twice, oh, God!" He didn't seem to be talking to me. "He's dead, isn't he?"

"It must have happened during the night," I said. "During the storm. He must have been caught by a wave or something, knocked against the rocks, maybe, and drowned."

"Why would he drown?" Theo said. "Thomas wouldn't drown, he could swim out of sight."

"Well, there's nothing we can do now, except call the police."

"I'll do that. Don't you leave him. Stay here, you stay here. I don't want him . . . I don't want him left."

He went back to the house while I stayed crouched by the body. I tried to brush some of the sand off Thomas's face while I waited, then I got up and walked to the water's edge to bathe my feet. I had cut myself on the broken glass during that first dash for help. As I swished my feet through the shallow water I saw something white floating close to the rocks. I bent to retrieve it. It was a small card and when I turned it over I saw that it was Mannix's visiting card, the one he'd given me at the party.

When Theo returned he brought a sheet with him that he placed over the body and weighted down with pieces of driftwood at each corner. Adrian appeared in the distance, but made no attempt to join us.

"Are the police coming?"

"Yes," Theo said. "I don't suppose they'll hurry. They never do."

"Well, I suppose there's not much to hurry for."

We had both smoked three or four cigarettes before a sergeant and a constable from the station at St. James' strolled across the beach. By then the sun was hot enough to be uncomfortable and the dead body was attracting flies. After the briefest of examinations the two policemen carried the body up the beach to the house and deposited it alongside Theo's car. Eventually an ambulance arrived and with it the inevitable crowd of sightseers, for the news did not have far to travel.

It took the best part of an hour for the sergeant to take down my statement, writing one word at a time. I thought he might have questioned Theo as well, but the effort of getting my statement seemed to have exhausted him, and when I had signed it he left us.

Adrian had spent most of the time in the bathroom during this; now he surfaced and immediately excused himself. "I'm sure you don't want me here," he said.

Theo didn't answer at once.

"I'll give you a call later, Theo. It's all been such a shock. Nice to meet you," he said to me.

"Don't you want a taxi?" Theo said.

"I think I'll walk. Fresh air'll do me good."

"I wouldn't talk too much about it. You know what this place is like."

"Oh, I won't. I won't say a word."

Theo made no attempt to see him to the door and he walked out of the house and presumably out of Theo's life, for I never saw him again, nor was his name ever mentioned.

"What did you mean out there?" I asked Theo during a sparse brunch we forced ourselves to eat. "You said 'twice'."

"I said what?"

"Twice. Has it happened before? Did somebody else drown out there?"

"I don't know what I meant. I don't even remember saying it. It was just too ghastly for words."

"I suppose there'll be a post-mortem?"

"I assume so."

"Does he have a family?"

"I believe so. I've never met them, but there's bound to be dozens of them. Practically everybody's related to everybody else."

329

"Well, quite a night, one way or another. What with the storm, and that girl getting burnt. I take it all back."

"Take what back?"

"What you told me. You predicted something like this."

"I wish to God I'd never brought that other creature back here."

"Well, that wouldn't have made any difference."

"It might. Thomas wouldn't have been out."

"Oh, I see."

"I'm such a bloody disaster." He got up from the table, and I was embarrassed for him. "Why can't I just be faithful to one thing, one person?" he said. "For what? I mean, for what?" He was close to tears, working himself into a bout of self-pity. "I didn't need it, I didn't enjoy it but I still make the same bloody mistakes time after time. And while I'm rutting in that bed with that bloodly little pouf my poor baby, my darling Thomas is dying out there. I wish you'd help me, I wish someone would help me sort it all out once and for all."

"Of course, I'll help."

He began to drink again. I took a few to keep him company, but the alcohol didn't touch either of us. I tried to put myself in his position, because it became more and more apparent that his relationship with Thomas had been a turning point in his life.

"You're the only one I can tell," he kept saying. "Nobody else would understand," but I didn't really understand, because even confronted with his anguish, part of me remained appalled.

"We all do stupid things for sex," I said.

"That's not what I'm talking about. I'm not talking about that. I should have protected him."

"You make it sound as though he was murdered or something. Was he promiscuous?"

Theo stared at me as though I had used a word he had never heard before.

"Is that all you ever think about us? Queers are promiscuous. Heteros aren't, I suppose? Christ, every bloody woman on this island is at it like knives."

"I was only asking. You've told me yourself you all pick up

strangers. Perhaps he picked up the wrong stranger."

"Perhaps." His burst of anger was over; he seemed crumpled again. "I'm sorry I shouted like that. Don't you turn against me, will you? I couldn't bear that. Just ignore me when I lash out . . . I can't really expect you to understand. He wasn't anything very special, poor Thomas, not to other people, but he never wanted anything from me. He was just a boy who was kind to me, and that's rare enough."

24

A S A RESULT of the tragedy I stayed longer than I had intended. There was a post-mortem, the verdict being,
predictably, death by drowning. I gave evidence of finding
the body, but nobody seemed unduly concerned. It was, after
all, only the death of a house-boy; an excuse for a colourful
funeral. Thomas appeared to have many friends and relatives, and the size of the cortège amazed me, since I was a
stranger to the customs of the island. The procession of cars
passed Theo's house along the coast road, preceded by a
band, a rather ragged band to be sure, but playing with gusto.
There must have been at least twenty cars following the
coffin, reminiscent of a Mafia ceremony, except for the
incongruous gaiety.

Theo did not go to the funeral or the wake. "They wouldn't
want me there," he said. "I'd only inhibit them.
They're very touchy about such things." He sent a generous
cheque to the family and a week later the father appeared,
dressed more sombrely on this occasion than anybody at the
actual funeral, to thank Theo and pay his respects.

He invited us both back for tea to meet his wife. We could
not refuse. His home was some ten miles away in a village
that bore no resemblance to the area around Theo's house.
Everything was on a miniature scale, doll's house versions of
Tara, built on precarious piles of rocks. I learnt from Theo
that this meant the occupants did not own the ground the
house was built on. If they couldn't pay the rent they moved
the whole house elsewhere; only those with freeholds built on
solid foundations.

The house, although a patched wooden wreck from the outside, was spotlessly clean within. We were shown into the
main room the size of an average British bathroom. Thomas's
mother and six or seven other children of various sizes and

ages stood clustered in a doorway while we were offered the only two chairs. There was a picture of the Queen on the wall, framed in gilt. Two odd cups and saucers had been laid on the table, together with a packet of Peak Frean's cream crackers. We were solemnly introduced to everybody present, but nobody spoke to us. Tea was poured and we drank it self-consciously, feeling, as Theo remarked afterwards, like the royal family at Versailles. Theo made a charming and I am sure sincere little speech about Thomas, extolling his virtues and saying what a good house-boy he had been. The mother smiled nervously, but none of the other children betrayed any emotion. And after a decent interval and one cream cracker each, we said our thanks and left.

"Do you think they really like us?" I asked on the journey home. "Politically this is a comparatively stable island, isn't it?"

"Yes. But change is on the way. I dare say in a few years all those charming little children will be making petrol bombs and throwing them in our direction. You can't blame them. They must see what we've got and what they haven't got. The only thing is, when we've gone they still won't have anything. Chances are they'll have even less. Still, that's progress these days."

He pulled into the side of the road to let an overladen cart of sugar-cane pass. It left a trail of green stalks in its wake.

"Something occurred to me the other day," Theo said. "I was watching two people on the beach, visitors, smothering themselves in sun-tan oil to fry quicker. And I thought, somewhere back in the States there are a lot of underpaid blacks making that stuff. There's irony for you, yes?"

"Yes. You should use it. Make a good short story."

"Too modern for me. You can have it."

In an effort to take his mind off recent events I suggested we dined out that evening, something we had studiously avoided until then. Theo was none too enthusiastic but allowed himself to be persuaded.

The restaurant was British-owned and like many similar establishments on the island hideously pretentious. The decor suggested that Butlins had been taken over by the Speer organisation – a mixture of plastic and Germanic wrought iron with a conflicting colour scheme of purple and orange.

"We must drink a great deal," I said. "And don't get the giggles. I've just spotted the Maître d'."

The gentleman in question was one of those Englishmen who can only succeed abroad, and had imposed a public school accent on top of Streatham Cockney, with the result that when he highlighted the *plats du jour* he sounded like a strangulated railway station announcer.

"If I maybe so bold, gentlemen, I think you'll find the veal done Viennese style with just a hint of garnish to your liking."

"How about the local fish?" I said.

"It's all fresh, sir, unless, of course you'd like the imported Dover sole which we have flown in from New York every day."

"That sounds enterprising."

"Then of course there is the boeuf Wellington, a speciality of the house."

"No, I think fish," Theo said, and kicked me under the table.

"We have dolphin, sir. Or flying fish."

"He doesn't mean our kind of dolphin," Theo said. "But it sounds off putting."

We settled for the plainest dish on the menu and ordered two bottles of Puligny Montrachet at a price that would have embarrassed the wine waiter at The Mirabelle.

As we ate bugs immolated themselves in the flame of the candle burning in the middle of the table, great green and brown things which stained the cloth with a strange charnel dust as they fluttered and died. The food when it came was tepid and the vegetables, overcooked, reminded me of childhood holidays in lodgings. But the wine was cold and had somehow weathered the long journey from the Côte d'Or. We made a determined effort to enjoy ourselves despite frequent visits from the proprietor. He was so obviously out of his depth that I began to like him. I wondered if he had been the author of the menu, which was prefaced by a greeting in Gothic Script which read: *Bon Ape Tit*.

"Now, how about dessert, gentlemen. I can personally recommend the pot au chocolat. Oh, wait a minute, that shouldn't be on the menu tonight."

"I think the crème caramel," Theo said.

"I cannot apologise enough, sir, but it's Friday and the man who comes in specially to make the crème caramel unfortunately didn't appear today."

"Right. Well, what about the ice cream, then?"

"Oh, yes, we have ice cream, sir."

"What do you have? What flavours?"

"Well, normally we have vanilla, strawberry, orange and cassata."

"What do you normally not have on a Friday?" Theo asked with a straight face.

"Tonight we've got the lime sherbert, sir."

"Just coffee," Theo said. "And another bottle of wine."

We were halfway through that third bottle when Theo's mood changed abruptly in the middle of an anecdote he was telling about his literary agent.

"Oh, God," he said. It was an involuntary exclamation.

"What?"

He was staring past me and I turned. Mannix was just entering the restaurant with a scrubby-looking young blonde tourist on his arm. Even from a distance I could see that she was a newcomer to the island, for she wore a topless dress which exposed the white strap-marks of her bikini on inflamed shoulders.

"Let's get out of here," Theo said. "There's somebody I want to avoid."

"You mean that man. I met him the other night at the party. Mannix. He gave me his card."

"That isn't his name," Theo said. "Look, do me a favour, will you? Pay the bill and let's get out."

He kept his face down, picking up the menu again to shield himself as Mannix was shown to a table on the far side of the now-crowded room. It didn't seem worth arguing about, so I called for the bill. Theo didn't wait for me to pay but got up and went outside. As I left, Mannix suddenly spotted me and waved, beckoning me to come over to his table.

"Thought any more about my offer?" he said. He made no attempt to introduce the young girl.

"I'm giving it a lot of thought."

"You on your own? Why don't you join us?"

"No, I am with somebody." I gestured vaguely. "Very nice to see you again."

Theo was already sitting in the car.

"Do you think he saw me?"

"No. Definitely."

"Thank God for that."

"Why the panic?"

"No panic. He's just one of the locals I try and avoid if possible."

"But he told me he'd only just arrived," I said.

"Well, he comes and goes. What else did he tell you? Did he mention me?"

"Yes, he did come to think of it. Nothing much. Just asked the odd question. He didn't seem to know you. He was mostly interested in me, wanted me to consider writing his biography, which seemed odd."

"Stay clear of him," Theo said.

"Well, I don't intend to take him up on the offer."

Theo drove very badly, mashing his gears and braking far too late on every blind corner. I found myself braced for the inevitable crash, though stupidly much too British to urge caution. About half a mile from the house our dim headlights picked out a group of natives far too late, and Theo reacted violently, swinging the wheel and hitting the accelerator instead of the brake pedal. We ended up in the ditch. It was not a serious accident and the natives pulled us on to the road again, but because I had been so tense I knew that I had pulled something in my back. When finally we reached home, the pain was intense and by the following morning I could hardly get out of bed. I asked Theo if he had a doctor.

"I don't use the local doctor," Theo said. "She's a woman and it puts me off. I always go to somebody in Bridgetown. He's a genius. Not everybody's cup of tea, but I swear by him. He's got healing hands. He's your man."

He ordered a taxi for me and gave complicated directions

to the driver, then watched us out of sight, which at the time I thought strangely touching.

We drove in sweltering heat for the best part of an hour, and at one point the heavy traffic forced us to stop by a lunatic asylum on the outskirts of Bridgetown. Half a dozen of the inmates rushed to the iron railings. They had demented, zoo-like faces, but seemed sadder even than the caged anthropoids they so closely resembled. They made no gestures, but just stared at us from a distance of ten feet.

The doctor's surgery was close to the harbour in a side street. It was a wooden building with a decrepit verandah running round it on three sides. There was a queue of patients waiting to be seen, most of them squatting against the slatted boards of the house. It was obvious that I had a long wait ahead of me, but having come that far and being still in pain, I told my taxi driver to park nearby.

It was a scene that closely resembled a television documentary on the life of some Schweitzer-like character. The biggest difference between the rich and the poor when they are sick is the attitude of resignation that most of the poor assume, like another symptom of the terminal diseases they carry. Nobody looked at me as I joined the back of the queue. We moved up one position every five minutes or so and I accepted the fact that my original estimate had been optimistic. There was a cinema opposite and I read the handwritten posters a dozen times, learning them off by heart. The programme being advertised was VILLAGE OF THE GIANT and THE TERRORNAUTS. There was an added encouragement, for the legend beneath one title read: *Teenagers Zoom. See them burst out of their clothes and bust up a town.*

I was sweating profusely from the combination of heat and the pain in my lower back. Looking at my wrist-watch I saw it had taken the best part of an hour for me to reach the entrance to the waiting room. There were still a dozen patients ahead of me, but at least I had gained my quota of shade. Ten minutes later I was inside the room and able to claim a cane chair. For the benefit of those waiting, there were some faded magazines mostly of a religious nature, and one tattered book. I picked it up, desperate for anything to take

337

my mind off the pain. Worms had eaten into the pages, making strange patterns, but I could still make out the title: *William Carey of India* by Percy H. Jones, Author of *The Young Browns Abroad*. I didn't have time to study the text, for the queue started to move at a faster pace, and we played a sort of crippled musical chairs. Now I could hear the doctor talking quietly in the surgery, for the fanlight above the door was broken. There would be a few muttered questions and responses and then a strange sound, like somebody faking a sneeze. It came at regular intervals. "Ha-shoo! . . . Ha-shoo!" I had no idea what it meant or who was responsible for it.

Finally I was at the head of the queue.

The surgery was no different from the rest of the building. It contained a rocking chair, a card-table, a couch, a tattered arm chair and some ancient green matting on the floor such as one finds in the pavilions of impoverished cricket clubs.

The man who greeted me was an old Bajan. I guessed him to be in his late seventies. He was wearing white American ducks with black shoes. When I came into the room he was sitting at the card-table writing something on the fly-leaf of a Bible. He motioned me to the couch. I sat looking at an eye-testing card on the wall opposite, but sweat, rather than poor eyesight, blurred the words. It was incredibly hot in the room and I became aware that it was windowless.

The doctor closed the Bible and moved to me.

"Where's the pain?" he said.

I put my hand on the tender region. He felt it, pressing hard into the spine so that I could not help crying out.

"Lie down," he said.

I climbed up on to the couch and lay on my back.

"Other way."

I turned over. Nothing happened. Then I heard the same noise again. "Ha-shoo!" and seconds later he seemed to jump on me with all his weight. I felt something crack in my back, and a pain so intense that my whole body poured with sweat. I waited, but nothing else happened.

"Five dollars," he said.

"Is that all? I mean is that all the treatment?"

"In a few hours, later this afternoon, you'll be better."

I paid him and he went back to the Bible and started to write again. As I left a woman with pendulous breasts under a cotton shift took my place.

The treatment seemed to have made the condition much worse, and it took me a few moments before I felt able to go in search of my taxi. I found the driver parked across the street. He was fast asleep and made no effort to assist me. The taxi itself was like an oven. I think I passed out the moment I was inside and when I next became conscious of my surroundings I found we were outside a native bar. My driver was nowhere to be seen, but before I could panic he appeared with a can of ice-cold beer. I drank half of it, wanting to die.

"I think I'm very ill," I said. "Drive very slowly. No bumps." Then I passed out again.

He must have taken me literally for it was late afternoon before we reached the house. Amazingly, I woke feeling almost normal. There was an ache in my back, but the blinding pain had gone and my legs, when I gingerly tested them, no longer felt as though they were joined to the pelvis by hot wires. I gave the taxi driver double what he asked for in an excess of gratitude.

I don't think I noticed anything particularly different about the house at first; ever since Thomas's death there had been little to disturb the normal quiet, for the garden foliage cushioned the traffic noise and the background of surf was so constant as to pass unheaded. The sudden absence of pain made me feel lightheaded and I could hardly wait to tell Theo the good news. He wasn't in his room as I had expected, so I walked down to the beach, since it was roughly the time when he took his afternoon dip. There were two or three people in the water, but no sign of Theo. I came back into the house to change into some clean clothes. Pinned to the door of my bedroom was a handwritten note.

Dear Tony,
Forgive me, but I've had to leave in somewhat of a hurry and there was no way of contacting you. Please don't be alarmed, and I'll explain when we meet up again in London. I had some urgent business to attend to in New

York, but I shall be moving around after that. Treat the place as your own for as long as you like. There's nothing worth stealing anyway. Excuse haste.

Ever,
Theo

I was reading the note a second time when a voice called from the living room.

"Anybody home?"

I walked into the room to find Mannix.

"I know it's not done to call without any invitation," he said. "I did ring but there hasn't been an answer all day."

"No, I've been out. I had to go to the doctor in Bridgetown."

"Nothing serious, I hope?"

"I don't think so. Not any longer anyway."

"Nasty business, being ill away from home. Something to avoid. Look, actually I came to apologise for my rudeness. I'd no idea that your cousin was such a distinguished literary figure. Somebody at the hotel told me and since I pride myself on being a keen student of literature, I wanted to pay my respects."

"What a pity," I said. "You've just missed him."

"Oh, he's not here?"

"No, he had to go away on business."

"You mean he's left the island?"

"Yes."

There had been something bogus about his reason for calling and something about his general manner which put me on my guard.

"Well, that really is a pity. I was really looking forward to meeting him. Do you know how long he'll be away?"

"I don't think he's coming back for some time. I shall be leaving myself shortly."

"That's too bad. Perhaps you'll tell him I called when next you see him."

"Of course."

"Tell him I'm always willing to pay a good price for original manuscripts. It's a hobby of mine."

340

"Yes, I'll tell him. I don't know that he ever parts with his manuscripts. We authors tend to feel very maternal about them."

"Well, you can always find me if he changes his mind."

He was staring at Theo's note in my hand.

"Take care of your health, Mr. Stern. You don't want to end up like me. You know what they say. Neglect your health and you end up dead. And once again, forgive me for coming in unannounced."

"That's all right. Have you made up your mind about buying a house here?"

"I think I've decided against it. There's not enough activity. Enjoy the rest of your stay, Mr. Stern."

He was surprisingly light on his feet for a man carrying that much weight. A few moments later I heard the sound of his car scattering the gravel on the drive, and poured myself a much needed Scotch. Perhaps it was only my novelist's mind at work, but Mannix's visit seemed more than coincidence. Reading Theo's note again, remembering his anxiety in the restaurant, there seemed reasonable cause for alarm.

There is something disconcerting about being left alone in a house that doesn't belong to you. One is tempted to do irrational, sometimes shameful things. An alien personality takes over. It becomes in one's mind, a hotel, impersonal, a place to which one will never return and therefore towards which one has no responsibility. I have to confess that disorientated by Theo's sudden exit, I examined his work room, sifting through the papers on his desk, opening drawers, behaving like some sneak thief. I found nothing that would explain his panic and after a while my behaviour shocked me.

I phoned the B.O.A.C. office in Bridgetown to make my own arrangements for departure, only to be told that the next available flight to London was in three days' time. I booked a seat, then spent those remaining days lazing about on the beach – which I mostly had to myself, the solitude being not unwelcome – and the enforced rest enabled my back fully to recover.

It was a night flight and before take-off the stewardess came round with an armful of English newspapers, the first I had seen for some weeks.

"They are today's, sir. They came out on this morning's flight."

I selected the *Telegraph* and the *Daily Mirror*, intending to break my fast with the best or worst of both worlds, settling down with seat-belt fastened in masochistic mood to enjoy what, in all honesty, I had not missed. News from England after an absence has a depressing sameness about it: the government and the T.U.C. were locked in one of their usual contortions, a former vicar of Balham had been charged with 'open and notorious sin', a Labour M.P. had made a speech criticising the cost of the Royal Family and the film of *Cleopatra* was still in difficulties following Elizabeth Taylor's illness. But the item which caught my eye was not given much prominence in the early editions. It was tucked away in a small paragraph at the bottom of page one and gave the first news that a Soviet spy named George Blake had been arrested.

25

I DON'T SUPPOSE I shall ever know for certain why Theo left Barbados in such unimagined anguish. At the time, of course, I made no sinister connections, inclined to the belief that the fat man was somehow part of that world of twilight sex which, without benefit of any reliable maps, I had neither the ability nor the inclination to explore in depth.

He seemed to have disappeared without trace, putting the island house on the market a few months later. I saw an advertisement for it in the pages of *Country Life* and noted that it was being sold complete with furniture and fittings through an agent. I contacted his British publishers, but they had no knowledge of his whereabouts and in fact were somewhat irritated by my enquiry; the editor I spoke to said they were anxiously awaiting delivery of his next manuscript. "We've announced it in our list," he said. "You've no idea what this does to our sales conference. It throws everybody out."

I was concerned for him, for I felt that we had once again grown closer, our relationship dovetailing as of old. My own life was not so stimulating that I could afford to dismiss the absence of somebody like Theo without a moment's thought. It was a period when I was drifting between two women, both of whom satisfied me in part, but both lacking that spark that might have led to a more permanent relationship. I sat down every day at my desk to fulfil my quota of words, but my writing lacked any real inspiration.

I followed the Blake trial with keen interest, for it touched upon some of my own wartime experiences, and perhaps because of this I was not so shocked as some at the apparent viciousness of British justice when his sentence was announced. I felt no pity for Blake, then or now. He was one of the coldest of operators, sending many of his colleagues to their death — a useful man, I suppose, if he's on your side, like one of those footballers who perform professional fouls with total indifference if their team is behind. Blake was a supreme cynic in a cynical game.

Now, of course, I am better placed to pull together most of the threads. I realise the significance of the word 'twice' and why Mannix's visiting card was floating close to Thomas's drowned body: it was just that – a social reminder to Theo as to who had come calling – except that, by chance, I found it and not Theo. At the time I had assumed it to be the card Mannix had given me in the restaurant, and which I must have dropped.

Then there was the phone call during the small hours of that same night. Blake's arrest had finally led the authorities to close in on Philby. He was in Beirut at that time, on the verge of flight, his well-documented bouts of drunken violence blurring his previous, ice-cold confidence. It could have been Philby, or somebody close to him, attempting to warn Theo. That seems plausible enough now.

I think Theo wanted out by then. He felt he'd paid his dues. His employers felt otherwise; they had to let him know he wasn't yet in line for a one-way ticket to Moscow. They'd left him alone for a few years, allowed him to put down roots on the island, cover his wartime tracks, and be lulled into believing that he was out of the wood. Now, with Philby spent, they reactivated him. I suspect the coincidence of my visit complicated matters. They hadn't bargained for me and for all they knew I might be there doing their business, with a brief to turn him a second time. So instead of the direct approach they killed Thomas to let Theo know they were in earnest.

None of these possible explanations occurred to me at the time. Why should they have done? Theo's behaviour may have been odd, but I didn't attribute anything sinister to it. Listening to him explain his way of life I realised it was something I could never fully comprehend so I didn't try. I had no strong moral views about his homosexuality, and I certainly understood his grief at the death of Thomas, even if it wasn't my sort of love.

No, I was too conventional in my outlook to harbour

344

deeper suspicions. I had left the war behind. It is only in recent weeks that I have begun to dredge my memory. Recalling the whole episode of Blake's escape, I've remembered an occasion, some years ago, when I was in Long Island researching a novel that I ultimately aborted when Mr. Mario Puzo's best seller about the Sicilian Forsyte Saga beat me to the post. I was tracked down to my motel by two men, one a lawyer who is still practising so I will not reveal his name. His companion was a man introduced to me as Herbert Hoover, which I thought was ironic. They came with a proposition for me to write a screenplay based on the Blake escape. It was all very businesslike. Their story was they were acting on behalf of a consortium stuffed with tax-haven money which could be used for financing a film. Until the United States Government passed new laws, it was perfectly legitimate a few years back. The idea was sufficiently intriguing for me to pursue it, but at the moment when formal contracts would normally have been exchanged the dialogue mysteriously came to an abrupt end, and I heard nothing further. In the interim, however, I had what facts were available and had made contact with several people who had been connected with the case. There was one detail, never satisfactorily explained at the time, which fascinated me.

Students of the case may recall that, oddly, Blake's mother and sister refused to provide him with the modest amount of capital necessary to finance his escape. Yet the money was eventually obtained and despite prior tip-offs to the authorities by an ex-safe-breaker that the attempt would be made, Blake walked out of his English prison with embarrassing ease. I felt that I needed to know more about this aspect and closely questioned my American contacts. For the first time during our dialogue they were curiously reticent. All I could extract from them was the admission that the identity of the benefactor would surprise me. "The person involved was a member of your artistic community," the lawyer said, using that curiously stiff vocabulary that Americans sometimes employ. I pressed them further, but that was as far as they would go. "A well-known name," they said with irritating smugness. Once the entire episode had petered out I took the trouble to look up one of my old colleagues who was still connected with the Special Branch. I told him what I knew and he thanked me for my trouble, but nothing ever came out and doubtless my information, together with other documents on the case, still await the statute of limitations on such matters.

Now when I think of it, I wonder if they were talking of Theo? The expression 'artistic circles' is loose enough and American legalese is just as obscure, if not more so, than its British counterpart. It could have been Theo. He was back in England by the time Blake made his escape.

Seemingly his old self and making no immediate reference to his long absence or the manner in which we had last parted, he turned up at the Garrick one day while I was having lunch. He'd been travelling, he said, doing what he had meant to do long ago. "I always regretted I'd never seen the Far East. So one day I just decided to take a boat and go."

I wasn't going to let him off the hook that easily.

"You did disappear rather quickly. I mean I went off to that witch doctor – and you were right by the way, he did have healing hands, though an alarmingly unorthodox technique – and when I came back, you'd gone. Not a trace."

"Yes." He smiled. "I felt badly at the time, but . . . well, anyway, I'm sure you've forgiven me, Tony; you were always of such a forgiving nature."

"I didn't at the time. I was frightfully worried. So were your publishers."

"They should worry. As a result of my trip they're going to have a best seller on their hands next autumn."

"Tell me something," I said. "Just to satisfy my insatiable curiosity, and then we'll forget it. Did your sudden exodus have anything to do with that gross character who called himself, Manic, no – Mannix? Do you remember who I mean? Looked like Sydney Greenstreet and boasted he had a plutonic device to boost his heart."

"What was your question again?"

"I'm asking whether he had anything to do with your headlong flight from the island."

"I doubt it. Did I ever give that impression?"

"You didn't give any impression. You just upped and went."

Theo merely smiled.

"He came looking for you on the day you left. I thought he was very bogus."

"So were most of the people on that island. I'm not sorry I sold the house. Got a reasonable price for it, too. I could never go back, of course, not after the way poor Thomas died."

"Was that the real reason?"

"Yes. I was very fond of Thomas. Very fond."

"And Mannix had nothing to do with it?"

"What a persistent character you are, Tony. You should have been called to the Bar. If you must know I once allowed Mannix to do me a favour. A great mistake, because he asked too much in return. He liked them very young. Much too young for my tastes. I draw the line at chickens. That's our slang for small children." He grinned at me. "I hope you're shocked but satisfied. Now let's talk about more fragrant subjects. I hear that the Duchess of Argyll is trying to stop her ex-husband publishing the secrets of their married life. This generation of aristocrats are such spoil-sports. Don't they realise that the only thing that keeps them from the tumbrils is the occasional really juicy scandal?"

There was a brittleness to his humour that almost made me suspect he was on drugs, but I was so delighted to have him back I refrained from further questioning. One sure way of losing friends is to criticise their morals.

He had taken a pleasant flat in some mews off Eaton Square and for the first few months after his return we again saw a lot of each other. Theo wanted to catch up on the theatre he had missed and seemed quietly confident that his new novel would surprise both his admirers and detractors. His confidence was not misplaced, for when *Pastoral with Rising Sun* was published he was 'rediscovered' and seemed not to have a care in the world, though like most of us he complained bitterly about income tax.

Reading his journal entries for the period confirms this, for they are mostly taken up with witty, often libellous accounts of his social activities. Fame in his case was a spur to a lighter view of human nature. He no longer tabulated his sexual encounters in such lurid detail. There are occasional references to brief affairs, but mostly he confines his sharp powers of observation to describing aspects of the so-called smart set.

Vogue is an obscene irrelevance, in itself a cause for revolution. Exclusive high camp, a strong lesbian influence in all the models who have mouths like sabre slashes, photographed in contrasting disaster areas, just to emphasise the fact that there are two worlds. There is also a monthly column purporting to be about People In The News, whereas in fact it is mostly about jet-setting layabouts famed for their unattractive behaviour. What fascinates me is the slavish way in which women allow themselves to be de-feminised annually by a few French poufs, paying through the nose for clothes that cannot be worn outside the fashion houses without arousing ridicule. Western civilisation deserves all it inevitably will get. To thumb through the pages of this and other similar magazines is to read advance news of the coming apocalypse – a glimpse of hell in which all the occupants will be condemned to the Royal Enclosure at Ascot for the rest of the time, dressed in last year's fashions, listening to readings of Jennifer's Diary given by a trendy Church of England bishop.

He moved in more exalted circles than I and the pages of his journals are dotted with references to Cabinet Ministers and the new plutocrats who made the headlines in the dizzy Sixties. I could wish that he had once attempted a contemporary novel, Trollope brought up to date, or a new look at the political scene. On one occasion he writes glowingly of having met the Beatles, his prose as awestruck as any teenage fan.

Lennon's remark about Christ is just, that is why they have turned on him. They *are* the new religion, and less harmful than the old. Their lyrics are the Gospel for the young, and at least they preach love and not pestilence and guilt. People cannot bear to be told the truth, especially when it is the young who are telling them. Reality is the ultimate outrage.

This was about the time I moved into Albany. We met fairly regularly and once a month went to the theatre together. I felt he was more relaxed, less inclinded to bridle at some imagined slight. His reputation as a major British novelist was now secure and since it was the age of instant punditry his opinion was often solicited to dispense wit and wisdom on a number of subjects about which, as privately he was the first to admit, he knew little or nothing. I remember him showing me a commissioned article he had written for one of the popular women's magazines. The piece was entitled *Why I Never Married*.

"It'll give you a laugh," he said. "It's in the great tradition of British fiction. Every queer writer I know has always responded to this particular call. I cribbed most of it from the collected writings of Godfrey Winn."

"I'm still impressed."

"My dear, if they're foolish enough to pay me four figures to tremble all those suburban wombs, who am I to reject them?"

Even allowing for the fact that his steady sales and such extra-curricular activities must have pushed him into the higher income brackets, I remember thinking that he seemed to enjoy a very affluent life style. It was a source of irritation, because I sold more copies of my own books, but lived on an overdraft.

"I have this amazing accountant," he said when I tackled him on the subject.

"How does he do it, then?"

"I never enquire. A little knowledge of tax affairs is a dangerous thing."

The explanation irritated me even further. My own accountant was a boring, pedantic little man, self-satisfied with his own lot, and a stickler for the fiscal truth.

Theo appeared to enjoy his money; there was no hint of the self-inflicted misery to come in Englefield Green, that last decade when he withdrew from everything and everybody. He must have been receiving regular payments from his Russian friends, for nothing else could explain the comparatively large sum that came to light when his Estate was proved. Novelists of the calibre of Theo are not in the habit of amassing small fortunes in modern-day Britain.

The paradox of his situation is that although blackmailed, he did not pay in money but in services rendered. He had no lovers to keep, no demanding kept boy with a wandering eye and a greed for Gucci trivia and Cartier cigarette lighters that seem the trademarks of their calling. It is true he always had to buy affection, but it was obtained from the bargain basement from creatures as driven as he was, who wrote on cheap notepaper and met with him in sad bed-sitting rooms. The last journal entries do not reveal a single splurge such as the lonely sometimes indulge in – money spent on an impulse in solitary desperation. On the contrary, the meticulous book-keeping is of a kind that would have impressed the small mind of my erstwhile accountant: every item detailed, journeys taken by public transport, depressingly ordinary meals taken in squalid restaurants, everything noted down to the last penny as though he was some old age pensioner too proud to ask for national assistance. I don't think he could have bought a new suit or shirt in the last ten years of his life, for all the clothes I found were out of fashion. The major expenses he incurred were all medical. He had a collection of patent medicines, many of them lethally deteriorated – infallible cures for what I suspect were mostly imaginary ailments. He subscribed to a number of nature-cure magazines, combining the orthodox with the unorthodox, backing every horse in the race as it were, and alongside the daily expense sums he recorded – sometimes hour by hour – his physical condition and the remedies he applied.

Perhaps nobody has ever prescribed a relief from deceit, and that is why he cast his net so wide, sampling herbal potions alongside the latest wonder drugs. I found homoeo-pathic powders in small white envelopes stiffened by the half-used contents, boxes of suppositories like bullets laid in for a long siege, pills for every organ, ointments for every joint, even a home enema kit. He kept careful note of his periodic and invariably unsuccessful attempts to give up smoking, recorded his own bowel movements – the list is hideously disconcerting, reading like one of those *Lives of The*

Saints that used to terrify me so much as a child, the pornography of the devout.

Those were the lost years I did not share in any part, for when he moved to Englefield Green he closed all previous accounts. By then, of course, Philby had surfaced in Moscow and the espionage fraternity were apparently happy to balance the books. The complicated game they all played had ended in a tie. Our side and the C.I.A. had given Philby a few years rope, a last attempt to save face by planting a final seed of doubt in Russian minds. Although nothing will ever surprise me again, I don't subscribe to the theory that we tried to turn Philby a third time: in the end, I think, we frightened him into defection. He was spent by then, just a husk, one of those old retainers who has been around too long and is an embarrassment to family and strangers alike: he couldn't lay table any more, or polish the silver, without making mistakes, and to top it all he was heavily into the wine cellar. A careful study of the journals reveals only one small reference to the event. 'It seems that Kim Philby has finally gone home to his elephants' graveyard' – that burial ground, a long way from Granchester, that was shortly to receive the remains of Guy Burgess. But old habits die ponderously, and shorn of his routine Philby kept his hand in with the oldest deceit in the world: stealing another man's wife.

I don't find it surprising, as some may well do if the truth ever comes out, that Theo escaped detection. The history of our security forces during that period is hardly one of continual success. The democracies have demonstrated time and time again how much they are prepared to conceal rather than admit to their political illiteracy and lack of foresight. By the time Philby had been granted Soviet citizenship there were juicier local scandals in the offing, plenty to divert the popular imagination, lurid tales of Cabinet ministers dressed as waitresses, orgies in high places, the very lifeblood of Fleet Street.

Theo, I believe, like Philby and the rest, had simply out-lived his usefulness, and if they knew him as well as I think they knew him, they realised he posed no threat. He retired himself, shuffling off into that backwater. Perhaps they

prodded him from time to time, just to keep fear one of his
ailments, something that none of his drugs could remove. And
in the end the remnants of a once distinguished life I found in
his cupboards were just as threadbare as the memorabilia
that Burgess left behind in that grace and favour flat he
occupied in Moscow – both exiled in their separate ways,
both broken in the last analysis by self-interrogation, a torture
that leaves no marks.

26

THERE HAVE BEEN many moments in my life when I have regretted my lack of perception, but never more so than now. Some people have no such worries; their minds work instantly, reminding me of that phenomenon occasionally witnessed at sunset in the West Indies. There is a fractional second which occurs just as the sun disappears below the horizon and the sky is slashed with an intense green light. It happens so quickly that the onlooker is often uncertain as to whether he has seen it or not. Theo introduced me to it, and often we stood on the sanded verandah of his house in Barbados to watch for it across the tranquil sea. I don't think I ever saw it.

Yesterday, on an impulse, not inspiration, I drove to Westfield, hoping I might resolve one of the imponderables that remain. I went unannounced.

The house seemed smaller than I remembered, but what was immediately obvious as I drove up to the front entrance was the neglect. The garden was unkempt, great clots of black ivy obscured some of the windows and the drive was scarred with pot-holes. As I rang the bell I realised I had no idea of Harry Gittings's second wife's Christian name. Water dripped on to the back of my neck from a broken guttering as I waited.

The door was finally opened and I came face to face with a woman who, although past her prime, had obviously been trim and attractive in earlier years. She had good bone structure and her face was still pert.

"Mrs. Gittings?" I said.

She nodded, but looked blank.

"You won't remember me . . . We did meet, once, many years ago, in somewhat sad circumstances. I'm Tony Stern . . . I was a cousin of Theo's."

"Oh, yes. Yes, at the funeral. I remember."

"I'm sorry I didn't warn you in advance. I should have done."

"That's no matter. Please come in. Have you driven up from London? The place is in a bit of a muddle, I'm afraid. I live alone and I sometimes don't bother."

I've noticed that women always make the same apology, no matter how tidy they keep their houses.

Something from those distant childhood years came back as I stepped into the hallway. Perhaps it was a certain scent, or the fact that the pictures on the walls were still hanging in the same places, but I had a rush of memory and could feel again that mixture of fear and excitement that always attended my visits there. The whole house had that chill that comes when many of the rooms are unused and unheated. I felt Gittings's presence still, the more so as his wife led me into his study. This was virtually unchanged except that I noted that the bound sets of Law Reports had been replaced with popular works of fiction from the Book Society. His desk stood where it always did, and beside it the brass spittoon Gittings had used for his cigars.

Mrs. Gittings bent to switch on an electric fire.

"I expect you'd like something warm after your long drive. What would you like, tea or coffee?"

"Coffee, I think. Thank you."

"Anything to eat?"

"No, I stopped and chanced my luck at one of those motor-way places. Just coffee will be fine, Mrs. Gittings."

"Call me Angela, please."

"Fine. If you'll call me Tony. Look, don't go to any trouble."

"No trouble. It's nice to have a visitor for a change. I shan't be a moment."

Left to myself I could not resist sitting at Harry's desk once again, and, taking care not to rattle the handle, opened the top drawer. It was empty. I looked around the room and I could see Theo's ghost, white-faced with adolescent concern, standing nervously in front of the desk that afternoon we made the great discovery. I got up, not wanting to be discovered there when Angela returned and passed the time examining the titles of the novels in the glass-fronted bookcase. I found one of Theo's, but none of my own.

"I don't know why I showed you in here," Angela said when she returned with a tray of coffee and chocolate biscuits. "It's not the most comfortable room in the house."

"No, it never was," I said honestly.

"Well, let's take our coffee in the sitting room."

She led the way. It was quite obvious that she had made the sitting room her own, for it was furnished in a taste entirely alien to Harry Gittings and for the first time since I had arrived I lost that feeling of unease.

"I was sorry about Theo," she said. "Not that I ever knew him. Harry wouldn't have his name mentioned."

"No, they really never got on," I said.

"He wasn't easy, Harry. He had many good qualities that perhaps other people didn't always see." She looked me straight in the eye. "But he left me comfortably off, and I went into it with my eyes open, so I've got no complaints." I had the feeling that she was warning me away from any criticism of him.

"You read the reports of Theo's death, I suppose?"

"No, I didn't. I'm somewhat cut off here. First I heard was when somebody from the local paper called. Just a young boy who'd been sent round to find out if I knew Theo."

I could imagine the young reporter bearing some resemblance to my old self – sent on one of those depressing assignments to the recently bereaved.

"I had to say I didn't know him at all, and he lost interest after that. How did he die?"

After I had told her the bare details I waited, but she did not pose the expected question. Most relatives, no matter how distant, usually cannot wait to ask the value of an estate.

"I suppose I should have contacted you before now."

"Why? No reason why you should. I'm not family."

"No, but it would have been polite. How long ago did Harry die?"

"Oh, about six years. Yes, be six years this coming March.

He suffered a lot towards the end, so I was glad I was here. I was trained as a nurse, you see."

"I'm sure you were a great comfort to him."

"I doubt that. He wasn't a man given to much happiness, as you probably know. He just wanted somebody to take care of his needs. And look after his cats. He had a thing about cats."

Again she stared straight at me.

"Yes, so did Theo."

"I haven't got any now. I had them all put down when Harry died. Not my favourite animals." She poured me a second cup of coffee.

"I expect you're wondering why I suddenly turned up like this, out of the blue? You've a perfect right to be curious."

"No," she said. "I had a feeling you'd show up one day."

"Why was that?"

"I don't know, I just did. Perhaps it had something to do with that man."

"What man?"

"Oh, about two weeks after Theo died it must have been, this man suddenly appeared on the doorstep. He mentioned your name, you see, otherwise I don't suppose I would have let him in."

"My name? Well, who was he?"

"He said he'd known you both. Something to do with the war, I think he said. About your age, I'd say. Now he did give me a name. Matlaw? I believe that was it. Does that mean anything?"

"Matlaw?" I said. "No, doesn't strike any bell. What did he want?"

"Well, that was the odd thing. He first of all said he was in the district and had merely called to convey his sympathy. I thought that was a bit odd, because why would he come here? Anyway, I suppose because I see so few people, I felt I ought to ask him in. Stupid of me, that's how people get murdered or robbed, so the local police say. Then, once he was inside he started asking questions."

"What sort of questions?"

"About Theo mostly. I mean, they weren't questions

exactly. How shall I put it, they weren't direct questions. Sort of, well, the way insurance men talk when they're trying to sell you a policy. But he kept mentioning your name, and he seemed genuine enough. I hope I didn't do anything wrong?"

"No," I said. "It's just that I can't think who he could have been. Did he leave any address where I could contact him? I mean, it's quite possible that I do know him. The war's a long time ago."

"No, I asked him to leave an address, but he said he was moving around a great deal and spent quite a bit of time abroad."

I must have looked anxious because her next question to me was right on target.

"There was something odd about Theo, wasn't there?"

"How d'you mean odd?"

"Oh, I don't know. It's none of my business. Just something Harry once said right at the beginning. You won't shock me, you know. I'm quite broadminded. Nurses usually are. I guess he was queer, wasn't he?"

"Yes," I said. There didn't seem much point in denying it to her.

"Harry couldn't wait to send them to jail. He was a J.P. you know, when he retired from his practice. And he had real malice on the bench towards anybody like that. That was the really evil side of him."

"Was this character, Matlaw . . . do you think he was queer or gay or whatever they call it now? Is that the connection?"

"No, I didn't think that. Very smooth, but, no, I wouldn't say anything else. He just said he was a great admirer of Theo's work and if I ever wanted to sell any of his first editions or papers, he'd be more than happy to pay a good price for them. But I didn't have anything. Harry wouldn't have Theo's books in the house. The only ones I've got I bought after Harry died."

"So he just went away, did he?"

"Yes. And I've never heard from him or seen him since. The only . . . well, I don't know whether I'm doing him an injustice, but about three weeks after that, after he called, the house was broken into. One afternoon, when I was at the

357

cinema. The curious thing is, nothing was taken. None of the silver or anything of value, which they could have had. Just the books and Harry's desk – they'd been gone through. Everything thrown all over the place. I can't imagine why, can you?"

"No," I said. "It does seem odd if they didn't take anything."

"It unnerved me for a while, and the police didn't find anything. I mean there weren't any fingerprints or anything. Still, that's something we have to live with these days. It must be worse in London."

"It seems general," I said. "Don't you find it lonely here?"

"Yes and no. I was lonely enough with him. So there isn't much difference." She smiled when she said this, as though to head off any more sympathy.

We chatted for another half hour and then I excused myself and left.

I drove back to London in obscuring rain, a sense of being on the brink of something keeping me alert, and when I woke the following morning the conviction was still with me. I set about trying to trace some of Theo's wartime colleagues. It was a difficult and mostly unrewarding quest, involving several long journeys with little to show for them at the end. Most of those I interviewed were seedy and suspicious; they were only really forthcoming about their present discontents, for almost without exception they were living on fixed and inadequate pensions. They remembered Theo, but as just another ghost from their shining pasts, and in any case the patterns of caution were too deeply engraved. The only time I felt close to the truth was when I managed to locate the woman who had originally interviewed him – the one he had called 'Miss Malcolm' in his would-be fictitious account.

Her real name was Upward, Dame Margaret Upward. She was a sprightly eighty-year-old living alone in a cottage in the Chalfonts. Her memory was still sharp, even though she was partially deaf and had cataracts on both eyes. She had been retired and made a Dame at the end of the Macmillan administration.

"Yes, I remember Mr. Gittings," she said. Her head

turned towards some dusty bookshelves. "You'll find a set of his novels over there somewhere. I used to read them a lot, when I could. He was one of my gentlemen. What's he doing these days?"

I broke the news of his death and explained my own background and relationship. "I've been thinking of writing a biography," I said. "But there are a lot of blank spaces. It's his wartime activities that interest me most and I can't discover much about them."

"Well, you wouldn't, would you?" Dame Margaret said. "And you won't now, I don't suppose."

When she chuckled she passed her hand over the top of her head, smoothing down the snow white hair which was cut in a severe, mannish style. Like many women of her ability and generation she had kept herself spruce even in ever-reducing circumstances. I don't suppose a grateful government allowed her much of a pension; in her day to be made a Dame Commander of the Order of the British Empire was considered reward enough. I noticed that she served me tea in odd cups. All that took the chill off her damp sitting room was a single-bar electric fire with a frayed lead.

After a few general questions, I guided the conversation around to the Burgess and Maclean episode.

"Never thought too much of Burgess," she said. "Something about the mouth. I used to go a lot by mouths. Very charming, of course. He could get around most people, but not me. I put in a report long before he took off. Got nowhere. He had friends in high places, or so I was told."

"What about Philby?"

"Ah, well, now you're talking about a thoroughbred. No, none of us suspected Mr. Philby." There were still traces of a grudging admiration in her thin voice.

"Did you ever believe in the Fourth Man theory?" I asked.

She took another sip of tea and her partially blind eyes came up to meet mine. "There had to be more than four," she said.

"Why d'you say that?"

"I've had a long time to think about it."

"Did you ever suspect anybody in particular?"

"I suspected everybody," she said slowly. "That was my job."

"Would it be anybody close to home?"

The question was out before I could stop myself and I knew at once it was a mistake. Dame Margaret was not the type to be put on the spot. She murmured something I did not catch.

"I'm sorry?"

"Dead," she said. "And if they're not, they should be."

I was committed now. "Theo's dead, my cousin's dead," I said. "Could it have been him?"

"More tea, Mr. Stern?" she said, and groped for the pot with the loose lid.

I tried to think of ways and means of putting the same question more obliquely, but she was not to be drawn again. Perhaps she was tired of the whole game. I couldn't blame her. I might even have misjudged her waning powers. All I know is that after my visit to her all further enquiries were discreetly blocked.

Denied any assistance from official sources I went back to the journals and papers yet again, hoping that I had overlooked something in previous searches that would provide the final answer. With a writer one can never be sure where deception begins, with what ease the practised author twists fact into fiction. And Theo had proved himself a master of the art.

The carefully hoarded contents of that room in Englefield Green reveal not only a man I never knew, but a man who, despite his many betrayals, is still deserving of my pity. Those fading cries for help, duplicated on cheap paper – box numbers answering box numbers, as though the war was still on and he had the need to communicate in code: I could take any one of them at random and be grateful for my own life of ordinary human despair.

Friday

Dear Friend, I still don't know your name, so it is a little difficult calling you anything when I write. I thought you might be disappointed when we didn't meet last Wednesday, and I'm sorry you had to be, but it couldn't be helped. You suggest

Monday. Can you come here at 6 p.m. or soon after? The flat I am in belongs to a Miss Harding – her name is on a card by the bell push. Ring this twice for me. If you only ring once it will bring her out. She is around most evenings which considerably restricts my activities and I must warn you of this, so do be prepared for disappointment in this respect. But we can always chat and for the rest just trust to luck. Will sign myself Charles which has always been a favourite name. I wish I'd been christened it. My own is a joke.

There is one phrase in that letter which haunts me. It seems to sum up Theo's last years, if not his whole life. 'Do be prepared for disappointment.' He was not given 'love with a capital L' that Philby once confessed to; no 'peace and stability at last'; no flight, no spurious glamour or sanctuary in a foreign country, just the slow working out of a familiar sad routine, passion with strangers who had to trust to luck.

The net was cast wide, some of the correspondence coming from the Continent from members of an organisation called The League of Pals. Across one such letter, originating in Germany, Theo had written *Where there is no hatred there is no need for forgiveness*. There were also glimpses of those serious charades played to an audience of the three cats. 'I can assure you I am prepared to be used for humiliation;' 'I am a practising Christian and always put Christ first;' 'I do not know from your letter whether your emphasis finally would be oral or anal (or both). I have become fully dentured within the past week and am anxious to know whether you would consider this a disadvantage;' 'I long for a true and sincere friendship and you will find that I love with a gentle strongness.' I found many of them unbearably poignant.

Then I came across a letter that at first I was inclined to skim through. The writing was miniscule and the opening page taken up with quasi-religious matters: 'What do you think about Montefiore's contention that we cannot rule out the possibility of Christ being homosexual?' There was much more in the same vein and I was just about to move on to the next when a name I had heard in recent weeks leapt at me from the page.

I thought I should warn you I'm almost certain I have seen a familiar face in the region of Temple Fortune on two occasions during the past month. If it was the person I think it was we both have reason to take care. I'm fairly certain he didn't recognise me either time. He was in the company of a younger man than himself – a foreigner from the look of him. I think you once knew him under the name of Mannix, but from my enquiries he uses a variety of aliases and now calls himself Matlaw. Please be on your guard. I suggest we don't meet again until I can be sure the coast is entirely clear. I will make contact when satisfied. Don't contact me.

The letter was signed 'A' and dated three weeks before Theo's death. I read it several times, then phoned Angela Gittings.

"Look, I'm sorry to bother you again, but that man you told me about – the one who came to the house, and called himself Matlaw, I think you said – how would you describe him? Would you call him fat man?"

"Yes and no," she answered. "Put it this way, he was a big man and his clothes hung on him. As if he'd once been much fatter, but had lost some weight. Why?"

"It's just that I do remember him . . . He was somebody I once met with Theo in Barbados. Have you been . . . has anybody worried you since?"

"No."

"Well, if they do, if anybody does, let me know."

I obviously hadn't kept the anxiety out of my voice. There was a slight pause and then she said: "You make it sound rather ominous."

"Did I? I didn't mean to. Forgive me."

"Theo wasn't mixed up in anything, was he?"

"No," I said quickly. "No, he just had a few odd hangers-on. People, strange people, sometimes latch on to writers, you know. They start out as fans and then sometimes they make our lives a misery. It's one of the hazards of the trade. Actors suffer in the same way."

"Well, I'll watch out," she said, "and let you know."

I regretted making the call the moment I put the phone down and hoped my explanation had sounded plausible. There was no point in embroiling a totally innocent person. I

362

think it was then I made up my mind to put an end to the whole business. After I had read the letter once more, I destroyed it, afterwards consigning the whole sorry mess to the dustbin. I hesitated over the journals, going back once more to read the final entries. A few of the pieces of the puzzle did fit. The letter mentioning Mannix tied in with the last page of the journal.

> Had difficulty finding A.'s address . . . He kept me waiting . . . said I could not stay . . . the whole thing was impossible and had to end . . . that it was madness, the place was being watched . . . I am past scaring.

I suppose I could have made more determined attempts to trace Mannix – but for what? By the end of his life Theo admitted he was past scaring. Why not take him at his word? For a writer there is no such thing as a happy ending, anyway: there are always more blank pages to fill, and others who come after me will undoubtedly fill them; the gaps in this story won't remain blank for ever.

All the rumours of a third man that preceded Philby's unmasking will one day be restitched to a fresh canvas. There had to be a fourth man. He wasn't Mannix; Mannix was just another pawn, like Theo. Perhaps if I had the resolve I could dig deeper and chance upon him, or then again, perhaps he, too, is dead and past scaring. But somewhere, at some time, in that Cambridge of the lost generation he placed the right advertisements and got the right replies; just as Theo, conditioned to the pattern, pursued his own converts to the very end. Politics, like sex, is so often the last resort of the lonely and unfulfilled – a conceit that few will admit to since 'duty' is a cleaner word than 'power'. He knew what he was about, that recruiter. Perhaps not always successful – for the proposals of marriage must sometimes have been rejected – but successful enough, claiming those we know of, promising them they could love, honour and obey the doctrine of deceit. As far as we can tell he confined his activities to Cambridge for selecting members of that 'élite force' Philby was so privileged to serve.

Is he there still – some cloistered, respected figure pointed out to visitors, made holy by the eccentricities of age so that what once would have betrayed him in turn is now accepted as wisdom? None of his converts ever gave him away, not even Theo who had greater cause than most, and from this we could deduce that his secret is still worth preserving, that the seductions still continue. There are, after all, future generations to betray, new privileges to bestow. Because we cling to our beliefs in a society he is dedicated to destroy, we shall never be proof against his kind. As long as we remain free, we are the prey.

Postscript

I THOUGHT I HAD written the finish to this story when I burnt Theo's journals, adding my own quota of treachery by destroying the evidence on Chobham Common – a necessary journey since Albany is now in a smokeless zone and my Adam fireplace houses a bogus log fire.

A week or so later I was sitting in Hatchard's Piccadilly bookshop signing copies of my latest novel. Such events do little for the ego. They can best be compared to feeding times at the zoo: the majority of the spectators merely come to gape, a few of the faithful actually buy copies, and the whole operation is conducted with painful embarrassment.

On the day in question I fared slightly better than usual, and in the course of three quarters of an hour managed to satisfy some forty customers. At one point there was a respectable queue of middle-aged ladies doubtless inflamed by a reference in one review to an isolated racy passage which, quoted out of context, gave the impression that I had written a sequel to *Tropic of Cancer*. Their gushing enthusiasm flustered me, so much so I found myself unable to look in their faces.

"How would you like it signed?" I asked the last of the few.

"You could put 'to Judy with love' if you felt like it," a voice said.

It was then that I looked up. Shock made me blotch the title page. Why is it that the sudden reappearance of someone we have once loved to excess has this power to destroy us? Seeing Judy standing there immediately made me feeble. Some of the old pain returned and my mind was swept back to our first meeting in that Cambridge tea room.

"I read in the evening papers you were going to be here," she said, "and I couldn't resist it."

She hadn't altered as much as me. There were no grey hairs and the face that smiled at me so guiselessly from under the permed perfection had retained all its old warmth

"I don't believe it," I said.

"I'm sorry if I gave you a shock."

By now there was a middle-aged man waiting his turn and slightly irritable at the delay. He thrust his copy at me. "Sign it 'To Marjorie'," he said. "Don't want it for myself." I winked at Judy and signed.

"Can I buy you lunch?" I asked, as Marjorie's copy was snatched from me. "I'll be through here in a few minutes. I don't think my services are going to be required much longer. We could go next door to Fortnum's "

"That would be nice. If you're sure you want to."

"Don't be ridiculous. Of course I want to."

"It'll be crowded," she said. "I'll go ahead and get a table."

I watched her leave the shop. She still walked the way I remembered, and although her waist had bowed to the inevitable her legs were shapely.

She was just as blunt as ever. The first words she said to me when I joined her in Fortnum's were typical of her old self. "I bet I know what you thought in there."

"What? What did I think?"

"You said to yourself, 'I'm glad I don't have to wake up and find that on the pillow every morning '"

"You're quite wrong."

"I always told you I'd go fat."

"Where?"

"Where it matters."

"Well, not as bad as me."

"As a matter of fact I was thinking just the opposite. Wondering what your secret was. I've given up trying. I went to one of those la-de-da health farms once, starved myself rotten for a week, then ruined it all by cramming down a pound of chocolates the moment I got home."

"Where is home now?"

"Nowhere special. I'm quite the traveller these days. I keep a small place in Dolphin Square, but I'm not there very often.

I'm mostly on the go, seeing the world, making up for lost time."

"Is . . . are you still married?"

She shook her head. "No, he's dead. George passed away, oh, nearly eight years now. Left me very comfortably off, mind. Enough to see me out anyway. How about you?"

"No, I'm not married."

"Were you ever?"

"Yes."

"Didn't work out?"

"It didn't have much of a chance," I said. "It was during the war . . . Was yours a happy marriage?" -

"I suppose so. Yes, happy as most. Least, he seemed happy enough and I kept my side of the bargain."

I touched her hand briefly as we shared looking at the menu. "It seems a long time ago since you took my order, Mrs. Fraser."

"Have you forgiven me?" she said. "I almost lost my nerve at the last moment. Walked past you twice. Guilty conscience, I suppose."

"No need to forgive when there's never been any hate."

"That's nice. You always said nice things. Did you write that?"

"No," I said. "So . . . tell me more about yourself."

"Not that much to tell. I go on cruises most of the year. Get in the warm, away from this bloody climate. I like cruises. You get a nice type of companion and it's never anything permanent. I mean, I still like a bit of that, if I can get it, even at my age. Isn't this nice? You and me sitting here. 'Course, bit different from where I first served you. That's gone now — it's a sodding great office block. Oh, I shouldn't swear in here, should I? No, it's all gone, your cinema, the lot. Still, I like change, keeps you young."

"The old cinema went in the war," I said.

"Were you in the war?"

"Sort of. I didn't do much fighting."

"Just as well. They might have killed you, then we wouldn't be here." She smiled. "You've got those white patches on your cheeks. You always got those."

"It's the effect you have on me. Where do you go on your cruises?"

"Oh, I'm not fussy, long as it's somewhere hot. Australia. all around there I've been, Hong Kong, then the other way round through the whatsit, that canal named after a hat, and round the Cape. I like the West Indies best, though. Ever been there?"

"Once," I said.

"I know what I had to tell you. Yes, that reminds me. On one of those trips down there, round the islands and that, I bumped into that cousin of yours."

"Theo?"

"Yes. Wasn't it a coincidence? Well, life's like that, isn't it? I mean, take us now. 'Course, I'd read about him from time to time. Used to get his books from the library. I never really understood them, but George was very taken. Bit deep for me."

"'Deep' was a good word for him."

"Was?"

"He's dead now," I said. "He died earlier this year."

For the first time in the conversation she didn't have an immediate answer. I wondered if she was thinking the same thing as I was.

"I'm sorry to hear that," she said, and her voice was quieter. "I expect that upset you. You were always so close."

"We shared a lot of things." I watched her face but her expression did not change.

"Got quite famous, didn't he? Well, you both did. Didn't mean to be rude . . . I don't suppose he ever married?"

"No."

"No, I didn't think so. As a matter of fact . . . I suppose I can say it now he's gone . . . there was a bit of trouble on the boat. One of the crew, some young boy he took a fancy to. He was a bit that way, wasn't he?"

"Yes, you could say that."

"Well, I didn't want to say it. Not come out with it like. Live and let live. Those sort of things never bothered me. People can't help the way they're made, and I was never the one to throw stones in glasshouses. As well you know. No, I don't care overmuch for the real whatsits, unless they're hair-dressers. Don't mind them. How did we get on to that?"

"You were telling me you bumped into Theo."

"Oh, yes. Yes, well, he was asked to leave the boat in Panama. I felt sorry for him really. Must be difficult if you can't say no. That's good, coming from me. But some of those cabin staff do flaunt it a bit. Very bold, some of them. Bring your breakfast at eight and stay for elevenses . . . It was all hushed up, being a British boat. If it'd been French they wouldn't have cared less. But I knew all about it. He came to me the night before we docked in Panama, told me all . . . I suppose he thought . . . well, after all, we weren't strangers."

She looked straight at me as she said this, and it was my turn not to betray anything.

"I think he just needed somebody to talk to, and you know me, never could resist a sob story."

"You resisted mine."

"I was right, though, wasn't I? You wouldn't be signing all those lovely books if you'd married me. We'd have both dragged each other down long before now. I'm right, aren't I?"

"I don't know," I said.

"Well, Theo agreed with me. We talked a lot about you that night. He was very fond of you. Said you were the only true friend he'd ever kept, that friendship was a fatal gift. Always remembered that."

"I wonder what he meant?" I said. "It's a quotation of Byron's, but he got it wrong. Theo, that is. I think the real quotation is 'the fatal gift of beauty'."

"Never mind, it was still nice, wasn't it? I know men like to keep their secrets, but it's always better to get it off your chest. He talked about so many things that night. Got himself in quite a state. Funny thing about you men, you can never quite bring yourselves to admit you're frightened, can you?"

"Was Theo frightened?"

"I thought so. I could be wrong. Not so much frightened about the trouble, but just things in general. Said he'd done everything wrong in life, that he could escape from what he was. 'Course, I'm not religious, I don't believe in all that afterlife stuff, so I couldn't help him much; I just listened."

"I'm sure you were a great help."

She dug her fork into a second slice of Black Forest cake. I stared at her, this woman whom I had once loved so obsessively. Don't, I thought. Don't remind me of the past any more. I've had my fill of love and betrayal.

"What's your new book about?" she said, changing the subject abruptly as though she had read my mind. "Will I like it?"

"Depends on your tastes. It's another thriller."

"Don't you ever write love stories?"

"Not for publication."

"Harold Robbins. He's my favourite. He gives you a slice of life. Well, that's what it's all about, isn't it? When I was young I used to give it away, then when I was older I sold it . . . Now? Now I'm buying it all back," she said, and laughed. "Fancy you and me, meeting like this after all these years. That's a book in itself."

She wiped her mouth with a tissue she took from a cluttered handbag, then reapplied her lipstick with generous strokes. "I gave him my address and he said he'd write one day and tell me the whole story, but he never did. Had better things to do, I expect."

We were practically the last to leave and the waitresses were anxious to go off duty. I paid the bill and bought Judy a box of hand-made chocolates. We said goodbye on the pavement in Jermyn Street. It was crowded with shoppers, their faces desperate with affluence. I asked her if she wanted a taxi.

"No, I think I'll walk. Shake down the lunch and get myself in shape for the chocolates." She leaned forward and kissed me. I could taste her lipstick.

"I'll let you know what I think of your book. If I finish it, that is," she said, with some of her old candour. "I usually cheat and turn to the last page first."

I watched her until she was lost amongst the crowd, then I walked back across the road to Albany. It was cold in my study. I switched on the electric fire and poured myself a drink. Somebody gave me a pocket calculator last Christmas.

It is only the size of a cigarette packet, but it has a memory and can tell the time in various parts of the world. By a process that is beyond my limited knowledge of modern technology it can also serve as an alarm clock. The source of power, like Mannix's pacemaker, is guaranteed to work the thing for years. For some reason at three-thirty every afternoon it repeats a bleeping sound for several seconds. It went off that day as usual to remind me of time passing, times past.

I thought of Judy as I had once known her and of that day we had all spent together on the river when the choices were simple and clear cut. It seemed like a way of life I had once invented for another of my fictions. But we can always cheat with fiction, turn to the last page first to find out if the solution fits our needs. We forget that it is the necessities of life – the need to be human and fallible – that determine ideas of right and wrong.

Theo's necessity was that he had to choose between the risk of betrayal and the risk of love. It seems now that I inherited that choice from him. It would be comforting to think that what he told Judy was finally reality, something that, for once in his life, he didn't have to betray for. But if all I gave him was only another fatal gift, then I doubt it. It will be my turn to sit here and listen to the warning note that sounds every day, if any of us care. Sit and wait for the batteries of conscience to run down. When that happens we shall need all our strength to remember we once had illusions – a deep innocence we thought we could protect forever.

Quicksand

The author would like to place on record
his indebtedness to
Professor Brian Simpson
for his generosity in making available
the research and scholarship contained in his definitive
work on the wartime 18b detainees

In The Highest Degree Odious

For
Michael Loxton MD and
Michael Powell FRCS
without whose skills
this book might never
have been finished

To betray you must first belong
                    - Kim Philby

Hate is the consequence of fear;
we fear something before we hate it
                    - Cyril Connolly

PROLOGUE

In 1909 the then Secretary of State for War came to be concerned about spies and set up a subcommittee to determine the steps to be taken to safeguard national security. The eventual report is said to be one of the more entertaining in the Public Records, rivalling in absurdity the file containing the Home Office Rules for the keeping of pet mice in HM Prisons. The subcommittee duly recommended establishing (in secret naturally) a Secret Service Bureau, the existence of which was not revealed until November 1914. It became what is now known as MI5.

The first head of the Bureau was a professional soldier with the splendid name of Vernon George Waldegrave Kell. In keeping with the British obsession with closed government, from the very outset the new department was structured in such a way that nobody could be held politically responsible for its operations. Kell and his staff immediately set about diligently collecting information about suspected subversives, but they did not act upon it if arrests, searches or interrogations were needed: such tasks, if required, were conducted by Special Branch and the CID, the final say resting with the Director of Public Prosecutions and the Law Officers. Thus the buck could be passed down a long line if there was any mishap, until, eventually, it was swept under a variety of Whitehall carpets.

The senior complement of the Bureau was exclusively recruited from the ranks of officers and gentlemen, the criteria being the right accent rather than any intellectual attainment or natural aptitude for intelligence work. From day one, Kell and his staff set about assembling a central index of every person ever suspected in any part of the world of anti-British activities. This index eventually contained an incredible 4,500,000 names, suggesting a global conspiracy the size of the entire German army.

By 1936, with the chance of a second European war moving inexorably from the possible to the probable, MI5 was instructed to prepare a new code. As a consequence of the immense extension of bureaucratic power during and after World War One, Whitehall assumed that a future conflagration could only be carried on in conditions in which civil liberty had, as a matter of law, been abolished. What the government now demanded was the authority to detain people simply as an instrument of political control, whether they were actively disloyal or not. Nothing was recorded of this decision, but the process of implementing it was commenced.

Thus, prior to 3 September 1939 covert steps had already been taken to widen the powers of MI5 and the Home Office. At 1 p.m. on the day Germany invaded Poland, the Privy Council caused regulation 18b to become law. It meant that anyone at all to whom the Home Secretary took exception could be locked up for an indefinite period. The prime purpose of the new Act was to round up and detain without trial members of the British Union, the neo-Fascist organisation that had Sir Oswald Mosley as its leader. This, despite the fact that the BU had not been proscribed, was a legitimate political party, and was fielding (with some irony it must be said) a candidate in a by-election due to go to the polls that very day.

Kell had supplied Special Branch with an initial list of thirty-six names, headed by Mosley, all of whom were deemed highly dangerous. A fortnight later the list had grown to 350 – a motley collection which in certain instances was more suggestive of a Ben Travers farce than any real threat to the nation, containing as it did such divers characters as a masseuse working for Elizabeth Arden, the wife of the Headmaster of Poole Grammar School, the Revd Montague Yates-Allen (dubbed the 'Nazi Vicar'), a former British heavyweight boxing champion and his wife, Prince Henry of Pless, an ex-Mayor of St. Pancras, and a name from the future – Kim Philby's father. Others, described as 'prominent persons', who were seriously considered for arrest but who escaped immediate *incarceration, included the Duke of Bedford, the eighth Duke of Buccleuch, Major General ('Boney') Fuller, Sir Jocelyn Lucas, Bt, MP, and Air Commodore Sir J. A. Chamier. Admiral Sir Barry Domvile, together with his wife and one of his sons, was detained at a later date.*

The granting of these powers to the executive was later to be described by Churchill as 'in the highest degree odious'.

1

LONDON 1940

Even in wartime it was highly unusual to find tanks in a side street close to Piccadilly, yet early on the morning of May 23rd 1940, a detachment of the Royal Tank Regiment took up their positions to seal off both ends of Albemarle Street, normally a peaceful thoroughfare where various traders flourished in less critical times.

Thus, on that morning of May 23rd, arrest for Carl Hain and his family came, as for others, without warning.

Hain, a specialist dealer in Viennese painters of the L'Apocalypse Joyeuse period, lived above his gallery in a comfortable two-bedroomed apartment. Until the outbreak of war he had made a modest living, some good years, some bad, depending on the always fickle tastes of his clientele, but he had the reputation for being honest and his expertise was widely respected in the trade. His paternal grandparents, originally from Hamburg, had settled in England during the 1860s, establishing a bespoke tailoring workshop in the East End of London. Their only son, Hain's father, had wider ambitions and was drawn to the artistic life. He attempted to make a living as a painter but, after marriage and the birth of Carl, was forced to accept that he had limited talent and turned his hand to the more lucrative pursuit of selling the works of others. Here he succeeded, for he was a natural salesman, and in time could afford to open his own gallery, which, after his death, passed to Carl.

May 23 was a day like any other for the Hain family. As usual, Hain was the first to be up and about. Still in his pyjamas and frayed dressing gown, he switched on the radio for the news. He was grinding fresh coffee beans, as was his habit, when the shop bell called him downstairs. He answered it, expecting to be greeted by the postman with a registered letter, only to be confronted by four large men in lounge suits, big boots and bowler hats – somewhat obviously policemen disguised as gentlemen. Beyond them he was amazed to see a tank with its gun swivelled to face his premises.

Hain had an academic appearance, accentuated by the fact that he wore strong bifocals and was prematurely stooped for his forty-five years. Now, unshaven, his sparse hair uncombed, he presented all the stereotypical characteristics of an alien to his unexpected callers.

He was brusquely asked to confirm his identity. Understandably perplexed, but not unduly alarmed, he gave his name. He was then quoted the authority for his immediate detention and advised of his scant rights, which in any case were later to be ignored. The police spokesman then informed him that his wife would also be detained, that his premises would be searched and any subversive material confiscated and removed.

'But why? What are you saying?' Hain protested, shocked and trembling from the suddenness of it all. 'What subversive material? I have none.'

'I think you know well enough, sir. Don't let's waste time on the obvious.'

Two of the policemen accompanied him upstairs to the living quarters, which, to their way of thinking, seemed to vindicate their visit. The lush trappings betokened foreign decadence: the rooms were furnished in a heavy, un-English style, for they included many pieces that had been handed down from Hain's parents. The walls were hung with his private stock of paintings, mostly examples of turn-of-the-century European works, including several by Klimt, Schiele and – his proudest possession – an exotic nude by Modigliani.

'Not only a traitor, but a pervert too, I see,' the senior policeman observed as he eyed the Modigliani.

'What right do you have to come into my home and call me by such names? That is a great painting. You have no reason to speak of it or me in those terms.'

Disturbed by the unfamiliar voices and likewise still in her dressing gown, Mrs Hain appeared in the doorway. It should have been immediately apparent to the searchers that she was pregnant, but her condition was not commented upon.

'Why are these men here, Carl? Who are they?'

'Policemen, dear.'

'Policemen? In our home? What are they looking for?'

'I don't know, dear, they seem to think I have forbidden material. All I know is I have been told we are to be detained.'

'What does it mean, detained?'

'My dear, I've told you, I have no idea.'

'Carl, you must telephone our solicitor. Get help, there must be some mistake.'

'No mistake, madam, and no calls are allowed,' one of the policemen answered, brushing past her to search the contents of a sideboard.

'Do you have a safe?' his companion asked.

'Yes,' Hain said. 'But there's nothing in it except documents concerning the provenance of the paintings.'

'Show me.'

Hain took him to a small closet where the safe was bolted to the floor.

'Open it.'

He did as he was told and took out a collection of files. The policeman placed these with other documents the search had produced.

'You must be aware that my wife is expecting a child,' Hain remonstrated. 'She has a delicate disposition and her doctor has told us she must not undergo any stress. All this is bound to affect her.'

'You should have thought of that before,' was the unsympathetic reply. 'If I had my way people like you would be put against a wall and shot.'

'What d'you mean,"people like us"? What have we done?'

'There's a war on, in case that escaped your notice. People who aren't for us, are against us.'

'I'm a loyal citizen. So is my wife.'

'Well, that remains to be seen, doesn't it? We're just here to carry out orders. You'll have a chance to state your case in front of the tribunal in due course.'

'Tribunal? What tribunal? This is monstrous. It's like Kafka.'

'And who might Kafka be?'

'A famous writer for your information.'

'But not a *British* writer from his name,' the policeman said, recording the exchange in his notebook. 'And now I must ask you both to dress.'

'What about our small son?' Mrs Hain said. 'We can't leave him alone here.'

'Your son, madam, will be taken into care by the authorities.'

Their further protests were ignored and they stood by helplessly as the apartment was turned over. All Hain's personal files, accounts and stock books were removed, together with a quantity of art brochures, many of them written in German. Particular interest was taken in a spiked, German army helmet, *circa* 1914, a trophy brought home from the trenches by Hain's father. The three members of the family were only allowed to pack one suitcase apiece. While helping to dress his small and frightened son, Hain managed to secrete over a hundred pounds on the child's person, the proceeds of a sale he had made the day before and had not had time to bank. The premises were then locked and the family driven to nearby Bow Street police station where they were again told of the authority for their arrest. Hain and his wife were documented, body-searched and fingerprinted before being separately interrogated by the CID.

Hain's interrogator was a Detective Inspector Mathews, a burly man with a face like a cratered landscape, the aftermath of adolescent acne.

7

'Don't try and bluff me, Hain,' Mathews began, 'because it won't wash. We know all about your hostile associations.'

Disorientated by the speed with which his entire life had been taken apart, Hain struggled to maintain his composure. A small part of him clung to the belief that he was in the grip of some terrible nightmare from which he would soon awake, yet the pockmarked face across the bare table, and the institutional, distempered walls of the room belied his last hopes. It seemed inconceivable that he and his family could have been plucked from the familiar warmth of their apartment without warning. As he answered his interrogator's barked questions he strove to recall anything in his past that could have had a double meaning, for he refused to accept that British justice could act in this manner. In other countries, yes, but even in wartime, not in Britain.

'What does that expression mean?' he said. '"Hostile associations"? It conveys nothing to me, and I demand to know who has laid these false charges against me and my wife.'

'We didn't need anybody to denounce the likes of you, Hain. We have a file on you. We know all about you, the company you keep, the trips you made to Germany before the war, your political views, you name it. So, you see, it wasn't necessary for anybody to lay charges, you were already in our bag.' Mathews tapped the file that lay between them. 'Let's begin with basics, shall we? We have it on record that you're a member of the British Union.'

'No.'

'Don't lie, Hain. Lying will only prolong matters, and I'm not a patient man. We have a copy of your membership card.'

'I am not lying. It is true that for a period, a short period, less than a year, I was interested in their aims. They represented themselves as a party dedicated to avoiding war.'

'And you became a paid member.'

'Was that illegal?'

'Just answer my question. Were you or were you not a member?'

'I've told you I joined to find out more, then I disassociated myself when Hitler annexed Czechoslovakia. I saw then that war was inevitable.'

'You sure you didn't go under cover so that some of your German friends could contact you later?'

'What German friends?'

Mathews opened the file and took out one of the documents. 'During the years 1929 to 1934 you made eleven visits to Germany.'

'They were not secret visits. Since you know so much about me you must know they are stamped in my passport. I went openly to make purchases in the legitimate pursuit of my business.'

'So you say now. Let's move on to something else. On at least two occasions your so-called "leader", Sir Oswald Mosley, came to your premises.'

'He was interested in my paintings.'

'Your *German* paintings,' Mathews said with heavy emphasis.

'Austrian, but what is odd about that? I specialise in such works.'

'Why not some good British paintings?'

'Art is not concerned with politics. The works I sell were painted long before the Nazi party came into being.'

'You don't deny, though, that you were on intimate terms with Mosley?'

'Certainly I deny it. That is an exaggeration. He was merely a potential customer. As it happens he admired my stock but did not buy anything.'

'At a time when you were a member of his Fascist organisation?'

'I was never a Fascist.'

'At a time when you were a member,' Mathews repeated. 'An active member. Just to refresh your memory, you were seen on Wanstead Flats in June 1936 when Mosley addressed a rally of the faithful.' He took a photograph from the file and passed it to Hain. It showed Mosley speaking from a van that had been adapted to his needs: a square had been cut out of the roof of the van and a raised steel cage installed. The van was flanked by two lines of black-shirted bully-boys facing the crowd; Hain was discernible in the second row of the crowd and his head had been ringed with red crayon.

'You don't deny that is you?'

Hain stared at the incriminating photograph but did not answer.

'I'm waiting.'

'Yes, that is me.'

'Progress at last. So at that time at least you hadn't "disassociated" yourself, correct?'

'I've told you my reason for leaving the party.'

'So you have, yes. Well, let me ask you something else. Your family name is Henke, is it not?'

'That was my grandfather's name, yes.'

'But not yours.'

'My father changed it by Deed Poll in 1915 because of the strong anti-German feelings prevalent at that time.'

'Conveniently, shall we say?'

'So did the Royal family,' Hain replied gamely. 'I take it you must also know that my father volunteered to serve in the British Army and was wounded at Ypres. He subsequently died from his wounds.'

'What have you volunteered for, might I ask?'

'I offered my services to the ARP but was rejected on account of my poor eyesight.'

'Well, we wouldn't want scum like you protecting us anyway. Right,' Mathews concluded, 'in view of the unsatisfactory answers you have given me in response to these questions, I am therefore informing you that you will be detained under Section 18b of the Emergency Powers (Defence) Act. Do you have anything further to add?'

'What about my wife and small son?'

'What about them?'

'I wish to know what is happening to them.'

'That's not my concern. Somebody else is handling your wife's case. Should she also be detained your son will be placed in care.'

Mathews closed the file and stood up.

'There is no case for us to answer,' Hain said. 'We are innocent, loyal people. A terrible mistake has been made.'

'Yes. You could say that. The mistake was to throw your lot in with the wrong side,' was Mathews's parting shot as he left the room.

An hour later, manacled to another detainee, and denied any further contact with his wife, Hain was taken to Brixton prison in a Black Maria. There he and other detainees were submitted to the pseudo-sanitary rituals of degradation: the bath and baring of privy parts; some were merely made to step into and out of an empty bath in order to keep the record straight. Only then, when the cell door closed on Hain, did the full realisation of his plight sink in.

Meanwhile, his wife, wrenched from her nine-year-old son, had given her stuttered and innocent responses to a similar interrogation, at the conclusion of which she had been removed to 'F' wing at Holloway, occupying a darkened cell, the blackout being rigidly enforced. Conditions in Holloway, where the staff were unprepared for the sudden influx of prisoners, were wholly inadequate. Largely unheated, the eleven by seven feet cells were infested with bed bugs and extremely dirty. Washing facilities were minimal and for many there was no toilet paper and no newspapers to use as a substitute. The issue blankets were made of canvas and disgusting.

On the third night after her incarceration, weakened and demoralised, she started to haemorrhage. Her condition was not discovered until the following morning. Taken to hospital too late, both she and her unborn child died later that day.

A week later and still in ignorance of his wife's death, Hain was transferred to Liverpool to be held in the disused women's prison where the decrepit accommodation had previously been the habitat of pigeons. Unlike Brixton, the prison staff in Liverpool were armed when supervising the infrequent exercise periods, for all the 18b detainees endured

11

long bouts of solitary confinement; even during air raids they were not moved to shelters. It was over a month before the ponderous wartime bureaucracy got around to informing Hain of his wife's death. Returned to his cell and convinced that he would never see his son again, he used his last razor blade to commit suicide.

Hain's now-orphaned son spent the remainder of the war with a variety of foster parents, finally ending up with a Quaker family in Swindon who legally adopted him. Not until he was in his teens and a scholarship student at Cambridge did he discover the true facts about his parents' incarceration and their subsequent fates.

ATLANTA 1997

It could scarcely have entered Dr Josef Freidler's reckoning that the last woman he would ever speak to would be a naked dancer at the Club Alpha with the improbable name of Starr Faithful. Like her siliconed breasts, which Dr Freidler was able to ogle but not touch, the name was a fake, chosen because an account of the real Starr Faithful – the victim of a salacious and never solved mystery which the dancer had read as a teenager – appealed to her sense of the romantic.

The Club Alpha was one of a growing number of similar establishments that had sprung up to satisfy American male fantasies in the age of safe sex. There was none of the sleaze of the older strip joints where bored showgirls gyrated their cellulite: the girls at Club Alpha were a superior breed, selected for their beauty, youth and an ability to put more than three words together. They were dressed in couturier gowns which, in the course of their duties, they were happy to discard. Their customers then paid to be treated to a tantalising display in the nude, termed 'lapdancing', for which the girls were handsomely rewarded, many of them taking home five figure earnings if they stayed the course, for at the end of their act the average punter placed fifty, even one hundred dollar bills in their garters, the only physical contact allowed. It was *Playboy* magazine brought to life, the voyeur's dream of the girl next door suddenly stepping out of the centrefold, exposing her perfect pneumatic breasts, the smooth stomach devoid of any blemishes, the carefully shaven pubic hair – all displayed at close proximity, the untouchable turn-on.

From the exterior, the club's premises had been designed to reassure – clean lines suggesting an up-market DIY store where all the family would be welcomed, except here they weren't: this was primarily aimed at men stalking sterilised sex, the very antithesis of DIY.

Dr Freidler, born in Israel but now a naturalised Swiss citizen, was President of a private Zurich merchant bank but maintained strong connections with his native land. In his early fifties, he was considered to be one of the most influential European financiers, his opinion sought by the Bundesbank, his manipulation of the markets noted on every board from London to Tokyo. It was said that what Freidler did today everybody else should have done yesterday. A multi-millionaire, he kept houses in the Hamptons, Cap Ferrat and his adopted Switzerland. Married over twenty years to the same wife, he had two teenage children and a discreet mistress in Monaco. His personal affairs were managed through a number of shell companies operating from tax havens. When at home, he entertained on the grand scale, his invitations being eagerly sought. An outstanding scholar, he had won a place at the Harvard Business School, and after graduating with honours had been swiftly recruited by the Kreditanstalt Bank in Austria. From there he was poached by Morgan Guaranty in New York, quickly rising to a position of authority, then resigning to form his own bank. Noted for his ruthlessness in dealing with competitors, he had the reputation of a man who brooked no interference with his dictates. He was not liked, but, as with most men in his position, his financial standing ensured that he was courted by those who feared him. Consummately vain, he had a personal hairdresser and a manicurist in daily attendance wherever he travelled, always wore pure silk shirts made for him in Jermyn Street and perfumed himself with Guerlain's *Eau de Cologne du Coq* at $300 a bottle. He moved in a closed international circle where money, and only money, talked and decided world economies. The inner sanctum he inhabited was seldom penetrated by outsiders, and although his legitimate activities were widely reported in the world's financial press, his other, more labyrinthine, deals were seldom traced to their source. He and his kind were the currency determinators who ensured the scales were always tipped in their favour.

Freidler was in Atlanta for his bank's annual convention. Like most similar jamborees, in reality it was merely an excuse for the senior officers to have a free holiday. They met every day to plot future strategy, but the really enjoyable business was conducted at night. On this particular trip Freidler's public relations man had arranged a visit to the Alpha Club on the last evening of the convention, promising a unique experience.

'I think you will be pleasantly surprised, sir,' he told his employer. 'This is like nothing you've seen before.'

'Really? Such as?'

'I'd prefer you to wait and see, sir.'

'I don't care for surprises.'

If there was one thing Freidler liked as much as money, it was the company of beautiful women. On this occasion his initial, venal anticipation was blunted when he became acquainted with the house rules, but once inside it was too late to turn back and lose face.

'What do you mean, we can't touch them?'

'I apologise, but they're very strict, sir. It's a new concept.'

'Only in America,' Freidler sneered. 'Only here could they get away with putting the goods in the shop window and then not let anybody buy them. What a way to do business, no wonder their economy is shot.'

Despite his initial disappointment, he was impressed with the ambience of the club; the decor was luxurious but discreet, the service impeccable. There was no raucous disco music and guests were not pressured. Freidler and his party were conducted to one of the private rooms, furnished with a number of sofas arranged in a semicircle. It was there, somewhat placated by the excellence of the champagne he was immediately served, that he was introduced to the girl who called herself Starr Faithful. She was twenty, blonde, with a full, sensuous mouth and impossibly long legs. Like the other hostesses she wore nothing under her expensive gown except a minute black G-string and garters. After conversing for ten minutes or so she asked him if he would like her to dance for him and taking his acceptance for granted, unzipped and stepped out of her single garment. Although Freidler was astounded by the sight of her body, he was conscious of his watching colleagues and maintained a bland expression while his eyes remained fixed on her impossibly perfect young breasts. (Later, in the shared dressing room, she compared him to earlier clients. 'I knew that fat old Jew was a tit man,' she said. 'I can always tell what melts their butter the moment I strip. Just watch their eyes. They either go straight to your legs, your butt or your boobs, don't they? He locked on to my boobs like somebody tracking Challenger.')

Although she had described it as 'dancing', the routine she performed for Freidler was not anything that would have impressed Bob Fosse. Removing her G-string she went through a series of writhing gyrations, gradually working closer to Freidler until, bending over him, she swept his face with her hair and brought her breasts tantalisingly close to his mouth so that it would have required the minimum effort on his part to lean forward an extra inch and kiss her prominent, rouged nipples. Very aware that his underlings were watching, he controlled his natural urges and maintained an outward composure. At the conclusion of her performance he placed three one hundred dollar bills in her garter, helped zip-up her gown and was rewarded by a chaste kiss on the cheek – the sole act of intimacy permitted under the house rules. Now that he had shown the way, others in his party paired off with their own choices. Starr sat down next to Freidler and sipped her soft drink.

'That was very beautiful. You dance very well. But what are you drinking? Wouldn't you rather have champagne?' Freidler asked.

'No, we're not permitted alcohol, Mr Freidler.'

'Please call me Josef. What else isn't encouraged?'

She had heard it all before, but pretended ignorance.

'How d'you mean, Josef?'

'A girl like you could have a different, easier life than this, surely?'

'I love this life.'

Freidler shrugged. 'I'm sure. But if you met the right person, somebody like me for instance, he could show you more of the world.'

The dialogue these old farts trot out, she thought, keeping her smile in place, it's out of the ark. 'No, I'm very happy here in Atlanta. It's my home town.'

'You wouldn't want to travel?'

'I do travel. Last year I went to Tahiti. You ever been to Tahiti?'

'No,' Freidler said. 'I was thinking more of Europe.'

Bending to place her glass on the coffee table Starr caught the eye of one of the security staff who were always discreetly situated and gave him the signal.

'If you'd allow me,' Freidler was saying, 'I could arrange for you to have a long holiday in Europe, show you my country.'

'That sounds very enticing, but unfortunately I have a contract here,' she said. The security man, who was wearing a well-cut dinner jacket, arrived by her side.

'Please excuse me, sir,' he said to Freidler, 'I'm so sorry to interrupt, but your companion has a regular client who has asked for her. Would you perhaps care for me to send another of our hostesses to keep you company?'

There was a warning note in his voice that did not escape Freidler. Although furious at being outsmarted, he controlled his anger. 'Thank you, no. I'm leaving.'

'So soon? I trust you enjoyed yourself, sir?'

Starr knew better than to linger. 'Thank you so much, Josef,' she said. 'It was my pleasure to meet you.'

'Likewise,' he said tersely.

He watched her cross the room, then beckoned to his public relations man. 'That girl who just left. I want you to bring her to my hotel suite later.'

His PR looked dubious. 'Well, I'll try, sir, but it's my understanding that the club rules strictly forbid these girls dating any of the customers.'

'I'm not talking about their rules, I'm talking about what I want. Just find who you need to bribe and get her for me. I don't care what it costs.'

'Yes, of course, sir.' He moved the coffee table to allow Freidler a free passage. 'You wish your car, sir?'

'Of course I wish my car. You think I'm going to walk?'

Freidler gestured to the others as he went out of the room. 'Stay and enjoy yourselves. I have to work, but don't let that deter you. Good-night.'

He returned to his hotel, stopping in the foyer to purchase a pair of diamond earrings which he took to his suite. There he rang room service and ordered two dozen oysters and a magnum of Cristal champagne. After changing into pyjamas and dressing gown, he sat in front of the oversized television and watched the stock market reports on CNN, confident that his instructions would be carried out. When his room service order arrived, he told the waiter to open the champagne and pour him a glass. Never one to let an opportunity for profit pass, having seen how the market had opened in London, he rang his broker and purchased ten million dollars worth of futures through one of his nominee companies. Later, another news item caught his attention. He made a second phone call, this time instructing his office to set in motion a hostile bid for a company he sensed was vulnerable.

He was still sitting in front of the television set when the door to his bedroom was opened with a pass key. He never heard or saw who entered behind him and the champagne glass was still at his lips when it was shattered by a single bullet from a silenced handgun which passed through his neck and blew away the lower part of his jaw, killing him immediately. Blood spurted on to the oysters, staining them in an imitation of the Tabasco sauce he never lived to enjoy.

3

ST PETERSBURG 1997

Afterwards, Hillsden was hard put to recall why he had given the man a second look, but from habit he had registered the face. One never knew when the blow might fall.

At the time he had been standing in a long line outside a bakery in a side street off Nevskiy Prospekt, resigned to his daily two-hour wait to purchase a loaf of bread. As the queue slowly shuffled forward he played his usual guessing game of trying to estimate how many noughts had been added to the price since the previous day.

The early March temperature hovered just above zero and Hillsden's fur coat, purchased with hard currency in the days when he had enjoyed the rank and salary of a Colonel in the GRU, attracted envious glances from his huddled companions. Even without the coat he stood out, for with his trim beard and tidy, greying hair there was an aloofness about his manner that set him apart. Shunning conversation with his neighbours, he also avoided eye contact as far as possible. He did not look his age, for since his new marriage he made an effort to keep in good shape. Only those few in St Petersburg who chanced to read the London *Times* might have noted a small item in the diary column a few weeks previously which listed *George Arthur (Alec) Hillsden, the ex-MI6 defector*, and even then, it was doubtful whether any would have made the connection. One of the British tabloids had picked up on the item a few days later under a headline

WHERE ARE THEY NOW? with an old, and now unrecognisable, photograph of Hillsden in British Army uniform standing with Margot, his wartime first wife. Rehashing some of his background, the accompanying story gave him the credit for exposing Glanville – the so-called 'Fourth Man' in the Cambridge spy ring made famous by Philby, Burgess and Maclean – but the main thrust of the piece gave greater emphasis to his own subsequent flight to the then Soviet bloc. The article concluded that, because of the new relationship between the two countries, it was possible that he could now be extradited to stand trial for the murder of the diplomat, Sir Charles Belfrage.

None of this was of interest to the bread queue: the past world of the Cold War did not figure hugely in their daily struggle to live with the new freedoms – freedoms which, for the majority, had not brought the promised, less-fearful future. Now, bemused by the constantly changing situation, most lived as best they could, taking life one day at a time. Like spring bulbs, past hatreds lay just beneath the surface ready to bloom.

Although more fortunate than his immediate companions, Hillsden shared their sense that nothing was permanent. Still one of the privileged by current Russian standards, he and his family enjoyed sole use of a four-room flat, gifted to him when finally he had been accepted as a genuine defector from British intelligence seven years previously. His GRU pension, eroded by inflation like everything else, had never been rescinded, somehow overlooked in the chaos left in the wake of the *coups* and counter-*coups*. Luck had played a part: many of the old guard of party bureaucrats had, of necessity, been left in place; Hillsden had no illusions that, without them, the entire edifice would have collapsed. The cumbersome machinery of Stalinist Russia, corrupt and terminally incompetent, had only been partially dismantled; many of the reinstated bureaucrats interpreted the new rules with a well-honed disregard for change. After a period when the novelty of broadcasting the truth after decades of calculated disinformation had proved counter-productive, the official Moscow news agency had reverted to its previous habits. There was a local joke: *only believe what they don't tell you.*

As part of the deal they had struck with him, Hillsden had been granted Russian citizenship and counted himself fortunate that, under the new regime, his position had not been reviewed by the authorities. Now, when he had nothing left to betray except memories, he lived in no man's land: he was no longer British and not truly Russian, just a non-person. He had learned that the recipe for survival was to keep a low profile. Thus far he had managed to provide for his Russian wife and small daughter, although every week saw a perceptible decline in their standard of living. There were luxury foods and Western goods available, but only at black-market prices: the emerging Russian mafia now controlled large sections of the economy; armed gangs of highly organised criminals either hijacked the supplies of food that came into the cities, or else cynically destroyed them in order to keep prices high. Whereas before everyday crimes such as the West had long become inured to had been ruthlessly suppressed, casual murders, muggings and robberies were now commonplace. Along with Western imports like Coca-Cola, Big Macs and the pop culture, the drug barons had become an integral part of the emerging, quasi-capitalist society. The old social order – feared, but at least familiar – had disintegrated, to be replaced by the gangster face of the new privileged.

That particular morning Hillsden was more than usually conscious of being alienated from his surroundings. Assuming he was successful in the bread queue, he faced having to join another line to attempt to buy some cheese – any cheese, for there was seldom a choice. On average he passed three hours every day in these quests. Once a week he used a portion of his sparse funds to try to purchase a small, black-market chicken or piece of meat which Galina, his Russian wife, had become adept at eking out over three or four meals. If he had anything left over he spent it on books, anxious to keep his brain alive, for in the past he had always apprehended the world through literature.

He and Galina had made few new friends since the collapse of the old regime and for obvious reasons Hillsden did not openly advertise his previous connection with the security services. Immediately following the revolution, members of the KGB and GRU had struggled to come to terms with their new status as reformed citizens, but few believed they would not, one day, return to power, called by another name, wearing different uniforms but once again finding their place in a country that, from the days of the Tsars, had tested the limits of fear. And so it had proved. Renamed, regrouped in a different form, they had crept back into the fabric of everyday life; it was as if, Hillsden thought, the Russian soul required an element of terror in order to function.

Now, as the bread line moved forward a few paces, Hillsden saw the same man again on the opposite side of the road. Their eyes met for a second, the man being the first to break contact. He was tall, clean-shaven, wearing an overcoat of obvious Western origin buttoned to the chin. Hillsden watched as the man consulted his wrist-watch and then moved off, his face dipped against the wind-swirled snow.

The only contact from the old days with whom Hillsden still kept in touch from time to time was his erstwhile controller, Victor Abramov. Denuded of his senior GRU rank, Abramov had secured a lucrative job as adviser to an American computer company. Paid in dollars, he now drove a Mercedes coupé and mixed with the foreign jet-set as an equal. He had made an effort to share some of his sudden affluence with Hillsden, often taking him for a meal in one of the starred hotels. Abramov was no longer the trim officer; easy living had given him a slight paunch and his complexion betrayed his conversion to claret.

'I could cut you in, Alec,' he said. 'There are so many openings. Somebody like you could be useful to my business acquaintances. They're always on the look-out for people with your know-how.'

But the offer held no attraction for Hillsden. 'I could never fathom computers. They terrify me.'

'You don't have to fathom them, you only have to sell them, my dear Alec. Today they're user-friendly, children master them in a few hours. Big bucks, Alec. It's the next quantum leap forward. Forget dead-letter drops and all that Cold War crap. Now, if you want to pass on stolen information, you do it instantly by electronic mail. Believe me.'

'I do believe you, but no thanks.'

'You're making a big mistake. Get on the gravy train, everybody else is, why miss out, buddy?'

The odd bits of Americanese slipped easily off his tongue. Victor now travelled widely, wore Armani suits and had already acquired the casual vernacular of the successful entrepreneur. Sitting across from him, carefully saving a portion of his meal to take home to Galina, Hillsden found it difficult to make the association with the time he had first been brought to Moscow; he had long since slaked off memories of the debriefing sessions Abramov had conducted in the Lubianka, when he had been forced to shed the skin of his old existence. Now it was only rarely that he recalled particular incidents. Mercifully, pain was not something one carried forward. Even so, the bond of a past, shared nightmare gave their relationship a special quality; they had been birds of a feather. It's just as well, Hillsden thought, that murder doesn't stay etched into a face. There had been murders along the way, episodes that he strove to forget but which, at intervals, entered both waking and dreaming thoughts. Often, when trimming his beard in the bathroom mirror, he wondered if Galina ever saw traces of the past in his face. He envied Abramov's indifference to those events, though whether it was assumed or genuine he could never be certain.

Save for Abramov's treats, Hillsden's life was uneventful, a backwater existence he had schooled himself to accept. Very occasionally the authorities asked his analysis of new developments in the West, but for the most part his presence in their midst seemed to be ignored. Like the Cold War, he had become history. Because of her past association with the university, Galina was given the odd commission to translate Western textbooks which Hillsden helped her revise. This supplemented their income and allowed them to buy extra clothes for Lara, their daughter. Occasionally they would pool their resources with one of Galina's old tutors and splash out on a dinner party. When the good weather came they picnicked in the Tauride Gardens which boasted an anti-quated fair-ground and was a favourite haunt of sunbathers and courting couples. Lara was bilingual and Hillsden's own Russian had become passably colloquial, though he still could not write it fluently.

Now, as he neared the head of the queue, he was able to see inside the bakery: he counted the loaves still remaining on the shelves and matched the total with the number of people still in front of him. There was a good chance his luck was in. It was at moments like this that England seemed as remote as a country he had never visited.

Abramov passed on his copies of *Time* and it was from one issue that Hillsden had been surprised to learn that the Firm had a woman as Director General who openly spoke to the press, a far cry from Lockfield who had studiously courted anonymity – a false entry in *Who's Who*, no photographs on file, his true character only penetrated after death. The existence of the Firm had finally been acknowledged, but only in the usual hedged-about British fashion – throw the public a few titbits, but never invite them to sit at the table and read the full menu. He wondered how the lady had fared in that previously male-dominated Disneyland, with its layer upon layer of intrigue and partisan back-stabbing. He was sure that, whatever the cosmetic changes, the major concern would still be to smother as much information as possible and ensure that the parliamentary estimates were kept high. Gone were the days of moles in royal circles, mavericks like old Peter Wright intent on mayhem, endless speculation about how far the Firm had been penetrated – that lucrative cottage industry of exposure feeding the media's insatiable appetite for scandal and keeping a score of novelists in clover. From a distance, the recent past now seemed like a film run out of sequence. Occasionally, anger (the useless sort that recognised his inability to change anything) made him replay the cycle of events that had condemned him to exile – how cynically he had been stitched-up and manipulated. Sometimes, in the middle of a sleepless night, bitterness welled up like bile. Now, when it was all too late, he could identify every wrong move he had made, allowing himself to be taken in like some guileless, unguarded innocent. 'Go back to where it all began,' Lockfield had urged, as though there was ever a beginning in the endless game they had all played in those days. Espionage was a shared ball of tangled string that was never completely unravelled by either side – the hunters or the hunted, the deceivers and the deceived – for the players' only object was to keep the game going at all costs. So he had gone back into the cold, severing his umbilical cord as he went, ensuring that he could never return home, driven by the need to solve the murder of a girl he had once loved. And, of course, betrayed from day one, since that had always been Lockfield's intention. Now all that lay ahead was a placid bourgeois existence in an alien country that neither claimed his imagination nor aroused any excitement – the flow of adrenalin in his veins was as frozen as the Russian winter landscape. He felt dulled and saw no end to the dullness. He had been a prisoner when he first arrived in Russia and now, despite a sort of freedom, he was a prisoner still.

Finally gaining entrance to the bakery he secured the last loaf but one. As he paid and left the shop, those denied surged forward to remonstrate with the bundled crone behind the counter. Hillsden tucked his prize inside his coat and hurried towards his second port of call. He felt curiously elated by his good fortune; it might be one of those days when he got lucky twice. The cheese shop was a few streets away and as he turned the last corner he was further encouraged to see that the line here was shorter than the last. That could mean that, for once, supplies were plentiful and those waiting were being satisfied quickly. He took his place and fumbled with his free hand to light a Camel cigarette, one from a carton Abramov had given him the last time they had met. The pungent odour of Virginia tobacco made several in the queue turn their heads and sniff appreciatively. Inhaling, the smoke warmed his lungs and for the first time since he had left the apartment he felt reasonably happy.

It was then that a voice behind him said, 'Ya angliskiy muzhchina' – 'I am an Englishman' – using that plummy accent some members of the British upper-class affect when speaking a foreign language, letting the locals know that although they have bothered to learn it, it really is rather inferior and tiresome.

Taken off guard by the sudden intrusion, Hillsden swung round and came face to face with the man he had seen earlier.

'So am I,' Hillsden replied for want of anything better to say.

'Oh, good. Took a chance. Sorry if I startled you. Look, awfully rude of me, but could I possibly cadge a cigarette?'

Hillsden hesitated a moment, then said: 'Yes, of course.' He proffered his packet. 'Do you have a light?'

'Thank you, yes.' The man, whom at close range Hillsden judged to be in his thirties, loosened his top coat to feel in an inside pocket, revealing as he did so an MCC tie.

'Awful thing to admit,' the man said, as he lit his own cigarette with a silver Dunhill lighter, 'I'm trying to give up, but catching a whiff of yours was too much temptation. The local brand are so filthy, aren't they? Bought a packet of Marlboro at the hotel only to find they were counterfeit. Fairly disgusting.'

'Yes,' Hillsden said guardedly, 'they usually are.'

'Reason I approached you was because you didn't look like one of the natives.'

Those immediately in front and behind Hillsden in the queue shifted uneasily. The exchange betokened a vague menace.

'Bit of luck then,' Hillsden said. Something about the man's accent alerted him: it was unmistakably Establishment, the sort that some politicians employ when caught out on a manifesto pledge. He was instantly on his guard. 'Are you here on holiday or business?' he asked, past instincts rather than mere politeness pushing him to find out more.

'Business. Of sorts. Yes. Just trying to get the feel of the place. You know how it is.'

'How what is?'

'The old economy back home. Still dicky, lurching from boom to bust as usual. So, thought I'd give it a whirl here. Emerging market and so forth, get in on the ground floor, nothing ventured et cetera, got to move with the times, don't you agree?'

'Yes, I suppose so.'

'Can't quite get the drift of this place. They haven't thrown off their past, have they?'

'No.'

'Wasn't expecting all the water. Don't know why. Reminds me of Seattle in a curious sort of way. Ever been there?'

'No.'

'Bit warmer than here.'

'Everywhere's warmer than here,' Hillsden said, by now tiring of the conversation. They all moved up a few paces.

'What're you queuing for this time?'

His use of the phrase 'this time' was a giveaway.

'Cheese, hopefully,' Hillsden replied.

'Cheese, eh?' There was a pause, as though the man was searching for a more entertaining comment. Then he said, 'Interested in cricket?'

The non sequitur threw Hillsden for a moment. 'Cricket? Yes, I used to be. Why?'

'I've got the latest Test score if you want it. The Aussies are taking our knickers down as usual. That young spin bowler has gone through the pack. Backs to the wall stuff. Ashes to ashes it looks like. Should have brought Gower back. He now does commentaries or something. Great loss to England, beautiful stroke player.'

'Yes,' Hillsden said as the line edged forward again.

The man stepped on to the road. 'Mustn't take somebody's place,' he said, 'might start a riot.' He smiled at the old woman immediately behind Hillsden, but got nothing but a blank stare in return. 'Look, can I return the favour, buy you a drink?'

Why would you? Hillsden thought, and took his time before answering. 'I have to go straight back with the shopping, I'm afraid. But thanks all the same.'

Something did not add up. In the ordinary course of events he would have welcomed a rare English voice, a chance to relax over a drink and learn the latest gossip about what was happening at home, but an icicle of suspicion had entered his mind from the very first moment the man had approached him.

'Fair do's,' the man said. He hovered on the edge of the kerb, then reached into his inside pocket and produced a wallet. 'Just in case, take my card. I'll be at the Grand for another three or four days. Give me a bell if you feel like it. Doesn't have to be a drink, we could make it a meal. Something better than bread and cheese. Thanks again for the cigarette, hope it hasn't launched me back on the downward path.'

When he left, Hillsden glanced at the business card he had been given. It read: *Gerald Pitchforth-Swanson, Managing Director, Beaver Enterprises Ltd. Enquiries welcomed.* The address was Orchard Mews in Hammersmith. It was printed rather than embossed. Studying it, Hillsden was taken back to the time when he had operated from the Firm's bogus wine business. It was from those fake premises that he had gone to old Hogg's post-mortem to learn how Caroline had been murdered and his journey back through the maze of deceit had begun. He put the card away and went into the cheese shop, still puzzled by the encounter, but more intent on getting his share of whatever was on offer that day.

4

ZURICH – LONDON 1997

Freidler's sudden death had sent shock waves through the financial world. One London paper made an attempt to connect his death to the still unsolved Calvi murder in order to make a splash headline, but the possibility of a link with the Vatican was discounted by most commentators. Bank shares generally were heavily marked down, the insiders hedging their bets against any incestuous fall-out. In times like these everybody looked over their shoulders. One tribute in *The Economist*, signed by Sir Raymond Charters, a prominent British figure, accorded Freidler near-sainthood, describing him as a gifted philanthropist with a social conscience whose loss would be felt throughout the Third World, whereas in truth he was just another successful predator who had exploited every financial loophole for his own gain.

His body was flown home to Switzerland in his private jet after the Atlanta authorities had conducted their post-mortem. It was established that the bullet had been fired from a standard German police automatic, readily obtainable over the counter in the United States. The identity of his assailant remained a mystery and there appeared to be no conventional motive for the murder; the newly acquired diamond earrings had not been stolen, nor were any of Freidler's possessions disturbed. The waiter who brought the champagne to the hotel suite, and Starr Faithful were dismissed from the case after being interviewed: it was established beyond any doubt that the girl had remained in Club Alpha until the early hours of the morning. She gave evidence that she had been approached by a member of Freidler's party and offered the sum of five thousand dollars to render services of a more intimate nature, and had refused, reporting the incident to the club management as she had been schooled to do. After a week or so, the story disappeared from the headlines until it was revived by a tabloid story claiming that the hotel housekeeper had seen a swastika sprayed on to the bathroom mirror. This was denied by the hotel management, anxious not to have the incident affect the tourist trade, and the housekeeper was subsequently dismissed.

The directors of Freidler's bank conducted their own internal investigation and were horrified to find more alarming skeletons in Freidler's cupboard. It appeared that their late president had made a number of unsecured loans to companies he controlled and that documentation concerning these transactions was, to say the least, sketchy. Far more disturbing to the senior officers entrusted with the task of opening and examining the contents of Freidler's private safe were damaging documents relating to undisclosed large sums being passed to parties in Israel, though the ultimate destination was unclear. What was not unclear was that he had used the bank's money and enhanced his own fortune to the tune of eight million dollars without the transaction appearing on any balance sheet. At a specially convened Board meeting, the directors took a decision to destroy the evidence.

. . .

Far from these developments the Rt Hon. Kenith Logan, the Home Secretary in Her Majesty's recently elected Labour government, sat in his huge office looking at the Lowry over the fireplace, pondering whether he had been handed a poisoned chalice.

Life had not dealt him an unbeatable hand, but until now he had always known in what order to play the cards he had been born with. He had studied and learned the rules of the power game from an early age; the first dictum he had taken to heart in the slums of Liverpool was that the poor and the meek, far from inheriting the earth, were lucky if they obtained anything more than beer money and a council flat. He was an observer as well as a doer, seldom wasting his time on envy, and had spent his formative years noting what made others tick and deciding that few actions taken were either objective or fair, but based on self-interest and advancement. A Geordie MP for fifteen of his fifty-two years, prior to entering the House he had played an active role in local politics, while at the same time amassing a modest fortune from a chain of DIY warehouses operating on a cash-only basis. ('I don't like the credit card companies milking my cows,' was one of his favourite expressions.) These efforts had enabled him to claw his way out of his working-class background and had given him a veneer of sophistication to complement his street-wise business acumen. He had long been able to suit his accent and manner to whatever company he kept, for he was an adept political chameleon who had carefully steered a path between both factions of the Party – a Jack-the-Lad when dealing with the unions, well equipped to hold his own at shop-floor level when required, while presenting a potentially ministerial face to the Whips and the Front Bench. He was popular with the faithful at Conference times, skilfully judging which motions openly to support and which to duck. Four years before Labour swept back to power he had been voted on to the National Executive Council and had first been rewarded with the post of Shadow Minister for Sport (as a schoolboy he had had a trial for Everton), before being promoted to Transport, acquitting himself well at the Dispatch Box against a lack-lustre Tory counterpart. Gaining in confidence, he had slowly honed the rough zircon of his basic personality until it shone in such a way that many took it to be the genuine article. He was always willing to talk off the record to the parliamentary lobbyists, but with a wink and a nod, knowing that there was a good chance his indiscretions would find their way into print. Nobody really knew him, but he was generally reckoned to be a coming man. He lived modestly, dressed conservatively and, covering his options, courted two Aids charities, was a life-member of the RSPCA, opposed blood sports, was pro-abortion and anti the House of Lords. In the last reshuffle before the General Election he had been moved up to Health and Welfare and had expected to retain that position in the Cabinet if Labour swept back into power. The sudden death of the incumbent Home Secretary a matter of days after the outcome of the election had meant a further panic reshuffle, and to everybody's surprise, including his own, Logan had found himself elevated to that well-known political graveyard, the Home Office.

In his first weeks as a senior Cabinet Minister, thrust into an office he had never expected to occupy, he frequently felt like a certified lunatic, completely cut off from ordinary life, protected by male and female trained nurses who, although behaving with every outward show of deference, had quickly hinted that sweeping changes were not on their agenda. He found the comparison with hospital routine apposite, for he was given a mental blanket-bath by his Private Secretary, his own ideas of what he might or might not do gently washed away, and his hesitant protests talcum-powdered with soothing Whitehall-speak. It seemed that the most important function he could perform for his servants was to allow their established routines to proceed without hindrance. The early pulse of his adrenalin soon slowed under their ministrations, for Logan was smart enough to acknowledge that in many cases he knew next to nothing of the brief he held.

He was still staring at the Lowry, at the myriad matchstick figures in a northern landscape so familiar from his own childhood, when Sir Charles Slade, his Permanent Private Secretary, knocked and entered the room. Slade would have been rejected by any film casting director as too obvious for the role he played, for he epitomised the urbane courtier who was aware that, whatever human flotsam the political tides deposited on his private beach, he would always secure the best deckchair. Beneath his impeccably tailored dark suit he wore a corset to help support a back injured in a hunting accident and flatten the old tummy. To those not in the know it gave him a ramrod appearance in keeping with his Guards background. In his middle fifties, with a moustache more like an upper lip smudge, he bore a passing resemblance to the late Ronald Colman.

'Good morning, Minister.'

'Morning, Charles. Is it going to be a good one?' The use of Slade's Christian name came out hesitantly. How to address Slade had given Logan problems at first. He still retained enough of his working-class background to be impressed by titles.

'Oh, I'm sure, Minister. The deputation is here, by the way,' Slade added, 'but it never hurts to keep them waiting a few minutes.'

He placed some cuttings he had extracted from that day's newspapers in Logan's in-tray, together with some letters prepared for signature. 'The deputation from Greenwich, Minister,' he added, noting that Logan's expression had gone blank. 'You've read the briefing, I'm sure.'

'Oh, that, yes. Yes. How many are they?'

'Three, Minister.' Slade discreetly edged a piece of notepaper in front of Logan.

'Tricky?'

'Not at all, Minister. I'm sure you've taken on board the department's ongoing view of these matters. Any multi-racial society is bound to throw up these incidents from time to time. Sadly, they are the unwelcome manifestations of the slow process of integration.'

Logan allowed himself to disagree. 'I hardly think murder is an acceptable part of the process and if you ask me progress has been minimal. I'm going to change all that,' he added allowing himself a rare statement of intent, 'so pass the good news down the line.'

'I'll certainly make sure it reaches the right ears, Minister. Of course,' he added with just a smidgen of caution in his voice, 'it's always best to take the House along slowly. And where these ethnic issues are concerned, history has shown us that no change is achieved without a measure of discontent.'

Logan frowned before looking down at his papers. It was never easy to decipher Sir Charles. From a study of his boxes the previous night Logan had discovered that Greenwich enjoyed the dubious accolade of being top of the league in racial murders. There had been three in the past month alone, attributed to the fact that First Legion, a breakaway section of the National Front, had recently set up its headquarters in a quiet residential area of Greenwich, provoking strong protests from the ethnic community. Popular feeling was strongly critical of the police, since so far no arrests had been made.

'Well, you'd better show them in, then.'

'Your next engagement is at eleven, Minister, so might I suggest giving them half an hour at the most? I shall have your speech to the Law Society ready when you return.'

'You saw the amendments I made?'

'Yes, indeed. If I may say so, pertinent though they were, they were at variance with the major policy decisions you'll be presenting in your White Paper in due course.'

He withdrew before Logan could respond. A few moments later three men were ushered into the office. One of them Logan immediately recognised as Luther Smith, a prominent black activist, who was frequently to be seen taking part in television debates. Articulate and with well-marshalled opinions, he belied his burly appearance. According to Slade's briefing notes, he was a graduate of the London School of Economics, had twice been arrested during protest marches, and was considered still to hanker for a return to old-fashioned Marxism. The second man was also black and introduced himself as the lawyer acting for the family of one of the murder victims. The last member of the party was an official of a local racial surveillance organisation named Streetwatch.

'Please sit down,' Logan said. 'And smoke if you wish. I do.'

They took the proffered seats.

Addressing Smith, whom he rightly assumed would be the principal spokesman, Logan began with, 'Let me say, Mr Smith, I'm fully aware of the purpose of your visit, and I share your concerns.'

'Perhaps what you're not aware of, Minister,' Smith broke in, 'is that another man was torched last night.'

'Torched?'

'Beaten up, doused in petrol and set on fire,' Smith said. He opened his briefcase and took out some photographs which he tossed on to Logan's desk. 'Take a look, Minister. They torched his crotch. And why? Because he dated a white girl. He was abducted by a group of fascist thugs whom your government has allowed to set up shop in my neighbourhood and terrorise the coloured population. Three murders, over sixty assaults, shit put through letter boxes, arson, ram-raiders, you name it, and I'd like to know what you intend to do about it.' He had not raised his voice, but there was no mistaking his hostility. 'I'm not just concerned with this latest outrage, hideous though it is, I'm asking you to take immediate action and proscribe First Legion. Shut them down before you have a full scale riot on your hands. You have the powers, use them.'

Taken off guard by the vehemence of Smith's opening attack, Logan stared at the graphic photographs while he searched for the right response. 'I'm not sure that you're correct on your last point. In the first instance, these are properly matters for the police and I have no doubt that they are already being dealt with by them.'

'Then let me disabuse you, Minister. So far no convictions have resulted from any of the murders.'

'Convictions depend on hard evidence.'

It was now that the lawyer interrupted. 'With great courage, my clients are prepared positively to identify two of the assailants if given the chance, but so far the police have done little or nothing. A fuse has been lit, Minister, and unless the authorities act quickly, I fear the consequences.'

Logan studied the photographs again. 'Is this man going to live?'

'He's in the intensive burns unit. They give him a fifty-fifty chance.'

Logan nodded. 'Quite hideous. Can you leave these with me? I shall personally take up the incident with the Commissioner at the earliest opportunity.'

'What about First Legion?' Smith asked.

'Do you have any direct evidence to link these atrocities with their members?'

'Isn't it obvious?' the lawyer said. 'The moment they set up shop in the area the number of racial attacks increased by some three hundred per cent. That can't be pure coincidence.'

'But proof? I have every sympathy with your situation, but for me or the police to take action, proof is required. Come to me with proof and I promise that I will act immediately.'

The three men on the opposite side of the desk exchanged glances. Smith said: 'What further proof do you need? Another three murders? Read your own manifesto again. You were voted in on a promise of justice for all.'

'I can assure you these issues are high on my agenda,' Logan replied stuffily. 'You have to remember we inherited a great number of problems, crimes of this nature being one of them, but they can't be dealt with in isolation. They're all part and parcel of a much wider social sickness. As you must know, we shall be publishing a number of White Papers designed to tackle the root causes.'

Smith got to his feet. 'Yeah, we've heard all that before. First from the Tories, now from your lot, but nothing ever happens.' He gathered up the photographs. 'I'll take these back, in case they gather dust, and before you publish your White Papers I'm going to spread them all over the tabloids.'

He made for the door. The other two followed him, only the lawyer making a lame attempt to exit on a placatory note. The last thing Logan heard was Smith's muttered, 'Another useless prick.'

Fifteen minutes later, still smarting from the exchange,

Logan got into his armoured Jaguar and, accompanied by his personal detective and a police back-up car, set off for his next appointment. What rankled most was the awareness that in dealing with the three men, all too soon, all too glibly, he had found himself using the bleak language of power and saying nothing.

5

ST PETERSBURG 1997

Galina said: 'Why, what makes you suspicious?'

Before answering Hillsden glanced at their small daughter who was concentrating on a jigsaw. 'Haven't I always been?' he said softly, 'ever since you've been unlucky enough to know me.'

'Don't say that. I hate it when you say things like that.'

'Well, if it wasn't for me, you could have a more interesting life now that the barriers have been lifted. You'd be free to travel, something you say you've always wanted to do. It isn't exactly an advantage being married to me. Because of who I am, you're trapped here.'

Now it was Galina's turn to shoot a look at their daughter. 'I know who you are and what you were, and I'm not trapped, I'm content.'

'Are you? Well, I'm not. It's a slow death here, and you and Lara deserve better.'

'What else happened this morning, something happened, didn't it? I want to know why you came back in such a funny mood. Was there something else you haven't told me?'

'No.'

'Then what was it about that man that made you suspicious?'

'I just don't believe it was a chance encounter. How did he pick me out as British in that queue?'

'You look British.'

'I don't think so. Not any longer. I certainly don't feel British. He was too pat.'

'Pat?'

'Yes. Meaning his dialogue came out as rehearsed.'

They sat opposite each other on either side of the stove. Through the thin walls of the apartment they could hear their drunken neighbour singing an old McCartney standard – 'Yesterday'. It seemed to be the only item in his repertoire and he repeated it endlessly, his sodden voice cracking whenever he reached for a high note. Hillsden had a sudden yearning for home, for different comforts, familiar landmarks. He was happy with Galina; not content, as she put it, but on the whole happy. At least he did not have to deceive her as he had been forced to deceive Margot, his first wife. Now, when he put his head on the pillow beside Galina, he no longer had to think twice before answering her night questions. Sometimes, denied sleep, he could see his past life so clearly; the suburban house where he had once lived, crammed with the kitsch trimmings that Margot had collected – all those special offers she had religiously answered, his marriage compiled from mail order catalogues, the outward signs, he now recognised, of her consuming loneliness. He had been forced to shut her out and the wonder of it was how he had managed to sustain the deception all those years, bound not by the vows exchanged in church, but the more monstrous ties of the Official Secrets Act.

Galina interrupted his memories. 'What else could he have wanted you for?'

'No idea.'

'Then why give him a second thought?'

'I explained why. I'm always expecting the past to catch up with me.'

'In a cheese queue?' Galina said, trying to make him see the humour of it.

'You didn't live the way I had to all those wasted years, never knowing what was round the corner.' He broke off as he became aware that his daughter had stopped doing the jigsaw and was listening to their conversation. 'Have you finished it, sweetheart?'

The child shook her head. 'Why are you and Mummy sad?' she said, her wide eyes boring through him.

'We're not sad. Let me see.' He picked up one of the spare pieces. 'The sky is always the difficult part. I could never do skies.'

He tried the piece in several places without success. 'What d'you know? I'm no better than you. Anyway, it's past your bedtime, young lady. We'll finish it in the morning. Off you go. Give me a kiss.'

She climbed on his knee and put her arms around his neck, planting multiple kisses on his cheek in quick succession.

'My word, how many is that?'

'A hundred, because I love you a hundred.'

'And I love you too.'

'How many?'

'Oh, three hundred at least.'

'Will we go to the park tomorrow?'

'If it's fine.'

'Promise.'

'I promise.'

She gave him one last kiss and then went to her room with her mother. Watching her go, Hillsden thought, by the time she's seventeen I'll be an old man, and the prospect chilled him. He put some more wood on the stove and poured himself a small measure of Scotch – another gift from Abramov and one that he rationed. Savouring the drink, he remembered the good gone times that he, Jock and Caroline had spent together in the old Austrian station. The preferred tipple then had been Hunter's Tea – local, home-made schnapps topped up with hot water – one of those lethal potions, like too many Pimm's downed on a hot summer's day, that floored you without warning. It all came flooding back, that past, foreign country where certainly we did things differently, he thought. Even his adultery with Caroline had had a sort of innocence about it, unjustified but nevertheless real, neither of them counting the true cost until it was too late. Was that the same with all lovers or just peculiar to them? He remembered the night walks by the dark, still lake at Anif, reliving those last days when, despite all his efforts, he had failed to dissuade Caroline from going back to East Berlin that final time. Within a few years, but all too late to save her, the Wall came down, the old futilities rubbled, Honecker's machinery of terror dismantled. Now, remembering the span of the Cold War, it was like looking at history through the wrong end of a telescope: the major players reduced to dwarfs. Were the deaths, the sacrifices worth it? he wondered. Did we make any difference to the inevitable outcome? In the end it wasn't our efforts but an act of spontaneous human combustion that overturned a whole continent. After Caroline's death he had attempted to build his own wall, to keep past and present separated, forgetting that memories had a way of jumping any barrier. Now, as he waited for Galina to return from putting the child to bed, those same, recurring memories touched the sciatic nerve of disloyalty. I should be happy, he thought. I have a good wife and child I love, I'm alive, be thankful for those mercies.

'D'you want a drink?' he asked when Galina came back.

'No, it's nearly finished and I know how much it means to you.'

'Have some, come on, I hate drinking alone.'

'I'm not that keen, really.'

'Vodka, then? Have a vodka.'

He got up to pour her one. 'Has she gone to sleep?'

'Yes, for once. Why is it that children never want to go to bed?'

'It's primeval,' Hillsden said. 'Fear of the dark, the unknown. Weren't you like that as a child? I know I was. I still am, sometimes.'

He paused as he went to hand her the drink, bending and kissing her on the lips.

'What's that for?'

'Can't a man kiss his wife when he feels like it?'

42

'I'm not complaining, I just asked why.'

'Because I fancy you.'

'Suddenly?'

'No, not suddenly.'

'Well, you're out of luck tonight, because my period just started.'

'Ah!' He handed her the drink. 'Then I'll have to settle for a cuddle. Come here. Sit on my lap.'

'Like daughter, like wife,' Galina said as she nuzzled him. 'You have two women who love you.'

'Yes, I'm a lucky sod, don't think I don't know it.'

They kissed.

'You're not really worried about that man, are you?' Galina said.

'No. You're probably right, maybe he did only want to cadge a cigarette. Did you read that in America there's a lobby gathering momentum to ban cigarettes altogether.'

'Pity they don't try the same here. I do so wish you'd give up.'

'Aren't I unbearable enough as it is? It's easy for you, you've never smoked.' Denied the ultimate intimacy, he stroked her hair, then dropped his hand to let it rest on her breast. 'Are you *really* content?' he asked as the same tuneless singing began again in the next apartment.

'Yes, I've told you.'

'But don't you long to get out of this city, escape the daily drudgery of it all? Maybe I should go and work for Victor, he keeps asking me to.'

'You'd hate that.'

'With the money he says I'd earn we could perhaps buy a *dacha*. It'd be good for Lara to be in the country when summer comes. I thought she looked pale tonight. You too, for that matter. We live like caged birds.' As he said it he was reminded of the canary Jock had once given him and nicknamed Gromyko, the only company he had had in that first cold-comfort Moscow apartment. Why did so many things from those days come back to haunt him? Although he had now made light of the chance encounter in the cheese queue, some unease remained. No matter how many changes had taken place, he believed that good old-fashioned evil still stalked the streets. There were past scores that remained to be settled. For all he knew, somebody in the Firm wanted to balance the books for personal reasons. He had never ceased to be on his guard.

. . .

As it happened he did not have long to wait.

Although the following morning it was still bitterly cold, the skies were clear and Hillsden gave in to Lara's repeated pleas for him to honour his promise. Swathed in extra layers of clothing they set out hand in hand to walk to the Tauride Gardens.

It had always seemed odd to Hillsden that, despite their love of the open air, Russians displayed little or no interest in gardening. He supposed this could partly be explained by the fact that few city dwellers had plots of their own, but even the communal gardens usually presented a pathetic sight. There would be spring flowers, of course, planted haphazardly, not in the meticulous patterns of London parks, and swiftly neglected except by weeds. Even the *dacha* plots were not given the slavish devotion the British lavished on their gardens; grass grew wild, trees were untamed, the idea of mowing a lawn anathema.

The Tauride Gardens looked particularly forlorn in winter, though Hillsden could appreciate why little or no maintenance was attempted: the frozen earth would have needed pneumatic drills to penetrate it. The only thing that could be said for the excursions he and Lara made was that they got him out of the apartment for a few hours. Lara had brought her skipping rope with her and he tied one end to a tree and patiently swung the other while she displayed her prowess. Hillsden went through the motions automatically, his thoughts elsewhere, and it wasn't until the man who called himself Pitchforth-Swanson was upon them that he was even aware of his presence.

'You play the good father, I see.'

Involuntarily, Hillsden stopped swinging the rope and Lara tripped over it. He rushed to pick her up before facing Swanson.

'Oh, dear, that was my fault,' Swanson said.

'No harm done.' Lara stayed close to her father's side.

'Well, we meet again.'

'Yes,' Hillsden said. 'But not by coincidence, I take it?'

'Well, I had rather hoped you'd take me up on my offer of a meal,' Swanson replied. He smiled as he said it, revealing bright, but uneven, teeth. 'You didn't call me, did you?'

'No.'

'I only ask because the hotel's not very good with messages.'

Irritation welled up in Hillsden. Why am I being so polite with this bullshit artist? he thought. He knew the Swansons of this world: lifted from a mould that had been in use since the days of the Empire, they looked down on anybody who hadn't been to the right school, condescending time-servers treading water until they received their mandatory K. Swanson had the sort of face that frequently adorned the social pages of *The Field*. 'What d'you really want?' he asked. 'I'm not so green as to think you turned up here on the off chance you might bum another cigarette.'

'I just want a chat, Alec.'

The use of his Christian name checked Hillsden momentarily.

'Just a friendly chat. To put a proposition to you.'

'Who sent you?'

'We'll get to that. Let's just say that it would be worth your time to have that chat.'

'I'm not going to talk in front of my daughter.'

Sensing a different note in her father's voice, Lara's grip tightened on his hand.

'No, I quite understand. Why not come to my hotel? It has

some of the best food around. My treat, of course.'

His smile, which Hillsden did not return, gave his mouth a lop-sided look.

'When?'

'Tonight?' Swanson said. 'Shall we say seven, in the foyer?'

Hillsden nodded.

'That's splendid, I look forward to it.'

Hillsden and Lara watched as he walked away towards the old fair-ground and was lost amongst the empty booths. Then Hillsden untied the skipping rope.

'Aren't we going to play some more?' Lara asked, her face puckered against a wind that had suddenly gusted.

'Not today, darling.'

'Is it because of that man?'

'No, nothing to do with him. It's getting too cold.'

'I didn't like that man,' the child said. 'You didn't like him either, did you?'

'Not over much,' Hillsden said.

'Then why are you having dinner with him?'

'That's enough questions.' He took her gloved hand. They walked slowly home while Hillsden tried to guess Swanson's real purpose in seeking him out.

. . .

Swanson was occupying a comfortable two-room suite. A table had been laid with drinks and a crystal bowl of imperial caviar on cracked ice, enough for half a dozen people.

'Are you expecting others to join us?' Hillsden asked. He shook the snow off his coat, folded it and placed it over the back of a chair.

'No, there's just you and me,' Swanson said. 'What's your tipple?'

'I prefer Scotch, but it doesn't sit well with the caviar, so I'll take the local poison.'

Swanson began: 'Well, you may be pleasantly surprised to

know that London are prepared to entertain a deal, all things being equal.'

'They never are, are they?'

Swanson paused from pouring the vodka and gave him a look. 'Sorry?'

'All things are never equal. In any deal one of the parties always comes out top.'

'Oh, I see, yes.' Swanson gave a short, mirthless laugh, but his face betrayed a trace of uncertainty. 'You want to help yourself to the feast?'

Hillsden moved to the table and spread caviar on the coarse brown bread rather than the blinis. 'I see the Firm can still push out the boat. I thought things were tight in dear old England.'

'For some. I'm sure the axe is poised to fall one day, given our new masters, but for the moment they need us. It's remarkable how power changes attitudes. Give a Minister an armour-plated Jaguar and a police escort and many of his liberal beliefs evaporate.'

Hillsden took the offered glass of vodka and waited until Swanson had poured for himself and heaped a dollop of caviar on to a blini. A few of the eggs dribbled out of Swanson's mouth on to his chin as he took a large bite.

'Who would have thought it?' Swanson said.

'Thought what?'

'Us being here together like this. Not so long ago it would have been unthinkable. I mean, being able to talk freely.'

'Are we talking freely?'

Swanson smiled. 'What a guarded character you are, Alec.' He spread another blini. 'Do have some more.'

'I don't have a large appetite these days,' Hillsden answered. He resisted the temptation to lean forward and wipe the caviar from Swanson's slack mouth with a napkin. 'You said you had a proposition to put to me, wasn't that the object of this meeting? Let's forgo the philosophic tiny talk and get down to that.'

'If you wish. I rather thought we could enjoy the meal first.'

At long last Swanson became aware of the state of his mouth and tidied it with a forefinger. 'Let's start by stating the obvious. You're quite right, I didn't come across you by chance.'

If he expected Hillsden to react he was disappointed. Taking another mouthful of caviar he continued, 'As you can imagine, this isn't somewhere I prefer to Henley, any more than you.'

'I've never been to Henley,' Hillsden said.

'Really? One of the few things that hasn't changed in England. Most everything else has. Changed for all of us. Different horses for different courses, different jockeys riding them.'

'Do me a favour,' Hillsden interrupted. 'I've had my fill of men of mystery. Just get to the point.' The belligerence in his voice was all too obviously not to Swanson's liking.

'Well, now, chummy, I don't think you're in a position to dictate.' The use of the word 'chummy' was deliberately offensive, but Hillsden remained impassive. 'If you want me to put my false teeth on the table, I'd suggest your situation is not so secure that you can afford to be cocky. As I said, times have changed, and that's true, but not in every respect. I hate to bring up the subject, but there's still a warrant out for your arrest and the long arm of the law can now reach this far . . . That isn't a threat, just a statement of fact. Equally, there are always ways and means of disposing of such inconveniences. Take the case . . . well, just suppose I was to tell you that in return for your co-operation you and your new family could kiss goodbye to cheese queues and go back to shopping at Tesco.'

If Hillsden felt any surprise he did not show it.

'You'd be buying a new life. The record wiped clean, a new identity, a home back in your own country, your daughter educated in a good private school, financial security for your wife. It's a good package, Alec.'

'And what's the price tag?' Hillsden asked after a slight pause. He reached to pour himself another vodka.

'Well, let's not call it a price, nothing so vulgar, just a return consideration.'

'Well, whatever you'd call it.'

'I happen to think your talents should not be allowed to rust. Somebody like you still has a lot of mileage in him. Alec Hillsden may be a burnt-out case, but give him an oil change, a totally new personality, and it's a different ball game as the Yanks say,' Swanson said in a flurry of mixed metaphors.

Hillsden downed his ice-cold vodka in one go, then shook his head. 'No, forget it. Not interested. I'm too old to go back in the game, and maybe too wise. You must have dozens of eager beavers to choose from. Why would you come all this way to head-hunt a burnt-out case like me?'

'But you don't know the game I have in mind, Alec. As it happens, your age, the fact that you're charred at the edges, fits the scenario I have in mind. I'm not looking for youthful brawn, I'm looking for guile born of long experience.'

'Well, there's plenty of that in this room.' Despite his antipathy towards Swanson, he found himself drawn into the cat and mouse tactics. 'Okay, tell me this "scenario" as you call it.'

'Oh, come on, Alec, you can't have forgotten how these things work? We don't accept post-dated cheques.'

'What I haven't forgotten is how I was stitched-up last time. What makes you think I should trust you or anybody else this time around? You want to trade, trade. You don't catch old fish with dead bait. How do I know you're not just the errand boy sent to snare me? Don't read the fine print, Alec, just sign on the dotted line and trust me. Bullshit! I've been there before.'

Swanson's face flushed but he did not reply in kind. 'That's where you're wrong, Alec. You haven't been there before. Nobody has. I can understand your caution, but it's misplaced, believe me. The deal I'm authorised to offer is a good one, but it won't come again.' His body language and tone softened – a Harrods salesman now urging a customer to take the suit he has suggested. 'I can't believe you want to spend your remaining years living on Russian charity, a forgotten dinosaur from a bygone age. Not a man of your abilities. So before you make a hasty judgement, why not hear me out? You see, I've studied your file very thoroughly, and you fit my role model. I want somebody with a burning need to get even. I've always thought nothing spurs one on like the prospect of revenge, don't you agree? You did your duty, Alec, served your country well, and in return got short shrift. I'm offering you a chance – a last chance – to go back and rehabilitate yourself.'

Hillsden listened without any change of expression, hearing an echo of Lockfield in Swanson's dialogue.

'I'll go this far with you,' Swanson continued in the same plummy tone. 'Because of the past I can well appreciate your caution . . . Let me tell you what's been happening in the real world. Labour swept in at the last general election on a manifesto they patently couldn't deliver, but the public bought it and the Tories were decimated, reduced to a rump. The "natural party of power", as they liked to think of themselves, now has to face a long stay in the wilderness. A small caucus of hard case right-wingers didn't take kindly to that. They split from the party and formed their own secret agenda with the aim of exploiting the race card and fomenting widespread social unrest. A motley crowd, Alec, with a hang-'em-and-flog-'em mentality, but not to be underestimated. They have a lot going for them despite Labour's attempt to paper over the cracks. The England of today is a tinder box waiting to be ignited. Many of the inner-cities have no-go ghetto areas, but as far as the new government is concerned it's politically unacceptable to admit the problem exists. Continuing high unemployment mostly amongst the ethnic minorities which, like the Tories, they can't solve without draconian measures, allied to a horrendous, drug-related crime rate, has stymied them. That gives the ultra-rights a lot of ammunition to play with. We believe they're biding their time until they can mount a *coup.*'

'It'll never happen.'

'You say that, but you've been away a long time, Alec. The England you knew no longer exists. We're edging closer to 1933 than drawing away from Orwell's '84.'

'Where does your role model fit into that?'

'Whether the enemy comes from the Left or the Right, Alec, some of us have to do what's required. Uncle Joe and company depart, enter the Fascists stage right. We know some of it, but not enough. We need to get closer, to infiltrate, stay ahead of them. There's the added factor, which you couldn't possibly be aware of, that, post Lockfield, certain elements within the Firm itself moved too far to the Right. Thatcher's long reign made sure of that.'

'Identified?'

'We sorted out two of them, but I suspect they were only the tip of the iceberg. The DG and I are convinced that some of the new intake are in contact with the Tory breakaway group and constitute a threat from within. Hence our need for somebody untainted to smoke them out . . . and who better than you, somebody from the old school who has such special qualities? You'd be working with a very small, hand-picked team, with me running the show. In return, your file would be wiped clean, deleted without trace. Doesn't that tempt you?'

'This team, do I know any of them?'

'One, I think.'

'Who?'

'Come home and find out,' Swanson said. He looked long and hard at Hillsden before helping himself to another drink. 'I can make it an attractive package, Alec.'

'What special qualities do I have? I'd like to know.'

'You're the man who never was, Alec. Part of the plan would be to arrange for you to die. By the time you arrive in England your obituaries will be wrapping fish and chips. We've thought of all the loose ends. I don't know why you're hesitating. Most people would jump at a chance of starting again with a clean sheet.'

'Except, I'm not alone, I have a wife and a daughter. And the fact that, in some ways, despite everything, familiarity has certain compensations,' Hillsden replied after a pause. 'Are you saying the murder charge would be dropped?'

'Absolutely. And eventually a pardon. That would have to be held over for obvious reasons.'

'I'd want a copper-bottomed guarantee before I leave here.'

'That can be arranged. What else?' Confident that, finally, he was winning the argument, Swanson returned to the caviar.

'A lump sum equivalent to back-dated salary for the past seven years, placed in my wife's name, in a Swiss numbered account.'

'I don't see any problem there. Officially you won't be listed in any of the Firm's accounts. You'll be paid from a secret slush fund not even the Select Committee know about.'

'I'll think about it,' Hillsden said after a long pause. He put his topcoat on, then picked up a bottle of Scotch and the half-finished bottle of vodka, together with the bowl of caviar. 'You don't mind, do you? Treat for the wife.'

He made for the door. 'I'll give you my answer two days from now. Let's meet in the park again and if there's anything still to talk about I'll take you back to our apartment. Eleven o'clock, by the fair-ground.'

'Why not give me your answer now?'

'Two days,' Hillsden repeated. 'I'm being generous. The Firm kept me waiting seven years.'

He left.

. . .

'Did you convince him?' the London voice asked.

'I don't know,' Swanson replied. 'He's not an easy customer.'

'What's the snag?'

'It's difficult to read him. He wants forty-eight hours to think it over. I still believe he's our best bet, for all the reasons we discussed.'

'How much did you tell him?'

'Just the bare essentials. Plus the offer, of course.'

'And that didn't sway him?'

'I think it interested him.'

'Well, if he finally says no, move to the contingency plan. Let's not leave anything to chance.'

'Understood.'

The line to London went dead.

. . .

'You know it means you becoming me, changing places,' Hillsden said. 'Relearning a life.'

'You did it,' Galina said.

'I had no choice.'

'Do I?'

'Yes. The choice is yours.'

'But you want to go home.'

'I haven't said that.'

'I know you do. It's in your face. If I spoilt it for you you'd always hold it against me.'

'You're wrong. Either way I'd only be doing it for you and Lara. You decide. It's your life I care about.'

6

ARKANSAS, USA

Marvin Schmidt had never witnessed an execution before, let alone a triple execution, but as the leading member of the FBI team that had brought the three murderers to justice, he felt a morbid compulsion to see it through to the end. God knows he had waited long enough: all three convicted men had been on Death Row for several years, their lawyers lodging appeal after appeal, but every legal loophole having been explored and rejected, the verdict of the court was finally going to be carried out.

Executions in the State of Arkansas being by lethal injection, the Governor of the prison had decreed that the three men would be terminated, in alphabetical order, during a two hour period commencing at midnight. At a press conference he stated his reasons: the procedure would be a cost efficient exercise, reducing overtime and stress on his staff. 'Executions ain't no picnic for those who have to carry them out and I have to think of that.'

It was out of character for Schmidt to become so emotionally involved in the aftermath of any case: some you lost and some you won, it more often than not depended on whether the defendant could afford a top lawyer; justice in the US of A was now just another adjunct of show business, he felt – trial by television in many cases. Normally, whatever the verdict, he tried to wipe it from memory, but this particular crime had never left him. A Jew himself, twelve years previously, being made aware of the anti-Semitic undertones in the case, he had put in a special request to be assigned to the Federal team handling the investigation. The crime in question was the brutal murder of a small town businessman killed, together with his wife and daughter, in what at first appeared to be a break-in that went horribly wrong. Then the Arkansas State police unearthed more sinister clues. The murdered man, Gerard Heinz, a Polish Jew, the only surviving member of a prominent Warsaw family, had been admitted to America as a refugee immediately after the war. He had married a Jewish girl, also a refugee, and after a period living in the Queens district of New York where they both worked long hours at menial tasks in order to amass some capital, they had moved to Arkansas and established a flourishing haberdashery store. The murderers had first tortured Heinz in front of his wife and daughter, then both women had been brutally raped before all three members of the family were shot at point blank range. The house and shop had been totally trashed, the murderers urinating in the beds, though, curiously, very little had been stolen. A respected, well-integrated member of the local community, Heinz had no known enemies and the initial investigation produced no leads. It wasn't until three weeks later that the State Prosecutor's office received an anonymous and crudely written communication.

> *Three of the scum eliminated. This is just the beginning.*
> *Soon the gas chambers will be back and the Jews*
> *will be made into soap which is all there (sic) fit for.*
> *By order of The SS Action Committee*

Curiously, the note had been posted in Chicago. Although it produced no fingerprints, forensic experts determined that the watermarked paper it was written on was manufactured by a small company in the Evanston district and only distributed and sold in Illinois. They checked all outlets but the trail went cold. Then an apparently unrelated incident attracted Schmidt's interest – a gun-dealer with known underworld connections was arrested on a charge of failing to keep proper records and an alert member of the Chicago police noticed that his invoices were printed on the same, suspect, notepaper. This in itself was not sufficient to tie in with the Arkansas murder, but in addition a quantity of anti-Semitic literature was found amongst the dealer's sequestered files, together with evidence of membership of a quasi-Fascist organisation calling itself Partisans of the New Front. Under interrogation Schmidt trapped the gun-dealer into revealing the name of a fellow member, a man called Mitchell who proved to have some form: he had once been arrested for attempted rape, but had been found not guilty for lack of corroborating evidence. He was currently on parole for a lesser offence.

Mitchell, a hardhat, was working on a construction site when tracked down. He was a thick-set man in his forties and carried a pronounced beer gut with a swaggering gait. His torso was extensively tattooed, including a small swastika on his right upper-arm. Schmidt went undercover, calling himself Joe Spader. After gaining a job on the same building site, he made it his business to get friendly with Mitchell during the lunch breaks, deliberately encouraging Mitchell's coarse sense of humour. They went bowling together and after a few weeks, the relationship cemented. Mitchell, who lived alone in a trailer park, invited 'Spader' back for a barbecue meal.

Schmidt was wired that evening. He sat in a plastic lounger, drinking beer out of a can watching Mitchell fuss over the charcoal.

'Take a look at these mothers,' Mitchell said. 'You ever seen T-bones like these? You can't buy these from a fucken market, you have to wait for them to fall off the back of a lorry.' He squeezed his empty beer can and reached for a second. 'I'll put you in touch with my supplier. Best fucken meat you ever tasted. Cheap, no questions asked.'

'Can't beat it,' Schmidt said.

'I don't pay those fancy Jew prices. No way. The kikes have got this country over a fucken barrel, know that?'

'You think so?'

'I know so,' Mitchell said as he basted the steaks with sauce and forked them on to the grill. 'Those Jew pricks control everything. You name it, they run it. The banks, movies, garment trade, supermarkets. Forget the Mafia, they ain't the threat.'

'Guess you're right. I never thought of it that way.'

'A few of us have got wise. How d'you like yours, rare or ruined?'

'Rare.'

'I like to see blood.' Mitchell flipped the steaks over. 'Couple more minutes and these beauties will melt in your mouth.'

Schmidt had to admit that the meat was exceptional, which gratified Mitchell. 'Listen, nothing but the best for a buddy. You married?'

'No. Was. No longer.'

'Me neither. Who needs it? Like they say, why keep a cow when you can buy milk at the K Mart? Ain't that the truth?'

'Ain't it just,' Schmidt agreed.

'I up and go wherever I please. Been all over. See, I got friends everywhere in the fraternity.'

'What fraternity's that? You mean the Elks?'

'Fuck, no! Fucken Elks are a bunch of nothings. I'm talkin' of real buddies, know what I mean? Guys who think alike, who see where this country's headed. Nothing but bleeding-heart liberals, fucken gays, blacks and rich Jew boys running our lives. But we're doing something about it. You wait.'

Schmidt nodded.

'Take Nixon, he was a prince and they fucken shafted him. Know who was behind Watergate? A whole bunch of Washington kikes.'

'Really? I didn't read that.'

'Course you didn't read it,' Mitchell said. He picked his teeth and hawked. 'Never got in the papers. But that's the bottom line, you'd better believe it. Some of us know and are doing something about it. Only a matter of time. Let me show you something.' He went inside his mobile home and emerged carrying a book. 'Take this back and read it. It'll open your eyes to what's really going on. But keep it to yourself, don't leave it lying around, that fucken book's a hand grenade.'

Schmidt studied the title, *The Only Solution,* before flicking through the pages. The chapter heading he stopped at read: 'The Purification of The Nation'.

'Looks interesting,' he said.

'Bet your fucken life it's interesting. That there's our bible.'

They had some more beers, though Schmidt was careful not to match Mitchell's consumption. When the mosquitoes began to bite they moved inside. The interior of the mobile home mirrored Mitchell's personality. Copies of *Hustler* lay on the unmade single bed, the pillow stained with the greasy hair preparation Mitchell used. The driver's swivel armchair and a matching companion were on a raised portion and behind them was a small dining table with bench seats either side, the table strewn with dirty crockery and a brimming ashtray. Schmidt noted a skeleton mascot dangling from under the rear-view mirror.

'Bet these are great pyjama wagons,' he commented.

'The best. Great for short-arm practice.' By now Mitchell's speech was getting slurred. 'You ever want to borrow it for a little goona-goona, just pass the word. No charge and you don't have to smuggle them past the landlord.'

Schmidt swivelled into the driving seat and fingered the steering wheel. There was a metal decal fixed to the centre of the wheel which he recognised as a Nazi SS insignia. 'And I bet this baby moves when you put your foot down.'

'Straight V-eight,' Mitchell answered through a belch. 'Taken her all over – Carolina, Texas, Arkansas, Arizona, just up and go.'

'I ain't never travelled far,' Schmidt said. 'Been to Texas once, Dallas, and I went to a funeral in Philly, but that's about it. What's Arkansas like? Ain't that where Clinton come from?'

'Clinton. What a dummy. You know who bankrolled him into the White House don'cha? Fucken Jew commies again. But we're getting around to him.' He belched again and went to use the small toilet, repeating 'fucken commies' several times as he urinated noisily. Schmidt used the moment quickly to rifle through some papers and road maps on the dashboard. Scrawled on a map of Arkansas were the words *Heinz tomato catsup* and a date. He pocketed this and was finishing his beer when Mitchell returned with his flies gaping. 'Say, listen, I've got to get some shut-eye. Thanks for the steak and beer.'

'Any time.'

'And you must tell me more about this fraternity.'

'Read the book. If you're hooked we'll get together on it.' Mitchell flopped on to the bunk. As Schmidt stepped outside he caught the rancid smell of burnt meat from the barbecue.

The date on the map was the date the Heinz family were murdered. Armed with this and his tape, Schmidt convinced his superiors that there was now sufficient circumstantial evidence to take it further. In the first instance, Mitchell was arrested on a charge of receiving stolen goods. While he was in custody the mobile home was taken apart. The search revealed two handguns, neither of which was registered, but little else, until a vigilant member of the search team noticed an irregularity in the ceiling over the shower. The removal of one of the tiles revealed a hidden compartment concealing an SS ceremonial dagger, which was subsequently proved to have been one of the murder weapons, a membership list of the Action Committee along with a quantity of violently anti-Semitic pamphlets and pornographic photographs.

Broken after prolonged interrogation, Mitchell finally confessed to being present at the murders, but blamed the actual killings on his two confederates. In preparing the State's case, the prosecution pieced together the journey to and from Arkansas through credit card vouchers from petrol stations along the murderers' route. Mitchell's attempt to plea-bargain was refused · and all three men ensured the verdicts of guilty by turning on each other.

Just before midnight on the night of the executions, Schmidt took his place with ten other witnesses in the observation booth. A panel of one-way glass allowed them to watch the proceedings in the execution chamber. The observers had been informed that the three men would be terminated at forty-five minute intervals, giving the officials time to carry the body out in a bag, clean the hospital trolley and change the needle before the next man was brought in. Since doctors were forbidden to administer the killing injection there were often difficulties in locating a vein for the catheter through which the sedative, paralytic agent and lethal chemical must flow. Since calculation of the dosage was not an exact science, especially when dealing with condemned men who had drug histories, mishaps were not uncommon.

Unsettled by these revelations, Schmidt braced himself amongst the other witnesses, but immediately after the first man was brought in and strapped to the trolley, he regretted his decision to attend. He had anticipated being present at the carrying out of a calm, judicial sentence that the law and society sanctioned as befitting the crime. Instead, he found himself a voyeur sickened by a tableau which brought to mind experiments on human bodies that, with disturbing irony for this particular case, had been a feature of Nazi Germany. The second man to die needed a venous cutdown before a clean opening could be made and by Schmidt's watch it took twelve minutes before the vein was pierced. The entire procedures overran the estimate by some thirty-seven minutes before Mitchell, the last of the three to die, was pronounced dead at 2.17 a.m.

Afterwards, the shaken witnesses assembled in the Governor's office for a drink. The Governor raised his glass of Jack Daniels. 'To Henry Ford,' he said.

'Henry Ford?' Schmidt queried.

'He invented the production line, didn't he?'

Schmidt downed his drink and left. Outside there was still a small batch of demonstrators kneeling in prayer. As he drove off, he said his own prayer in Hebrew for all the Jews who had taken longer than twelve minutes to die at the hands of their oppressors.

7

ST PETERSBURG AGAIN

'Robert Bartlett,' Hillsden said, reading the name in his new passport. 'Who chose that?'

'Who knows?'

Swanson had a slightly peeved expression and was in a more subdued mood than on their previous meetings.

'Does it really matter what you're called in future?' Swanson asked. 'I would have thought that was the least of your worries.'

'No, probably not, except there used to be a Bartlett in the Firm years ago, that's all. One of the men that fancy old queen Glanville betrayed. Of course they sent a different breed into the field in those days,' he added pointedly.

'We have to have a new photograph taken. They want you to dye your hair a different colour. Shave your beard but leave the moustache. I shall take it with a Polaroid camera.'

'They think age will take care of the rest, do they? I've had a facial before, you know, courtesy of the GRU. Maybe you'll end up employing Dorian Gray,' Hillsden said with glacial humour. 'I hope you take flattering pictures, since it'll probably be my last likeness.' He put his own passport to one side and examined the ones for Galina and his daughter. 'I see they've changed the format while I've been away.'

'Yes, as I warned before a lot of things have changed,' Swanson snapped. 'Most of them at the behest of those overpaid bureaucrats in Brussels.'

'These look a very cheap job compared to the old type, more like driving licences. No longer does Her Britannic Majesty request and require all those whom it may concern to allow me to pass freely. Still, I dare say nobody touches the forelock these days when you present them.' He noted that Galina was now to be known as Georgina Bartlett and their daughter had been renamed Laura.

'They'll have to be rehearsed,' Hillsden said.

'Who will?'

'My wife and daughter. It won't be that easy for them to get used to new names.'

'Have they been told?'

'I've discussed it with my wife, yes. There was no sense in worrying my daughter until everything was agreed. So let's check the rest of my shopping list, shall we? The money. Let's begin with that.'

Swanson laid a document in front of him. 'As requested, a numbered account in Credit Suisse, Geneva, in your wife's new name, so they'll require a specimen signature.'

Hillsden nodded. 'Yes, we'll both have to practise those.' He studied the document closely.

'You'll see that the numbered code they chose is her birthday – seven, three, fifty six – day, month and year – as being the easiest to remember without it being written anywhere.'

'Good idea.' Hillsden looked at the amount and tried to work out if it was correct. Seven years back pay meant over two hundred and forty thousand pounds expressed in Swiss Francs – enough, he calculated, to take care of Galina and Lara if and when he fell or was pushed off the perch.

'Yes, that seems in order. Next thing. Has it been decided where we're to be relocated in England?'

'We chose a small village in Suffolk, near to Bury St Edmunds, and reasonably out of the way.'

'Isolated?'

'Yes, I suppose so, but isn't that a good thing?'

'In one way, but I have to think of my wife.' Now that the

plan was no longer conjecture but becoming reality, a splinter of doubt crept back.

'Assuming we're in business,' Swanson said, searching Hillsden's face, 'the procedure is that once the passports are complete our man at the Embassy here will take care of the exit. You'll fly to Paris, spend a week or so there, during which time all three of you will be provided with pocket money, kitted out with new clothes and various other day-to-day essentials, all British, naturally. Then enter the UK via Heathrow normally, as though a family returning from a holiday in France. What is vital is that, apart from what you stand up in, everything else has to be left here. You must divest yourselves of anything that could be traced back to Russia. Burn all personal papers. The Embassy will dispose of the rest once you've left and our Paris man will get rid of the stuff you arrive in.'

Hillsden took this in. 'Understood. Fine. Except for one thing.'

Swanson frowned. 'What?'

'The small question of my pardon.'

'Oh, that, yes.'

'That, yes. Where is it?'

'I can confirm it's in hand,' Swanson said, looking away. 'These things take time.'

Hillsden shook his head. 'Not good enough. I spelled it out for you. No pardon, no deal.'

'They're waiting for the Home Secretary to approve the wording. The latest information I have is it will be signed and given to you in Paris.'

Again Hillsden shook his head. 'No way. I want it here before we leave. Get back to them and tell them they're wasting their time.'

'I'll do what I can,' Swanson said.

'No, do better than that. Get it here or forget the whole deal. Another question, has anybody given any thought to how our disappearance from here will be explained? Although I only have one contact worth bothering about, Galina has a number

64

of friends at the university who'll notice she's gone.'

'I don't see that as a problem. You've moved to France leaving no forwarding address. Who is this contact of yours?'

'Oh, come on, Swanson, you know my file. His name's Abramov, ex-high-ranking GRU, the man who handled me when I first arrived. I guess you might say he's been my only friend. We shared a lot.'

'So? He can be told the same story,' Swanson said.

'He might not believe it.'

'Then don't tell him, just disappear.'

'That would be a mistake. You don't know my man as well as I do. A disappearance would make him suspicious, he'd follow it through. Not for any sinister motive either, just habit. You'll find this difficult to believe, Swanson, but he cares about me. We drank from the same cup, you see. Since the *coup* he's become a high-flyer, moves around a lot, dresses rather smarter than you as a matter of fact. And he was never a man you could fool for long.'

'Except that at one time you did.'

'Ah, yes,' Hillsden said, 'but then, it was life and death in those days. I didn't arrive here with a Business Class return ticket like you. It wouldn't do to disappear without saying goodbye. But leave my friend Victor to me, I'll deal with it.'

Swanson looked dubious. 'I'll have to get clearance on that. There can be no question of telling him the truth.'

Hillsden said, 'Do either of us know what that is any more? And for your information, how I tell him and what I tell him is my business.'

'This is a delicate operation. If there was any leak, the whole thing would be called off. You can't want to risk that.'

'You think risk vanishes because one shaves off a beard and moves house? You've got a lot to learn. Take-offs and landings are the moments of maximum danger, any experienced traveller knows that. Don't try and get clearance, Swanson, just stay on the ground. As you say, a delicate operation. Ask London for clearance and if anything goes wrong, your card will be marked, you'll take the can back. A promising career blighted.'

Swanson stared at him, his cheeks suddenly mottled, like a schoolboy reprimanded by the head. 'Well, I realise I lack your superior experience, but don't ever forget who's running this show.'

'My superior experience wasn't much use when the Firm decided to shaft me. I want sight of that pardon so that Galina can lodge it in her Swiss bank. Otherwise your journey was wasted.'

Swanson looked as though he was searching for a suitable, face-saving rejoinder, then thought better of it.

When Swanson left and while he waited for Galina and Lara to return from a shopping expedition, Hillsden took stock. Looking around the apartment he saw, as though for the first time, how dingy it was. At the same time it had the comfortable dinginess of familiarity and he acknowledged that part of him would miss it. One stupendous error, one blind act of belief, a belief that he needed to repay a debt of love, had altered the course of his life and brought him to this alien city, and now he was about to leave it to journey back to a place he had once counted as home. He wondered how Galina would react to their changed circumstances. Suffolk, he thought, trying to picture what it would be like. Was it flat like Norfolk and the black fen country where once he had cornered Glanville? Had they selected a picturesque cottage of a sort photographed from the best angle for *Country Life*, or one of those hideous, nondescript post-war red brick horrors with their cramped metal windows and poky rooms? He wasn't so concerned about Lara (*Laura*, I must start getting used to that) – children adapted more easily and he could picture her in the playground of some village school amongst new friends. As for Galina – correction, *Georgina* – undoubtedly she would find it more difficult, especially if I'm not around all the time, he thought. The British were curious about foreigners, never really tolerant towards anything that was outside their immediate comprehension, condescending, addressing them in louder-than-normal voices as though in addition to being foreign they were also deaf. On the credit side he would now be able to give *Georgina* (God! that would never have been his choice) some of the luxuries she had always been denied: she would get a kick out of the promised week in Paris – hotel rooms, abundant hot water – and he would enjoy showing them both around, introducing them to the uniqueness of Paris, a relief from the grimness of Russian streets. He suddenly felt light-headed, and the mood stayed with him as he went through the apartment and for the second time in his life began the task of destroying traces of his old self.

8

WUNSIEDEL, GERMANY – LONDON

A few days after Swanson returned to London, a procession of young far-Right skinheads, estimated by the police to number three hundred, and distinguished from the Red skinheads by the white laces in their Doc Marten boots, marched through the narrow streets of Wunsiedel, a small town not far from Bayreuth.

The burial place of Rudolf Hess, Wunsiedel now attracted a flow of pilgrims from the radical Right. This day, the procession, headed by standard bearers carrying banners honouring Hess as a martyr for Germany, was the object of a counter-demonstration by elements of the anti-Fascist organisation, Antifa. White-helmeted police walked alongside, keeping the two groups apart, while a police helicopter hovered overhead. Most of the Hitler disciples wore a quasi-uniform – black or brown shirts, heavy, studded belts. From time to time some of them left the procession to attack the Antifa supporters. The ensuing scuffles were quickly broken up by the police, although, surprisingly, no arrests were made. Groups of elderly local inhabitants watched with mixed feelings, as the evocative chants of 'Fatherland, we are coming' were repeated over and over again. Press photographers ran alongside; one, a British freelance journalist named O'Neill, had his Nikon knocked to the ground and, as he bent to retrieve it, he was kicked in the head, but again his assailant was not arrested, but merely pushed back into the procession. The marchers finally halted and assembled in the town square, where they were addressed by a man later identified as Gottfried Sonntag, a one-time native of East Berlin, author of *Das Zweites Deutschland (The Second Germany)* and a spokesman for the *Hilfsorganisation für Nationale Politische Gefangene und deren Angehörige e. V. (Relief Agency for National Political Prisoners and their Dependants).* Unlike his audience, Sonntag was dressed in a smart suit and had a conventional haircut. Using a megaphone to drown out the noise of the helicopter, he launched into a denunciation of the authorities, his voice often shrill and incoherent with hatred.

'The rabble who have come to mock this homage to a great patriot and peace-lover, who once stood side by side with the Führer, have renounced their German consciousness. This collection of two-legged rats shelters under the protection of the police, since, like rats, they are scared to meet us one on one. We, who are proud to display our pure Aryan blood and affirm our German stock, will one day sweep these vermin from our streets. We think of them as devils from the deepest hell conjured by Dürer. They will be left behind when we are the only rulers, marching into the future under the flag which will lead us to the end of time . . . '

His speech was punctuated by frequent outbursts of cheering and the waving of banners, while the counter-demonstrators kept up a constant barrage of taunts. The police maintained a passive role, positioned at the rear of the assembly keeping the opposing factions apart.

After the meeting ended, small groups of skinheads separated themselves from the main body, acting on a pre-arranged plan designed to put the police at full stretch, and roamed the streets looking for trouble, openly declaring their intention of 'fucking up some niggers'.

Coming across a lone foreign worker, a nineteen-year-old Kurd, they attacked him with baseball bats, stabbed him and jumped on his head. He was left lying in a pool of blood in the street a few yards from the immigrant hostel where he lodged. It was only when the skinheads had disappeared from the scene that the victim's friends, who had witnessed the beating, ventured from the hostel to recover his body. When the police and ambulance finally arrived the young Kurd was pronounced dead. Later the witnesses could only positively identify one of the attackers. Brought before the courts, the accused skinhead, the same age as the dead man, was arraigned on the lesser charge of 'second-degree murder with qualified criminal intent', his lawyer successfully pleading, as grounds for the qualification, the extraordinary defence that 'the victim's skin colour significantly contributed to the crime'.

The court accepted this and the accused youth was given a cursory sentence of five years detention in a reformatory.

Although the incident aroused little comment beyond a few regional newspapers, a monitoring unit in Copenhagen staffed by members of Amnesty logged a report broadcast on a German radio station. Sonntag's name was included in the report. In due course, along with details of other atrocities perpetrated on ethnic minorities, this was circulated in one of Amnesty's regular bulletins and, via Interpol, reached Special Branch in London, since Sonntag's movements and activities were already of interest to police forces in several European countries. The British Home Office had twice refused him entry to the United Kingdom, though on at least one occasion, using a false passport, he had managed to slip in to address a meeting of The British Movement in Wolverhampton. It was one of a number of similar incidents brought to the Home Secretary's notice in a lengthy study commissioned by the European Parliament on the plight of ethnic minorities and the growing resurgence of Fascist organisations.

Having been briefed on this and other matters, Logan chaired the regular monthly meeting of the Combined Security Committee, a homogenous collection which took in elements of MI5 and MI6, including Swanson and a Commander Pearson, together with the RUC, the SAS, the GPO Letter and Telephone Interception units, as well as the

Commissioner of the Metropolitan Police. Sir Charles Slade was also in attendance.

Logan entered the committee room without a greeting to those present, sat in the centre of the long table and poured himself some coffee from one of the Thermos flasks placed at intervals along the table. His bad mood stemmed from a hangover and his wife's revelation at breakfast that she believed their teenage son was on drugs.

'Right,' he said. 'I take it the minutes of the last meeting have been circulated? May I sign them as correct?'

There was a murmur of assent.

'Matters arising?'

'Item seven,' the Secretary prompted. Everybody turned to the page. 'The question of protection for the minor Royals.'

Logan looked up at the Commissioner. 'Hasn't that been dealt with yet?'

'Not entirely, Minister.'

'Well, either it has or it hasn't. Which is it?'

'We have a meeting at the Palace scheduled for next Tuesday. It's a question of striking a delicate balance between available manpower and cost. As you're aware, Minister, there's continuing hysteria in the tabloids on this subject.'

'Well, you know my views. In the present climate I consider there are better ways of spending public money. I doubt if any of them are in any danger, unless they act true to form and shoot themselves in the foot.' Logan sipped his coffee and grimaced. 'Who buys this stuff?'

'Central Requisitions, sir.'

'Well, it's filthy. In future we'll buy our own. I'll tell you where to go. There's a wonderful little place in Soho.' He pushed his cup to one side. 'Right, let's take the rest of the agenda. Ignore the first item for the moment and go to item two. Which department requested we should put a phone tap on this man Attenborough? Why would we tap a distinguished actor?'

'No, it isn't him, sir. Not Lord Attenborough. Our man is a northern industrialist, owns a machine tool factory.'

'I see. Well, I'll repeat the question, who requested it?'

'We did, Minister,' Commander Pearson answered.

Logan looked down the table to the speaker. 'Why?'

'We were approached by the Yanks to aid them in an investigation.'

'You mean the CIA?'

'Yes, Minister'

'Well, say so. What were the grounds?'

'They suspect he could have a connection with the supply of detonators of a type used in the Oklahoma bombing.'

Logan stared around the table. 'So we jump, do we, every time the Yanks want us to fish in our waters?'

'I don't think that's quite the position in this case, Minister,' Slade murmured when Pearson looked across the table to him.

'No? What is the position then?'

'They think they have reasonable cause to make the request.' Slade produced documentation. 'As you will note, he was previously questioned during the investigation into the Iraqi super-gun case.'

Logan scanned the document. 'Questioned, but not charged, I see.'

'No, sir. At the time, you recall, there were certain irregularities in the procedures.'

'A cock-up, you mean? Well, let's be clear about one thing, shall we? You won't find me as easy to persuade as my predecessor. While I'm sitting in this chair phone taps will only be authorised on grounds of proven national security. And I'm certainly not going to be dictated to by the Americans. I don't consider this application falls within that category. Refused. Item three.'

A few looks were exchanged before they moved on. Logan prided himself in demolishing an agenda quicker than some of his Cabinet colleagues. He was constantly sending his department reminders to keep the paperwork down and their memoranda as concise and brief as possible. This didn't apply to his own verbose papers, which were often collectors' items. He worked through the rest of the agenda and set the date of the next month's meeting.

Swanson gave a discreet cough. 'We still haven't dealt with item one, Minister.'

'I'm aware of that. I wish to take that in a more closed session. If you and Commander Pearson and the Commissioner would care to remain. Thank you, gentlemen,' he nodded to the others, who gathered up their papers and left. Sir Charles remained where he was.

'Now,' Logan began once the door had closed, 'this other business. What's the man's name?'

'Hillsden,' Swanson answered.

'Yes, well I've studied the papers very thoroughly and I have grave misgivings. You'll have to make out a very strong case to convince me. The man is a defector and wanted for murder.'

'I think if it ever came to trial, Minister, we'd all be very embarrassed.'

'In what way?'

'Evidence which came to light subsequently would lead us to believe that he was innocent of both charges.' Swanson produced a document from his briefcase and passed it across. 'Because of the nature of the material I thought this should be for your eyes only.'

Logan took the document and began to read. The other three men waited. Finally Logan looked up. 'This reference to Hillsden's memoirs. Were they ever authenticated?'

'They were instrumental in exposing Lockfield,' Swanson answered.

'Remind me. Was he the ex-Director General of MI6 who topped himself?'

'Yes.'

'Your section has always had a murky past,' Logan said testily, 'let's hope we're not subjected to any repeat performances. From this sordid little history, which reflects no credit on anybody, your lot seem to have been penetrated more times than a whore. I'm amazed you don't have a permanent plumber on the staff to plug the leaks. What makes you think this man Hillsden is now reliable? If he was wrongly accused all those years ago, he must be harbouring a considerable resentment.'

'I think that was true, Minister.'

'Why "was"?'

'I interviewed him on a number of occasions in St Petersburg and gained the firm impression that he could be appeased by the offer we're making him.'

'Money doesn't buy loyalty. I would have thought your outfit would have learned that by now.'

'Agreed, Minister. But the terms reflect a legitimate entitlement. If he chose to fight it in court a jury might well treble the damages in view of what he has suffered.'

'We could block anything like that under the Official Secrets Act,' Logan snapped.

'Not if he stayed beyond our jurisdiction.'

'Well, I don't like it. I'm being asked to give him a *carte blanche* pardon. What if it all blows up in our faces? The last thing I want is another security scandal. Let's be quite clear, this government is not going to be made to look incompetent like the Tories were. Let me ask you this, why risk somebody like Hillsden? Why take such a chance?'

It was Pearson who now took over. 'It was felt that if we are to infiltrate this organisation, Hillsden is one of the few, if not the only operative with the necessary field experience to undertake something as delicate as this. You will have noted that we intend to give him a new identity, but, more importantly, because he has been out of circulation over a long period he will have the added advantage of being an unknown quantity. I might add that prior to his incarceration in Russia he was considered one of our top operatives.'

Logan opened the document file again and stared at it afresh before turning to the Commissioner. 'What's your view?'

'Well, I agree, sir. I've studied the papers, as has the DPP and we're both convinced the murder prosecution wouldn't stand up in court. The case was based almost entirely on Lockfield's evidence. The word of a dead traitor would be demolished by any competent defence lawyer. Plus it would inevitably mean washing a lot of dirty linen.'

'Who took over from Lockfield?'

'Keating, Minister.'

'Did you get his views?'

Swanson coughed again. 'That would be somewhat difficult, Minister. He died of a heart attack some years ago.'

Logan tapped on the table, then got up and walked to the window, his back to them, 'So, what you're actually saying is that your department, despite its inflated budget, can't put its hands on any other suitable candidate? I'm still waiting for you to advance a compelling reason why I should rubber stamp this man.'

Swanson looked at the other two before answering. 'If I might say so, I think you've already answered the question yourself, Minister. It would be a disaster for the government to risk a security scandal so early in its term. We know Hillsden is an angry man – this way we buy his silence and at the same time avail ourselves of his considerable expertise. Obviously, we *could* use somebody else, but this kills two birds with one stone.'

There was a long pause before Logan spoke again. 'Has he accepted all the terms and conditions?'

'Subject to your final word, yes.'

'It'll have to come under the fifty-year rule, of course,' Logan said as he returned to the table. He felt inside his jacket pocket but before he could produce his own pen, Sir Charles handed him his.

'I'd like you to minute my misgivings, Charles. I won't say I'm signing under duress, but I remain dubious about the whole operation. There's a lot that could go wrong. *Should* it go wrong quite a few people will be staring at early retirement. Perhaps you'll bear that in mind, gentlemen.' He unscrewed the top of the pen and signed the document that Swanson now slid in front of him.

'Thank you, Minister.'

'I expect to be kept fully informed.' He emphasised the

75

word 'fully' and laid down the pen. With Sir Charles following, he left the room without another word, leaving behind an air of disapproval as pungent as stale cigar smoke.

'Finally,' the Commissioner said. 'I must say there are times when early retirement doesn't sound all that unattractive.'

Swanson gathered his papers together. 'Join the club.'

'Now all we have to do is get him home,' Pearson said.

9

CLOSE ENCOUNTERS – ST PETERSBURG

'Why tell me?' Abramov asked. His face was half in shadow, making it difficult for Hillsden to judge his expression.

'Because I trust you, Victor, and because I need an insurance policy. I thought if you kept a copy of the pardon and they ever reneged on the deal, you could make it public. For all I know it's just a trick to get me back within their jurisdiction, and then spring the trap. It's happened before, as you have good cause to know.'

They were sitting in Abramov's new Mercedes coupé, parked in a side street on the outskirts of the city. Abramov switched on the interior light to study the piece of paper he had been given. 'What an Alice-in-Disneyland world we live in, Alec. Such a generous favour they're granting you – forgiveness for a murder they committed and blamed you for. That's more Russian than British! You're right to be suspicious.'

Sitting there beside him as Abramov extinguished the light, Hillsden had a sudden feeling of *déjà vu.* 'Doesn't this remind you of something?' he said.

'Remind me? What of?'

'Moscow, that time in Gorky Park? We sat together in a car then, admittedly an inferior model, and you asked something of me. You can't have forgotten, surely?'

'Alec, my friend, we don't talk of those days any more, or the things we had to do.'

'You might not talk of them, but I don't forget them.'

Abramov shrugged and adjusted the heater fan to clear the windscreen. Hillsden leaned forward and before the efficient demister had time to work he wrote the word 'Jock' on the steamed glass. 'Does that bring it back? You used that ploy when you revealed the last piece in the puzzle, remember? That's how you finally told me who was responsible for Caroline's death.'

'Did I? What a memory you've got, Alec.'

'Should I forget that I killed a man who had once been my friend? That was what you demanded of me in return, the quid pro quo, a murder I *could* have swung for.'

'Ah, Alec, my friend, at that time we were both condemned to play out the same cynical game.' He added something in Russian – an oath, a curse? – that was unfamiliar to Hillsden. 'We had no choice. What had to be done, had to be done.'

'Meaning, you had got used to it?'

'Used to what?'

'Murder.'

Abramov brushed some ash from the lapel of his jacket. 'I obeyed orders.'

'That's what they said at Nuremberg.'

'Semantics, Alec. You have no real idea what it was like to live under our old regime. You saw only the tip of the iceberg in the dying years. But I was born under it, grew up under it and never for one moment could I ignore it. The only way to survive was to accept everything without question.'

'Everything?'

'You want a confession from me? Let me tell you something that I've never told anybody before.' He paused to light a cigarette, staring straight ahead as he exhaled the first intake of smoke. 'I turned in my brother, my younger brother.'

'How d'you mean?'

'What I say. I reported him to the authorities for distributing subversive literature. Why? Because it was him or me. I could have been tarred with his crime if I hadn't. That's how they operated. Collective guilt. One member of a

78

family was guilty, all of the family was guilty. You're a well-read man, Alec, so you know the way people disappeared without trace into the Gulags. Millions. Labour camps for homosexuals, the old, the mentally sick, the dissidents. My brother was homosexual, very pretty – he could have passed for a girl. Pretty and arrogant like so many of the people he kept company with. No, perhaps "arrogant" is the wrong word, unfair to his memory. He thought he was smart enough to beat the system, and he wasn't, nobody was, not even Beria himself.' He stubbed out the rest of the cigarette, as though the acrid taste accentuated these memories. 'I loved him, but I suppose I did not love him enough. I loved myself more. So don't think you're the only one with something to haunt you. What did you do? You disposed of a useless individual – your friend Jock was a drunken, burnt-out case, somebody who had killed many times, not only your Caroline, but others, half a dozen others – he isn't worth losing sleep over. You did everybody a service.'

'Except myself,' Hillsden said. He did not speak for a few moments, then asked: 'What happened to your brother?'

'I don't know. I never saw him again.'

'But you were safe?'

'Safe? No, it didn't work like that. I was still tainted by association, under suspicion, watched all the time. I had to work extra hard to establish my reliability. You helped my rehabilitation. Turning you was a feather in my cap.'

He took out his gold cigarette case again, this time offering Hillsden one and lighting it for him. 'Go home by all means, Alec, but forget the past. Of course I'll take care of this for you, you know that. I'm offended you ever doubted me.'

He smiled and patted Hillsden on the thigh, but Hillsden was still digesting what he had just been told. As he jolted his lungs with a shot of nicotine he felt bile at the back of his throat. It was a long trail they had both travelled to a dead end. Future generations would study the KGB's and the Firm's Dead Sea Scrolls of betrayals and be stupefied, not only at the horrors revealed, but the sheer futility of it all. The meek never inherited the earth – that was just a sop hawked by the Jesus salesmen – the real world was run by men who looked like janitors in a tenement block: no casting director would have given Stalin a leading role other than as a small-time thug; the hideous Ceausescu and his wife were bit players in a Hammer movie; Lenin, only fit for playing the town schoolmaster who molested children; Honecker, perfect for a grubby little pimp. The list was endless – Dzerzhinsky, Himmler, Beria, Idi Amin, Papa Doc – how did they achieve and hang on to power for so long, all these squalid nonentities who kept whole countries in chains, the rest of the world on edge? It was as if some mad scientist had produced a race of mutants and programmed them to be leaders, having first removed the compassion factor and substituted a quartz-driven mechanism of terror.

'Wasn't there ever a moment when you questioned what you were doing?' he asked. 'In the still, small hours of the night, when you weren't wearing the uniform, what thoughts did you have?'

'One had night thoughts, yes. Bad dreams, very bad dreams. But, you see, when you woke up there was no door you could open which led out. You in the West have never known that. There was always an escape route for you. Isn't that true?'

Hillsden nodded. 'You're right. We always took the high moral ground. Officially, we were incapable of acting in the same way as you. Crap, of course. All prisons have to have warders. Had the Nazis conquered us in '40, we'd have produced our own crop of gauleiters, depend on it. It was just that we were never put to the test. Look at the French, it's only now that they are acknowledging some of their skeletons. And we weren't as white as the driven snow. We arrested and interned without trial.'

'I didn't know that.'

'Oh, yes. We had something called regulation 18b . . . Isn't it funny how all such laws hide behind numbers?'

'But you didn't have a deliberate policy of killing your own people.'

Hillsden said, 'Oh, we didn't shoot them and bury them in mass graves, we just shortened their lives in other ways.'

While he talked he fiddled with the glove compartment. It sprang open to reveal a revolver clipped to the shelf. He took it out to examine it.

'I see you don't leave anything to chance, Victor.'

'Not the way things are here.'

'Perhaps you should leave as well?'

'In time, in time maybe, when I've made enough.'

He took the gun from Hillsden and checked the magazine. 'People like us, Alec, who led double lives . . . what d'you think now? You have regrets? I sense you do.'

'More a feeling of waste. There must have been a moment – maybe it was, I don't know, Yalta perhaps – when three old men, one near death in a wheelchair, one exhausted and the third a certified monster – and between them they fucked up. All the effort, all the millions of dead, the bombed cities, for what? There was that moment when they could have changed it all, but instead they condemned us to another forty years of horror. You were fooled, I was fooled, the madness went on in a different form. The wealth that could have transformed the world spent on the ultimate weapon.'

'Which kept the peace,' Abramov interrupted.

'What peace? The killing didn't stop.'

'All the same, Alec, we're still here.'

'And a new monster waiting in the wings.'

'Of course, what else do you expect?' Abramov said, placing the gun on the top of the dashboard. 'Remember that story we all told? If the bomb wiped out the world and there were only a hundred people left alive, within twenty-four hours somebody would have appointed himself leader and claimed privileges.' He stroked the soft leather upholstery. 'Of course, if you're still undecided, then stay here, join forces with me and you could be driving one of these babies. It's all here for the taking. Make clay while the sun shines.'

'Hay,' Hillsden corrected. 'Make hay. You always did get those things wrong.' There was a fug of cigarette smoke in the car and he pressed the switch to let down the window on his side.

'Whatever. Listen, have you any idea of the opportunities out there? Give you an example. Yesterday, I did a deal with an ex-nuclear physicist for a truckload of Levis. A year ago he was running a whole plant in the Ukraine, now he's happy to take ten per cent on black-market jeans, no questions asked. I'll have off-loaded the entire lot by the end of the week and made myself another Mercedes. That's the only game in town, Alec.'

'What about protection?'

'What about it?'

'Do you have to pay?'

Abramov smiled. 'Put it this way. I didn't sever all contacts with my past. Memories are long here, Alec, and nobody's quite sure that the old order is completely dead and buried. I have my own protection – files I smuggled out ahead of the mob, safely hidden, as will be the insurance policy you've just given me.'

He turned the ignition key. 'Don't you just love the noise of that engine? I used to dream of owning one of these.'

'I've never cared much for cars,' Hillsden said. 'Except as a means of getting from one place to another.'

'That's because you've always had a choice.'

'Probably.'

'You said yourself you're not sure of London's true motive. So what is yours?'

'That's a good question. Maybe I don't have one beyond a homing instinct.'

'How about your wife, how does she feel?'

'Perhaps she's the reverse of what you told me. Maybe, like your brother, she loves me more than she loves herself . . . And that's ironic in a way. It was love that brought me here in the first place. Love's always a risk, isn't it?'

'So they tell me. I wouldn't know. Emotional involvements get in the way, I've found.'

He was just about to put the Mercedes into gear when two shadowy figures appeared on either side of the car. Abramov reacted fast, hitting the power button which locked all the doors automatically. 'Close your window,' he shouted, but as Hillsden fumbled to find the right button a hand reached in and jerked his head back. Abramov did not hesitate, but fired across Hillsden at point blank range. The unknown assailant was blown backwards into the darkness as though whisked away on a stage trick-wire. Abramov threw the gun into Hillsden's lap and slammed the gear shift into drive. The Mercedes surged forward, catching the second attacker a glancing blow before he could jump out of the way. The whole sequence of events had taken less than twenty seconds and as Hillsden recovered from the shock and suddenness of it all Abramov shouted: 'Use the gun if any more of them come at us. They usually hunt in packs. My fault for stopping there so long.'

'You think you killed him?'

'I hope so.' Abramov was smiling. 'One less.'

As they sped on back into the centre of the city, Hillsden knew that whatever unknowns lay ahead a choice had been made for him.

10

LONDON NIGHT LIFE

Sir Raymond Charters stepped out of his custom-made, private London taxi in front of the Ritz Hotel, Piccadilly. He wore a wide-brimmed black trilby and dark glasses, even though it was evening. Like the taxi, this was a personal idiosyncrasy, two trademarks which, together with the suits he had hand-made in Rome, he felt set him apart. Some passers-by might have glanced twice at his chauffeur and wondered why a gent like Charters had a uniformed bruiser to drive him around: the two did not seem to go together, although the London of 1997 had seen a marked increase in the number of private security companies who supplied bodyguards to the great and the good.

The Chairman and Chief Executive of Charters International, a company owning a score of European newspapers and magazines, together with a Dutch publishing house, stakes in satellite television and a tele-communication network, Charters carried his fifty-nine years well, helped by daily work-outs with a personal trainer in the company's health club and a clever tailor. Knighted during the Thatcher years after some pointed donations to the Tory coffers, he had enjoyed the Iron Lady's approval as a man not afraid to take on the unions. He was well regarded by City analysts and the larger institutional investors, and was courted by the gossip columnists for his flamboyant life style. As well as owning a London town house in the Boltons, he farmed a large estate in

Yorkshire, travelled everywhere in the company's private jet (which included a Maxwellian device he had purloined from the late Captain Bob, namely a switch above his seat that enabled him to bypass his pilot and speak directly to air traffic controllers, berating them if he was kept in a holding pattern for too long). But so far his wealth had not bought him the total social acceptance he craved.

Ignoring the hotel commissionaire who stepped forward, he was saluted by the doorman at the adjacent Ritz Casino. As a frequent visitor to the tables he was a welcome high-roller and treated with the staff's customary courtesy. Signing in downstairs he first looked to see whether the gambling salon was busy before going to the cloakroom. He had a fetish about cleanliness, often showering three times a day, and now he scrubbed his hands after relieving himself and applied some Dunhill cologne to his face. The cloakroom attendant brushed his jacket and was rewarded with a five-pound tip.

Charters entered the salon and was annoyed to find that the table he normally played was occupied by a group of foreign gamblers. One of the assistant managers came forward to greet him and offered to open another table for him. Charters accepted with ill grace and asked to be given twenty thousand pounds. He changed one of the five-thousand pound lozenges into hundred pound chips, and began playing, using a system that allegedly had been Winston Churchill's – betting on alternate spins of the wheel and then placing a maximum neighbour bet on the last but one winning number. Like most systems it was fallible, but Charters used it religiously and he won sufficiently often not to lose faith in it.

This was not to be one of his successful nights. After one win early in the session, he lost steadily, going through his first twenty thousand and calling for a further twenty, signing the cheque brought to him with a scrawl. A senior manager appeared to keep a watching brief and when other less affluent players drifted in from the dining room, they were tactfully diverted to other tables. When Charters was down to a few thousand, he switched from his favoured system and began to back single numbers *en plein* with maximum bets. He struck lucky once, then went cold again. He got up abruptly, scattering his remaining chips. 'Cash me in.' He flung the words at the cashier.

While waiting for his money, he wandered to the next table and there, like many an unsuccessful gambler, he could not resist a final bet, placing a hundred pounds cash bet on his favourite number, twenty-three. It lost. The manager appeared by his side and Charters pocketed the six sealed packets of brand-new notes for his cashed chips and walked out without a word. Win or lose he was always the same, showing neither pleasure nor annoyance, for he prided himself on never letting anybody know his true feelings.

His taxi was waiting outside and Harry, his driver, was the recipient of his ill-humour. 'D'you know a club called Tudor's?' Charters snapped.

'Yes, sir. Greek Street.'

'Your style, no doubt. Well, take me there.'

They set off in the direction of Hyde Park Corner.

'Not that way, you stupid oaf. Make a U-turn. I haven't got all night.'

Harry complied. He had been on call without a break since ten o'clock that morning, but Charters's staff were expected to suffer such inconveniences without complaint.

The amplified sound hit Charters like a wall. There were three couples clinging to each other on Tudor's small dance floor. When his eyes had become accustomed to the darkness he made his way to a table in a corner where a man called Carstairs, middle-aged, of nondescript appearance, rose to greet him as he approached.

'Good evening, Sir Raymond.'

There was something more than servility in his voice, something approaching fear.

The owner of the club came up. 'This is a great pleasure, Sir Raymond. Are we eating tonight, sir? Can I send a waitress?'

'Yes, do that.'

'Something to drink meantime?'

'A bottle of Chablis, if it's really chilled.'

'Of course, Sir Raymond. Right away.'

Charters eyed the couples on the floor, picking out an American actress who had once achieved a certain notoriety in a long-running sit-com. She was dancing with a long-haired youth half her age who looked more feminine than she did.

'I used to follow her series,' Carstairs said, seeing Charters studying the couple.

'Mutton dressed as lamb.'

'Oh, do you think so? I'd say she's worn rather well.'

'In this light, maybe. I wouldn't fancy waking up and finding it on my pillow.'

A waitress arrived with the drinks at this point. She was wearing a scanty Tudor-style dress which revealed a lot of cleavage. When she had opened the wine and Charters had sampled it without comment, just a nod of the head, she waited for the meal order.

'Bring me a plate of smoked salmon and scrambled eggs. I want the salmon cut wafer thin and the eggs runny.'

'And for you, sir?'

'Nothing, thank you,' Carstairs said. He was drinking whisky. When the waitress left he raised his glass to Charters, but the toast was ignored. There was a certain sad seediness about Carstairs – flecks of dandruff on the shoulders of his blue suit, a creased shirt collar.

'So, what did you want to see me about so urgently?'

Carstairs framed his reply carefully. 'Well, we've run into a slight problem, sir.' His hand clutching the whisky glass had nails bitten to the quick.

'What sort of problem?'

Although there was no need, given the loud music, Carstairs lowered his voice. 'Nothing that can't be speedily rectified, sir, but I thought it best to bring it to your personal attention.'

'What sort of problem?' Charters repeated.

'Well, unfortunately the consignment of Sonntag's book

was seized at Harwich.'

'You call that slight? Why was it ever sent to Harwich? I gave orders for it to be flown in at night to the usual drop.'

'Yes, I agree, sir. Somehow, your instructions were not relayed to the right person. An unfortunate misunderstanding. By the time I discovered what had happened the shipment was already *en route*.' Carstairs took a large gulp of Scotch.

'Who made the mistake?'

'Van Elst. Usually so reliable.'

'Can they be traced to us?'

'Oh, no, sir. They were documented as fax rolls and the shipper's name was false. I ordered another print-run immediately.'

'Well, cancel it. Have them put the text on disc and brought over by courier. Better still, bring it yourself.'

Some of the Scotch dribbled down Carstairs's chin. 'Me?'

'Yes. And get it here by Monday.'

'I don't think that's possible.'

'Make it possible. And find out who leaked it.'

The hapless Carstairs made an attempt to defend himself. 'I'd be amazed if it was a leak, sir. More Customs being unusually vigilant in my opinion.'

'I'm not interested in your opinion. Somebody must have tipped them off. Who? I want to know.'

'I have the utmost trust in everybody.'

'That's where you're a fool,' Charters said. He broke off as his food was served, waiting until it was placed in front of him before continuing. 'You think I trust you? I trust you until a mistake like this, then I start to ask whether that trust is misplaced.'

'You've no reason to doubt me,' Carstairs said. He looked around the dance floor as though expecting someone to challenge the statement. The actress and her young boyfriend drifted close, kissing each other and trailing a heady perfume.

'Don't depend on it,' Charters said. 'There's no room for mistakes in our operation.' He forked some scrambled eggs into his mouth, grimaced and pushed the plate to one side. 'Put this right or your days are numbered. And another time, don't drag me to a place like this even for good news. Just deal with the problem and deal with it fast. I want that disc here Monday first thing.' He got up abruptly and pushed his way across the dance floor, bumping into a couple. Concerned at seeing him leave so abruptly, the club owner stopped him on the way out.

'Leaving so soon? Nothing wrong I hope, Sir Raymond?'

'No, everything's fine,' Charters said without stopping. The owner went over to Carstairs.

'Was there a problem with Sir Raymond's food?'

'No, nothing like that, it was just that he was late for another meeting,' Carstairs answered, but there was no conviction in his voice.

'Can we bring you another drink?'

'No, thank you. I have to be going myself.' He waited for the bill and settled it with cash, and was halfway to the door when he went back and picked up the receipt.

Outside in the street he looked both ways before walking to Soho Square where he had parked his car. He sat behind the steering wheel for several minutes, trying to stifle a rising nausea. Then he opened the door and vomited into the gutter.

11

HOMECOMING

Swanson met them in Heathrow's Terminal 4 arrivals hall, wearing his peeved expression – presumably, Hillsden thought, to signify that such a menial assignment was beneath him.

They had passed through passport control without incident, although, approaching the desk, Hillsden had felt suddenly naked without his beard.

Greeting them abruptly with, 'Heathrow is a nightmare,' Swanson shepherded them across the road to the car park. 'It's about time they scrapped the lot and began again.' He led them to a black Ford Mondeo. A much younger man who was seated behind the wheel got out as they arrived and opened the boot to take their hand luggage. He nodded at Hillsden, but said nothing by way of greeting.

'This is Hadley,' Swanson said. 'One of the team. He's driving you part of the way. I'll contact you once you've settled in. No snags, I hope?'

'No,' Hillsden said. 'I'm just getting used to the smell again.'

'What smell?'

'England.'

After helping Galina and Lara into the rear seats, Hillsden climbed in the front. As Hadley reversed out he saw Swanson walk to a Jaguar saloon.

'We don't rate a Jag, I see,' Hillsden said, breaking the ice with the silent Hadley.

'No. There's only one in the car pool and Swanson claims it as his own. Anyway, this is less conspicuous.'

'It's odd for me, sitting on this side.'

'How's that?'

'Driving on the left again.'

'Oh, I see. Yes, of course.'

Once clear of the airport they crawled towards London, negotiating the snaking avenues of cones that transformed the M4 into an assault course for formula one drivers.

The new clothes Hillsden had been provided with in Paris still felt stiff, reminding him of the one time, aeons ago, when he had taken part in some amateur theatricals (a now almost-forgotten play, *The Passing of the Third Floor Back*). On that occasion, forced to wear a hired suit reeking of cleaning fluid, he had experienced the same feeling of being detached from his normal self. Sitting in the front passenger seat, he fingered his now soft, beardless chin as though that, too, belonged to a stranger. It was curious, he thought, but when you shaved off a beard the revealed skin looked as though you had lived for a period under a stone.

'Where are we heading for?' he asked.

'Ultimately, Suffolk.'

'Yes, I know that, but where in Suffolk?'

'A place called Walsham le Willows.'

Hillsden repeated the name. 'Never heard of it, but it sounds romantic.' He swivelled to look at his wife. 'Hear that, sweetheart?'

'It's just a small village,' Hadley said.

'Swanson didn't really introduce us, did he?'

'No, he's not given to politeness.'

'But it's Hadley, is it?'

'Yes.'

'How long have you been with the Firm?'

'Seven years.'

'As long as I've been away,' Hillsden said. He felt suddenly elated, like somebody waking after a long illness to find himself recovered, taking in every passing scene, anxious not to miss anything. At intervals they passed signs informing road users that 'Construction Operatives Are At Work'.

'What do they signify?'

'Oh, that's the new, politically correct term for what used to be called "navvies",' Hadley replied.

'Where are they? Can't see any.'

'No, that's another innovation, you'll find. Nearly every road in the country is under repair, but nobody actually mends them, they just put out lots of cones.'

Hillsden turned to see if Galina and Lara were sharing his excitement. His daughter was wide-eyed, taking in her first glimpses of a landscape that had hitherto only been a name in a school textbook, but Galina seemed withdrawn.

'Okay, darling?' he asked.

Galina nodded. During the week they had spent in Paris, Hillsden had urged her to spoil herself with hair and beauty treatments, a luxury she had been denied for years. Looking at her he thought how much he loved her, suddenly conscious of the sacrifice she had made for his sake. I'm home, he thought, but she's homeless.

When they finally reached the Hammersmith flyover Hillsden looked for known landmarks, but he recognised little except the old Victorian church standing in the Broadway island. Now it was surrounded and dwarfed by new office blocks, on one side a gaunt pink monolith and on the other an extraordinary bulbous, glass structure.

'What the hell's that?'

'It's called the Ark, it apparently slipped through without Prince Charles noticing.' The comment went over Hillsden's head.

'Like the Bible?' Lara chirped, head poking between the two front seats. 'Are there animals in it?' But Hadley had to brake sharply and did not respond.

More roadworks slowed their progress again. Examples of graffiti were everywhere: faded exhortations to *Ban Trident* which recalled memories of the once annual march from Aldermaston – how remote that moral gesture now seemed,

Hillsden thought. Further along a humorist had been at work, modifying *God so loved the world He gave His only Son* to *He gave His only Sony*. A group of winos sprawled on a thin patch of grass by the roadside, passing each other a shared bottle, mirroring the derelicts Hillsden had left behind in St Petersburg, while above them revolving hoardings advertised aspects of a life style they would never know. At the traffic lights Hadley waved away a youth with a Mohican haircut who attempted to wash the windscreen. The youth thumped his annoyance on a side panel as he went to the next car.

Progressing towards Knightsbridge, they entered the world of anonymous hotels: once elegant town houses now displayed torn signs on their flaking porticoes: *Room for the Night £25, Vacancies, Open 24 Hours.* Further down the Brompton Road, outside the modern hospital, elderly Arab men wearing slippers shuffled along the pavement, their veiled wives a few, dutiful paces behind. Watching the flow of pedestrians as they passed Harrods, it seemed to Hillsden that the majority of young girls had opted to dress as medieval troubadours, wearing abbreviated tunics over thick black tights that accentuated their arses, their tights ending in heavy boots that had once been the hallmark of Teddy Boys, as though they were determined to obliterate all traces of their sex.

Compared to the French capital, it seemed to Hillsden that London was cramped, pushed in on all sides and he felt cheated. His initial elation – like that of a lover keeping a long-delayed reunion – began to slip away.

'Wouldn't it have been quicker to miss the centre of London?' he asked.

'Like Swanson said, I'm only taking you part of the way,' Hadley answered.

'So where are we going now?'

'East End. Forest Gate. There's a safe house there. Then Rotherby's taking you the rest of the way.'

Hillsden could not keep the surprise out of his voice. 'You mean *Colonel* Rotherby? Is he still with us? I imagined he'd have fallen off the perch by now.'

'No. The Firm still enjoys his presence.'

'God! Dear old Rotherby, eh? We used to call him Lawrence of Wapping because he owned up to a turgid admiration of T.E.'

'T.E.?'

'Aircraftman Shaw, if you prefer.' Then, when Hadley still did not get it, he elaborated. 'Lawrence of Arabia.'

'Oh. Why him?'

'Never quite figured it out. We used to put it down to a romantic streak. I think he served in the desert during the war. Well, it'll be great to see old Rothers again. That's cheered me up no end.'

Hadley had to stop at traffic lights. 'And why Lawrence of *Wapping*? What's the connection?'

'Ah, well, the time I'm talking about we operated from a bogus wine importers in that part of the world. Rather a good cover in that we could help ourselves to some of the stock. Just plonk of course – there was an economy drive on even then.'

Passing under Admiralty Arch from the Mall, Hadley edged between cars coming from all directions as he manoeuvred the Ford around Trafalgar Square and headed for the Strand. It was getting dark by now and grey clouds of pigeons rose and headed for their night roosts. This sight brought a cry of excitement from Lara.

'Look, Papa!' she exclaimed in Russian.

'In English, sweetheart. From now onwards, always in English, remember?'

'Sorry, sorry, I forgot. But look how many there are!'

'Bloody sky rats,' Hadley muttered. 'They're diseased, you know, foul everything with their droppings. Breed as fast as rabbits. Completely ruined the window boxes outside my office. I want the Firm to recruit some hawks.'

Hillsden noticed that the drifters still gathered on the steps of St Martin's, and, in the Strand, where yet more roadworks again slowed their progress, the homeless were already taking up their positions in shop doorways, arranging their cardboard bedding as the commuters passed with heads averted, hurrying towards Charing Cross Station and the comforts of suburbia.

They picked up speed again as they reached the Aldwych and passed Bush House, where once a foreign journalist had been murdered by the tip of a poisoned umbrella, like an expendable featured player in a James Bond movie. They eventually gained the Mile End Road, making the transition from the anonymous office blocks and modern architectural glitz to the shabby wasteland of the East End with its boarded-up shops and general air of decay. The Luftwaffe had done its best to obliterate the old, tight-knit Cockney communities, and for fifty years bureaucracy and the speculators' greed had combined to squander the opportunity for a renaissance. There was little glitz here, just crumbling squalor punctuated by fenced vacant lots. Even the parked cars revealed the class divisions that England had never been able to renounce; gone were the Mercedes and BMWs that choked the West End, here there were only battered relics, their sides blotched with amateur repairs like vivid birthmarks. The pavements were strewn with junk-food cartons and plastic bags of refuse that awaited collection. Aimless groups of youths slouched on street corners, impatient for the night's violence.

As they reached the outskirts of Forest Gate in the gloom, Hadley asked him to check a street map. 'Ridley Road is what we're looking for. Close to Wanstead Flats.'

The parallel, tree-lined streets of Forest Gate had once boasted rows of genteel terraced houses but, thinned out early in the Blitz, their scars had long since been built over with a variety of nondescript post-war dwellings, some of which had already begun to self-destruct. Here and there, the lower windows were crudely shuttered against squatters; in many, the front gardens had been concreted over to provide off-street parking for rusting hulks. Turbaned Sikhs trod the uneven pavements with an air of sadness; bands of children still played a makeshift game of football in the gloom, using rolled-up coats for goals, their amusement constantly interrupted by passing traffic.

With Hillsden acting as navigator, they finally arrived at their destination. The safe house in Ridley Road backed on to an old cemetery and once might well have been a vicarage, for it stood alone and was larger than its neighbours, though it shared their look of neglect. A pollarded plane tree stood in the front garden behind a moth-eaten privet hedge. The railings had been shorn off close to the ground; only the iron gate remained, hanging at an angle from the one remaining hinge.

Hadley parked the Ford a short distance away and, having made sure no bystanders were paying any attention, motioned for Hillsden and his family to get out. They traced an uneven path to the rear of the house. Light from a street lamp glistened on the broken glass of a derelict greenhouse and an emaciated black cat scurried away at their approach. Hadley led the way and knocked four times on the frosted glass of the kitchen door, giving what Hillsden took to be a prearranged signal. There was a pause and then a light went on inside and the outline of a figure was projected on to the glass. Hadley repeated the same knock. The light was extinguished before the door was opened.

'Welcome back,' a voice said, and they stepped forward into darkness.

A torchlight came on and Hillsden turned to confront a familiar face.

'Well, who would have thought it, Colonel?'

'Who indeed!' Rotherby embraced him, kissing him on both cheeks, in a rare show of emotion. 'Go on through, all of you.' Using the torch, he ushered them through the kitchen and a small hallway into the living room. The inside of the house belied the exterior, for it was comfortably, though not luxuriously furnished, like the home of some white-collar worker forced by reason of his job to live in a location not of his choosing.

'I thought,' Rotherby said, going straight to the drinks

table, 'that the occasion demanded something a little special, Alec . . . My God! Listen to me, a bloomer straight off . . . Robert, Robert, Robert! Get your act together Rotherby, you stupid twit.' He turned to Galina. 'Forgive me, Mrs Bartlett, completely forgetting my manners, but seeing your husband again after such a long time . . . Welcome to England. And you, my dear,' bending to pat Lara on the head, 'I've got something you might like.' He produced a box containing a doll. Lara looked to her father to get his approval before taking the gift. 'Such a beautiful little face,' Rotherby said. 'You must be proud of her, Robert. God damn it! It's ridiculous calling you Robert, you're Alec to me and you always will be. Don't worry,' he added, as he caught Hadley's warning glance, 'I won't forget when we're outside, but this place is safe enough, swept once a week. Now then.' He produced a bottle. 'Johnnie Walker. Not Red label, not Black label, but *Blue* label, old son. I told housekeeping to lay in the best. Don't suppose you've seen one of these for a while.'

'Not ever,' Hillsden said. 'Didn't know it existed, Colonel.'

'You haven't changed.'

'That's not what I wanted to hear,' Hillsden said. 'I thought I'd returned a master of disguise.'

'I meant about calling me Colonel. You always did take the micky. No, the appearance is very good. Wouldn't exactly fool me, but it'd pass muster to strangers. However,' he said, unscrewing the bottle, 'let's baptise this. How about you, Georgina . . . There! Got that one right . . . Would you care for whisky?'

'Not really,' Galina said, 'but thank you all the same.'

'A glass of wine perhaps?'

'That would be nice.'

'Red or white, we've got both.'

'Red, please.'

'And what about the young lady?'

'Have you got a Coke?' Hillsden asked.

'Ah! That could be beyond us. Lime juice perhaps?'

'Try her.'

'Could I use the bathroom?' Galina asked.

'Of course, yes, sorry. Hadley show them where, will you? Second on the left.'

The moment Hadley left the room with Galina and Lara, Rotherby dropped his voice. 'Can't get used to them being so young. And what did you make of our friend Swanson?' Before Hillsden could answer, he added, 'Too tight-arsed for me. Not my style. Not like the old team, not like Jock and old Wadders.'

'No,' Hillsden said, accepting the glass of whisky.

'Let's drink to them. And Caroline. Three of the best.'

'Yes,' Hillsden said.

'While you were over there, did you ever find out what happened to Jock in the end? I know he was meant to be dead, but then somebody reported a sighting.'

Hillsden hesitated before answering. Was Rotherby ferreting? Had the truth ever filtered back? 'No, he was dead. I got that at first hand,' he said flatly.

'Betrayed, like Caroline, by that bastard Lockfield. And for what? Now that it's all over, for what? Cat and mouse, Alec, old son, but did the cat get the mouse or vice versa?'

'Who knows?'

'And mind you, Keating wasn't exactly another Rebecca of Sunnybrook Farm, he was another devious bastard. It's made me very cynical in my old age. Now I'm just treading water until pension time. Roll on the bus pass.'

'You never took a bus in your life, Colonel.'

'True, true. How well you know me. God! It's good to have you back. What was it like over there?'

'Not too hot.'

'I can imagine. I never believed you were a scrimshanker, needless to say. I always figured that Lockfield had it in for you. Events proved me right. But at least you came home in one piece, and with a wife.'

'Yes.'

'And a daughter.'

'Yes.'

'Well, that's more than I've got. Cecily died.' He downed his whisky and looked past Hillsden. 'And we never had any children. Well, that's a lie. I had a child once. Not by Cecily and not in the sight of God. Happened when I was stationed out in Malaysia. Took up with a girl there. Rotherby's gone native was the word. Sweet girl, much younger than me. Never told Cecily, of course. No point, didn't want to rock the boat. I sent money for ten years or more when I got home. Then, one day, word got back she and the child had been murdered by guerrillas. I often think about it.' He went to pour himself another drink, then stopped. 'Better not. I'm driving and the Old Bill's very hot on that these days. Course the pubs stay open longer now and you can shop on Sundays. Progress, old son.'

'I never thought of you as an adulterer,' Hillsden said, then immediately regretted the remark. He tried to retrieve his embarrassment by adding. 'Me, yes, but not you.'

'Well, you can't go by appearances.'

Now that he had a chance to study Rotherby more intently, Hillsden saw remains of the man he had once worked alongside: thinner now, the cheeks hollowed, the sparse hair swept straight across to hide the balding crown and the hand gripping the whisky glass mottled with age spots. It was like being at a school reunion, where you come face to face with your contemporaries after a long separation and are amazed how much they have aged. It never occurs to you that undoubtedly they are thinking the same thing about you.

The others returned at that point and as soon as everybody had finished their drinks Hadley looked at his wrist-watch. 'Don't leave it too late,' he cautioned. 'You've still got a long journey, and I expect the child's tired.'

Lara looked up from playing with her new doll. 'No, I'm not,' she said.

'Yes, you're right,' Rotherby agreed. 'Just a couple more things I have to discuss with Alec, and then we'll get on our way.'

Hillsden followed him out of the room and was led into a

small study off the hallway. Rotherby went to a desk and took out a wallet. 'Lovely money, chum. Five hundred in used notes as a float. Have to sign for them, I'm afraid. Driving licence. There'll be a car registered in your name waiting in Suffolk. Credit cards. I had one done for the wife, too. Is she familiar with how they work?'

'I'll show her.'

'Never found Cecily had any problem grasping their use. And don't worry about how the accounts get paid, they'll be automatically debited to the Firm's closed account.'

'Oh, good.'

'Then deducted from your pay,' Rotherby added as he opened another drawer in the desk and removed a handgun and a leather shoulder holster. 'And lastly . . .'

'I need that, do I? I've never carried one before.'

'The rules have changed, old son. Quite a few of the police forces go around armed now. When you get settled in they'll give you some practice on the range.'

Hillsden took the gun from him and examined it.

'Magazine releases from the bottom. Safety catch here. Two trigger pressures. German. Very reliable, stop anything.' He watched as Hillsden detached the magazine and put it in a pocket.

'What am I?' Hillsden asked. 'Has that been decided? I notice the new style passports don't give occupations like the old ones.'

'No. Well, I don't have the answer to that. That hasn't come down from on high yet. I think that's the lot. Put everything in this holdall. Oh, and sign the receipt. Our new masters are sticklers for bloody paperwork. Gone are the days when we used to get paid in golden sovs, no questions asked.'

'Are you filing reports nowadays? What happened to your philosophy?'

'Did I ever have one?'

'Yes, don't you remember? You used to say, "If you don't write it, they can't read it. If they can't read it, they can't copy it. If they can't copy it, they can't steal it, and if they can't steal it, they can never hang you for it. " Or words to that effect.'

'Did I say that?'

'Frequently . . . How different are things at the Firm?'

'Well, the wind of change blew through the corridors for a while. They appointed a headmistress.'

'Yes, so I read. How was that?'

'Interesting. I was all for her. A big improvement on that other old woman, Lockfield. Didn't last though. I think she frightened the Establishment. The biggest change is we're no longer looking for Reds under the beds.'

'So what occupies the Firm these days?'

'Well, we've got the Islamic fundamentalists, the anti-Turks, followed by the anti-Cypriots, nuclear smugglers, and the neo-Nazis to keep us in business. Trade is still quite brisk.'

'And you've no idea what they've got in mind for me, why they brought me back?'

Rotherby looked him straight in the eye. 'Truthfully, no, and I wouldn't hesitate to tell you if I had. Hey, we'd better get going! Don't want to make Hadley late for his Horlicks.'

They rejoined the others and after telling Hadley to lock up the house when he left, Rotherby took them through the unkempt garden and through a gate in the wall. This led to an alleyway where another car, this time a Volvo, was parked. 'We're lucky,' he said.

'Why lucky?'

'Lucky it's still got four wheels. They say a car is stolen every thirteen seconds in the Greater London area.'

He de-activated the alarm and they transferred the luggage from the Ford. Lara was asleep as soon as they were under way.

'How long will it take?' Hillsden asked.

'Shouldn't be too bad at this time of night, and I know a few short cuts. Lived in that neck of the woods myself once. Cecily kept dogs then. Bred them. Setters. Lethal halitosis, farted a lot as they got older, bed always covered in hairs. Substitute children. Prefer cats myself.'

They drove on in silence for a while. When Hillsden

glanced over his shoulder he saw that Galina, too, was asleep.

'Thanks for buying Laura that doll. Thoughtful of you.'

'My pleasure. How d'you feel?' Rotherby asked.

'D'you mean, am I tired?'

'No, how d'you feel about being home?'

'Strange. Rather like *The Passing of the Third Floor Back*.'

Rotherby gave him a look.

'It's a play I once acted in, for my sins,' Hillsden explained. 'That was the title.'

'You always were a literary man, Alec. Never saw it myself. What was it about?'

'The second coming,' Hillsden said, staring beyond the headlight beams into the darkness.

12

COUNTRY FOLK

It was the silence that woke Hillsden the first morning in the new house. For a few moments he had no idea where he was. Thin sunlight slanted across the uneven bare walls and a moth fluttered against a window pane. There were age-blackened beams above his head and a scent he could not place immediately – heady and sweet, unlike the smells of the St. Petersburg apartment – but as he sat up in the bed he saw that somebody (had Rotherby mentioned a housekeeper?) had placed a bunch of freesias in a vase on the chest of drawers. Galina was still asleep and he eased back the duvet carefully and swung his bare feet on to the peg-boarded floor, padding his way to the window. It had been too dark for him to get any clear idea of the countryside when they arrived, but now he saw scattered cottages, smoke from their chimneys drifting straight upwards. The vista reminded him of the posters that used to adorn pre-war railway stations. This is the England I've missed, he thought, and emotions he had hidden surfaced, so that, for a moment, he could easily have given way to tears. He remained by the window a long time, noting that it was double-glazed and had security locks fitted

Leaving the bedroom, he used the bathroom, with its old-fashioned taps and deep cast-iron bath, stained with lime scale where the tap had leaked. Then he looked inside Lara's room; like her mother she was still fast asleep, one arm thrown across the new doll that Rotherby had given her. Have

I done the right thing for them both, bringing them here? he thought, the innocence of his sleeping daughter reviving doubts.

He went downstairs to the kitchen which was warm and well stocked with all the basics and made himself a cup of coffee, boiling the water on a gas-fired Aga which, thoughtfully, had been left ignited. The rest of the kitchen was fairly rustic and he went around opening cupboards and trying sink taps, finding the water had a silky, country softness to it when he splashed his face. Leading off the kitchen was a utility room equipped with a deep-freeze, a washing machine and dryer, which he knew would please Galina. Taking his coffee mug with him, he went on a tour of the rest of the downstairs. There were two adjoining living rooms, both with low ceilings, the larger of the two having an inglenook fireplace. What pleased him most were bookshelves on either side of the fireplace housing a small library. He lingered in front of them and was somewhat surprised to find a section devoted to the global resurgence of neo-Nazi movements, with titles such as *The Fourth Reich* and *The Coming Racial War*. Surveying the rest of the room, he took in the nondescript, but comfortable furniture, the matching sofa and chairs covered in flowered chintz. Whoever had been responsible for the freesias in the bedroom had placed another bunch on the windowsill. Ducking his head under a slanting doorway he went into the hallway. There was a double porch to a front door fitted with two Chubb, double-mortice locks, the frame reinforced with a steel surround. He was still inspecting this when he heard a sound from the kitchen and a voice behind him said: 'Mr Bartlett?'

Hillsden turned, conscious that he was only wearing pyjamas and instinctively looked to see if his flies were gaping. He found himself facing a well-built, middle-aged woman with smart, greying, cropped hair and wearing a green tartan skirt and Norfolk tweed jacket. Her stocky legs were covered with knee-high woollen stockings and on her feet she had chunky, rubber-soled mountain boots. She looked, if anything, like a jolly hockey mistress and his immediate reaction was to take her for a lesbian of the old school.

'Sorry if I startled you,' she said. 'Came in the back way and didn't expect you up this early. I'm Audrey, though some people call me Major. I answer to both,' she added with a short, smoker's laugh that ended in a cough, 'although I think clinging to rank is a bit orff unless you're still at it. Don't you agree?'

'Doesn't bother me one way or the other,' Hillsden said, taken aback.

'Well, it's a bit la-di-fucking-da. Sorry about that, just slipped out, won't do it in front of the wife. I was a convent girl and we all swore like troopers so we had something to confess. Slept well, I hope? I tried to get the house warm. Didn't show my face last night, know what it's like after a long journey, last thing you want is to be social. You've got coffee, I see, what about breakfast? I've brought some fresh bread, bloody good local bakery, not that packaged muck. I'm not much of a cook, but I can do passable bacon and eggs.'

'Sounds good,' Hillsden said. 'My wife and daughter are still asleep, but you've sold me.'

He followed her back into the kitchen. 'Was it you who put the flowers in the rooms?'

'Yes. The place was like a bloody morgue when I took up residence. I doss down in the annexe, by the way. Converted stables.' She busied herself preparing his breakfast. 'They got me out of semi-retirement for this. Not that I mind, it was becoming a bloody drag babysitting other people's pets, which seemed to be my main function in life since I was put on the reserve list, and quite frankly Audrey can do with the extra dosh, so I was more than happy when this came up. The house has been swept, in case you were going to ask, and I've been round it myself, just to make sure.'

'What's the form going to be here?' Hillsden asked.

'With me? Well, officially, I'm your housekeeper. Been with you for years. Story is, which I've put about in the village shops, you decided to move the family here because you didn't think London was safe any more, and I came on ahead to get the house straight.'

'Sounds plausible. Are the natives friendly?'

'On the whole, yes, those I've met. Usual mixture for these days. Majority born and bred hereabouts, I suspect, with a touch of the Archers here and there.'

'They're not still going, are they?' Hillsden asked.

'Good God, yes. Part of our heritage, like Coronation Street. Then we have a sprinkling of outsiders with second homes – you know the type, vote Lib-Dem, recycle everything including their wives, have this dream of living under a thatched roof with tits nesting over the front door until the patter of rats' feet in the eaves sends them scurrying back to Chelsea.'

Hillsden nodded. 'How much were you told about me?'

'All they thought necessary. The fact that you've been out of circulation for some time, and that your missus and child will find everything a bit strange to begin with. You can tell Audrey more if you want to, or not as you think fit, suit yourself. Old Rotherby likes you and that's good enough for me. He's a card. One egg or two?'

'Yes, isn't he?' Hillsden said. 'Er, two, please.'

'Oh, shit, Audrey, you've broken that one, you silly mare. Still, all goes down the same way, doesn't it? Yes, Rotherby and I go back a while too. I got to know him on a couple of other jobs, not as well as he would have liked I might add.' She looked up from the frying pan and winked. 'Got a roving hand. Bit of a taxi tiger.'

'Really? That's a side of him I haven't come across.'

'Well no, you wouldn't, would you? Lonely, that's his problem. Wife died about four years back. Easy to handle though. Slap his wrists and he's quite harmless. Told him if his old wink stirred to put a hat over it and smuggle it up West. He rather went for that, though I think it was a touch of down-memory-lane. How about some fried bread?'

'Fried bread! God, I haven't had that for ages.'

'Well, you look as though you could do with putting on a

bit of weight. Unlike some. I've tried every bloody diet, but our Audrey's given up now and lets it all hang out.'

Hillsden had forgotten how delicious the pungent aroma of bacon was and he stood mesmerised, watching the sizzling pan.

'Doesn't seem to be a dining room, so d'you mind it on the kitchen table?'

'Anywhere's fine,' he said. Audrey placed the heaped plate in front of him. 'Mustard?'

'Mustard! Yes, please.'

She watched as he studied the small yellow bottle, turning it round and round in his hand. It was as if she had given him a jewel. 'Colman's,' he said. 'I haven't seen that in nearly eight years.' He cut a piece of fried bread and dipped it in the egg yolk, then took the first bite.

'How is it?'

'Unbelievably delicious.'

'Now, look,' Audrey said. 'You and I must establish a working arrangement.' She took a tin of small cheroots from one of the kitchen shelves and sat opposite him. 'This won't make you gag, will it?'

'No, go ahead.'

'Tried everything to kick the habit – acupuncture, the patch, hypnotism, but then I decided that life was such a crock anyway one might as well stick to vice. Do you smoke?'

Hillsden nodded.

'That's two things we have in common then.'

'Two? What's the other one?'

'Well, we're both birds of a feather. I did a stint in Belfast, working undercover as the manageress in a restaurant, then my cover got blown and they had to get me out fast. Nothing as exotic as you, I'm sure.'

'Oh, my past wasn't exotic,' Hillsden said. 'Not even dangerous for long periods, just dull.' He savoured his meal while Audrey got up to make a fresh pot of coffee. 'Any idea what they've got in mind for me?'

Audrey rested her cigar on the lip of a saucer and poured

the coffee. 'Haven't they told you? That's so bloody typical of the Firm. Well, they told me, so it can't be a state secret. My brief was you're an insurance broker.'

Hillsden grimaced. 'What genius thought that up? The only thing I know about insurance is that the premiums used to go up every year and that they questioned every claim. What about Galina, my wife, how is she explained?'

'Georgina, you mean, don't you?'

'Yes, sorry.'

'We should start using the new names. Make them second nature. If we get used to it in private there's less likelihood of a slip up in front of strangers.'

'Yes, quite right, remiss of me.'

'What's your wife's English like?'

'Pretty good. A trace of an accent still.'

'And Laura?'

'The same.'

'What do their passports say?'

'Born in Belgium.'

'Fair enough. As for schooling, I made discreet enquiries and there is a local church school, but I'd be happy to tutor if you think that's safer until she's really settled in. I can manage the basics.'

'Wouldn't that arouse comment?'

'I don't see why.'

'I mean, is that allowed?'

'Wait until anybody enquires. By then she'll have found her feet.' Audrey lit a second cheroot. 'Two with coffee,' she explained. 'Two after lunch and two with a nightcap. That's my ration.' She offered the tin to Hillsden. 'Want to try one?'

'No, I'll stick to cigarettes.'

'What's your usual brand?'

'I don't have one. I used to smoke Red Dunhills. Where I came from I smoked anything I could lay my hands on.'

'I'll get you a carton next time I'm out.' She got up suddenly and took down a biscuit tin from one of the shelves. 'Nearly forgot.' Opening the tin she produced a sealed envelope and a pair of spectacles. 'I had to give you these.'

Hillsden examined the spectacles. 'What am I supposed to do with these?' He held them up to the light, then put them on. 'Non-prescription.' Next he opened the envelope. Inside was a plain piece of paper with a London address typed on it – *Flat 6, 440, Bickenhall Street, W1* – a date two days hence and a time.

'Bickenhall Street,' he said, showing the note to Audrey. 'That's a new one. What goes on there?'

'No idea, new one on me. Can you remember the details?'

'Yes,' Hillsden said after studying the note again.

Audrey took the paper from him and tore it into small pieces, then put them in her ashtray and burned them. 'I remember when I was first recruited I had to report to a shop off the Marylebone Road. Had some very odd stuff in the window – breast supporters and artificial limbs. Very kinky, Audrey, I thought, what have you got yourself in for here? I take it they supplied you with a pea-shooter?' she added, letting the sentences slide into each other.

'Yes. I hate the bloody things.'

'Likewise, but all too necessary these days. They gave me a refresher course, and although I'll never be chosen for Bisley I can handle myself, so when you're not here don't worry, I've got no moral objection to using one if necessary. Funny old game we're in,' she added. 'Never quite believe it myself, but at least it's less boring than doing needlepoints, which is what my mother did. Every bloody room was crammed with them. Never got on with my parents. Mostly my fault, but they were paralysingly dull.'

Hillsden wiped his plate with his last piece of bread. 'God, that was good.'

'Now, what else have I got to tell you?' Audrey asked, pouring him a second cup of coffee. 'Transport. With what I can only believe was a sudden rush of blood to the head, they've given us two cars, a Rover for you and something called a Clio for me. Your keys are on the mantelpiece. Don't forget to drive on the left and watch out for the boys in blue, they're very keen these days. I bought you a road atlas, since I thought you'd need one.'

'I expect it'll all come back to me, given time.'

'Oh, and most important, you don't have to give me any housekeeping, that's taken care of, paid into a bank in Bury St Edmunds. But what I'll need to know from the wife is what she and your daughter like to eat, what they're used to.'

'No, don't give them what they're used to,' Hillsden said, with a smile.

'Your wife cooks, I take it?'

'Yes, she became a dab hand at producing miracles from nothing.'

'I got her this,' Audrey said, picking up a copy of Delia Smith's latest. 'Thought it might come in handy. No recipes for caviar, though,' she added, letting slip she knew more than she had professed. 'Anything else I should mention?'

'Your surname, I ought to know that.'

'I was hoping you wouldn't ask. Daddy was double-barrelled and possibly double-gated as well, always had my suspicions. The family name was Warrington-Smythe, can you believe? I never use the last bit, too fucking la-de-bloody-da – there you go again, Audrey, now watch it, don't go blotting your copybook the first day. Daddy was a manic snob, kept his one invitation to the Buck House garden party framed on the Bechstein. Can you imagine?'

'What did Daddy do?'

'Oh, Foreign Office, how else d'you think I got involved?'

'It's just Warrington then? You never married, Audrey?'

'No,' she said, taking his dirty plate and putting it in the sink. 'Plenty of hot water you'll be glad to hear,' she continued in the same breath in an obvious change of subject.

Hillsden got up from the table. 'I'll check whether my two are awake yet and have a bath. Then take a stroll, get acquainted with what's outside. Thanks for breakfast, Audrey. I think we'll all get along famously.'

He mounted the bare, creaking stairs, thinking, so it all begins again – the deceits, the nightmare of love, trusting my

110

life to strangers – nothing's different, just a new set of characters in a changed landscape. He lingered in the doorway of Lara's room, staring at her unmarked, sleeping face, wondering how long it would be before the age of innocence ended for her.

13

WHITEHALL DOUBLE-SPEAK

'You'd better come up with some answers fast, Kenith,' the Prime Minister said pointedly across the Cabinet table. 'Put some firecrackers up the Commissioner's arse, and tell him to get his men out of their bloody Panda cars and on the streets. Those are our people getting hurt out there.'

Logan's fellow ministers shuffled their papers, not displeased that he was taking most of the flak that morning.

'Well, not entirely *ours*,' Logan said with a whisper of emphasis, for once letting his prejudices show. 'Half of them don't vote for anybody.'

'It can't have escaped your notice, Kenith, that we've got a by-election coming up which I don't want to lose,' the PM snapped. 'Imagine what play the Tory press would make of that so soon after we got in. We promised a new era of law and order and we've got to start delivering.' Much younger than his colleagues, he was at some pains to assert his authority.

Instinctively, Logan reached for his cigar case, then, just in time, remembered that smoking was off limits in the Cabinet room. During the election campaign the image-makers and spin doctors had been brought in – gone was the pipe-smoking informality of the Wilson days, now everybody wore suits and sober ties when appearing on the goggle-box, reliable respectability was the order of the day in an attempt to lull the electorate into believing that the Party was safe, forward looking and squeaky clean.

Logan cleared his throat. 'In my view, we should not dismiss the option of proscribing this First Legion outfit,' he said, employing his ministerial voice.

The PM shook his head. 'No, forget that, smacks of panic measures. Looks as though we've lost our nerve overnight. The existing laws are quite sufficient to handle it providing they're enforced, but all I ever get from the Commissioner are bleatings about lack of manpower and resources. If you ask me he's not quite sixteen annas to the rupee,' he said, expecting and getting a smile from most of the faces around the table. It was an expression he had purloined from the Permanent Secretary to the Treasury. 'Find out when he's due for retirement.'

Logan took this reproach and diligently made a note. 'I think one of the difficulties we face is that a lot of people out there don't give a toss whether Salman Rushdie and his kind get their comeuppance. Regrettable, but true.'

There was a moment's silence around the table before the PM said: 'Don't minute that,' to the Cabinet secretary and flashed a warning look at Logan. 'Yes, well, let's not open that can of worms.' He switched topics abruptly. 'Have we selected a candidate for the by-election?'

'Yes, after some heart-searching,' replied his Deputy.

'Is he any good?'

'Well, he's black. Or rather, West Indian. A solicitor. Very active in civil liberties.'

'I'd better see him. Fix it with my diary.' He returned to Logan. 'So, Kenith, I think you should do a little PR, visit the worst areas, get yourself photographed in hospitals wearing your compassionate face.'

'You mean the one I wear all the time?' Logan said, using his charm in an attempt to defuse the charged atmosphere.

Logan refused to dwell upon the PM's veiled sarcasm when the Cabinet meeting finished. Given time, and given the fact that nobody else wanted the job, he was confident he could produce results. He cancelled the rest of the day's appointments and that afternoon travelled to Slough, where the previous day a mosque had been burnt to the ground and the leader of the Muslim community savagely beaten up. In retaliation, well-organised groups of Asians had smashed and looted a dozen shops in the high street before the situation had been brought under control.

Ignoring the more pressing documents in his red box, he relaxed by reading an article in *The Economist* about the fall-out following Freidler's murder. High-flyers in the financial world had always intrigued Logan, for like most socialists in power he did not want to spend the rest of his days practising what he preached to others.

'Bet your life there's more to come out yet,' he muttered.

Andrews, his armed, Special Branch detective, turned round from the front passenger seat of the Jaguar. 'Sorry, sir?'

'Nothing. Just talking to myself,' Logan said. 'There's more to the murder of this banker, Freidler, than has come out yet, you mark my words. Have you been following it?'

'No, can't say I have, sir.'

'Bound to have had his hands in the till and salted away millions. The whole banking system is corrupt. They're all morally bankrupt.' Logan put the magazine to one side as he noticed something ahead. 'What's this we're driving into?'

'Looks like some sort of demonstration, sir.'

Logan's driver slowed down and allowed the police back-up car to overtake them.

'Can we turn off anywhere and avoid it?'

'Not off this road, sir,' the driver said. He checked that the door locks were on.

'Well, go on, don't stop.'

The driver exchanged a glance with Andrews. Fat chance, he thought.

Despite the fact that the back-up car had activated its lights and siren, the crowd refused to give ground. Very soon both cars were surrounded and although half a dozen local policemen tried to clear a path they were overwhelmed by the sheer numbers and the small convoy was forced to a standstill. Angry faces pressed close up against the windows of Logan's car, shouting slogans; one of the demonstrators wielding a wooden stave threw himself on to the bonnet and attempted to smash the windscreen before being thrown off.

'Drive on,' Logan shouted, 'get us out of here.'

'Can't, sir,' the driver said. 'There are kids lying down in the road.'

Andrews put out an alarm call on his radio as the Jaguar was violently rocked. 'Try reversing out,' he ordered. The driver did as he was told, but it was soon obvious that this would not work.

'Bloody people, don't they know I'm here to try and help?' Logan said. He sat in the centre of the rear seat, hardly able to make himself heard over the noise on all sides. 'This is ridiculous! The police are supposed to have this sorted out.'

'Not always that easy, sir,' Andrews said, defending his own.

'Well, I shall want a full explanation from the Chief Constable and the ringleaders prosecuted.'

Three more police cars arrived on the scene, together with a van-load of officers in riot gear. Those demonstrators lying in the roadway were forcibly dragged to one side and eventually the convoy was able to proceed. The incident was filmed by a newsreel camera team who had appeared from nowhere.

'How do those bastards always turn up when they're least wanted?' Logan muttered. 'Who tips them off?'

'You're news, sir,' Andrews said with just a touch of irony.

On arrival at the hospital, a still ruffled Logan was relieved to find that word had preceded him and there was a large police presence holding back another crowd of demonstrators. As he got out of the Jaguar the obligatory smile was wiped off his face as an egg just missed him, splattering the roof of the car. He was quickly hustled inside.

After being introduced to the senior hospital staff, he was conducted to the ward where two victims of racial attacks were recovering. Visiting the first bed, he arranged his face and spoke words of comfort to an elderly Sikh who had extensive head wounds.

'I'm afraid he speaks very little English,' one of the hospital officials said when Logan got no response from the old man. 'We believe there's also some brain damage.'

'Ah, yes. Tragic,' Logan said. He smiled at the old man and moved to the next bed where a young West Indian had both arms in plaster.

'What's your name?' Logan asked.

'Montgomery.'

'After General Montgomery, eh?'

'Who's he?' the young man asked.

Logan ploughed through this. 'Comfortable, are you?'

'Not very. Got a bleeding headache.'

'Well, I'm sure these good people are looking after you and you'll soon be back at work.'

'Haven't got any work to go back to.'

'Well, we must do something about that.'

'Yeah, well don't leave it too long, willya?'

Logan managed to keep his compassionate expression in place, conscious that the cameras were turning again. Nothing, that day, was turning out as he had hoped. In order to avoid a second clash with the demonstration he slipped out of a side entrance and was taken to the town hall where a reception committee hosted by the mayor and including senior police officers from the Thames Valley force had been assembled.

The mayor was a woman and Logan was unsure how to address her – the gender vocabulary had become an issue which always confused and irritated him – should she be addressed as the Lady Mayor, or, ludicrously, as Mayor Person? A somewhat dumpy little woman, weighed down by her chain of office, he drew some comfort from the fact that in this case she was also the leader of a Labour Council. Some tea, cakes and a variety of desultory sandwiches had been prepared for his visit, and Logan made a short speech to the assembled great and good, stressing the need for calm and assuring them that all those responsible for the racial attacks would be hunted down and subjected to the full severity of the courts. Afterwards, he buttonholed the local police Commander.

'I'd like your current evaluation, Commander. Are your men prepared for any further backlash?'

'Well, the situation's still extremely volatile, Home Secretary. Emotions are running high amongst the ethnic community, and we're stretched very thin on the ground in some places.'

'Well, don't lay that at my door,' Logan flared. 'Blame that on the Tories. You have armed units, I understand. Have they been deployed?'

'Deployed, but not used. Hopefully they never will be, except as a last resort.'

Balancing his cup of tea, Logan bit on a tinned-salmon sandwich and frowned – a small piece of bone had lodged between two of his lower front teeth. He used a fingernail to extract it. 'Is there going to be a last resort?'

'Weapons are easily come by these days. You doubtless saw the Commissioner's report to Conference, Minister. Armed attacks on us have gone up by six hundred per cent in a year.'

Logan's frown stayed in place. 'Yes, yes, I'm aware of the statistics, they're being analysed by my department.'

'The riot squads have the availability of rubber bullets, which I shall authorise if necessary. I've already had four officers and a WPC injured.'

'Well, the last thing we want is another Broadwater Farm.'

'That goes without saying, sir.'

'Have you arrested anybody for this latest incident?'

'Not yet, Minister.'

'Any suspects?'

'Everything points to it being an outside job. The only witnesses we have are the man's two small children. All they could tell us was that whoever attacked their father went off in a red car, but children are notoriously unreliable, especially when they're in shock.'

117

'Have you come across this organisation called First Legion?'

'Not directly,' the Commander said. 'I'm aware it exists, but so far they haven't set up shop here. That's not to say that they won't.'

'I intend to convene a meeting with all the Chief Constables in the near future to discuss what further steps can be taken to stamp out these outrages before they escalate further.'

'What many of us would like to have taken on board, Minister, is a return to capital punishment for certain capital crimes. Today's villains will kill for a few pence.'

Logan flushed and shook his head. 'No, the death penalty's not the answer. My government will never countenance that. We must never lose sight of the sanctity of human life. Better that ten guilty men go free than one innocent man be hanged.'

'Yes,' the Commander answered, still keeping his voice even, 'I am familiar with that argument, Minister. Curiously, it doesn't go down too well with widows and orphans. I've often thought our society has double standards. Where the death penalty's concerned, I mean.' He fixed Logan with unblinking eyes throughout this speech. 'It never seems to come up in times of war, does it? Then we cheerfully send off our young men as sacrificial victims. One could say that the majority of those who die are innocents. The sanctity of human life seems to be forgotten in wartime.'

None of this was to Logan's liking. He gave a thin smile and looked around for means of escape, caught his private detective's eye and gave him the nod. 'Well, don't relax. We want results. And when you catch them, make sure your case is watertight. We don't want another conviction overturned. Good talking with you.'

'Thank you for your time, Minister.'

The Commander watched him impassively as he walked away, then raised his eyebrows at his second-in-command.

Logan stayed another ten minutes making small-talk and then excused himself and left. He was silent on the journey back to Whitehall, conscious that not only had he lost the argument, but that once again he had no compelling answers.

14

EYE CONTACT

Carstairs knew they would kill him; it was only a matter of time. He told himself, I mustn't give way, there has to be a way out, but fear was batting to and fro in his mind, like a shuttlecock. His future was etched with the acid of the inevitable.

He lay, fully clothed, on the single bed in the anonymous Bayswater hotel he had chosen as a last refuge, registering under a false name. There was an illustrated tourist guide on the bedside table, alongside a soiled handkerchief, the bottle of Valium and his car keys. The photograph on the cover of the guide showed a big-breasted girl in a bikini lying on an inflated Lilo in impossibly blue water. *Affordable Luxury Holidays*, the legend said, *Your unique made-to-measure experience. Discount fares if you book early.* Just another lie, Carstairs thought. There were no bargains to be had in the world he had chosen to inhabit, no return tickets, only a last painful journey. 'You'll be set up for life,' Charters had said, and he had believed it. 'Just a few telephone calls to this number at the right times, that's all you have to do, there's no risk, nothing can go wrong.'

I didn't do it for myself, I did it for her, so I could give her the good life, the life she craves, he said to himself, and thinking of the love he was about to lose for ever brought a stab of pain to his chest. If only God could take the final step for me, he thought, but it was too late to rely on God. He shook a handful of Valium capsules into his palm and went into the small bathroom. A notice pasted on to the mirror reminded him that the management took no responsibility for articles of value left in the rooms. He filled the toothpaste glass with tap water and after a moment's hesitation, swallowed the capsules, staring at a stranger's face in the mirror. Then he went back into the bedroom and lay down once more. He tried to remember a childhood prayer, one last insurance policy, but his mind wandered as an unaccustomed calm began to sweep over him. Before he slipped further into the abyss, he reached under the pillow and took out a .25 calibre automatic pistol. Turning on his side, he rested the cold metal against his left temple. 'Forgive me, darling,' he murmured. He stared one last time at the holiday brochure before he gave himself the unique made-to-measure experience of blowing his head apart.

. . .

The Bickenhall Street address Hillsden had been given proved to be an ornate mansion block close to the area in London, bordering Harley and Wimpole streets, that had long been the province of the medical profession. He was wearing the plain-glass spectacles he had been given and made a show of peering at the panel listing the residents, most of whom appeared to be foreign with medical credentials after their names. Pressing the requisite bell on the panel and waiting for a response on the entry-phone, he recalled an A.J. Cronin novel he had read long ago – *The Citadel* – that in its time had aroused a certain amount of controversy, pulling aside, as it did, some of the veils doctors hid behind. It seemed to him appropriate that the Firm would choose to operate cheek by jowl with another profession that thrived on secrecy.

A muffled male voice said 'Yes?'

Hillsden answered close to the microphone. 'Mr Bartlett,' he said, 'I have an appointment.'

'Third floor,' the voice responded.

There was a pause and then the automatic lock clicked open and he pushed the heavy door inward. The carpeted entrance hall was spotless, bare of furniture except for a console table with some uncollected mail on it. He walked up a short flight of stairs to the lift: there was a distant clunk from above as the pulley mechanism engaged, then he heard it stop again. When eventually it reached the ground floor, the doors slid open to reveal a middle-aged couple. Confronted by Hillsden, both ignored him, but before the woman averted her head he saw she was crying.

The third floor was as characterless as the entrance, the same patterned carpet and absence of furniture. There were brass panels on all the doors. The one on number six was engraved *Mr C. Smith FRCS, Ophthalmologist.* Hillsden knocked and again the lock was opened automatically. He entered an empty waiting room. This was decorated in a different style from the rest of the building: stipple-painted walls hung with a few posters for contact lenses, a cabinet containing a variety of spectacle frames, a modern sofa and desk. There was a closed door to one side of the desk. After a slight pause this door opened and Swanson appeared.

'You found it all right, then,' Swanson said.

'No Mr Smith?'

'Ah! No, out to lunch I'm afraid,' with a flickered smile. 'Permanently.'

'Can I dispense with these?' Hillsden asked, removing the fake spectacles. 'I take it I'm not here to have my eyes tested?'

'God no! Had somebody press our bell by mistake last week. Threw me for a loop. Had to pretend Mr Smith was away sick and I was the secretary. Anyway, let's go into my den.' He pressed a switch on the desk and Hillsden heard the door lock behind him as he entered the second room where there was another desk with an Anglepoise lamp on it, together with three telephones, two comfortable leather chairs and a filing cabinet. On the far wall was a test chart with diminishing lines of letters and, opposite, the elaborate testing equipment eye-specialists use.

Swanson took the chair behind the desk. 'Necessary window dressing. Sit you down. Too early for a drop of Vera Lynn?' He swivelled to open the top drawer of the filing cabinet and took out a bottle of gin and two glasses.

'Why not?' Hillsden said. This was a more relaxed, altogether more pleasant Swanson, less guarded now that he was on home ground. 'Haven't heard it called that in a long time.'

'Got some tonic somewhere.' Swanson searched the back of the filing drawer. 'Here we are. No ice, I'm afraid. Say when.'

'When.'

Swanson slid a glass across the desk. 'Well, here's to your new life. How did you find our Audrey?'

'Fine.'

'Formidable creature. The word is, don't mess with Audrey. She's part of the team, together with Rotherby – I included him to make you comfortable – Hadley, Commander Pearson and his side-kick.'

'Who's Pearson?'

'You never came across the good Commander?'

'I don't think so.'

'George Medal, and two Queen's commendations, all earned in Belfast. And that's it. I kept the numbers down for obvious reasons, as I'm sure you would agree.'

Hillsden nodded.

'Everything else tickety-boo in darkest Suffolk?'

'The house seems very comfortable.'

'What about the wife? Happy?'

'Well, everything's bound to be strange for her at first, but I'm sure she'll soon adapt. It's strange for me, too, come to that.'

'Bound to be.' Swanson took out a gold fob-watch from his waistcoat, consulted it and then polished the face with a silk handkerchief before putting it back. 'I suppose we should get down to the nitty-gritty. We'd better start with you signing this.' He took a sheet of paper from a file.

'I thought the Official Secrets Act stayed in force for the rest of my natural life?'

'This is something else, preventing you from ever publishing your second volume of memoirs.' Swanson handed him a pen and waited for Hillsden to read what was before him. 'Okay?'

'Well, I don't have any choice, do I?'

'Not if the pay cheques are to come in regularly,' Swanson said evenly.

Hillsden took the pen and signed.

'Right,' Swanson said, 'onwards and upwards. Well, now, new name, new game'. He savoured a sip of gin, looking at Hillsden over the rim of the glass. 'Recently it was deemed expedient to ginger up the anti-Fascist section of F Division. The sound of jackboots is being heard again in the land. There's always been a latent Fascist element – apologists, Hitler-worshippers, Holocaust sceptics, unrepentant Jew-haters, all tumbled together with your Paki-bashers – but until recently they didn't pose any real threat. Too scattered, all doing their own thing. But what we're now facing is something much more organised and well funded – an international fraternity with various groups colluding to exploit mutual hatreds.'

Swanson took another sip of his gin. 'My old physics master used to say that once you create a vacuum, something always fills it. Politically, that certainly holds true.'

Hillsden nodded agreement, then said: 'In St Petersburg you talked about an undercover operation.'

'Yes, after a great deal of thought, I've devised a fairly elaborate scheme.'

'I gather I've got a new career as an insurance broker.'

Swanson looked miffed. 'Who told you that?'

'Audrey.'

'I wish people wouldn't jump the gun,' Swanson said. 'None of her bloody business. Your age presented a problem – I had to come up with something that was as watertight as I could make it. I hit upon insurance, then decided to narrow it down to car insurance. Premiums are at an all-time high, but recently a number of new firms have come on the market offering cut-price rates, so one more shouldn't arouse any suspicion. Your operation has been designed as the genuine article, able to issue policies at attractive rates and, if necessary, pay claims – there's a separate slush fund set up.'

'How am I meant to operate?'

'This is where I think your age is an advantage.'

'Ah, I wondered when you'd explain that,' Hillsden said.

'As I told you, I wasn't looking for brawn. The scenario is, you were unable to make ends meet on your pension, so you took up part-time work as an independent insurance agent. I've prepared a fake CV for you to study and learn, which gives Robert Bartlett's family history.' He passed another document across the desk. 'You'll note you're a widower.'

'Yes, I saw that.'

'Sensible precaution, I thought. We don't want the little woman put in the line of fire.'

'Nor my daughter. How much should my wife know?'

'The minimum you can get away with. From time to time it may be necessary for you to use the safe house in Forest Gate. Does that worry you?'

'It'll need explaining to my wife.'

'I'm sure you're good at that sort of thing,' Swanson said blandly. 'The way I see it is you start with a mail shot which will include half a dozen names of known players. Hopefully, one or more will take the bait and contact you to hear more. Then it's up to you to secure their business and establish an ongoing relationship. You'll be interested in their lives, sympathetic towards their political views because, as you will discover in your CV, you were made redundant in your previous job for voicing racial slurs against a fellow worker. Are you with me so far?'

'More or less. What if we don't get any of the right takers?'

Swanson flashed his annoyance at this quibble. 'I've put a lot of thought into this and I'm assuming you will come up with at least one positive response.'

'But, assuming you're wrong, obviously the operation's not repeatable. What happens to me then?'

'Let's not look on the black side. No pun intended,' Swanson said with his thin smile, but he could not keep the annoyance out of his voice.

'From where I'm sitting, I have to.'

'Well, yes, should the operation prove negative, you couldn't be used again. We'd have to have a rethink. Let's cross that bridge when we come to it, shall we?'

'These "known players", who are they?'

'Mostly small fry Special Branch have been keeping an eye on. Until recently they've been operating solo without any discernible pattern, doing their own thing locally, but then we noted a change in their activities. Suddenly they seemed to become organised. They had access to funds, they could afford premises, produce literature, field political candidates – echoes of Mosley and his blackshirts. But beyond that, we started to notice a new trend which suggests the nature of terrorism itself has changed.'

'In what way?'

'In your field days, terrorists mostly had nation-states as patrons: Libya, Iran, Palestine and, of course, Russia itself. The Yanks, too, for that matter, with their covert operations which frequently backfired. The targets were usually heads of state, or symbols of state power. Now the focus has shifted. There seems to be a common political end that crosses frontiers closer to home, the threat coming from extreme right-wing groups and always racially motivated. Jewish cemeteries desecrated here, foreign immigrants attacked and murdered in Germany and France, a Fascist revival in Italy, not forgetting the growing armies of militiamen in the States prepared to take the law into their own hands. Study the press now you're home, you'll find examples any day of the week. Have a look at this thing. Acting on a tip-off from our man in Copenhagen, Customs at Harwich confiscated several hundreds.'

Taking a booklet from the desk drawer he swivelled it

126

across the desk. 'Written by a certain Gottfried Sonntag, a prominent German Jew-baiter, although he uses a pseudonym for the English translation. It's the usual filth, on the same lines as that *Protocols of the Elders of Zion* thing old Henry Ford treated as the gospel. The title tells it all – *Sin of the Blood.*' Taking back the book, Swanson flicked through the pages. 'Open it anywhere, the message is the same.' He read aloud: '"*With satanic joy in his face, the black-haired Jewish youth lurks in wait for the unsuspecting girl whom he defiles with his blood.*"' Turning to another page, 'And listen to this, "*The Jew virus constitutes a far greater threat than Aids. We shall regain our political and social health only by eliminating the Jew.*" We're dealing with animals. Animals,' he repeated. 'You aren't going to find this a pleasant assignment because to be accepted you're going to have to speak their language. Are you up to that?'

'I guess I'll have to be,' Hillsden said. He looked straight at Swanson. 'But you seem to have paid a high price for my temporary services. Should I be flattered?'

'From what I know of you, Hillsden, you've always known your way around the maze. I depend on you to deliver and lead us to whoever's at the top. That's the objective.'

'Where do I run the operation from?'

'You'll operate out of an office we've set up for you in Docklands, with an assistant to handle enquiries and mail. I should have mentioned her before.'

'Her?'

'Yes, girl called Sarah, ex WPC in the Met. It's all equal opportunities now. Official Labour policy. When you've studied all the material, I'll have Hadley take you down to Docklands and get you acclimatised there. After that you work to your own timetable. If you need to contact me or Pearson, use this number and it'll be automatically patched through to one or the other of us on a scrambler. Just ask for another eye appointment.'

He finished his gin. 'I won't pretend it isn't a dangerous assignment. What's out there is not a game of ring-a-roses.

What has changed is England itself. Make the wrong move and A-tishoo, A-tishoo, we all fall down.'

15

COUNTRY FOLK CONTINUED

'Is it dangerous, what they've asked you to do?' Galina asked.

Lying beside her in bed, Hillsden looked up from reading the fake CV. 'To do what?' he said, his brain momentarily refusing to work.

'Don't keep it from me if it is.'

'Why d'you say that? I told you, they've given me an office job.'

'And you expect me to believe that's all there is to it?'

'I promise you.'

'You've changed,' she said. 'Don't you know you've changed?'

'I'm home,' Hillsden said. 'Home after a long time away. I'm sure I seem different, but then who wouldn't be? You're different too. We've got to get acclimatised. I don't say it's as difficult for me as it is for you and Lara, but all the same I'm not finding it easy.'

'Except to lie to me.'

'Who's lying?'

'You don't have to shield me. I'd rather know. Just tell me, so I'm prepared: is it dangerous, this work you're involved in?'

'No. I'm more likely to be run over crossing the road. I'm still having to think twice about which side we drive on.' He closed his book and put his arm under her, drawing her closer so that her head nestled on his shoulder and he caught the scent of the shampoo she had used.

'When I first met you,' Galina murmured, 'you told me it was all over, what you did, and I didn't mind the past, there was nothing to be afraid of in the past. Now it's all started again, I know it has, and I need to prepare myself.'

'You are a silly creature. Prepare yourself for what?'

'Losing you.'

'You're not going to lose me. Whatever put that in your head? This is a better life than the one we left, isn't it? We have a home, your first real home, no money worries, you can go out and buy things you never dreamed of, anything you want.'

'All except one thing,' she said.

'What's that?'

'Peace of mind.'

To give himself time to frame his next answers, Hillsden leaned across to the bedside table to take a cigarette.

'Don't smoke in the bedroom,' Galina said.

'Sorry.' He left the packet where it was.

'That's an indication. You always reach for a cigarette when you're worried.'

'No, I'm a lifelong addict. Tell you what, tomorrow, why don't we drive into Bury St Edmunds, have lunch in some posh hotel, and then I'll take you and Lara to buy some new clothes? How does that sound?'

'That you don't want to tell me the truth.'

'There's nothing to tell.'

'Then why are you studying all those books about Nazis? You left one in the bathroom. And why don't you tell me what you do when you go to London?'

'I sit behind a desk and read files.'

He attempted to stifle her concern with a kiss, but she avoided his mouth. With despair he could see their life ahead. Galina was right, he had been trapped once more. What a fool I was, he thought, what a fool to believe that the Firm ever give you the best of a bargain. The only winners were those who acted from conviction, idealism, the certainty, however mistaken, that theirs was the only true faith. I never had that,

I was driven by the one emotion we all betray sooner or later.

He kept his arm under Galina until the rhythm of her breathing told him she was asleep, then slowly eased it free. 'I love you,' he said softly, hoping it would penetrate her dream. It came to him then, as he turned over and closed his eyes, that nobody deceived as well as lovers.

. . .

The Chinese chambermaid was puzzled. For over thirty-six hours a 'Do Not Disturb' notice had swung from the door of Room 18. In such cases there was normally a tray of used coffee cups and empty wine bottles left outside, for the hotel catered mostly for clandestine one-nighters and their girlfriends.

Putting her ear to the door she listened for any sounds from within, but all was silent. Next she knocked, and said 'Room service', but there was no response. After knocking again, she decided to risk it and used her master key. She pushed the door open a fraction and said, 'Maid, please.' Nothing. She allowed the door to open fully and looked inside. Then she screamed.

. . .

'You'll have to excuse me,' Hillsden said, 'if I sometimes appear to be a fossil from a bygone age, but I've been out of circulation for a while. Did they tell you that?'

The young woman looked at him from across her desk. 'The story I had was you'd been brought out of retirement for a special job.'

'That's about it. Well, I'd like to get off on the right foot, so how d'you like to be addressed? Is it Mrs Carter, Miss or Ms? I'm told it's important these days.'

'Well, certainly not Mrs because I've never walked up the

aisle,' his new assistant said. 'Not for want of trying, I might add. Why don't you just call me Sarah, Mr Bartlett? I don't give a toss about all that feminist lark, so don't worry, you'll never be greeted by the smell of burning bras.'

There was just a hint of a long-buried Cockney accent in Sarah's voice. Hillsden guessed she was in her late twenties, possibly a year or two older, smartly dressed, her short blonde hair neatly arranged. A waft of perfume reached him as she handed him a cup of freshly brewed coffee.

'Oh, thanks. You already figured out one of my weaknesses.'

'Have you got many?'

'More than is good for me.'

'It hasn't got sugar.'

'I don't take it.'

'Well, that's one on the plus side, Mr Bartlett.'

'Look, Sarah, when there's nobody here, for God's sake call me Robert.' The assumed name still came uneasily to him. 'As far as I'm concerned, you and I are working for each other. What's that perfume you're wearing?'

'Poison.'

'Poison? There's a perfume called Poison?'

'Oh, sure. There's also a cigarette called Death.'

'Do you smoke those?'

'I don't smoke,' Sarah said.

'Oh, dear, is that going to be a problem, because I do?'

'No sweat. My boyfriend smokes.'

'I'll try and cut it down while I'm here. What does your boyfriend do?'

'He's in the Met. Diplomatic protection. He gets to wear a suit, but I guess you could say that the relationship isn't exactly tailored for romance. They work him all hours.'

Hillsden was studying the layout of the office as they conversed. It was impersonal but functional: two desks, two PCs, laser printer, filing cabinets, fax and copying machines, three telephones ('The red one's the scrambler,' Sarah told him). A small kitchen and a bathroom led off the main room.

'And you, what brought you into the Firm?'

'I was in the Met, too, did eight years with them, ended up working for the anti-terrorist squad, personal assistant to the boss man.'

'Who was that?'

'Commander Pearson. He's been seconded to our team.'

'Yes, Swanson told me.'

'When this came up, he was the one who thought my face might fit in here.'

'Mine too, apparently.' Hillsden sat at his desk and rifled through a stack of the insurance brochures. 'He thought you might make an insurance agent, did he?'

'Always willing to learn. It's a pretty neat scam if we can work it.'

'Well, we're going to try. At least it's original,' Hillsden said. He brandished one of the insurance brochures. 'Have you had a chance to study these?'

'Yes, I was impressed. They've done a professional job. If that came through my letter box I'd give it a second look. Matter of fact, the rates are so good I wondered whether I could write a policy for my own car. D'you think they'd wear it?'

'Maybe not. Is there a list of the first mailing shot?'

'Top left-hand drawer, but I've already put everything on both computers while I was waiting for you to arrive.'

'That was very efficient. Don't expect me to use one of these things, I haven't got a clue. You're a whiz, no doubt?'

'Not bad. Well, very good actually, no point in being modest. You needn't worry, I programmed it to be really easy, but you have to key in the code word to get started . . . I thought "Hitler" was appropriate. Okay?'

'Yes, I think I can manage to remember that. It's what comes after the code.'

'It's simple. When the menu comes up, you type the first letter of whichever heading you want. Let me show you.' She came behind him and put in the code. 'They're really fast these machines,' she said as the menu came on screen. '486s with a Pentium chip and turbo drive.'

'That's good, is it?'

'State-of-the-art. Now then, you see how I've categorised it. Names: so supposing you typed "N", you'd get a complete list in alphabetical order. Date when contacted. Reply. Action taken, et cetera. If you get your knickers in a twist, don't worry. Both machines are linked and I'll be doing all the spade work. When we're bored we can play games.'

'We can?'

'Sure. Go to Windows in the menu. Watch.' She used the mouse and clicked twice on an icon. 'Have to use the mouse though.'

'Mouse, windows, it's all a foreign language.'

'Click twice for Solitaire. That's the one I like best.'

Hillsden stared in amazement as a deck of coloured playing cards appeared and Sarah began to manipulate the mouse with great dexterity. 'Here,' she said, 'you try. But I warn you, once you get hooked, it's a great time waster. Move the red six over to the black seven. That's it. Now go to the pack for the next card.'

'This might prove my undoing, you should never have shown me.' He relinquished the mouse. 'Shouldn't we make a start?'

'I already did.' Sarah went to her own desk and picked up a stack of stamped and addressed envelopes. 'The priority twenty names on the list are ready to go.'

Hillsden examined the envelopes.

'Okay to post them?'

'Why not? Let's cast our bread upon the waters and see if any of the fish bite.'

As she passed him, he got another whiff of her heady perfume.

'Poison, you say? I must remember that and get some for my wife.'

'Not mad about it myself, but it turns my boyfriend on. Every little helps. Gives him all sorts of ideas,' she said. 'All except wedding bells.'

When she left to catch the post, Hillsden could not resist

resuming the computer game. Engrossed, it was some moments before he became aware of the reflection of a red dot blinking on the monitor screen. He swivelled round to see the call-light signalling on his scrambler phone. He picked up.

'Bartlett?' a voice said.

'Yes. Swanson?'

'No, Hadley. You took your time.'

'I was in the loo.'

'Isn't Sarah there?'

'She's gone out to the post.'

'Oh, right. You're up and running then?'

'Yes, all stations go.'

'Good. Just checking. Any problems?'

'Not so far.'

'Good. Keep me in the picture, won't you? If I'm left in the dark I can't be much help,' Hadley said.

'I'll make it my life's work,' Hillsden said.

He put the phone down and sat looking at it for a time, wondering why he had reacted in such a prickly manner. Hadley probably meant well, it was just that he was young and gung-ho, anxious to prove his worth. It was funny how old suspicions still lurked just below the surface, immediately activated by a chance remark. Resuming the game of Solitaire, he came close to getting it out, but was denied success by one card – the ace of spades.

16

A MURDER INVESTIGATION

'Why do we have to be involved?' Commander George Pearson said to Lloyd, his number two. 'Can't the bloody CID sort out their own problems?'

He searched in the glove compartment of their unmarked car for his bottle of antacid tablets. They had been stalled in the heavy traffic around Hyde Park Corner for the past five minutes.

'Who asked for us?'

'Gilbert.'

'Oh, that useless sod.' Pearson shook two tablets into his palm and mouthed them. 'He couldn't solve the *Standard* crossword. Traffic warden, that's all he's good for.'

'I've always got on well with him.'

'Yes, well you're going to end up in the *Guinness Book of Records* for kissing the most number of arses.'

Lloyd tapped a drumbeat on the steering wheel rather than respond, an action which seemed to fuel Pearson's irritation. He was frequently on a short fuse these days. The vehicle in front of them jerked forward a few feet.

'Got kangaroo petrol in his tank,' Lloyd observed.

'What's that mean?'

'Just an expression. Haven't you heard that before?'

'No. Put the siren on,' Pearson said, 'otherwise we'll be here all day.'

'Well, what good will that do? I can't drive over the top of

136

them.'

'Never any police here when you need them,' Pearson said with conscious irony. He crunched the tablets noisily. 'God, I can't wait for retirement. Only six more months and I'm out of it. Out of it,' he repeated, reaching under the dashboard to activate the siren. 'Roll on the Costa bloody Brava. You meet a better class of criminal there.'

'Told you,' Lloyd said. 'Siren doesn't make any difference. We're in a gridlock.' But, even as he spoke, miraculously, the traffic began to move again, though he couldn't decide whether it was the shock of their siren or one of those unfathomable occurrences that every day managed, at the last moment, to unclog London's jammed streets. With the siren still blaring, they shot round the war memorial and cut across into the park.

'Where're we making for?' Pearson asked.

'Hereford Road. Hotel Methos.'

'What is it, Greek?'

'Who knows?'

They weaved in and out of another jam on the Bayswater Road, sometimes using the right lane, as Lloyd put his foot down.

'Don't go mad!' Pearson said.

'Thought you were in a hurry.'

'I'm not in a hurry to be dead. We're going to a homicide, remember, not a premature birth.'

They came to a stop in front of the hotel where already two squad cars and an ambulance were parked. A small crowd of onlookers was grouped round the entrance.

'Where's the incident?' Pearson said to the officer standing at the door.

'Second floor, sir.'

They went inside. The dilapidated foyer was typical of the hotels in the area. Mostly owned and run by Asians, many of them charged exorbitant rates to foreign students during term time, and relied on prostitutes for the rest of the year.

'Don't imagine Egon Ronay gave this any stars,' Pearson observed as they mounted the stairway. They wound their way up to the next landing, passing through the obligatory fire door into a dimly-lit corridor. Room 18 was the last they came to. Pearson and Lloyd entered and took in the scene. The fingerprint and forensic teams were still busy around the single bed where the body of a fully clothed male lay on top of the tired floral bedspread. One side of his face had been shot away; the lower jaw lay on his chest, the stiffened left arm outstretched at an angle as though its last act had been to ward off a blow. Cobwebs of blood and hair, mixed with dried brains, had spattered the faded striped paper of the wall behind the bedhead.

'So what's all this about, Archie?' Pearson said.

Detective Superintendent Gilbert, kneeling by the side of the bed, turned at Pearson's voice.

'You took your time, George,' he said.

'I hope it wasn't a waste of time. What've you got?'

'On the face of it suicide, but time will tell.'

'So, why would I be interested?'

'Couple of things. Come outside.' He ushered them out into the corridor. 'I'm reasonably certain he was a suicide, but chummy in there doesn't conform to type. He left too many clues behind. My theory is that a lot of them choose dumps like this for it because they want to do an ostrich act. Know what I mean?'

'Not really, no, but tell me,' Pearson said, and Lloyd recognised the boredom in his voice.

'Well, like they feel they're anonymous, that's the way I'd put it. Head in the sand stuff.'

Pearson lit a cigarette. 'Oh, that. Yes. Not too many documented cases of ostriches being able to use a handgun, though.'

'George, I'm doing you a favour bringing you here, don't give me a hard time. In my experience, the majority think they've covered their tracks. Usually there's nothing on them to identity them. But chummy was the exception. If you ask me, he wanted us to know exactly who he was.'

'And who was he?'

'One of yours, George, one of yours, on the face of it.' He opened his hand and revealed a plastic security pass for Century House.

It was Gilbert's big moment and he enjoyed the brief look of surprise on Pearson's face. Pearson took the pass from him and examined it.

'Know him?'

Pearson shook his head. 'No, but that doesn't mean anything.'

'Can I see?' Lloyd asked.

'I'm not saying it belonged to him,' Gilbert continued. 'Have to rely on fingerprints for a positive identification, given what he did to his face, but it was found on him.'

Lloyd also examined the pass but, taking his cue from Pearson, was also non-committal. 'Looks genuine enough, but you never know. They can fake anything these days. I got passed a dud twenty-pound note yesterday.'

'Could he be one of your mob?'

'I'll certainly check,' Pearson said.

'Well, I thought it was worth putting you in the picture,' Gilbert said, waiting for a pat on the back.

'Yes, thanks,' Pearson replied. 'I'll owe you one. Can we keep this?'

'If you sign for it.'

'What did he use?'

'Not regulation issue. Point twenty-five. But they're easy to come by.'

'Who found him?'

'Chinese chambermaid. She went in because she thought he'd done a runner without paying his bill.'

'How long had he been dead?'

'The doc made it a day and a half.'

'Sometime on Wednesday then,' Pearson said. 'Any note?'

'Haven't found one. The only other thing in his pockets was a bill from Tudor's. That's a night club, as you probably know.'

'Why would I know that?' Pearson said. 'I don't have your

exotic lifestyle, Archie. That's one of your regular haunts, I'm sure.'

'Ha ha. Chance would be a good thing.'

'So, nothing else?'

'Not so far, but we're still working on it. D'you want to take another look?'

'I don't think so. I'll let you have all the fun stuff. Well, thanks again, Archie, glad to see somebody's on the ball. You're not just a pretty face, after all. I'll get back to you when I've made my own enquiries. Let me know if the forensic boys come up with anything else of interest.'

The repeated use of his first name appeared to gratify Gilbert.

'Will do,' he said. 'Thought it was worth bringing you in.'

Once they were back in their car Lloyd and Pearson looked at each other.

'Carstairs,' Pearson mused. 'Glad you played dumb as well. Doesn't do to let the Yard know all our secrets. Question is, why? Why would he top himself, *if* he topped himself?' He crunched on another antacid tablet.

'Maybe he was getting a bit on the side. The night club receipt might be a pointer. I know he was married, but maybe he put it around.'

'Did you ever meet him? Not exactly Richard Gere.'

'I thought he was working out of Copenhagen.'

'He was.'

'So how come he ends up stiff in a Greek hotel here?'

'Perhaps he had some air miles he wanted to use. Don't keep asking me bloody silly questions. I'm not taking part in *Mastermind*.'

'God, you've got the hump today. Everything I say, you jump down my throat. Entitled to voice my thoughts.'

Pearson didn't answer, but continued to study Carstairs's security pass. 'How to play this,' he said.

'Well, one thing, we could do the decent thing and be the ones to break it to his wife,' Lloyd ventured, still smarting from the last exchange. He got no response from Pearson.

'Yes? Good idea? Have I said something right for once?'

'Let me get his address.' Pearson picked up the car phone and dialled.

'Messy way of doing it,' Lloyd said as he executed a U-turn and headed for the Bayswater Road.

'Messy, but usually conclusive.' Pearson spoke into the mouthpiece. 'Commander Pearson here. Give me records.' He waited. 'I mean, if you've made up your mind to do it, don't take chances it won't work and end up a vegetable. That seems to me the worst of all possible worlds.' He took out Carstairs's security pass again. 'Oh, records. This is Commander Pearson. Can you give me a home address for somebody. Serial number seven two four zero eight seven.'

He clicked his fingers at Lloyd. 'Pen.'

Lloyd handed him one and he scribbled the information. 'Thanks.'

'Where is it?' Lloyd asked.

'Putney. Deodar Road.'

'God, that takes me back. I used to date somebody who lived there. Stunning little number, a dancer in that show . . . what was it called?' He hummed a few bars of a well-known tune. '*A Chorus Line*, that was it. She was very keen.'

'Keen on you?'

'Keen on *it*. And keen on me, too, I have to admit. For a time, anyway. The gardens lead down to the river. Nice in summer. Those houses are pricey these days.'

'How pricey?'

'You wouldn't get much change out of four hundred thousand.'

'Sounds a bit rich for Carstairs. Unless he was on the take. So what happened?'

'What happened to what?'

'Your dancer?'

'Well, you know me, the jealous type. She was too career-minded.'

'You should have taken up ballet and joined her. Broke your heart, I expect?'

'Did, as a matter of fact. Funnily enough, I dreamed about her the other night. It's the ones who get away we remember, isn't it?'

'True,' Pearson said. He burped.

'D'you remember your first?' Lloyd asked after a pause.

'Yes and I remember the venue too. I booked us for a dirty weekend in some hotel in Midhurst. Ghastly place as I remember. Flock wallpaper everywhere and full of County types drinking double gins before breakfast. I checked us in under separate names and gave the night porter a hefty tip. Crept along to her room at midnight.'

'Very Agatha Christie.'

'You're not far wrong. It was the sort of hotel where you expected the vicar to have done it. Unfortunately my lady friend got the curse the moment she stepped over the threshold. Nerves, I expect. Anyway, it was a complete disaster. Rained the entire time and she cried her eyes out.'

'Well, it wasn't your first then.'

'It was the first *attempt*,' Pearson said with a tinge of nostalgia in his voice. 'You're heading in the wrong direction, by the way.'

'How come?'

'Putney.'

'We're going there, are we? You didn't say.'

'Yes, I did. Or if I didn't I meant to, start reading my mind.'

'Jesus!' Lloyd activated the siren again and swung across the oncoming traffic to go in the opposite direction. 'D'you ever wonder what happened to her?'

'Who?' Pearson asked.

'The bird you took down to Midhurst.'

'No.'

'That's not normal.'

'I'm not normal. Haven't been normal for years. How can you be normal in our job? Stands to reason.'

They both pondered these and other inescapable truths for the rest of the journey to Deodar Road.

Carstairs's house had a somewhat gloomy aspect; the front

garden had a mixed holly and laurel hedge instead of the smartly painted iron railings of its immediate neighbours.

'Well, if he was taking the dropsy,' Lloyd said, 'he certainly didn't spend it on the paintwork.'

They walked to the front door and pressed the bell. There was a *Vote Lib-Dem* sticker fixed to the inside of the downstairs bay window. A dog started to yap, one of those croaky barks peculiar to very small dogs. Then a woman's voice said, 'Now go back, Monty, go in your basket. Go on, do as you're told and shut up.'

The door was not opened immediately. Instead the woman spoke from behind the frosted glass panel. 'Yes? Who is it?'

'Colleagues of your husband, Mrs Carstairs.'

'He's not at home,' the woman answered guardedly.

'No, it's you we wanted to see, Mrs Carstairs.'

Mrs Carstairs opened the door a fraction, but it was still held on a security chain.

'D'you have any identification?'

'Of course.' Pearson handed her his wallet through the crack in the door, the wallet opened to reveal his plastic security pass.

After a slight pause, Carstairs's wife closed the door again and released the chain. When she opened it, she wasn't what either of them had expected. Not in the least. Had they been asked, they'd have guessed she'd be middle-aged and mousy, a gender clone of her late husband, but Pearson and Lloyd were confronted by somebody who looked as though she might have been cast as a barmaid in some sit-com. Of indeterminate age, probably late thirties, blonde, heavily made-up, painted fingernails, numerous gold bracelets, wearing a tight sweater and smart slacks. An Aids bow was pinned to the sweater. Her breasts, whether true or false, pointed at them like twin shell cones.

'Sorry to put you through the rigmarole,' she said, 'but you can't be too careful these days, can you?'

'Absolutely right,' Pearson said as she stood to one side and allowed them both to enter.

'You read such dreadful things in the papers. Seems as though serial killers are on the increase. I was reading about that American chap who kept the bodies in his fridge ... And that film! I didn't think that nice Tony Hopkins should have played that part. I like it best when he's a butler. I walked out, couldn't take it after a while. Come on through into the lounge.' She spoke in a strange, little girl's voice, with an accent that suggested she had taken a correspondence course in posh, but had failed to complete the curriculum. 'Wasn't expecting company, so you'll have to excuse the mess. My daily had one of her turns and didn't show up.'

The dog started to bark again as she led them into an over-heated room that had been extended by a conservatory and looked out on to the garden and the river beyond. The main suite of furniture was in leather, arranged in front of a fake log fire. Various women's magazines and dirty coffee cups were strewn around and there was an open box of chocolates on the hearth.

'Can I offer you a drink?' Mrs Carstairs asked.

'A bit early for me,' Pearson said.

'And, no, thank you, I'm driving,' Lloyd replied.

'Quite sure? Well, do you mind if I do? I could just kill for a crème de menthe. My weakness,' she said with a flirty smile, adding 'one of them anyway.' She helped herself from a garish drinks trolley that held a formidable array of bottles. At that moment, the small dog – a minute Yorkshire terrier – crept into the room, took in Pearson and Lloyd, and gave a solitary yap before scurrying to a distant corner of the conservatory.

'Oh, don't be so silly, Monty, come and make friends, come on. Proper little poof, you are.' But the dog stayed put, quivering. 'Funny, dogs, aren't they? Some people they take to straightaway and others make them go all peculiar. As if they sense something, bad vibes or something. You'll have to excuse him. Well, now, what can I do for you? Do sit down. Sling those magazines off the chairs.'

They all sat in an uneasy semicircle. Pearson cleared his

throat. The dog finally crept to its mistress and she picked him up on to her lap.

'Well, I don't know whether your little dog picked up bad vibes from us, Mrs Carstairs,' Pearson began. 'They do say animals have premonitions . . . I'm afraid the reason for our visit is we don't have good news concerning your husband.'

About to take a sip of her drink, Mrs Carstairs paused. Her eyes, heavily outlined in mascara, opened wider.

'I'm sorry I have to tell you this, but he's met with an accident,' Pearson continued in an attempt to cushion the blow.

'What sort of accident?'

'A bad one, I'm afraid.'

'How bad?'

'I'm sure this will come as a terrible shock to you, but it was a fatal accident, Mrs Carstairs.'

'Fatal? Oh, my God! Don't say that. Not my darling, not my Freddie?' She put her drink down clumsily on the coffee table, spilling it across a magazine cover showing Princess Diana. 'How? What sort of accident?'

'He was found dead in a Bayswater hotel.'

'What d'you mean, a hotel? How could he be in a hotel? He couldn't be in Bayswater. He telephoned me on Wednesday from Copenhagen.'

'You're sure of that?' Pearson asked gently.

'Course I'm sure. He'd been delayed over there, said he'd be back today.' She hugged the dog to her bosom. Although obviously distressed, no tears came, but her voice got huskier.

'Well, it appears he changed his plans, Mrs Carstairs, and we were wondering whether you could tell us why.'

She ignored the question. 'Was it . . . Did he have a heart attack? I mean, how did it happen?'

Pearson exchanged a look with Lloyd before answering. 'No, it wasn't a heart attack . . . at the moment, and it's by no means confirmed, it looks as though he took his own life.'

She stared at him without comprehension, then buried her face against the dog. 'He couldn't, why would he do that?' she said in a muffled voice.

Pearson waited, then said: 'I know how distressing this is for you, but anything you can tell us about your husband's state of mind the last time you saw him would help us. Was he depressed about anything?'

She shook her head, her mouth pressed against the dog. 'Not more than usual.'

'What does that mean?'

'Well, he was never what you'd call, how shall I put it? . . . You know, chirpy.'

Lloyd and Pearson avoided each other's eyes. 'Can I ask you if you were aware of the sort of job he was engaged in?' Pearson continued. 'Or, put it this way, did he discuss things with you?'

'All he ever told me was it was sort of police work. Not murders, mostly investigating financial people and that.'

'Nothing else?'

'No. Not anything that comes to mind.' She downed the crème de menthe and poured herself another.

'Well, of course, any police work carries an element of risk these days. And . . . Some of the jobs put us in danger because we're fishing in murky waters. I'm sorry to press you at a time like this, but he never mentioned names, did he? Names of people he was investigating. If you could think back.'

She shook her head. 'Oh, no. My Freddie was very conscientious like that. Not that I ever probed. We kept that part of our lives very separate.'

'Was it money?' Lloyd put in. 'Did he have money worries?'

'Not that I know of. We always had enough. He never kept me short. I could have anything I wanted, I only had to ask.'

'So you can't think why he would do a thing like that?'

'I don't believe he did. Not my Freddie.' She reached for her drink and spilt it again.

'Let me,' Lloyd said, going to the rescue. 'The same, or would you like something stronger?'

'Yes, I'll have a snifter of brandy.' It was only now that her face began to fall apart. A trickle of mascara started to edge

146

down both cheeks.

Lloyd got up and poured the drink for her. As he came back from the trolley he noticed stray black hairs on the nape of her neck protruding from under what he now realised was a blonde wig. Handing her the brandy he shot a quizzical look at Pearson, but Pearson failed to pick up on it.

'What're you saying? I mean, tell me, I can take it now I've got over the first shock. Did he take pills or what?'

'Not pills,' Pearson said gently. 'He used a gun.'

'Oh, my God!' Brandy seeped from the corners of her red mouth, and she choked back a sob.

'D'you have any relatives or friends who could stay with you tonight?' Lloyd asked.

'No relatives, but I've got a friend.'

'Would you like us to contact her for you?'

'Him. No, I'll do it when I've pulled myself together. Where's my Freddie now?'

'I imagine he's been taken to the mortuary.'

'Will I have to go there to identify him?'

Pearson and Lloyd looked at each other before Pearson answered. 'Well, I'm sure somebody else from the department could spare you that. Leave that with me, we wouldn't want you to be more distressed than you obviously are. I'm sorry we had to be the bearers of such sad tidings.'

'No, I'm grateful. Excuse me a minute.'

She put the dog down and left the room. It started to quiver again, then jumped off the sofa and scurried after her.

'Clock the hair when she gets back,' Lloyd whispered.

'What?'

'The hair. It's an Irish.'

'What're you talking about, Irish?'

'Irish jig . . . wig. Doesn't matter. I'll explain later. Let's go, shall we? We're not going to get anything more out of her in the state she's in.'

They stood as Mrs Carstairs returned, having partially repaired her face.

'Look, Mrs Carstairs, if you assure us you won't be on your

own tonight, we won't bother you any more. If you need to contact me or Mr Lloyd here, I'll leave a number where we can both be reached at any time.' He scribbled it on a notepad and left it on the coffee table.

'Thank you. You've both been very kind.'

'We'll see ourselves out. Don't you bother.' As they went into the hallway they heard the chink of a bottle against glass.

Once back inside their car Pearson said, 'What were you trying to tell me in there?'

'Her hair. It's a wig.'

'So? A lot of women wear wigs.'

'Know what I think? I don't think she's a bird. She's a bloke.'

'Come off it!'

'I'm telling you. That's a bloke. I studied her very closely. From the moment she opened her mouth I thought there was something odd about the voice. Didn't you notice it got deeper?'

'Well, she was upset.'

'And she crossed her legs.'

'What does that prove?'

'Okay, then, what about the Aids bow?'

'What about it?'

'Another pointer. It's mostly men who wear those.'

'Mostly, but women aren't excluded, are they?'

'All right, you have it your way,' Lloyd said as he turned the ignition key. 'But I'll take a bet I'm right.'

'You've always had a thing about poofters. Bloody homophobia.'

'Okay, okay, time will tell.'

'You seriously telling me that Carstairs was gay and shacked up with a cross-dresser?'

'Well, it's not exactly unknown,' Lloyd said, increasingly irritated that his judgement was being questioned at every turn. 'Given the moral climate of this country, I'm amazed you're so naive about certain matters.'

'Who said I'm naive? I just don't happen to buy it, that's all.'

They both remained silent until Lloyd said: 'Never really fathomed it.'

'What?'

'The gay scene.'

'What's there to fathom? Some are, some aren't. Some are born like it, some are converted. Some are butch, some are camp, some are screaming. Same building we all inhabit, some just enter by the back door is how I think about it.'

Lloyd took his eyes off the road and glanced at Pearson.

'I've never heard it described like that before.'

'Well, stay around me and you learn something every day.'

17

DOWNING STREET

'I can't say that I'm happy about bringing this Hillsden fellow back,' the Prime Minister said as the sound of Big Ben striking midnight penetrated No. 10's living quarters. 'I made my views clear to the DG yesterday.'

Swanson sat somewhat awkwardly on the edge of a sofa, nursing a gin and tonic. It was the first time he had been received in the inner-sanctum and he felt uncharacteristically nervous. He cleared his throat and started to respond but the Prime Minister cut him short.

'What has to be emphasized . . . excuse me . . . is that we can't afford for there to be any slip-ups. It seems to me that the previous lot were constantly dropping the government of the day in the shit. In the past the word "security" was usually a contradiction in terms.'

'Following the Home Secretary's guide lines, procedures have been considerably tightened, Prime Minister.'

'Well, long may it continue. This whole racist business is as explosive as Semtex. The tabloids – in fact the media in general – give it too much bloody prominence, helped along by some monumental police fuck-ups.' He looked to see how Swanson reacted to the expletives. Relaxed, sure of himself, conscious that he enjoyed the reputation of being somebody who had finally tamed the loony Left wing of the Party, he had a tendency to use shock tactics with anybody he could push around.

'I'm sure that some of the legislation you introduced in the Queen's speech will go a long way to damp down the situation,' Swanson said at his most unctuous.

'Let's hope so. Getting back to this man Hillsden. I've now had a chance to study the papers. I should have got to them before, but for some reason I was kept in the dark about his past. If he was turned once – isn't that the expression you lot use? – what's to say he can't be turned again?'

'Well, since you've now studied the papers, you will have seen that he was deliberately framed by Lockfield.'

'Yes, well, we can't disinter Lockfield, can we? So his side of the story will never be told. In any event, that whole sorry era is best left buried. What I'm saying is, why should we take Hillsden's version as gospel? Philby's autobiography was exposed as a tissue of lies. Spies live by concealing the truth.' Before Swanson could reply, the PM continued: 'I might add that the Home Secretary also had considerable reservations about signing the pardon.'

'I'm aware of that, sir.'

'But you forced it through, right?'

'It was our view, sir, that we needed a highly experienced officer with a low profile – in Hillsden's case, no profile at all, having been out of circulation for seven years. I'm sure you've been told we've also given him a totally new identity as an added safeguard. I believe we've covered all the bases.'

The PM topped-up his own brandy glass. 'So what is the overall aim of this exercise?' he asked. 'Give it to me in a few words, I've got my boxes to do.'

'The plan is for Hillsden to infiltrate – in the same way that undercover intelligence agents infiltrated the IRA with notable results.'

'I wouldn't call them notable,' the PM snapped. 'We had twenty-five years of it and three thousand dead. Let's not equate the Irish situation with something that hasn't even happened.'

'Well, I think we have to,' Swanson said with a flash of spirit, but then immediately used a more placatory tone. 'In many ways it could be even more threatening to mainland Britain than the Irish situation was. There are shades of the 1930s here. My father always used to say that had we had the will then we could have stopped Hitler with one brigade of Guards. Sadly, we didn't have the will. I hope we don't make the same mistake again. The compulsive purifier is the most dangerous extremist.'

'"Compulsive purifier"? What does that mean?'

'You haven't heard that expression, Prime Minister?'

'No, I haven't.'

'Somebody who divides the human race into the ideally good and the intrinsically evil. The more generally used expression is "ethnic cleansing".'

'You're not saying that we face that?'

'It's a logical extension of what these people in our midst believe.'

'I refuse to countenance that. Unthinkable.'

'I'm sure you're right, Prime Minister. But I'm sure you agree we should maintain vigilance. The last thing we would wish would be to lay your government open to the charge of complacency in security matters.'

'Um. Well, provided we don't have any loose cannons as in the past, I'm prepared to give you a limited amount of rope, but I'm not too keen on any American involvement. I don't trust them. Their "special relationship" with us usually means whatever is in their best interests, rather than ours. That's off the record, of course.'

'Of course. I have to say that their co-operation is useful. They recently supplied us with a hit list of prominent Jews as a result of their investigation into the Freidler murder.'

'Freidler?'

'The banker who was murdered in Atlanta.'

'I'm not *au fait* with that.'

'There was a *Panorama* programme about it a few weeks back.'

'I don't watch television if I can help it. More important things to do.'

'According to the FBI, he was murdered by the National Socialist Action Front, a neo-Nazi group banned by the West Germans in '83, but who have since been operating out of Chile.'

'When you say "hit list", you mean it included names on this side of the water?'

Swanson nodded, delighted at being able to score a point. 'Including a member of your Cabinet.'

For the first time the Prime Minister was visibly disconcerted. 'Who?'

'Montague,' Swanson answered, giving the name of the Minister for Social Services.

'Does he know?'

'We thought it best not to alarm him, but the police are providing extra protection.'

'Well, I insist he's told. That's exactly what I mean. You people are a law unto yourselves, and I'm not prepared to be surprised at Question Time in the House. I shall raise it with the DG.' He got up and made a note in his diary.

'We believed we were acting in the Minister's best interests.'

'God forbid you have to say that to his widow. I insist that the Home Secretary and myself are kept fully informed at all times. Is that understood?'

'Of course, Prime Minister.' Swanson got up and placed his empty glass on the coffee-table. 'I'll take personal responsibility for keeping you up-to-date, and I'm most grateful to you for finding time to see me.'

Winding his way down the staircase, he glanced at the framed photographs of past holders of the highest office, most of them looking like average bank managers staring fixedly into camera, their expressions as blank as their achievements. He thought how much he despised the entire political arena. Politicians came and went, relishing their moments of power, but never solving the eternal problems, merely handing down the ragged legacy of their mistakes to those who replaced them.

18

DOCKLANDS

Hillsden had spent the morning on the police firing range testing his rusty skills.

'Either aim at the head or the balls,' his instructor advised. 'If you ever have to use that thing make sure they go down and stay down. You don't get a second chance these days and you're not exactly in line for taking home a coconut at the moment. Here, try another magazine.'

At the third attempt, Hillsden landed a few shots on target. 'That's more like it, but you're still jerking the trigger. Squeeze it gently. And it's got to be instinctive, like this.' The instructor took the gun from him and fired an entire magazine in rapid succession, scoring every time. 'See what I mean?'

'I see what you mean, but I doubt whether I shall ever be a top gun.'

'You don't have to be that good. Just be accurate.'

Hillsden went back to his office in Docklands in chastened mood.

'Any takers, Sarah?' he asked.

'Well, maybe our first customer.' She held up a letter.

'Who is it?'

'Would you believe, a Mr Hyde?'

'I won't make the obvious comment. Is he one of our specimens?'

'Yes, as luck would have it. Lives in Wolverhampton, drives a 1992 Honda Legend, three years no claims bonus and wants us to give him a quote.'

'What other details?'

'Gives his age as thirty, unmarried, and says he has a clean licence and no previous convictions. Which is a lie because he has some form. I ran him through the central computer and came up with two entries. He was bound over for uttering threats against a neighbour in 1988, and then got two weeks for assault in 1990.'

Hillsden took the man's reply from her and studied it. 'Wouldn't win any awards for calligraphy. What was the assault charge?'

'Arrested during a cup tie. In possession of a dangerous weapon, to wit a bowie knife.'

'Just your average football fan out for a quiet afternoon's fun. What are we quoting on a 1992 Honda Legend? Have you looked up the scales they gave us?'

Sarah gave him another sheet of paper. 'Yes, but I'd like you to check it. Does that seem right to you?'

'Very reasonable. Over a hundred pounds less than he's paying on his existing policy.'

'So, shall I write back and give him a quote?'

'No, better still, phone him. I need to get face to face. Thank him for his reply and say you're sure we can quote a substantially reduced rate. Say that, as it happens, one of our representatives, a Mr Bartlett, covers his area and would be pleased to call on him. Ask when it would be convenient and fix it. Use your charm. We're a friendly company, don't forget. That's our image.'

'Is it?'

'Absolutely. Ring him now. And if you get him and he agrees, try and fix an appointment for tomorrow. Oh, and look up the trains to Wolverhampton and see if I can make a connection from Suffolk.'

'Won't you drive up?'

'No. According to the news every bloody motorway to the North is under repair for months, probably years. I'll pick up a hire car when I get there. Oh, and I'll need a street map of the area.'

The next day as he was preparing to leave, Galina said, 'It's not like I thought.'

'In what way?'

'I thought we'd be together more, but you're always away in London.'

'Isn't Audrey good company?'

'She's all right, but I don't understand half the things she says to me. Her accent.'

'Well, early days yet. But you're happy, aren't you? You like this house?'

'I'm not unhappy. Just lonely. How long will you be away in this place you're going to?'

'Only a day. I'll be back tomorrow. Why don't you ask Audrey to drive you into Bury St Edmunds?'

She shrugged.

'D'you have enough money?'

'Yes, I have money. It's not money.'

'What then?' Hillsden said, keeping his voice even, though he was anxious to get away. 'I thought, later on, you should have lessons and take a driving test. Then you could drive yourself around, explore the countryside. No?' when she shook her head. 'Isn't that a good idea?'

'Perhaps. I don't know.' Then she added, 'Lara has nightmares, too. And every day she asks why we've all got different names. She doesn't like her new name. She's only tiny, she doesn't understand, and I don't know how to explain it to her. Can you think of something?'

'I'll try. What did you mean, you have nightmares, too?' He kept the question casual.

'Well, I do.'

'Why didn't you tell me?'

'You've always said you hated hearing about other people's dreams, that they bore you.'

'Well, maybe as a general thing, yes, but nightmares are

156

different,' Hillsden said with a quick glance to the mantelpiece clock. 'If you're troubled you should tell me, that's what I'm here for,' then, as her expression changed, he immediately wished he had put it another way, softened the obvious.

'It's always the same nightmare,' Galina said. 'I'm being questioned by you in a bare room and you're in uniform, like the KGB. You're very angry and you keep shouting at me, but I can't hear the questions so I can't answer you. And then you take out a gun and Lara's there . . . and you shoot her in front of me. That's when it ends.'

Hillsden put his arms around her. 'Oh, sweetheart, that's horrible and I'm sure it's upsetting, but it is just a dream. I wouldn't harm Lara, I love her, I love you and this is a bad time we've got to get through. I wish you could make some friends in the village. Somebody with children of Lara's age. There seem to be plenty about.'

But, even as he spoke the words, he thought, what have I condemned her to? There were fault-lines running through any advice he gave her, since he knew the immediate future held nothing but further loneliness for her. Village life, he thought, why should she get a thrill out of that? I know I wouldn't. The minutia of over-the-hedge gossip, the everlasting British obsession with the weather, local politics that were even more boring than the national variety, elderly women exercising equally elderly dogs, the vicar chatting up church-going spinsters after communion – why am I trying to pretend any of it holds the slightest interest to a Russian girl dumped down in the back of beyond? He remembered a line of Larkin's – *Life is first boredom, then fear.*

'The reason I haven't made friends is because I'm scared.'

'Scared of making friends?'

'No, I'm worried that Lara might say something . . . See, even I use the wrong name . . . Not that she'd mean to, but because she doesn't understand the situation, she might put us in danger.'

'You're not scared living here, are you?'

She shook her head. 'But I only feel safe when you're here.'

'Nobody'll get past Audrey, she's better than a Rottweiler.' He looked at the clock again. 'Darling, I have to go now, otherwise I'll miss the train, but I'll be back tomorrow evening at the latest, and I'll ring you as soon as I get there. When I get back we'll have a proper talk about it and work something out. I can't bear to leave you like this.'

'I'm probably just being silly. Forget it. You get off.'

'No, I can't forget it, and I'll make it right somehow.'

They kissed and he made his escape. Audrey was in the kitchen, swearing to herself, as he appeared downstairs.

'What's wrong?' Hillsden asked.

'Audrey's made a cock-up of these waffles. Thought they'd be a treat for Laura's breakfast. I read somewhere kids like them, but you could re-tile the kitchen with these.' She indicated a stack of rejects on the kitchen table.

'Never mind. The thought's the thing. Do me a favour, try and think of something to amuse them both while I'm away. Georgina seems very depressed this morning. See if there's a good film on. But nothing scary.'

'I'll look in the local paper. Good luck with your trip.'

As he reversed the car out, he realised how swiftly he had once again been absorbed into a world he had thought he had renounced for ever, a world where ordinary emotions were pushed into second place – no time for endearments, no time to make love, just the necessity of the treadmill. On the surface everything was normal: to a casual onlooker in the village he would appear to be a man leaving to go to work, another breadwinner with all the usual worries the struggle for survival imposed. How easily I lie, he thought with a sense of revulsion. To myself, to her. Half of my life has always been hidden. The only person I was ever able to speak to without prudence was Caroline. 'You poor sod,' he said aloud to himself as he adjusted the rear mirror and hit the de-mister button, 'you're back in the game with a vengeance.'

. . .

When he arrived at the station he was greeted with a notice crudely chalked on a blackboard announcing a number of train cancellations due to lack of staff, including the one he had intended to catch. His enquiry at the ticket office produced only a surly and non-committal answer from a fat, unshaven youth wearing what looked like a cast-off uniform several sizes too small for him. The station itself seemed, to his unaccustomed eyes to have been assembled from building blocks. In his memory, he had always retained an image of simple, well-proportioned country stations such as Betjeman had spent a lifetime extolling. Now there was only a plastic uniformity copied from the Siberian model and announcements made in an unintelligible language so that one might as well be an alien visiting earth for the first time. He waited, pacing the platform with fellow disgruntled travellers, until finally the loudspeakers crackled another announcement.

'What did that say?' he asked the man next to him.

'Where are you trying to get to?'

'Wolverhampton.'

'We have to change at the next stop. That is if we ever make the next stop,' the man added with that cheerful fatalism programmed into those who daily entrusted their lives to the British rail system. 'This one terminates there.'

When the train arrived, he and the man got into the same dusty carriage. Discarded beer cans rolled backwards and forwards with the jerky motion and although there were prominent 'No Smoking' notices, Hillsden saw that the floor was littered with butts. He made an effort to put Galina's anxieties out of his mind and to concentrate on what lay ahead. His companion opened his newspaper and Hillsden stared at the headline: *Revealed: the secret thoughts of Harold Macmillan.* As if, he pondered, secret or otherwise, they have any relevance now, except to fill a few column inches, but then he remembered that, when put out to pasture, politicians were always brimming with hindsight. It was a British failing always to hark back to a halcyon past that never existed – to a time when, allegedly, we exerted a benign moral influence, whereas in truth we had always been the bad schoolboys of Europe, breaking the rules with a chilling superiority, Harry Wharton and Co. with an X-rating.

It was mid-morning before he finally arrived at Wolverhampton. He organised a hire car, then checked into the motel that Sarah had booked, paying for it with his credit card and managing to write a decent copy of his well-practised new signature. Like many of its kind, the motel had been designed like the lower decks of a cruise ship – endless narrow corridors, intersected every twenty yards with fire doors, giving access to the identical cubicles. Hillsden opened the door to his room with the plastic security lozenge. Inside it was clean and functional, providing the necessary minimal comforts – a double bed, dressing table unit, a television, trouser press and a tray containing an electric kettle together with a basket full of tea bags, sachets of coffee, sugar and small cartons of long-life milk noted for their resistance to being opened. The framed print above the bed was screwed to the wall, he noticed. Although an improvement on what used to pass for a modest British hotel, there was a sterile gloom about it, betraying the fact that most of those who used it were just passing through. Maybe, Hillsden thought as he unpacked, the very anonymity is a sort of refuge: you bring no memories to it and take away none.

After consulting the notes Sarah had typed for him, he sat on the edge of the bed and dialled Hyde's number, letting it ring half a dozen times before deciding that he would probably have to wait until Hyde returned from work. He spent the next hour going over the sort of questions he would be expected to answer, then switched on the television. The only channel that held his interest for a while was showing an old black and white movie – Jack Warner epitomising the British bobby and meeting his maker at the hands of Dirk Bogarde. Later, he left the room and wandered the streets, amazed by the proliferation and variety of restaurants that had sprung up since last he had been in middle England. The contrast between the present reality and the make-believe world once inhabited by gentle Jack Warner and company brought home how great the change had been. But what surprised him most was the difference in dress: with few exceptions even the middle-aged of both sexes now sported trainers and crumpled jeans – the Americanisation of England being firmly established at all levels, just as the days of Ealing films were over, obliterated by the nihilistic fantasies of Hollywood. It was as though the inhabitants were determined to ape a culture few of them had ever experienced at first-hand, but were brainwashed by the imported sit-coms and mini-series to the point that they no longer had any faith in their native identity.

He had a snack meal then rang Hyde again from a public phone. This time Hyde answered.

'Oh, good afternoon,' Hillsden said. 'My name is Robert Bartlett. Can I speak to Mr Hyde please?'

'Who are you?'

'Bartlett. From Avalon Insurance. My company wrote to you and then I believe you kindly agreed to let me pay you a visit.'

'Oh, yeah, that's right.'

'From what you've told us I think we'd be able to reduce your car insurance substantially. I'm in the area and wondered if it'd be convenient to call on you.'

'When?'

'You say.'

'Now, you mean?'

'If that suits you.'

'Well, I just got in . . . Yeah, okay, but give me a couple of hours.'

'Around seven then,' Hillsden said, consulting his watch. 'Thank you, Mr Hyde. I look forward to meeting you.'

Hyde hung up first. Returning to the hotel, Hillsden showered and, before dressing, rang Galina. Audrey answered.

'Audrey, it's me. How's Georgina?' he asked, remembering

but still finding it strange to use her new name.

'Seems fine.'

'Did you go out?'

'No, she decided against it.'

'I see. Well, let me talk to her.'

When Galina came on the line he willed tenderness into his voice. 'Had a good day, darling?'

'Not too bad.'

'Did you go to the cinema?'

'No.'

'Oh, nothing good you wanted to see? *The Jungle Book* is showing up here, that's something Lara would like.'

'Has your day gone well?'

'Lousy train journey and this hotel's not up to much. I shall be glad to be back in my own bed with you. I miss you. Listen, darling, I'm just off to keep a business appointment, but I'll ring you again. What time are you going to sleep, I don't want to wake you.'

'I don't know, but it doesn't matter if you wake me. Promise you'll ring.'

'Of course I will. Is Lara still up?'

'Yes.'

'Let me say good night.' He heard her shout for the child to come to the phone and a moment later his daughter's squeaky voice was in his ear. Why were children always out of breath when they spoke on the phone? 'Hello, precious. What have you been up to?'

'I saw a fox.'

'You did?'

'Yes, he walked through our garden.'

'Well, that was something, wasn't it?'

'And the cat that lives across the road. He was sick.'

'Was he? Oh, dear.'

'Lots of it. Bye.'

She went. Galina picked up the phone again. 'That was short and sweet,' he said.

'She's watching television.'

'Talk to you later then. Okay? Love you.'

'Love you.'

Before putting on his shirt, he wired himself, using a roll of flesh-coloured surgical tape first to attach the battery to his waist, then strapped the miniaturised recorder under his left arm. Once he had finished dressing, he carefully checked his appearance in the mirror, then left the room. It was raining when he got to the car park and the wipers on the rented car smeared the windscreen. Aiming to give himself plenty of time to find Hyde's house, he consulted his street map again before driving off. His route took him out of the city to what looked like a recently built housing estate – row upon row of neat, characterless boxes arranged back to back. He finally located Hyde's house and, as he was still early, drove on past it, noting a dozen or more 'For Sale' boards, a pointer to the long recession that was still depressing the market, Thatcher's dream of a house-owning society in ruins. Here and there, satellite dishes were stuck to the side walls, their phallic centre stamens aimed skyward to capture Murdoch's electronic Babel. Circling the estate by a different route he came upon a mosque, its dull gold minarets outlined against the turbulent clouds, and close by a wooden structure advertising itself as the local Labour Party Club – one sacred alongside one profane? Hillsden wondered. Retracing his route at a deliberately slow speed (he felt it was probably a good thing not to appear too keen), he arrived outside Hyde's house eight minutes after seven. Hyde's Honda was parked on the small forecourt. Before leaving his own car he activated the tape recorder.

Hyde opened the front door after the second ring. He was a burly man with tight, wavy hair which clung close to his scalp, clean shaven, wearing a smart denim shirt and jogging trousers, and seemed at first glance older than the age he had given on his reply form.

'Mr Hyde?'

'That's right.'

'Bartlett. Sorry I'm slightly late. These streets all look alike and I took a couple of wrong turnings.'

'Yeah, it happens. You want to come in?'

'Thank you.'

Hillsden was led into a neat, open-plan living room-cum-kitchen, furnished with a collection of matching Habitat pieces. There were no feminine touches and the only decoration was a large, framed map of the world, illuminated from behind, which showed the time zones.

'Let's sit at the table,' Hyde said. 'Can I give you a beer?'

'That's kind of you but, no, I'd better not. I'm driving.'

'Suit yourself,' Hyde replied laconically. He moved to the fridge and took out a can for himself. 'So, what have you got for me?' There was no trace of a provincial undertone in his voice. If anything, Hillsden would have placed it as a flat, London accent.

Hillsden opened his briefcase and took out the necessary papers. 'Well, now, let's see, I'll just run through your letter. You own a '92 Honda, which I take it is the one outside?'

'Yeah.'

'And under your current policy you're paying four hundred and forty for full comprehensive, with a hundred pounds excess. You have a clean licence, correct?'

'Correct.'

'Good.' Hillsden made a tick on the form. 'Anything pending I should know about?'

'Couple of parking tickets.'

'Well, we won't bother about those. I had four in the last month. They work on commission, you know, those cowboys.'

'You don't have to tell me. I hate the pigs.'

'I see you give your occupation as company director. What sort of company is it?'

'Private security. We patrol this estate, looking after the whites.'

Hillsden made no reaction to the use of the word 'whites', but said, 'It's terrible, isn't it, the way we all have to live now? And getting worse. I shouldn't complain, I suppose, because it's good for my business, but everywhere I go I see the same thing. The only growth industry in this country seems to be crime.'

'Yeah, you can say that again.'

'You're much younger than me, but I can remember when I grew up my parents never locked the front door. They kept the key on a piece of string through the letter box. Things have certainly changed since those days.'

'Yeah. So, what're you offering?'

'Sorry. Didn't mean to get on my hobby-horse. Well, now, taking into account your clean bill of health, the age of the car and the fact that you're not engaged in any of the restricted occupations – actors and jockeys are high on the list, believe it or not – I can quote you a very keen price.'

'How keen?' Hyde took another drink from the beer can.

'Give me a minute.' Hillsden took out a pocket calculator and punched in some numbers, then paused. 'I'll be frank with you, Mr Hyde. In order to compete with the big boys we have to cut our overheads down to the bone, which in turn means we can pass on the savings to our customers. Plus the fact we want your business. And since you're my first in this area, I'm going to bend over backwards.' He resumed his calculations, then paused again. 'One thing I should have asked. You have a current MOT on the car, I take it?'

'Yeah. Want to see it?'

'No, I'll accept your word ... Now then, what comes up for full comprehensive, excess slashed from a hundred to fifty, plus free windscreen replacement for one year, is a saving to you of a hundred and eight pounds. Your premium would be three thirty-two, payable in one lump sum or, if you prefer, twenty-seven and a bit a month plus two per cent interest. If you stay with us and don't have a claim we guarantee the rate for three years.' He was enjoying himself and was secretly pleased that he had mastered the patter.

'Three thirty-two?' Hyde repeated.

'That's what I said. How does that seem to you?'

'What's the catch?'

'No catch. We want the business from reliable people like yourself.'

Hyde got up from the table and went for a second can of beer. 'Sure you won't change your mind?'

'Okay,' Hillsden said, 'you twisted my arm.'

'This is good stuff. Chum of mine goes over to France every week. Nice to get something back from the frogs for a change.'

He opened Hillsden's can before passing it to him. 'Yes, okay,' he said, 'I'll go for it.'

'You will? Wonderful. I assure you, you won't regret it. Cheers.' He drank some of the beer and relaxed for the first time since he had entered the house. 'Excuse me asking, but is that real?' He pointed to a parrot perched on top of the television set.

Hyde laughed. 'No. Fools everybody though. A girlfriend gave it to me for Christmas. Watch. Listen to this.' Projecting his voice louder in the direction of the parrot, he said: 'Pakis out.'

There was a slight pause and then the parrot repeated, 'Pakis out.'

'Cute, huh?'

'Incredible. Will it say anything else?'

'Sure. Repeats everything. Try it.'

Hillsden spoke at the bird. 'Pretty Polly.'

The parrot repeated the words.

'How the hell does it work?'

'Who knows?'

'What a novelty. I must get one of those for the office. Be a talking point with clients.' He returned to his papers. 'So, we're in business, are we? I've filled in all the necessary details, all it needs is your signature here . . . and for you to initial there and there. Did you want to pay monthly?'

'I think maybe, yeah.'

'Then you'll need to fill in a bank mandate.' He passed the papers and a pen across the table to Hyde. 'Keep the pen, by the way, it's got our telephone number on in case you need us for any emergencies.'

Hillsden watched as Hyde completed and handed back the

papers. 'I'll send you the policy later this week. You have seven days to study it before you're committed. I think that's everything, and thank you once again.' He drank some of his beer before saying casually, 'Do you get much aggro on this estate in your line of business?'

'You'd better believe it. This place is a ghetto, swarming with coloureds. What you said about your parents is true. Are they alive?'

'No, they both passed on some years ago.'

'They're well out of it. They wouldn't recognise this country. There's no Great Britain any more. Unless we're very careful we whites are going to be in a minority.'

Hillsden fingered his beer can and avoided looking at Hyde when he answered. I need to pitch my response very carefully, he thought. 'Sadly, I think you're probably right.'

'I know I'm right. Look at the birth rate, theirs and ours. We're on the decline, they're breeding like rabbits.'

Hillsden nodded. 'Nothing we can do about it, unfortunately. We've left it too late.'

'Not us – them, those useless wankers up in Whitehall. They're the ones who've sold us down the river.' Hyde crumpled his beer can and tossed it with accurate aim into the sink. 'But some of us are doing something about it,' he said loudly and the repetition came back from the parrot: 'But some of us are doing something about it.'

Hyde said, 'Where do you live?'

'Forest Gate, East London.'

'Married?'

'I was. My wife died.'

'Any kids?'

'Unfortunately no.'

'Well, maybe that's no bad thing. I've got two kids, boy and girl. So what's their life going to be? They're already outnumbered by coloureds in the classroom. Listen, my view is they're entitled to their own lives, but not here, not in our country. They should ship them all back to where they belong. Overnight you'd wipe out the drug scene, most of the crime and unemployment.'

It was the usual bigot's dialogue, Hillsden thought, belonging to the some-of-my-best-friends-are-Jews school. 'Of course, many of them are second and third generation,' he said, playing devil's advocate.

'So? Don't change their colour, does it? Listen, it isn't just us. Happening all over Europe. The Germans have got the right idea.'

'How's that?'

'I'll show you.' Hyde got up and rummaged in one of the kitchen drawers, producing a magazine. 'Take this with you. It'll open your eyes, believe me.'

Hillsden glanced at the magazine which seemed to have been crudely produced on a computer. It was headed *Action Now!*

'That tells it like it is,' Hyde said. 'The Germans are our natural allies if you study history like I have. I mean, time has shown we should never have declared war on them. If we'd have thrown our lot in with them in '39, we wouldn't be in this mess now. Together we could have taken Russia out just like that,' he snapped his fingers, 'saved ourselves the Cold War.'

'Would that have saved the Jews, do you think?'

'Well, who knows? That's something else. You ever read anything of David Irving's?'

Hillsden shook his head.

'You should. It's an education. He's got his own theories on that subject. But take that copy if you like, read it, might give you something to think about.'

'Thank you, I will.' Hillsden stood up. 'It's been a pleasure to do business with you, Mr Hyde. Enjoy cheaper motoring.'

'Enjoy cheaper motoring,' the parrot said as he left the room.

19

CONVERSATIONS

'Do you ever think about dying?' Lloyd asked. He and Pearson were eating a pizza on their knees in their unmarked car.

'What brought that up, apart from this junk?'

'I don't know, I go to sleep every night wondering whether I'll ever wake next morning. Does it take you like that?'

'No. You must have a guilty conscience about something. Been cheating on the wife?'

'What d'you think about at night then?'

Pearson put the remains of his pizza back in the box and closed the lid. He wiped his mouth on a tissue. 'God, that was revolting. I don't know how this country got hooked on pizzas. It's like the Italians slipped in a new disease when we weren't looking.'

'Mine's okay,' Lloyd said. 'So tell me.'

'Tell you what?'

'At night, what d'you think about?'

'You really want to know? Last night, I wondered whether my eldest grandson was on crack, whether the dishwasher would last out the week and whether my wife had remembered to buy a lottery ticket.'

'And had she?'

'Don't know. Slipped my mind this morning.'

'That's a reason for suicide. Imagine, you use the same numbers every week, you finally hit the jackpot, and then find it's the one time you forgot. Be worse than death, wouldn't it?'

'Cheer me up, won't you?'

'Tell you something else. You were talking about retirement the other day. That's on my mind, too. But I've worked out what I'm going to do, I've already put out feelers. I'm going to get myself a job on one of those crime-reconstruction series on the telly. They've got more police on those than there are on the beat some weeks.'

'And a better success rate,' Pearson said gloomily. 'Notice they always get their man.' He took an antacid tablet and washed it down with a diet Coke. He stared through the windscreen at the passing scene in Queensway. At that moment a traffic warden, nattily attired in one of the new uniforms, arrived by the car and took out his charge pad. Pearson wound down his window.

'You can put that away, sunshine.'

The man went on writing. 'You're on a yellow line.'

'No, what we're on is duty. Now, unless you want to be arrested for perverting the course of justice, I suggest you tear that up. We're here on official business.'

'They all try and pull that one.'

'Do they? Well, perhaps they don't all carry one of these.' Pearson produced his identity card. The warden glanced at it without a change of expression.

'You're still on a yellow line.' He tore off the parking ticket and put it behind the windscreen wipers before moving off.

'Now that has given me thoughts of death,' Pearson said. 'His death.' He put his hand around the side of the window and retrieved the ticket. He gave it to Lloyd. 'You're the driver, you pay it. I'll tell you what does occupy me at night: why did Carstairs top himself?'

'And why was he having a drink with a tycoon?'

'If he was. The owner wasn't positive.'

'Shouldn't we question Charters?'

'Gilbert already has.'

'And?'

'Strongly denies he ever met Carstairs.'

'No harm in us having a second go.'

'Swanson's adamant we don't.'

'Why?'

'Charters is very litigious, issues writs like most people tear off toilet paper. Plus Swanson doesn't want anyone smelling around our Copenhagen operation. I must admit Charters's name cropping up intrigues me though,' Pearson mused. 'I wouldn't have thought Tudor's was his scene. He's not your average disco dancer.'

'Have you seen the waitresses? All dressed like Anne Boleyn with a lot of tit showing.'

'Maybe he's like you, a keen student of history. I must admit this whole Carstairs business has me foxed. Especially since we met Mrs Carstairs. Something doesn't add up.'

'Blackmail maybe?'

'Crossed my mind. Doubt it. No money worries that we know of.'

'The autopsy didn't give us any other clues, did it?'

Pearson shook his head. 'Unless you want confirmation that his idea of a good time was anal penetration.'

'Do me a favour,' Lloyd said with a grimace. 'I don't like hearing those things. Was he HIV positive?'

Pearson shook his head. 'Clean as a whistle. One of the lucky ones.'

'What's the form with our master sleuth, Mr Gilbert then?'

'Cut and dried suicide. No further interest, over to us if we wish to pursue it. You know what they're like at the Yard, they haven't got time to solve crimes, too busy sorting out rogue coppers.'

The traffic warden passed them again. 'And if you're still here when I come back, you'll get another one,' he threw in.

Pearson checked his watch. 'May as well move off, that ponce means what he says. Drop me in Docklands before you take that meeting with the FBI at the embassy. Play it cautiously with them. Word has come down that we're to keep our cards to ourselves.'

'What's this American guy's name?' Lloyd asked as he turned the ignition key.

'Schmidt. Might be a good idea if you went over to Copenhagen on the quiet. Carstairs was getting his information from a character called Van Elst. You could lean on him, no harm done now that Carstairs is out of it.'

Just before they arrived in Docklands, Pearson remarked: 'I'm looking forward to meeting Hillsden at last. Anybody who helped torpedo Lockfield deserves our gratitude. Hillsden was a legend in his time.'

'Aren't we all?' Lloyd said.

. . .

'Hold it there,' Pearson said as he listened to Hillsden's tapes. 'Who was that, who said that?'

'A parrot.'

'A parrot?!'

'It was a mechanical parrot,' Hillsden said, enjoying Pearson's look of surprise, 'repeats everything anybody says.'

'Maybe we should subpoena it as a material witness. Switch off for a moment. Seems to me all you've got so far is fairly tame and predictable.'

'Yes, I agree. You can pick up that sort of dialogue in any pub.'

'Have you contacted him again as he suggested?'

'No, not yet,' Hillsden replied. 'Swanson thought it might look too keen. You seen this rag before?' He picked up *Action Now!*

'Seen varieties of it.'

'Any idea as to where it originates?'

Pearson shook his head. 'Could be any one of a million computers. Did Hyde have a computer?'

'Not that I saw. Didn't seem the computer type to me. Tell me, how come he's allowed to run a security outfit? He has form. Don't they vet these characters?'

'Not that you'd know of.'

'Jesus!'

'How is the rest of the operation going? Have you got any response from any of the other targets on the list?'

'Not so far. We've sent out just under a hundred brochures and so far issued seven policies to genuine customers.'

'Disappointing. Still. Want to ask you something,' Pearson said, switching subjects. 'In the old days did you ever come across one of our chaps called Carstairs?'

'Carstairs? . . . No, don't think so. What was he in?'

'D Section.'

'Doesn't ring a bell. Why?'

'He was transferred to Swanson's operation and sent to Copenhagen to plug a hole there. Weird little character. Weirder than we thought as it turns out. He tipped us off about a consignment of anti-Semitic literature coming our way, then a few days later blew his brains out.'

'What did you mean when you said "weirder than we thought"?'

'Well, as far as we knew he was a happily married man. And in the wider sense that was true. But it turns out that Mrs Carstairs is a drag queen.'

'That's a new one. Even Blunt never went that far,' Hillsden said. 'Maybe we're in for a new cycle of memoirs.'

'I read yours,' Pearson said casually. 'How did you remain sane?'

'What makes you think I did? D'you ever wonder that maybe the reason some of us go off the edge or round the bend is because the job is too awful or too ridiculous to endure?'

'Probably. I've known a few who finally can't take the loneliness and duplicity . . . That might have been Carstairs' problem. Did you ever think of ending it while you were over there?'

'There were times,' Hillsden said. 'I could have drunk myself to death at one point. I guess what saved me when I was staring into the abyss was my wife. I owe her everything. It was a bad time for her, too, until the *coup*. Having our daughter made it all possible.'

'And when this offer came, did you hesitate?'

'Yes.'

'What made you bite the bullet a second time?'

'Money. By the law of averages I'll be under the sod before my daughter's twenty-one. I wanted to leave her and my wife something I never had. Security. That sounds funny, bearing in mind our jobs.'

'And to clear your name?' Pearson asked.

'That too. Again mainly because of my daughter.'

'Are you bitter? I'd be bloody bitter if it'd been me.'

'I'm getting over it. I'd like to have the wasted years back, and lose a few memories . . . ' Anxious to get off the subject, Hillsden said: 'This man Carstairs, was he working on his own or do you have a network out there?'

'On his own. Networks are a thing of the past with the exception of the Middle East . . . ' Pearson broke off and asked: 'Do you have a glass of water?'

'Sure.'

'I need to take a tablet.'

Hillsden went into the small kitchen. 'Tap water okay?'

'Anything.'

Handed the glass, Pearson palmed two tablets into his mouth and swallowed them. 'Occupational condition. I've got one of those stomachs that produces pure prussic acid. What were you saying?'

'I was thinking if Carstairs was flying solo and his cover was blown, couldn't that be the answer?'

'Except they didn't kill him. He came home and topped himself.'

'That's confirmed, is it?'

'Yeah, I don't think there's any room for doubt.'

'How rough do these boys play? They've given me a pea-shooter, presumably with good reason?'

'I think we're looking at a future scenario that could get very rough. The signs are all there. Not that the politicians are prepared to admit it, they're more concerned with deciding where the fucking Channel Tunnel rail link ends up. The truth is governments don't work any more, they promise too much

174

and then can't deliver. And when that happens over a long enough period, the die has been cast, and the reactionaries start moving in. There's a madman waiting in the wings in Russia, Italy's just about ready for somebody to drain the Pontine marshes again, old familiar tunes are being played in Germany . . . and we poor sods are meant to sort it all out with our hands tied behind our backs.'

Pearson's monologue had brought the blood to his cheeks and he seemed embarrassed by his own vehemence. 'Still, I expect we'll muddle through like we always do. Lose all the battles, but win the war.' He stared morosely at the tape recorder, then pressed the rewind button. 'Let me listen to this again. Did you watch television last night by any chance?'

'No, 'fraid not.'

'By coincidence, there was a documentary about Mosley. Impressive speaker. I could understand why people followed him. Odd to think that at one time he was being spoken of as a possible Prime Minister. He might have made it if he hadn't changed his colours. That's a thought, isn't it?'

20

A KILLING IN THE NIGHT

It was the first dead body PC Walters had ever seen. Now, as he stared in some disbelief at the Rt Honourable Emanuel Montague's mutilated corpse he struggled to remember correct procedures. Fumbling with his cellular phone, he twice misdialled before getting through to the station.

'728 PC Walters. Give me the duty officer.'

'What's your problem, Walters?' the station Sergeant asked.

'I'm not sure, Sergeant. Looks like a murder.'

'Hang on, son. First things first. Where are you?'

'Hamilton Terrace,' Walters stammered.

'What number?'

'What's its . . . Montague's house.'

'Shit! Who's dead?'

'Him, himself, the Minister.'

'Oh, shit!' the Sergeant repeated. 'Right, son, don't touch anything, go outside, stay there and I'll get you back-up.'

Before he had stumbled from the scene of the crime Walters had tried mentally to Polaroid his initial impressions. *If you're first on the scene be sure to register details*, had been drummed into him during training, but now he found his mind was a blank. Had he touched anything, disturbed any evidence? He couldn't remember. But he knew that for the rest of his life he would never forget Montague's dead face.

Although Montague, like the rest of the Cabinet, was entitled to police protection, it had not been thought necessary to give him round-the-clock armed protection, since the post of Minister for Social Services was not considered to be high risk. Instead, at night, his London house in this fashionable and expensive area was patrolled every hour. In addition, like his Cabinet colleagues, he had been hooked up to British Telecom's Red Care system, which ensured that if the line to his burglar alarm was ever cut, a signal would be automatically flashed to the police. It was subsequently determined that no such signal had ever been received, the control box digital print-out establishing that the installation had not been operative at the time of the murder.

During the course of his tour of duty that night Walters had twice assured himself that all was well, once at eleven p.m. and again at one a.m. It wasn't until he returned a third time, just before he was due to hand over the beat to his relief, that he noticed something different: a red swastika had been sprayed on to the front garden perimeter wall close to the entrance gate. He directed his torch to examine it more closely, then aimed the beam towards the house. The light picked out another swastika on the front door. He opened the gate to take a closer look and as he advanced up the forecourt he saw that the front door was ajar. There was a closed circuit television camera fixed above the portico, but the lens had been obliterated with black foam. He hesitated, unsure what to do next, then tentatively pushed the door wider and called, 'Sir? Mr Montague, sir?'

There was no reply. He had never met Montague, but had been told that the Minister lived alone when in London, his only staff being a housekeeper who came in on a daily basis, and a government chauffeur who picked him up every morning.

The hallway was in darkness, but he saw a faint light coming from one of the rooms leading off the hallway.

'Police, Mr Montague. Is everything all right?'

Walters took one step inside, then paused, wondering whether such a move would activate an alarm, but nothing happened. He walked slowly towards the light, careful to tread lightly on the marble floor and said, 'PC Walters, sir. Just checking. Your front door was open.' His voice sounded unreal to him, as though coming from a stranger.

He stood outside the room for fully half a minute, weighing up the options open to him. He reached behind and released his truncheon, the only weapon he carried. Listening for and hearing no sign from within, he took a deep breath and pushed the door wide open. He found himself looking into a library. The light source was an overturned lamp which lay on its side close to a leather-topped partner's desk, the crumpled shade a short distance away. He could see no sign of Montague, but he became aware of a sharp, pungent odour he could not identify but would later be told was a mixture of bodily fluids, blood and cordite. Venturing further towards the broken lamp, it was then that he saw Montague, pitched backwards in his armchair, very obviously dead even to Walters's inexperienced eyes, for his throat had been cut from ear to ear so that the head now hung at an angle. A large quantity of blood darkened the front of his torso and ran all the way down to the thick pile carpet. The Minister's red box had been placed on his chest and a notice taped to it. Walters managed not to gag and shone his torch down on the body. Even from a distance he could read the words on the notice. Wavy capitals, almost certainly sprayed from the same can that had produced the swastikas outside, spelled out: *ANOTHER JEW LESS*. What he failed to notice and omitted from his subsequent written account, was that Montague had also been shot twice; the pathologist later determined that two .22 bullets had been fired from less than three feet away, the first shearing off Montague's top set of dentures, the second entering his left cheek. Fired in pairs known in police jargon as 'double taps', they were the hallmark of a professional assassin.

Out of his depth, and with rising nausea, Walters backed out of the room without making any closer examination. Once in the fresh air again he had retched into a flower bed before being able to phone for assistance.

Three squad cars and an ambulance arrived in quick

succession, the lead car containing two CID officers, one he recognised as a Superintendent Goodwin, a character remote to Walters, with the reputation of being a martinet.

'Who are you?'

'PC Walters, sir.' Walters stood to attention.

'Did you originate the call?'

'Yes, sir.'

'So, show us, where is he?'

Walters led the way into the house. 'In there, sir.' He indicated the murder room. Goodwin and his team went inside. Uncertain as to what was now required of him, Walters hovered in the doorway for a few moments, but when nobody paid him any further attention, he retreated outside. Other cars arrived bringing another CID team. They brushed past him as he stood by the gate wishing he had the courage to have a cigarette. Lights went on in the houses across the street and a man appeared in a dressing-gown.

'What's going on?' the man shouted. 'Somebody hurt?'

'Nothing, sir,' Walters replied. 'Nothing to worry about,' hoping this was the correct response, 'just investigating an alarm call.'

'Pity we don't all get that sort of response,' the man said pithily. 'I waited twenty minutes the other night when mine went off. One law for them, another for us.' He stood surveying the scene for a while, then went back into his house, still muttering.

Walters's relief arrived at that moment, a taciturn older Constable named Cooper, who prided himself for never being fazed by anything.

'What's this flap about then?' Cooper asked.

'Murder, Coop.' Glad to have one of his own kind for company and beginning to recover from the shock of his discovery, Walters made the most of his moment of revelation. 'Somebody's killed the Minister.'

'Oh, yes? Was it you who found him?'

'Yes.'

'Lucky you. Glad it wasn't me. You're in for a long night,

son, writing that up.' Flashing lights from the various squad cars illuminated his smile. 'It's certainly brought out the heavy mob. Who's in charge?'

'The Super. Goodwin.'

'Oh, Christ! Well, I'll make myself scarce.'

'You're meant to relieve me.'

Cooper shook his head. 'No, son. You've got a lot to learn. First on the scene stays until the incident officer dismisses him. You can report that I arrived at the correct time, judged that the situation did not require my presence and went about my proper business, namely policing the rest of the neighbourhood as per.'

He walked away.

Mindful of what Cooper had said, Walters took out his notebook, consulted his watch and was about to begin writing up his report when Goodwin came out of the house.

'You, Constable.'

Walters straightened and turned. 'Sir?'

'What can you tell me?'

'Arriving here to make my hourly inspection, sir, I first noticed the painted signs on the wall and door.'

'What time was that?'

Walters consulted his empty notebook, hoping this would impress Goodwin. 'I have it down as 02.05, sir.'

'And?'

'Well, sir, seeing as how the front door was open, I entered the premises and called out for the occupant – the Minister, sir. Getting no response, I then proceeded further into the house where I saw a light. I then discovered the body.'

'Did you search the rest of the house?'

'No, sir, I immediately phoned the station.'

'But *after* you phoned the station?' Goodwin snapped.

'No, sir, I was told to stay outside.'

'While you were away on your beat, did you see anything suspicious, any cars cruising around?'

'No, sir, the only person I encountered during the previous two hours was a foreign lady who wanted to be directed to

Notting Hill Gate tube.'

'Uh-huh. Well, have a full report on my desk first thing tomorrow.' Goodwin gave no sign that the account had impressed him and went back into the house. Walters felt sweat trickling down from his armpits. He remained at his post for a further two hours until Montague's bagged body was removed. Goodwin and his team walked past him and drove off without a word, leaving the forensic boys to continue working. Still uncertain as to what he should do, Walters had to wait until Cooper finally returned.

'How did you make out with his nibs? Has he gone?'

'Yes. Don't know. Told him all I knew. What d'you think I should do now?'

'Piss off, if I was you, and sell your story to the papers.'

'Don't be daft. Can I go?'

'Far as I'm concerned you can.'

'Will you take over then?'

'Yeah, long as I've missed him.'

As Walters walked back to the station he went over the night's events, hoping that his luck held, that he had not committed any major gaffe. Nothing in his training or the handbooks had prepared him for finding a Minister of the Crown with his throat cut.

21

POST-MORTEMS

The story broke the following day, the first editions of *The Standard* giving it front-page headlines and devoting many column inches inside to an account of Montague's life and achievements. He was described as a devoted family man, proud of his humble origins, an astute politician and passionate supporter of the State of Israel, to which he had donated substantial funds over the years. The lunchtime television news bulletins were extended; Members of Parliament of all persuasions were united in singing his praises as well as deploring his hideous death; the Prime Minister recorded a personal tribute which was televised in all the evening news programmes. A message of sympathy from the Queen was sent to his family, and word was received that the Israeli Foreign Secretary would fly to England for the funeral. It possibly came as a surprise to many that a relatively obscure member of the Cabinet who, while alive, had never attracted undue media attention, should now be painted as a latter-day saint, whose loss immeasurably impoverished the nation's future.

Immediately after he had been informed, the Prime Minister called an emergency meeting of the Cabinet and arranged a reshuffle. Coming as it did not long after he had been deprived of Logan's predecessor, he was conscious that his original, carefully positioned team was now in disarray. When the Cabinet dispersed he had a further session with

Logan and the Commissioner of police.

'It's obvious that the security arrangements were totally inadequate. A good and valuable man is struck down in his own home simply because your people weren't capable of protecting him.'

'We do all we can, Prime Minister,' the Commissioner replied, 'but without introducing draconian measures which would restrict everybody's freedom, I think we have to accept the fact that, in a democracy, a determined terrorist, striking at random, will often succeed, whatever steps we take.'

Logan cleared his throat. 'I have to agree with the Commissioner, regrettable though it is.'

'Well, I don't accept it,' the PM said. He brandished a memo at them. 'I don't call a young, unarmed and inexperienced policeman – who's only been in the Force four months – adequate protection for a member of Cabinet. And how is it that the left hand doesn't know what the right hand is doing? A week or so ago MI5 told me that the Yanks had warned us that a hit list existed and that poor Montague's name was on it. I told them to tell you. Did either of you know that? And if not, why not?'

Logan and the Commissioner looked at each other. Neither wished to be the first to answer, but Logan was forced to. 'I wasn't aware of that particular piece of information,' he said, 'but, of course, the Home Office receives a great number of similar reports, most of which turn out to be the work of hoaxers. Every one has to be investigated and faithfully followed up, but there's a limit, as the Commissioner rightly says, to what his stretched resources can do.'

'That's always the excuse, and I don't wear it. We've poured money into the police and security services, and to be fair, so did the Tories, and yet nothing changes. We were elected on a promise to reverse the trend and something like this makes us a laughing stock. You mark my words, when the media have stopped crying crocodile tears over Manny, they'll turn on us, I've no illusions about that.'

'With all due respect, Prime Minister,' the Commissioner

began, 'the police are always used as a political football. One moment I'm being told to provide more community policing, the bobbies-on-bicycles syndrome, and the next moment asked to take a tougher line. I'm in a no-win situation. Are you saying that I should openly arm every one of my men, a Belfast scenario? Because that's the road we'd be going down. I accept that the tragic affair of last night means we must take a hard look at what went wrong and learn the lesson. However, sir, if you think it appropriate, I am prepared to let the buck stop with me and offer my resignation.' He said all this quietly, but there was no mistaking the ice in his voice.

'I don't want your resignation, Commissioner, though I applaud your integrity. But you have to shake a few rotten apples out of the tree.'

The Commissioner was dismissed, but Logan was asked to stay behind. The moment they were alone the PM turned on him. 'That advice goes for your department too. Tell everybody to pull their finger out. I gave you the bloody job, and I can just as soon take it away. I didn't drag the Party into the twenty-first century to have it brought down by a few neo-Fascists. Root them out or I'll appoint somebody who can.'

. . .

While this dialogue was taking place, a jet-lagged Marvin Schmidt woke up in his London hotel with the phone ringing. It took him several seconds to grasp which country he was in.

'Sorry? Who is this?'

'Commander Pearson. You met with my colleague, Lloyd, yesterday.'

'Oh, yeah.'

'I think you and I should meet urgently in view of what happened last night.'

'What did happen?'

'Haven't you heard?'

'No, I'm sorry, I'm still in the sack. I overslept.'

'One of our politicians, a Minister, was assassinated. He was on that hit list you brought us.'

By now Schmidt had swung his legs over the side of the bed and was coming to. 'Jesus! Right. Give me half an hour and I'll be with you. Where are you?'

'No, I'll come to you. You're at the Hilton, aren't you? I'll pick you up in the coffee shop and take you to Swanson's club.'

'Club?'

'Yes, he thinks our comings and goings will attract less attention there.'

'Okay.'

On his way to the bathroom Schmidt switched on the television. Having put his head under a cold shower he returned to the bedroom and gleaned the facts about Montague's murder while he dressed.

. . .

Equally unaware of the night's events, Hillsden was working at his office, going through the latest batch of replies they had received when he became aware that the light on his scrambler phone was blinking. He picked up.

Swanson wasted no time on social niceties: 'Pearson thinks we should all meet in view of this latest thing.'

'What's that?'

'Haven't you seen the papers?'

'Not yet.'

'Switch on your television then.'

'I haven't got one here. What're we talking about?'

Swanson told him.

. . .

'This is some place,' Schmidt said. From the moment he had walked in with Pearson, he had been impressed by the polished furniture, the vast portraits of departed luminaries, the reverential atmosphere.

'Yes,' Swanson said, 'we've got some very good kit here.'

'What's it take to join a club like this?'

'A long time,' Swanson replied with a stab at humour.

He settled back into an ancient leather armchair once the drinks had been served. 'Do we look like the Five Just Men? I hope not. This place is very discreet.'

'Four,' Hillsden murmured.

'Come again?'

'The book was called *The Four Just Men*. Sorry, I get very pedantic sometimes.'

'Drank a lot of tea,' Lloyd said.

'What are we talking about now?' Swanson asked.

'Edgar Wallace, the man who wrote it. I read he had his staff put cups of tea all over the house while he dictated. So wherever he walked around he could always find a fresh cup of Rosy handy.'

'That's enough trivia, let's get down to business. Do we have any preliminary details of the autopsy?'

'Yes, basics,' Pearson said. 'He was shot twice by a point twenty-two automatic, and according to Hogg, our pathologist, the throat cutting was done afterwards.'

'Was it a Ruger?' Schmidt interjected.

'The gun? Not sure. They're still carrying out ballistic tests.'

'Freidler was killed by a Ruger, same calibre. The bullets have a low mass and velocity, seldom produce an exit wound but sure make a mess of your insides.'

'What puzzled even Hogg were a number of small foam particles he found in Montague's head.'

'The killer probably used a home-made silencer.' The other four men looked blank and he elaborated: 'An empty Pepsi can fitted over the barrel and filled with plastic is very effective with a Ruger. The smart operators prefer it to the real thing – instantly disposable.'

'New one on me,' Pearson said.

'They found the same traces when they opened up Freidler.'

'You're not suggesting it was the same man who did both jobs, are you?' Swanson said, irritated that the American was airing his superior knowledge.

'No, just that the similarity's there. In both cases it was a professional gun for hire, depend on it. But that's no great surprise, there are plenty of wet boys around when you need one.'

'What's that expression mean?' Swanson asked.

'Agency-speak for assassin.'

Pearson turned to Schmidt. 'Was Freidler on that list the Bureau supplied us with? I can't remember off-hand.'

'No. But, as you must know, he was a very prominent member of the Jewish banking community. Wall Street and Zurich felt that bullet going in.'

'Well, because of some inter-departmental fuck-up,' Pearson continued, 'the police didn't get sight of that list in time. Logan got bollocked by the PM and I got an earful from the Commissioner. Not our bloody responsibility, yet we get the blame.' He turned to Swanson. 'How come the Met were left out?'

'I've no idea. I certainly passed it on.'

'Well, we'd better tighten up all round.'

It was not to Swanson's liking that Pearson had taken over the meeting. He cleared his throat. 'I've gone through it again very carefully and as far as I can ascertain, apart from Montague, there are only two other names on the list that are our immediate concern, the first being Lord Miller, Chairman of Trans-Continental.'

Schmidt asked: 'Jewish?'

'Yes. Original name was Muller, I believe. Pillar of society. Not short of a few million. Was once a member of Maggie's think tank, serves part-time on the Race Relations Board. The other name is Paul Sheenham,' Swanson continued, 'which sounds as if it's from this part of the world, but I could be wrong.'

Schmidt shook his head. 'Yes, you are. He's an ex-basketball star. Went through the drug scene in the sixties, then became a, quote, born-again Christian, unquote. Now has his own church and a television show out of Georgia.'

'Black?' Swanson asked.

'Yes. Another one who's into the religious scam industry. You guys wait until you get some of our holy-rollers here on satellite.'

'Why would he be singled out?'

'He nightly castigates the Right, preaches that the day is dawning when the blacks will take over and has announced his intention of running for President. He's coming your way soon.'

The other four listened intently as he gave the backgrounds to the rest of the names on the list. It included two Democrat Senators noted for their liberal views, a lecturer in political science at the University of Hamburg, a New York rabbi, a prominent French sociologist, two female gay activists, several Afro-American notables, one of whom was a Supreme Court judge, and finally the Jewish head of a Hollywood studio.

'Shades of McCarthy?'

'This year's model. Hollywood is more and more the public conception of what's wrong with America.'

'I would have thought the current trend in violent films suited their purpose. Art anticipating reality.'

Schmidt said: 'Reality's the word. They're not interested in fantasy *Batman* violence. The *Godfather* syndrome is their role model.'

'Are you saying the Mob's involved?'

'Bet your life the Mob are looking to become involved somewhere along the line, ready for any rich pickings that fall by the roadside.'

'Well,' Swanson said, 'a very catholic selection from all accounts, catholic with a small c, that is. Where did the list surface?'

'It came to light during the course of an investigation into another racist murder in Arkansas. We know it originated in Germany.'

'How?'

'It was intercepted by the US mail addressed to one of the men convicted in the Arkansas case, postmarked Frankfurt.'

'What action is the Bureau taking to protect those named?'

'We've got surveillance on every American name.'

'I remember,' Pearson said, 'that when the Jackal came to London and had one of his rare failures when he attempted to assassinate a very prominent member of our Jewish community . . . he left behind a similar list which fortunately he didn't have a chance to work through.'

Swanson took over again. 'Given the steam rising over Downing Street, we can't take any chances where Miller is concerned. Are we moving on that?'

'It's done. Already in place.'

'I take it Marvin knows Robert has gone undercover?'

'Yes, I'm up to date on that,' Schmidt said. He gave a look to Hillsden. 'That's one tough assignment. I went undercover myself once. Two years. Bitched my marriage. Are wire taps allowed over here?'

'Difficult to get officially. Of course we don't always play by the rules,' Pearson answered.

'Nobody heard that,' Swanson said and switched the conversation. 'I should also tell you that a Mossad team are flying in today with the Israeli Foreign Secretary. Not something I welcome, because they're loose cannons usually.' Once again he addressed Schmidt. 'I'd like to know what your brief is. We don't want to get lines crossed.'

'This was just a stop-over to exchange information. I'm on my way to Munich, then Rome and Israel, to see if the scattered pieces of the jigsaw fit together. The murder of your man last night has moved the goal posts.'

'What d'you want from us?'

'Full details of last night's murder and any background you can give me.'

'You say you're going to Munich,' Pearson said. 'How seriously do the Germans take all this?'

'Langley's view is, not seriously enough. Despite what's been happening recently, their courts have been handing out some pretty lenient sentences. They'd like us to think it's not a big problem. Anything that reminds them of the past, they try and brush under the carpet.'

'It's difficult to read our new allies,' Swanson said, leaning back and staring at the ceiling. 'Since the reunification we've seen some ominous signs that they're beginning to flex their muscles again. And don't forget they wrote the original text book. My view is, that for all their big talk, they bit off more than they could chew when the Wall came down. Now they're having second thoughts. And they're less and less willing to admit they should feel guilt for the past. They frighten the hell out of me. Officially, of course, we have to co-operate, but I think we can interpret the rules with a certain amount of discretion. It is, after all, our show.'

Hillsden studied Swanson's bland face. He and his kind never change, he thought. Like Palace courtiers, they rebuff with studied ease any menace to the *status quo*, any threat which might reduce their influence.

22

WONDERFUL, WONDERFUL COPENHAGEN

By the time Lloyd arrived in Copenhagen it was too late for him to begin what he was there for, and in any case he felt he was owed a night off at the Firm's expense. After showering in his hotel, he strolled the pedestrian precincts, finally choosing a restaurant on the waterfront at Nyhavn to have dinner. Oddly, he was not that seasoned a traveller, having only taken occasional family holidays in Spain, and, like many of his countrymen, was disconcerted by the first sight of a foreign menu. On this occasion he studied it without comprehension until rescued by a pert young waitress who guided him to marinated salmon, followed by roast pork and red cabbage. 'And you must have a glass of *kande* with it,' she said.

'Anything you say,' Lloyd responded. When it appeared, the drink proved to be a sort of black and tan – a mixture of two beers, plus aquavit, Pernod and lemonade. After two refills, Lloyd felt no pain and required a taxi to return to his hotel.

He was hungover the following morning, and it wasn't until he had suffered a prolonged cold shower and several cups of black coffee that he felt able to face the world. While dressing he went over what Hadley had told him.

'Van Elst owns a locksmith's in an area called Stroget. You can't miss it apparently. According to Carstairs the shop window has nothing but thousands of keys in it.'

'What cover did Carstairs use?'

'Ostensibly he was on an exchange programme from our

Natural History Museum to theirs, preparing a study on the transmigration of flora for the EEC.'

'How did he feed his stuff back to us?'

'He used a book code based on a seed catalogue.'

'Jesus!' Lloyd exclaimed. 'That's out of the ark. I didn't know anybody still used that. He'd have been safer phoning it in.'

'He was old fashioned, preferred the traditional ways.'

'Not in his sex life, he didn't. What name did he go under?'

'Professor Paul Chandler.'

'Professor?'

'He felt it gave him more authority.'

'Okay, and this Van Elst was his source?'

'Yes.'

'His only source?'

'Yes. He never penetrated further.'

'Tell me about Van Elst.'

'Active member of the Danish chapter of Wiking-Jugend – Viking Youth – just a name for another neo-Nazi outfit.'

'And how did Carstairs make the connection?'

'Through a shared love of nudism.'

'What?'

'Van Elst is a fanatical health freak.'

'You telling me Carstairs went in for that?'

'Apparently, yes,' Hadley said.

'Did you ever meet Carstairs?'

'No.'

'Well, he was hardly Mr Universe. God, that's a grisly thought – Carstairs starkers with a lot of naked Viking youth. Greater love hath no agent than that he bared his all for Queen and country.'

'Well, it takes all sorts in our line of business, doesn't it?' Hadley said. 'The man's dead, so we shouldn't hold that against him. He sent back some useful stuff while he was there.'

Lloyd still carried that disquieting image of the dead Carstairs as he set out from the hotel armed with a tourist street map. On the way he stopped at a news kiosk and bought a health magazine which bordered on soft porn, thinking it might serve a useful purpose when he met Van Elst. Stroget proved to be a popular shopping centre, with the longest pedestrian zone in Europe, and he walked nearly a mile before he located the shop, its unobtrusive front tucked between two more splendid establishments. As Hadley had said, the window was inches deep in keys of all description – old and new, large, small, modern, antique, rusty, gold-plated, you name it, all heaped together.

He stood studying the display for several minutes, then moved to enter by the glass door. It was locked. He peered into the shop and could see two men. Rapping on the glass he caught their attention and mouthed 'Are you open?' One of the men came forward and unlocked the door.

'Ja? Kan jeg hjaelpe dem?'

'I'm sorry,' Lloyd said, 'I don't speak Danish. D'you understand English?'

'Yes, I understand enough.'

'Oh, good. Are you Mr Van Elst, by any chance?'

'No. Was he expecting you?'

'Not really. It's just that we have a mutual friend who asked me to come by and say hello. We share the same interests, apparently.' Lloyd allowed the health magazine to come into view.

'I see. Please step inside,' the man said.

Lloyd went past him into the shop. He smiled at the other man behind the counter but got nothing in return. He heard the shop door being locked again. He turned back and found he was looking straight down the barrel of a handgun.

'Now,' the first man said, 'what is the real purpose of your visit?'

23

PARROT TALK

Hillsden allowed six days to go by before deciding to contact Hyde again, making the excuse that he wanted to deliver the policy in person and go away with a completely satisfied client. 'It means a lot to me to get your business,' he said. 'I'll be frank with you, Mr Hyde, I've been out of work for over two years and getting this job saved my life. I'm the wrong side of the hill and not too many people were willing to give me a chance.'

Hyde readily accepted the explanation and indeed was sympathetic. 'Where are you staying?' he asked once the policy had been handed over.

'This time I'm in a motel on the other side of town.'

'Have you eaten?'

'Not yet, no.'

'Want to come out for a bite?'

'Well, I don't want to put you to any inconvenience, Mr Hyde.'

'I never eat in. Not since my wife took off.'

'You sure now? I must admit it's a bit depressing to eat on my own every evening.'

Hyde took him to one of a chain of steak houses he was obviously familiar with. 'Go for the prime rib, that's always good.'

Conditioned by years of hard drinking in Russia, Hillsden's head remained clear as they polished off a bottle of the house red wine. Facing Hyde across the patterned Formica table in the plastic-covered booth he was careful to keep the conversation away from the topic that occupied him most, and it wasn't until Hyde had finished his second helping of 'home-made' apple pie that had been microwaved into oblivion, that he casually mentioned he had read the copy of *Action Now!*

'Oh, yeah. What did you make of it?'

Acting a role, Hillsden looked round at the adjacent booth before answering in a lowered voice, 'It certainly opened my eyes.'

'I knew it would.'

'I mean, I'm no great student of politics, but in recent years I've lost all faith in governments. I didn't even vote in the last election.'

'You were out of work, right? And nobody gave a toss about you.'

Hillsden nodded. 'I don't want to give you a sob story, because I'm only one amongst many, but I lost my house – that was repossessed because I couldn't keep up with the payments – then my wife got sick, needed an operation, but of course there was a waiting list and by the time they found a bed for her it was too late. She died. Cancer.' He felt conscience-stricken at the ease with which the glib lies passed across the table, thinking, Oh God, how quickly I've slipped into my old clothes.

'That's too bad. What we stand for is not only the truth, but it's patriotic. We want to preserve the old British way of life.'

'You're actively involved, are you?'

'I play my part. Can't just lie down and let them walk all over us. Otherwise we'll end up like bleeding Rhodesia. It was all right for them to come over and fight in the Battle of Britain, wasn't it? Welcomed them with open arms then, didn't we? Then sold them down the river to that black git. Were you in the war?'

'Last two years, yes.'

'Well, then, you know. You were going to come back to a

land fit for heroes, right? You shouldn't have to work at your age. You should be enjoying the fruits of your labours. Instead you're having to graft for a living just to keep a lot of fucking jungle bunnies and druggies on welfare.'

He looked around the restaurant as though daring anybody to question his convictions, then drained his glass of wine. 'Am I right? You know I'm right. Everybody's too shit scared to come out and tell it like it is. But not us. We're going to make changes. Big changes. And those who aren't with us are going to be swept away, and when the time's right we're going to strike. You look surprised.' He beckoned Hillsden to lean closer. 'Know how many people we've already got in the movement? Twenty-eight thousand and growing every day. Not just people like you and me, but important people, people capable of taking over government when the push comes.' His speech was slightly slurred now and he leaned closer, knocking over a plastic bottle of tomato ketchup. 'Can I trust you?'

'I hope so.'

'If you're really anxious to know more . . . I'm going to do something for you. You did me a favour, I'm going to do you one. Got a pencil?'

Hillsden produced a company pen which he handed across.

'Ring this number, ask for Tony and say I suggested you call him to discuss joining the snooker club.' He scribbled the number and address on a paper napkin and handed it to Hillsden.

'Snooker club?'

'That's where our London group meets. I'll tell Tony to expect your call. Have a word with him, he can explain it more.'

'Don't have to play snooker, do I?' Hillsden said. 'Not one of my games.'

'You can always learn,' Hyde said, as he paid the bill. He had ketchup on his hand, like blood.

24

MOVING IT ALONG

It was just gone midnight when the telephone rang. It woke both Galina and Hillsden and he let it ring several times hoping that Audrey would pick up on her extension as she normally did. When nothing happened he reluctantly fumbled to switch on the bedside lamp, knocking over a glass of water in the process.

'Oh, Jesus!' he muttered, as next he dropped the instrument, the cord snaking it out of his reach. When he finally untwisted it and got the receiver to his ear a voice was saying, 'Robert?'

'Who wants him?'

'Is that seven double-nine four?' The delivery was vaguely recognisable.

'Yes,' tersely. 'Who is this?'

'It's me, the Colonel.'

It took a second or two before the name registered. 'God, Colonel, have you any idea what time it is? You've woken the whole household.'

'Yes, do forgive me, old chap, but I thought it important and this is the first chance I've had,' Rotherby said.

Galina sat up in bed. 'Who is it?' she whispered.

Hillsden put his hand over the mouthpiece. Looking at her naked, worried face, he knew her fears: in Russia midnight calls had always carried menace. 'Nothing, sweetheart, just a friend, go back to sleep.'

'Hello, you still there?'

'Yes. What's happened?'

'Reason I disturbed you is I stumbled across something I thought I should alert you to. I'll cut it short because I haven't got any more change. Your car's been bugged.'

Fully conscious now, Hillsden reached for a cigarette.

'You sure?'

'I was on my own on late shift this evening and to pass the time I was shunting around the computer, updating myself on our current wire taps. Your car phone was listed. So, watch your back, old son.'

'Why would the Firm bug me?' Hillsden said, but before Rotherby could answer, the bleeps sounded and he was abruptly cut off.

As Hillsden was untwisting the cord again there was a cry from Lara's room across the passage, and the next moment her small figure appeared in the doorway.

'What was that noise, there was a noise?' she said.

'Just the telephone, baby. Go back to bed, you'll get cold.'

'I had one of those nasty dreams.' She padded closer to the bed. 'Can I sleep with you and Mama?'

Galina roused herself again, 'Yes, come and get in here.'

The child climbed over Hillsden and settled herself between them. Hillsden felt the smallness of her as she nestled against them, twining her legs around his. He switched out the light and thought about what Rotherby had just told him. There was total trust in the little body lying beside him, but that was where trust ended, everything beyond the four walls of the bedroom carried old threats. Surprise at the news gave way to anger. Well, two can play that game, he thought, I've been there before.

When eventually he managed to get back to sleep, he dreamed he was in an unfamiliar room, playing snooker with Hadley, when two men in SS uniforms entered and Hadley denounced him. One of the SS wore dark glasses and as he was being marched away he tore the glasses from this man and found he was staring at Jock's smiling, sardonic face.

Then Jock's features peeled away revealing the skull and a maggot crawled out of one empty eye socket.

. . .

While Audrey cooked breakfast the following morning he made a casual reference to the late-night call. 'Did the phone wake you as well last night?'

'Phone? I didn't hear it.'

'It rang around midnight.'

'I'm sorry, I was listening to a concert on my Walkman,' she apologised. 'Who was it?'

'No idea. By the time I picked up whoever it was had rung off,' he lied. Now caution would have to dictate his every move.

He drove off but stopped the car in one of the lanes a mile or so from the house and, using the tool kit, searched the car, eventually finding the bug hidden behind the speaker grille in the driver's door and wired to be activated by the ignition key. He carefully replaced the grille without disturbing anything. A sliver of ice entered his mind. Was perhaps Audrey, the compliant token woman, a plant? According to her, Hadley had delivered the car prior to the family's arrival, but that in itself proved nothing. What was obvious was that somebody in the Firm still didn't trust him.

Continuing his journey to the railway station, his thoughts were more for Galina's and Lara's safety than his own. For good or bad, Russia was all they had ever known and even for prisoners there was a strange kind of comfort in the familiar. He had moved them from one prison to another, just to exact a stale revenge.

'You bloody fool,' he said aloud, as his concentration lapsed and he had to brake suddenly, his anger directed more at himself than the cyclist he had narrowly avoided.

The anger stayed with him on the slow journey into London. Staring out of the grimed windows as the train crawled past a stretch of track that was being repaired, other regrets surfaced. He remembered Abramov's offer and thought, Victor had the right idea. Don't get even, get rich. At every turn in my life, he thought, I've betrayed those closest to me: Margot, Caroline and now Galina and Lara. Abramov's unasked for confession about his brother also came back. *I loved him, but I suppose I didn't love him enough. I loved myself more . . .* Is that true of me? Is that true of me, he repeatedly thought as the train finally arrived at the terminal and he walked amongst the hurrying commuters to the barrier, then made his way to a public phone booth and dialled the number of the snooker hall that Hyde had given him.

The line rang at least half a dozen times before it was answered.

'Yes?'

'Could I speak to Tony, please?'

'Not here. He'll be in around two o'clock.'

'Can I leave a message for him?'

'We don't take messages,' the voice said and hung up.

Having left the station forecourt for the underground, Hillsden stood on the platform deciding his next move as a sudden rush of cold air signalled that somewhere in the darkness a train was approaching. Then he heard the sound of a woman crying out and seconds later two youths ran past, scattering other passengers and laughing as they took the exit stairs two at a time. The woman shouted: 'My bag! Stop them, they've stolen my bag!' but her anguished voice was blotted out by the noise of the train as it emerged from the tunnel. The waiting crowd pushed against those alighting as soon as the doors slid open, buffeting each other in their determination not to become involved. Hillsden held back, searching for the woman as the mêlée thinned. She was middle-aged, smartly dressed in a pale grey outfit, an absurd little hat perched on freshly permed hair. Not a regular, Hillsden thought, but somebody up in town for a day's shopping. As she approached he saw that the make-up on her cheeks was streaked with tears.

'They took my bag,' she said in a voice that contained no hope. 'All my credit cards, money, everything. What will I tell my husband?'

'I can give you some money to get home with,' Hillsden offered. 'If that would help.'

She recoiled from him as though such a gesture held further menace.

'Please, take this,' Hillsden said, holding out a note.

She shook her head. 'My husband wouldn't approve, I don't know you.'

As a train swooshed out of the parallel tunnel she began to walk in small circles like some clockwork toy that had malfunctioned, at one moment veering dangerously near to the edge of the platform. Hillsden put out a hand to save her and again she recoiled, raising her hand as if to ward off a blow and managing to knock her hat askew.

'I think you should go up top and report it,' he said, but she ignored him, saying as she backed away: 'Why did it have to be me? I was meeting my friend in Harvey Nichols,' as if this was the sole reason she had been singled out. She took the same exit as the youths who had ruined her day. Hillsden saw that she had a plaster on the back of one ankle where her new shoes had rubbed.

Taking the next crowded train, he stood holding on to a support bar in the swaying carriage, thinking, Should I have done more, chased the thieves, insisted she take the money? He noticed that most of the hanging straps were either broken or missing and recalled that he had been told that they were used as coshes. As a deserted station flashed into view and then was gone again, a memory of a favourite film he had seen as a child, *The Ghost Train*, came into his mind. That and *Oh, Mr Porter* – reminders of a time when travelling, like going to a Saturday matinée, had been a placid adventure. The annual family holidays in Weymouth during summers that he only remembered as hot under unblemished skies. A vision of his father, collarless shirt, braces, trousers rolled up to the knee, a handkerchief knotted at four corners and stuck on his balding head to prevent sunburn. He and his kind seldom bared more of their bodies in those pre-war days, so that when they returned home their arms and necks were burnished with russet tidemarks. Hillsden saw it all again: sepia snapshots taken with a box Brownie, faces from the past squinting into the sun, himself beside sand castles destined to be swirled away by evening and built again the next day, sad donkeys with wary infants on their backs clutching the stiffened manes, the only violence played out in Punch and Judy shows.

It came to him that what had prompted these images was the woman whose bag had been stolen. She had had the same gentle features as his mother, her make-up applied in the same inexpert way. What had his mother always worn? Yardley's face powder, that was it, and a dab of *Evening in Paris* perfume, the poor's version of Chanel No. 5. Her best clothes, too, never quite in fashion, always a few years out of date, but carefully put away after any special occasion so that a faint smell of camphor always lingered. He could see all that so clearly, but wondered what had he ever known of his parents' inner lives? Had it been good, bad, both by turns? The most he had been conscious of then was that there was always food on the table, nothing fancy, but adequate: tinned salmon for Sunday tea, followed by lardy cake that none of his women had ever been able to make since, the recipe dying with his mother. Today, looking at television talk shows, reading articles in the Sunday supplements, it seemed that anybody who had ever been famous for five minutes could be relied upon to trot out examples of their parents having failed them: naked, personal hatreds exposed for profit. *I need to find myself*, most of them said, as if anybody ever found themselves or others. We only tell what we want to tell,

Hillsden thought, we only see what we want to see, and, bringing his thoughts back to himself, he recognised that, although he knew next to nothing about his dead parents, he had never felt abandoned or disaffected because of that. Perhaps they too died knowing little of him, wishing that they could have had dialogues that went beyond a recitation of the day's events, something more than a glimpse into a life they had produced but had never understood.

Coming out of these thoughts he glanced up as the train stopped and saw that he had gone past his station. He just made it on to the platform before the doors hissed closed. Emerging irritated and disorientated into the street, he was at a loss to get his bearings. The snooker hall he had to locate was in Shepherd's Bush, an area he had once been familiar with: East Acton was an unknown country. He cursed himself for not bringing a street map. Nothing in the immediate vicinity gave him a clue as to which direction he should take. He stopped an old man pushing a stolen supermarket trolley overflowing with plastic flotsam.

'Can you help me, please? I have to get to Shepherd's Bush. Which way do I go?'

'Who did?' the old man said. His face was encrusted with dirt.

'Me. I'm trying to get to Shepherd's Bush.'

'The Lord Jesus is your only Saviour,' was the reply, delivered with the old man's eyes fixed on something in the distance that only he could see.

'Doesn't matter, sorry to bother you,' Hillsden said. He walked to a main road and was lucky enough to find a cruising taxi. He was careful not to give the exact address, just the street; people remembered taxis.

Once he had arrived, he waited until the taxi drove away, then walked to the snooker hall. It had a plain brick exterior which, inevitably, was disfigured with graffiti, and three square windows made of thick glass blocks. There was a flickering neon sign over the entrance which should have read GARRATY'S but the first three letters were dead. There was nobody on the door and he went inside to find it more spacious than the façade suggested. He guessed that at one time it had either been a car repair shop or a warehouse for it lacked any pronounced architectural features, being merely a long rectangular room, painted in a dark colour and housing a dozen full-size snooker tables under canopied lights. There was a bar down one side and a few one-armed bandits. A large notice behind the bar stated 'No Credit' and, underneath, gave a price list of the hourly rates for the tables. A trophy shield stood on a bracket in the centre of the opposite wall, surrounded by tattered photographs of past recipients. All the billiard tables were in use, the regular click of the balls being the most noticeable sound: this was a venue for serious players, not a haunt of casuals.

Some of the spectators glanced at him as he entered and went to the bar, but otherwise he attracted little attention.

'A Heineken, if you've got it,' he said to the barman.

'Budweiser or Fosters,' the barman said without looking at him, being far too engrossed by a tricky shot on the nearest table.

'Budweiser then,' Hillsden said.

Without taking his eyes off the game, the barman reached down, produced the can of beer and placed it on the counter top. 'One sixty,' he said. Only when the shot had been accomplished did he turn his attention to Hillsden. 'If you're looking for a game, you've got a long wait.'

'That's okay. I actually came in to see Tony. Is he about?'

'Table eleven,' the barman said. 'But don't put him off his stroke. He's on a break.'

Hillsden took his drink and wandered down the line of tables. Finding table eleven, he took a seat next to the player sitting it out while the man he took to be Tony made all the running. Ball after ball was dispatched into the pockets with deadly accuracy as Tony moved around the table, chalking his cue, picking his angles, then completing the execution. He was a well-built man in his thirties, wearing a checkered shirt and jeans held up by an oversized leather belt with an imposing silver buckle.

Money changed hands when the final ball found its home and the disgruntled loser drifted away. As he pocketed his winnings, Tony took in Hillsden. 'You looking for a game? Tenner a frame if you're interested. Best of three. Double or quits for the third.'

'I don't play I'm afraid. If you're Tony, a friend of yours, Les Hyde, suggested I looked you up.'

'Yeah?'

'Yes, he thought I might like to join the club.'

Tony looked him up and down. 'We don't take non-players.'

'I think he had something else in mind.'

'Such as?'

'He said you'd tell me.'

Tony stared at him and lit a cigarette American style, shaking the cigarette out of the packet. 'Oh, yeah. And who are you?'

'Robert Bartlett.'

'Where did you meet Les?'

'At his home in Wolverhampton.'

'How come?'

'In the course of business.'

'What business is that?'

'I'm an insurance agent. I sold him a policy on his car. Let me give you my card.'

Tony took the card and examined it in a way that suggested he was not impressed. 'So what did he tell you?'

'He gave me a magazine to read which explained certain things I hadn't realised before. Then we met again, had a meal together, and that's when he suggested I find out more from you.'

'Yeah, well then, he must have told you that magazine isn't available to the general public. Did he tell you that?'

'Yes, he did.'

'You appreciate anybody could come in here and say they're a friend of a friend of mine.'

'Yes, I understand,' Hillsden said.

'Given the nature of what he told you, be easy to make a mistake. I'm not saying you're not who you say you are, but I have to be careful.'

'Oh, I agree. You're quite right.'

Tony looked hard at Hillsden again. 'Pity you don't play, otherwise we could talk here. But I think it best you come back to my place. Finish your beer, I'll meet you outside.'

'Right. Thank you.'

Hillsden watched Tony walk to the bar and pick up the phone. He remained seated, watching another game until he had downed his beer, then got up and left the room, passing Tony who was still at the bar but didn't look at him.

A few minutes later, Tony joined him in the street and led him to a nearby vacant lot where half a dozen cars were parked. He went up to a battered Nissan hatchback and unlocked it.

'Want to give me a quote for this heap?'

'Sure.'

'Just kidding. Any car I drive would put you out of business.' He reversed out of the parking lot and drove through a series of back streets, eventually pulling up in front of a tower block. 'Welcome to Alcatraz,' he said, as he fixed a steel security bar to the steering wheel. 'How's your ticker?'

'My ticker? Oh, my heart, you mean? Okay, I think.'

'Needs to be because, as usual, the fucking lift isn't working. We've got to walk up seven floors.'

There was a smell of urine in the stairwell and the bare concrete walls were stained with damp and graffiti. On the third landing they were confronted with a used condom. 'Somebody had a safe knee-trembler, ha ha,' Tony said as they climbed higher. 'This dump wants blowing up, and I might just be the one to do it.'

Finally reaching the seventh floor, which was indistinguishable from the rest, Tony took him along a covered way until they reached a door at the far end. Before putting his key into the mortise lock, Tony thumped on the door: it gave back a dull, metallic sound. 'Steel,' he informed Hillsden. 'I had it specially made after three break-ins, plus the frame's reinforced. I'm just waiting for the cruds to come back with an acetylene torch.'

'Why d'you stay here? Why not move somewhere else?'

'You live on another planet or something? I'm lucky I can afford this shit-hole.'

Once inside, he locked the door again. The layout of his flat was typical of most of those in the tower blocks thrown up to relieve the post-war housing shortage: living room, kitchen, bathroom and bedroom. Made of prefabricated concrete sections of questionable durability, owned by local councils with little money to spare for regular maintenance, the flats had long since exceeded their shelf-life. Badly heated, if heated at all, many of them were now infested with cockroaches and other vermin. Only the elderly and those unable to escape out of the poverty trap endured such conditions. Drug-pushers, pimps and prostitutes who weren't bothered about *House and Garden* surroundings moved in whenever one fell vacant.

Tony's rooms had a musty smell to them and Hillsden noticed crumbling plaster on the ceilings and window surrounds. There was an unmade sofa bed in one corner of the living room, a small television set on a chest of drawers with a bra hung over the portable aerial. Seeing Hillsden's eye go to this, Tony volunteered: 'Gives it a better reception,' then said, 'just stand there.' He ran his hands over Hillsden's body in a professional search.

'Sorry about that, but I had to make sure you weren't wired.'

'Wired? What does that mean?'

'Carrying a tape recorder. You could be working for the old Bill.'

'Oh, I see. That's what you call wired, is it? I didn't know.'

'As it happens I checked your story with Les, but I was just being extra careful. Some of our people have been caught out. You want another beer?'

'If you're having one.'

'I'm having one.'

When he disappeared into the kitchen Hillsden took the opportunity to examine the rest of the room, now noticing that in contrast with the general poverty of the surroundings, there was a laptop computer on a small table, together with a stack of *Action Now!* On the wall above was a poster advertising the previous year's Notting Hill Carnival.

'So, sit yourself down and tell me more about yourself,' Tony said, tossing a can of beer to Hillsden as he returned. He cleared some clothes off the only chair while he himself sat on the sofa bed. 'You met Les . . . and what?'

'Well, we got talking about things in general . . . and like I told you, he gave me a copy of that . . .' indicating the pile of *Action Now!*, 'which I hadn't come across before. I took it home and read it and it seemed to me to spell out some home truths. Things that worry me.'

'What sort of things?'

'Crime. The way ordinary people are pushed around, made to feel they're living in a foreign country.'

'Foreign's right. Look outside. You could be anywhere. Fucking Chinese takeaways, curry parlours, Paki grocers, you name it. So go on, you got talking with Les, did you?'

'Yes.'

'He's a deep thinker is Les. I bet you found that.'

Hillsden nodded in agreement. 'He made me think. So when we met the second time I said I'd made up my mind to find out more and that's when he suggested I should contact you.'

Tony's next question took him off guard and he realised that he was not home and dry yet.

'So why do I look at you and think you don't fit?'

'How d'you mean?'

'Well, you're a bit old for a punch-up in the street.'

'Oh, I see. Is that what you do?'

'We don't look for fights, but sometimes it's necessary. If we let you in, you won't be joining the Salvation Army. And once you're in, you're in for good. We don't like people wasting our time. People who join, learn about us, then decide it's not for them . . . they cause problems, problems for us and sometimes bigger problems for them.' He crumpled his empty beer can and tossed it to one side. 'But don't get the wrong idea. You'd be joining a legit political party, but maybe some of the things we stand for might not be everybody's way of looking at things. I'm sure you gathered that from Les.'

'Yes.'

'He feels very strongly about the state this country's in.'

'Don't we all?'

'No, we don't, that's the trouble. Most people don't give a toss. We have to change all that. What I have to know is, how far d'you want to get involved?'

'All the way.'

'We have a process, see. Everybody who applies to join has to go through it. No exceptions. I have my say, but I'm not the last word. Assuming I decide you're somebody we'd like to have with us, you still have to be okayed by somebody above me. Chain of command.'

'Yes, I understand.'

Tony took Hillsden's business card out of his jeans pocket. 'This the best place to get you?'

'Yes.'

'Okay, well, if we decide to contact you again I'll send you a message just saying the snooker championship is on and tell you when and where. We don't use names over the phone. But you'll know what it means, right?'

'Yes. Snooker championship.'

He looked at his wrist-watch and for the first time Hillsden noticed a skull and crossbones tattoo on his arm. 'Listen I've got somebody else coming, so I'll have to ask you to scarper.'

'Oh, right,' Hillsden said, standing up. 'Well, I appreciate you giving me this time, Tony, and, believe me, I'm dead serious, so I hope your people take me on.'

'We'll see,' Tony said. He unlocked the door and looked out. 'Until next time, if there is a next time. Otherwise, you never met Les, you never met me.'

'Yes, I understand.'

'Make sure you do.'

On the way down, Hillsden paused to let a blade-faced girl dressed in black leather and with a Mohican hair-style go past him. She stared at him aggressively, as though, because he looked out of place, he could only be somebody she was against – a rent collector, a council official? Hillsden held his own look a fraction too long for her liking, 'What you staring at, Grandpa?' she said. 'Get lost.' She continued on her way up, her heavy, steel-tipped boots hitting each concrete step with a precise rhythm.

Hillsden continued on down. He felt as dirty as the grimed walls.

25

STRENGTH THROUGH JOY

None too pleased at being locked in a cell while the Danish authorities contacted London and satisfied themselves that he was who he said he was, Lloyd was slightly mollified when a senior officer from PET, the Danish State Police Intelligence Unit, released him and apologised for any inconvenience suffered.

Captain Mulder introduced himself and extended a large hand that gripped like a vice. He was a burly man, at least six inches taller than Lloyd, with a physique that suggested he spent his leisure hours pumping iron. 'Come and have a drink, I'm sure that would be welcome.'

He led the way to his office. 'Your colleague, Commander Pearson, thought it all highly amusing. He told me to say it would be instructive for you to see how the other half of the world lives.'

'Yes, I bet he did.'

'Is he always that cheerful?'

'Oh, he's a natural bundle of laughs.'

'Your native sense of humour.'

'Not really. He's the exception to the rule.'

Mulder took a bottle of aquavit out of the small refrigerator behind his desk and poured two generous tots. 'It's probably always a mistake, don't you agree,' Mulder said, 'to arrive unannounced?'

'Yes, being wise after the event.'

'The men who arrested you were expecting somebody else to turn up. We've had a stake-out there ever since the murder.'

'Whose murder are we talking about?'

Mulder topped up both glasses. 'I suspect the man you came to find. You were a week too late. The *Fromandskorpset* fished him out of the water,' he said, naming the combat swimmers who provide anti-terrorist capability for Danish ports. 'Tell me, what was London's interest in him?'

'We are talking about Van Elst?' Lloyd asked as the double shot of aquavit thawed his previous mood.

'Yes.'

'We had a man over here, working undercover, tracing the source of neo-Nazi literature that's currently flooding into England. Van Elst was his informant.'

'You say "had". Have you withdrawn him?'

'He's dead, like Van Elst.'

'How?'

'All the evidence so far points to suicide, which I must say has us puzzled.'

Mulder picked up the aquavit bottle again, but Lloyd put a hand over his glass. 'Not for me, it's already reached my feet.'

'Why does it puzzle you?'

'He came back to London unofficially, checked into a hotel and blew his brains out, but a short time before his death he passed on information which enabled our Customs to intercept a large consignment of a book by this man Sonntag.'

'Ah, Sonntag,' Mulder said. 'He's somebody we'd like to get our hands on if he ever surfaces here. You think there's a direct link between that incident and your man's suicide?'

'On the face of it, no. There could be a more mundane explanation. We discovered that his personal life was fairly bizarre. He was homosexual, lived with a sex-change "wife". Perhaps we're only looking at a lovers' quarrel with a tragic end.'

Mulder permitted himself a grin. 'He sounds as though he was very thoroughly vetted.'

Lloyd returned the grin. 'Well, as you know, we've made a

speciality of choosing the wrong people. Do you have any leads on Van Elst's murder? He was a member of the Wiking-Jugend, wasn't he?'

'Yes, but we don't think it was their doing. So far, they haven't shown their hand in that way. They keep a low profile. Your man, what was his name?'

'His real name was Carstairs, but he operated here under an alias . . . called himself Professor Chandler and was working on an exchange programme at your Natural History Museum.'

Mulder thought about this, then said: 'How much simpler our lives would be if we weren't so suspicious of our friends. A word in my ear and your man might be alive today.' He took out a file from a drawer in his desk. 'This was Van Elst. Mean anything to you?' He offered Lloyd two photographs. The first showed a good-looking blond in his late twenties, wearing a quasi boy scout uniform, a role model for Aryan male beauty. The death shot, taken in the autopsy room, made Lloyd grimace.

'No,' he said. 'Never seen him before.'

'As you will note,' Mulder observed, 'he wasn't drowned.'

Van Elst's neck gaped open, the bloodless flesh wound reminding Lloyd of a gutted fish on the slab.

'Shot first,' Mulder continued, 'then had his throat cut, as if they wanted to make doubly sure. Afterwards the body was stripped and dumped in the harbour. Maybe that was their little joke.'

'Joke?'

'He was a member of a nudist club. The body washed up near the beach they frequent.'

'Ah, yes. Carstairs was also a member apparently. Perhaps we should question a few of his fellow skinny-dippers.'

'First, let's pay a visit to the museum, see what they can tell us,' Mulder said. 'And then search where he lived.'

. . .

Pearson and Schmidt sat in the gardens of *The Bells of Ouzeley*, a popular pub on the outskirts of Old Windsor, killing an hour before Schmidt had to catch a plane at Heathrow. Sipping a glass of warm beer, Schmidt studied a trim cabin cruiser chugging past on the nearby Thames, its engines throttled back.

Pearson said: 'What brought you into this?'

Schmidt turned back to him. 'Sorry?'

'I wondered how you got into our line of business.'

'Oh, I joined the NYPD as soon as I was old enough. New York's finest, as they say . . . except they don't say it so often these days . . . and became a housing cop for five years.'

'A "housing cop"? You mean you handled real estate?'

Schmidt smiled. 'If only! No. Policing public housing projects. You didn't find any Joe Friday or Kojak volunteering for that shift. You were patrolling the living dead. No shortage of action. I stopped a bullet in my leg during a drug bust and figured enough was enough. So I quit, put in some time working for a government agency in Washington, found I missed the adrenalin and joined the Bureau.'

'Does the adrenalin still flow?'

'Not so often since my marriage broke up.'

'It's a wonder mine has lasted,' Pearson said. 'My wife has been on at me for ages to quit. Gives me a lot of grief. I've been hanging on for retirement and my pension.'

'How long have you got?'

'Six months.'

'It's a crock of shit, this game,' Schmidt said, sipping his beer. 'We're the fall guys led by the unqualified to do the unthinkable for the ungrateful.'

'That's good, I must remember that.'

'It's all about ass, don't you find?'

'Ass?' Pearson replied, interpreting the word as 'arse'.

'Yeah. You're either kissing it or licking it. Don't get me on the subject of politics and politicians.'

They both fell silent as a large cabin cruiser came into view. It had a flying bridge and the man at the wheel wore spotless whites and a naval cap. His passengers, three young girls waved as they passed.

'Now, that's my idea of retirement,' Schmidt said.

'Provided you win the lottery. Some joker over here collected eighteen million the other week. Eighteen million. And know what he said? "I'm not going to change my life style." He was already a millionaire, apparently.' The thought of such wealth switched Pearson to another topic. 'I don't suppose the name "Charters" means anything to you, does it?'

'Charters? No.'

'Sir Raymond Charters, to give him his full title?'

'No. Who is he?'

'A big operator on this side of the pond. Has his fingers in a lot of pies, especially publishing. Owns several newspapers.'

'And?'

'Something keeps niggling at me. When you're on a case, do you ever get the feeling that something doesn't fit and you're compelled to get to the bottom of it? The last time anybody saw Carstairs alive was in a night club and this guy Charters was also there. That much we know. Now, Charters was way out of Carstairs's league, and yet something tells me they met that night. Why? I don't like coincidences when there are corpses around. So far I've got no corroboration but, like my mother used to say, "My corns ache so it's going to rain tomorrow." Well, my corns start to bother me when I ask myself what was Carstairs doing in London when everybody, including his so-called "wife", thought he was in Copenhagen? And why would he be in that particular night club? Or Charters for that matter? There's something there that doesn't add up, if only I could discover what. If I put together a hypothetical scenario, my suspicious mind would say that Sonntag's piece of shit has to have been published somewhere on the Continent. Who owns printing works all over Europe? Our friend Charters. Two men who in the ordinary course of events would never cross paths, yet they were both in an unusual venue at the same time and later the same night our man does away with himself. It bothers me.'

'What do you have on him?'

'Charters? Nothing. He's one of the great and good. A captain of industry. The sort who got rich under Thatcher. Or richer, in his case.'

'Want me to run him through Langley's computer? Never know, we might have something you've missed.'

'Sure. You never know.'

Schmidt took out a pocket notebook and jotted down the name. 'As soon as I get to Munich, I'll make a call. Take this fax number and get your office to send the most recent photo of him you have.'

'I appreciate it.'

'I'm a Jew, remember? I hate these bastards.'

At that moment, two startlingly pretty girls seated themselves at a nearby table. Schmidt swivelled to get a better view of them. 'Think we might score there?'

'You might. I hate rejection. Come on, duty calls, you've got a plane to catch.'

'Don't know why it is,' Schmidt said as they made their way to Pearson's car, 'but whenever I see somebody I could fall for, I'm always on my way to an airport.'

. . .

The Copenhagen apartment Carstairs had been using was on the top floor of an old building close to the Natural History Museum. Gaining entry, Lloyd and Mulder were both immediately struck by the scent of trapped tobacco smoke in the sealed and airless rooms just below the roof. It looked as though Carstairs had left in a hurry, for the bed was unmade, the kitchen sink full of unwashed crockery and in the bathroom there was an enamel basin containing soiled underwear which had been left to soak – all the sad signs of a man unaccustomed to fending for himself. His life was laid bare in the unemptied ashtrays on the table that had served for a desk, the international editions of *The Daily Telegraph* which littered both his bedroom and living room, together with nudist magazines, the empty bottles of Scotch dotted around the kitchen, the drip-dry shirts with their crumpled collars hung over the bath. There were bottles of vitamin pills alongside a ragged toothbrush and a squeezed tube of KY jelly on the shelf above the washbasin, the bathroom itself giving off yet another stale odour which reminded Lloyd of the repellent smell of the home of a bachelor uncle he had visited as a child.

'Is this the wife you were telling me about?' Mulder asked, picking up one of three framed photographs of the same person.

'Yes, that's her, or him, as you prefer.'

'Not unattractive, if you didn't know.'

They searched the apartment thoroughly, going about it in methodical fashion. Since it was just under the roof they were soon sweating profusely from their exertions.

'Let's see if he kept any beer in his fridge,' Lloyd said.

He went to look and came back with a single bottle that they shared.

'It's funny, you can tell a lot from what a man leaves behind,' Mulder said, 'and yet the final answer is always missing. There are no text books that lead you to a man's secret thoughts, and it's those secret thoughts that determine the choice between good and evil. Had you not told me, for example, of your man's double identity, what would I have deduced from all this? A family man in love with his wife, somebody living away from home, untidy, unable to deal with domestic chores. A masturbator, perhaps, missing a regular sexual outlet, but frightened to take his pleasures elsewhere. Nothing too out of the ordinary. Just a man with average problems.'

'Perhaps we're all double-agents of a sort,' Lloyd said. He was rummaging through a chest of drawers and suddenly came across a bank deposit book tucked into a laundered shirt. He opened it and studied the contents.

'Not exactly a poor man, though. Look at this.' He handed the book to Mulder. 'I don't know the rate of exchange, but it seems he kept a healthy bank balance in Luxembourg. Regular credit entries and no withdrawals.'

'Interesting,' Mulder said. 'Very interesting. Van Elst maintained an account with the same bank. He also received large regular payments, and the likelihood is from the same source. We must both track them down.'

'Do Luxembourg banks divulge that sort of information?'

'Given a murder case, I imagine they would bend the rules.' He handed back Carstairs's deposit book. Lloyd examined it again before pocketing it. 'Both hoarding the spoils for the old age they never reached.'

'Tell me,' Mulder said. 'How did he communicate with London?'

'He was old-fashioned. Preferred the simplest of letter codes. Used a seed catalogue.'

'We should look for that then.'

They continued the search but found no trace of the code book. His library consisted mainly of cheap paperbacks. Tucked into one of them they found a photograph of Van Elst, nude like the bevy of youths surrounding him, taken on a beach.

'The lost leader would not have approved,' Mulder said. 'He had Roehm murdered for embracing pure Aryan youth too literally. Everything comes full circle, don't you agree? Fascism didn't die in 1945, nothing died except the dead.'

26

FURTHER DEVELOPMENTS

It subsequently emerged that Marvin Schmidt never arrived in Munich. The Lufthansa plane developed engine trouble just as it was passed to German air traffic control and the Captain judged it serious enough to divert. He was given permission to put down in Frankfurt. For some reason, Schmidt apparently decided not to resume his journey on the replacement aircraft but checked into a hotel for the night. It was confirmed that he took a taxi into the city and obtained a room in the *Neue Krame*, a moderately priced hotel in the old section. At which point the trail went cold.

. . .

Back in London, the tenuous association between Carstairs and Sir Raymond Charters continued to nag at Pearson.

'You're driving yourself against a brick wall,' moaned Lloyd, who was tired of going over the same old ground. 'You'd be better off trolling the gay bars.'

'Well, okay, but you know me, once I get a bee in my bonnet. What else do we know about Charters? Langley came up with a blank. Just humour me, look him up on our database.'

Lloyd keyed in their desk computer to the mainframe and punched in a series of codes. They waited. When the required menu came up on the monitor, he typed in a further series of commands, followed by Charters's name. Almost immediately the words *Nothing Found – Abort, Retry, Fail?* appeared.

'I thought that bloody thing was supposed to be definitive?' Pearson said.

'Tell me something in the Firm that is.'

'Try *Who's Who*. He must be in that.'

'Have we got one?'

'I've seen a copy on old Rotherby's desk. He loves anything to do with the famous.'

When Lloyd returned Pearson flicked to the requisite page. 'Here we are, Charters, Raymond . . . Quite a sizeable entry. Born 1931, London . . . now that's odd.'

'What is?'

'Doesn't give his parents.'

'Conceived on the wrong side of the blanket maybe. Or else he's ashamed of them, now that he's made it.'

Pearson read on: '*Educated Swindon Grammar School, subsequently won a scholarship to Sherborne. Married to Catherine Pitt-Saunders, no issue. Marriage dissolved 1977 . . . blah, blah blah . . . CBE 1982, knighted 1989 . . .* Then a long list of his directorships *. . . hobbies: shooting, golf and study of contemporary history.*' He snapped the book shut. 'Guess you're right, just one of my quirks. Forget it. It's just that . . .'

'What?'

'This.' Pearson picked up a file and took out the receipt from Tudor's found on Carstairs. 'Look at this again. What does it tell you?'

Lloyd peered at it. 'Various drinks and an order of scrambled eggs and smoked salmon. So?'

'The autopsy found only traces of valium and alcohol in Carstairs's stomach.'

'Well, you know what the old saying is.'

'No, what?'

'Doesn't matter what you eat, if you're sick, all you ever throw up is diced carrots and tomato skins.'

'How bloody disgusting.'

'True, though.'

'What's that got to do with Carstairs?'

'Just an interesting piece of information.'

'Keep to the subject. He must have gone to that place for a purpose. Don't forget his, quote, wife, unquote, had no idea he was in England. Nor did we for that matter. That in itself is odd enough. And I also think it's odd that a man of Charters's standing would go there on the off-chance. That's not his style. He doesn't need to ogle tits.'

'Now, there I disagree,' Lloyd said. 'He and his kind have kept the tabloids in business. The bigger they are, the more they seem to fancy a bit of rough trade. Maybe the thrill of getting caught turns them on.'

Pearson grunted. 'Well,' he replied, determined to have the last word, 'that certainly didn't apply to Carstairs. He had a bit of rough waiting for him at home. But he didn't go home, did he? He blew his bloody brains out.'

. . .

The Prime Minister had insisted on a good turn-out for Montague's funeral. With the exception of the Foreign Secretary and the Chancellor, who were both in Brussels trying to frustrate yet another Franco-German move to speed the introduction of a common Euro-currency, the rest of the Cabinet, together with the Leaders of the Opposition Parties, attended the service held in North London. The Chief Rabbi officiated and the eulogy was delivered by the Prime Minister. The occasion received respectable coverage on television, despite being overshadowed by the news that England's football manager had resigned following a humiliating defeat by the Americans.

After spending some time with Montague's widow and intimating that he had it in mind to mark her husband's distinguished career by offering her a life peerage, the PM asked Logan to accompany him back to Whitehall.

'Ever been to a Jewish funeral before?' he asked the moment they got under way.

'No, can't say I have.'

'Different.'

'Yes,' Logan said. 'Rather moving, I thought. Relief at not having to listen to those droning Church of England voices.'

'Did you get a chance to talk to the Israeli Ambassador?'

'Yes, I did.'

'And?'

'Well, naturally he's very concerned by events, but I assured him that every step is being taken to find who was responsible.'

'With a singular lack of success so far,' the PM said acidly.

'The Ambassador told me that Mossad is convinced it was the work of Al-Sharqi.'

'Who's he for God's sake?'

'Them,' Logan corrected. 'A Palestinian group calling themselves Pioneers of the Popular War of Liberation, an element of the Syrian Ba'ath Party.'

'Have they cropped up here before?'

'Who knows? There are so many bloody terrorist splinter groups, one loses track.'

'Well, when, or *if* I suppose I should say, they charge anybody let's make sure the thing goes through without a hitch. And let's hope he or they are from this Al-something lot, and not home grown.'

'He did ask a favour, by the way.'

'What sort of favour?'

'The Israeli Cabinet is anxious that nothing derails the current round of peace talks. They'd like to step up the Mossad presence over here, bring in some specialists.'

The Prime Minister frowned. 'We can't have foreign bods stationed here and meddling in our internal security.'

'Well, to be realistic, I dare say they already are. Or put it another way, they always have been. The Israelis are allies, after all.'

'They're also trigger-happy in my experience. What did you tell him?'

'I said we'd consider it.'

'Get back and say I've considered it and that I'm confident our security forces are able to deal with the situation. And make sure my answer's carefully minuted.'

Anxious to change the subject, Logan said, 'Absolutely. You've seen the latest poll have you? On the by-election, I mean. It's neck and neck, but we should hold the seat.'

'Yes. I'm more concerned about the selection for Montague's old seat. He only just scraped in at the General Election.'

'Has it been decided who'll stand?'

'Not yet. I let it be known that I would favour another Jewish prospect, but so far that's been resisted at local level. Just a selection of deadbeats as far as I can see. And you know how touchy the grass roots are if we try and plant somebody on them.'

'Yes. Have these early days been very different from what you expected?'

The PM frowned before answering. 'I expected having to sort out a bloody mess, if that's what you mean. And I wasn't far wrong. My main concern is to weaken the grip of the Establishment, to ensure that, beneath the surface, the same people don't continue to run the country as before. Too many of them are still in place. I need to get at their throats, and anybody else's if they don't share my views and get results.'

Logan stared straight ahead, thinking it best not to probe any further, and it wasn't until they turned into Trafalgar Square that the PM offered words of sparse comfort, as though reading his thoughts.

'Nothing personal in what I said, Ken, don't think that. I'm sure you'll eventually pull your department round.'

. . .

It was Sarah who took the call. She greeted Hillsden with the news the moment he walked into the office. 'He rang ten minutes ago, you just missed him.'

'Who?'

'Your friend the snooker player. The game's on.'

'When?'

'Tonight.'

'Nothing else?'

'Yes, he said the championship was being played in a different hall and you're to meet him outside Hampstead tube station at nine o'clock.'

Hillsden immediately dialled Swanson on the scrambler phone and gave him the details.

'No clue as to where he's taking you?'

'No.'

'I'll have somebody there at the tube station.'

'Is that clever?'

'Minimum presence,' Swanson said 'Have you got problems with that?'

'Yes, I have problems with that. Problems concerning my health if it goes wrong.'

'Well, we'll need corroborating evidence at a later date to identify this man Tony.' He waited. 'Wouldn't you agree? Jesus, we've got little enough to go on so far. You can't go in with a camera or a tape recorder, can you?' he asked rhetorically.

'No.'

'Well, then?'

'Okay,' Hillsden said. 'Put a man there, just one, but make sure he's good. And by good I mean invisible.'

When the conversation ended he dialled his home number. While waiting for somebody to respond he made a face at Sarah. 'Don't look so worried, I'm too old to do anything really dangerous. This is kids' stuff compared to Russia. Get me a bed somewhere for the night,' he added as Audrey came on the line.

'Audrey, it's me. Do me a favour, sleep in the house tonight.

224

I won't be back.'

'Understood.'

'Everything okay?'

'Everything's fine.'

'That's good. Buzz Georgina will you?' Putting a hand over the mouthpiece, he turned back to Sarah and threw her his credit card. 'Use this and get a confirmed booking. Whatever else, I don't want to spend a night on the streets.' Then he heard his wife's voice saying, 'Robert?'

'Yes, darling. How are you both?'

'We're just about to go visit the school.'

'The school?'

'Yes. I've decided she must have proper lessons. Audrey does her best, but I worry that Laura will fall behind.'

'I see. How does Laura feel about it?'

'Oh, she wants to go to school. She doesn't have anybody of her own age. This way she might make friends.'

'Well, I'm sure you're right.'

'You don't sound too sure.'

'No. I think it's a good decision. Look, darling, something's cropped up, a meeting I have to go to this evening which I can't get out of. And it means I shall almost certainly miss the last train. So, if it's okay with you I think I'll stay in town, get a hotel. I've asked Audrey if she'll sleep in the house tonight . . . Hello, you still there?'

'Yes,' Galina said.

'I'm sorry about it.'

'Yes. I was looking forward to telling you what we thought about the school.'

'Well, I'll be back tomorrow, you can tell me then.'

Again there was a silence.

'It'll only be tonight,' Hillsden said. 'And if you both like the school, I'll go and see for myself. Don't be cross, it's something I have to do.'

'I'm not cross.'

'You sound it.'

'No. I'll see you tomorrow then.'

'I love you.'

The line went dead.

'I envy you,' Sarah said as he replaced the receiver.

'What for?'

'Being able to lie so easily.'

'Necessary trick of the trade,' Hillsden said. 'If you can't lie you don't last long. Not that I enjoy lying to my wife. Make that booking will you?'

Sarah hesitated. 'Why bother with a hotel? Why don't you stay at my place? I've got a spare room.'

Hillsden glanced at her before answering, but there was nothing in her face to suggest the thought that came immediately to his mind. 'It's kind of you, Sarah, but I don't know what time I'll be through. A hotel's less complicated.'

While she rifled through the Yellow pages, he turned out the contents of his pockets, making sure that he carried nothing that might condemn him.

27

A DIFFERENT GAME OF SNOOKER

A sudden flurry of cold rain stung Hillsden's face as he emerged from the tube station entrance ten minutes before the appointed time, having decided that, if Tony was already there ahead of him, it was probably a good thing to show keenness, but he saw no sign of him and took shelter in a nearby shop doorway. Even at this hour there was plenty of traffic. One of the things he had noticed since his return was that London now seemed to have a continuous rush hour; there were very few hours in the day and night when the streets were not choked with cars.

He kept close watch, but the blur of headlights in the rain dazzled him. A young man, not dressed for the weather, joined him in the shop doorway. Hillsden saw he was selling copies of *The Big Issue*, a broadsheet by and for the homeless. More to appear normal than from any philanthropic motive, Hillsden asked the price.

'Sixty p, or what you like,' the young man said.

Hillsden gave him a pound coin. 'I don't want any change,' he said.

'Oh, thanks. Appreciated.'

'How're you doing? Have you sold many?'

'In Hampstead? You're joking. They're all Socialists up here,' he said, smiling at his own joke.

At nine o'clock, Hillsden braved the rain and paced outside the station. Now it begins again, he thought, his mind going back to the moment when Lockfield had first sprung the trap and the direction of his life had been irrevocably changed. As he stamped his feet against the cold and turned up his coat collar, he saw, as though in a bright mirror, his past self: beaten-up, a fake derelict in jail; a fake alcoholic acting out rehabilitation in the Brothers of Mercy's retreat; waiting, as now, for a messenger to arrive and lead him into an unknown country. The big issue then, he thought, was whether I'd ever come out alive. Was this to be a repetition?

The young man selling the broadsheet came to join him, the rain having eased off. 'I might pack it in soon,' he remarked as he proffered his wares to a passing couple who avoided eye-contact as though what he was offering was a contagious reminder that their turn would come. 'See what I mean?'

Hillsden nodded, but was too intent on his own mission to become involved in a dialogue. By now it was ten minutes past nine and there was still no sign of Tony. Would he come alone if he came at all, or was this just a trial run to keep him guessing – the familiar-cat-and-mouse routine that had been standard procedure for dead-letter drops in the days of the Cold War? He thought: what schoolboy games we all played then with our secret codes and miniature cameras — the toys of betrayal.

Another five minutes ticked away and he became convinced that Tony was not going to show. 'I'll have one last try,' the young man said. 'Hope your date shows up. Enjoy your snooker game.'

Before Hillsden could react the young man moved out and stood on the central traffic island in order to approach motorists halted at the traffic lights. As the signal turned green and the waiting cars cleared, Hillsden saw Tony start to cross towards him. He was forced to pause on the traffic island as a solitary motorcyclist jumped the amber. Gaining the pavement, he passed close to Hillsden. 'Follow me,' he said without stopping and disappeared around the corner. Hillsden made a show of looking at his watch again, his body language signalling a man who had been stood up. Then he made off in the same direction as Tony. Out of the corner of his eye, he saw the young man leave the traffic island.

There was no sign of Tony when he rounded the corner, but a hundred yards ahead there was a white transit van parked at a meter. As he drew level with it Tony leaned across from the driving seat and opened the passenger door.

'I'd almost given you up,' Hillsden said as he climbed in. 'I was there on time. Ahead of time, actually,' he added, trying to strike the right conversational note. 'Different car tonight.' He took a quick look in the side mirror, but the street lighting was patchy and he could not see any sign of the young man.

'Yeah. I use this one for business.'

They headed off in the direction of Swiss Cottage, but almost immediately Tony turned off and took a complicated route through a series of back streets. Hillsden concentrated on noting any prominent landmarks, such as the names of pubs, but it soon became apparent that Tony was doubling back in rather obvious fashion, unaware that his passenger was an old hand at such manœuvres. They eventually entered Regent's Park, passing London Zoo on the perimeter road.

'How is business these days?'

'Up and down.' He showed no inclination to elaborate and Hillsden did not pursue it.

They travelled for perhaps another fifteen minutes. The rain started again, coming down heavier this time and the wipers on the transit van left a smeared arc. Oncoming headlights further obscured Hillsden's view so that for the last stage of the journey he had no clear idea where they were. When they finally stopped, he saw that they were in a wide, tree-lined road, but he looked in vain for a street name. Before getting out of the van Tony said: 'From now on, do exactly as I say. Stay where you are until I give the word that it's all clear. Then follow me to the house.'

'Whose house is it?'

'Don't ask. If you're accepted, you'll find out. If not, you'd be smart to forget you ever went near it.'

Tony scouted the street, then indicated for Hillsden to get

out. They walked for some fifty yards until they reached the well-kept front garden of a three-storeyed, detached house. A flight of steps led up to an ornate front door. Like the plethora of Mercedes and Range Rovers parked along the street, it smacked of money.

They were admitted by a youth dressed in black jeans, a black shirt with epaulets, and, incongruously, a Paisley scarf around his neck, knotted cowboy-style.

He acknowledged Tony, studied Hillsden intently, but said nothing by way of greeting. He conducted them both across the large hallway where the walls were hung with abstract art of no particular distinction, the paintings crammed together so that none were shown to advantage. Opening one side of a pair of mahogany doors, the youth preceded them into the room. 'Tony's here,' he announced, but at first glance Hillsden could not see whom he was addressing. He found himself in what he took to be a library, dimly lit. Those walls that were not bookcased held another art collection, this time revealing a more eclectic taste, a mixture of styles and period: he recognised some choice examples of kitsch from the Nazi era – Aryan men in heroic poses, heavy blonde *Mädchen*, one suckling a babe at her breast. There was an elaborate stone fireplace in which a fake log fire burned and over it a large painting, this time a nude Rhine maiden embracing a wounded German soldier. Twin bookcases housing leather-bound sets flanked each side of the fireplace.

The voice which now greeted Tony came from behind a decorated screen to the left of the fire.

'Tony, come and warm yourselves.'

It was a fruity voice, bringing to mind the voice of an actor conscious that he should give equal value to all the vowel sounds.

As they went forward, the owner of the voice came into view. Although his unlined face belonged to somebody in his forties, the thick hair was snow white so that it was difficult to guess his true age. He was sitting in a metal wheelchair, his lower half covered by a tartan blanket and was smoking a cigarette in a gold holder which he waved at them both, an affectation that again seemed to Hillsden theatrical.

'So, this is the Mr Bartlett you talked about, Tony? Do sit down, Mr Bartlett. I apologise for not getting up to greet you, but this is one of my bad days. Can I offer you a drink?'

'Thank you.' Hillsden perched on the edge of a sofa on the opposite side of the fireplace.

'What will it be?'

'A Scotch, please.'

'How about you, Tony? Or are you being a good boy and don't drink and drive?'

'I could handle a beer.'

'I think we can run to that, can't we Johnny, dear,' he said, addressing the youth. 'Pour our guest a Scotch . . . I forgot to ask, what is your preference, Mr Bartlett, blended or malt?'

'Malt, I think.'

'A man after my own heart. The same for me, Johnny. So, pour ours, then get Tony a beer.' Throughout this exchange he never took his eyes off Hillsden. 'How d'you take it?'

'Oh, straight, please.'

'Very civilised. I had an American guest once,' his host said, removing the spent cigarette from the holder and immediately lighting another, 'who drank my best Isle of Islay mixed with Coca-Cola. I was somewhat stretched to be polite. They do have the most extraordinary tastes in food and drink, don't they? Some of which, unfortunately, they've exported to us. Have you ever been over there?'

'No, I never have,' Hillsden replied as the youth handed him his drink.

'You don't travel much?'

'I travel a lot in England on business. And I've been across to France on holidays.'

'You're in the insurance business Tony tells me.'

'Yes.'

'I'm a great believer in insurance.' He smiled, revealing a brace on his lower row of teeth, the sort that children wear for correction, the firelight glinting on the metal.

Johnny returned with Tony's beer already poured into a crystal brandy glass.

'A little outré for beer, Johnny dear, but we all make mistakes from time to time. Why don't you take yourself off and watch the ten o'clock news? Let me know if Arsenal won tonight. I've got money on it.'

Johnny withdrew, but not without a pout.

'Your good health, Mr Bartlett. It was kind of you to come out on a cold night, I hope you weren't inconvenienced?'

'Not at all.'

'Do relax, this isn't going to be a third degree, just a social chat to explore certain common interests. As I'm sure Tony has told you, we have to consider every new applicant with a degree of caution for the simple reason that our views on certain matters don't command universal support. That will change as we gather strength and the true facts get wider distribution.' He glanced up at the painting above the fireplace, gesturing with his cigarette holder. 'The mistake others made . . . was to identify the wrong enemy. They should never have gone to war with us. For centuries they were our allies, right up to the time of Waterloo. We have so many blood ties, as you doubtless realise . . . our royal family, for instance, were related to the Kaiser. The Third Reich was a brave, much needed venture which sadly was prevented from achieving its final mission. Unless we are very diligent, our own, once great, country is in danger of making the same mistake . . . Your first name's Robert, isn't it?'

Hillsden nodded.

'Well, Robert, not wishing to preach to you, but if history teaches us anything, it shows that when the purity of a race – any race, and I could give you numerous examples, starting with the Romans and Greeks – becomes corrupted by indolence, inter-marriage with inferior, ethnic blood, then we are staring into the abyss. If we add to this a total moral collapse, such as exists today in all sections of society, which allows the degenerates amongst us openly to flaunt their vices, condoned by the churches and with those who rule us too craven to take a stand, then it's beholden on the chosen to act before it is too late. It won't be an easy task, any more than the road from Munich was easy. I have no doubt that blood will have to be spilt along the way. We must cross that rubicon without flinching. The electorate has been systematically brainwashed into believing that our Anglo-Saxon heritage will somehow be enhanced by a transition to a multi-racial society. It is one of the great lies of this century.'

Hillsden nodded, leaning forward to show his interest.

'Furthermore, it spells the end of everything we hold dear. Unless this lemming-like rush is halted, the white population of this island will become an oppressed minority. Those are the facts, Robert, and we ignore them at our peril.'

Hillsden could not bring himself to answer in kind. Instead, sipping his whisky, he said: 'It's a sobering thought.'

'But we're going to change all, aren't we, sir?' Tony said, anxious to make his presence felt.

'We are indeed, Tony. Now, Robert, I take you to be an intelligent and caring man. You care about your country, am I right?'

'Yes.'

'Certainly you care enough to come here and find out more. Am I correct?'

'Yes,' Hillsden repeated.

'That's very heartening. We need more people like you – caring, intelligent people of your age and background – so that we can dispel the false impression that we are nothing more than a bunch of yobbos and Fascists. Oh, yes, that's the word you'll hear a lot of – the usual parrot response from those who can't face the truth. That'll be thrown at you once your involvement with our movement becomes known. Are you prepared for that?'

'Well, it's not true, is it?' Hillsden responded carefully. 'I'm not a Fascist any more than you are, or Tony here.'

'Of course you're not. But let me hear your own views, Robert.'

Hillsden began a rehearsed dialogue, starting slowly. 'Well,

'I suppose, like a lot of people of my generation, I've seen the changes taking place and I haven't liked what is happening. Drug pushers outside schools, perverts everywhere, old people afraid to walk the streets, our police, whom I was brought up to respect, made to look the villains while the real villains get their wrists slapped. That seems all wrong to me.'

'That's very well put, isn't it, Tony? What a lot of people think, but are too scared to say. And isn't it sad that so many have been too frightened to speak their own minds like Robert here, tyrannised by minorities.' He paused to light yet another cigarette, using the holder flamboyantly, like a character in a Noël Coward play. 'I confess to bouts of feeling useless, confined as I am to this chair. I'd like to be in the forefront, leading the way, but fate has dictated that I must sit on the sidelines. Now, Robert, I have to ask you this. By joining us, you must be aware that your life will change. It will include an actual degree of danger from now on. The police you rightly used to admire will not be on your side. They will be used against you. Heads will be broken, perhaps your own. You may end up in jail for your convictions. I want you to be aware of that.'

'No room for second thoughts, is there, sir?' Tony interjected.

'No room at all.'

'I have to give an answer now, do I?' Hillsden said, deliberately playing the novice.

'Before you leave this room. Should you have even the slightest doubts as to the commitment I hope you'll give, then now's the time to voice them. We don't take kindly to part-time followers. It's all or nothing, Robert.'

'Can I ask you one thing?'

'Please do.'

'I find what you've told me exciting, but I don't know much about politics. Does that go against me?'

'Not at all. We lead, you obey.'

'Well, I definitely would like to join,' Hillsden said.

'You're prepared to be openly identified with our aims?'

'Yes.'

'To be bound by our oath of allegiance and faithfully perform any tasks you're given?'

'Yes.'

'Regardless of the consequences?'

'Yes.'

'Then I congratulate you on your acceptance into our ranks.' Again the thin, metallic smile that had no real warmth in it. 'You have joined the élite, Robert, as the future will prove.'

The expression reminded Hillsden of somebody else who thought he knew all the answers: Philby had used the same words to proclaim his allegiance to a different cause. The spoilers always quoted from the same text, convinced that they alone were right, that any means justified their end. The man who sat opposite him, chain-smoking beneath the tacky depiction of another madman's dream, mouthing an old recipe for a new chaos, had an all-too familiar face: trust me, his smile said, I have all the answers and will lead the way to dusty death.

'You've been at a disadvantage so far, Robert, in that I haven't introduced myself. I hope you didn't take that as deliberate rudeness. Just natural caution, which I urge you to copy from now on, especially when you come in contact with those who aren't sympathetic to our cause . . . My name's Fadiman, Graham Fadiman . . . and I'm delighted you're going to be with us.'

'Likewise, Mr Fadiman.'

'I find it very gratifying that, more and more, we're able to attract people like yourself. We're gathering strength every day, Robert, and soon we're going to be on the march.' He looked at his wrist-watch. 'Oh, dear. You must excuse me, but it's time for me to take my medicine.' He leaned out of his wheelchair and pressed a bell switch at the side of the fireplace. 'I hope it doesn't disturb you, but you're in the presence of a morphine addict. A registered one, I hasten to add. One of the crosses I have to bear. Fortunately, Johnny has become very adept at administering to my needs.'

Hillsden finished the last of his drink and stood up.

'Of course, I understand. Well, it's been a very illuminating meeting for me, Mr Fadiman. I appreciate you explaining everything so clearly and I promise you I've taken it to heart. Thank you very much.'

'No, thank you, Robert. I look forward to the next time.'

As Hillsden and Tony moved towards the door, Johnny wheeled in a small hospital trolley. He was wearing surgical gloves and as they passed each other Hillsden noted an array of sealed hypodermics and vials of the drug.

'We'll see ourselves out,' Tony said.

'What an impressive man,' Hillsden remarked as they drove off. His eyes sought a street sign, but, as in the majority of London roads, the identifying plaques were placed too high on the corner buildings and were impossible for him to read without craning round and drawing attention to the action.

'Very impressive,' he repeated.

'Yeah,' Tony agreed. 'He's brilliant. Course, there are others behind him, the money men, but he's the one who decodes strategy. He's the brains.'

'That condition of his . . . being in a wheelchair, I mean . . . did he catch something like polio?'

'No. He was mugged a few years back. Two blacks jumped him one night. He was brave enough to take them on, but they stomped him, the bastards, broke both his legs with iron bars. He'll never walk again.'

'God! How terrible.'

'Don't worry, he'll get even one day. We all will. Listen, I've things to do, got another meeting to go to, so I can't take you all the way. Where d'you want to be dropped?'

'Oh, anywhere near a tube station. Where are we now?'

Tony shot him a look. 'For a Londoner you don't know your own city very well, do you?'

'I get confused sometimes at night,' Hillsden said quickly, realising the blunder. 'All these new one-way streets. I'm fine in the daytime.'

'We're in the Holloway Road. I'll put you off at King's Cross, that suit you?'

'Fine . . . When d'you think I'll hear from anybody?'

'When we've got something for you to do.'

'What'll that be?'

'Depends.' Tony fished in the glove compartment and took out a small notebook. 'Reminds me, one other thing, better we don't use your office number from now on. Write your home address and stuff.'

It was the one thing that Hillsden had not anticipated and he thought quickly. There was no question of giving the Walsham le Willows address, but what else could he put? He tried a bluff. 'D'you think that's wise, bearing in mind what Mr Fadiman drummed into me? Putting anything in writing, I mean? Why don't I ring you at the snooker place tomorrow and give you it over the phone. Will you be there?'

'Yeah, okay, good point. Try me around three o'clock.'

Hillsden's heart was still racing from the narrow escape when Tony left him at King's Cross. The moment he was inside the station he went to a public phone and dialled Rotherby.

'Colonel, it's me.' He could hear soft music in the background.

'Who is it?'

'Who else calls you Colonel?'

'Oh. Right, got it.'

'I've got a problem that needs sorting out urgently. Can you meet me?'

'Now, you mean?'

'Yes.'

Rotherby's voice dropped to a whisper. 'Bit delicate tonight, old son. I'm "entertaining".' He gave the word a special intonation. 'Been nurturing this one for a couple of months, and it's just coming to the boil. Can't it wait until tomorrow?'

'No, I need to see you now. Make some excuse and leave her with another bottle of shampoo, I'm sure she'll still be hot when you get back. I wouldn't ask if it wasn't urgent. It won't take long.'

'Where are you?'

'King's Cross. I'll wait by the bookstall.'

There was a slight pause. 'You're a shit, you know that,' Rotherby said. 'Okay. I'll be about twenty minutes though.'

Hillsden killed the wait having a cup of nameless liquid masquerading as coffee and finessing the idea he intended to put to Rotherby. It was half an hour before Rotherby came into the station forecourt.

'So, what's the panic?' he asked.

Hillsden brought him up to date. 'What I thought of was this . . . The safe house in Forest Gate. Can you get an answering machine installed there by lunchtime tomorrow? Get the type that has a remote bleeper, so I can activate it to pick up any messages. Can that be done?'

'Bit short notice, but I suppose so.'

'Get the machine first thing, then bring it to my office and I'll record a message. It'll have to be connected to a separate line, of course – will that present a problem?'

'No, there's already a spare. The whole place is wired for anything.'

'Good. You're a chum, Colonel. Here.' Hillsden felt in his pocket and took out some money.

'Don't be stupid, I don't want that. It'll be paid for out of stores.'

'No, this is for you. For your taxi fare and some condoms. I want to be sure you're going to practise safe sex.'

'Oh, very funny. I'll be lucky if I can find it after all this time.'

'Listen, I hope I didn't ruin anything. See you tomorrow, and thanks again.'

When Rotherby had gone he went to the taxi rank and gave the driver the name of the hotel Sarah had booked for him.

28

A SEARCH

Even without Lloyd pouring cold water on his suspicions, Pearson harboured his own doubts about Charters's involvement. The connection between Charters and Carstairs which had set him on the trail was tenuous, to say the least, and part of him accepted Lloyd's scepticism, but he could be pig-headed when it suited him. The time he had spent in Northern Ireland had convinced him that his instincts deserved to be trusted – on more than one occasion in that tragic country, instinct had kept him alive. Trust nobody, be pig-headed, test every doubt, follow every lead, however obscure; in his experience somewhere in every haystack a needle lay buried. He had persuaded himself that the omission about Charters's parentage in *Who's Who* was worth following up and it was the reference to Charters's early schooling that now put him on the road to Swindon. What the hell? he thought, even if I draw a blank it's a day out.

Without telling Lloyd the purpose of his trip, he made an early start, but the inevitable road works and several accidents slowed his progress and it was gone eleven before he reached the outskirts of the town. By then his empty stomach was playing up and he pulled into a roadside café frequented by long-distance lorry drivers and had an enjoyable, but immediately regretted, greasy breakfast.

The obvious starting point was the electoral register, and his first call was to the town council offices. He gave his name as Chalmers so that he obtained the right volume. There were two Charters listed: *John* and *Pauline*. He made a note of the address and returned the volume to the librarian. Next he went to a post office to get directions.

The house, when he located it, was unprepossessing, a stucco-fronted, post-war semi-detached that would never win any architectural awards. There was a child's plastic bike lying on its side in the front garden and a bedraggled teddy bear on the porch.

When Pearson's ring was answered, the door, held on a security chain, was opened a fraction by a young woman clutching a small boy in her arms. She was wearing yellow household gloves and had a harassed look.

'Sorry to disturb you, Mrs Charters, but I wonder if you can help me?' Pearson said.

'Mrs who?'

'Aren't you Mrs Charters?'

'No, our name's Mather.'

'Oh, I'm sorry.'

'They must have been the last lot.' The small boy slid down to the floor and tucked himself behind his mother, staring wide-eyed at Pearson. 'Can't help you I'm afraid. The house was empty when we bought it.'

'Well, I apologise for troubling you, Mrs Mather. It's just that they're distant relatives I'm trying to trace.'

'You could try the estate agent's, they might know. Chancellor's in the high street,' she said, her voice still tinged with suspicion.

'Yes, that's a good idea, thank you.' Pearson bent down to pick up the teddy bear and handed it through the crack in the door. 'Here, poor teddy got left out.'

Her gloved hand took it from him. 'Ta,' she said and closed the door.

The girl in the estate agent's was only able to tell him that the house had been repossessed by the building society three months previously, and as far as she knew the Charters had left the district.

'You wouldn't know where they went, would you? They're relatives of mine.'

'I wouldn't have a clue.' She turned to a male colleague. 'This gentleman's enquiring about that couple who lived in number forty-eight Marpleton Street. You handled that, didn't you?'

'What's the problem?'

'No problem,' Pearson said. 'Just wondered where they moved to. I'm a cousin of theirs.'

'Well, I'll see if we kept any record.' He went to a filing cabinet and pulled out a folder. 'No, nothing here. The only thing I can remember is the wife was very upset. There's a bank reference. Barclays, you could ask there. But other than that, can't help I'm afraid.' He replaced the folder and went back to his desk.

'Is that the local Barclays?'

'Yes. Two blocks down on your left.'

'Well, thanks for your help.'

He went to the bank and after a wait was shown into the Manager's office. 'I know you can't give out confidential information, but all I'm trying to discover is whether Mr and Mrs Charters, who were customers of yours before they moved out, left any forwarding address.'

'Who are you from?' the Manager said stiffly.

'I'm not from anybody. They're family and I've only just found out they lost their home. Thought I might be able to help in some way. Did they transfer their account when they left?'

The Manager frowned and showed no disposition to be forthcoming.

'Well, I remember them, yes. They defaulted on their mortgage. Doubt if there was anything to transfer, given the circumstances.'

'No, well, I just thought I'd ask, having made the journey.'

'You understand one has to be careful in my position.' He tapped a silver pen on his blotter. 'However, I dare say I could take a look, but I doubt I have anything.' He punched something into his computer and peered at the screen. 'No, I was wrong. There was a small balance which we transferred to our branch in Yeovil. That's all I can tell you.'

'Well, that's something to go on,' Pearson said. 'I'm most grateful. Awful when you lose touch.'

'Yes. Depends, I suppose. I'd be happy to lose touch with some of my relatives.' He gave a thin smile, momentarily becoming human.

Before driving back to London Pearson decided to make one further search at the main cemetery's chapel. There he examined the Book of Remembrance and was rewarded by finding two entries. A Martha Charters had died in 1954 and alongside her name was written: *Beloved wife of William Paul Charters, who went to Jesus June 17th, may her soul rest in peace.* Leafing forward he came across a second reference: in 1962 this same William Paul Charters met his maker. Against this was written: *Much missed father of John and Janet.*

Although disappointed that there was no mention of a Raymond Charters, Pearson noted these details. He considered travelling on to Yeovil, but then remembered that he had promised to take his wife to the theatre for a delayed birthday treat. On the return journey to London he felt the day had not been entirely wasted.

. . .

Once he had ensured that the answering machine had been installed in the safe house, Hillsden contacted Swanson to give him a blow by blow account of his meeting with Fadiman. For some reason it did not produce the reaction he had expected.

'Yes, it's progress of a sort, I suppose, but again nothing we can immediately act upon. Fanatics spouting off about the purity of the race from a wheelchair hardly justify sending in the cavalry. I'm much more concerned about a report from our man in Munich.'

'What about?' Hillsden asked.

'That Bureau chap we met, Schmidt. He's been found dead.'

'Dead?'

'Yes.'

'In Munich?'

'No, Frankfurt apparently. I'm waiting for more details, but he was discovered in an underground hotel parking lot, stabbed to death.'

'Poor bastard,' Hillsden said.

'Yes, one of the few Yanks I've ever got on with. It's a bloody pity because he could have been very useful to us,' he added with no real sympathy in his voice, just annoyance. 'I've been trying to get hold of Pearson all morning, but he seems to have gone walkabout without telling anybody. He saw Schmidt again after us, maybe he knows something more.'

'That was a nightmare I often had in Russia.'

'What was?'

'Dying in a foreign country. Why Frankfurt, I wonder? He told us he was flying direct to Munich.'

'Yes, well that's part of the mystery that has to be solved. I wish to God something would go our way for a change. I get nothing but aggro from the Home Office. One has to have balls of steel to survive in this job. I wrote my resignation the last time Logan balled me out, then thought why give the little creep the pleasure? He had the nerve to ask whether I felt I was in the right job. You had the best of it, Alec.'

'Robert,' Hillsden corrected.

'Yes, "Robert", sorry.'

'What makes you think that?'

'Well, you chaps always knew who the enemy was.'

'Did we? The enemy without perhaps, but not always the enemy within.'

Swanson ignored the veiled reference. 'Nowadays they come at us from all directions, and we're expected to operate as before but on half the budget. The last Interpol symposium

I attended in Paris, I had my hotel expenses questioned. Next thing you know with this lot they'll be asking what school I'm sending my children to.' Then he made another subject U-turn. 'D'you have any idea where you were taken last night? Although our chaps got the number of the van, they weren't quick enough off the mark and lost him.'

'Chaps?' Hillsden said. 'You promised me there'd only be one.'

'Did I? Well, I changed my mind.'

'Thanks for telling me.'

This was ignored. 'So, do you know where you were taken?'

'I looked at a street map this morning and tried to fathom the route. At a reasonable guess I'd put it somewhere in the Islington area. There's a certain amateurism about the way they operate, though I suppose we said that about the IRA in the beginning. Doesn't make them less dangerous.'

'Well, unless this Fadiman's using a phoney name, it shouldn't be difficult to trace him. We'll run him through the computer, see what comes up.'

'The character named Tony mentioned there are money men behind Lionel Barrymore in the wheelchair.'

'Lionel Barrymore?'

'Don't you remember those old films?'

'I don't even remember new films,' Swanson replied testily. 'And by the way I don't like hearing things second-hand. I'm running you, not Rotherby.'

'If you're referring to the answering machine, I had to think of something quickly.'

'Even so.'

It was the cue for Hillsden to reveal the existence of a bug in his car, but once again he said nothing.

. . .

As far as London was concerned, Schmidt's unsolved murder

was put on the back burner. It was decided that the Yanks should be left to solve their own problems. Certain disturbing incidents closer to home proved more pressing. There was a sudden spate of synagogues being firebombed; London, Bristol and Leeds were the selected targets though, miraculously, there was no loss of life in any of them despite extensive damage to property. This was followed by a number of prominent Jewish and Pakistani businessmen receiving letter bombs, posted in various parts of the country. Most of these were intercepted and defused, but one slipped through the net and a secretary in Marks and Spencer's head office had her right hand blown off. The IRA and Animal Rights were ruled out and it was the opinion of Special Branch that a new Libyan terrorist cell was responsible. Several media commentators questioned this, in view of the fact that the attacks had not been confined to Jewish targets. Others argued the diversity of the targets was a clever tactic to confuse the issue and throw the security forces off the scent. Correspondence columns in the press printed the usual quota of letters from the flog-'em-and-hang-'em school. This new campaign, coming as it did on the eve of the two by-elections, embarrassed the government, forcing it on the defensive. Logan was savaged by the Opposition in the House, the Tories having put down an emergency motion on law and order. The debate was still in progress when a serious riot broke out in Manchester as the result of a badly mismanaged drugs bust, though this was subsequently considered to have no connection with the bombing attacks. *The Times*, in a front-page leader, thundered against the increasing number of no-go areas that had become a disturbing feature of the inner-cities, saying that it was intolerable that a siege mentality had been forced on ordinary citizens who now could not walk the streets without being in fear of their lives. Various armchair pundits monopolised the television talk shows with their panaceas and the polls immediately showed diminished support for the government.

It was during this volatile period that Hillsden received the summons to meet Tony again. The message on the machine invited him to another game of snooker in two days' time, with the added emphasis that 'it was in preparation for a big match'.

Since Hillsden's first visit to the snooker hall, it had been under surveillance, with anybody entering or leaving the building being photographed by an around-the-clock team concealed in a derelict shop opposite, but, apart from Tony, nobody had been positively identified.

'He obviously passed the first test then,' Pearson said when Swanson called him to discuss this latest development and to plot a response. 'Do we have anything on Fadiman?'

'Clean as a whistle, apart from one conviction for dangerous driving ten years ago. He's a bachelor, wealthy background, only son of a man who made his pile in South Africa. The father died and the mother, who was American, appears to have returned home. The only item of possible significance is that he spent a period in Germany before his accident. While he was there, he bought a lot of Nazi art at auction, including a couple of paintings purported to have once belonged to Goering.'

'That figures – Hillsden said they were mostly crap. When is this meeting?'

'Thursday night. Tell me, are the police aware of our surveillance team?'

'No,' Pearson said. 'Tell them too much and they're likely to blow the whole thing by parking a Panda car right outside. But Lloyd and I will be around. Disguised as Stormtroopers,' he added, but Swanson did not smile.

'Let's cut the humour, shall we? I'm not in the mood.'

. . .

That evening while Galina was putting Lara to bed, Hillsden

took Audrey to one side.

'How well do you know the locals now?' he asked.

'Oh, I'm on first name terms with a lot of them. Why?'

'Are they curious about me?'

'Not especially. One or two have asked what you do. I tell them you have to be away on business a great deal of the time. And – this'll make you laugh – when they learned you were in insurance, a couple of them said they might give you a chance to quote. Do you handle bona fide customers?'

'Yes, gives me an air of legitimacy. But don't encourage them. Look out for any strangers suddenly putting in an appearance. From now on we need to be extra careful.'

'Is it hotting up?'

'Well, they've taken the bait. Whether they've swallowed it remains to be seen.'

'And how are you making out with our friend Hadley?' she asked a little too casually.

Hillsden looked at her pointedly. 'Did you ever hear that story about two people who met in the street and one asked where the other was going. "To see a friend," was the reply. "Ah!" the first one commented, "You remind me of the Frenchman who received the same answer and said, 'Take me along, I never saw one.' "'

'What're you laughing at?' Galina asked as she returned.

'Oh, just some joke I heard on the radio,' Hillsden lied, not wishing to get into it.

'Will you go and read a story to Laura. Just one, I want her to go to sleep early tonight.'

'Sure. Put the coffee on, Audrey, and we'll all have a cup together. I like your brew.'

He went upstairs and read a chapter of *Charlie and the Chocolate Factory*, Lara having just discovered Roald Dahl.

'Are we always going to be here?' Lara asked when he was about to tuck her in.

'Don't you like it here? It's nice, isn't it?'

She wrinkled her nose. 'I liked it best when we were other people and you were always at home.'

'Daddy has to work so that he's got the money to buy food.'

'You didn't used to. Tell me again why Audrey calls Mama and me something different.'

'Just that we're in England and that's the way people speak.'

'It's not a nice name, though, is it? I think it's a silly name to call Mama,' she said as her eyes fluttered and closed with that enviable suddenness peculiar to small children. Looking at her, Hillsden felt his age and still couldn't reconcile himself to the fact that she was his; she seemed so tiny and vulnerable, especially at night.

Galina joined him in their bedroom before he went downstairs.

'Do you think she's too thin?' Hillsden asked.

'Laura? No, she eats like a horse. Why d'you say that?'

'Just asking. I'm not used to little girls, remember.'

'You get on well with big ones though.' She made it sound casual, but from the way she looked at him he sensed an undercurrent.

'What does that mean?'

'You and Audrey are always whispering together.'

'Darling, that's a total exaggeration. If you mean a few moments ago, I was just telling her a joke.' Galina's face did not change. 'What's wrong?'

'I want you to tell me jokes,' she said. 'We don't have laughs any more, you and me. Back home we shared everything, now there's somebody else.' The word 'home' hung between them and Hillsden thought, she's never thrown that at me before. It was the first step over a dangerous threshold into a room he did not want to enter. 'Audrey isn't "somebody else". She's here so that you're not alone when I have to be away. It's a difficult role for her, too, remember, thrown together with a family of strangers.'

'That's what we've become, a family of strangers.'

He saw that tears were forming and went to her. Her arms tightened around his neck. 'I'm sorry,' she said. 'But I'm so mixed up.'

'What are you mixed up about?'

'About you and everything, the way we live. I thought it would always be the same, but that was probably silly of me. It's just that I'm so frightened sometimes. In St Petersburg I always knew where you were, what you were doing. We had less there, but we had more too. I sometimes wish . . .' She didn't finish.

'What?' Hillsden said gently. 'Tell me.'

'I know you came back because you wanted me and Laura to have the things we'd missed . . . but I don't know what's meant by happiness any more. I went to church the other day, on my own, just to see if that made any difference . . . it's meant to, isn't it? You're meant to find comfort from faith . . . and I stared up at Him, on the cross, and all I could think of was . . . why do we worship suffering? Isn't there enough down here on earth without all that? Why can't we believe in a God who doesn't bleed for us? Do you ever think that?'

'I'm the last person to ask,' Hillsden said. 'I haven't been inside a church since I buried my parents.' He kissed her. 'But, darling, listen to me. This episode we're living through, it won't last for ever. I have to settle my account, but once it's finished, it'll just be the three of us again.'

'Will we have to stay here for ever?'

'No, we can go anywhere you like.'

'D'you promise?'

'I promise.'

Audrey called from the foot of the stairs: 'The coffee's ready if you still want it.'

'We'll be right down,' Hillsden answered. He kissed Galina again, wishing he could say something of real comfort to her, but his mind was filled with old thoughts, a scrapbook of memories they could not share.

29

A SECOND FRAME

This time Tony conducted Hillsden through the snooker hall to a windowless rear room where he found himself joining some twenty or more unfamiliar faces. He was regarded with a certain wariness as Tony, using only Christian names, made a few introductions. With one exception, the others present were considerably younger than Hillsden. The exception was an olive-skinned character, forty or thereabouts, introduced as Harry, whose beard-line suggested that he had forgotten to shave that day but, as Hillsden had recently discovered, the look was now dignified with the term 'designer stubble'. Some of the group wore variations of a quasi-uniform – bomber jackets, black trousers and heavy boots; his off-the-peg suit stood out in contrast. None were stereotype skinheads, though many sported hair cropped army-fashion and sat, feet sprawled, on the chairs arranged in a semi-circle, exchanging macho anecdotes which he guessed were intended both to isolate and impress him as the newcomer. A crate of beer stood on a trestle table and Hillsden was invited to help himself, which he did, drinking out of the bottle like everybody else. He took a seat next to the man called Harry.

'Your first meeting, Dad?' Harry said. There was a hint of derision in the way he addressed Hillsden.

'Yes.'

'Well, you're never too old to get wise.' It was a guttural, smoker's voice, with a polyglot accent, which, to Hillsden's ear, suggested a sandwich of Cockney and assumed American. 'And you've joined at the right time. Those who aren't with us now are going to miss out. The word is we're moving into top gear.' Harry drained his beer bottle, then volunteered in a boastful non sequitur, 'I just got back from the fatherland. You ever been over there?'

'No, I haven't.'

'Those Germans, they know what the score is, always have, we've got a lot more to learn from them, and the sooner we take a leaf outta their book the better.'

'Too bloody right,' Hillsden said, coarsening his own dialogue to suit the situation. 'That's what we're here for, isn't it?'

'You got it, Dad!'

It was then that a door at the rear of the room opened and Johnny wheeled in Fadiman. Immediately everybody stood up and shuffled to attention in a show of military discipline, Hillsden following their lead. Fadiman was wearing a green Tyrolean jacket, the collar and cuffs trimmed with leather. He lifted an arm that stopped just short of a Nazi salute.

'At ease, gentlemen. My apologies for keeping you waiting,' he said as Johnny wheeled him into the centre of the semi-circle and applied the brakes.

'A drink, sir?' Tony asked.

'Thank you, no. Cold beer doesn't sit well with me.'

'Something else then, sir?'

'No, nothing, thank you,' he said as his eyes swept around the gathering. He nodded at Harry, then fixed, momentarily, on Hillsden. 'Ah! We have our new recruit, I see. Good. I'm sure we're all pleased to welcome Robert, representing the older generation, somebody who has lived through the folly of our times.' He reached into his jacket pocket and took out a cigarette. Tony immediately struck a match, but Johnny, standing behind the wheelchair, already had a lighter poised.

Fadiman expelled the first inhale. The smoke hovered in the air and, for a few seconds before it dispersed, haloed his head. 'Well, gentlemen, the purpose of calling you together was to share some good news, news I'm sure will excite you as much as it does me. We are poised to make our presence felt.' He paused for effect. 'We are to be favoured with a rare visit from a comrade in the forefront of our movement, a man who, in his writings and speeches, has consistently shown the way forward. His name will be familiar to you . . . 'He smiled, and the braces on his lower teeth glinted in the light from the bare bulb above him. 'For some inexplicable reason, our authorities have never been over-anxious to welcome him to our shores and therefore his occasional visits must, of necessity, be carefully prepared for and carefully concealed from those who misguidedly don't share our reverence . . . I refer, of course, to Herr Gottfried Sonntag.'

His listeners leaned forward, and Fadiman smiled and nodded. 'I thought that news would excite you. Not only is he the author of several enlightened instruction manuals, he is undoubtedly a man of destiny. He sees where the mistakes of the past have landed us, and he has a vision of how to lead us out of the present morass.'

Fadiman paused again, flicking his cigarette ash on the floor, the act of a man who was accustomed to having somebody else clean up after him.

'We live in momentous times,' he continued, 'and we are the privileged few who share his vision. What I've brought you here for is to outline the purpose of his visit. In the very near future he will be recreating a flight first undertaken by the last inhabitant of Spandau . . . need I spell that out? No, I can see from your faces that you have grasped the symbolism . . . the only difference being that he will not be arriving in a Luftwaffe fighter, but, of necessity, in something more modest.' Fadiman nodded as his joke received a murmur of laughter.

'From start to finish of his visit it's imperative that we maintain the strictest security. His presence in our midst means he must take a considerable personal risk, and any breach of security would put his freedom in jeopardy. Therefore we must take every safeguard. Should anybody abuse the trust he expects from us, they will suffer swift and decisive punishment.' His eyes flicked to Harry, who nodded. 'We have our own final solution for those who betray our cause.

'Now then, I'm sure you're anxious to know the object of his visit. Apart from wanting to reach a wider audience in this country, the intention is to make the authorities look incompetent. Plans have been prepared for him to speak at the largest rally we have yet mounted. That's all I wish to tell you at the moment. All of you present tonight have been chosen for special responsibilities. On the day, you will act as marshals for the units coming from various parts of the country. I want this to be a public relations exercise, so you will all leave your modified Doc Martens at home. And let it be written in stone, on no account is anybody to carry anything that could be described as an offensive weapon. Is that clear?' All heads nodded. 'Let's not give the police any excuse on our behalf.'

'Can I put a question, sir?' somebody asked.

'Please.'

'Is he always going to be a secret? I mean, once it's all over, aren't we going to get some publicity out of it?'

'That's a good question and I was coming to that. Once he's safely out of the country again we shall certainly maximise the publicity. His speech will be video recorded and printed copies will be given wide distribution.' He dropped his cigarette butt on the floor and Johnny stepped on it for him. 'Any other questions?'

Nobody spoke. 'We're all quite clear then. I thank you for your attention, gentlemen.' He released the two brakes on the wheelchair but before Johnny could swivel him round he issued one last instruction. 'Be sure to leave singly at odd intervals, not in groups. Good night, gentlemen.'

Fadiman's audience stood up and, led by Tony, they gave the Nazi salute as he was wheeled out. There was a rush to the beer and an excited exchange the moment Fadiman had left. Hillsden mingled with the others and let his fake enthusiasm show on his face.

'Brilliant,' Tony said. 'If he pulls this off we'll scare the shit out of them.'

'*When* we pull it off, not *if*,' Harry said.

'I meant when.'

'Then say it.' Harry turned to Hillsden. 'What did I tell you, Dad? That guy is crackerjack. Fucking brilliant dodge to fly him in like Hess. You know they murdered Hess, doncha? He was a peace-maker, but they kept the poor bastard locked up long after the others had gone, and then they murdered him.'

'Yes, it was inhuman the way he was treated.'

'Well, this'll show them. Glad you joined?'

'Definitely.'

'Want to know my motto? Some of my best friends was Jews. Neat, eh?' He laughed, beer spilling out of his mouth and staining the front of his jacket. 'You want to stay on and play pool?'

'I never learned how to play.'

'That's okay by me, I've no objection to taking money off beginners.' He laughed again, then drifted away with some of the others into the snooker hall.

'Fadiman's a bloody good speaker, isn't he?' Tony said.

'Yes, he certainly knows how to hold your attention.'

'You can see if he hadn't been done up, he could have been another Mosley. Mosley had the same gift, apparently. Too bad I never saw him. Did you?'

'I saw him on newsreels,' Hillsden said.

'You wait, we're going to have rallies like that very soon. When I get the word I'll be in touch. Make sure you're available. You're one of the chosen now.'

'Where can I get some of Sonntag's books? I'd like to read one before the day.'

'You can't buy them in a shop and the fucking Customs impounded our last shipment, but I know where there's a few. Leave it with me.'

'Les Hyde wasn't with us tonight,' Hillsden said casually.

'No, he was organising something else. We've got a lot on the boil, and Les is a key player.'

'I'm lucky to have got to know him.'

'Well, you did him a good turn and now he's done you one.

Right?'

'Yes.'

Hillsden said his goodbyes and went through the snooker hall to the front entrance, glancing up at the dark windows of the shop opposite where, he knew, hidden cameras were recording the various departures.

30

A MEAL OUT OF TOWN

That same evening another meeting was taking place in a fashionable watering hole frequented by the affluent, Le Manoir aux Quat' Saisons. Sir Raymond Charters was entertaining a reluctant guest.

'Ralph,' he said between mouthfuls, 'let's put our false teeth on the table. You know and I know this is something that's going to happen sooner or later. You can't stop it, so why don't you bow to the inevitable? Get in bed with somebody you know rather than somebody you don't know and can't trust to do the right thing.'

His guest, Lord Miller, stared down at the meal on his plate, an item of *nouvelle cuisine* colourfully arranged like an edible drawing by Matisse. Unlike the other diners he had little appetite for what was before him or what was being said. Charters, on the other hand, was enjoying both the occasion and the meal. Like many corporate predators he was never so happy as when, having identified a potential victim, he moved in for the kill.

'We've done our homework, and you're highly vulnerable, don't pretend you're not. Your company's a dinosaur and it's haemorrhaging. The banks don't give you second chances these days, and they're ready to move in. You've got big cash-flow problems, the pre-tax profits for the year end were sixty-eight per cent down, you only held the dividend by digging into the reserves. You know your · mistake? You caught a cold going into too many wacky diversification schemes and you haven't helped the situation by paying yourself too much by way of salary. That wasn't politically correct in today's climate.' He forked the last of his food into his mouth.

'I've always made it clear I'd fight a hostile bid,' Miller replied.

'Fight! Who wants a fight? The only people who benefit are the lawyers. And I'm not offering you a hostile bid. How can it be hostile when I'm sitting here across the table making it easy? You go the route I'm suggesting, you walk away with a generous handshake for past services, we cosmetic it, invite you to stay on the Board for a year as an adviser, and you can enjoy the rest of your life.'

'I enjoy it now,' Miller said.

A waiter came up to the table and looked at Miller's uneaten dinner. 'Is everything to your liking, my Lord?'

'Yes, it's fine. I'm just not hungry.'

'Can I get you anything else?'

'No, thank you. Just some more mineral water.'

Charters returned to the attack the moment the waiter removed the plates and left. 'Doesn't that make sense?'

'To you, maybe.'

'Ralph, what d'you need it for? You've got all the honours. You've got your health, the best shoot in Wiltshire, nice house, grandchildren . . . and this way, the way I've laid it out, we take all the worries off you.'

Miller answered deliberately. 'I accept that, on the face of it, it's an attractive offer and I dare say a lot of people in my position would take it and run. But I built up this company from scratch, it's been my whole life, and while we might be going through a bad cycle, the banks are staying loyal, they still have confidence that, given some breathing space, I can retrieve the current situation.'

Charters shook his head. 'Don't depend on it. They'd pull the plug on their own grandmothers if it suited them. Charlie Gillard went around saying the same thing,' he added, naming a man whose business had recently collapsed in spectacular fashion, 'and look what they did to him. He ended up with nothing but his soiled underpants.'

Miller grimaced at the crudity of the remark as the waiter returned and poured him some mineral water.

'Can I describe the desserts we have this evening, my Lord?'

'Not for me.'

'How about you, sir?'

'Perhaps later,' Charters snapped. 'We'll tell you when we're ready.' He went back on the attack. 'Listen, Ralph, I'm sure you'll make up your own mind, no matter what I say, but I'm telling you you're running out of time. The institutions are in our camp, plus we've already got a forty-two per cent favourable response from shareholders. It's all over bar the shouting. But, as a personal gesture to you, I've come here tonight to say I'm willing to up the cash offer for the A shares to four twenty. That puts another million two in your pocket. Take it and smile.'

'Yes, that is generous, but my answer's still no.'

'How can you sit there and say that?'

'Because I'm an obstinate man who believes you're wrong.'

A note of exasperation crept into Charters's voice for the first time. 'Don't talk like an old Jew.'

'I am an old Jew,' Miller said quietly, 'and proud of it. And you just made your first mistake.'

'Oh, where's your sense of humour? It wasn't said to give offence.'

'Perhaps not, but you said it.'

'Ralph, listen to me. Believe your own Board. Both Anderson and Stanhope,' he said, naming two of Trans-Continental's executive directors, 'have come out publicly and said our bid is the only one that makes sense.'

'They can say what they like. I'm not interested in what they say.'

'You need friends at times like this. I'm your friend, Ralph. I'm thinking of you.'

'Yes, I'm sure you're acting from the very highest motives. I'm thinking of me, too. That's why I'm saying no thank you. If I lose –'

'Which you will – '

' – then it won't be for want of trying. I still have some cards I haven't played.' Miller folded his napkin. 'Now, if you'll excuse me, I'll let you enjoy your dessert. I've swallowed enough for one evening.' He stood up and made his way out.

Charters watched him go, holding a fixed smile on his face for the benefit of anybody who might be observing him. He finished his claret, wishing to give an interval before his own departure. Then he beckoned the waiter for his bill.

'Lord Miller took care of it, sir. He particularly asked us to say that he only accepts hospitality from his closest friends.'

· · ·

In his tenth-storey Frankfurt office, Walter Hekelmann, a senior officer in the Bundeskriminalamt, Germany's equivalent of the FBI, studied the autopsy photographs of Marvin Schmidt on his desk, then looked up at the CIA man attached to the American Embassy. 'This violence is new violence,' he said gloomily. 'We've got used to skins killing the *Immigranten* since the renunciation, but killing tourists is something different. Well, he wasn't a tourist, I know, but to them he probably looked like one. Why was he here?'

'He wasn't meant to be,' the Agency man said. 'He was on his way to meetings in Munich, following a lead on the Freidler case amongst other things. We know he was on that Lufthansa flight that got diverted, but that's it. He made no phone calls, right?'

'Not any from his room.'

'Did he receive any?'

'He might have done. The hotel doesn't log them.'

'Was he seen with anybody else in the hotel?'

'No. Only three of the staff remember him at all. The

reception clerk, the room maid and the night manager.'

'Did he eat in the hotel?'

'He ordered room service, but when it came up he wasn't in the room.' He lifted a piece of paper. 'Here's the docket. Hamburger, French fries and a piece of Black Forest cake. The food was uneaten.'

'Something, somebody caused him to leave his room soon after he checked in. Who, why, for what reason?'

Hekelmann threw his arms wide. 'It's a blank sheet. We know nothing from the time he rang down for room service until the time he was discovered the following morning when somebody moved their car . . . He was Jewish, wasn't he?'

'Yes. Not obviously so, as you can see.'

'Well, that's another thing that puzzles me. If he was "sidewalk-cracked" by the skins, their usual targets are Turks, gypsies, Kurds, the ones who *look* different, dress differently, don't speak the language, keep to their own quarters, eat in certain restaurants and bars.'

'Can we find out who else was on his plane? Have you got a passenger indent?'

'Yes, take a look.' Hekelmann handed over a computer print-out. 'Only two other people didn't fly on to Munich. I've marked them. One was a woman, as you can see. We checked and she was sick, seen by a doctor at the airport, diagnosed as having a stomach virus. She had relatives here who collected her. The other one . . . You've got the name there . . . Thompson.'

'Thompson. Do we know anything about him?'

'Nothing much. Travelling on an EC passport. Those are the details there.'

'Has he been located since?'

'No,' Hekelmann said. 'He checked into the Savoy for one night, then left the following morning, and took a flight to Copenhagen.'

'Why do people suddenly decide to get off a plane?'

'Are you asking me?'

'I'm thinking aloud,' the agent said. 'They get off because

they've had a bad experience . . . well, that flight came in with reported engine trouble . . . or they're genuinely sick like this woman . . . But neither of those marry with Schmidt. He flew all the time, once told me he'd clocked up enough air miles to fly twice round the world by Concorde. And he sure as hell didn't have stomach trouble if he ordered a burger. But he got off that plane.'

'Perhaps,' Hekelmann suggested hesitantly, 'and I'm not trying to be smart . . . but there's one other possible explanation you didn't mention. Maybe he got friendly with somebody on the plane – one of the hostesses perhaps? – it's happened before . . . and decided to have a little fun before resuming business.'

The agent considered the idea. 'Yeah, it's happened before. But somehow it doesn't sit with Schmidt.'

'We're all tempted – away from home, foreign country, the opportunity presents itself and . . . '

'Okay, well, no harm in interviewing the crew.'

'I have that on my list. But it has to wait. That crew flew out to Los Angeles before I could get to them.'

'Could be there's no real lead to follow. Could be the poor bastard just happened to have an appointment in Samarra.'

The agent picked up a plastic bag of belongings found on Schmidt's dead body and turned the contents out on to Hekelmann's desk. 'You've been through all this I imagine?'

'Of course. They're all labelled as you can see.'

The agent picked up a small pocket diary and rifled through it. He stopped at the last reference. 'He was found on the eighteenth, wasn't he?'

'Correct.'

'There is a reference here on the eighteenth, did you notice?'

Hekelmann took the diary from him and studied the page. 'Yes, we saw that, but it meant nothing.' He handed the diary back.

'Three names: Carstairs, Chandler and Van Elst. Mind if I keep this?'

'I assumed the Bureau would take the lot and return them to his next of kin.'

Reverting to their earlier topic, the Agency man asked: 'They just kill, do they, for the fun of it? They don't rob?'

'No, they're not interested in property, only people.'

'How organised are they?'

'If you mean is there one dominant group, the answer's no, we haven't found that. They're what we call "actively connected" on occasions. Various groups will often come together at events like Oi pop concerts.'

'What's Oi, for God's sake?'

'Heavy metal rock about genocide. You never heard of it?'

'No, that's a new one on me.'

'Not to us. Want to hear one of their favourites?' He walked across the office to a radio and tape player, switched it on and inserted a cassette. 'This is "Turken Raus", played by a local outfit called Onkelz. The sound on this is lousy, but the lyric goes "Turkish cunt shaved naked, Turkish cunt shaved away".' He turned up the volume and the American listened with a stunned expression.

'How do they get away with it?'

'We try to stop them,' Hekelmann replied, turning the machine off. 'It's banned, they're banned, but there are enough pirate copies floating around.' He removed the cassette and juggled with it in his hand. 'You're looking at one cynical German agent, my friend. This isn't the cause, it's just another symptom of our problem, your problem, Britain's problem, France's, Italy's and, any moment now, Russia's. The wolves are coming out of the forest, raiding the trash cans in our backyards. How did we lose it all, can you tell me?'

'I guess we can do precision bombing or just about everything else, but we ain't found a way to destroy hate.'

'Your man's a case in point,' Hekelmann said. 'They didn't kill him for a cause, they killed because they're mindless, they were just looking for some way to pass the time between the next pizza, the next beer, the next fix. They've got shit in the head, and that's tough to destroy, too.'

Everybody was waiting for the next development.

Hillsden had reported the content of Fadiman's briefing: 'He was so careful, all he gave away was the fact that this Sonntag would be coming. No date, no time, no location.'

'Light aircraft that come in low are not always picked up on radar,' Hadley commented, and Swanson gave him a look which implied that his input was not welcome.

'If indeed he uses an aircraft. Fadiman could have invented that to throw everybody off the scent,' Pearson said. 'On the other hand, the Hess factor would be a good piece of one-upmanship if they pull it off. Are the German police keeping close tabs on Sonntag?'

'I believe so.'

'Where is he now?'

'In his home town,' Swanson answered. 'He's a window cleaner, by the way. Correction, he runs a window cleaning firm. Earning an honest living.'

'Well, Hitler was a house painter, so he's in good company.' Pearson laughed at his own joke.

Swanson frowned, 'Actually, that's a myth. He wanted to be an artist and according to some reports had a certain talent.' He changed the subject and picked up a sheaf of photographs. 'Disappointingly, only one of the men caught on camera by the surveillance team outside the snooker hall proved to have any previous form. He served three months for grievous bodily harm in a pub brawl during the height of the IRA's mainland campaign.'

'Patriotic type though,' Pearson observed, studying the report. 'He slugged an Irishman.'

This time he got a laugh from Hadley.

'But nothing on the man called Harry?' Swanson asked.

'No. Were you counting on something?'

'Yes.'

'Why?'

'Well, it's not a golden rule, but in the past I've found that people who volunteer information to strangers either feel the need to boast or have something to hide. He told Hillsden he'd just come back from Germany.'

Pearson looked through the set of photographs again. 'I think we should all be aware that Hillsden is uneasy about the way it's going. He feels they accepted him too readily. The way he put it to me was he has the gut instinct that they were expecting him. Anybody share that view?' He looked around the room. Nobody spoke until Swanson broke the silence.

'Well, he's in and we can't take him out now.'

31

PEARSON GETS WARM

At the earliest opportunity and still concealing his intent from Lloyd and Swanson, Pearson drove to Yeovil, determined either to eliminate Charters from the reckoning or prove his point.

Yeovil, in Somerset, had once been a centre of the British glove industry, a town where the pungent, sour odour of the tanneries had always been present. Now, due to foreign competition, the local glove industry had all but disappeared, though the town still retained its friendly, sleepy atmosphere so characteristic of the land of Cheddar cheese and butter where, in summer, leather hit the willow on verdant village greens and ladies played bowls in blazers and soft linen hats.

On arrival, Pearson located the branch of Barclays Bank he had been given in Swindon. He saw no reason to conceal his identity on this occasion.

'It's nothing sinister,' he said, when he revealed who he wanted to trace, making up a plausible story as to why. 'The Charters are not in any sort of trouble. Just that, in the course of another investigation we came across some important information regarding a relative of theirs. It's possible they may be entitled to a sum of money.'

'Oh, I see,' the Bank Manager said. 'Well, I'm sure they'd welcome that, if it proves true.' He produced their address, writing it down for Pearson, together with directions showing how to get to the house.

The Charters lived in the lower half of a house in Woodland Grove, a hilly street close to a local landmark, the Nine Springs. He was greeted by a tall, depressed-looking man, who peered at him through John Lennon spectacles.

'Mr Charters?'

'Who wants him?'

'Mr John Charters?'

'What's it in connection with?'

'I'm making enquiries about a relative of your family who I believe once lived in Swindon.'

'We don't have any relatives in Swindon.'

'But you are Mr John Charters?'

'Maybe. Who are you?'

'I'm sorry, I should have shown you some identification.' Pearson produced a bogus business card he carried in addition to his official pass. This merely stated: *Commander A.G. Pearson (Rtd) Loss Adjuster*, together with the name and address of a fictitious company. He handed this to Charters who examined it closely.

'This isn't some try-on, is it?'

'Try-on?'

'You from the credit company? Because if you are you're wasting your time.'

'No, I promise you.'

'Loss Adjuster's a joke where we're concerned. We've lost everything. And my wife and I have to be careful.'

'I understand.'

'I doubt it. Those people never let up. Leave you with nothing.'

'But I have got the right person? You are Mr Charters?'

'Yes.' His initial suspicions having been partly allayed, he now seemed willing to unburden himself of past grievances. 'I was off work for a few months and for the first time got behind with the payments. Next thing you know they walk in and repossess the house. Just like that. So you can understand I'm very cautious these days.'

'Yes, that sort of thing happens to a lot of people, I'm

afraid,' Pearson said. 'I sympathise.'

'So, tell me again, what're you asking?'

'Well, it's just a long shot, but since you're a Charters, and, I believe, from Swindon, I thought it worth looking you up.'

'Something to do with a will, is it?'

'Sort of, yes,' Pearson lied, feeling mean.

'Well, I could be wrong, of course, but I can't think of any close relatives still living. I had a sister, but she died . . . must be ten years ago. And there was a cousin who moved to Australia, but I've no idea whether he's still around.'

The possibility of there being some money behind the enquiry had brought about a change in Charters's attitude. 'Why don't you come in for a minute, can't talk standing on the doorstep. You'll have to excuse the place.'

Charters showed him into a room denuded of everything but essentials. A few sticks of furniture and, the only luxury, a small black and white television which Charters now switched off. 'You see what I mean, this is all they left us with.'

'Awful . . . Is your wife at home?'

'No, she does part-time at Sainsbury's. I'm still under the doctor, you see. Got a dicky heart. I'm on the waiting list for a pacemaker.'

Pearson nodded. 'Well, they do wonderful things these days . . . You mentioned a sister.'

'Janet, yes.'

'You didn't have a brother?'

'No, only the two of us.'

'Well, obviously it's just a coincidence, but I came across another Charters who was a pupil at Swindon Grammar School during the war.'

Charters frowned. 'During the war? That's going back a long way. Not me, you mean?'

'No, not you, another male member of your family.'

'Weren't any. Just me and my sister.'

'Oh, well, I'm sorry I troubled you. I must have been given the wrong information.'

'Looks like it . . . Oh, now, hold on, wait a minute. The old brain doesn't work as fast as it used to. I've an idea who you might be talking about. One of our evacuees. My late parents were Quakers, you see, wonderful people, hearts of gold. I never kept up with it after they passed away . . . life has dealt me a few duff cards and I guess I couldn't live up to my folks' standards. They turned the other cheek, but I find that difficult.' He cocked his head on one side, inviting Pearson's understanding.

'Yes, it isn't always easy to play the good Samaritan,' Pearson said. 'You were about to say?'

'Yes, what got me on that?'

'You mentioned evacuees.'

'Ah, that's right. Yes, they took in a couple of East End kids at the start of the war, real little tearaways, I might add – no manners, didn't know how to hold a knife and fork, not that I'm being critical, just a question of upbringing I'm sure . . . But after the . . . what did they call it? . . . the phoney war, when nothing happened, their parents took them back. Then, later, when the French capitulated, there was another exodus and after the Blitz started my parents took in another boy. He was an orphan we were told, his parents had been killed in the air raids I think . . . not sure about that, the old memory's a bit hazy. I seem to remember he'd been shunted all over the place until he found his way to us.'

Pearson cut in to his rambling as politely as he could: 'Your parents were obviously very good people.'

'Salt of the earth. How funny, you've brought it all back. I hadn't thought of him in ages.'

'Who are we talking about now?'

'This other boy. Carl. He went to the same school as us.'

'Carl? Not a very common name. What was his surname?'

'Ah, now you've got me. Let me think . . . What was it? Gone. I do remember my father talked about legally adopting him at one point, Carl being an orphan and that.'

'And did he?'

'Well, now, did he? No, I don't think he did in the end for

268

some reason, although Carl did use our family name. There's something called a Deed Poll, isn't there?'

'Yes.'

'Maybe that was it. Seems to strike a bell. Something to do with identity cards, ration books and that. Knowing my father, he probably didn't want the boy to feel set apart, if you get my meaning. So he went to school under our name. They used to call out the names at morning prayers, that's how I remember. Maybe you could find out whether it was done properly, I can't help you there. He was older than us two and children don't bother about those things, do they?'

'Did he stay with you all after the war?'

'No. No, he left. He was bright, clever at his lessons, cleverer than us, I suppose, because he got a scholarship and left. And that was the last we heard of him. Not that our parents wanted to lose touch, it was him, he never bothered to write or anything. Just went out of our lives. Upset my parents at the time. Not a very nice way to repay their kindness, was it? My sister and I weren't too bothered, because we didn't like him overmuch. Gave himself airs. How funny, it's all coming back now. Haven't thought about him in donkey's years.'

'Well, it was a long time ago,' Pearson said.

'Now, hang on, wait a minute. Let me see if I can put my hands on something that might help.'

He disappeared into another part of the house. Pearson heard him rummaging about, closing and opening drawers. He returned carrying a somewhat tattered album of the sort that families once treasured and hoarded mementoes in. 'Here we are,' Charters said. 'Found it.' He opened it and some loose snapshots fluttered out. 'Coming to pieces.' He retrieved them and having examined them, handed one to Pearson. 'That's the three of us.' The photograph showed three children standing by a concrete pillbox.

'There's me, that's my sister, and that's him, that's Carl. Here he is again. Bit older there. Taken at Wookey Hole caves. You ever seen them?'

'No, I haven't.'

'Well worth a visit. Now this one must have been taken on VE Day. There was a big party, bonfire, fireworks, the lot. Doesn't it seem an age ago? I suppose he could be dead by now, couldn't he?'

'That's what I'm trying to establish,' Pearson replied.

'If he is dead, I suppose you're looking to trace anybody entitled to benefit? . . . If he left anything that is. And, of course, there is a family connection, in a manner of speaking, wouldn't you say?'

'From what you've told me there's a link, certainly. Though how it would stand up in law, I don't know.'

'Don't mention the law to me. I've had enough of the law, thank you . . . By the way, I wouldn't want you to take away the wrong idea. When I say me and my sister didn't get on with him, there was no bad blood or anything, wouldn't like you to think that. Just that we were kids and he was a stranger thrown amongst us and I suppose we resented it, as kids do.'

'Understood.'

'Did you want to take any of these snapshots?'

'No, that won't be necessary. Thank you so much for letting me take up your time.'

'Hope it's been worthwhile.'

'Oh, it has. You've told me a lot I didn't know.'

'Well, feel free to come again if you want to. I could show you around the caves if you had more time.'

'Yes, that would be nice.'

Pearson hesitated, then said casually, 'You do have one rich namesake, of course.'

'Do I? Who's that?'

'Sir Raymond Charters. You've heard of him I dare say?'

'No, can't say I have. We live in a bit of a backwater here, you know.'

'You don't think he's a distant relative?'

'I'd like to think so, but I doubt it. Never heard it mentioned.'

He accompanied Pearson to the front door. 'Sorry the wife

wasn't here. She'll be very intrigued.'

They shook hands. 'Thanks once again. I hope you don't have to wait too long for your operation,' Pearson said.

'The doctor says I'll be a new man once it's done.'

Pearson had much to mull over on his way back to London. In one sense he had inched closer, but now there was a new trail to follow. He doubted whether any records of evacuees still existed after half a century; the mass exodus, first in 1939 and then again in 1940, would almost certainly have been organised at local authority level and if one was talking about a London Borough so much archive material had been destroyed in the Blitz.

Where to begin again? The name Carl, with its vaguely Germanic ring, intrigued him, but it was the original surname he needed to discover. Even so, he felt vindicated.

. . .

'I've had your favourite detective on the line,' Lloyd said the moment Pearson returned to his office.

'Who's that?'

'Gilbert the filbert.'

'Oh, yes, what's he want? I had an interesting day I have to talk to you about.'

'They pulled in Carstairs's, quote, wife, unquote, last night, looking like that actress in *Absolutely Fabulous*, apparently. Pissed out of his/her mind, and shouting his/her mouth off that her husband had been murdered because he was a spy.'

'Tell me some good news. Hey-bloody-ho! We needed that. Where're they holding him?'

'West End Central.'

'We'd better go deal with it then. We don't want Carstairs's domestic arrangements splattered all over the tabloids. By the way, you might still owe me one on Charters,' he said as they went down to the car park. 'I found out something of interest today. I don't think it's his born name.'

'Really?'

Lloyd's continued boredom with the subject irked Pearson and he did not conceal it. 'Show some enthusiasm, won't you? I don't like talking to myself. Proves I could be on the right track about him.'

'Proves nothing. A lot of people change their names.'

They argued all the way to West End Central police station with neither giving ground.

Pearson greeted the Duty Sergeant with 'I gather you've got an hysterical queen on your hands? We got the message from Inspector Gilbert.'

'Yes, he thought it best if you dealt with her.'

'Where was she picked up?'

'Legless and screaming outside a pub at World's End. She's only just quietened down. It was bloody mayhem during the night. You're welcome to her.'

'Okay, we'll sort it out. Take it from me you'll have Gilbert's okay for you to let her off with a caution.'

They were shown to the cell where 'Mrs Carstairs' was being held. Her clothes were torn and the blonde wig looked like an abandoned bird's nest. She had a bruise over the left eye and mascara had streaked her make-up. You poor old cow, Pearson thought and wondered what sort of existence lay ahead for somebody like her. He tried not to show the disdain he felt. The moment she saw him and Lloyd she began to cry.

'Oh, thank God! Thank God! Get me out of here for Chrissake! I couldn't take another night.'

'All right, all right. Don't make yourself upset again. First of all, tell us what brought this on.'

'Have you got a cigarette, please?'

Lloyd produced one and lit it for her.

'Now, we gather you've been making accusations,' Pearson said. 'What made you do that?'

'Because I want the truth to come out.'

'What truth?'

'My darling Freddie didn't commit suicide, he was

murdered. And I know why.'

'Calm down, take it gently. What d'you know?'

'He was a spy, wasn't he? He wasn't doing police work like you said. You were lying to me. You're all the same lying bloody devious lot.'

'Well, now, that's the saucepan calling the kettle black. You're not exactly straight, are you, if we're trading insults? We didn't lie to you, if anything we were trying to protect you.'

'Oh, some protection.' Her voice climbed higher. 'You sent one of your men to threaten me.'

'I did *what*?'

'I got a visit, didn't I? Told I'd end up the same way as my Freddie if I didn't keep my mouth shut.'

'Somebody from my department threatened you?'

'Yes.'

'Who?'

'Well, he didn't give a name, did he? But he must have come from your lot, otherwise how did he know where we lived an' all?'

Pearson and Lloyd exchanged looks. 'Now listen,' Pearson said, 'and listen carefully. Just quieten down for a moment and listen. Nobody – I repeat, nobody – from my department could have paid you a visit without my knowing. So let's put that out of the way before we go further.'

'Why should I trust you?' Mrs Carstairs sniffed.

'Because it's in your own best interest. If you say somebody came to the house, I believe you. But I want more details. Can you give us a description of this man?'

'Poncy, evil little sod, I thought.'

'Yes, fine, but what did he look like, what sort of age?'

'I don't know. Forty maybe.'

'Any distinguishing features?'

'Dark hair. Not very well dressed. About your height.'

'Would you recognise him again?'

'I bloody would. Won't forget that face in a hurry.'

'And how exactly did he threaten you?'

'He had bad breath when he got close.'

'I see, but what did he say?'

'Well, he rang first, said he had some important news to give me which he couldn't talk about over the phone. He sounded kosher, and I was taken in. He said it was urgent and would I be in if he came round right away.'

'What time was that?'

'I'd just given Monty his tea, so it'd be about, oh, six o'clock.'

'Just him? Nobody else?'

'No, just him.'

'Did he show you any identification?'

'No.'

'Didn't you ask him for some?'

'No, he was fine on the doorstep, wasn't he? Seemed what he said he was. It was only when he got inside that he changed.'

'Stop there. *Who* did he say he was?'

'Said he worked for the same people as my darling Freddie.'

'Go on.'

'Then he said . . . "Your Freddie, as you call him, was a double-crosser, did you know that?" And of course I said I knew nothing, that Freddie never discussed his work with me. Which he didn't. Then he started to slap me around, gave me this.' She fingered her bruised eye. 'Called me a lying whore. Well, you can say a lot of things about me, and fucking sticks and stones don't break my bones, but I've never been on the game, I was always faithful to my Freddie. I swore blind I didn't know anything, but he kept it up, knocked me about something savage, and all the time he was saying, "Who did he shop us to?" Then, when he couldn't get anything out of me, because I had nothing to tell him, he killed him. He killed my Monty, stepped on him and broke his little neck.' Tears streamed down her face. '"That's just a taste of what you'll get," he said. "We took care of your Freddie and we'll take care of you, so you'd better try and remember something I want to hear, because I'll be back ."'

'Here,' Pearson offered her a handkerchief. 'Look, whatever else, let me assure you of one thing. Your husband . . .' he got the word out with the barest hesitation, 'wasn't murdered. He took his own life. There is absolutely no doubt about that, so this character was lying.'

'That's no bloody comfort, is it? He's dead whichever way.'

'Yes, I agree. We can't bring him back. So now we have to think about you . . . This is what I want you to do for me. First, we'll get you out of here and take you home.'

'I couldn't, I couldn't go back there.'

'Wait, I haven't finished. You know we're genuine, don't you?'

'Suppose so.'

'Well, the police wouldn't have let us see you if we weren't. You'll be given protection and if this character pays a second visit, we'll nab him. Then, tomorrow, I'll bring you some mug shots to look at, you might be able to recognise him from a photograph. How does that sound?'

'Haven't got much choice, have I?'

'Trust me. I know you've had a terrible shock, but I promise you that man was nothing to do with us. We don't work like that. If we thought you were holding something back, either me or Mr Lloyd here would have questioned you. There's just one other thing I want to ask you before we take you home. Did your husband ever mention the name Charters to you?'

'No. Never heard of him.'

'Okay, just wait here a moment or two until I get you signed out and make a phone call. Then we'll be on our way.'

He and Lloyd went back to the desk.

'You make me laugh, you do,' Lloyd said.

'Laugh? What about.'

'When you said "husband" in there. Sounded so bloody funny.'

'Well, what else was I going to call him? She'd had a rough enough time from all accounts.'

'There you go again – "she".'

'Oh, give it a rest,' Pearson said. 'Just take care of the paperwork while I get some protection organised.'

. . .

Sitting across from his wife and daughter at the dinner table, Hillsden felt soiled. While he listened to Lara's chatter about what had happened on her first day at school, part of his mind kept returning to his secret life. Already, he thought, I have been trained by the Fadimans of this world, forced to speak their language, assume their hatreds, echo their prejudices. It was a heavier price for freedom than he wanted to pay. He stared into his daughter's excited face and tried to concentrate on what she was saying.

' . . . and we made clay models. I'm doing something special and secret for you, Dada.'

'Are you? I can't wait.'

'I nearly finished it and then it broke. Mummy knows what it is, but she mustn't tell you.'

'Oh, no, it's got to be a secret.'

Lara looked down at her plate for a moment, then said in the mumbled speech children use when troubled: 'We have a lot of secrets, don't we?'

'Do we?'

'Yes, tell me again why I had to change my name.'

Hillsden and Galina exchanged glances.

'Just that it's easier to spell it the English way now that we're in England,' Galina said. 'I told you that before.'

'But Dada was always English and he's changed his name too.'

'Now, not so much talking, young lady, just finish what's on your plate and then it's bedtime.'

Later, when Lara had been put to bed, Galina said: 'She's always asking me that question. It didn't matter so much before she went to school, but now I'm worried she might let something slip amongst her friends. And you couldn't blame her, because she's confused. I get confused. I nearly gave myself away the other day when I was signing for something in a shop . . . I almost wrote "Hillsden", just stopped myself in time. You're used to leading a double life, we're not.'

'I know, darling,'

'You find it easy though.'

'No,' Hillsden said.

'We've burdened her with our lives. She's fearful, too fearful about things. She shouldn't be fearful of life at her age. That'll come soon enough. The other thing she asked me today was whether it was all right for her to be in the class photograph.'

'Did you say yes?'

'Yes, but then I thought, is it safe, would you turn round and tell me I'd done the wrong thing?' She waited for him to answer. 'Should I have said, no, that's not a good idea?'

'You couldn't have said that. That would only have led to more questions.'

'I can tell from your expression though that you'd rather she didn't.'

'No. As a matter of fact I was thinking of something else you said. That we've burdened her with our lives. You could have put it another way, that I've burdened you both with my life. Isn't that the truth of the matter?'

'If only you'd tell me what the truth is.'

'Galina, my darling,' Hillsden said, 'd'you think I want to involve you any further than I have already? It's enough that I brought you both here . . . I was so anxious to give you what I thought would be a better life that I didn't think it through. Whatever else you blame me for, don't blame me for that because I did it out of love.'

'I don't blame you,' she said. 'I just didn't want you to change.'

'Have I changed?'

'Not towards us, I don't mean that. I know you love us, but I don't think you love yourself any more.'

Hillsden was jolted. It was as if, throughout dinner, she had been reading his thoughts with that startling perception women, and especially mothers, often had.

'You once said to me "I'm safe now",' she continued.

'Did I?'

'Not so long after we met. And I believed you. Should I still believe you?'

Instead of answering her, Hillsden said, 'Then do you remember that when you told me you were expecting Lara, you asked if I was pleased, and I think I said to you that I'd only been trained to recognise hatred, that love always took me by surprise. Or words to that effect. Do you remember that?'

Galina nodded.

'Well, that's still true. I often wonder why it is you still love me.'

'And you haven't answered me,' she said.

'I'm safe with you,' Hillsden replied, 'if that's what you want to hear.'

32

THE TROUBLE WITH HARRY

The first day of the following week Hillsden sat at a corner table in one of the many sandwich bars in Docklands eating a snatched lunch. From boredom he was reading somebody's discarded copy of *The News of The World*. It had been a dull Sunday: no ex-employee of the Royal family had sold the serial rights to their memoirs. He leafed through the pages wondering what gave the British press its unique facility of maximising the instantly forgettable. He turned to the financial pages and studied the advertisements for PEPs as he pondered whether he should invest some of the money he had set aside for Galina and Lara. Alongside one of the ads there was a photograph of a couple taken at a race meeting. The caption under the photograph read: *You win some and you lose some. Although his champion three-year-old 'India Rose' was ridden to victory at Kempton Park yesterday, millionaire businessman, Sir Raymond Charters, recently failed in his take-over bid for Trans-Continental.*

He looked up from the paper to find Sarah standing beside him with a worried face.

'What is it?'

She sat down opposite him. 'Somebody arrived at the office.'

'Who?'

'I don't know, he wouldn't give me his name, but he said he knew you. I told him you were out to lunch and he said he'd call back in an hour. So I locked up and came to find you.'

'Well, get your breath back. Do you want a coffee, something to eat?'

She shook her head.

'He said he knew me?'

'Yes.'

'But didn't say how or where?'

'No. I asked him if he was interested in car insurance, but he said, no, it was a personal matter.'

'How long ago?'

Sarah looked at her watch. 'I'd say twenty minutes.'

'Okay, now, I'll tell you what you do. Go back to the office and I'll join you there. I want to make a phone call first. If he gets back before I do, give him brochures, chat him up with some sales talk. Off you go. I'll be there as soon as I can.'

'Right.'

They got up together and Sarah left while Hillsden paid his bill. Outside he had to walk two blocks before he found a public phone box. It was occupied and he fretted outside while two girls, jammed together inside the box, shared a lengthy conversation. The moment the box was free again he dialled Pearson's number. Hadley answered.

'He's isn't here,' Hadley said. 'What's up?'

Hillsden gave him the brief details. 'It could be nothing, but let's not take chances. How soon can you get down here?'

'I'm on my way.'

'Just come in as if you were another customer. Whoever it is, I'll try and keep him there until you arrive so you get a look.'

He hurried back to the office and the moment he got inside Sarah said: 'Oh Mr Bartlett, you're back. There's a friend of yours here to see you,' and as he turned from closing the door he saw who it was.

'Harry!' he said warmly. 'To what do I owe this honour? Don't tell me I'm going to get your business after all?'

'No, don't get excited, I was down this way and I thought I'd pay you a call. See where you hang your hat.'

'Has Sarah offered you a coffee?'

'She did, but I said no.'

'Come into my office so we can talk. I'll have one, Sarah, but no calls.'

He escorted Harry into the inner office and closed the door. 'Do you have any news?' he asked in a lowered voice.

'News?'

'The news we're waiting for?'

'No, like I said, this is just a social call. Our friend in the wheelchair thought we ought to get to know each other better.' He looked around the room, taking everything in. 'Nice set-up. How's business?'

'Not bad.'

Harry said: 'Useful little earner, insurance, I'm told.'

They were interrupted by Sarah bringing in the coffee. Putting it down on Hillsden's desk, she turned to Harry. 'Are you sure you wouldn't like one, Mr . . . ? I'm sorry, I don't know your name.'

'No, I'll pass.'

'I know you said no calls, Mr Bartlett, but there is another gentleman waiting outside.'

'Well, apologise, say I'm with a client and I'll be with him shortly.'

Sarah withdrew, closing the door after her.

'I'm surprised to see you,' Hillsden said when it was safe again. 'Tony felt I shouldn't be contacted here.'

'That so? Yeah, well, Tony has his own ideas, I go about things in a different way.' He picked up one of the brochures on the desk and looked through it while talking. 'You still got your health?'

'My health? Yes, I think so.'

'Great thing health.' He put the brochure down again and gave a thin smile. 'We all need to stay healthy. Not take chances. But, you'd know that, being in the insurance game. I don't take risks. I don't even drink coffee. Yours is getting cold, by the way.' He walked around the room. 'You landed a nice little set-up in your old age.'

'Yes, I got lucky.'

'Twice,' Harry said.

'Twice?'

'You joined us. You never know when your luck may change, though.'

'No,' Hillsden agreed. 'Not these days. What d'you do for a living, Harry?'

'Me? Nothing much. Do a bit of chauffeuring, never been one for the nine to five routine. I make a living.' He moved to the door. 'Anyway, nice to see somebody else hard at it.'

Hillsden went with him through the outer office. Hadley sat reading a brochure and looked up as they appeared. Harry gave him a passing glance.

'Be with you in a minute, sir,' Hillsden said to Hadley, following Harry into the corridor and closing the outer door.

'I'll see you on the great day then.'

'Yeah, let's hope so,' Harry said enigmatically, as he departed down the stairwell. 'I'll keep in touch, depend on it.'

Back in his office, Hillsden found Hadley using a small two-way radio. 'Leaving the building now. Medium build, brown jacket and blue jeans.'

'Are you having him followed?'

'I thought we might as well.' Hadley saw Hillsden's dubious expression. 'Don't worry. Be interesting to see what his next port of call is. Did he tell you anything new?'

'No'

'He didn't give you the date when Sonntag arrives?'

Hillsden shook his head. 'No, he just fingered my collar.'

'What's that mean?'

'You make me feel my age, Hadley. It's an expression they used to use when the police gave you a caution.'

'You think he had an ulterior motive coming here?'

'I'm sure of it. People like Harry don't make social calls. They always have a purpose. Put that in your book and learn it by heart.'

. . .

They met in one of the service stations on the M4 motorway, arriving in separate cars. Hillsden found Rotherby in the sparsely populated smoking section of the restaurant.

'You still do, don't you?' Rotherby asked, balancing a cigarette on the edge of the ashtray while he dunked a digestive biscuit in his coffee.

'Smoke? Yes, of course.'

'I was sitting here trying to think of the brand that used to have silk flags of all nations on the packets.'

'Kensitas,' Hillsden said. He opened a small plastic bucket of milk and emptied it into his tea. 'My father doted on them.'

'How brilliant of you to remember. Pity I didn't save them, a complete set goes for a fortune at auction.' A segment of his soggy biscuit fell into his coffee but he seemed not to notice. 'So what's worrying you that we had to meet in secret?'

Hillsden hesitated. He felt like a writer staring at a blank page, knowing the plot but unable to conjure up the dialogue. 'More and more,' he said finally, 'I think I've been set up. You telling me my car was bugged planted the idea and somewhat late in the day I've become convinced that I've been chosen as the patsy. I think the Fascist mob were expecting me.'

'What makes you think that?'

'Because it's all gone too smoothly. Doesn't it strike you that way?'

'Yes, to be honest. Didn't mention it to you, which was a mistake, but put that down to the general euphoria of seeing you again. What has been in my mind all along is something Masterman wrote in his last will and testament,' Rotherby replied, referring to a once banned book by a now dead member of the Firm. 'He laid down that a double-agent can't be produced out of thin air and set upon the stage ready at once to play a leading role. Which is what they did with you. He maintained that the double-agent had to be steadily "built up", as he put it, over a long period, and that in the beginning he is never an asset but always a liability. You were flung into it and it always puzzled me that you didn't protest and ask for more time.'

Hillsden took a moment before answering. 'I don't have a simple reason. Perhaps the truth is that, having been out of the game for all those years I'd become careless. Tell me, who first floated the idea of bringing me back?'

'I've never been able to track it to its source. I first heard it talked about just before Keating died. Then it didn't surface again until they started to beef up the anti-Fascist section of F Division. That was when Pearson and I got moved over.'

'What d'you make of Pearson and his Man Friday?'

'Two examples of the old school. Not too much imagination, maybe, but get there in the end. They both spent time in Northern Ireland, so they know a trick or two, but they never struck me as being plotters against their own kind.'

'So you'd rule them out?'

'I don't rule anybody out, but they seem unlikely casting.'

'How about Hadley?'

'Ah! Difficult to read our friend Hadley. Touch of La Gioconda.'

'Which comes back to Swanson. How d'you read him?'

'Sees himself as future DG. I think he'd piss on my grave if he thought it would push him another two rungs up the ladder.'

'How about my grave?' Hillsden said.

'No, you're his man. He was the one who recruited you, don't forget. You pull this off and he takes the credit for masterminding the operation.'

'So who else is there?'

'There's me, of course,' Rotherby said, draining his coffee cup.

'I trust you, Colonel.'

'Is that wise? Why trust anybody?'

'Why else would you tip me off about the car?'

'Perhaps that was a double-bluff to put you off the scent.'

Without changing his tone of voice, Hillsden said: 'If I really entertained that I'd have to get rid of you.'

'Not you, old son. You're not cut out for the rough stuff.'

'You think not?' Hillsden paused as though taking a decision, then said: 'I thought that until I had to kill Jock.'

Rotherby stared at him. 'Jock was murdered by the KGB. He was buried in Vienna, the British Council put up a headstone. I've seen the photographs.'

Hillsden shook his head. 'No, he was never buried there. That was a KGB fake. He was turned. They turned him. I killed Jock in Moscow. I smothered him with a pillow while he was drunk.'

'Are you kidding me?'

'Unfortunately, no.'

'Why?'

'Why? I had to. You see, we're all faced with having to make the ultimate choice between love and hatred sooner or later. Something Caroline said to me just before she went back into East Berlin for the last time. She said, "That's the game we're in. Not the love game, the hate game." It was the last conversation we ever had. And I had a good reason to hate Jock. He murdered Caroline.'

Rotherby's jaw dropped another inch.

'How could he have done?'

'He was sent back here for that express purpose. Caroline was the one who held the last piece in the jigsaw that could bring down Lockfield and the whole pack of cards . . . sorry about the jumbled metaphor . . . When they traded her she came back from the Lubianka a vegetable, but they still weren't taking any chances.'

Rotherby started to say, 'But you three . . . '

'Yes,' Hillsden finished for him. 'I know what you're going to say. We were the Austrian Holy Trinity until it broke up. I came back, Caroline went to Berlin, Jock was taken and like you, I grieved for him when the report of his death filtered through. But he fooled us all, and nobody more than me . . . and he was the one who betrayed Caroline in the first place.'

Rotherby was silent for an appreciable time, unable to grasp what he had just been told. 'Then you met again, obviously.'

Hillsden nodded as various ghosts flitted in and out of his memory. 'I had a GRU handler in Moscow, somebody who curiously became a friend, remains a friend as it happens. When finally they were sure of me, he thought I needed company, so he brought Jock to Moscow and put him in my apartment block. As far as Jock was concerned, he and I now were two of a kind, we'd both been turned. He was an alcoholic by then, he'd gone the way of Burgess, and with good reason, given what he'd done. And one night when he was sloshed, the whole story came out. He admitted he betrayed Caroline to save his own skin. The way he told it, he had no choice, but we always have a choice, don't we? He thought I'd forgive him, but I couldn't even forgive myself.'

'How d'you mean?'

'When they traded Caroline, when she came back and the Firm put her in that home to rot, I also betrayed her.'

'In what way?'

'I never went to see her. I was too bloody scared of what it would do to me. Oh, I pretended to myself I was the reformed adulterer, acting nobly for Margot's sake, but the truth was I couldn't face seeing what they'd done to her. Wouldn't you call that a betrayal?' Despite the passage of time, his voice cracked slightly and he reached for a cigarette which Rotherby lit for him. 'I loved her, you see.'

'Then you disappeared.'

'Yes. After that, all I had was hatred. I became so consumed with hatred I made a stupid mistake, I gave Lockfield the opening he was looking for. That devious old queen, Glanville, remember? They granted him immunity in return for his silence. He was supposed to be off limits, a burnt-out case with nothing else to offer, but I didn't give a fuck about that, I was sure I could squeeze some more out of him, and I was right. He revealed a lot more. Shortly afterwards he was found dead and suspicion fell on me since I was the last person to see him alive. Lockfield must have thought I was getting too close, and now he had the excuse he had been waiting for to silence me once and for all. He played the

Caroline card, knowing I couldn't resist it, and sent me back into the cold. Afterwards, he bolted the door by pinning a murder on me. It was neat, very neat, I'll give him that.'

'Does it ever leave you? The thought that you've killed somebody?'

'No. It's there, nudging you like an exposed nerve in a tooth. You go for a while without feeling anything, and then suddenly you bite down on it and it jolts you.'

'God, Alec, old son, rather you than me . . . And what now?'

'I have to go through with it, I can't back out now, but keep your ears to the ground for me.'

'Of course. But if you've been set up, what have you been set up for?'

'That's what I haven't been able to figure out. Somebody, somewhere is playing with me.'

33

THE CLOCK STARTS TICKING

Immediately following the first intimation of Sonntag's impending arrival, a plan of action had been agreed by the combined security forces. After obtaining Cabinet approval, Logan issued a carefully worded letter, written on Ministry of National Heritage notepaper, requiring every police authority to supply details of any venue that had been booked for large public meetings over the next two months. The phoney reason given was that the Minister wished to ascertain the depth of public opinion on conservation in preparation for issuing a White Paper.

A list of some thirty-seven such meetings, widely scattered across England, and one in Scotland, had come back. All had been investigated. In the majority of cases the meetings had been organised by either charities or local councils and were established as being genuine. Three remained questionable, including the one in Glasgow, and were further scrutinised, especially the Scottish venue in view of the Hess factor. Of the two in England, both were in the Home Counties, within reasonable distance of the centre of London; one was in Amersham, and the other in Luton. In the case of Amersham, a British Legion hall had been booked by an organisation calling itself C.A.D.R.E. (Campaign Against the Destruction of Rural England), with a registered office in Harringay. The one in Luton had been booked by a similar protest group, this time under the banner Nature Comes First. Although the

Scottish venue had been booked by the SNP, it was still considered suspicious by elements of MI5, though the consensus amongst Special Branch favoured one of the two local locations nearer to London.

The offices of C.A.D.R.E. and Nature Comes First, the latter proving to be above a fish and chip shop, were covertly inspected. Both appeared to be staffed by earnest middle-aged citizens who in earlier times would have been found in the ranks of those who made the yearly pilgrimage from Aldermaston. On the surface, both organisations seemed to be outlets for legitimate protest, with no apparent connections to either the far Right or far Left.

'They both seem too good to be true,' Pearson observed.

The actual venues were carefully reconnoitred by Special Branch men, who went in under the guise of Health Inspectors. The large bingo hall in Luton which had at least six exit points was considered to be the most difficult to police, whereas the Amersham meeting in the British Legion hall was thought to be an easier prospect. The dates for all three meetings were contained within a time frame of ten days. Police leave in all three locations was cancelled during that period and extra supplies of riot gear were issued. Detachments of the Special Patrol Group were also alerted and detailed instructions issued to their senior officers. The most recent photographs of Sonntag were obtained from the German authorities and circulated to all concerned. RAF radar stations on the East coast were given phoney orders about a non-existent Nato exercise and told to be extra vigilant about tracking any unidentified aircraft. All that could be anticipated was thought to have been covered.

. . .

Much calmer now and, if the truth were told, mollified by the presence of a young Special Branch detective as a house guest, the man who passed himself off as Mrs Carstairs studied the collection of mug shots that Lloyd put in front of him.

'No ... No, nothing like ... No ...' He paused and lingered over the next. 'That's getting warmer, except the hair was different ... No ...' This time he placed a hand over the eyes and nose. 'That's his mouth, he had a thin, cruel mouth, no lips to speak of.' One by one he rejected the selection. 'Sorry, don't recognise any of them.'

'Never mind,' Lloyd said. 'Have a look at this batch. They're not as clear as the others, but use this magnifying glass.'

He produced a batch of photographs taken with a telephoto lens, the work of the surveillance team keeping watch on the snooker hall. A good number of them had been taken in poor light.

'Take your time, no hurry. Study each one.'

Standing close beside him, Lloyd was conscious of a cloying perfume; not for the first time, he found himself speculating about the initial decision that led to such a life. Was it something, half-comprehended in childhood, that crept up on you? What single act forced the final realisation, and what kind of resolve was needed to make that first purchase of feminine clothes, the step that took you into make-believe land?

These thoughts were disturbed as 'Mrs Carstairs' suddenly gave a tiny, involuntary gasp, clapping a hand to his mouth. 'Him!' he said. 'That's him.'

'Which one? Show me.'

'Mrs Carstairs' pointed with a manicured finger, tipped with bright nail varnish. Lloyd took the magnifying glass. He saw that the man picked out was the one they knew as Harry.

. . .

Pearson was in gloomy mode. Lloyd found him hunched over a pile of annual reports obtained from Companies House, all concerned with companies either owned or controlled by

Charters.

'Well, our first break,' Lloyd said.

'What?'

'"Mrs Carstairs" identified Harry as the one who came to the house and duffed him up.'

'We've got to stop calling him Mrs Carstairs. He isn't Mrs Carstairs. He's a woofter in drag.'

'Okay, okay, don't get excited. Shall we get the Met to pull Harry in?'

'No, bad idea. Think what that does. It tips them off and puts Hillsden and the whole operation at risk. We can have him when the time's right for us. Meanwhile, Swanson's decided that Hillsden should move out of Suffolk and into the safe house at Forest Gate for the time being.'

'The whole family?'

'No, just use your loaf for once. Are we likely to move the whole family? For one thing, Hillsden's cover story is that his wife's dead. Swanson feels that since Harry paid a visit to Docklands there's always a chance that one of them might check out Forest Gate.'

'How did Hillsden take it?'

'He hasn't been told yet.'

'He won't like it.'

'Probably not. But it's safer than them tracking him to Suffolk.'

'What's that you're reading?' Lloyd said, anxious to get off the subject.

'Annual reports of Charters's various companies.'

'Thinking of buying shares, are you?'

Pearson looked at him with disdain. 'I sometimes wonder how you and I have survived as a team this long. For your information, I'm to establish whether any of his various enterprises trade out of Luxembourg. Carstairs's bank account, remember?'

'Oh, I see, yes. You're still flogging that dead horse, are you?'

'Do yourself a favour. Don't antagonise me.'

. . .

Ghosts reappeared in the Forest Gate house. Whether it was the confession he had made to Rotherby, or the fact that he was on his own, denied even the comfort of a telephone call to Galina except from an outside call box, more and more Hillsden found himself pulled back into the past. He frequently woke from a nightmare, unable to place himself in the strange bed, the unfamiliar room, on one occasion thinking he could hear the canary that Jock had given him as a pet, the dream so real that he reached for the bedside light switch to reassure himself that he wasn't still in that Moscow apartment where the cage had stood by the window. Another night, he awoke convinced that he had heard somebody trying the handle of the back door. He felt for the service handgun he now kept under his pillow and checked the magazine, wondering, as he slipped the safety catch, whether he would ever be able to fire it in self-defence. There was an unreality about his life; for the second time he had been divorced from everything that mattered to him. He missed Galina and Lara and feared for them, silently berating himself for his stupidity. How had Swanson described him? *You're the man who never was. We've arranged for you to die.* I feel dead, he thought, if only I could believe in something other than the past.

For the rest it was a waiting game until finally, late in the evening of the tenth day the phone rang and Tony's voice said: 'Robert?'

'Yes.'

'The party's on. Thursday, the twenty-second, five o'clock sharp, leaving from the usual place.'

'To where?'

'Don't ask. You'll find out on the day.'

The line went dead.

Thursday 22nd was in eight days' time.

34

THE ARRIVAL

Eight days later, the man who arrived at Plymouth airport on the flight from Jersey, mingled amongst returning holidaymakers and attracted no attention. Tanned, his normal flaxen hair dyed a much darker shade and wearing thin-rimmed Granny spectacles, he bore scant resemblance to the photographs that had been circulated by Interpol. The only luggage he carried was a small overnight case and a Duty Free plastic bag. Presenting a valid British passport, which gave his name as Arthur Clarke, he passed through Immigration, then took the green customs exit without being challenged. Outside, he queued for a bus into the city centre. Once there, he went into a large department store, entering by one door and leaving fifteen minutes later by another, accompanied now by a woman roughly his own age – one of those anonymous, working-class, British women who, pretty in their teens, had lost their early bloom: with her frizzed hair and coat of unfashionable length, she could have passed for any harassed housewife out for a shopping trip with her husband. The only item about her which caught the eye was a silk rose pinned to the lapel of her coat, by which the man had identified her at their pre-arranged rendezvous point. Threading their way along the crowded pavements they walked, arm in arm, to a multi-storey car park, avoiding the lifts and climbing two flights. There the woman led the way to a nondescript Volvo. It was only when they were both inside the car that any words were exchanged.

'No problems?' the woman asked.

'No, everything as planned,' Sonntag said. 'So far,' he added.

The woman turned the ignition key, backed out of the narrow bay, and drove out of the car park. Sonntag lit a cigarette, then, just before putting the packet away, he made a hissing sound. 'How stupid can I get?' Extinguishing the cigarette and crumpling the packet, he wound down his window and threw them both into the street.

'What's up?' the woman asked.

'I brought a packet of German cigarettes with me.'

'Well throwing them out was stupid, too,' the woman said, pleased she could score a point. 'You can get done for littering our streets.'

'Never mind that. Take a good look, is there anything about me that seems odd to you? I look British, yes?'

'Yeah, of a sort.'

'What d'you mean, "of a sort"?'

'Well, I know you're not British, but probably others wouldn't give you a second glance. Have a look around – don't go by the colour of their skin – everybody's British now.'

The reply seemed to please him. He fished inside the Duty Free bag and took out some Dunhills. 'For the rest of my visit I must get used to these.'

'Or you could give up,' the woman said, winding down her window.

'Don't you smoke?'

'I quit two years ago.'

Sonntag shrugged. 'It's a mistake not to retain at least one vice.' He lit the Dunhill. 'Why give up? We all have to die sooner or later. Anything you have to tell me?'

'No. Everything's in place.'

'There have been no changes?'

'No.'

'That's good. How long will it take us to get there?'

'About two hours, the way I drive.'

'You will drive carefully, if you know what's good for you.'

The woman shrugged, changing gear and accelerating. 'I meant I shall be avoiding the motorways and taking the back roads.'

Travelling through the centre of Plymouth, they passed the shell of a church.

'They left it standing like that after the bombing raids,' the woman said.

'It's good we're still remembered.'

'Oh, you're remembered here all right. How did you manage to give your lot the slip?'

Sonntag grinned, lighting a second cigarette from the first and ignoring her grimace. 'Simple. I'm a window cleaner, remember? We have a contract to do a large office block at night. I went in with my team, but left before they finished. *Schmutz* the world over have their minds fixed in a groove.' He used the Nazi slang for 'dirt' to describe the police. 'They assumed because we entered by the service entrance we would leave the same way. I didn't.'

'And from there?'

'Why're you asking so many questions?'

'Just curious. Suit yourself. Don't tell me if you don't want to.'

'I prefer not,' he said stiffly, and for the first time she caught a hint of his true accent. 'It was the same with this trip – I was convinced they'd be looking in one direction, so I came from another. I was right, of course.'

He gave off an air of self-satisfaction, as real to her as the cigarette smoke that now made her nauseous. She was not drawn to him, having expected somebody immediately charismatic; instead he was like any other man who had entered her life. They all thought a lot of themselves, and this one, flabby and overweight, left her cold.

'I knew if we planted the Hess rumour they'd fall for it. Your authorities have always had a thing about Hess. You know why? Because too many of your countrymen would have liked him to have succeeded. Did you know that?'

'I wasn't even born during the war,' she said.

295

'Don't you know the history of our movement?'

'Some of it.'

'So, what makes you one of us now?'

'I hate the fucking Jews,' she said in a matter of fact way, her eyes on the road, 'they put my father out of business.' She eased her foot off the accelerator as she spotted a police car waiting in a side turning. 'Turn your head towards me.'

'What?'

'Do as I say. We're just passing a police car.'

Sonntag did as she told him. 'Do the *Schmutz* worry you?' he asked, again using the slang term.

'Why take chances? Is that your word for them?'

'Yes. Filth. What d'you call them?'

'Pigs.'

'Your pigs aren't even armed, are they? Pathetic.'

'That's changing,' she said. 'Are you worried they might arrest you tonight?' she asked, her eyes going to the rear-view mirror.

'No. I might even welcome it, for all you know. We all have to pay our dues. Going to jail for the cause is an honour. We must be willing to pay the price if necessary. Are you prepared for that?'

'I'm here, aren't I?' the woman replied with sudden vehemence. 'Driving you. Okay, you can relax now.' Her foot went on the pedal again and she pushed their speed to forty.

'Can't we go any faster?'

'Not yet. Not until we're on the dual carriageway. They've got speed cameras on this section.'

Sonntag pushed his seat back and stretched himself. 'Hess is my role model. He never renounced the leader. Not like that apologist Speer.' He looked at the countryside they were passing through. 'Such a small country, England. You ever been to Germany?'

'No.'

'You should. Visit our shrines, like the Luitpold Hall.'

'What's that?'

'You don't know?' he snapped with scornful emphasis.

'You don't know Nuremberg?'

'Of course I've heard of it. It's where they held the trials.'

His tone had made her lose concentration and she passed a turn-off and had to reverse back.

'What sort of person have they sent to meet me?' Sonntag said, as though addressing a third party. 'Listen, woman, it was famous before the trials. It was the place where the Führer held his great rallies. Try as they might, they couldn't destroy all of it, it was built for a thousand years. And one day we'll rebuild it exactly as it was.'

Sonntag lapsed into silence for the next few miles, only stirring himself as they passed through a belt of farmland. He suddenly pointed. 'What is that called?'

'What is what called?' the woman asked.

'That yellow.'

'Rape.'

For a reason she could not comprehend, this amused Sonntag and he repeated the word 'rape' several times, then said, 'A field of rape. That sounds very funny. Your language is absurd sometimes. Don't you think it's funny?'

'Not particularly. It's what it is. What else should they call it?'

He half-stubbed out his cigarette in the ashtray where it remained smouldering. The woman pulled a face and deliberately coughed, but Sonntag made no effort to put it out completely.

Sonntag's mood switched abruptly. 'Yes, you must come to Germany one day. Complete your education. Things are going astonishingly well for us. We are on our way, leading as always. It will take time, of course, but history is on our side, and we are not going to strew ashes over our heads for ever. We are not prepared to be humiliated any further.'

A police Range Rover going in the opposite direction passed them and the woman watched it carefully in her rear-view mirror. Sonntag followed her look. Then he said: 'Tonight we start to make history. The important thing is to leave a scar on the world.'

Once Hillsden had relayed the date, a crucial meeting had been convened, chaired by Logan. Those present were faced with a critical decision: none of the three previously suspect venues were scheduled for the twenty-second, and were thus ruled out. A further urgent search had revealed a derisory list: the few large events due to take place on the twenty-second were a meeting called to oppose blood sports in Cheltenham, an anti-abortion rally in Newcastle, a farewell concert by The Stones at Wembley and an appearance by the American evangelist, Paul Sheenham, at Earls Court. Only the latter provoked any serious discussion.

'We can't ignore the fact that Sheenham was one of the names on the CIA hit list that Schmidt gave us,' Pearson said.

'Yes, but you can't have two star performers, can you?' Swanson pointed out. 'It's absurd to think they would inject Sonntag into a mass of born-again Christians. Just doesn't add up.'

'I have to agree,' the Police Commissioner said. 'And if they were intending to assassinate Sheenham they'd hardly want Sonntag around.'

'So what do we have?' Logan interjected. 'If the information given by this man . . . remind me of his name . . .'

'His undercover name is Bartlett, Minister.'

'Well, if the date Bartlett has supplied is genuine and if their object is to obtain maximum publicity when they produce Sonntag, then it follows that at some point they have to reveal the venue. Where haven't you looked?'

The others allowed the buck to be passed to the Commissioner. 'Taking the point you've just made, Minister – namely, that we must assume they are hoping to gain publicity – we've acted on the premise they would choose a public venue. That would seem the logical course, but as you know we have uncovered no evidence that fits that scenario.'

'Are we still maintaining a strict watch on all airports and ports?'

'All immigration controls have been tightened, Minister. And that includes the Channel Tunnel, of course.'

'And?'

'Over forty suspects have been detained and questioned without success, including one individual piloting a private plane who made a landing in a field just outside Edinburgh. For a few hours we thought we had our man, but it was subsequently established that it was a genuine forced landing due to engine failure.'

'Well, this is a ludicrous situation,' Logan said. 'Here we have the entire police force, strongly supported by the security service, outguessed and out-manœuvred by a ragbag gang of Fascists. I gave my permission for this undercover operation to go ahead with considerable misgivings. It seemed to me at the time that it was unlikely to produce the desired results, but I was persuaded against my better judgement. I should warn you all that if it ends in humiliation, the government will not hesitate to ask for resignations.'

Again the Commissioner was the only one who found his voice. 'With all due respect, Minister, it's never an easy task to detect a crime that has not yet been committed. We still have forty-eight hours. Everybody concerned is aware of the urgency and renewed efforts will be made by the combined police forces. All Chief Constables are ready to move their forces into position the moment we get a break.'

'And if we don't get a break?'

'Well, I'm not God, Minister, I'm just a policeman.'

He met Logan's penetrating stare, but he had gone too far and he knew it. Logan rounded on Swanson. 'I don't want any further excuses, I want answers. What d'you propose to do in the forty-eight hours remaining? Can't this Bartlett man whom you have so much faith in provide the vital information?' There was no mistaking the venom in his voice.

'They have been ultra careful, Minister. All he has been able to discover is the actual date and the rendezvous point.'

Logan pounced on this. 'Rendezvous point? What

rendezvous point?'

'The London cell meets in a snooker hall, which we've been keeping under surveillance, and according to Bartlett, certain elements are to assemble there on the night to be transported to the, as yet unknown, venue.'

The impact of what he had just said took a second or two to sink in. The Commissioner turned on him. 'That's news to me. Why wasn't that brought to my attention sooner?'

Swanson looked flustered. 'Wasn't that passed on?'

'No.'

'I apologise and I shall certainly make it my business to find out who was at fault.'

'Well, this changes the whole situation,' the Commissioner said. 'They can be followed in unmarked cars in constant radio contact and the moment we know in which direction they are heading a massive police net can be drawn around them, ready to converge on the ultimate destination.' He looked at Logan, prepared to accept some appreciation.

'Yes,' Logan said. 'For the first time I've heard something that makes sense. However, I'm not prepared to tolerate or defend any subsequent charges of police provocation. I want it to succeed, obviously, but it must succeed without comebacks.'

There was further discussion and it was agreed that, unless they were fortunate enough to apprehend Sonntag prior to the meeting, he was to be taken by police snatch squads before he could address the faithful.

That was the plan. It remained to be seen whether it would work.

35

HIDE AND SEEK

A few minutes after five o'clock on the afternoon of the twenty-second, the minibus carrying Hillsden, Hyde, Harry and the other selected crowd marshals drove out of the parking area at the rear of the snooker hall. Acting on Fadiman's instructions, the occupants had modified their usual way of dressing; the majority had dispensed with their Harrington jackets and wore suits; some wore caps.

During the previous night a second police surveillance team had taken up position in a disused warehouse which overlooked the parking area. In addition an armed unit of the Special Patrol Group had been placed on the roof of the warehouse. Unmarked police cars were parked in all the exit routes from the snooker hall, each car linked by radio, communicating by code. The minibus was to be identified by the code-name 'Ambulance', while Sonntag was code-named 'Sharon' – a name suggested by Lloyd who had never recovered from seeing *Basic Instinct*. Some thirty other unmarked cars were positioned at various points in the Greater London area, ready to tail the minibus on a relay system once it had been determined which route it was taking. Each car had one armed officer and all personnel wore civilian clothes. It had also been decided that, as an extra precaution, none of the police cars should continue the tail for more than two miles.

Before the minibus had moved out of the car park, its

description and registration number had been radioed to all units. In order to preserve his cover, none of the ordinary police taking part had been told of Hillsden's role.

The first pursuit car, a battered Volkswagen Golf, moved off, keeping the minibus in sight as it crossed Shepherd's Bush and headed north on Wood Lane, past the BBC Television Centre. At the intersection it made a left turn on to Westway. The first car followed it as far as Hanger Lane where it passed the tail to a second car. A radio message was sent to the Command room in Scotland Yard: *Ambulance heading west on Western Avenue.* Western Avenue being a dual-carriageway with an uninterrupted central crash barrier for long stretches, an immediate decision was taken to bring in cars belonging to the Thames Valley force with instructions to take over at the Northolt intersection. The pursuit continued without incident, the minibus turning left into Denham Road just before the beginning of the M40 motorway. It made a right turn shortly afterwards and headed for Fulmer Common, skirting the north perimeter of the common before going in the direction of Amersham. There another police car took over. It was still impossible to determine the ultimate destination, but the command room alerted the main back-up units, and these started to converge on Westway, following the identical route to the minibus, some twenty miles behind it. Pearson and Lloyd were in one of this group of vehicles.

. . .

Hillsden had to admit that whoever had planned the operation (and he assumed it was Fadiman) had done so with considerable skill. The moment the minibus was under way, Hyde stood up in the front of the bus and briefed them.

'First of all, I have a message from the Deputy Leader, saying he regrets he's not with us tonight, but he felt that discretion was the better part of valour. However, as he told us, the meeting will be videoed and he looks forward to the pleasure of viewing it at a later date.'

Two or three of the men applauded and Hyde held up a hand to silence them.

'Right. Now, listen carefully, and take this in, because I shall only say it once. We have it on good authority that the police, like you at this moment, don't have a clue where we're going. Because of the way this has been planned they've been looking in quite the wrong direction, expecting us to have hired some public hall for our comrade's visit. Well, we didn't. The Deputy Leader is too fly for that. Our journey tonight will take us to a large country house which until recently was operating as a health farm where rich parasites, a fair number of them flabby Jews I have no doubt, paid through the nose to lose their unwanted fat. It was purchased by one of our powerful backers who prefers to remain anonymous for the moment, and in due course it will become our national headquarters.'

He paused and consulted his watch, then turned to the driver. 'How are we for time?'

'Spot on,' the driver said.

'Keep to the speed limits and keep your eyes peeled for any sign of the fuzz.'

'Nothing so far.'

'Good. Don't want any slip-ups at this stage.' Hyde resumed his address to the troops, smug with self-importance in his role as the only one in the know. 'So, that's our destination, but before we get there we have to rendezvous with the rest of the comrades who have come from all over the country to take part.' He looked at his watch again. 'If we keep to schedule we should be meeting up in seventeen minutes time.' He glanced out of a side window as a small car overtook them. 'There will be several coachloads waiting for us. I want four of you in each coach, to act as stewards. You will make sure everybody behaves in orderly fashion. This has been planned as a military operation and it's up to you to see that everything goes off smoothly. Understood?'

He received general assent. A voice from the back asked:

'Did he fly in as promised?'

'Yeah, he flew in,' Hyde said and sat down beside the driver.

. . .

Pearson listened to the voice in his headphones: 'Ambulance now heading for Chalfont St Giles.'

'Any sign of Sharon?' he radioed back.

'Negative.'

'Nothing new,' Pearson reported to Lloyd, who was driving.

'Want to take a guess as to where we end up? My bet is somewhere in the Midlands.'

'Who knows at this stage. They're certainly taking us on a scenic tour. Funny the attraction Fascism has for so many different types. The rich are attracted because they believe it will protect their wealth, the middle-class because it feeds their prejudices and at the lower end of the scale it's a honey pot for the bully boys.'

'Taken up philosophy in your old age, have you?'

'Yes, well, some of us think about the state of the world. I've made a study of fanatics.'

'So have I,' Lloyd said. 'Many of them Chief Constables.'

'Listen. Fanatics aim their appeal towards those who are imperfectly balanced. I always remember something that John Buchan wrote. Buchan defined a fanatic as somebody who has no logical gaps in his creed. He wrote that you can't say there is any one thing abnormal about him, because he is all abnormal. Basically insane, of course, but believes his claims are brilliantly sane. Those are the ones, like Hitler, who pose the greatest threat.'

Lloyd permitted himself a nod of the head, though by now he had lost the thread of Pearson's reasoning.

'It's when he appeals to the sane and the sane respond, that's when you get revolution,' Pearson continued. 'You follow me?'

'Interesting.'

'We're facing something like that now. The time is ripe. People the world over have to have a bogey-man, somebody, something to hate. That may be a jaundiced view of human nature, but history bears it out. We had fifty years of being frightened of Russia, now the pendulum is starting to swing over to the other extreme. Communism has never been able to get more than a toehold over here, but Fascism might well.'

Lloyd just had time to say, 'Cheer me up, won't you?' when another message came through. 'Have lost Ambulance. Repeat: Have lost Ambulance. Last grid reference zero four A-for-apple seven.'

'Shit!' Pearson said. 'How the hell can those silly sods have lost them?' He consulted his map. 'Zero four A seven, that's somewhere between Chalfont and Chorleywood. Mostly woods, open countryside, a few farms.'

'Can't be holding the bloody meeting in a farm, can they?' Lloyd said.

'No, but the Ambulance could have led us on a fake run away from the main event. Oh, bollocks! Hold it here for a moment.'

He got out of the car and walked to the lead police van in the convoy to confer.

.   .   .

From his window seat in the Happy Eater, Tony had a clear view of the road and parking lot. He was wearing standard motorcycle gear: black leather bomber jacket and trousers. His gloves and two crash helmets with smoked-glass visors were on the chair beside him.

'Can I clear away?' the young waitress asked.

Tony spun round. 'What?'

'You finished?'

'Oh, yeah.'

'That your BMW out there?'

'Yeah.'

'Bet that moves. Don't want to give me a ride, do you? I finish in twenty minutes.'

'Another time, darling.'

The girl gave him a look as she removed the dirty plate and coffee cup. 'I see you've got a spare helmet.'

'Yeah, I'm waiting for a friend.'

At that moment the car he had been waiting for pulled into the parking lot. The woman driver flashed her headlights once. Tony got up, left a fifty pence tip on the table, paid his bill, and sauntered out. Ignoring the car, he went to his BMW motorbike, started it, and went alongside the car on the passenger side. Sonntag got out, took the spare helmet Tony offered him, donned it, and sat astride the pillion seat. No words were spoken during the change-over. Tony opened the throttle and they roared out.

The woman watched them go without expression, then took a mobile phone from the glove compartment and dialled a number she had only used once before.

. . .

The farm outbuildings, surrounded by a brick wall, were hidden from the road, and the driver of the minibus, having determined that there was nothing following him, had done an abrupt turn into the pot-holed drive and parked out of sight. As Hyde had promised, there were a number of coaches full of comrades parked behind the walls that shielded the farm from the road.

As per Hyde's instructions, Hillsden and the others divided up and immediately boarded the coaches. It was only now that Hyde revealed the final destination to the coach drivers. He travelled in the lead coach as the convoy moved out, leaving the minibus behind.

Meanwhile, Pearson and the police units were still stationary, frustrated and unable to decide on their next best move. There was still no report of any further trace of the minibus. The use of a helicopter was ruled out by the command room on the grounds that it would almost certainly be a tip-off. The existence of the convoy of coaches had been noted, and aroused no undue suspicion at first, until an alert officer in one of the unmarked cars searching for the elusive minibus spotted that all of them came from different parts of the country and reported this to the command room.

When this was radioed back, Pearson was quick to grasp the possible significance. He took a decision: 'Radio all cars to tail them and give us a map reference.' He then went over to the Chief Superintendent to share the information. 'It's a long shot, but all we've got at the moment, so leave a token force here and have the rest follow us.'

. . .

The ex-health farm had operated from a building best described as thirties nondescript, almost certainly one of those oversized country houses, with little or no architectural merit, built between the wars to satisfy the pretensions of the *nouveaux riches*. Whoever had converted it into a health farm had grafted on various additions – an indoor swimming pool, a large conservatory and, incongruously, a clock tower – the final effect guaranteed to make Betjeman turn in his grave.

Hillsden got his first view of its irregular outline as the convoy of coaches drew up in front of the closed main gates. Hyde got out and spoke into the entry-phone and shortly afterwards the gates were automatically opened and the convoy drove through.

Inside, the house had been denuded of most of its fixtures but still retained a faint, antiseptic atmosphere reminiscent of an abandoned hospital. Sonntag's audience trooped in and was directed by Hyde to what at one time had been the ballroom, and later the health farm restaurant, where the dedicated had sipped such elixirs as bottled water with a slice of lemon and nibbled the odd organic carrot. A stage had been erected at the far end with a lectern and a public address system, with Nazi flags draped on either side. Martial music was playing as the audience entered and took their seats.

Hyde mounted the platform and tested the microphone. 'I think congratulations are in order. By arriving here without mishap we have achieved a major victory over those whom we know would like to spike our guns. So be patient for a little while longer. Our distinguished guest from the fatherland will arrive shortly and I know you will join me in giving him an enthusiastic welcome.' He raised his right arm in the Nazi salute by way of illustration. 'Listen carefully to the message he brings, because it is a message we, the torch-bearers, must pass on. Tonight is a watershed in our journey towards Valhalla and in coming here we recognise the role played by another generation, those who were so shamefully betrayed. We have gathered to demonstrate to our guest that the Führer's historic struggle to establish a world order was not in vain.' He was just about to leave the stage when he returned to the microphone for an afterthought. 'At the conclusion of the meeting refreshments will be served.' This announcement was greeted with cheers.

Hillsden, seated in the body of the hall, surveyed the audience as a murmur of anticipation went through the ranks. He was conscious that the majority were considerably younger than himself. A proportion, perhaps a third, were stereotypical Fascists – chunky, with cropped hair, clean shaven, many sporting a ring in one ear; they had the cocky self-assurance of those who only find an arrogant courage when part of a gang. The rest seemed to him to have been recruited from the ranks of ordinary men willing to follow any cause that promised some excitement hitherto missing from their drab lives.

The coaches had been tailed to their destination and the information radioed back to the main police force; all units were now converging on the spot. Now, as Pearson and Lloyd, in the lead car, rounded a corner a mile or so from the final location, Lloyd was forced to brake sharply, only just stopping short of a motorbike which lay on its side in a pool of petrol and oil. There was a crash helmet a short distance away but, curiously, no skid marks on the tarmac.

Pearson reached for the hazard lights switch. Shouting, 'Go and stop the others and get them to whistle up an ambulance,' he ran to the fallen bike and found the engine was still hot. He stared around for any sign of the rider. He did not have far to look, but instead of one there were two men sprawled in the roadside ditch. Pearson's brief examination established that both were dead. Again, curiously, there were no obvious signs of injury. One man, dressed in civilian clothes, had fallen face upwards; bent stalks of foxgloves and Bishop's weed criss-crossed his chest and one of the blooms, stained with a trickle of blood rested in his gaped mouth. The second man, dressed in standard leather gear and still wearing his crash helmet, was head down in the ditch. One arm was thrust out, the hand clutching a tuft of coarse grass with stiffened fingers.

Having halted the rest of the convoy, Lloyd came back accompanied by half a dozen police officers.

'What have we got?' the Chief Superintendent asked.

'Two dead,' Pearson answered. He gestured to the ditch.

'Did they hit something?'

'No sign of anything. As you can see there are no skid marks, no obstruction, nothing. It's as if one moment they were going along normally, and then bingo. The only thing I can think of is that the brakes must have seized up, although that's rare, specially with a new job like that.'

The Superintendent told his men to remove the bike from the road and see if it started. The engine fired immediately.

'Take a closer look at the bodies,' Pearson said, 'because at first glance I couldn't see any injuries. If it wasn't so far-fetched and daft you could almost believe they both died of simultaneous heart attacks.'

'You didn't see any other vehicles?'

'No. We came round the corner and there it was. Only just missed it ourselves.'

'Right, well we can't afford to hang around here. Leave this mess for Traffic to sort out.' The Superintendent detailed two of his men to remain until the ambulance arrived.

. . .

The recorded martial music was repeated a third time. Although the audience was not openly impatient with the delay, a certain degree of restlessness had begun to manifest itself.

'Keeping us waiting long enough,' the man next to Hillsden said.

'Building up the suspense. It's an old trick,' Hillsden replied.

'Yeah, expect you're right. They always did that, didn't they? I've seen news reels of those torchlight parades.'

Hyde came from the back of the room and mounted the stage again.

'I know you're all wondering what is happening, but I can assure you that our guest is in the country and will be with us shortly. This has been a very difficult operation to mount and we couldn't afford to leave anything to chance or take any risks with the safety of our German comrade. So I do ask you to be patient, for I am sure the wait will be . . .' but he never finished, for at that moment the French windows on one side of the hall were smashed open and snatch squads from the Special Patrol Group broke in. At the same time, other squads raced in from the rear of the hall, encircling the audience and cutting off all escape routes in a text-book manœuvre that achieved complete surprise. Using a loud hailer, the Chief Superintendent issued a warning: 'Everybody will remain seated and be required to establish their identities. This is an illegal assembly and I am empowered to arrest and detain anybody who does not co-operate.'

But there was to be no co-operation. A chair was hurled at the Superintendent and this was taken as a signal for whole sections of the audience to attempt to break through the police cordon. Within minutes, the hall was the scene of a dozen or more fights with chairs being broken and used as rough and ready weapons. The initial police squads were swiftly reinforced as a hard core of the younger skinheads tried to fight their way to the stage and claim the Nazi flags. Many on both sides went down and it was some twenty minutes before any semblance of order was restored. Hillsden was struck by a flying chair early in the proceedings. Stunned and bleeding from a cut on the back of his skull, he recovered sufficiently to crawl to safety under the platform. Some time later he was dragged out by the police and put with the rest of the casualties.

Then began the long process of sorting out the mess. A few of the faithful gave their real names, but the majority, taking their lead from Hyde, gave Mickey Mouse-type pseudonyms. All were videoed by a police cameraman. Hyde was given special attention. Handcuffed, he was taken to a separate room to be interrogated by Pearson.

Pearson started on him with: 'I should formally tell you that you and others are going to be charged with having conspired to bring an illegal alien into the United Kingdom, namely one Gottfried Sonntag, a German national. It would be to your advantage if you identified him to me.'

'Get stuffed. I don't know any Gottfried Sonntag,' Hyde replied. 'This was a lawful, private meeting to debate conservation issues. I'm going to lay charges against you for unprovoked police brutality.'

Pearson stared through him. 'What were you trying to conserve, the Nazi flag ? Listen, chummy, you're out of your league, and don't make the mistake of thinking you're dealing with the local CID and can get some tricky lawyer to get you off the hook. I've got ways and means of keeping you out of circulation for a very long time. So let's try again, shall we? Herr Sonntag is a prominent neo-Nazi your mob brought over. We know that for a fact. He was going to speak here tonight, wasn't he? Tell you bedtime stories about the great Third Reich and how the Holocaust was invented Jewish propaganda. So, if you know what's good for you, you'll point him out to me. That'll go in your favour.'

'I don't need any favours. And I don't know who Sonntag is.'

'What I'm talking about, if you don't help me, chummy, is a very long stretch of porridge. You see, added to the conspiracy charge we can tack on assault on a police officer.'

'I never touched any of the pigs.'

'Wrong. I saw you myself.'

'Lying bastard.'

'But who will they believe, you or me? I rather fancy my chances. So I'll ask you for the last time, where is Sonntag?'

'Go fuck yourself.'

'No, you're the one who's fucked, chummy. We won the last war, remember?' He turned to the police escort. 'Take him out and put him with the others.'

'I'll have you one day,' Hyde said as he was led away. 'Depend on it.'

'Don't frighten me,' Pearson said. 'I'm near retirement.' He went outside just as Hillsden, handcuffed to another man, was about to board one of the charabancs, now impounded by the police. He came face to face with Hillsden, but neither of them betrayed any sign of recognition. Hillsden spat down on Pearson's feet as he passed and was cuffed by the escorting police officer.

Tipped off by a local resident intrigued by the unusual amount of police activity in what was normally a quiet backwater, the local paper rushed somebody to the scene.

'Better give him some bland story,' Pearson urged the Chief Superintendent. 'Nip it in the bud, before he starts smelling around.' The Superintendent went outside to the young reporter.

'Understand you've had some trouble here, sir?'

'Well, yes, very minor. A public meeting was disrupted by a hooligan element, but we quickly restored order.'

'A political meeting was it?'

'I don't think so. I'm told it had something to do with conservation issues.'

'Like Greenpeace?'

The Superintendent looked beyond the young reporter, affecting casualness. 'Something like that. Animal rights, I believe.'

'Yeah, that's a subject that gets people stirred up. Did you make any arrests?'

'We shall be charging some people, yes.'

'Just that it seems a very large police presence for somewhere like this. Would you say the police over-reacted?'

'No. I'm sure you agree it's much better to be safe than sorry.'

'Anybody hurt?'

'There were some minor casualties, yes.'

'How many?'

'A dozen perhaps.'

'Amongst the police?'

'Three of my officers were hit by missiles. None seriously, I'm happy to say.'

'Can I know who I'm speaking to, sir?'

'Chief Superintendent Walsham.'

'And you're the officer in charge?'

'Yes.'

'Well, thank you, you've been very helpful, sir. Just one last thing, I was told that members of the Special Patrol Group took part, the heavy mob, as it were. That's unusual, isn't it?'

'It would be if it was true. I don't know where you got that rumour. Now, if you'll excuse me . . .'

He rejoined Pearson.

'How was it?'

'Usual tricky little customer,' the Superintendent said. 'I

wouldn't be surprised if he's ringing one of the nationals right now, out to make his name. I don't think I fooled him.'

'The press are all the same. You win some and you lose some. And we lost Sonntag.'

'Definitely no trace?'

Pearson shook his head. 'No, the building's been searched from top to bottom. Might be as well to leave some men here overnight, just in case he makes a late appearance.'

'Yes, I've already taken care of that.'

'In due course I shall find out whether he ever showed from our man. But there's nothing I can do at the moment because he was taken off with the rest of them.'

'I can have him isolated.'

'No, don't do that. His cover has to be preserved at all costs. Anyway, thanks, I thought your chaps did a good job, too bad we didn't get what we came for.'

Pearson went to his car where Lloyd was waiting.

'What a pisser,' Lloyd said. 'What will you tell Swanson? He's going to go spare.'

'So, he'll have to go spare. We did what was required of us, not our fault that the target didn't show.'

'D'you think Sonntag's actually in the country?'

'Your guess. They obviously expected him to be, otherwise why bring people here? Anyway, let's go.'

Lloyd started the engine. 'Poor old Hillsden copped one. Did you see him?'

'Yes.'

'Don't envy him his lot.'

'I don't envy any of us,' Pearson said.

. . .

'Name?' a weary Sergeant asked as he booked yet another one.

'Bartlett,' Hillsden said.

'First name?'

'Robert.'

314

'Address?'

'No fixed address.'

'Employed?'

'No.'

The particulars were quickly noted. He was read his rights and told that he would be charged with taking part in an affray and would be brought before the magistrate the following morning. Then he was led to the cells.

'Can I make a phone call?' Hillsden asked.

'No,' the escorting police officer said.

'Why not?'

'Because the phones are out of order.'

'I'm entitled.'

'If I were you, Dad, I'd keep my mouth shut and thank your lucky stars you got off lightly with just a bash to the head. You should know better at your age than to get mixed up with that slag.'

'I was only there as a spectator.'

'Yeah? Well, next time stick to bingo.'

The cell door closed and Hillsden found he was sharing it with Hyde.

'You okay, Robert?'

'I caught a couple on the head.'

'Bastards.'

'What went wrong, d'you think?'

'I wish I knew. What I can't understand is why Tony didn't get any word to us. Our friend was picked up at Plymouth all right, that I do know. Listen, as soon as you get out, get word to Fadiman as to what happened. Go see him, don't phone. Here's his address. Memorise it, then destroy it, okay?'

'Right. What d'you think they'll do to us? Will it mean prison?'

'You? No. You'll get a fine and be bound over. They may have something else in mind for me.'

'Why d'you say that?'

'Because I know these things. They've already given me a going-over, not the police, some other mob, either Special Branch or the spooks.'

'Spooks?'

'I forget, you're a bloody innocent, aren't you? Spooks are the MI5 boys. So just plead guilty tomorrow and play dumb. You know nothing, whatever they ask you.'

'Right, understood. Just as well he never showed. At least they didn't get him. That's something.'

'Yes,' Hyde said. 'But the question is, where is he?'

. . .

Lloyd took the same route back and as they reached the stretch of road where they had discovered the two dead bodies Pearson suddenly ordered him to stop.

'What's up?'

'That accident. Something's been preying on my mind ever since. The whole thing was bloody odd.' He reached for the radio phone on an impulse. 'Get me the Amersham police, will you?'

'What're you ringing them for?'

Pearson waved a hand for him to be quiet as he spoke into the phone. 'Give me the Duty Officer, please . . . Commander Pearson, Scotland Yard . . . Who am I talking to? Inspector Grant? I wonder if you can help me, Inspector? We were in your manor tonight on a special job and happened to come across a road accident. Two men on a motorbike. Did you lot deal with that? . . . I see. Where are the bodies now? Have they been identified? . . . Only one. Give me that name again. Arthur Clarke. I see . . . Look, there could be some connection with another case I'm working on, so I'd appreciate it if you could let me come and take a look. Not trying to poach on your territory, but I need to check out something . . . Thanks a lot. Hope I can return the favour one day.'

He replaced the phone. 'Turn round. We're going to Amersham.'

'What for?'

'To take another look at a corpse.'

36

A GAME OF DARTS

The following morning, together with fifteen others, Hillsden was fined twenty-five pounds and bound over for one year after pleading guilty to taking part in an affray. The police objected to bail in Hyde's case and he was remanded in custody for seven days.

Hillsden's first action after leaving the court was to ring Galina and to his relief Audrey answered.

'Thank God you've phoned. Your wife's been frantic with worry. I made up some excuse, said you were probably tied up in some business meeting. What happened?'

'I was involved in a minor road accident,' Hillsden said. 'Suffered some concussion and they kept me in hospital overnight.'

'Are you all right now?'

'Yes. Bit of a headache. Put her on, will you?'

Waiting in the public box, Hillsden heard Audrey shout for Galina and a few moments later he heard his wife's reproachful voice. 'Where were you last night?'

'Darling, I'm truly sorry I caused you so much worry,' Hillsden said as he began his rehearsed lie, 'but there was no way I could phone. I had to make a trip out of town and somebody else was driving, took a corner too fast and we hit another car. Nobody was seriously hurt, but I got a knock on the head and had to spend the night in hospital.'

'I thought you were dead,' Galina said.

'Why would you think that?'

'What else could I think?' A note of anger was mingled with her relief. 'You could have been dead.'

'Well, darling, I'm not, so stop worrying. Was Laura upset too?'

'No, I lied to her, made up some story that Papa had been working late and that you were still asleep when she went to school this morning.'

'That was clever.'

'No,' Galina said. 'It was just another of the lies we live with. Are you ever coming home?'

Hillsden thought quickly. 'As soon as I've given a statement to the police about the accident, I'll try and get back. Please don't upset yourself any more, I'm fine, no real damage done. I'll be back as soon as I can.'

He bought a selection of the morning's papers but only one of the tabloids carried anything about the incident and that was on the inside pages, although the headline – *Police use Sledgehammer to Crack Small Nut* – was predictably inflammatory. The accompanying story asked why it had been thought necessary to invade a small rural community in such numbers in order to disperse what their correspondent understood to be *'a peaceful meeting called to protest against the export of live animals to the EEC'*.

Hillsden walked to a nearby McDonald's for some much-needed breakfast, giving himself time to think what his next move should be. Afterwards, he made his way to Docklands. Greeted by an over-solicitous Sarah, he was uncharacteristically brusque with her. 'I'm fine, I'm fine. Get me Pearson and ask him to hold while I ring Swanson.' He did not want sympathy, he wanted solutions.

But both Pearson and Swanson were unavailable.

. . .

Pearson, like Hillsden, had had an eventful night. After viewing 'Arthur Clarke' in the mortuary and comparing his features with the latest photograph of Sonntag supplied by the German authorities, he felt his hunch could prove right. The police surgeon who had carried out preliminary examinations on the two dead men and had signed the death certificates had been unable to determine the exact cause of death and listed an open verdict until such time as the autopsies were performed. 'Arthur Clarke' carried a valid British passport in that name, but the other man had nothing on his person to establish his identity.

'The bike was in perfect working order,' Inspector Grant told him, 'brakes hundred per cent, tank full of petrol, no skid marks on the road, no reports of anything untoward. In fact, the only thing we've come up with is this.' He handed over two small pieces of paper. The Star of David was stamped on both. 'We found one on each of the men, tucked into their clothing.'

Pearson feigned casualness. 'Weird,' he said. 'If I sign for these can I take them away?'

Inspector Grant hesitated. 'Yes, I suppose so. You mentioned you were in the area investigating something, Commander. Can I ask what?'

'Not for the moment,' Pearson said in a tone that precluded further discussion. 'I think, with your further co-operation, I'd like to transfer the bodies to our forensic lab for autopsies.'

'I'd need to get authorisation for that.'

'Yes, of course. If I can use your phone, I'll make sure you're in the clear.'

The Inspector still looked dubious. 'Perhaps whoever you're ringing should talk to the Chief Constable. This is all getting a bit rich for me.'

'No problem,' Pearson said. 'Just one other thing. That place down the road, used to be a health farm I believe, d'you happen to know who owns it now?'

'I think it changed hands twice after the receiver moved in. I can find out for you from the local council in the morning.'

'Would you do that and let me know personally.'

'Where will I get you?'

'Ring me at Century House.'

The name of MI6's headquarters stopped Grant in his tracks. 'Ah! Fine, yes. Will do, Commander.'

. . .

When Hillsden finally made contact with Swanson he was immediately treated to an earful of rancour. 'I've just had the mother of all meetings with Logan, wanting to know why the whole operation was bungled. What the hell went wrong?'

'What went wrong was that the man didn't show.'

'So instead, the police acted as though they were putting out a forest fire. Why did they have to be so heavy-handed? It got into one of the tabloids, which did nothing for Logan's blood pressure.'

'Well, don't shout at me, I was just a spectator. All I got out of it was a crack on the head and a night in the cells. My most urgent problem is to let Fadiman know what happened.'

'That's out of the question. I can't risk that. Much too dangerous at the present time.'

'It'll be more dangerous if I don't. Calm down and let me explain.' He related the conversation he had had with Hyde. 'So, I have to go through with it, otherwise I'm a dead man. Fadiman may tell me what we want to know about Sonntag, there's always a chance of that.'

'When do you intend to do this?'

'Today, soon as possible, assuming he's there.'

He waited for Swanson to answer. After an appreciable pause Swanson said, 'I can't say I'm happy about it.'

'Well, neither am I, but what's the alternative?'

'Have you told Pearson?'

'I couldn't get him this morning. You're the only one I've spoken to.'

'I'll deal with Pearson then. But be sure to report back to me at the first opportunity. It's vital I know every development.'

The autopsy on the man Pearson believed was Sonntag was carried out by Dr Colin Hogg, CBE, for many years the senior Home Office pathologist. A martinet in his own 'kitchen' – as he liked to call it – his many idiosyncrasies, acquired over fifty years laying bare human remains, had been elevated to heroic status amongst the small circle of his closed profession. By rights he should have retired at the statutory age, for he was now seventy, arthritic, cranky and in many ways resembled a cadaver himself. But there was a darting alertness about him whenever he operated. 'I come to life in death,' he would tell any new acquaintance, deliberately seeking to shock, for there was something of the schoolboy about him and he could not resist showing off. He might have given the appearance of age, but his faculties were unimpaired and his eyesight was keen; he boasted that he needed reading glasses only to study the obituaries in *The Times* over his usual breakfast of devilled kidneys and grilled tomatoes. An inveterate and unrepentant smoker, in his usual contentious manner he insisted that he owed the retention of his still formidable mental powers to his addiction to nicotine. It was a theory which did not commend him to the BMA, yet what could not be challenged was his uncanny skill at spotting what others missed and, despite Hogg's age and acerbic opinions, Pearson's department always requested his services whenever they wanted a definitive report.

Hogg made no apologies for scorning the regulation surgical gloves and invariably wore thick orange ones of the kitchen-sink variety, which offered greater protection against HIV infection. 'Imagine what a speculative field day the tabloids would have if the plague claimed me. I'd be bracketed with Burke and Hare in the history books. Hogg, the necrophiliac Aids victim. No thank you, I can do without that.'

Now, stooped over the corpse on the stainless steel table, watched closely by his two regular assistants, both of whom he had trained to his own meticulous standards, he dictated his findings and frequent asides into a microphone suspended over the corpse. 'Good God, he was nothing but blubber,' he said as he completed an incision and peeled back the abdomen. 'Fat, not age, shall wither a man, advice you would do well to observe, Charles.' Charles was the assistant who tended to stutter whenever Hogg asked for confirmation of an opinion. 'I notice you are still a slave to junk food and were careless enough to leave the evidence in the waste bin outside. Ah! Now that's interesting,' he continued in the same breath as his scalpel uncovered another layer. 'Take a good look both of you, you won't see a better epithelial tumour of the liver than that. Magnificent. This little beauty would have done for him in less than a year.' Charles and Graham murmured their appreciation. 'As I keep telling you, there's no such thing as natural death. Open up anybody and the horoscope is there.'

An hour later, having scrubbed up, he came out to give his findings to the waiting Pearson, lighting a cigarette before warming to the task. 'I smoke Turkish, you know. Always have, but the damn things are difficult to get. Fortunately I have an admirer in Cairo who keeps me supplied. Splendid chap, does sex-change operations. Not my idea of a career, but fascinating all the same. Now then,' he said, having expelled the first heady intake, 'eliminations first. He was not shot, he was not stabbed, he didn't die from a heart attack, nor choke to death on a surfeit of lampreys.'

Pearson waited, letting him have his moment.

Hogg went to his locker and took out his jacket. The cigarette was kept in his mouth while he put his arms in the sleeves. 'What I did discover, however, was a mark on the upper right arm made by a needle of some sort, not necessarily a hypodermic needle, more likely some form of dart fired with considerable force judging by the depth of penetration. It is my belief, which I am absolutely sure will be judged correct by further tests, that this was used to introduce a lethal toxin capable of producing death in a very short time.'

'Cyanide?'

Hogg gave him a faint, condescending smile. 'No, nothing as mundane as that, which in any case would normally be self-administered orally, a somewhat difficult feat I imagine whilst riding on a motorcycle and wearing a crash helmet.' He produced a brush and comb from the locker and arranged his sparse hair. 'I believe that, when identified, the substance will prove to belong to the family of poisons used to put down pet animals. They react extremely fast, bringing on total respiratory failure in less than half a minute. Effective little buggers. Pity the NHS is not allowed to use them on us when we're ready to fall off the perch. Sort of thing I shall give myself when the time comes. No intention of becoming a vegetable.'

'Can you do me a favour?' Pearson said.

'I thought I'd already done you one.'

'Can we take a look at the other man? Just to establish whether he died in the same way.'

Hogg gave him a long look.

'It's important.'

'Tell me what isn't with you chaps. I must be getting soft in my old age.' He turned and shouted. 'Charles!'

His assistant appeared with a worried look. 'Sir?'

'Wheel out the other one.'

As Charles disappeared Hogg said: 'Come and see for yourself. And don't worry, I'm not going to cut anything.'

A reluctant Pearson followed him into the laboratory and stood to one side as Charles and the other assistant lifted Tony's body on to the stainless steel table. Dousing his cigarette in the sink, Hogg removed his jacket, put on a new pair of gloves and started to examine the corpse. Pearson stood back.

'Tell me,' Hogg said, 'any idea what this one was wearing?'

'Some sort of leather gear.'

'Yes, that would account for it.'

323

'Account for what?'

'The indentation is not so deep . . . Give me a marker, Charles.'

Charles handed him one and Hogg drew a circle on Tony's flesh on the right shoulder. 'There it is, same thing. Take a look.'

Pearson stepped to the table. Hogg had circled a small discoloured area.

'That's all there is to show?'

'If I'm right, it was enough to make him shuffle off his mortal coil in a hurry.'

Before leaving the laboratory Pearson rang Inspector Grant at Amersham.

'I'd like your men to carry out another search in the area surrounding the scene of the accident. Tell them to look for two darts.'

'Darts?'

'Not the kind used in pubs, the sort that can be fired from a rifle. And tell them to be extremely careful if they find them, because they could be lethal.'

. . .

'I hope I did the right thing in coming here,' Hillsden said, 'but Mr Hyde insisted I got the news to you as soon as possible and I didn't want to trust the phone . . . in case, well, one never knows who's listening in.'

'Quite right, Robert,' Fadiman said. 'You acted very sensibly.' He manipulated the wheelchair and propelled himself round so that his back was to the light. 'We have suffered a setback, no doubt about that, but we shall recover and strike hard in return. Do sit down. Pull up that chair. Let me get you some refreshment, ring that bell for me, please. I'm sure that bruise on your head is painful. Your first wound in the cause, Robert. Think of it that way.'

'Yes.'

Johnny appeared in the doorway

'What would you like, Robert?'

'Just coffee would be fine.'

'Coffee for Robert, and I'll have a glass of champagne. That always revives my spirits. Now then,' Fadiman continued as Johnny withdrew without a word, 'tell me exactly what happened, stage by stage.'

While Hillsden was describing the events of the night before, Johnny returned and served coffee and champagne in a surly manner. When the door closed behind him, Fadiman confided: 'He's in a bad mood because I've grounded him for a week to teach him a lesson. I'm afraid his sexual tastes lean to the bizarre and I can't have this house used as a male brothel. He may have outlived his usefulness. But, go on. Hyde, you say, was remanded for seven days?'

'Yes, whereas the rest of us were let off with a fine.' Hillsden picked up his coffee cup and spoke into it. 'Do we know if Sonntag actually arrived in the country?'

'Oh, yes. We can trace his movements to the moment when he was transferred to Tony. After that, nothing.'

'And you haven't received any reports of an accident?'

'No, but then, on the other hand, I wouldn't expect any.'

'What d'you think happened to Tony?'

'For the moment I have no idea. The police were there in force, you say?'

'Yes, I've never seen so many. Had Sonntag got to the venue he would have been taken, no doubt about it.'

'On the journey there, did you notice anything untoward?'

'Untoward? No.'

Hillsden could not see Fadiman's eyes, but there was no mistaking the steel in his voice. 'We have been betrayed, Robert. There is no other answer. Somebody in our midst must be rooted out and eliminated.'

'Could it be Tony?'

'That's a good question, Robert, but only time will tell. We shall have to make many changes in the way we operate. But rest assured that this temporary setback will not go unanswered. Watch your newspapers, Robert. You'll soon be reading about the ways in which we can reply and destabilise their world. They have underestimated us, roused a sleeping tiger.'

. . .

'Let's find out whether Sonntag was ever fingerprinted by the Germans,' Pearson said the moment he returned to Century House. 'And if he was have them send us a set, together with any dental records if they have them.'

'You're still convinced it's him?' asked Lloyd, putting in his usual lugubrious two-cents worth of doubt.

'Yes, and I'll tell you my other theory, too. If it is him, and if Hogg is right, I think it's highly probable that they were both taken out by Mossad, and those bits of paper with the Star of David were their visiting cards.'

'Well, assuming you're right, if *we* couldn't trace whether Sonntag was in the country, how come they did?'

'Maybe they're smarter. If it was them, you might say they did us a good turn.'

'Or landed us in deep shit.'

'I bet you were a depressing little sod as a child. The sort that never gave anybody their ball back if it landed in your garden.'

'We never had a garden,' Lloyd said.

Pearson reached for his antacid tablets.

37

NIGHT TRUTHS

Hillsden's brief reunion with his family had not been as smooth as he had hoped, for Galina did not conceal her resentment at the way in which their lives were being manipulated. At one moment during an argument which developed after Lara had been put to bed, she said: 'And if the next call I receive is to say you're dead, what then? What happens to Lara and me?'

'It's not going to happen.'

'Oh, Alec, don't you see how it's changed us? We never argued in St Petersburg. I'm your wife, why don't you tell me what's really going on? All last night I lay awake, it was like the bad times in Russia when people you loved were never seen again.'

'And here I am, right as rain.'

'But it's in your face. I can read it in your face. You just pretend for me.'

'I'm tired, that's all. Tiredness, that's all you can see. Like you, I spent a sleepless night.'

'Stay here tonight.'

'I can't do that, sweetheart.'

'And you can't tell me why, can you?'

They were suddenly interrupted by the sound of a car approaching; a moment later the headlights beamed on to the far wall of the living room before being extinguished. Next they heard a car door slam and two voices – Audrey's and a man's. Shortly afterwards Audrey came inside and pulled a face as she spoke.

'You've got a visitor,' she said, then whispered, 'Hadley,' again with a grimace. 'Do I show him in?'

Hillsden glanced at Galina. 'I guess so. Just give us a second or two.'

Galina said: 'Why would he come here?'

'Darling, I don't know, do I?'

'I thought you told me they'd leave us alone here.'

'That's what they promised.'

'Some promise – broken like all the others. Well, I don't want to see him.'

She left the room and went upstairs just before Audrey ushered Hadley inside.

'Why, Hadley,' Hillsden said, putting on a friendly face. 'Is this a social visit or have you come to read the gas meter in case I'm fiddling the Firm's expenses? Can I offer you a drink, cup of coffee?'

'I'll take a cup of coffee,' Hadley said. 'Decaf if you have it.'

'Audrey, do we run to decaf?'

'Have to be instant,' Audrey replied, going into the kitchen, but not without some heavy body language. 'Do sit down, Hadley, make yourself at home,' Hillsden said, settling into an armchair.

Hadley sat on the sofa. 'Look, I'm sorry I turned up without warning . . .' he began, then seemed to lose confidence in how to continue. He started again. 'But I wanted to get certain things out in the open, things which have been on my mind for some time now and which I don't understand.' Again he hesitated, searching, it seemed to Hillsden, for a way to lessen some blow. 'I guess, when I was invited to join . . . I had a romantic notion of how the Firm now operated. I thought, naïvely, I'm sure, that everything would have changed.'

'Changed in what way?'

Audrey returned with the coffee before Hadley could reply. She put the cup and saucer down on a small side table and turned to Hillsden, ignoring Hadley. 'Anything else I can do?'

'I don't think so, Audrey, thank you very much.'

'I'll be next door if you want me.'

After they heard the front door close, Hillsden repeated: 'Changed in what way?'

Hadley picked up his coffee and stared at it before answering. 'I felt sure that because of the past exposures and resulting scandals the age of dirty tricks was over,' he said slowly. 'I suppose I was being naïve.'

'It's always been a dirty business that we're engaged in, Hadley . . . Sorry, what's your first name, I ought to know, but I don't and it's rude of me.'

'Christopher . . . My mother had a thing about A. A. Milne . . . Thank God she left out the "Robin".' For the first time his features lost their set look. 'I prefer Chris,' he finished.

'So what're you trying to tell me, Chris? I don't imagine you drove all this way for the pleasure of it or to give me a history of the Firm.'

'I think . . . and I can't be positive at the moment, but certain things have occurred to me that don't add up.'

'*What* certain things?'

'About your situation . . . The way in which you're being used. If you must know, I think you've been set up, and I thought I should warn you.'

'Why would you go out of your way to do that, assuming you're right?'

'Because I've made it my business to find out more about you, things I never knew before, such as what really happened to you in the past. See, I never had the entire picture, I was only given an edited version. When I realised the full extent of what Lockfield and others did to you, it was only then that I began to put two and two together on the present scenario . . . I became convinced it was happening again, and it didn't seem fair.'

'Fair?'

'Yes.'

Hillsden put his whisky down. 'Forgive me, Chris, I'm not mocking you, don't think that, but "fair" isn't a word I've heard too often around the Firm. "Fair game", yes. We're all fair game, as you'll discover for yourself. But I get your meaning . . . Tell me one thing before you go on, was bugging my car your idea?'

Hadley coloured. 'Yes.'

'Can I ask why?'

'I thought it was a way of keeping one step ahead of them. That I might glean something that was being kept from me. But it didn't work as I planned. You don't talk much in the car.'

Hillsden gave a wry smile. 'No, for good reasons . . . But "them"? Who are we talking about?'

'I wish I could answer that . . . it all seems too preposterous.' His coffee cup started to rattle and he put it down carefully. 'For instance, what first puzzled me was the ease with which you were established. They gave you a bogus set-up and supplied a list of names.'

'Who prepared the list? D'you know?'

'Well, it didn't come from Pearson, that I do know. I had to be careful about how I made enquiries, but as far as I could tell somebody in D Section put it together, that's where it first surfaced.'

'Go on,' Hillsden said, listening intently.

'Well, I wonder, weren't you surprised you got a response almost immediately? And that, without too much trouble, this character, Hyde, started the ball rolling? He arranges for you to meet Tony, and, bingo, you're taken to see Fadiman who quickly gives his blessing and shares some of their secrets. Doesn't all that seem a bit too pat to you?'

'It crossed my mind, yes.'

'And?'

'It's like quicksand,' Hillsden said. 'Once you've taken the first step into it, it's too late to turn back, you can only hope that you get out eventually.'

'And there are other things,' Hadley said, unstoppable now. 'What about Schmidt's murder? According to Pearson he was going to check on Carstairs for us, but he's dead before he can do anything. Then Lloyd goes to Copenhagen and again he's too late, there's another dead body. To me that suggests somebody is one step ahead of us at every turn. Even Mossad.'

'Mossad? What have they got to do with it?'

'Pearson's convinced that Sonntag's dead and that Mossad took him out.'

'Why does he think that?'

'He and Lloyd came across a road accident a short way from the meeting place, two men dead in a ditch, but no sign that they crashed or anything. He had an autopsy carried out by that old guy he always uses if he can.'

'Not Hogg, surely?'

'Yes, that's the name.'

Hillsden gave himself a whisky, lingering over the action so that Hadley would not see his changed expression as the past returned to choke him. Why was it that everything led him back to Caroline sooner or later? 'I never thought he could still be around,' he said.

'According to this Hogg, both men were killed by poisoned darts.'

'I still don't understand why Pearson suspects Mossad.'

'They found the Star of David on both bodies.'

'I see . . . Going back to my situation, have you discussed this with anybody else?'

'Of course not, what d'you take me for?'

'Well, I guess I have to take you at face value for the time being.'

'Meaning, you don't trust me?'

'Meaning, what you've just told me says I should be on my guard. I've been out of it for a long time, I don't know you, or Pearson, or Swanson, or any of the present gang. The only link with my past is Rotherby. And Rotherby is somebody I do trust. So, since it's obviously too risky for you to make a habit of contacting me direct, assuming your suspicions are right, maybe it would be a good idea to share any future developments with Rotherby.'

Hadley hesitated, then said: 'There is something else that I have to tell you . . . I don't think it could have any connection with what we've been talking about, but you never know . . . Your Russian friend is in town.'

Hillsden reacted. 'You mean Victor Abramov?'

'Yes. The man who once controlled you. I bumped into him at a reception given at the German Embassy. He told me he was over here looking to buy a house with his new-found wealth and was anxious to see you.'

'He knew who you were?'

'He knew I worked for the Firm. It seems he still has good contacts.'

'So what did you tell him?'

'Nothing. I wanted to speak to you first. All I said was I'd try and get a message to you. He's staying at Grosvenor House.'

'Under his own name?'

'Yes, as far as I know.'

'Why the German Embassy?'

'He said he had an ongoing contract to supply them with Korean computer hardware.'

'Well, well. So old Victor finally made the big time,' Hillsden said. 'Capitalism does work.'

'Would it be safe for you to get in touch?'

'Possibly not, but friendship is worth a few risks. I'll think of a way.'

Hadley got up. 'I think I should push off now.'

'Give me a lift back to Forest Gate. We can talk some more on the way. I just want five minutes to say good-night to my wife.'

Galina had already undressed for bed; the white cotton nightgown clung to her figure, her nipples like dark stains on the fabric, and he thought, why is it that lies and guilt turn us so quickly towards lust, as though only a physical act can save us? There was so much mystery to women, whole areas that a man could never reach. They loved with their minds first, it was their minds that made the first declaration and decided when love was over.

'What did that man want?'

'He came to tell me Victor is in London.'

'He drove all this way just for that? There must have been another reason.'

Hillsden shook his head, trying to appear relaxed for her. 'I think he just wanted an excuse to give his new car a spin . . . Exciting that Victor's over here, isn't it? I just hope I can find a way of seeing him.' The words were out of his mouth before he could stop them.

'Why wouldn't you be able to see him?'

'Depends on my work.'

'Or whether you're telling the truth. Every time you tell me something different. I don't even believe you were in a car accident.' She sat on the edge of the bed. 'Are you having an affair?'

'An affair?'

'Is it the girl in your office?'

'Sarah, you mean?'

'Is that her name?'

'Of course I'm not having an affair. With Sarah or anybody else. Why on earth would you think that?'

It was the truth between them, something that for once he did not have to lie about and yet it sounded like a lie. Perhaps, he thought, adultery was preferable to deceit for a cause. Trust between them had been disconnected.

'Because you haven't made love to me in weeks.'

'That's proof of an affair?'

'It's proof of something,' she answered.

'Only of the life I'm forced to lead. And, anyway, I haven't been here.'

She looked at him defiantly. 'Give them their money back, we'll survive. I can take a job in the hours that Lara's at school. We don't have to live here, we could get somewhere smaller in a town, where there's some life. There's no life here. I pretend there's life, but there's none in this house and none outside. I have to live your lies, too, with my new name, the

333

pretence that I'm somebody else with a husband who sells insurance policies. Why don't you tell me what's really happening to us, what you really do when you leave here? I could take the truth, but I can't go on living with a stranger.'

Hillsden knelt in front of her and took her hands. They were cold and he folded them in his own and took them to his mouth, brushing his lips across her fingertips. 'When it's over,' he began, but she pulled her hands away.

'How long are you going to go on saying that? Whenever I face you with it, that's the only thing you ever say. I'm not a child, and I was born in a country where one expected to live in fear.'

'Darling, I don't have a choice,' Hillsden said, and heard Caroline's voice saying the same thing to him by the lake at Anif. You could change names, change the country you lived in, change the woman you slept beside, but there was always a premium on happiness.

When he came downstairs, burdened with fresh guilt, he found Hadley was waiting for him in a new Nissan 400SX.

'Don't tell me the Firm runs to one of these?'

'No. Actually it was a present from my mother.' He gave a sheepish grin and Hillsden could suddenly see Hadley's whole life unfold: only son, wealth, public school, doors opening for him at every stage, always drawing the long straw of privilege. And, given all that, why this? Hillsden thought. Why, if the going was so good, choose to work for the Firm?

As Hadley let in the clutch the headlights picked out a rabbit in the middle of the road, momentarily frozen in terror. For an instant Hillsden lived with the certainty that they were going to hit it, but Hadley pulled the wheel over and they bumped up on to the grass verge. Behind them the rooks shuffled uneasily in the trees, complaining at the disturbance.

38

A DIPLOMATIC EXERCISE

'It *was* Sonntag we found by the roadside,' Pearson said. 'The prints and dental records match. The other man was a character called Tony Fuller, one of the group who screened Hillsden. We traced him easily enough because he had some past form.'

Swanson made a strange movement with his jaws and cleared his throat. 'And you're still sticking to your theory that the killings were carried out by a Mossad team?'

'Well, *we* certainly didn't take them out. It was a very sophisticated hit, they go in for that sort of thing. And let's not forget the visiting cards left on the bodies.'

'I don't attach much importance to those. They could have been planted to point us in the wrong direction.'

'Okay, who else had a motive? Not any of the Middle East boys – Sonntag was aiming to do their job for them.'

'Well, if you're right, it's quite monstrous. If it leaked out, it'd be a major embarrassment for the government, and a heap of grief for us. We'd have to admit that Israeli intelligence is superior to ours.'

'So what's new? There's nothing we can do. Let the diplomatic boys do their usual cover-up if need be. More urgently, did Hillsden get anything out of Fadiman?'

'Just vague threats of revenge. As far as Hillsden could tell, Fadiman knew even less than us.'

'And you still don't want to bring him in for questioning?'

'What would we achieve by that? He wasn't at the meeting, he'd just deny all knowledge of it, plus any interest in him on our part would almost certainly lead straight back to Hillsden.'

Pearson accepted this. 'The only other item to report is that we've traced the ownership of the former health farm. It's currently listed as belonging to a shell company registered in Luxembourg. That's some progress and I'm having a further search done. If Fadiman proved to be one of the directors, that would give us an opening.'

'Yes,' Swanson agreed, but he had the look of a man waiting to hear confirmation of a terminal illness.

. . .

When Logan put down the phone after speaking with Swanson he was in an even fouler mood than before and immediately dialled another extension.

'Logan here, give me the Foreign Secretary . . . I don't care, get him out of the meeting, this is urgent . . . No, don't have him ring me back, get him to the phone now.'

He paced to the full extent of the telephone cord, at one point getting it twisted which added to his frustrations. 'Reggie . . . Kenith . . . Yes, I'm sorry, but you'll appreciate why in a minute. We've got a very tricky situation staring us in the face and I need your help. Our security chaps are convinced that a Mossad squad, operating here illegally, carried out a political assassination a couple of nights ago . . . some neo-Nazi. What? . . . Yes, bloody unbelievable on our doorstep . . . so we'd better get on top of it as soon as possible. Can you have an off-the-record talk with the Israeli Ambassador . . . you're on good terms, aren't you? . . . I thought so, yes . . . Oh, that's a good idea, use the Security Council Vote next week as a quid pro quo . . . Look, I'm sorry to push it on to your plate, but I thought you'd be our best bet. I'll send over such details as we have, so that you go into the meeting briefed. Thanks,

Reggie, I shan't forget the favour.'

He hung up.

Like Logan, Telford, the Foreign Secretary, had not had an easy ride in his new office since the Labour government had taken power, and many of his preconceived notions of the changes he would bring about had proved non-starters. He had quickly found that shuffling the pack of faces that constituted the British government did not alter the state of play; other world leaders continued to further their own nationalistic aims regardless of Britain. It had come as a shock to Telford to realise that H.M. Principal Secretary for Foreign Affairs was often reduced to the role of spectator around the international poker table – allowed to sit in on the game but frequently unable to match the high stakes.

That morning, when Logan dragged him out of a meeting, he had been attempting to formulate a strategy for his forthcoming summit in Peking on human rights, and the death of a neo-Nazi demagogue did not figure high on his list of priorities. However, he was a great champion of Cabinet loyalty and requested the Israeli Ambassador to pay a call as soon as possible. He gave no details to the Embassy, but said the matter was one of urgency. The request was acted upon later that same day.

'I do apologise for summoning you at short notice, Yoram, but it seems you and I could have a shared problem of some delicacy.'

'Tell me a problem that isn't delicate these days,' the Ambassador said.

'Perhaps you'd be good enough to read this report from MI6. Can I get you a drink?'

The Ambassador looked at his watch. 'Why not, the sun's nearly over the yard-arm. I'll have a gin and tonic, if I may. Plenty of ice.' While Telford prepared the drinks, the Israeli Ambassador studied the papers he had been given. 'Interesting,' he said, as he finished and waited for Telford to make the first move in the chess game they were about to play.

'As you've just read,' Telford said, 'our security boys have come up with the theory – possibility, rather – that Mossad could have carried out the assassination. D'you think such a possibility is credible?'

'Well, of course it's unthinkable that my government would sanction such an action by any of our agents within the boundaries of another sovereign state.'

'Of course,' Telford readily agreed.

'Therefore, on behalf of my government, I must formally register a strong protest regarding such an implication and refute it.'

'Yoram, I understand your position totally, and it's noted.'

'However,' the Ambassador continued, and his features relaxed slightly, 'having said that, it's not beyond the bounds of possibility that certain individuals – who may or may not have a connection with our security forces, I'm certainly not in a position to confirm that – could have taken it upon themselves, without my government's authority or knowledge, to act unilaterally. Such things have happened before and doubtless will happen again, given the legitimate feelings still harboured by those whose families suffered in the Holocaust.'

'Always on the cards, I suppose. And for our part we haven't admitted that this Nazi was ever in the country. Nor will we.'

'That's helpful. And, naturally, it would be quite wrong for my government to interfere or influence your judicial processes, nor would we attempt to do so, but I can't help thinking that it would serve no great purpose – if we accept the hypothesis in these papers – to create a situation whereby both our governments were unnecessarily embarrassed. Don't you agree?'

'Absolutely.'

'Much cleaner if the whole thing could be discreetly buried. One could imagine that in certain quarters the death of this man, however achieved, might actually be welcome news.'

'I'm sure you're right,' Telford said, thinking quickly as he

338

saw the door the Ambassador was opening. 'It's delicate, of course.'

'These things always are at the time, but they tend to get papered over by more important issues.'

'Yes, yes,' Telford answered gravely. 'So, how best to handle it, d'you think?'

'All this on the understanding that I am not admitting that any member of Mossad was involved . . . '

'Take that as read.'

'However, I shall make the necessary enquiries and if it transpires that two of our operatives entered the UK illegally we will deal with them in our own way. And, in the unlikely event you were ever called upon to make a statement, you could say quite openly that the Israeli Embassy denied all knowledge and you were content to accept our assurances that we were in no way involved.' He smiled. 'Which of course we weren't.'

Telford returned the Ambassador's smile. 'Absolutely. No good purpose would be served by raising dead issues. Much the cleanest solution from both our standpoints.'

'As to the man himself,' the Ambassador said, 'he's your concern. And since you tell me there's no documented evidence that he ever entered the country, and since we didn't kill him, I don't imagine his disposal will present any insuperable problems.'

'I'm sure you're right. Let me top up that gin. And while we're here together, Yoram, Shelagh keeps reminding me that it's about time we returned your hospitality. How about you and Rachel coming to dinner on the eighteenth? What's your diary like?'

.   .   .

The following day, two Israeli citizens were taken in a closed car straight on to the tarmac at Heathrow and put on an El Al aircraft prior to the rest of the passengers boarding. All previous references to their presence in England were destroyed following a regrettable administrative error.

That problem out of the way, the question of how to dispose of Sonntag's body remained. It was Rotherby who came up with the answer. 'Sonntag never entered the country, did he? "Arthur Clarke" was the one who set foot on this sceptred isle. Let Mr Clarke be the one who departs. Who are we to take away a man's name?'

So, with the full co-operation of the Bundeskriminalamt, the remains of the erstwhile 'Arthur Clarke' were put aboard a night cargo flight to Frankfurt. Rather than risk having any paperwork that could be traced back to Hogg, a second death certificate was prepared by MI6 and presented to Customs at Heathrow. It was judged to be sufficiently accurate in that it gave the cause of death as cardiac arrest and aroused no suspicion. The coffin was collected in Frankfurt by plain-clothed members of the German police posing as undertakers acting on the instructions of 'Clarke's' relatives. Instead of being removed to a mortuary to await burial, the coffin was taken to a remote country area. There the body was removed from it, placed behind the driving wheel of a previously wrecked car and doused in petrol. The vehicle was then set on fire. The burnt-out shell and charred remains of the occupant were discovered the following morning by a farmer. After a suitable interval, the authorities issued a press release stating that, with the help of dental records, their investigations had identified the victim as Sonntag, and that tests on the vehicle had established that the probable cause of the accident was a faulty brake cable. No witnesses had come forward and they had been unable to establish why Sonntag had been travelling on that particular stretch of road, which was a notorious black spot.

A funeral took place shortly afterwards in Sonntag's home town, attended by over two hundred sympathisers, many of them wearing swastikas. Although the police kept a low profile, skirmishes broke out when an attempt was made to drape the coffin with the Nazi flag, and several arrests were made.

The paperwork in England and Germany relating to a man named 'Arthur Clarke' vanished from the files. Only Hogg's original post-mortem report was deemed protected under the Official Secrets Act and locked away marked 'never to be revealed'.

Tony Fuller's nearest and dearest were informed that he skidded and died in a road accident whilst travelling at excessive speed.

39

FOREIGN BODIES

Following his usual routine, Pearson lay soaking in the bath, listening to the early morning news bulletin on a portable radio, wondering why it was that he felt scarcely human these days. The news seemed to be confined to social minutiae: a well-known soap opera performer had been outed, a pit-bull terrier on death row had been granted a seven-day stay of execution, and the Bishop of somewhere had questioned the validity of the Virgin birth.

Pearson lifted a soapy hand to switch the radio off when the bulletin continued with, 'The death was announced this morning of Lord Miller, the Chairman of one of Britain's largest companies, Trans-Continental. His body was found by his chauffeur and it appears that he died as a result of gunshot wounds. Foul play is not suspected. Lord Miller was seventy-three, and was created a Life Peer in 1987. Trans-Continental was recently the target of a take-over bid, following the collapse of its share price.'

Pearson heaved himself out of the bath, grabbed a towel and went downstairs to his study and dialled Lloyd's home number.

'Did you hear the news just now?'

'No, I didn't have it on.'

'Old Lord Miller has copped it.'

'Christ! He was on Schmidt's list, wasn't he?'

'Yes. How many does that make?'

'Three,' Lloyd answered. 'Did they say how Miller snuffed it?'

'Just that he died of gunshot wounds. Foul play not suspected, but that's just the local CID. I'll find out more.'

The obituaries were respectful, recording the passing of one of the old school of entrepreneurs who, in recent years, had failed to move with the times and diversify. Comment in the financial columns concentrated on the most likely outcome being a management buy-out, funded by a yet undisclosed white knight. The shares rose by twenty-seven pence in expectation.

Later that same week there was a small story tucked away on the inside pages of two papers stating that the body of a middle-aged woman had been washed up on the Devon coast and identified as Miriam Cohen, a resident of Plymouth. Even if Pearson had noticed the item, which he did not, he could have been excused for not making any connection.

. . .

Still harbouring thoughts of Galina's unhappiness and the wounding exchanges of the previous night, Hillsden walked up South Audley Street, heading for Grosvenor House. He had decided that, come what may, he had to see Abramov again, the magnet of the years they had shared in Russia powerful enough for him to put the possible risks to one side.

It was one of those rare, perfect days when parts of the centre of London make an attempt to take on the characteristics of a Mediterranean resort. Chairs and tables appear outside pubs and sandwich bars, swiftly occupied by coatless businessmen braving lethal concentrations of carbon monoxide to sip warm beer. Policemen shed their jackets, workmen on building sites strip to the waist, St James's Park is transformed into a grassy beach for mating rituals, bewildered tourists wrongly dressed for the expected Arctic conditions adjust their light meters, young girls stream out from the offices and shops at lunchtime to perambulate in the sunshine of Regent Street with figures alarmingly revealed, strangers exchange smirks as they pass on the hot pavements and while it lasts a sort of unnatural gaiety persists as though a performance of *King Lear* having been announced, the curtain goes up to reveal *A Midsummer-Night's Dream*.

As he turned into the hotel forecourt he came face to face with a devastatingly pretty girl, obviously bra-less, and in all probability American for she had that clean, long-limbed, shamefully healthy look seemingly made for magazine covers. Momentarily stunned, Hillsden stepped off the pavement to let her pass and caught the scent of her perfume. The chance encounter stayed with him as he entered the hotel foyer. As he made his way to the reception desk, he suddenly caught sight of Fadiman in his wheelchair, attended by Johnny. Fadiman was engaged in earnest conversation with a man Hillsden did not recognise: stocky, with the florid complexion that possibly indicated a heavy drinker, wearing an impeccably cut suit. Rather than risk drawing attention to himself by suddenly turning about, Hillsden proceeded at a leisurely pace to the concierge's desk. There he changed his intended enquiry about Abramov and instead asked for a Mr and Mrs Pearson. The concierge consulted the list of guests.

'We don't appear to have a Mr and Mrs Pearson, sir. Did they have a reservation?'

'I thought they did.'

'I'll check the forward bookings.' The concierge tapped an instruction into the computer. 'No, sir, nothing in the future either.'

'How odd. I must have misunderstood them. Sorry to have troubled you.'

'No trouble, sir.'

Hillsden lingered by the desk, picked up a free tourist brochure, and while making the pretence of studying it, shot a glance to where he had last seen Fadiman. The other man had disappeared and Johnny was releasing the brakes on the wheelchair preparatory to conducting his employer to the exit. Hillsden let them go out of sight before crossing the foyer to one of the house phones.

'Mr Victor Abramov's room, please,' he requested when the switchboard answered. After the room phone had rung at least half a dozen times the operator came back on the line.

'Mr Abramov is not answering, sir. Would you care to leave a message?'

'No, it doesn't matter. I'll try him again later.'

As he recrossed the foyer he saw the man that Fadiman had been talking to. He was now sitting in the middle of an all-male group taking coffee. From their uniformly smart suits he took them to be business executives. He continued on through the foyer and out into the hot street, pausing in front of a shop selling all manner of surveillance devices – briefcases with miniature cameras built in, night sights, phones that could not be tapped – and was still staring in the window when somebody called out 'Robert'. Momentarily he paid no attention, then when the name was repeated he turned to find a taxicab by the kerbside. The passenger window was open and Fadiman beckoned him.

'I thought I recognised you,' Fadiman said as Hillsden approached. 'Can we give you a lift?'

It was then that Hillsden saw that it was not a taxi for hire and that Johnny was driving.

'That's very kind.'

Johnny got out and opened the door and Hillsden climbed inside.

'Can you ease yourself past my chair?' Fadiman asked. Hillsden took the jump seat and sat facing him.

'Where're you making for?'

'I've got a call to make in Pimlico,' he said, choosing a location at random. 'Ebury Street.'

'A famous address,' Fadiman said. 'Did you know Mozart once resided there, as did Noël Coward, George Moore and, more importantly, Sir Oswald Mosley.'

'Really?'

'Oh, yes. Well, I can drop you at Victoria, it's on my way, no

345

problem.'

'Is this your personal taxi?'

'Rather smart, eh? No, a friend lends it to me. It's one of the few vehicles able to take my chair.'

'That's the sort of friend to have.'

The traffic was halted around Hyde Park Corner as a troop of mounted Life Guards, escorted by police, clopped their usual diagonal path across the island towards Buckingham Palace.

'Tourist fodder celebrating a dying dynasty,' Fadiman remarked, then added, 'Toytown stuff.'

By the time the mounted troop had disappeared, the traffic was backed up as far as Knightsbridge and Piccadilly and it took another five minutes before it was unsnarled.

'Have you found out anything more?' Hillsden ventured.

Fadiman nodded. 'Some of it, yes. But as I promised you, we've already struck back.' He took out a packet of cigarettes and his holder, then clicked his fingers. 'Decisively, in the only way they understand,' Fadiman said. Johnny pressed the cigarette lighter on the dashboard and a few seconds later passed it back over his shoulder. Hillsden handed it on. Fadiman lit his cigarette and gave back the lighter before continuing, 'We eliminated the informer.'

'Who was it?'

'Nobody you would know, Robert. A dirty little Jewess, who played a double game, but she wasn't a very clever little Jewess . . . I'm sorry, I'm blowing smoke in your face . . . You're new to it all, Robert, but you've had your baptism, and the price you paid was to be beaten over the head and thrown in jail. I did warn you, however, that the road ahead was not going to be easy for any of us.'

'How did you discover this . . . this Jewish woman was the one?'

'How? That wasn't difficult once Harry had a talk with her. He's rather single-minded, our Harry. Doesn't make friends easily, but he was fond of Tony. He took Tony's death very personally.'

'Tony's dead?'

'Regrettably, yes. Both he and Comrade Sonntag were killed by an Israeli murder squad, doubtless in collusion with MI6. They'd be only too happy for somebody else to do their squalid work.'

Still presenting himself as a man unable to take in such revelations, Hillsden stared at Fadiman open-mouthed. 'But there was nothing in the papers.'

Fadiman flicked his ash towards the ashtray in the door and missed. 'Doesn't that make my point? There was no mention of it. To me that proves they were hand in hand. It was a blow, Robert, I don't conceal that from you. We shall have to be more ruthless in future, and rest assured we're already planning to widen the scope of our operations. There'll be a role for you to play when we get even. I'm sure you'd welcome that.'

'Yes, I would,' Hillsden said. 'I never knew such things went on.'

Fadiman patted him on the knee. 'But now you do. You've been given your first experience of the sort of people we're up against.' He looked out of the window as the taxi pulled into the kerb. 'This is as far as I can take you . . .'

'Well, thank you again for the lift.'

'My pleasure.'

Hillsden closed the taxi door and watched as Johnny pulled out into the traffic, then he took the precaution of walking in the direction of Ebury Street for a hundred yards or so before doubling back and going into Victoria Station to ring Swanson.

. . .

'It's the Kell files I'm particularly interested in,' Pearson said. 'Can you dig those out?'

Harrison, the keeper of the Firm's archives, whose bald and pointed head gave him the appearance of a garden gnome, fixed him with a pained expression.

'You sure you mean Kell?'

'Yes.'

'Are you serious? You do know what you're asking for, do you? You couldn't live long enough to get through all of those. There was a moment when those upstairs thought it would be useful to put the whole lot on our database, but we did a time and motion study and calculated it would take somebody working seven days a week the best part of five years. The man was barking, a human squirrel. I pointed out that of the four million plus names he collected, ninety per cent were dead.'

'Do squirrels bark?'

Harrison, not noted for his sense of humour, glided past this and pursued his own line of thought. 'Unless you've got time to waste, I suggest you think again.'

'I don't want all of them. Just the war years will do if you can put your hands on them without too much trouble.'

'I can put my hands on anything,' Harrison said archly, immediately offended that anybody would question his system. He led the way between the parallel rows of shelving housing his dusty charges. 'The man was obsessed, of course. Saw subversives everywhere, made McCarthy look like Pollyanna. The early years are written in copperplate. Works of art in their way, I suppose . . . Now then . . . they should be around this section as I recall . . . Yes, here we are. My system seldom fails me. Nineteen thirty-eight, thirty-nine . . . Haven't been touched in ages, hence the dust. They were restricted until a few years ago, God knows why.' He extracted a series of box files, and plonked them on a table. 'Help yourself. I think you'll find them dull reading. Anything else you require?'

'I wouldn't mind a cup of instant coffee.'

'Don't insult me. I grind my own beans,' Harrison said. 'And only best Colombian,' as he walked away trailing the reproach like a cloak.

Harry had a strong feeling that he would soon be asked to kill again. It didn't occupy him overmuch either way. One did it, one got paid and moved on. He had always failed to understand why others got so het up. He never selected the targets so there was no personal involvement, it was just a shopping list he worked through. The phone call came, a name was given, it was left to him to work out the details, which was how he preferred to work. He never wanted to know the reason, and he never exceeded his instructions. Others might be tempted, but then others weren't as careful as he was, maybe they got some extra pleasure out of it. Harry wasn't in it for pleasure, he was a professional doing a job for money. Once the phone call was received he went into training: no alcohol, no sex, no new acquaintances; everything concentrated on the detailed when and how of the event until it was over. Afterwards there was plenty of time for extra stimuli.

He waited to see if his hunch was right and hoped that the next one would give him more of a challenge: the last two had hardly tested him.

. . .

Pearson couldn't help being impressed by the opulence of Sir Raymond Charters's office and lifestyle, especially since reading that Charters had received a £1.4 million bonus in addition to his monster salary as Chief Executive of the company. He had calculated that in the highly unlikely event that Charters's tax lawyers didn't shelter any of it and the Revenue took forty per cent, he would still be left with well over a million. Sitting on the deep leather couch sipping the cup of excellent coffee provided by the receptionist, he passed the time working out that it would take him a good forty years to earn that amount.

Making a show of consulting his wrist-watch, he deliberately caught the receptionist's eye. She smiled sympathetically.

'I'm so sorry about this', she said. 'We try our best to keep Sir Raymond's diary straight, but it doesn't always work out.'

'Happens to us all.'

Pearson had observed that keeping underlings waiting was one of the prerogatives of power, and Charters was certainly exercising that power in his case. He had arrived a few minutes before the appointed time and had been made to cool his heels for the best part of thirty minutes. Maybe, he thought, men like Charters had a graduated scale for these things. Equals were admitted immediately, others according to their social status or usefulness.

'Can I get you another coffee?'

'No, thank you.'

'Would you care to see today's *Financial Times*?'

Testing her sense of humour, Pearson said: 'I'm not playing the market at the moment', and saw that she was uncertain how to interpret this.

'Oh, right.'

The door to Charters's office finally opened and his secretary came out. 'I do apologise, Commander. Sir Raymond will see you now.'

'Thank you.'

She held the door open and closed it behind him. Charters's office was furnished in matching rosewood: his desk with its array of telephones, fax machine and personal computer, the fitted bookshelves with their sets of leather-bound volumes, the coffee table and side chairs, all were fashioned in the same rich wood, presumably as a symbol of their owner's taste and wealth. He was making a statement, as the Americans put it. There were several oil paintings on the walls, and Pearson trod an elaborately patterned Oriental carpet as he went forward to greet Charters.

'Commander, please forgive me for making you hang about. I hope my people took care of you?'

350

'Yes, I was well looked after, thank you.'

Charters took a seat by the coffee table and Pearson did likewise.

'Some days are sheer hell.'

'I know the feeling,' Pearson said.

'Do you smoke?' Charters pushed a silver cigarette box towards Pearson. 'Feel free if you do.'

'I won't at the moment, thank you.'

'So, to what do I owe this honour from somebody of your eminence?'

'I can't say I'm conscious of having any eminence.'

'Well, it's not every day that one has a visit from a senior officer of MI6. How can I help you?'

'Well, it's just a general enquiry really, to ask if you could throw any light on the death of Lord Miller.'

Charters nodded. 'Oh dear, yes, that. A very sad business from all accounts. I always think it must be quite terrible for the families of a suicide. Death should always have some dignity.'

'You knew him, of course?'

'Yes. I won't say he was a close friend, but we certainly socialised. Birds of a feather, you know, we tend to frequent the same watering holes and talk the same shop. I mean, in one sense I suppose, we were antagonists.'

'In what sense is that?'

'As business rivals. We overlapped in certain areas. I'm sure I don't have to tell you it's very cut-throat these days, especially since Black Monday. The stock market has never been the same. Then we've had the Maxwell scandal, all those unfortunate Names at Lloyds, Barings going under . . . things which were unthinkable a few years back.'

'Yes, I understand . . . Am I right in saying that you dined with him not long before his death?'

If Charters was surprised by this question, he concealed it. 'I believe I did, yes.'

'Did you notice any change in him on that occasion?'

'Not that I can recall. Old Ralph was very much a one-man

band. Kept his thoughts to himself.'

'And at the time, if the papers are to be believed, you were in the process of making a bid for his company?'

'We were looking at his company, certainly.'

'It was described at the time as a "hostile bid". I'm not quite sure what that means.'

'It's just City jargon. Roughly, it means that the bid is not entirely welcome.'

'So do I take it that he wasn't keen?'

'No, and I understood why. He'd built up the company from scratch, it was very much his baby. He knew he was vulnerable, but he wanted to hang on as long as possible.'

'And it didn't go through?'

'No, we analysed the numbers and decided they didn't add up from our point of view. Happens all the time, we're always looking for companies that could be useful. Diversify or die is the word today.'

'That could have been a factor then?'

Charters took a surreptitious glance at his watch. 'Factor?' he queried.

'The state of his business. Being aware that predators were stalking him.'

'I don't think I'd describe myself as a predator,' Charters said with a ghost of a smile.

'No, nor would I. That's just a word I've picked up from the tabloids.'

'Ah, the tabloids! They're the bane of everybody's life. But to answer you, I dare say that he did have concerns about whether he would have to bow to the inevitable. There's no doubt his business was going through a rough patch. That was obvious to anybody from the share price.'

'But apart from that you didn't get the impression of anything out of the ordinary the last time you saw him?'

'Forgive me, Commander,' Charters said, 'but what is the purpose of these questions?'

'Just to find out as much as we can about the state of his mind prior to his death.'

'Who knows what goes through a man's mind before he decides to commit suicide?'

Pearson did not answer immediately. Instead he reached for the cigarette box on the coffee table. 'D'you mind if I change my mind?'

'Please. I'm a cigar man myself, but I try to hold out until after lunch. Here, let me get you a lighter.' Charters got up and went to his desk, picking up a lighter in the shape of a pistol.

Once his cigarette was alight, Pearson said: 'What if he didn't commit suicide, Sir Raymond? What if he was murdered?'

Charters stared at him. 'Am I to take that remark seriously?'

'I certainly meant it seriously, sir.'

'Good God. That's shocking news, if it's true. Is there any evidence to that effect?'

'Certain things about his death aren't crystal-clear.'

'But that's a matter for the police, surely, not your department?'

'You're absolutely right, sir, and the police are handling that end. The reason we were called in to assist is that matters of security could be involved.'

'Security? What're we talking about? Industrial espionage?'

'I wouldn't like to speculate at this point,' Pearson said.

'It would surprise me if his company had anything worth stealing in this day and age. He didn't have any defence contracts as far as I know. Are you implying that he was mixed up in something else?'

'I wouldn't imply anything, sir, until we've got much further.'

'You've really shocked me, you know. I take it that what you've told me is not common knowledge?'

'I'd appreciate you treating it in confidence for the time being, yes. For the sake of his family as much as anything else.'

'Are they in the picture?'

'Not entirely.'

'I must write to his widow. Meant to do it before.' Charters went to his desk and scribbled a reminder. 'Only wish I could be more helpful. God, we live in strange times, don't we?'

'We certainly do, sir.' Pearson extinguished his cigarette and got to his feet. 'Thank you for your time and I'm sorry I gave you a shock.'

He paused in front of one of the paintings depicting small boats in a fishing harbour as he went towards the door. 'You've got some very nice paintings. I particularly like this. Who's it by?'

'Kit Wood,' Charters said. 'He died young unfortunately. Yes, it's very pleasant. Bought it years ago.'

'I wish I knew more about painting. This reminds me of Devon where I was evacuated during the war. That all seems another world now. Life was a lot simpler in many ways. Were you an evacuee yourself?' he added, still studying the painting.

'Yes, I was. Didn't end up anywhere as nice as Devon though. I got shunted down to Swindon.'

'They pushed us all over the place, didn't they? The war changed a lot of lives, mine included. I lost both my parents in the Blitz.'

'Likewise,' Charters said.

'In London?'

'Yes.'

'We're both orphans of the storm then. Well, thank you once again, Sir Raymond.'

They shook hands and Pearson was halfway out of the door when he paused. 'There was just one other thing. Does the name Carstairs mean anything to you?'

Charters's face did not alter. 'Carstairs? Carstairs?' he repeated. 'Can't say it does. Should it?'

'Only that his name cropped up in connection with this affair. I thought possibly it might ring a bell. As you said, you businessmen of a feather tend to frequent the same watering holes. It was just a thought.'

The moment Pearson had left the room Charters dialled a number.

'What're you playing at?' he said angrily when the line was answered. He listened for a few seconds, then interrupted with, 'I couldn't care less about your problems. Just get these people off my back.'

. . .

'Did you ever stop to consider that we're not the romantic heroes of fiction?' Hillsden said. 'I'll tell you what our fiction is: it's tales told to idiots about little men serving little causes, just expendable pawns out in a no-man's land between two sets of barbarians, minor players in a game we didn't start, half the time don't understand and which most of us will never live to finish. If I had my time over again, I wouldn't waste my life on it.'

'You realise that sort of dialogue could condemn you as a bad risk,' Swanson replied.

'Then do me a favour, have me reclassified. I was condemned long ago.'

'Yes, I keep forgetting that . . . But right now you're an invaluable member of the team. Tell me about this man you saw with Fadiman in Grosvenor House – that interests me. Had you ever seen him before?'

'Not that I can recall.'

'Would you recognise him again?'

'I think so.'

'Why were you in Grosvenor House?'

Caution determined Hillsden's answer. 'I'm an insurance agent, remember? One of the enquiries we got was from a character who runs a car-hire business in Manchester who wanted us to quote for a fleet of Rovers.'

'Somebody connected with Fadiman?'

'Could have been. But he didn't keep the appointment.

355

What I don't understand is why we haven't pulled in this Harry character.'

'I prefer the waiting game,' Swanson said with no change of expression. 'There's more to be gained by letting them think we're still in the dark.'

'Think? I thought we were,' Hillsden said.

. . .

'Back again?' Harrison said.

'Let me see the Kell files for 1939 and '40 again.'

'You writing the old bugger's biography, or something?' Harrison asked. 'You're the second one who's asked for them in the space of a week. The bloody things gather dust for fifty years, suddenly they're on the best-seller list.'

Pearson kept the surprise out of his face and voice. 'Who was that?'

'No idea. I was off sick. Our Ethel would know. I'll ask her.'

'Well, it's not important. I only wanted those two particular years, if you'd be kind enough to get them for me. And I wouldn't say no to another cup of your freshly ground Colombian. That went down a treat last time. Gave me a kick-start.'

'Oh, good, I've made a convert, have I?' Harrison looked gratified that his expert knowledge of the bean had been recognised. 'The secret is to keep them in the fridge until you need them. It brings out the flavour. To my mind the aroma of fresh coffee is intensely erotic. You don't take sugar, do you?'

'No, haven't you noticed, I'm sweet enough?' Pearson said and was ashamed of having said it, but the news had rattled him.

It was too much of a coincidence, he thought, as Harrison shuffled away. Even without being told, it had been obvious from his first visit that the files had remained untouched for half a century, lying dormant there like some Dead Sea Scrolls. Why the sudden interest immediately following his own enquiry? Giving himself time to think before Harrison returned, he reached for his cigarettes, then remembered smoking was no longer permitted in Archives. Authority was needed by anybody outside the Firm before they were allowed to examine classified information, and for some pointless reason the Kell material had always been regarded as ultra-sensitive. Probably, he thought, because in the wrong hands they could confirm the utter uselessness of most of the collected information – from Sarajevo to the Somme, to Munich, many of the guesses had been disastrous, setting the pattern for disasters to come.

Harrison returned empty-handed. 'Well, I'm sorry, but you're out of luck, Commander,' he said. 'The two years you wanted are out. Any others interest you?'

'Not at the moment,' Pearson said, getting up. 'I'll come back on another day.'

'Oh, aren't you going to wait for your coffee?' Harrison said, aggrieved.

'No, just been called on my bleeper,' Pearson said. 'Thanks all the same.'

'Oh, what a pity, I've got the kettle on.' But Pearson had already gone. On his way out, he stopped in at Ethel's cubbyhole. With her immaculate starched blouse and severely neat hair, Ethel brought to mind the days when hospital matrons ruled the roost, and indeed there was a sterilised air to her office: nothing was ever out of place. Although forced reluctantly to accept the electronic age, she still considered her own filing system, compiled over the thirty years or more she had been a fixture in Archives, to be superior. The computer, like the absence of men in her life, was merely another cross she bore with fortitude.

'Ethel, my darling,' Pearson said, 'if you'll forgive my blatant sexual harassment so early in the day . . . those Kell files. How long are they likely to be out?'

'I've no idea, Commander. They didn't say.'

'Well, it's not that vital. Who took them, by the way?'

'Somebody from your lot,' Ethel said. She flicked a large Rotadex. 'Young Mr Hadley.'

'Ah! Hadley,' Pearson said. 'That explains it. I'll get them from him. May I say, you're looking radiant this morning, Ethel. You must have a new lover.'

'Really, Commander, whatever next? The things you come out with.' Her hand fluttered to the small locket around her neck, but as she watched him go she thought, always such a gentleman, unlike some. She reached down below her desk and took a small compact out of her handbag and powdered her nose, her morning made.

40

LINKS IN THE CHAIN

'Rotherby, you belong to the London Library, don't you?' Pearson said.

'I certainly do. Best library in existence.'

'Well, in that case, could you do me a small favour? I'm trying to trace something and our records are very sparse on a certain subject.'

'What subject's that?'

'The history of 18b. Well, actually, anything to do with the emergence of the British Union.'

'Battle of Cable Street and so forth?'

'Yes, but with particular reference to 18b.'

'I'll go today.'

Pearson lingered a moment longer. 'That a picture of your cat?' he said, pointing to a photograph on Rotherby's desk of a grossly overweight Persian that resembled a furry Buddha.

'Yes, that's Mr Pooter. The wife was maniacally doggie, but I was never keen myself, much prefer the pussies. Fastidious, fascinating creatures, altogether superior to dogs. Cleaner habits all round. I read somewhere that two thousand tons of dog poo is left on London streets every day.'

'I've stepped in half of it,' Pearson said as he departed again.

. . .

The call Harry expected came after midnight and he recognised the voice immediately. He listened, smiling, as he was told a name.

'When?' he asked.

'I leave that to you. The sooner the better,' the voice said. 'But vary it this time. Your trademark is becoming too familiar.'

'Understood.'

The line went dead.

. . .

'Run an errand for me,' Pearson said. 'Go ask Hadley if he's finished with the Kell files.'

'Why don't you just ring him?' Lloyd said. 'He was at his desk when I went past just now.'

'I have my reasons.'

Lloyd went into his Watson impersonation. 'What a man of mystery you've become, Holmes.'

'Just tell me what he says.'

When Lloyd left the room, Pearson stared down at the four volumes Rotherby had obtained from the London Library. They had not provided the information he was looking for. Reaching for the phone, he dialled Scotland Yard and asked for Gilbert.

'Archie, you thought I'd forgotten, right?'

'Forgotten what?'

'That I owe you a dinner. How about tonight?'

'What's the catch?'

'No catch. God, life has really soured you. You did us a good turn over Carstairs's suicide, remember? I like to pay my debts.'

'I can't tonight.'

'Okay, then pick another day.'

'Is it just you and me, stag?'

'No, doesn't have to be. My treat, let's include the wives.

360

Amaze them.'

'We could do Saturday.'

'Saturday it is. I'll make the booking and let you know.'

'Well, thanks, sorry I jumped to the wrong conclusion.'

'Story of your life, Archie, that's why so many crimes go unsolved. By the way, how good are the Yard's wartime files?'

'I knew it, I knew it,' Gilbert said. 'You didn't ring just to invite me out to dinner, you crafty sod.'

'What d'you mean, we've just made a date.'

'Come on, don't give me that. What d'you want?'

'I may be on a false trail, but you know me, if I'm chasing a fox, I've got to run it to earth. I need to find out details of 18b detainees. From the little I've been able to discover, we didn't handle the arrests, that was left to Special Branch. D'you have any idea whether those files still exist?'

'Come over and take an unofficial look.'

'Archie, you're a prince.'

'That dinner had better be good.'

'You can order à la carte, not the set menu, how's that?'

'Drop dead, George.'

. . .

Examining the Yard's files, Pearson was astounded by many of the names and cases documented. It was no surprise to find all the prominent members of the British Union, but the inclusion of others such as a masseuse from Elizabeth Arden smacked more of hysteria than any considered effort to safeguard national security; it seemed highly improbable that such a motley collection, unarmed, unorganised and having no discernible relationship with each other, could have presented any real threat.

Pearson knew what he *had* to find if his supposition was to prove correct, but after two fruitless hours he began to feel that once again he would go away empty-handed. Rather than admit defeat, he concentrated on that week in May 1940 when the new powers had first been used, looking for cross-references of detainees sharing the same name. It was during this second search that he singled out a family named Hain who had been arrested in Albemarle Street, London, on May 23rd. A footnote indicated that Hain and his wife had both died within a month of each other. Against Hain's name the word 'suicide' was appended in red ink. The fate of their child was not given, there was merely a notation that he had been taken into care by an official of the Westminster Council on May 27th 1940. Pearson took copies of all the relevant entries, then left the Yard and returned to his office.

'So, what happened to you?' Lloyd questioned him. 'You ask me to run an errand, then disappear.'

Pearson brandished the Xerox copies. 'I'm getting close to Charters at last,' he said.

'Oh, God!' Lloyd said. 'Here we go again.'

'Just read these,' Pearson pushed the Xerox copies at him.

When he'd finished, Lloyd looked up, unimpressed. 'So? A family called Hain. Where does Charters come into the reckoning?'

'I think he was the son, that Hain was his given name. I traced a connection that led me first to Swindon and then to Yeovil down in Somerset. If I'm right, Charters was born Hain, the only son of Carl Hain, described there as an art dealer and listed as a Nazi supporter. The parents were both arrested under 18b shortly after the fall of France, then both died within a very short space of time afterwards, Hain committing suicide as you can see from the footnote.'

'Yeah, okay, well?'

'Well, you remember that, significantly, Charters's entry in *Who's Who* omits his parentage.'

'So what? Most people doctor their entries. Women always omit their real ages if they can get away with it.'

'Wait, hear me out. I traced a surviving member of the

genuine Charters clan to Yeovil and this guy told me his parents had taken in various evacuees during the war, including an orphan boy he only remembered as Carl. They lived in Swindon at the time. Subsequently, this Carl took their name, left his foster home at the end of the war and they never heard from him again. When I went to see Charters ostensibly enquiring about Lord Miller's death, I got him to admit that he was an evacuee . . . And guess where? Swindon! You have to admit the facts start to slot together. Tell me you're impressed for once.'

'Yeah,' Lloyd said reluctantly, 'you're beginning to make a case.'

'You perverse bastard, is that all you can say?'

'It still contains a strong element of the coincidental.'

'Well, think back, how did Charters come into our reckoning? Carstairs's suicide, yes? And, okay, coincidence, but men have been hanged for less. Then ask yourself what was Carstairs doing in Copenhagen. Tracking down the source of all that Fascist literature flooding into the country, right? Who owns printing presses on the Continent? Friend Charters. Who's well-heeled enough to be payrolling Fadiman and company? Charters again. And we know that both Carstairs and Van Elst were on somebody's payroll, getting regular sums from Luxembourg. I checked with the CAA, Charters's private jet logged eleven flights to Luxembourg in the past eight months.'

'My, you have been a busy little beaver. The big question mark is how d'you prove Charters was once an evacuee named Carl? So he changed his name. Big deal. So did Cary Grant. It's not a criminal offence. Give me a motive.'

'It's staring you in the face. Revenge. Parents arrested under notorious wartime legislation, imprisoned without trial, and both died in prison. Years later orphaned son decides to get even.'

Lloyd grimaced. 'Is that why you were so keen to see the Kell files?'

'God! I'd forgotten them. What did Hadley say? Why did he want them?'

'He didn't', Lloyd said. 'Swanson asked for them.'

They looked at each other.

41

A DEATH IN THE FAMILY

'What do you think?' Abramov said as he gunned the new Lexus from the slip road on to the motorway, the needle moving effortlessly to seventy-five as they headed for Suffolk.

'I don't have your thing about cars, Victor. All I care about is whether they start when I turn the key,' Hillsden replied.

'When I ship this home, it'll sell in a flash.'

'If it's so good why would you sell it?'

'Because I'll treble my money. You're no businessman like me.'

'Is that what brought you over here, to buy a car?'

'No, I'm looking at property. You've no idea how much Russian money is pouring into your impoverished country. A lot of it being washed, of course, but I'm clean, a legitimate capitalist at last. We always said we'd take you with our bare hands.'

'Don't tell me you're going to buy a grouse moor and wear tweeds? I somehow don't see you playing the lord of the manor.'

'Why not?'

'Because you'd be bored stiff.'

'How's Galina? Is she bored stiff?'

The question touched a raw nerve and Hillsden edged around it. 'I think she hasn't found it easy.'

'And how about your little daughter?'

'She's settled in better than I expected. In fact, she's staying with a little friend tonight.'

'And you? How does it feel to be back in harness? Is it like the old days?'

'Same chessboard, different players. I hope you've still got my insurance policy in a safe place.'

'Of course. Listen. I know you turned me down before, but once you've fulfilled your part of the bargain here, let me cut you in on my operation. I'm making so much money it scares me. I can't spend it fast enough. And I want to widen my business, because I don't intend to be trapped in Russia when the next *coup* comes. And believe me, it will come. Think about it.'

After a pause, Hillsden said: 'Maybe I'm not that ambitious. If I survive this one, we've got enough to live the way I want.'

The Lexus made little sound as it drove down Walsham le Willows's deserted main street and turned off into the long lane leading to the house. As they approached they could see lights burning in Audrey's annexe but curiously the house itself was in darkness.

Victor got out and stood savouring the clean air. 'It's so quiet out here,' he said.

'Yes, took some getting used to at first.'

But as Abramov collected the gifts he had brought for Galina and Lara, Hillsden became conscious that the stillness had a different quality from usual. Normally he would have expected to hear Audrey's radio – she seldom switched it off, saying that although she didn't listen all the time, she liked the background sound for company – but that night it was missing, although he noticed that the door to her annexe was ajar. He led the way towards the house and called out to let Galina know they had arrived. There was no response. The fact that there were no lights on anywhere puzzled him.

'Where is everybody?' he said. Above him in the chestnut tree the rooks answered him with a rustling of wings. He turned the handle on the front door but it was locked, and he found he didn't have his key.

'Darling?' he shouted. 'Hello . . . We're here.'

They waited, but again there was no response.

'Sorry about this,' he said to Victor. 'Not much of a welcome. Let me go find out where they are.'

He went towards the half-open doorway of the annexe. 'Audrey, you there?' It was at that moment that he knew with absolute certainty that something was horribly wrong. He pushed the door wide open and saw that the room had been trashed, the furniture overturned, lamps and Audrey's collection of china ornaments smashed. He went no further, but called Victor, at the same time giving him a cautionary gesture.

Victor put the parcels on the bonnet of the Lexus and joined him.

'Something wrong?'

'Take a look.'

'Jesus!' Victor said in the open doorway. 'Have you got a gun?'

Hillsden nodded and produced it. He motioned for Victor to accompany him and together they walked to the rear of the cottage. There they found the kitchen door open and could smell burning. Reaching inside, Hillsden felt for the light switch. As the light came on the first thing they both saw was Audrey's dead body. She was lying face upwards at a right-angle to the Aga cooker. There was an acrid smell originating from a saucepan on the Aga which had burnt dry and close to her body another, smaller saucepan that had contained a sauce; the contents had spilled in a pool close to Audrey's head and at first they mistook it for blood. Hillsden knelt to examine her and could find no wounds, but from the bruising circling her neck there appeared little doubt that she had been strangled. From her position, Hillsden's immediate thought was that she must have been taken from behind.

Finding a torch on one of the kitchen shelves, Hillsden led the way as they cautiously approached the living room. Switching on another light they saw that apparently nothing had been disturbed here. Continuing to the stairwell they climbed to the first floor, pausing on the landing to listen for any sounds that somebody was still in the house. All was quiet, too quiet. The door to his and Galina's bedroom was wide open, the room beyond in darkness. Hillsden edged to one side of the door, silently indicating to Victor to move to the other side. He shone his torch around the room but could see nothing untoward.

'Galina?' he said softly. 'Darling? It's okay, it's only me and Victor.'

Getting no answer, he steeled himself to go inside the room. Everything was undisturbed, the bed made, nothing out of place. He handed his gun to Victor. 'You have it,' he said. 'You're more useful with them than I am.'

They checked the bathroom, all the closets and Lara's room, but found nothing, eventually going downstairs again and conducting a more thorough search there, including the garage where they found both cars but still no sign of Galina.

'Let's look around the garden,' Victor said.

Using the torch, they first scanned the area around the house before moving to the large patch of lawn and shrubbery at the rear. There was a lean-to greenhouse at the end of the garden, with a number of panes of glass missing. Hillsden had intended to repair it but had never found the time. The previous owner had given the glass a wash of paint to reduce the heat during the hot summer months. A grapevine had once flourished inside, but now only a few dead tentacles poked through the holes. One of the hinges on the door had rusted and the door hung at an angle.

Hillsden and Victor approached the greenhouse from opposite ends, and while Hillsden shone his torch through a broken pane, Victor, gun in hand, pulled the door open so that he could enter. The torchlight beam swept across the dusty wooden staging, taking in a galvanised watering can and a collection of earthenware pots containing withered plants. Hillsden angled the beam downwards and it was then that he saw part of Galina's body under the staging at the blind end.

Hillsden thought: 'Oh, God, don't let her be dead, not that.'

He said as calmly as he could, 'Darling, it's me, don't be afraid, you're safe now.' And as he spoke he saw a movement and a moment later her face came into view, streaked with dirt, her hair cobwebbed. Victor went forward to help her up and bring her to Hillsden at the door. She clung to her husband without being able to speak.

'It's okay, it's okay,' he soothed. 'All over.' He carried her up the garden and round to the front of the house to Victor's car. Once there, he put her into the back seat and got in beside her, cradling her in his arms. Her whole body shook against him, attacked by a sudden ague. Victor opened one of the parcels he had left on the bonnet and took out a bottle of malt whisky.

'Let her have a sip of this.'

Hillsden held the bottle to Galina's lips. 'Just take a little, sweetheart, it'll warm you.' Then to Victor, 'See if you can find a rug or a blanket inside.' While Victor went to search, Hillsden massaged her cold hands, all the time murmuring words of comfort, but it was some time before she stopped shuddering. The first thing she said as she came out of shock was, 'Audrey, where's Audrey?'

'Don't worry about Audrey, she's fine,' he lied. 'When you're able, tell me something of what happened. But take your time, there's no hurry, everything's all right now.' He offered the bottle of whisky again, but she waved it away.

'I was outside,' she began, 'getting some herbs for the dinner, when I heard a car. I thought it was you . . . and . . . and I was just about . . . just about to come back to the house . . . when I heard Audrey cry out . . .' She stopped and the tears came, damming her breath.

'Take your time,' Hillsden repeated. He wiped some of the dirt from her cheeks with a handkerchief. Victor returned with a blanket and between them they tucked it around her.

'I stopped halfway,' Galina said when she was able to get her breath again. 'Then there were lots of crashes, things breaking . . . and the radio, Audrey's radio, that suddenly stopped. And after that it went quiet . . . something warned me not to call out . . . I just crouched down on the path . . . and in the light from Audrey's window, I saw a man come round the corner of the house and I lay flat and didn't move . . . When he disappeared again, I crawled to the greenhouse and hid myself in there. I was so frightened.'

Hillsden said, 'How long ago was this?'

'I don't know. An hour maybe. It seemed for ever.'

'Then did he drive away?'

'I don't know.'

Hillsden and Victor looked at each other across her.

'Where's Audrey, what happened to her?'

'She's okay, just resting like you,' Hillsden lied again.

'She's dead, isn't she? I know she's dead, you're just saying that.' For the first time she became aware of Victor, turning to stare at him, not making the connection.

'Hello, Galina,' Victor said, smiling.

'It's Victor, darling. Remember?'

'Oh, Victor . . . yes,' Galina said, then returned to the thought uppermost in her mind: 'The man did something to Audrey, didn't he?' Galina said, more insistent now that she was recovering.

'No. He just trashed the place. Burglars always do that if they can't find anything worth stealing. I think the best thing is to get you away from here. Victor will drive you to London, won't you Victor?'

'Sure.'

'I don't want to go to London.'

'Listen. Listen. I'll stay here and take care of Audrey, then I'll collect Lara from her friend's and we'll all spend the night in Victor's hotel. I can pack some clothes and overnight things for you both and bring them up with me.'

He hoped he had persuaded her, but she wasn't having it.

'What d'you mean, you'll take care of Audrey? Tell me the truth.'

'I am telling you the truth. Audrey's like you, she had a shock.'

'Then why isn't she with us?'

370

'Darling, just do as I suggest, be a good girl. The important thing right now is to get you away and into bed somewhere you'll feel safe. You know Victor, and you know he'll look after you until I get there. Right, Victor?'

'Absolutely.'

He seemed to have persuaded her at last.

'You promise you'll bring Lara?'

'Of course I will. I'll join you as soon as I can.' He kissed her, then eased himself out of the back seat. As he and Victor met by the driver's door, Victor slipped him the gun which he quickly slid into a pocket. 'Can you remember the way back?'

'Yes, I think so.'

'Just keep straight on out of the village. About two miles and you'll hit a main road. Make a left and you'll pick up the signs to the motorway. Go south.'

'South.'

Hillsden gave Galina a last look; her eyes were closed, but her face was still taut. He watched the Lexus until it was out of sight, then went into the house to do all the things that needed to be done quickly. The first thing was to call Rotherby. The line was busy when he dialled it, but he had the operator interrupt for an emergency. A concerned Rotherby finally answered.

'Don't ask questions, Colonel, just listen. We've had some bad news here in Suffolk. Poor Audrey's met with a fatal accident and I'm going to need help. Get Pearson down here and tell him that it's something Hogg will have to deal with. Got that?'

'Right. You want me, too?'

'Yes, because you know the way.'

'Anybody else hurt?'

'No, thank God. Don't waste time talking, just get here.'

When he put down the phone he steeled himself to go back into the kitchen. Avoiding the pool of sauce, he knelt beside Audrey again and gently closed her staring eyes. Then he made a careful search of the surroundings in the hope that he might find some clue, but whoever had killed her had left nothing that was obvious. After securing all the downstairs doors and windows and drawing the curtains, he went up to the bedrooms to pack toiletries and clothes for Galina and Lara. He had a last look around their own bedroom, wondering if he would ever see it again. Afterwards he went down into the living room, poured himself a stiff whisky, turned out the lights and with the gun close to hand, settled down to wait for help to arrive.

The house was still, but, from across the fields, he heard a vixen scream.

. . .

Three hours later, he was still sitting in the darkness going over all the possible permutations of what lay ahead, when the headlights of two cars briefly pierced the drawn curtains. Opening the front door he saw Pearson coming towards him, followed by Lloyd and Rotherby.

'You did well, made good time,' he said.

'The roads are deserted at this time of night. What've we got?' Pearson asked as Hillsden led them inside the house to the kitchen. The three arrivals stared down at Audrey's body.

'She didn't deserve that,' Pearson said. 'She was a trooper, our Audrey. One of a kind.'

'The best,' Rotherby agreed softly.

Lloyd and Pearson went closer to the body. 'Looks as though they used rope,' Lloyd said. 'Wire would have cut into the neck.'

'He,' Hillsden corrected. 'According to Galina there was only one.'

'The wife's okay, though?'

'She hid herself in the garden, thank God, and fortunately our daughter is away, staying with a friend. I had Galina taken to London.' He became conscious that he had stopped using their phoney names.

'What's that mean?' Pearson asked.

'A friend took her.' Then seeing the blank looks: 'I drove down here with a friend we'd invited to dinner.'

'Don't scare me,' Pearson said. 'What sort of friend?'

'Somebody I got to know in Russia.'

'A Russian?'

'Yes.'

'Oh, great, that's all we need with this mess. How could you bring a Russian down here?'

'Don't panic. If you must know, he ran me there, but he's out of the game now, and I'd trust him with anything. We both know each other's secrets.'

Pearson looked very dubious.

'George, I promise you, he's okay.'

'He'd better be. We're in deep enough shit as it is. You didn't ring the police?'

'No. The only call I made was to the Colonel here. What do we do about the police?'

'Nothing. We deal with this ourselves.'

I've been away so long, Hillsden thought, I'd almost forgotten that the Firm is a law unto itself when it comes to protecting its own interests.

'The urgent thing is to get things cleaned up and get out of here,' Pearson continued. 'Apart from this room, where else did he go?'

'He turned over Audrey's annexe, presumably to make it look like a burglary.'

'Nowhere else?'

'No. I've checked. The rest of the house wasn't disturbed.'

'Right, well you and Rotherby take care of her place while we do what's needed in here.' He turned to Lloyd. 'Back your car up as close as you can to the door, and fetch in the necessary.'

By the time Hillsden and Rotherby came back Audrey's corpse had been put into a body bag and the kitchen made tidy. 'Lucky we didn't have any blood to deal with,' Lloyd said. 'We don't want any DNA tests coming back to haunt us.'

Between them they carried the bagged body and put it on the back seat of Pearson's car, then covered it with a blanket.

'Let's make one last check,' Pearson said, 'because you and the family are not coming back.' He registered Hillsden's quick look of concern. 'This place is history.'

'I agree,' Hillsden said, 'but I'm wondering how best to deal with that. We'll have to have some story for the village. The neighbours are not unduly nosey, but they're bound to wonder why we did a moonlight flit.'

'No problem. Tomorrow you ring a couple of the local stores and tell them your firm's relocated you suddenly and you're having to put the house up for sale. Cancel the newspapers and milk. Happens all the time. We'll make sure the furniture and the rest of your belongings are removed.'

Hillsden still looked dubious. 'Somebody will have to notify Laura's school as well.'

'Fine, whatever's necessary will be done,' Pearson said, a note of irritation creeping into his voice.

'It's not just me, remember. I have a wife and child to think about. Where they're going to be dumped next.'

'We'll decide that in the morning, just get out of here. You and Rothers make a last check before you go.'

He drove off, with Lloyd following in Audrey's car.

'Never seen him edgy like that,' Rotherby said.

'No. Easy for him. I've still got to concoct some story for Laura when I collect her . . . How do you explain any of this to a child?'

They went back into the house and made sure nothing had been overlooked. Hillsden collected a few more personal belongings, including the doll Rotherby had given Lara the night they had arrived in England. Then he switched off everything and locked up.

'You get off,' Hillsden said. He stood and watched Rotherby drive away, then turned and had a last look at the house, trying to collect his thoughts and frame the right

words to say to Lara before he, too, left for the last time.

When the disturbed rooks had settled, the night was still again.

42

SHADOW BOXING

Hillsden woke after a few hours' fitful sleep. It was some moments before he could relate to where he was, taking in the unfamiliar wallpaper, a different lamp and telephone on the bedside table, furniture that he did not recognise. The bed he found himself in, that was strange too, larger, softer, with white linen sheets. He turned his head, for a moment totally disorientated, then, as he saw Galina curled and sleeping beside him, his fogged mind began to clear. There was also a single bed in the room with Lara asleep in it and he remembered that Victor had arranged for this knowing that the child would not want to wake in an alien hotel room and find herself alone. Victor, he now recalled, had taken care of everything, somehow achieving what Hillsden had been dreading – breaking the news of the murder to Galina.

He became aware of a faint rumble of traffic, again odd after the silence of the house in Walsham le Willows. He looked at his watch and found that it had gone ten o'clock. Not wanting to wake Galina and the child, he padded to the bathroom and closed the door. The marble floor struck cold on his bare feet as he stood and urinated. There was a telephone on the wall adjacent to the toilet and when he had sluiced his hands and face in cold water, he rang the operator and asked to be connected to Victor's room.

'Oh, good, I was afraid you might have gone out,' he said when Victor answered.

'No, I deliberately stayed in my room until you called.'

'Thanks so much for all you did last night.'

'Listen, what are friends for? Are they both okay?'

'They're still asleep. The other thing I have to thank you for is telling Galina about Audrey. I wasn't looking forward to that.'

'Well, she kept asking me. I guess in her heart she knew the truth, so in the end I told her. She cried at first, but we sat talking – in Russian as a matter of fact, we slipped back into that – and I gradually calmed her.'

'Victor, I can't thank you enough. You must let me know what I owe you for the room.'

'Forget it, all taken care of. I love any excuse to use my new American Express card. I feel like the man in the TV ads.'

'Well, I have to ask you another favour. Can you look after them today until I've sorted things out?'

'Sure, no problem. Tell Galina to ring me when she's ready, I'll be here.'

Hillsden hung up and went back into the bedroom. Galina was now awake, although Lara hadn't stirred.

She whispered: 'Oh, darling, I thought you'd gone without saying anything.'

'As if I'd do that.' He sat on the side of the bed and she clung to him.

'I imagined I'd dreamed it all until I woke up in this room.'

'I know.'

'Poor Audrey,' Galina said, and cried silently. Hillsden held her close and let her cry. 'What's going to happen to us?'

'I'll deal with everything as soon as I can. You're quite safe here and Victor's waiting in his room for you to call him. How will you explain it to Lara when she wakes up?'

'I'll tell her you've decided to give us all a treat. Children don't question those things.'

Hillsden gently eased himself out of her embrace. 'Here,' he picked up the room service menu and gave it to her. 'Order the works, spoil yourself for once.'

'We won't have to go back there, will we?'

'No,' Hillsden said and kissed her. 'That's over.' He left the room, closing the door quietly.

. . .

Pearson said: 'Are we agreed then that Alec's cover is blown?'

'No. Why d'you say that?' Swanson sounded edgy. He frequently sounded edgy these days and was quick to take offence. He went to the window and made a show of examining his bonsai tree, prodding the soil around the small trunk.

'Audrey was murdered last night. You don't imagine they were just after Audrey, do you?'

'I'm keeping an open mind.' He poured a small amount of water around the base of the tree from a bottle he kept for this purpose. 'Unlike some, I don't jump to immediate conclusions, and I'd remind you I'm running Hillsden, not you.' Now, he fiddled with his wrist-watch strap and Pearson noticed the watch was one he hadn't seen before, an expensive chronometer, the type that showed the date, phases of the moon and God knows what else. 'It's always possible the unfortunate woman surprised a burglar and was killed as a result. That's a familiar occurrence these days, they've got nothing to lose since the death penalty was abolished. Violence isn't confined to the inner cities, in fact research shows people are just as likely to be attacked in out of the way villages.'

'If it was just a burglar, how come nothing was stolen?'

'Was there anything *worth* stealing? You say her room was trashed, which rather proves my point. It's another well-known fact that thieves smash up everything if they discover they're going to go away empty-handed. I'm told they often defecate in beds, like dogs marking their territory.'

Pearson and Lloyd exchanged looks.

'I think it would be fatal to make a hasty decision on Hillsden,' Swanson continued. 'Wait and see what their next move is.'

'We're playing with his life,' Pearson said, the image of Audrey's sprawled body in front of the Aga still vivid in his mind.

'He knew the risks when he took the job. It's what he's getting paid for.'

'And what happens about poor Audrey?'

'Already taken care of. Cremation, tomorrow, before questions are asked. Fortunately, she didn't have family. It was thought best to deal with it as though she died of natural causes.'

'How does that fit in with your other theory?'

'Meaning?'

'Meaning, if she was murdered by some casual intruder, shouldn't the police be looking for her killer?'

'The police won't be looking for anybody,' Swanson said at his blandest, fingering a small shaving nick on the side of his usually immaculate face. 'You played a part in that, by acting as you did and removing all traces. What you don't seem to appreciate is that there is a great deal more at stake than the regrettable murder of one minor operative.'

'Oh, I do appreciate that,' Pearson answered, the sarcasm unconcealed. 'It's always good to know that the Firm hasn't lost its touch in dealing with embarrassments. It's something we can all look forward to, should we meet with an accident.'

Before Swanson could frame a reply, the light on his scrambler phone started to blink. He picked up and immediately said: 'Ah, Alec, I'm glad you contacted me. We were just talking about you . . . Yes, awful, she'll be sadly missed.' His eyes flicked to Pearson as he said this. 'Everything's been taken care of, have no worries on that score, there'll be no comebacks where you're concerned, that episode is finished . . . They have? When? . . . That's very interesting. It bears out what I believe. I'm firmly of the opinion that last night's events had no connection. I think it's important you make the meeting . . . No, I disagree . . . I share your concern for your family's safety . . . but not to go to the meeting would leave us in the dark as to their future intentions. If they're planning a reply to Sonntag's death, it's vital we find out what . . . We need all the help we can get at this stage and you're the only one we have on the inside track . . . You have my word, the family will be taken care of . . .' Now he listened again. 'I'm sorry, no, we can't abort the operation on what I consider is speculation and not proven . . . I have to insist . . . What condition?' He listened, frowning. 'Well, that may be difficult, but I'll try. I can't promise, of course, you know how sticky the Yanks are . . . But I'll keep my side of the bargain if you do likewise. Good. I'll wait to hear from you.'

He replaced the receiver. 'Fadiman has contacted him and wants a meeting. I consider that a good sign.'

'A good sign?' Pearson said.

'Yes.'

'Unless they intend to make sure of him this time. Having failed last night.'

'Are you saying he shouldn't go to the meeting?'

'Well, we can't let him go in unprotected. Where is the meeting?'

'At Fadiman's place.'

'When?'

'Tomorrow night.'

'Then we'd better make arrangements to be around.'

Swanson's face clouded again. 'What d'you mean by "around"?'

'Close by. Let him go in wired with a panic button.'

'That's a risk.'

'The whole bloody thing's a risk. We should have moved in on them long ago. Leaving Fadiman aside, we've got enough circumstantial evidence on Charters for me to have another go at him.'

'I didn't take kindly to you seeing him the first time without my knowledge,' Swanson said airily.

'I thought we were a team working for the same end.'

'A team with me at the head.'

'Okay, I chalked up a black, but that doesn't alter the fact that I believe I can make a case against him.'

'And if you're wrong,' Swanson said with real venom, 'he'll have a case against us. I would remind you that I'm answerable to the PM himself if this operation self-destructs. You may be near retirement, but I'm not.'

Lloyd stepped in before the dialogue became more heated. 'Can I ask what else Hillsden was saying about his family?'

'He wants them out of harm's way, otherwise he won't go along.'

'And you agreed to that?'

'I agreed to think about it.'

It was Pearson's turn to harden his voice. 'No, you agreed to it, I heard you.'

'Then you also heard me say it would be difficult to implement his request.'

'And what was his request?'

'He wants them to be sent out of the country, to the States, under the witness protection scheme.'

'Why not?'

'Again, it may be against policy.' Swanson fingered the tiny scab on his face and it started to bleed again. He went to his desk and took out a tissue, dabbed it and examined the stain.

'I don't see why the Yanks wouldn't agree to that. They owe us a couple of favours.'

'Cost,' Swanson said. 'Who pays? One can't expect the American taxpayer to take in our lodgers.'

'Oh, bull! You think the American taxpayer gets a monthly audit of everything Langley spends?' He turned away motioning Lloyd to follow him as he moved to the door. 'You concentrate on policy. I'll concentrate on protecting Hillsden.'

Once outside the office he slammed his fist into his palm. 'What is it with Swanson?'

'You questioned his judgement.'

'What judgement? He hasn't made any. You know his game-plan? He's desperate for the old blade on his shoulder, so he's going to kiss arse all the way to Downing

Street and back.'
'So, what's new?' Lloyd said.

43

ARRIVALS AND DEPARTURES

It was unusual for a London taxi to be seen in the small Oxfordshire village of North Stoke, which was more accustomed to Land Rovers and Mercedes estates, but late that evening one drew up outside the closed gates of Sir Raymond Charters's listed Grade II Queen Anne mansion. Harry got out and spoke into the entry-phone. A moment later, the gates swung open and he drove inside and parked alongside a number of other cars. Helped by Harry, Johnny manhandled Fadiman's chair up the flight of porch steps. The impressive front door had already been opened for them by a manservant who then took over and wheeled Fadiman inside.

He was trundled across a marble hallway past busts of Wagner and Nietzsche and conducted into one of the rooms at the rear of the house where a group of a dozen men were already assembled.

'Ah, Graham,' Charters said, coming forward to greet him. 'Sorry to drag you out at night, but I thought it was important for us all to meet. You know most of our comrades, of course, but we also have two new faces.' He singled out the newcomers. 'Charles Doyle from Belfast, and I'm particularly pleased to welcome Colin Adamson from Combat 18.' The introductions made, Fadiman nodded at Hyde and others he knew by sight.

Charters took the centre of the room and stared around. His eyes were clear to the point of blankness. In his own residence, surrounded by his own possessions, he had the assurance of a man who knows that money buys most things, especially people. 'I called this meeting,' he began, 'in order to update our strategy and regain the initiative. As you're all too aware, we recently suffered the loss of our distinguished German comrade, Gottfried Sonntag. Gottfried is dead, but his spirit and writings live on.' He paused to acknowledge the murmur of approval. 'He was murdered because we had an informer in our ranks. That informer was speedily detected and eliminated. Because we have a mole in position, our intelligence usually keeps us one step ahead, but we had not reckoned on the Jews, on Mossad. They were ruthless and clever, I give them that. Clever in the way the killing was carried out and clever, too, in the way they acted in collusion with the security forces to conceal the true facts. In the future, we must match that ruthlessness and cleverness.' He let this sink in before continuing.

'I am not somebody prepared endlessly to finance a lost cause. I have funded this organisation for the past three years and now I want a return on my money. Isolated acts, such as disposing of the odd Jew, killing a few ethnics and instigating riots in the ghettos have achieved very little. At best they have merely caused the authorities temporary concern. I want to explode their smug complacency, make them tremble in their beds. The example of the IRA struggle is before us. Violence pays. Violence makes the headlines. Violence means you are taken seriously. So, the time has come to put that example to work. That is the primary reason for bringing you here tonight. We have the money, and we have the brains . . .' Charters waved a hand towards Fadiman. 'Our chair-bound comrade has ample reason, as I have, to get even. Tonight, he will outline a brilliant plan which I am confident will change our destiny. He has studied the tactics used by allied organisations in America, Germany and Japan, and adapted them for our uses. We cannot establish a new political order with speeches. Like the Führer before me, I consider democratic politics a historical irrelevance. If the hour demands it, we must build a new order on corpses.'

He spoke in a terse, but modulated voice, making eye contact with his audience. If any of those present found his words melodramatic they showed no sign.

'No more pinpricks. We need to bring off something as big as Oklahoma and Tokyo, something that cannot be concealed and commands the attention of the world media. I shall not elaborate further, but hand over to the architect of the plan, Comrade Fadiman.'

He relinquished his position as Fadiman wheeled himself in front of the ornate fireplace.

'I don't know that I deserve full credit,' he began. 'As our leader has intimated, I have merely borrowed something old, something new from abroad. My real contribution was to zero in on a particular event that is due to take place very shortly. It is an event ideally suited to the purpose we have in mind and if we bring it off, as I am confident we will, it could change the course of history. Every year, the character of London, our capital city, is traduced and transformed by a celebration so repulsive that words fail me. It is that celebration that we intend to finish once and for all, and regain our national sovereignty . . .'

Outside, in the illuminated grounds, Harry and Johnny leaned against the bonnet of the taxi, enjoying a joint.

'Something big in the offing, right?' Johnny said.

'You said it.'

''Bout time.'

'Yeah. Look forward to a bit of real action for a change.'

. . .

When the briefing finished, Fadiman remained behind for a private meeting with Charters.

'You intend to use this man . . . remind me again of his name,' Charters said.

'Hillsden. But he goes under the name of Bartlett,

Robert Bartlett.'

'Is that a wise move? I thought he'd outlived his usefulness.'

'Not quite. By involving him directly one last time we achieve two things. First, we ensure that he becomes the prime culprit should -- God forbid – anything go wrong.'

'You say "God forbid", but what are the risks?'

'Negligible. Second, we need a courier, but once the things are safely delivered back here, he's expendable. He'll have served his purpose, as we always intended, and can then be eliminated. As you will recall, when I first came up with the idea, we needed somebody inside their network who would report to our mole, and at the same time protect our mole . . . It's worked very well so far.'

'Except they're smelling around, getting too close for my comfort. This man, Pearson, for example, hasn't been idle.'

'Well, Carstairs caused a problem, I admit. I was never happy about Carstairs, but you overruled me.'

'I wasn't to know he'd commit suicide. That started the whole investigation,' Charters said. 'You promised me Harry would take care of him.'

'And he would have done. It was just that Carstairs took matters into his own hands before Harry could get to him. Nobody could have foreseen that.'

'How far has this man Pearson gone?'

'We know that he's been down to the West country and questioned one member of your wartime foster family, but that produced very little.'

'But you reported he'd also been tracing back through the Kell files. That's the danger area.'

'Raymond, my dear, relax,' Fadiman said, lighting a fresh cigarette. 'That's a dead issue. The pertinent files, the ones concerning you, met with an unfortunate mishap and were inadvertently shredded. We have a safe pair of hands in the right place when they're needed. Where, if you will allow me to say so, I think you should be more careful is in some of your business pursuits. Forget going after Miller's old company.'

This was not to Charters's liking. 'It represents a very quick profit.'

'But what shall it profit a man if he gains Miller and loses the main prize?' Fadiman said unctuously.

'Perhaps you're right,' was the grudging response.

'I know I'm right in this instance. Always distance yourself. We are on the brink of a breakthrough.' His cigarette ash was just about to fall and Charters reached for an ashtray. 'Thank you. Tell me one thing, because I've never been quite certain. Is it just revenge that drives you on, or is it something more? I was taken by something you said tonight.'

'What was that?'

'About politics being an irrelevance. Surely, you don't really believe that? After all, when we come to power, won't you be seeking the ultimate office? I know I would, if I was in your place.'

Charters did not answer immediately. 'If there was no alternative, I would have to consider it seriously,' he said.

. . .

From the rear windows of the unmarked surveillance van, Pearson had an unrestricted view of Fadiman's house. He and Lloyd were in position early on the evening of the following day, equipped with cameras and state-of-the-art listening devices. Deliberately flouting Swanson's orders, Pearson had ensured that this time Hillsden went in wired: a minute, but highly efficient microphone and micro-transmitter had been built into the arms of Hillsden's spectacles.

Hillsden arrived outside the house by taxi shortly after nine o'clock and was admitted by Johnny. The watchers in the van had no idea whether there were others inside. They heard Hillsden say, 'I'm sorry I'm a little late. I had trouble getting a taxi,' and Johnny's uninterested response, 'Too bad,' as he conducted Hillsden into Fadiman's presence.

'Reception's good,' Pearson said as Fadiman greeted his

visitor with, 'You've recovered, I hope?'

'Recovered, sir?' Hillsden's voice sounded cautious.

'From that blow on the head you suffered for the cause.'

'Oh, that, yes. It wasn't anything too serious. The only after-effect was that my eyesight blurs from time to time. I shall have to get stronger glasses.'

'Good man,' Pearson muttered.

'Your first wound stripe, Robert,' Fadiman replied. 'You proved your worth. I flatter myself that I'm a good judge of character, and I was immediately taken by your positive attitude the first time we met. Did you know that?'

'Well, I hoped you were, yes.'

'Some of our flock are none too bright. We've made mistakes in the past . . . early on, when we were feeling our way. But you weren't one of them. I saw at once that you have a brain, Robert. That's what I was looking for. There is a time and place for brawn, and a time for guile.'

The expression struck a chord in Hillsden's memory and while he listened to Fadiman he strove to remember who had first said that to him.

'That's why,' Fadiman continued, 'I've brought you here tonight, to discuss a special mission. You're not married, are you, Robert?'

'Not any longer. My wife died.' He almost stumbled over the three words, wondering when, if ever, he would be free of the Judas factor.

'Perhaps it's not a bad thing to be unencumbered. I never married either. I've always felt it simplifies one's life not to have human emotional entanglements. That was Hitler's great strength, you know. It enabled him to see his destiny with crystal clarity. I know he married in the final hours, but the bunker ceremony was simply a symbolic act. Wagnerian in its beauty. He wished to show those who had abandoned him – that gross Goering especially, who revealed his true colours when the end was in sight – that there was still one person who would follow him to the grave. Do you appreciate that?'

'No,' Hillsden momentarily lost concentration, then recovered. 'Now you've explained it, I can see what you mean.'

Earphones on, Pearson grimaced. He gesticulated to Lloyd to put on his headset.

'Have you ever stopped to think, Robert, what our world would be like today if this country had been led by somebody of our vision? Instead of whole cities being polluted by the dregs of Africa and the Caribbean and television corrupting our minds with Hollywood's Jewish filth and Communist propaganda, we would have been cleansed of all that. You fought in the war, I believe?'

'Yes, towards the end.'

'I'm sure you were brainwashed to believe that it was a righteous war, like we all were. That we would triumphantly emerge into a brighter, more glorious future. But what did we get for our sacrifices? Fifty years of living under the threat of Stalinism, ourselves governed by crypto-Communists, the wealth of the Empire given away to black illiterates while we lived on handouts from the Americans. Do you wonder why I and others like me strive to keep the flame alight? You and I may not live to see the final solution, but at least we shall have played our part.'

There was a pause and then the listeners in the van heard Fadiman say, 'Can you hand me that lighter. Thank you.' His intake of breath as he dragged cigarette smoke into his lungs was clearly audible. 'You must forgive me. I have so much time, confined as I am, to think of what might have been. It obsesses me, Robert. I have these two wasted limbs but I am determined not to allow my grey matter to go the same way. The years are not on my side, that is why I have devoted myself to the furtherance of the cause . . . Forgive me, I'm forgetting my manners. Please pour yourself a drink.'

Pearson and Lloyd heard the sound of Hillsden's chair being scraped back and then the chink of a glass.

'How about you, sir?'

'Thank you, no. Alcohol doesn't sit well with the new drug

I'm taking. Now, I'm sure you're wondering why I asked you here alone. I have a purpose, Robert.'

Pearson checked the recording machine and adjusted the volume.

'For some time now, I and others have been seeking a way of destabilising the present government. Our aim has always been to foment the sort of social unrest that would pave the way for our alternative. It's the classic route, Robert, as I'm sure you know, and I have studied the lessons of the masters. We've had our successes, but nothing that truly achieved the desired results. However, at long last I believe I have found the answer, but there is still some way to go before it can be put into effect. There is a role for you to play, Robert. An important . . . no, a vital role if you're prepared to accept it.'

'What does it involve?'

'I'm coming to that. Tony's death was a great loss to us, he was a key member of the planning committee. I have chosen you to take his place. You're going on a journey, Robert. To Copenhagen. There you will be met by our friend Harry and told the second part of the operation.'

'What exactly do I have to do?'

'Harry will tell you. It's a question of security, you appreciate.'

'Press him, press him,' Pearson muttered in the van.

'When do I go?'

'Tomorrow. We are working to a very tight schedule. I hope that doesn't present any problems?'

'No, I can report sick. How long will I be away?'

'Not long. If all goes well, you'll be back in two days. Your air ticket and a generous sum of money are on that table . . . You look worried, Robert.'

'No,' Hillsden said. 'Just taking it in. I'm just amazed, stunned that I've been chosen.'

'Yes, I thought you might be. But then, you see, you have special qualities for the return journey . . . An honest face, Robert.'

· · ·

Hillsden thought: One can go for months without mishap – never breaking even a fingernail, never nicking the sleep-swollen flesh when shaving, living a placid, uneventful life – and then the razor slips, a hammer strikes a glancing blow, one trips on a loose paving stone, or there is a sudden stab of pain, and life changes.

Now, as he watched Galina and Lara drive away from the hotel in the American Embassy limousine, he asked himself: Am I for ever to carry an image of the faces of those I love disfigured by the agony of separation? I believed I was buying peace for all of us, but always there are deceptions to be practised, goodbyes to be said: peace was taking a late flight to Washington.

'You say you love us,' Galina had said, hunched on the hotel bed, 'and yet you do this to us.'

'Not me, them. They gave me no choices.'

'Them, it's always them. Couldn't you tell them that you've had enough, that you've done your bit?'

'My dear, it's not like that, not as simple as that,' he had said, and her pain travelled through him as though they were both touching the same electric wire. 'Don't let's quarrel in the little time we have left. I did what I thought was best for you. I wanted you both to be safe. And it won't be for ever, this agony will finish one day and then we'll be free.' The banality of his words, words that he had used too often to give comfort, sickened him; it seemed as though all he could ever give them both was not love but his own despair.

'If you're ever free,' Galina said.

Having watched the limousine pull out into the traffic, its darkened windows denying him a last glimpse of his wife and child, he carried the loss of them back into the hotel like excess luggage. He waited by the lifts in the crowded lobby, oblivious to those intent on the evening's pleasures, thinking back to what Galina had once said: *I don't know what's meant by happiness any more*. The lift doors slid open noiselessly.

Entering, he pressed the button that would take him to an empty room.

A few minutes later, he stood staring at reminders of their hurried departure – one of Lara's dolls lying on the floor in a position that reminded him of Audrey.

He began to pack a small overnight bag when there was a knock on the door and he admitted Victor.

'Did they get off?' Victor asked.

'Yes, they've gone.'

'I'm sure it was the best and wisest thing.'

'Yes.'

Victor looked at the half-packed bag. 'You don't have to go. Stay. You can stay here as long as you like. You need company at a time like this.'

Hillsden looked at him. 'No, I can't stay. Funny, isn't it, that you and I should end up friends, seeing as how we began?'

'Has something else happened?'

'Yes, but don't ask me what. You're a free man now, and you've done enough, don't get involved any further.'

Abramov embraced him. 'Alec, we're two of a kind, don't forget that. When we meet again, as we will, I'll make sure you get smart like me.'

. . .

For the umpteenth time Harry stared up at the arrivals board in Copenhagen's airport, searching for the latest information on the delayed British Airways flight. As he watched, the details were scrambled then rearranged, and to his relief he saw that it had finally landed. He took up a position by the barrier but it was still some twenty minutes before Hillsden came out of the customs hall.

'Christ! You gave me a bleedin' heart attack,' Harry said as they met. 'Come on, we've got to make up for lost time. Do you have luggage to collect?'

'No, only this.' Hillsden indicated his hand baggage.

'Good. You're learning. Luggage can be traced back to you.'
They threaded their way through the crowds and walked to a parking lot.

With Harry at the wheel of a British licensed Ford estate they took the scenic coast road, heading for Gilleleje, the small fishing port on the northern tip of Sealand.

During the journey Hillsden several times attempted to find out details of the next stage but Harry was deliberately vague. 'How long have you been over here then?'

'Enough to do the necessary.'

'And this place, what're we going there for?'

'We're meeting somebody who'll hand over a package which you'll be taking back to London.'

'Just me? You're not coming with me?'

'No. You'll be on your tod. Driving this.'

'Why's that then?'

'Because that's the way it's been planned.'

'What happens to you?'

'I make my own way back. Just follow the map, make sure we don't lose the way.'

They drove on into the gathering gloom and it was dark by the time they reached the outskirts of Gilleleje. 'We're meeting at a restaurant. I can't pronounce it, but it's marked in that guide, so keep your eyes peeled.'

'Hos Karen og Marie,' Hillsden read out an approximation of the name. 'It's got a good write-up, let's hope it lives up to it. I couldn't eat any of that plastic airline muck.'

'Eating's the least of our worries. Keep looking.'

They drove around until Hillsden spotted a sign giving the name of the restaurant on a two-storey, unpretentious wooden building facing the harbour. After parking the Ford on the quay, they went inside.

'What're you going to have?' Hillsden asked when they were seated. He studied the menu which featured a variety of fish dishes. 'Want to go for the house speciality?'

'What is it?'

'Fish.'

'Don't they have a burger?'

'Doesn't look like it.'

'Well, order that whatever it is then.'

'Want a beer with it?'

'I don't drink when I'm on a job. Nor do you.'

'Oh, right.'

When the meal came, Harry stared at the unfamiliar fish on his plate with deep suspicion. 'What is this?'

'No idea, smells good, though.' Hillsden tucked in. 'Any special reason why you chose this place?'

'I didn't choose it, dummy. Fadiman did. According to him it's got symbolic associations.'

'Really, how's that then?'

'During the war the Jews used it as an escape route to Sweden. That appealed to him.'

'He's clever, isn't he?' Hillsden said, wiping his mouth. 'Generous, too. You should see the money he gave me, just for a couple of days.'

'Not his dosh, is it? He just hands it on.' All the time Harry's eyes were on the entrance. He looked at his watch. 'He should have been here by now.'

'D'you know what he looks like?'

'No idea.'

'How will you recognise him then?'

'How d'you think? He'll make himself known with a password.'

Always careful to portray himself as a novice in such matters, yet at the same time wanting to gain Harry's approval by flattering him, Hillsden nodded sagely. 'I see. Of course, I should have known you'd have thought of everything.'

The flattery worked and for the first time since they had set out from Copenhagen, Harry dropped his bombastic pose. 'Well, some of us have done this sort of thing before, you know.'

After a pause and while wiping his plate with a piece of bread, Hillsden tried to capitalise on this opening. 'Whose money is it then, any idea? Stands to reason, running an organisation like this must cost a bomb.'

'Yeah, you can say that again. Know how much I've got on me?'

'No. Tell me.'

'Fifty grand.'

'Get away!'

Harry nodded and patted his waist.

'And you got it through? You were lucky not to be searched when you left.'

'I didn't have it when I left, did I? Picked it up in Luxembourg.'

'Fifty grand!' Hillsden said. 'God, they must trust you.'

'Yeah, well, I'm part of the inner-circle, aren't I?'

'Who keeps that sort of money in his bank account?'

'Somebody who isn't short of a few. Ever heard of a man called Charters?' Harry asked, now unable to resist airing his superior knowledge.

'No.'

'Very big and out of your league. Goes everywhere by private jet.'

'And is he the one who bankrolls us?'

'He's our principal backer, yeah. But that's not for everybody to know.'

'No, of course not. It's safe with me.'

Suddenly Harry's expression changed. 'Hold it, this could be our man. Don't look round, just act normal.'

A man roughly the same age as Harry, blond, Nordic, tanned, approached their table and then seemed inadvertently to knock against it as he passed. He stopped and apologised, first in Swedish and then in sing-song English. 'Please, excuse my clumsiness.'

Harry replied: 'You're welcome.' and the man continued on to the bar. As soon as he had gone Harry motioned for Hillsden to get up and leave. They paid the bill and went outside to the van to wait. Some ten minutes later the man joined them and climbed inside.

'Any problems?' Harry asked him.

'No problems, but I must explain,' he said. He took two four-packs of lager from his plastic bag, handling them with care. Upturning the packs he displayed them to Harry and Hillsden. All eight cans were marked with a black cross. 'Important precaution. They've been primed then resealed under high pressure, but they're completely safe until opened. Even so, always treat them with respect.'

Harry took the packs from him and examined them gingerly, studying the authentic Tuborg logo. 'Neat. Very neat,' he said. 'Your people do a good job.' He put the packs beside him on the seat, unzipped his security belt and took out a wad of notes. 'Fifty thousand, as agreed.'

The man checked them slowly. 'Yes,' he said finally. 'Correct. Thank you. Have a safe journey home.'

He opened the passenger door and was gone.

'What exactly did he mean when he said, "primed"?' Hillsden asked. 'Are they bombs?'

'Of a kind.' Harry placed both packs inside a cardboard box filled with wood shavings and made sure they were secure. 'A very special kind, so treat them with respect.'

'Semtex?'

'You don't know much, do you? That's plastic, you don't need to put that in tins under pressure.'

'I thought perhaps it had been done like that so that we could smuggle it in.'

'No, Semtex is yesterday's news. This is canned gas. You've heard of Sarin, haven't you?'

'The stuff they used on the Tokyo underground?'

'Ten out of ten.'

'Christ! For us to use?'

'That's the idea. So, let's get going.' He checked the box once more. 'And you can drive the first leg, but take it easy.'

On the return journey to Copenhagen, Hillsden kept his questions down to the minimum, anxious not to press too hard, but wanting to find out as much as he could while Harry was in his current expansive mode. 'They must want this stuff for something special if they've paid fifty thousand for it,' he said at one point.

'Yeah, they haven't told me the exact details yet, but it's big, I know that. Fadiman dreamed it up, apparently, or so Johnny told me.'

'He seems a bit out of place, that Johnny. I mean, he's not like the rest of us.'

'He's an iron, if you ask me.'

'Iron?'

'Iron hoof – poof. Haven't you heard that before?'

'I see. D'you think Fadiman is, too, then?'

'Doubt it. I don't think he does anything except sit there and dream up ideas.'

'Like this one. Wonder what he's got in mind?'

'We'll find out soon enough,' Harry said.

They parted company at Copenhagen airport where, for the second time, Harry went over the details for the rest of Hillsden's journey. 'So, have you got it straight? Here's your ticket and the booking for the hovercraft. Be sure you make that particular time. That's important, because you'll be met at Dover.'

'By you?'

'Maybe, maybe not. Here's the money, some Deutschmarks, most of it in Francs to buy the rest of the beer. You know how to pack it?'

'Yes,' Hillsden said. 'I take out two packs and replace them with the phoney ones, then reseal the case.'

'You got it.'

'If I'm asked in Customs, I came over to buy stuff for my granddaughter's wedding.'

'Good. If you stop anywhere for a bite, make sure the car's locked and parked where you can see it all the time.'

'Will do.'

'Good luck.'

Harry disappeared into the airport terminal.

. . .

Hillsden drove at a steady speed until he crossed the border into Germany and took the autobahn. He kept careful watch in his mirrors all the time in case Harry was having him tailed, but saw nothing to arouse his suspicions. He stopped at the first service station he came to, locked the van, purchased coffee and food, then made a telephone call from a public booth.

Swanson answered. As briefly as he could, Hillsden gave him details of his return trip to Dover, together with a description and registration number of the car. 'The cargo is volatile, so needs careful handling at your end.'

'Understood,' Swanson said. 'Are you on your own?'

'At the moment, yes. My companion flew back earlier. But he or somebody else will meet me on arrival.'

'Nothing else?'

'Yes, tell Pearson I finally found out who paid for my trip. Tell him his hunch was right.'

'You've done well. Good man, congratulations. Travel safely.'

It was only after he had resumed his journey that it occurred to Hillsden that praise coming from Swanson was out of character.

44

A GAS LEAK

'I think it would be dangerous to take them in the actual terminal, in view of what Hillsden said.' Swanson looked around the assembled company. 'He described the cargo as "volatile" and my reading of that is they're bringing in some type of explosive. I would have thought – and, of course, I defer to you, Commissioner – that our best bet would be to set up road blocks a mile or so out on all roads leading from Dover, and intercept them there. Less danger to the public. I think it's a fair assumption they'll be heading for London.'

The Commissioner of Police considered this. 'Yes, I think that's probably a wise move. D'you agree, Commander?'

Pearson nodded. 'Yes. Yes, I do.' He looked to Lloyd, seeking his approval too. For once, he thought, Swanson has had a good idea.

'I'll put Robertson in the picture immediately,' the Commissioner added, naming the Chief Constable of the Kent constabulary, 'and ask him to put a maximum force at your disposal, including armed units.' He went to the map. 'They'll need to cover the A2, the A20 and the A256. Is he coming across by ferry or hovercraft?'

'Hovercraft.'

'They'd better post somebody in Customs who can confirm he's arrived.'

'You should also inform the Kent lot that it's our man driving the car. If it comes to a shooting match, we don't want

Hillsden taken out,' Pearson warned.

'No, that's a very good point,' Swanson said. 'But let's hope it won't turn into a shooting match.'

'Since our team are the only ones who can identify Hillsden,' Pearson added, 'one of us should be at every road block.'

'And at Customs,' Lloyd interjected.

Swanson said, 'I'll take Customs.'

'How long have we got?'

'Just over fourteen hours. Hillsden's booking is for the last departure of the day from Calais.'

'Then I suggest we get cracking,' the Commissioner said. 'Commander, if you'd like to come with me, we'll start to put this thing together.'

Pearson paused at the door. 'That's all Hillsden told you, is it?'

'Yes, just the bare details. He obviously didn't want to elaborate over the phone,' Swanson said evenly.

'Right,' Pearson said after a pause, then followed the Commissioner out.

'It seems we're near the end,' Swanson said.

'Let's hope so,' Lloyd answered but, like Pearson, there was a note of uncertainty in his reply.

. . .

Hillsden arrived at Calais with nearly two hours to spare before his hovercraft departure. As instructed, he visited one of the numerous warehouses selling discounted beer and wine to eager day-trippers out for a bargain. There he purchased a quantity of Tuborg four-packs, together with two crates of sparkling wine, before joining the line of cars and trucks awaiting to board the *Princess Margaret*.

As luck would have it, the Channel was like a mill pond and the crossing remarkably smooth. Spot checks were being carried out by Customs at Dover and he was one of those stopped. The Preventive Officer had the look of a man who had heard and seen it all before. Opening the tailgate, he examined the crates of beer and wine.

'These for personal use?'

'Yes. Not that I'm going to drink the lot,' Hillsden said, 'though I dare say I'll have my fair share. Got my granddaughter's wedding coming off next week and this is my contribution. Grandads always have to cough up, don't they?'

'I wouldn't know,' the Preventive Officer said, 'I'm not even a father. Anything else?'

'No.'

He walked around the vehicle and peered inside. 'Okay, good luck next week.' He moved to the next vehicle.

As Hillsden climbed back behind the driving wheel he thought he saw Swanson standing in the window of the Customs shed, but with other cars behind him anxious to get going, he couldn't be certain. Just outside the Customs area he spotted Harry waiting for him and pulled alongside.

'You made it then?'

'Yes. That was a good tip of yours about the wedding.'

'Trust me and you won't go far wrong.' Harry got into the passenger seat. 'I'm full of good ideas,' he said. 'Come on, don't let's hang about.' He looked into the back of the car as they moved off. 'Where did you put the stuff?'

'The crate next to the wine.'

'Right, do just as I say and keep alert.'

'Where are we heading for?'

'Just do as I say,' Harry repeated in a flat voice, 'take a left here.'

Hillsden did as instructed. His eyes flicked to the rear-view mirror. A motorcycle seemed to be hanging on their tail some hundred yards behind.

'Now take another left,' Harry commanded. Hillsden noted that Harry's eyes never left the side mirror.

When they reached a large intersection, instead of taking one of the main roads out of Dover, Harry ordered him to turn left on to the secondary B2011, heading in the direction of Folkestone. Checking his mirror again, Hillsden saw that the motorcycle was still following them.

They proceeded through the suburbs with Hillsden keeping to the reduced speed limits. He sensed that Harry was tensed, waiting for something to happen. They went another half a mile, entering a stretch of road where the speed limit was increased to forty mph.

'Put your foot down,' Harry commanded. 'Go!'

The car lurched forward as Hillsden did as he was told.

'Be ready to make a fast turn to the right in about a hundred yards, after the next set of lights.'

Hillsden checked his mirror again: the motorcyclist was still behind them in the stream of traffic. The traffic lights changed to amber as they approached.

'Keep going, jump the lights,' Harry said, and Hillsden obeyed, crossing the intersection on red. He noted that the traffic behind them was stationary.

'Now!' Harry shouted, 'and flash your headlights twice.'

Hillsden made an acute right turn and found they were in a cul-de-sac. Straight ahead were two large wooden gates. Seconds after he gave the signal with his headlights, the gates were opened.

'Drive straight in and up the ramp into the truck.'

Now they were inside the forecourt of what appeared to be a factory where several men stood waiting beside a large furniture pantechnicon, with its rear doors open. Two wooden planks formed a ramp leading up into the belly of the pantechnicon. Hillsden gunned the car up and drove inside. The doors were immediately closed behind them.

'Out you get,' Harry said. He dived into the back of the car to lift the crate containing the doctored beer cans.

Climbing out of the estate and exiting through the cabin of the pantechnicon, Hillsden now saw that a Bentley turbo with darkened windows was parked nearby. It faced the exit, had its engine running and the boot open. The ramp was already being removed as Harry joined him and placed the crate in the boot.

'Get behind the wheel, and put that chauffeur's cap on,' Harry said, as he got into the rear of the Bentley.

Somebody shouted, 'All clear.'

'Let's go.'

Unaccustomed to the power of the Bentley, Hillsden shot forward and only just missed hitting one of the main gates. He righted it with a touch of the power steering and they surged clear.

'Turn right,' Harry instructed. 'And head for Folkestone, but ease off, keep to the limits. Act like a fucking chauffeur.'

'Jesus,' Hillsden said, 'this thing has a mind of its own.'

'Bet you never thought you'd be driving something like this.'

'No.'

'He's got two.'

'Who has?'

'Charters. Know what they cost? With the extras he's got on this, you don't get any change out of a hundred and eighty. So make sure you don't bang it.'

'That was neat back there,' Hillsden said.

'Yeah. Worked a treat. And the last thing they'll be looking for is a Bentley.'

. . .

'What d'you mean, you've lost them?' Swanson shouted into the phone. 'It's pathetic.'

The Kent Superintendent at the other end of the line did his best to remain polite. 'All I can say is, sir, they didn't pass any of our road blocks. The car was tailed but contact was lost on the Folkestone Road, which we were not instructed to cover. Immediately we were informed we cordoned off the entire area, and are still carrying out searches. But so far nothing.'

'Well, you'd better come up with something, that's all I can say.' Swanson slammed down the phone.

Once on the M20 motorway, Hillsden was urged to put his foot down, and despite the situation he found himself in he derived some pleasure from the joy of driving the Bentley. He was forced to slacken speed again when they joined the heavier traffic on the M25 and headed north.

'Where are we aiming for?' he questioned.

'You'll see soon enough. Pull into the next service station, I have to make a phone call.'

'Why stop? Use the car phone.'

'They can be tapped. Don't you know anything?'

If Hillsden thought he would have a chance to make use of the car phone himself, he was immediately denied this when they pulled into the service area.

'Give me the key,' Harry said when they both got out. He locked the car and pocketed the key. 'Stay with it.' He walked inside. Hillsden thought quickly. Taking a discarded wrapper from a rubbish bin he wrote Pearson's telephone number and in capitals underneath, POLICE EMERGENCY. RING THIS NUMBER AND GIVE MESSAGE: 'GET CHARTERS, YOU WERE RIGHT'. He stuck this on the windscreen of a nearby saloon car, securing it under the wiper blade. It was a forlorn hope, but the best he could do.

Harry returned a few minutes later and they resumed their journey.

'There's been a change of plan. We're not going into town, it's considered too risky. Seems somebody tipped them off. Keep going until you hit the M4, then head for Reading to begin with.'

'Who could have tipped them off?'

'That's a good question which needs to be answered,' Harry said flatly. 'Keep your eyes peeled for any sign of the fuzz.'

'I've been doing that already,' Hillsden said.

. . . .

404

'Don't take it out on me,' Pearson said. 'None of us fucked up. You say you definitely saw him come off the hovercraft.'

'Yes,' Swanson said.

'Was he on his own?'

'At that point, yes.'

'Nobody met him?'

'I didn't see anybody.'

'It seems likely somebody did. Otherwise Hillsden would have acted on his own initiative.'

'You think so?'

'Don't you?'

'I'm not sure. I've had doubts about Hillsden in recent weeks. What if they've got to him?'

'If they've got to him why would he contact you to arrange a reception committee? That doesn't add up.'

'Nothing adds up at the moment except I shall be carrying the can back for a total cock-up. It just seems too fortuitous that they elected to take the one route we didn't have covered, and apparently the Kent police only put one unmarked motorcycle cop on his tail. The bloody fool lost him.'

'Perhaps the idea of road blocks wasn't so good after all.'

'We can all be wise after the event. I acted as I thought the situation demanded.'

'Absolutely. But as you've often remarked, you're running the show and the buck stops with you,' Pearson said, finally sticking his own knife in. 'So, is it back to the old drawing board? What's your next move?'

'The priority is to find Hillsden, I should have thought that was obvious.'

'Yes,' Pearson replied, 'but it's the obvious we often overlook, isn't it?'

. . .

The Bentley eased its way past the electric gates of Charters's mansion and parked next to a London taxi.

'Some pad,' Hillsden said admiringly as he switched off the engine and applied the brake.

'Yeah. Don't forget when you meet him, he's a fucking Knight, so be respectful. Open the boot.'

Harry went to the rear of the car and removed the carton containing the cans of Sarin, treating it with respect. To Hillsden's surprise the front door was opened by Hyde.

'Oh, good, you're out,' Hillsden said.

'Yes, been out some time. They dropped all charges in the end. Course, I was provided with a good lawyer.' He admitted them into the hallway. 'How are you after your travels?'

'Fine.'

'Mission accomplished, we understand. Is that the cargo?'

'Yeah, eight of the little beauties,' Harry replied. 'They should put a few to sleep come the day.'

Hyde escorted them across the hallway to Charters's study, allowing Harry to precede him into the room. As Hillsden followed the other two he saw Fadiman swing round in his wheelchair and beyond him another man he took to be Charters.

'Raymond, I don't think you've met Harry and Robert before,' Fadiman said, making the introductions.

'No. But I understand congratulations are in order.'

'Thank you, Sir Raymond,' Harry spoke for both of them. 'Where would you like me to put these, sir?'

'Oh, on that table. Let me make room.'

Harry put the carton down on a round Georgian gaming table which held several piles of leatherbound books. He took out one of the beer cans as Charters, Fadiman and Hyde gathered round.

'They look harmless enough,' Charters said. 'And very authentic.'

'I thought they'd do a good job,' Fadiman leaned in and picked up the can. 'Our German comrades said the Swedish chapter could be relied upon. I think we're going to make history with these.'

'Don't shake it,' Charters admonished, and took a step backwards.

'Oh, they're quite safe until opened, sir.'

'Even so, let's not press our luck.'

'Any problems on the way here?' Hyde asked.

'No. It all worked a treat.'

'And you Robert . . . ' Fadiman turned to Hillsden, 'did you enjoy the trip?'

'Yes. Especially driving the Bentley.'

'Ah, yes, that was an extra perk, I'm sure. You performed admirably . . . except in one respect.'

He was still smiling, but Hillsden became conscious that the other three men in the room were staring at him.

'What was that, Mr Fadiman?'

'I think you know, Robert.'

Hillsden felt somebody else come into the room behind him.

'A certain phone call you made, Robert, which had it not been received by the right person would have damned all our plans.'

'Phone call? I didn't make a phone call, that was Harry, wasn't it, Harry?'

But Harry just stared at him without answering. Harry knew his place.

'It's somewhat too late for bluffing, Alec,' Fadiman continued, and the first use of his real name hung in the air between them. 'You see, we know who you are, we've always known. But we thought it a pity not to make some use of you before we discarded you. This seemed an appropriate occasion, an extra precaution on our side should anything go wrong . . . Being in the insurance business, Alec, you should have anticipated that.'

Hillsden took a step backwards and turned, only to find the ubiquitous Johnny in the doorway with a gun in his hand.

'Good try, dear,' Johnny said.

. . .

Pearson and Lloyd had not been back in the office long when the phone rang. Pearson picked up the receiver.

'I'm sorry, who d'you want? . . . Yes, you have the right number, but who d'you want to speak to, Madam? . . . I can't say until you tell me what this call is about . . .' He gesticulated at Lloyd and put the call on the speaker phone.

'I see . . . and where was this you say?'

The woman's voice answered: 'At a service station on the M25. I found it stuck on my windscreen when I came out. I thought it was a joke, but when I got home my husband said I should ring, seeing as how it said police.'

'No, you did quite right. Tell me again what was written.' Pearson reached for a pen.

'Police emergency. Ring this number and give message: "Get Charters, you were right." '

'Charters?'

'Yes.'

'Spelt C-h-a-r-t-e-r-s?'

'Yes.'

'Nothing else?'

'No, that's all there was.'

'And how long ago was this?'

'About three hours ago.' They heard her saying something to her husband. 'Yes, that would be about it.'

'Well, I'm most grateful. You did the right thing.'

'*Are* you the police?'

'Yes, we are. My name is Commander Pearson. Could I have your name, Madam?'

'Thomas. Mrs Thomas.'

'And your number, should we wish to contact you again?' He wrote it down. 'I more than appreciate your co-operation, Mrs Thomas, very public-spirited of you. Thank you so much, you did the right thing.'

He hung up.

'It has to have been Hillsden.'

'Yes,' Lloyd said. 'The timing fits.'

'So what about an apology?'

'Okay, so your hunch about Charters was correct.'

'Don't overwhelm me with congratulations, will you?'

'Okay,' Lloyd repeated. 'I admit you're a genius, Holmes, I'm just slow on the uptake.'

'The fact that Alec resorted to such a chancy, desperate tactic means he wasn't alone. By a piece of good luck he stuck the message on the right windshield and our Mrs Thomas came through . . . But where is the poor sod now? And what were they bringing over?' Pearson asked, thinking aloud.

45

SOLUTIONS

Rendered secure and immobile, bound and gagged with nearly an entire roll of wide-gauge industrial tape, Hillsden was locked in a wooden gazebo that stood at the end of a herbaceous border in Charters's extensive grounds.

'However you dispose of him, I want no knowledge of it,' Charters said. 'There can be no question of any connection with me or this house, is that clearly understood?'

'Totally,' Fadiman said. 'I think you know me better than that, Raymond.'

'I'll leave you to it, then. I've got other business to attend to. Help yourselves to drinks, but make it quick. The sooner he's off the premises, the better. Whatever you decide, I want it done tonight.'

About to leave the room, he paused, looking at the cans on his Georgian table. 'Those too. I want those removed.'

'Of course, Raymond.'

'The first question we have to ask,' Fadiman began when Charters had gone, 'is whether Hillsden is worth more to us alive or dead?'

'Dead,' Harry said.

'Yes, just curb your natural instincts, Harry, and think it through. Swanson's original plan, which we all went along with, and which had a certain logic to it, was cunning in the extreme. Give me a light, Harry, I think better with a cigarette in my mouth.'

Harry obliged.

'In order to service us, he needed a go-between. That protected him and also was intended to provide a scapegoat if necessary. This Hillsden fitted the bill perfectly. A man with a history of defection. A man at one time wanted for murder. A man, it could easily be believed, intent on revenge against an establishment that had deprived him of his freedom. Swanson parlayed that through with his superiors employing his usual skill, and it certainly worked as intended. We were always kept fully informed of any progress they made. Admittedly, there was a blip.'

'Remind me, what was that?' Hyde asked.

'Carstairs committing suicide.'

'Oh, yeah, that's right.'

'Had Harry taken care of him we would have been spared Pearson's enquiries. Sir Raymond ordered him to return to Copenhagen, and Harry would have taken him out there, as he did Van Elst. That way it would have looked like just another homosexual murder, no big deal. Dying here led the danger man, Pearson, to instigate a line of enquiries which could well have led back to our host. He got very close. Only quick thinking on Swanson's part prevented him finding the last pieces of the puzzle.'

'Let's get back to Hillsden,' Harry said. 'You heard what Sir said, he wants him out of here.'

'All right, Harry, all right, don't tell me what to do. A hasty decision now could ruin everything.'

'Top him, that's the best thing.'

'You could be right, but where and how?'

'I know what I'd do.'

'So tell us.'

'Test one of these cans on him. We've got eight, more than enough, let's see if they work. Better find out now rather than later.'

Fadiman waved his cigarette holder and Hyde was immediately there with an ashtray. 'You've got such an evil mind, Harry. That must be why I'm fond of you, despite your obvious shortcomings. Well, now, let's consider that. Where?'

'That's no problem. I know places.'

'Such as?'

'Disused lock-up garage. Plenty of those around. Or better still, a condemned tower block. Put him in one of those, they wouldn't find him for months. Probably blow it up before they found him.'

Fadiman nodded. 'And you'd take care of it?'

'Be a pleasure.'

'Let me be devil's advocate. Bear with me, I'm not pouring cold water on your solution, I think it has considerable merit. But let me go back to my original question: is he worth more to us alive?'

He looked from Harry to Hyde, but neither ventured an opinion. 'You're not sure. Neither am I. On balance, I think he's better dead. My only concern is a worst scenario, where Swanson is exposed. The contingency in his plan was always that, in such a scenario, he could hide behind Hillsden, reveal him as the mole.'

'If Hillsden's dead that could still work,' Hyde said.

'Yes, you're right. Well, now, do we vote on it?' Fadiman extinguished his cigarette. 'Harry?'

'Well, you know my vote. Whichever way you look at it, alive, he's a liability. Just leave it to me.'

'Very well, I'll go along with that. We do, after all, have other pressing matters. And I agree it would be highly sensible to test the material before the day.'

'What is the day?' Hyde asked. 'Am I entitled to know now?'

'It's a special day,' Fadiman said. 'The start of the Notting Hill Carnival. Where better to make our statement?'

'Oh, boner!' Hyde said. 'Brilliant!'

'Thank you. Now, before you deal with our friend Hillsden, let's remove those. Hyde, you'd better take charge of them and arrange distribution.'

'Except two,' Harry put in. 'One for him outside and one for me.'

'Yes, fine. One last thing, Harry. As an extra precaution, I don't want you to go back to your own place until this is over.' He produced some keys from a pocket. 'I keep a small cubbyhole in Greek Street, which I want you to use. Stay out of sight until the day. We'll get all the final details to you there.' He held out the keys. 'The number's on the tag; one key for the front door, the other for my flat on the top floor. You'll find everything you need there, Johnny keeps it well stocked.'

He watched as both men carefully removed the cans. 'Oh, and Harry,' he said as they reached the door, 'don't forget, I shall be anxiously awaiting your call about the result of the test. A lot hangs on it.'

. . .

'Now what?' Lloyd asked. 'Why're you undecided? Let's go.'

'Just had a thought. Why did he give my number, not Swanson's?'

'First one he thought of probably.'

'I wonder,' Pearson mused. 'Something Swanson said keeps coming back to me. That he was having doubts about Hillsden. Yet he was happy for Hillsden to go back into the lion's den. The two things don't add up. Unless . . . '

'What?'

'Let me think. What if he knows more than we do?'

'Who're we talking about now?'

'Hillsden. Keep up with me. What if he deliberately contacted me, instead of Swanson? What does that tell you?'

'I don't know what you're getting at.'

'It makes me think he had a good reason. Who has consistently kept us from moving on Fadiman and Charters?' He looked straight at Lloyd. 'Swanson, right? Who thought of the road block scheme and then put himself at the point of entry? Swanson again.'

'But the whole scheme was Swanson's baby from the start. Like you said, he's an arse-licker out for number one. Why would he sabotage it when we're in sight of the end? Much more likely he wants to grab all the kudos for himself.'

Pearson took two of his stomach tablets, always a sign, Lloyd recognised, that he was agitated. 'I know what first sent the warning lights flashing, but stupidly I put it out of my mind.'

'What?'

'The missing Kell files. Who had them last? Swanson again.' Pearson strode across the room and hit his forehead with an open palm somewhat melodramatically. 'I'm so bloody dense, no wonder I'm near retirement . . . Of course, of course . . . Get the DG on the blower.'

'The DG?'

'Never mind, I'll do it myself.' He picked up the phone and dialled an unlisted number.

'What're you ringing him for?'

'If I can convince him I'm right I'll need his authority to obtain the warrants.'

'Convince him about what?'

'That we've been leaking like a sieve,' Pearson said as he fretted for his call to be answered.

. . .

Trussed like a chicken, Hillsden lay face downwards on the warehouse floor, painfully inching his way towards the sheet of corrugated iron. At the back of his mind was the hope that he could find a jagged edge against which he could scrape away at his bonds. The effort cost him dear and he had to rest and recover after every heave. He persisted until he was only a foot or so away from the door, his clothes soaked in what, from the smell, he took to be diesel oil. It was now that he felt something cold fall on the back of his head; the sensation was repeated a few seconds later, then at closer intervals. He managed to roll over on to his back after three attempts and stared up at the corrugated iron roof. There were gaps in it and he could see a glow in the night sky. It was raining and water dripped down, now splattering his face.

At that moment the door was unlocked; it struck him a glancing blow as it was pushed inwards.

'Oh, trying to make a run for it, were you, Dad?' Harry said. 'Bit late for that. You're not going anywhere.' He bent down and carefully placed a beer can containing the Sarin on the floor, then dragged Hillsden to the far end of the warehouse, turning him over on to his stomach again.

'I've brought you your Horlicks, to make sure you get a good night.'

He laughed at his own joke and, grabbing Hillsden by the hair, twisted his head round so that he could see the can.

'There it is. I thought we'd test whether it's past its sell-by date. Want to be sure that the carnival goes with a swing, don't we? Put all those nig-nogs to sleep. Pity you won't be there to see it.'

Harry retrieved the can, then produced a dampened teacloth with which he covered his mouth and nose. Taking a deep breath and holding it, he knelt down, gripped the can with one hand and pulled the catch open. There was a hiss as the pressure was released. Harry quickly got to his feet and backed out.

. . .

After a stall of nearly two hours, during which time there were a series of urgent debates between the DG and an extremely dubious Home Secretary who refused to take a decision until the matter had been agreed by Downing Street, authority was finally given and warrants issued for Pearson and his teams to go into action. Backed by armed units from the Met and three county police forces, the raids were to be carried out simultaneously once Pearson, who had claimed the right to arrest Charters, had his unit in position in North Stoke. Rotherby headed those going after Fadiman, while

Lloyd and Hadley accompanied the units seeking to take Hyde and Harry. At top level it had been agreed that, to thwart any possible tip-off, no move would be taken against Swanson until the first swoops had netted the other players. Swanson's apartment block in Pimlico was cordoned off by a force from Special Branch who were poised to go in once the signal had been given. It was emphasised to all concerned that the number two priority was to locate Hillsden. In every case, the warrants had been issued on conspiracy charges under The Defence of the Realm Act.

It was raining steadily when Pearson's group, numbering twenty men, arrived in North Stoke. All but one of their vehicles were parked at a discreet distance from Charters's house, and half the force dispersed to cover the walled perimeter of the grounds. Pearson, together with four armed policemen, including a Chief Inspector, was poised outside the main gates in a Range Rover. To achieve maximum surprise the wall was scaled and the automatic gate mechanism activated from the inside. As the gates began to swing open, security lights illuminated the entire area and alarm sirens sounded. The Range Rover accelerated through and surged towards the house, followed by the remainder of the police.

Pearson was first out as the Range Rover scattered the gravel drive by the entrance to the house. A startled manservant was brushed aside the moment he opened the front door, and as Pearson and the Inspector entered the hallway Charters, in a dressing gown, appeared at the top of the staircase. He stopped, staring at the armed police confronting him and his manservant spreadeagled on the hall floor.

'What's this all about? How dare you come bursting in like this.'

The Chief Inspector stepped forward. 'Sir Raymond Charters?'

'Yes, what of it?'

'I hold a warrant for your arrest, sir, and must duly caution you that you have the right to remain silent, but that anything you do say can be . . . '

Charters cut him short. 'Don't spout that garbage at me. This is an outrage. You'll be chopped for this, all of you.'

Unimpressed, the Chief Inspector went back over the same ground. 'Anything you do say can be used in evidence against you. Do you understand your rights?'

'I bloody well do and I demand the right to ring my solicitor.'

'You'll be granted facilities at the station, sir, once you've been formally charged.'

'Charged with what?'

'Conspiracy under The Defence of the Realm Act, sir. Now, if you'd like to get dressed and accompany us . . . '

'And what if I refuse?'

'Then I'll have no alternative but to handcuff you, sir, and take you as you are.' He nodded to two of his men who moved to the staircase. It was only now that Charters appeared to recognise Pearson.

'I know you, you're that bloody MI6 type who came to my office.'

'How good of you to remember a face on such short acquaintance, Carl,' Pearson said evenly. 'Perhaps you'd prefer to be charged under your born name of Hain?' He turned and spoke into his mobile phone, 'North Stoke achieved, all units go.'

As Charters went back up the stairway followed by the two armed officers, Pearson addressed him again.

'There is one thing that would stand in your favour. We're anxious to know the present whereabouts of one of my officers, Alec Hillsden. You know him as Robert Bartlett.'

Charters paused halfway up the staircase. 'You're wasting your time. I have no knowledge of the man under either name.'

'Just as you have no knowledge of making payments to the late Mr Carstairs,' Pearson answered, getting in the last word.

Hadley and his team were not so lucky: they found Harry's flat bare and despite being relentlessly turned over it offered up no clues as to the whereabouts of its absent owner. Apart from a few soiled articles of clothing discarded on the bathroom floor, there was little to indicate human habitation. The small refrigerator encrusted with ice in the sordid kitchen contained only a stiffened portion of pizza and a carton of stale milk. There wasn't even a torn piece of paper in the waste bin.

Deflated by the lack of success, Hadley ordered the broken door to be secured and returned to base.

Rotherby, on the other hand, encountered no problems when arresting Fadiman and Johnny. In view of his disability, once charged Fadiman was remanded to the hospital wing at Brixton. After being allowed to consult his lawyers, he declined to answer any questions. Bail was refused.

Once confirmation had been relayed to the Yard that both Fadiman and Charters were in custody, two senior officers from MI5 detained Swanson. He offered no resistance and was taken to a house in the Home Counties to begin prolonged sessions of interrogation.

. . .

Meanwhile it was Lloyd and his team who came away with the most valuable piece of the puzzle.

Arriving outside Hyde's house, they were relieved to find the area deserted save for two stray dogs circling each other around a broken street lamp, bent over the road like a wilted sunflower.

Drawing their guns, the team went past Hyde's parked car to the front door, treading carefully. Lloyd had already detailed two of his men to cover the rear of the house. Two more took up positions on either side of the front door before he hammered on it. After a pause a light came on and they heard the sound of somebody descending the stairs.

A voice said: 'Who is it?'

'Me, Harry,' Lloyd answered in a passable Cockney accent. 'Let me in, I'm in trouble.'

A bolt was shot back, then a key turned in the lock. As the door opened a fraction the two armed policemen lunged forward, knocking Hyde backwards. Before he could recover, they and Lloyd were inside and had slammed the door shut.

'What the fuck?' Hyde exclaimed. He was wearing only a pair of striped boxer shorts.

'Check the upstairs,' Lloyd ordered, and one of the men went in search.

'Now then, sunshine,' Lloyd pushed Hyde against the wall. 'We want to know what happened to Bartlett.'

'I don't know any fucking Bartlett.'

'I have a warrant here which says you do, that you're part of a conspiracy aimed at threatening Her Majesty's realm. Shall I read you your rights?'

'Get lost!'

'No, let's do it by the book.' Lloyd recited the statutory caution, then they backed Hyde at gunpoint into the living room. 'Sit down. Now if you tell us what we want to know I might be persuaded to give you a character reference.'

'I don't have to tell you pricks anything.'

'It's all over, sunshine. Nobody's going to help you but me. So start thinking of yourself, use what little grey matter you possess and do yourself a favour.'

'Go fuck yourself.'

'You're becoming monotonous.'

The policeman returned from searching the upstairs area. 'No sign of him up there.'

'Right, well, tear the rest of the place apart and have your chums outside go over the garden.'

'I'll have you lot for this,' Hyde snarled.

'Don't bank on it. You won't be out in time to get me. I'll be dead before you breathe fresh air again. You're looking at life and no remissions.'

'That meant to frighten me?'

'Where's Bartlett?'

'I've told you, I've never heard of him.'

'But you've heard of Gauleiter Fadiman, haven't you? And Reich Chancellor Sir Raymond.'

'No, nor them neither.'

'That's funny, they know you.'

'You can bluff all night, you won't get anything out of me,' Hyde said, but a hint of uncertainty had crept into his voice.

'Well, I'm in no hurry. You keep a pet parrot I see. Bartlett told us about that. Looks as though its battery's dead. Shall we try again? Where's Bartlett? The sooner you tell me the sooner we can get you tucked up in a nice warm cell.'

'Get fucked.'

'You know, sooner or later we're going to have to teach you some manners. I'm starting to be offended. But I'm a patient man and I've got nowhere else to go. Matter of fact I could do with a drink while I'm waiting. D'you mind if I help myself to something?' He went to the fridge. 'Oh, dear, proper old Mother Hubbard, aren't you? Just one can of beer, so I can't ask you to join me.'

Lloyd took the can out of the fridge and curled a finger inside the ring on the lid. Hyde jumped up, gabbling. 'Don't touch that! Please, for fuck's sake don't open that thing . . . I'll tell you everything, just put that down! Put it down!' The startling change in him and the sheer panic in his voice as he backed away into a corner took Lloyd by surprise. Puzzled by the hysterical reaction, he studied the can more closely.

'What have we here then?'

'Don't mess with it, please. Do as I say, for God's sake . . . I will talk, but first put it down.' All his previous bravado had disappeared and his shout suddenly activated the mechanical parrot: the beak opened and closed and it repeated 'put it down'.

Lloyd placed the can on the coffee table between them. It was only now that Hyde visibly relaxed.

'Okay, sunshine, how's that? Now, start talking.'

. . .

Events moved quickly.

Following Hyde's confession, the suspect beer can was rushed to the Ministry of Defence's laboratories, Porton Down, where it was confirmed as containing Sarin.

In the early hours of the following morning a further number of arrests were made by armed teams drawn from the Thames Valley, West Midland and Hampshire police forces. Quantities of neo-Nazi literature were recovered from the premises raided and specialist personnel wearing full protective clothing and respirators removed five other cans of Sarin. They were subsequently rendered harmless. D Notices had been issued to the media and no mention of these operations reached the public.

. . .

Playing hide and seek in a condemned warehouse close to St Pancras Station, Charlie Bostock, aged eight, desperately sought a place to conceal himself before his friend finished counting to twenty. Clambering over some old packing cases, he hid behind some sheets of corrugated iron and ducked low. He heard his friend shouting 'I'm coming,' and lay as flat as he could. It was then that he saw the man's body a few feet away, and it wasn't just an ordinary man, but somebody lying at a curious angle, tied like a parcel, with black tape wound around his face. There was a puddle of oily water close to the man's head and the man did not move. His eyes seemed to be staring right at Charlie. Panicked, Charlie scrambled to his feet and cried out for his friend. 'Pax!' he shouted. 'Come here quick!'

His friend came into view. 'What's up?'

'Look! This bloke.'

Both children stared at the body as their small world

changed for ever.

'Why's he like that?'

'Don't know.'

'Is he dead?'

Charlie took a small step nearer.

'Don't touch him.'

'Not going to.'

'We'd better go fetch yer Mum.'

Not taking their eyes away from the silent body, they backed away, then turned and ran.

. . .

Pearson kept vigil outside the intensive care unit where frantic efforts were being made to keep Hillsden alive, but as the hours passed without any discernible change in his condition it became obvious that the battle was being lost.

Shortly before dawn the Staff Nurse in charge of the unit called Pearson to the bedside. 'I think it's any moment,' she said.

'Can it do any harm now if I talk to him?'

'No.'

Pearson lifted the plastic sheeting enveloping the bed and put his face close to Hillsden's. 'Alec, it's me, Pearson. Can you hear me?'

Hillsden's eyelids fluttered briefly.

'Did-you-find-out-anything-else?'

Again there was the slightest of reactions.

'Alec-try-and-remember,' Pearson said, louder this time.

Hillsden's lips moved and Pearson bent closer still.

'What? Say again . . . !'

Hillsden made a sound, but whether it was a last, dying breath or a partly formed word, Pearson could not be sure. It sounded to him like 'calm' or perhaps 'carn'.

A second later the screen for the machine monitoring Hillsden's heart went blank. The Staff Nurse tapped Pearson

on the shoulder.

'You're too late,' she said. 'He's gone.

46

REVELATIONS

There was little time for grief. The consensus was that the eighth, and, as far as anybody knew, last can of Sarin, must be in Harry's possession, though none of those arrested was prepared to grass on him. After Hyde's initial willingness to save his skin, once in safe custody, he had clamped up. All Harry's known haunts were being kept under close observation, and computer enhanced close-ups of the photos identified by Carstairs's companion were displayed in all police stations and post offices. But Harry had gone to earth. A further and more extensive search of his flat revealed a Ruger automatic concealed behind a panel in the bathroom, together with a home-made silencer fashioned, as Schmidt had once described, from a Pepsi Cola can. The crime of murder was now added to the warrant for his arrest.

'You're good at crosswords, Rotherby,' Pearson said as he once again tried to read a meaning into Hillsden's dying word. They were gathered together with Sarah in Hillsden's Docklands office, going through the files for a third time in the hope that they could turn up a clue to the mystery.

'He either said "calm" or "carn" but it was so faint that I can't be certain. Can you think what he might have been trying to tell me?'

'Could it have been Calne, the place?'

'I don't know.'

'Maybe it was just "calm",' Hadley offered. 'You know, he

was saying that he felt calm dying.' He looked at the others. 'No?'

'Yes, I suppose that's possible,' Pearson said.

Rotherby was jotting words down on a notepad: '*Cairn, Carmine, Carnage, Carnation, Carnal* . . . any of those suggest anything?'

They pondered, but nobody could think of anything.

'What about "Carnival"?' Sarah said suddenly.

The four men looked at her.

'Just a thought, but the annual Notting Hill do begins at the end of next week,' she said.

'"Carnival",' Pearson repeated. 'You could be right. You could indeed. Why didn't we think of that?'

'Because men are not as bright as women,' Sarah said perkily.

Pearson rounded on Lloyd. 'That meeting Alec had with Fadiman which we bugged – did Fadiman ever mention Notting Hill?'

'Not that I remember, no.'

'Jesus! If Sarah's right, it figures, though, doesn't it? If they're planning to revenge Sonntag's death, what better opportunity? Oh, Christ! You don't need much imagination to visualise what would be the result if any of that bloody stuff was released in the middle of that crowd. Carnage and panic on a frightening scale. The police are anticipating well over a million people. All those bastards would have to do is plonk the cans down in the crowd and walk away. Dear God, dear God.'

The thought that he might, at last, be close to the truth, made him almost incoherent. 'When it was used in Tokyo it was in a confined space and therefore more hideously effective, but according to reports, even released in the open air it's lethal to those in the immediate vicinity.'

'How effective would just one can be?' Lloyd asked.

'One killed Alec, didn't it? And until we find Harry, we don't know there *is* only one. We've only got Hyde's word for it. We'd better move fast.' He rounded on Rotherby. 'Get on to

Control straightaway, tell them we have good reason to believe the carnival's the target and that it's vital to track down Harry. Tell them we want every available man they can give us. And, Sarah, you alert the bods at Porton Down that we're going to need their expertise. Find out what precautions, if any, we can take. Do it now, both of you.'

After they had left the room, Hadley said: 'That cold, calculating bastard.'

'Who?'

'Swanson. I had my suspicions from the start. If only I'd acted on them earlier, but I was the new boy, I didn't have any real proof and I didn't want to speak out of turn. I did talk to Hillsden once, but only in a roundabout way, warning him to be on his guard. Now I wish to God I'd gone further, I wish I'd had the courage of my convictions; if I had Alec might still be alive. That'll be on my conscience for ever. When I think of the way Swanson snared poor old Alec – to promise a man freedom, knowing you are taking him to his death. That's the action of a man steeped in shit.' His vehemence brought a flush to his face. 'The prick wanted revenge, I suppose. It all falls into place now.'

'What's that mean? Revenge for what? He didn't know Alec before this.'

'Oh, it goes back a long way. I never had any real proof until I stumbled on something. But even then it was only hearsay, I needed to dig deeper . . . It was at a party of my mother's. She's something of a fag hag I suppose . . . Since my father died she collects gays, finds them amusing and no threat . . . About two weeks ago she persuaded me to host one of her soirées. There was a character there I hadn't seen before, titled, the sort of prat you see in those arse-paralysing features in *Tatler*, not obviously gay, but his mask slipped after two or three of my mother's Martinis. He got me on my own at one point and made a pass . . .' Hadley's face went a darker shade of red. 'Nothing I couldn't cope with . . . Mother and I had a major row about it afterwards . . . Turned out this queen had been in the Firm during Lockfield's time . . . Mother knew all about him, she loves dishing the dirt . . . Anyway, during the course of the row, she let slip that Lockfield was gay. "I don't know why you're so stuffy about my friends," she said. "That place where you work has always been a hot-bed, as you must know." I couldn't argue about that, but then she said: "And that man who's your boss, well he's no wallflower. Timmy told me . . ." that was the name of the character who made the pass at me . . . "he was Lockfield's toy-boy as a teenager. Lockfield left him all his money."'

'You're sure she meant Swanson?'

'Definitely. I questioned her at length. Then I made it my business to check Lockfield's will. My mother was right. Swanson was the sole beneficiary.'

'But where does revenge come in? I'm still not with you.'

'Think about it. It was Alec who fingered Lockfield and as a result Lockfield topped himself. What better motive than a lover's grief?'

'Dear God,' Pearson said finally. 'Now I've heard it all. I thank my lucky stars I'm getting out.'

'Well, I don't have your experience,' Hadley replied, 'but I've already come to the conclusion that in this game we've never heard it all.'

47

A CALYPSO FOR THE DEPARTED

Just before six a.m. on the first day of the carnival, Pearson and a group of senior officers from Special Branch stood outside the Elgin Arms on the deserted corner of Elgin Crescent and Ladbroke Grove in the Notting Hill Gate area. They were being briefed by the police Commander with overall operational responsibility for the event. While their discussion took place, squads of uniformed police started putting crash barriers into position. Other teams, wearing protective clothing, rubber gloves and boots, lifted manhole covers and descended into the sewers, sealing the manholes with heavy tape once they had been declared clean. There were fewer parked cars than usual in the surrounding streets, since many of the local inhabitants had followed their custom of giving the celebrations a wide berth.

'If what we are prepared for does happen,' the Operational Commander said, 'and the device or devices are activated, then our task will be to saturate and contain the immediate areas and attempt to minimise the number of casualties. I've studied the lessons learned from Tokyo. There they had three separate incidents resulting in eight dead and nearly five thousand injured. I'm not making comparisons because here the gas will not be released in a confined space. That having been said, nobody can predict for sure how this substance will perform, or for how long it constitutes a lethal threat. In the opinion of the Army experts much depends on the prevailing weather conditions. It's one of those times when we might welcome thunderstorms, since one body of opinion is that heavy rain reduces the penetration, but storms are not predicted. In fact we are expecting a long day of fine, humid weather with temperatures above the average. We shall be getting hourly reports on the air quality from the Met Office. I'm no expert, gentlemen, I'm a fatalist who believes in planning for the worst scenario.'

He addressed Pearson. 'How many of your people have ever come face to face with this man?'

'Only two, I'm afraid.'

'Hmm. So the majority will have to rely on the photograph.'

'I'm sure you've thought of it,' Pearson said, 'but the likelihood is he'll be wearing some disguise . . . even a carnival mask.'

'Yes. Don't depress me any further.' He looked around at the sombre group. 'That being so, gentlemen, what we could be facing before this day is over, is wholesale panic. It will be our task to prevent that panic turning into a full scale riot. The history of this carnival in recent years has been a happy one. Excellent relations with the organisers and crime kept within containable limits. But it only takes a spark. The use of poisonous gas has always carried a particular dread for most people, understandably so. It's happily been an unknown country up until now. Let's hope it remains so. I suggest that we use the time still at our disposal to check and check again that every possible or probable risk has been anticipated. I want all divisional officers to assemble again at the command post at twelve noon. Thank you and good luck.'

He walked away to his car.

. . .

By ten a.m. the green coaches of emergency police were in position all over the area, the occupants equipped with gas masks in addition to riot gear. The number of spotter video cameras had been trebled from the previous year's event; two-man teams of police marksmen armed with high-velocity rifles occupied rooftop vantage points overlooking the carnival route. In addition to the regular police presence, three Army Disposal Squads and units trained in chemical warfare had been brought in. Plain-clothed officers were stationed at Latimer Road, Notting Hill Gate, Royal Oak and Westbourne Park underground stations and on all main bus routes. In all, over twelve hundred officers were deployed.

By noon, upwards of a million revellers were converging on the area and the numerous steel bands were already vying to be heard above each other. The first of the elaborately decorated floats began its stately progress to the assembly areas escorted by bedecked, plumed and altogether magnificent dancers. Food vendors had fired up their jerk chicken stalls and the carnival was under way, gaining in momentum every minute and conducted in an atmosphere of good humour. There were few incidents other than the arrests of half-a-dozen pickpockets, a few lost children and one heart attack. The sun shone, the floats amazed, the street dancing was frenzied and the general mood of the vast and ever-swelling crowd had never been better.

. . .

It was shortly after seven p.m. when Harry left Fadiman's hideout and cut through the back streets to Tottenham Court Road. He took a bus as far as Queensway, alighting there and walking to Westbourne Grove, losing himself in the crowds as he proceeded to Chepstow Road. Because of the news embargo he was still unaware that Hyde and the others were to play no further part, and, despite Pearson's fear, he had not bothered with any disguise, relying on the dense crowds to conceal him. By the time he arrived, the police had estimated there were still in excess of one million people on the carnival streets.

Harry stopped and purchased a leg of barbecued chicken. The can of gas was secured in a pouch attached to his trouser belt and concealed under his jacket. While eating the chicken, he threaded his way through the unsuspecting crowds, looking for the ideal spot to use his device. It had been decided that the can would be activated shortly after nine o'clock, when the tired police would be fully occupied with shepherding the revellers home. He finally chose a location at the junction of St Luke's Road and Tavistock Road, where six or seven of the huge sound systems were in close competition. The cacophony of sound, he felt, would add to the panic he hoped to produce and at the same time hinder the police. Having made his choice, he next carefully studied which escape route he would use. His usual confidence never deserted him.

. . .

As the day progressed without alarm, Pearson's apprehension mounted rather than diminished. The only two members of his own team who had ever come face to face with Harry were Hadley and Hillsden's erstwhile assistant, Sarah, and he knew the odds were stacked against them. Both had been circulating in the crowds all day, Hadley with an armed plain-clothes man, and Sarah with her police boyfriend. At intervals they had reported back to him, always in the negative. With the memory of Hillsden's last moments still vivid, Pearson could not bring himself to believe that their luck would hold. The effort of concentration as he made slow progress through the raucous and increasingly ragged, but seemingly inexhaustible revellers, studying every face he passed, caused his stomach to spasm. He was forced to rest, leaning up against the railings of a house until the pain subsided. A grotesquely masked dancer offered him a drink from a bottle of rum, but he declined with a forced smile. The dancer consumed the rest of the contents in front of him, then suddenly fell, insensible, to the pavement, a happy look on his face, out to the world.

Pearson waited until the spasm eased and looked at his watch. It was just before nine o'clock.

. . .

Half a mile away from where Pearson was resting, Sarah and her boyfriend approached the junction of Tavistock Road and St Luke's Road. The crowds were still thick here, but good-natured, and several times Sarah had to refuse an offer to join in the dancing. The steel bands were still going full blast. It was at this moment that further back in the crowd three teenagers, petty thieves from the Brixton area, started to ram-raid through the crowd, bag-snatching as they went, relying on speed and brute force to achieve their getaway. At precisely this moment Sarah and Harry were separated by less than ten yards. A few minutes earlier Harry had removed the can from the pouch. He now held it firmly in his right hand, pressed closely to his body at thigh height, and was edging his way to the spot he had pre-selected.

At the end of their run the three bag-snatchers scattered in different directions, cannoning off anybody unfortunate enough to obstruct their flight. One of them ran straight into Harry, sending him crashing to the ground. Then this same youth changed direction and this time hit Sarah, knocking her over as he made his escape.

It was while she was lying, semi-stunned, on the ground that Sarah glimpsed a prone Harry through a sea of legs. He was a few feet away from her and the hand that still clutched the can was momentarily in her eyeline. She saw him start to clamber upright and screamed, 'There! That's him! Get him!' but her voice was lost in the hip-hop, jungle sounds bursting from the mammoth speakers.

She crawled towards Harry and managed to hook an arm around one of his legs. Harry hit down at her with his free hand, but she hung on. He chopped another blow on her forearm, forcing her to release her grip, then pushed his way into the crowd. It was only then that Sarah's boyfriend grasped what was happening and dived for him, bringing him down in a clumsy tackle. Both men engaged in a frenzied, confined struggle, now egged on by the crowd who believed that one of the thieves had been apprehended. With his free hand Harry landed a karate chop to the throat and as her boyfriend doubled in pain, Sarah saw Harry go for the release catch on the can. She screamed, 'Stop him!' and a burly onlooker wrenched Harry's head back causing him to relinquish his grip on the can. It flew out of his hands and rolled beneath one of the steel drums. Sarah scrambled to reach it, wrapping her bloodied knuckles around it and hanging on for dear life. When police reinforcements arrived it was with some difficulty that they prised her fingers loose.

POSTSCRIPT

Galina never remarried. She and Lara now have American citizenship and live in Phoenix, Arizona, where she manages a computer warehouse owned and financed by Victor Abramov.

Hadley left the Firm without regret and joined a merchant bank where he is very successful.

'Mrs Carstairs' sold her story to the *Sun* and is now cohabiting with a plastic surgeon in Miami.

Pearson retired and bought a house on Gozo. In the last Birthday Honours he was awarded a CBE in the Civil List.

Lloyd took early retirement and found he had a talent for writing detective stories, several of which have been sold to television.

Rotherby died of a heart attack and left all his money to a feline charity.

Even with remission, Swanson was not expected to be released until the year 2010.

Fadiman served two years of a seven-year sentence in an open prison and was then paroled on compassionate grounds. He is working on his memoirs.

Sir Raymond Charters was acquitted on appeal, but stripped of his knighthood. He sold all his companies in England and emigrated to Chile.

Hyde was killed in a prison brawl, while Harry was given two concurrent life sentences for the murders of Montague and Lord Miller.

Victor Abramov purchased an estate in the Cotswolds having made a killing in the currency market. He enjoyed the English way of life, even to the extent of learning to play cricket.

NEWS ITEMS

Adolf Hitler's legacy is proving hard to kill in Austria, the country of his birth. For the second time in a year the country is being terrorised by a wave of neo-Nazi letter bombs. The Mayor of Vienna, Helmet Zilk, lost half his left hand and almost died of loss of blood after opening a letter bomb sent to his home. The current campaign coincides with the retrial of the man seen as the leader of neo-Nazis in Austria, Gottfried Kussel, thirty-six, currently appealing against a ten-year sentence for his Fascist activities.
— Sunday Express, 1994

Israeli agents are mounting a major undercover operation to 'contain' the threat to London's Jewish community posed by Sunday's rally of Muslim fundamentalists at Wembley. The team from Mossad will work with the full approval of MI5 and MI6.
— The Standard, 1994

German police raided fifty homes across the country after an attempt to hold a neo-Nazi rally in Triptis, in the eastern state of Thuringia. Arms, ammunition, chemicals and propaganda were seized.
— Independent on Sunday, 1995

Two brothers, aged sixteen and seventeen, neo-Nazis from Salisbury Township, Pa., are accused of beating their parents and brother, eleven, to death. Victims were beaten until their faces were unrecognisable.
— Arizona Republic, 1995

British Jews Suffer 'World Tide Of Hatred'.
— Headline, 1995